SIGNATURE PAGE

HEALING IN THE HOLLOW

HER ENEMIES AIN'T A HUCKLEBERRY COMPARED TO HER.

INTERNATIONAL BESTSELLING AUTHOR

CASSANDRA FEATHERSTONE

Content Information

This is a *paranormal whychoose romance with poly elements*—our FMC, Jolene, will not have to choose between love interests.

There are many situations included that are intended for mature audiences (18+).

In these books, there may be instances/references (be they small or lengthy) that could trigger some individuals such as:

- liberal use of appropriate consent
- the fucking Fae
- group scenes
- MMF, MM, MFM, MF, MFMMM, and more
- poison
- assassination attempts
- alphahole/possessive MMCs
- cinnamon roll MMCs
- bargains made by asshole Fae
- slightly unhinged chaotic MMC
- unhealthy coping mechanisms
- spoiled, selfish gods, goddesses, and royalty
- extremely aggressive boundaries
- group sex
- age gap (from 10 yrs to immeasurable)

- weird Fae drugs and tricks
- magically enhanced sex
- oral sex
- anal sex
- DVP
- BDSM
- raw sex
- shifted sex
- breeding kink (talk, not actual attempts)
- traumatic childhood
- alcohol use and abuse
- threats of bodily harm
- death
- body modifications
- mile high sex
- fancy genitalia
- side character death
- mate knots/barbs
- the goddamn Fates meddling
- bullying (in person and on social media)
- PTSD
- blood
- emotional abuse from outside poly group
- body dysmorphia
- adult language
- pop culture references
- literary references
- emotional manipulation
- power play
- adorable nicknames
- physical intimidation
- emotionally abusive/manipulative parents (MMCs)
- voyeurism
- rough sex
- wings/tails/horns/magic in sex
- masturbation play
- markings/tattoos
- Easter egg character cameos from other series in the universe
- lawyers (ugh, but Jackson is a doll)

- family dysfunction
- super awesome BFF and her poly group
- animal companions
- absolute disrespect for shitty parents
- brief mentions of non-body positive dieting culture
- brief mentions of parental death
- very liberal re-imagining of history
- ancient secret society who only cares about bigger picture
- official corruption
- discussion of arranged marriages
- name calling
- occasional misogyny
- shitty mothers
- absent fathers
- exhibitionism
- hand necklaces
- adult bullying
- magical kinks
- winged sex
- clawed sex
- discussion of parent in mental health facility
- visit to a mental health facility
- parent with mental health issue on page
- impact play
- elitism
- bribery
- corpses
- fat shaming (not by MCs)
- drama
- physical threats to FMC and others
- species-ism

No sexual practices in this book should be taken as safe or appropriate for real life application.

Content information is important and I don't ever want to harm a reader with inaccurate information.

Stalk Cassandra Featherstone in the Dark Corners of the Web

Join my Facebook group and follow me everywhere!

Want More?

Sign up for my bi-weekly

manifesto for
a free series sampler:

*Join my Ream as a **FREE** follower or exclusive subscriber to get access to cover reveals, WIPs, Serial Stories, and personal chats from me!*

CASSANDRA FEATHERSTONE
QUEEN OF SWORDS, FRESH SPICE

Reader's Note
A few things you should know...

Healing the Hollow contains books 2-3.5 (Realizations in the Hollow is 3.5 and cannot be found outside of this omnibus.)

The world in which our characters live is set up in those books and you will be very confused if you do not read them. This is technically book ***five*** in the series, but I write dummy *thicc* books and they will not fit in a single omnibus. Books 4-5.5 will appear in another omnibus (hopefully, this next winter) to complete the series.

The series is planned to have five ***whole*** books and several ***bonuses and gap novels***. I always recommend reading those because they often contain info you'll want later on.

This is a multi-book series, so *everything will not be revealed at once*. Some plot lines will continue through series in a larger arc and not get resolved in the first or even the third book.

I write lengthy books with intricate world building, strong character development, and *lots* of tiny threads that stretch throughout a series that may not always seem important at first glance. However, I promise nothing I put to paper and leave in the book is unimportant; it may simply become *more* important later on. There is no 'throw-away' detail in my worlds, so every scene will mean something eventually.

I promise it will all get tied up and have a HEA; don't worry!

Healing in the Hollow is a why choose/poly romance, which means our FMC will not have to choose.

I would consider it a medium burn, slow build family group. It will continue to get spicier in the following books. If you're looking for porn with little to no plot, no judgment, but this isn't the series for you. It's also not closed door or FTB, so I believe the spice will be worth the wait. I realize spice scales are subjective and everyone has different opinions on it, so forgive me if mine and yours aren't totally aligned.

There are some characters and creatures that speak in other languages. I made the *translations clickable end of chapter notes* to help.

There are some words that are slang, jargon, or foreign that may seem to be spelled wrong—*please email the author or find her on social media rather than report to Amazon* if you think something is wrong. This has been proofed and edited *several* times since release; if you believe you found errors, you may not be correct. It could be a stylistic choice or a dialect choice. Please do not assume the two ARC teams, betas, alphas, and several proofers missed everything you believe is incorrect. Contact me if you find things; I want to make sure it doesn't get taken down so everyone can read!

If you see this book *anywhere besides major retailers or my website in ebook format*, please reach out to me via social media or email. Pirating kills my ability to write full time and I am so grateful for your help.

Contact Cass for issues or to report piracy: teamcassandra@cassandrafeatherstone.com

Author Ramblings

Readers, your love for our sassy Southern woman is beyond amazing.

As I said in the last note, there are Easter eggs for those of you who are inclined to read the heavier PNR/SFF series *Rise of the Resistance* and some for *Villains & Vixens*, but if you don't, those references won't leave you behind the curve.

Jolene will encounter more obstacles and enemies in *Revenge in the Hollow*, but for now, I've brought you a lovely omnibus that includes *Rejected in the Hollow*, *Revealed in the Hollow*, and a **new, full-length novel** *Realizations in the Hollow*.

As usual, I've done a lot of research and added quite bit of mythology, depth, and information to my rich world. Hopefully, you enjoy seeing a point of view you didn't get in the previous books.

Thank you to everyone who has read and recommended on Facebook, Instagram, TikTok, on Goodreads, and on Amazon. Your recs in groups and continued support help me get closer to my indie muppet dream of going full time.

In a world where there are hidden pitfalls and people that smile to your face and slide the knife in your back when you aren't looking, I want to thank my author besties who support me every day, my PA, my street/ARC team, and all the others who chat and help me every day.

Finding true support that doesn't require me to give up part of myself has been a goddess blessed event. I feel more and more like the confidence I had when I first entered this genre has returned and the abuse that caused me to falter is fading.

For that, I can never repay you.

However, I never give up and I never back down, so I'm going to be here with silly puns and smart FMCs who aren't afraid to show how big their hearts, libidos, *and* brains are.

Enjoy the world of the genteel South where the women—like me—are filled with *sugar, spice, and steel.*

Blood and guts,

Cassandra Featherstone
QUEEN OF SMART, SASSY SPICE

A Note To My Loving Family Members and Their Friends...

THANK YOU for supporting me by buying this book!

It appears I have to simply warn y'all for forever and forever, amen.

I'm still getting sneaky little questions to which I send response links and put my hands in the air in supplication that I won't have to answer further.

Stop that.

Now, Goddess willing and the creek don't rise, I may have gotten into through our thick Southern skulls that it is NOT appropriate table conversation.

If not, I'm gonna crack some heads.

CAVEAT: If you choose to keep reading, know that at no time will I explain terms, positions, themes, tropes, or any other part of this novel at family events, in group chats, or on social media.

DON'T ASK.

Rejected in the Hollow Playlist

CHAPTER TITLE SONGS

Rejected in the Hollow Chapter Playlist

BONUS PLAYLIST

The Hollow European Travel Playlist

Revealed in the Hollow Playlists

CHAPTER TITLE SONGS

Revealed in the Hollow Playlist

BONUS PLAYLIST

Fucking Fae Playlist

Healing in the Hollow Playlist

CHAPTER TITLE SONGS

Realizations in the Hollow Chapter Playlist

*Sweet girl,
you control the vibes
that occupy your space.
Don't be afraid
to open a few windows
and let the trash take itself out.*

~Stephanie Bennett-Henry

WAIT!

My series typically have prequels, gap novellas/novels, and bonus material that are integral to your having a satisfying reading experience.

If you have not read the other pieces in this series, you may feel as though you have missed critical details, developments, plot points, and other information. This will cause the book to appear to have continuity gaps that it does not have.

If you have not read the bonus material for this series, it is available online here, in audio versions (if applicable), and in print special editions (if applicable).

I highly recommend consulting the bonus page prior to reading this new title so you're up to speed on all the things going on in this world.

Happy reading!

RICH PEOPLE
NEIGHBORHOOD

CITY HALL
MAYOR NELIA'S HOUSE

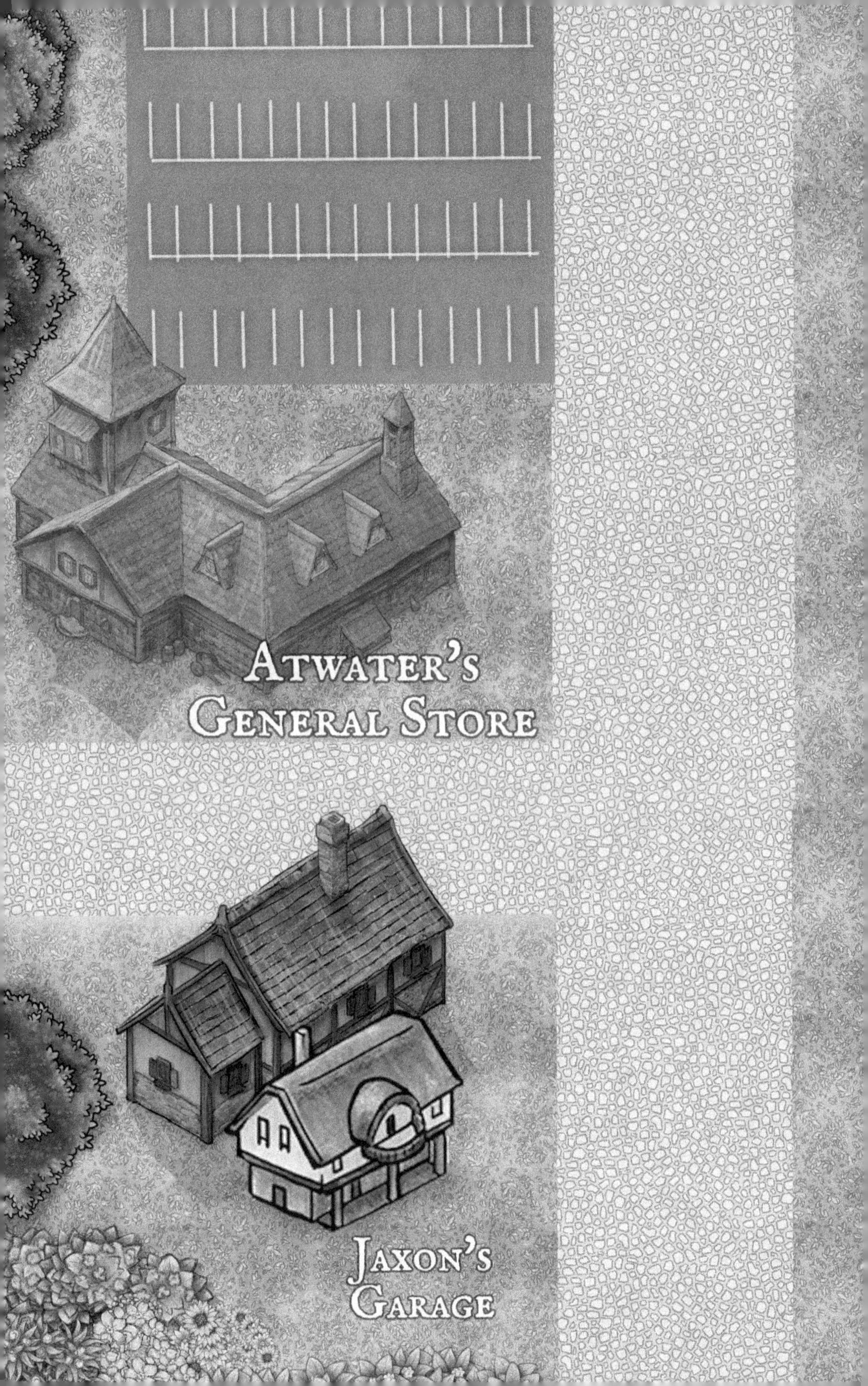

Atwater's General Store
Jaxon's Garage

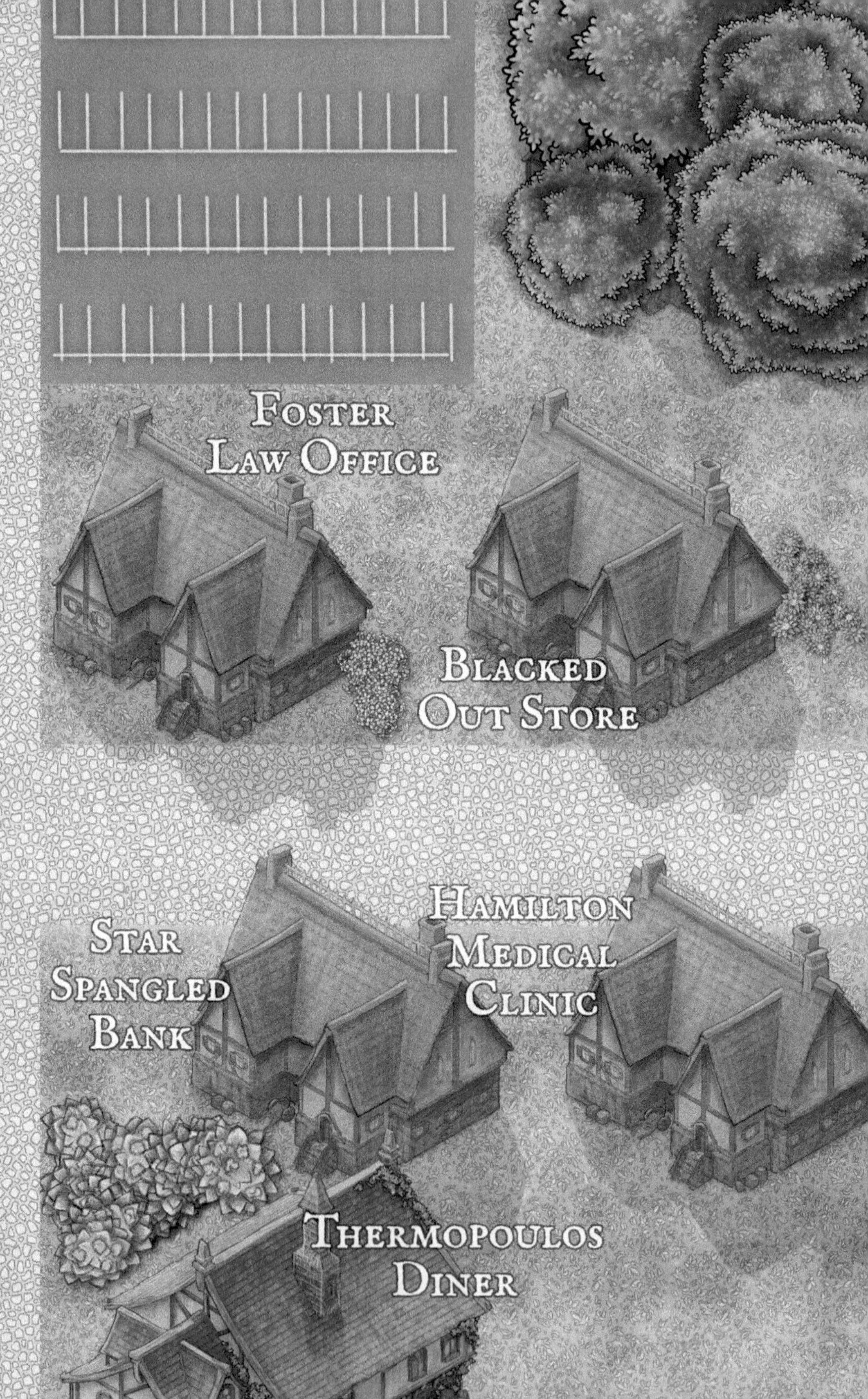

Foster
Law Office
Blacked
Out Store
Star
Spangled
Bank
Hamilton
Medical
Clinic
Thermopoulos
Diner

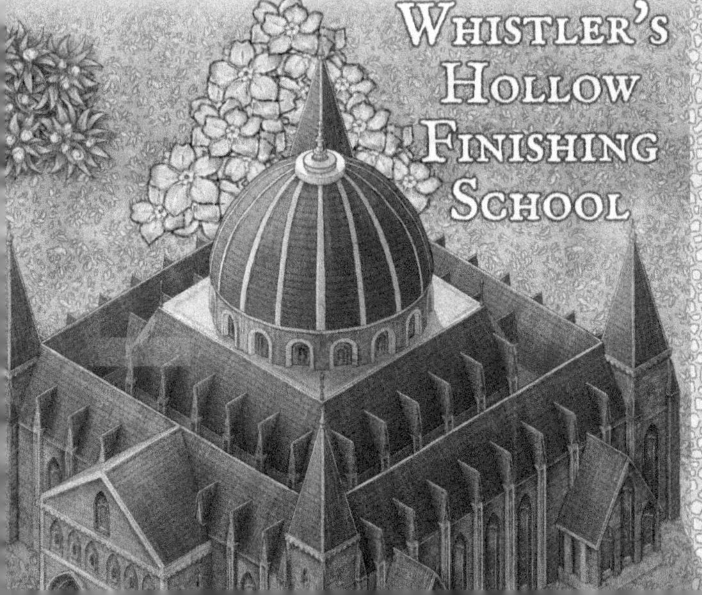

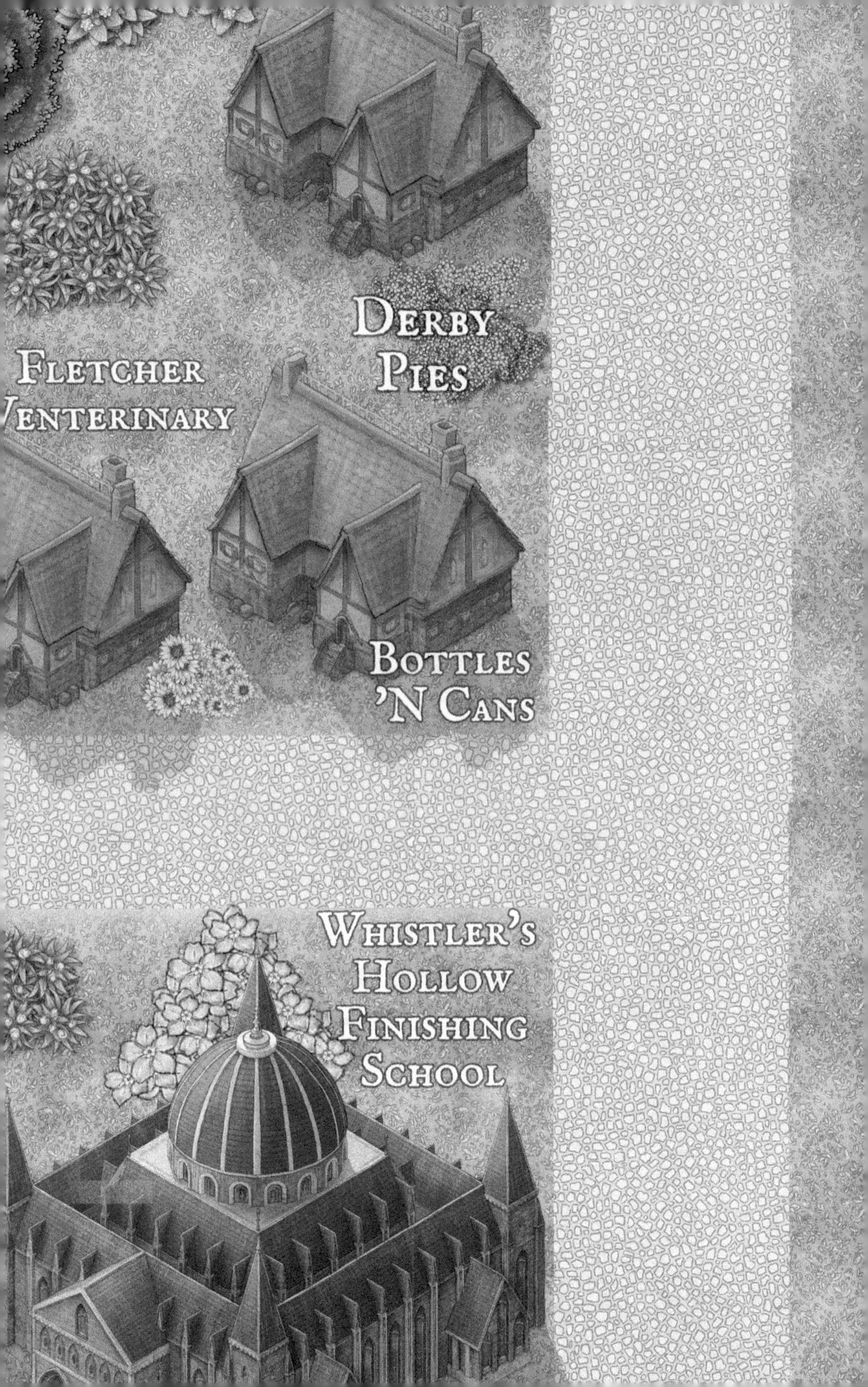

Fletcher Venterinary
Derby Pies
Bottles 'N Cans
Whistler's Hollow Finishing School

GRANT HOME FURNISHINGS
WILD ASTOR PLANTS
DRESS ME UP BUTTERCUP
WHITLEY GALLERY
WHISTLER'S HOLLOW PARK

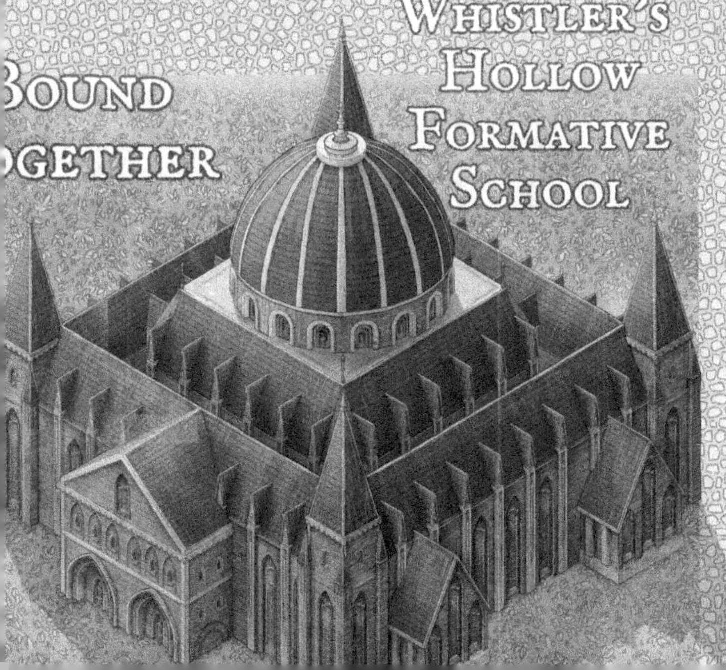

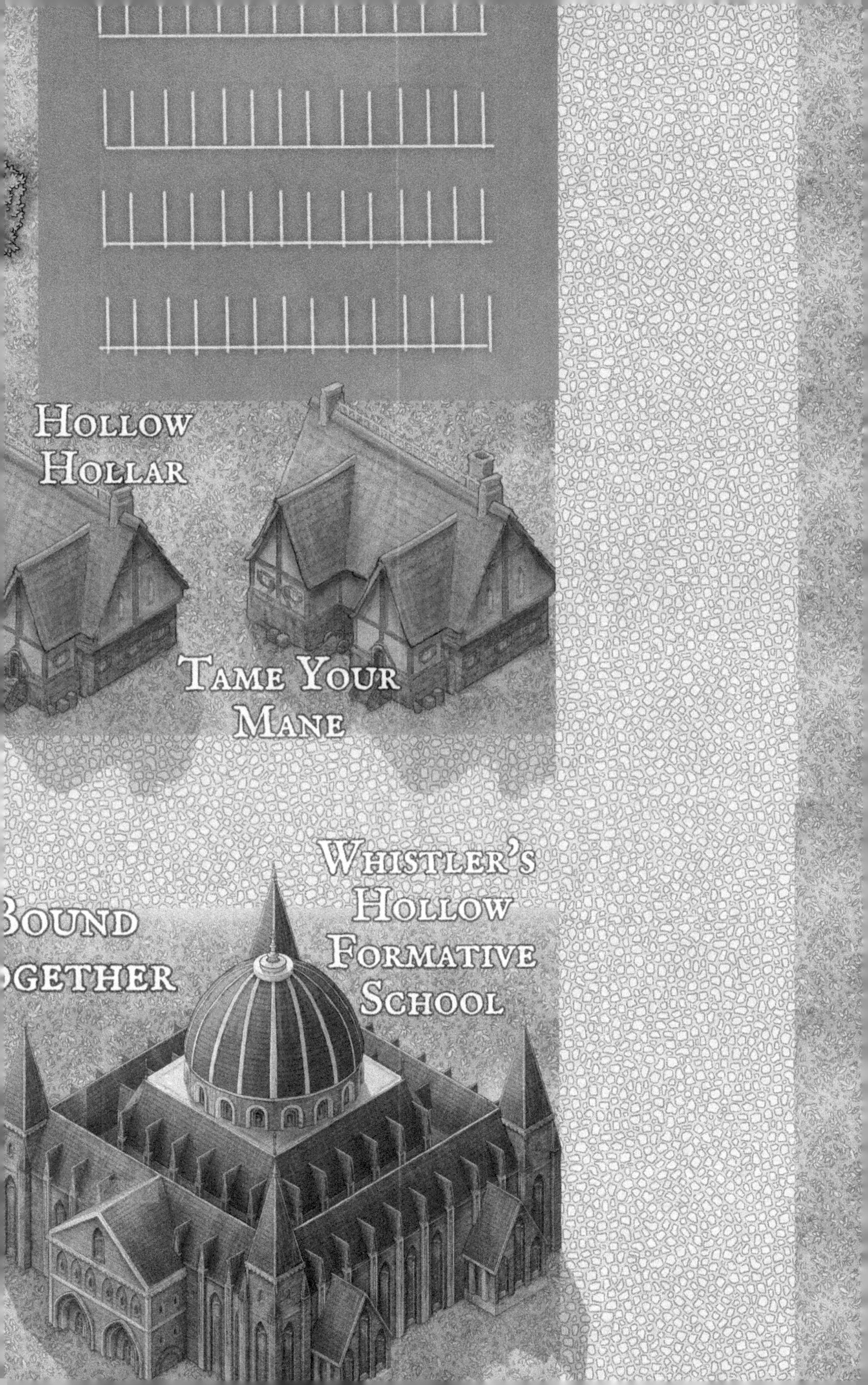

HOLLOW
HOLLAR

TAME YOUR
MANE

BOUND
TOGETHER

WHISTLER'S
HOLLOW
FORMATIVE
SCHOOL

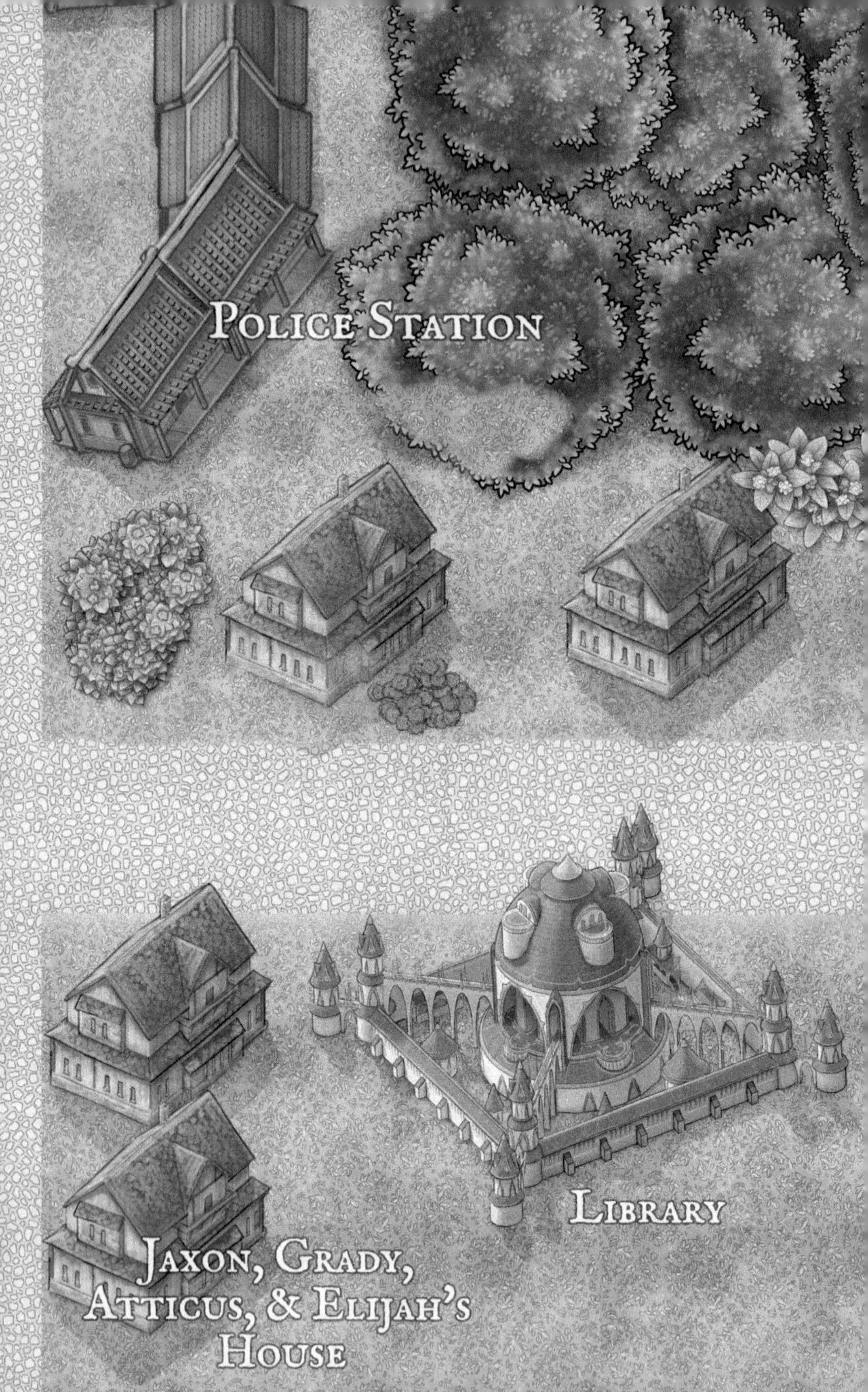

POLICE STATION
LIBRARY
JAXON, GRADY, ATTICUS, & ELIJAH'S HOUSE

LORELEI'S
HOUSE
LONGWORTH
FAMILY
MORTUARY

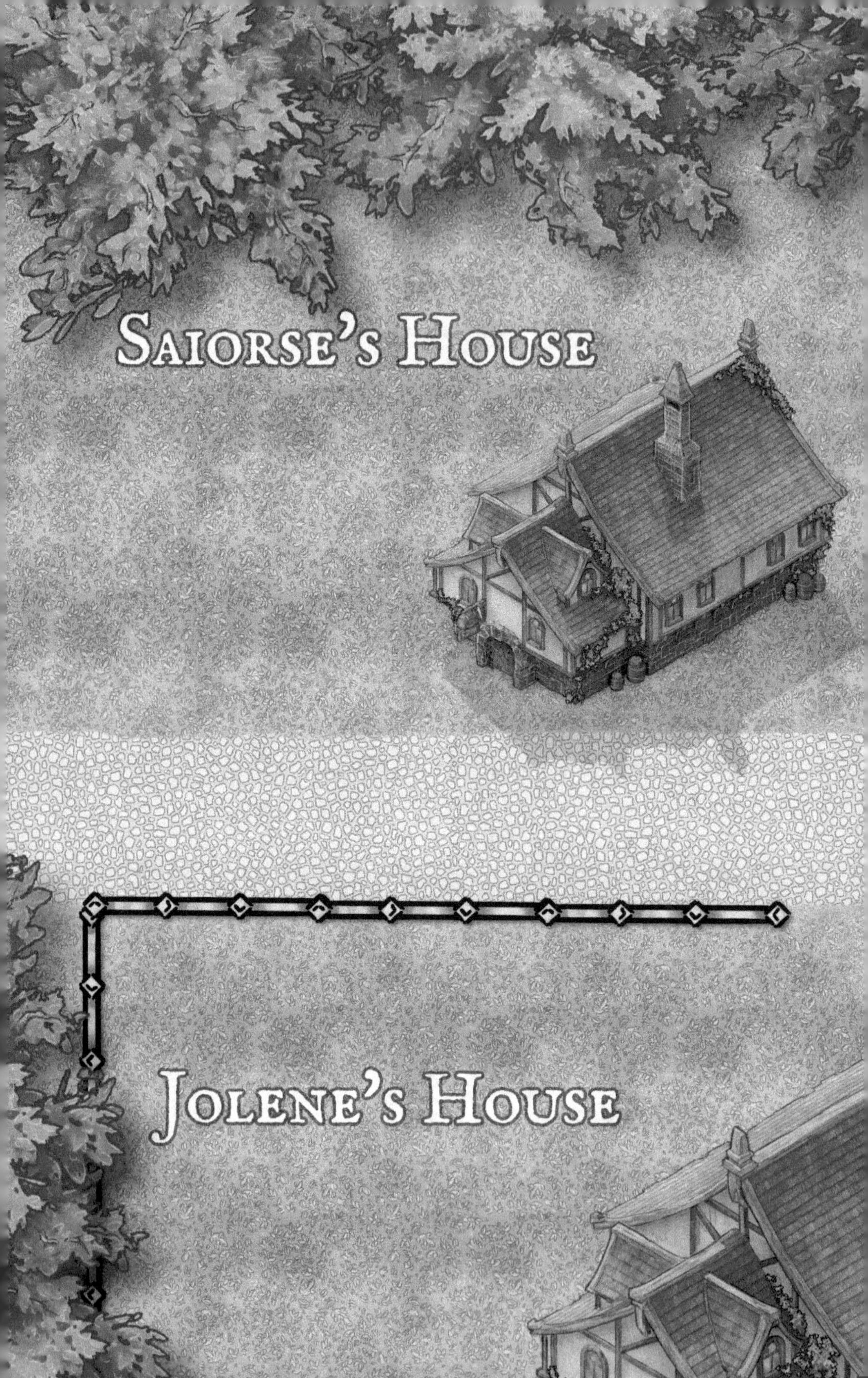

Saiorse's House
Jolene's House

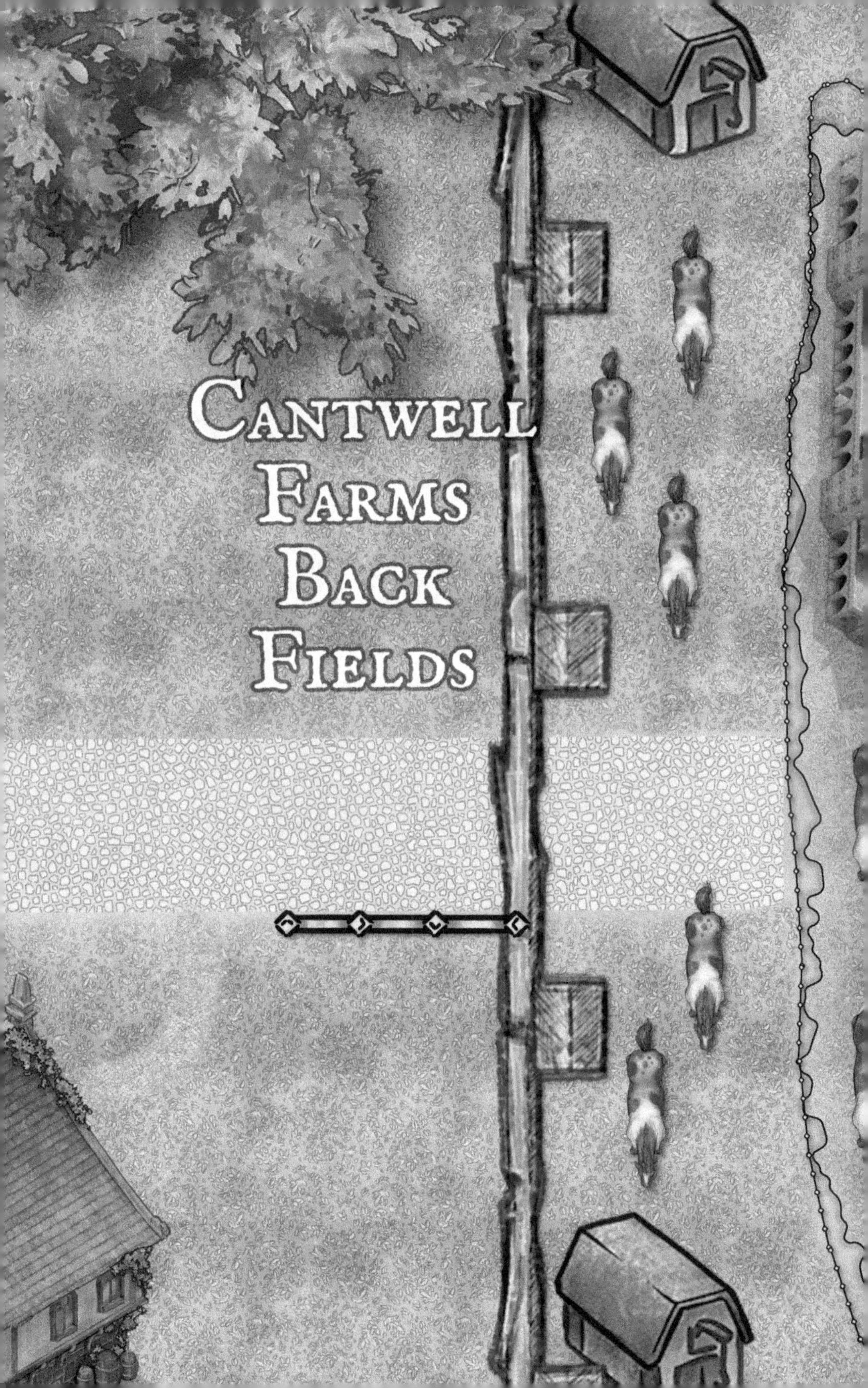

Cantwell
Farms
Back
Fields

REJECTED

FAMILY ISN'T JUST BLOOD

IN THE

IT'S WHO YOU CHOOSE TO WATCH YOUR BACK

HOLLOW

INTERNATIONAL BESTSELLING AUTHOR

CASSANDRA FEATHERSTONE

I Knew You Were Trouble

Jolene

The silver-haired woman walks in slowly, her brow arched as she notes my raised fists. I don't look very threatening in a hospital gown and connected to tubes and wires, but cornered animals are the most dangerous.

"I'm not a threat. Not to you or your friendship with my girl," Julia says softly. She continues moving closer, making certain I can see her hands.

I'll be damned if she gets to see how terrified I am about this situation.

I snort, raising my chin. "Tell me something I don't know."

"You will not get the answers you want yet. It's going to piss you off and you'll have to make peace with it. We all know that."

Blinking, I gape at her. She's as blunt as I am and in this situation, I appreciate it. No wonder they sent her instead of Seer or one of the guys—Julia has no intention of coddling me. I drop my dukes in my lap and jerk my head at the chair next to the bed. "Fine. Have a seat and tell me why I'm going to be angry."

To my surprise, she complies without an argument. Propping her elbows on her knees, she looks at me with a serious expression. "Jolene, there's so much you don't know and much of it, I cannot share with you. Your men and our girl are similarly bound by rules and obligations so deeply woven into our beings that you cannot comprehend them."

"Oh, please. If this is some Southern Skull & Bones shit, I'm not buying it. Whatever happened at the ball put me in a fucking hospital and I'm not even sure which one or how much time has passed. I don't have 'clearance' will not cut it."

Not to mention my heart is splintering into pieces as we talk. I haven't let *anyone* besides Seer in since Trevor until I came home and now look where I am. Everyone I care about is lying to me and I'm hashing it out with someone I've only met a few times. I'm so numb that all I can access is the fury inside of me, burning like a righteous sword held by an angel.

"Whoa!" Julia holds her hand out in a 'stop,' gesture. "Whatever you were just thinking, you need to *calm down.*"

Who the hell does she think she is telling me how to feel?!!

My joints ache, and my heartbeat speeds up, blood thumping in my veins like fire. I've felt like this before, but it's part of yet another memory I can't access. A primal scream rips from my throat as I bury my hands in my hair and yank, unable to bear all the emotions assaulting me at once.

"Jolene, control your anger. Feel the waves and soothe them. Picture the fury as a red ball and gather it up, then cup it in your hands. When you're holding it, the colors will fade…"

The soothing voice penetrates the haze in my mind and I follow the instructions, forcing myself to get a grip on the feelings that seem to engulf me. I breathe slowly, closing my eyes as Seer's girlfriend continues murmuring to me, and after a few minutes, my brain reactivates. I've never felt anything like this and no doctor or shrink has ever pulled me back from a blackout.

She's a fucking wizard, that's what.

"How… how did you do that?" I ask shakily. My eyes open and I look at Julia in shock. "No one has ever kept me from going into the blackness—not even Andromeda."

Raking a hand through her rainbow highlights, she shrugs. "I've had a lot of training. Hard cases are a specialty of mine."

I frown, lying back against the pillows. My body feels beaten and bruised, but I don't see any visible marks. The ache is bone deep, though, and it's why I haven't tried to get out of the bed and leave. "Where am I, Julia? How did I get here? You have to be able to tell me that much."

She nods, settling back once she realizes I'm calm. "You're at State U Medical Center in a private wing. When you… blacked out… after Antigone showed up, you got transported here. The entire group followed, and we've been here ever since."

"Jesus. How long was I out this time?" The room doesn't have windows and I can't get a read on the passage of time. Julia looks rumpled, but she's not in her costume.

"Five days," she murmurs. "Zasha and Tharin went out to get supplies for us after the first night. Clothes, toiletries… all that shit. I couldn't get any of your men or Saoirse to leave the waiting area. Your sweet vet had to be sent to pee; he was that inconsolable."

My chest tightens at the mention of Wolfie, and I have to turn my head and bite my lip. If I keep thinking about their betrayal, I'm going to cry and I do *not* cry in front of people. But the pain is slicing through my soul like a hot knife through butter and my eyes sting with unshed tears.

I trusted them instinctively, and I was wrong.

"Jolene, they all care deeply about you. I daresay they love you, even if some of them haven't realized it yet." I don't turn around, nor do I answer, so Julia continues. "Everyone has secrets. We all have things we aren't ready or able to share, even with loved ones. The reason your family hasn't told you everything is because people have died for breaking this vow."

The rage bubbles up again, competing with the sorrow for domination. Her excuses aren't helping and I still know next to nothing about what happened to me. Whirling around, I glare at her.

"Julia, I don't give a flying pig's balls about anyone's vow. You *all* have information I do not and it's about *me*. I don't know if it explains why

I black out or what's wrong with me, but I'm never going to be okay with being lied to."

She steeples her fingers and nods, looking pensive. "That's fair. It would frustrate anyone in your place. I won't justify their actions, but I *can* tell that you won't be able to resist hearing them out."

This woman has lost her goddamn mind.

"I have no interest in hearing lies. I hope you have a lot of room for houseguests. Stock up on groceries," I mutter. "My house is a no-fly zone from now on."

She sighs. "I can't tell you why that's an incredibly poor decision, but if need be, I'll accept the burden."

"Why? Why is it bad? You admit my best friend and the men I… they're *all* lying to me! They have no plans to stop, according to you, until some mythical moment when everything will become clear. What about that makes my decision to hold them accountable wrong?"

"Shit. Dancing in the fire," Julia says as she rolls to her feet and paces across the room. "It is not wrong to want those who have behaved poorly to make amends for their actions. However, it is very difficult to maintain that distance, regardless of what your mind wants."

Arching a brow, I cross my arms over my chest. "I'm pretty sure I can live without jumping anyone's bones, especially when they refuse to admit they're hurting me."

Her eyes widen as she stares at me. "Hades' bells, Jolene! They *know* it hurts you; every single one of them is beating their own ass over it. Taking responsibility isn't the issue here."

Is she kidding me? They know and I'm supposed to forgive them?

"I don't… I don't even know how to respond to that."

Stalking over to the wall, Julia puts her hand on it and leans in. "I think they need to talk to you themselves. Whether they wanted or meant to hurt you, Seer and your men need to make their amends for their errors. You won't be able to see this clearly until they apologize for betraying your trust."

"No shit, Sherlock." I huff the sarcasm at her with bite, but inside, I know she's right. If I'm ever going to get past this, I need them all to admit they were assholes and apologize. I can't even comprehend forgiveness until they admit what they did was wrong.

When she turns back to me, the silver-haired woman gives me a sheepish grin. "That's the spirit. No one said having a good reason for behaving badly prevents you from being angry. You have every right to feel hurt and betrayed."

"Thanks for giving me permission," I grunt. "But it doesn't change the fact that you've clarified that the lying won't stop. How am I supposed to look at my friends or… lovers… when I know they aren't being honest? How can I trust them with anything else?"

"I can't answer that for you, Jolene. I can only tell you that your family would tell you if it didn't put them or you in imminent danger. And I don't mean 'get fired' danger—I mean death and disfigurement."

How is that even possible?

I close my eyes, trying to sort through all the emotions coursing through me. After Trevor, I swore I would never allow anyone to abuse my trust in that way again. I was young and naïve, too starry-eyed, to pay attention to all the giant red flags waving around him. Until the ball, I didn't know the woman he cheated with was Antigone. I was too mired in self-pity after he broke up with me to even ask who he'd left me for.

I don't know if I can let these people lie to me every day and not relive that trauma.

"Did the 'special guest' leave after I…" I open my eyes and look at her, pushing the revulsion down.

Her laugh echoes off the walls. "Oh, she definitely left. I don't know if she'll stay gone or if you have a new enemy to contend with when you get home. I have sequestered us far from that mess while we waited for you to awaken."

"Where do I go from here? Am I even able to leave? Have the doctors cleared me?"

"Well, *your* doctors haven't, but the staff here have. No one was allowed in until we checked you from head to toe. I have clothes for you and your animals are waiting outside, just as anxious as your men."

Why the hell didn't she start with that?

"Bring me the clothes and let the animals in—and *only* the animals. I want out of here."

"Aye, aye, Captain," she mutters.

This is going to be a fun ride home, I can tell.

Don't Give Up On

Edgar

My *drugar*[1] is not speaking to any of us and she rode home with the pixie's tribe and her animals. Before our girl came out of the room, Julia warned us that the truth did not sway her. Our idea of sending her to smooth the waters didn't work as well as we'd hoped.

The hound is howling inside and I feel like tearing something to pieces.

"She knows we don't have a choice, right?" Wolfie whispers from the back seat.

The pup is wrapped in the doc's arms, looking about as fragile as I've ever seen him. It makes the beast inside of me growl louder and I slam my palm on the steering wheel in frustration. Benjy tilts his head at me from his seat at shotgun, his eyes knowing. My old friend recognizes when I'm struggling with one of my sides, but I've never felt it this keenly before.

My other sides are eerily silent and I don't know what that means, but it's not good.

"Lucy, she just needs some time. It will be okay," Prez murmurs as he strokes his hair.

Doyle is quiet for once, but he sighs and nods. "Aye. Knowing you're the only person who's on the outside and you can't come in is hard on the psyche."

"It's going to take longer than any of you think," Saoirse whispers. She's crunched between Prez and Doyle, looking about as miserable as a person can. "Because of Trevor, yeah? That right arsehole tore her to pieces and this will reawaken that dragon."

"Dragon? That guy from the dance? No way," Benjy mutters. "He smelled human."

Saoirse snorts and shakes her head. "You're right—sort of. Of course, Peanut had no idea, but once she told me about her days at State U, I did my diligence. He's a low level mage from a moderately wealthy family in another state."

"Our girl deserves better than a tool like that," I growl. "He couldn't even look her in the eye *before* she shifted."

Presley grins at me in the rearview mirror. "If only she could remember it, we'd be golden. It was majestic—a perfect shift for such a newly emerged supe."

I nod, feeling the fire within spark as I recall. "The way she pinned that witch that betrayed her in high school was hotter than shit. Almost hotter than doing it myself."

"Antigone is the one who stole Trevor at SU," Seer says. "Jolene might have let go of the high school bullshit and made peace with her if not for the targeted campaign to steal her fiancé. Those queen bees from high school packed their bullshit up with their dorm supplies."

I was too busy drinking and fucking my way through sorority row to notice what Sherilynn and her cronies were up to.

"Don't beat yourself up, Edgar. It wasn't your job to monitor those harpies."

"That's true," Wolfie finally speaks again. "None of us can change what happened in the past. If we want to fix this, we have to go to Sugarplum by ourselves and own up to our mistakes. It's not her responsibility to come to us; we fucked up by not starting this conversation sooner."

Doyle sighs dramatically and thumps his head on the seat. "Can't we just fuck it out of each other? Hate sex is not only cathartic but calorie burning."

The sound of multiple fists hitting skin followed by a yelp makes me grin a little. "As appealing as rough, angry group activities sound, I don't think that will get us out of the doghouse. No pun intended."

"Who's going first?" Seer asks as she leans forward. "We'll be on our own, regardless, because Peanut will not let anyone make excuses for anyone else. She's got boundaries for days after that quack in London hypnotized her."

"I'm sorry… what?"

The tiny woman looks guilty for a moment when she realizes she's accidentally betrayed a confidence. "We were visiting one of her mates from 6 and she had a big episode. She was out for two weeks that time and when she woke up, she went to see this 'hypnotist to the stars' that one of our clients recommended at an embassy party. Her reasoning was if doctors couldn't fix her, maybe voodoo woohoo— her words, not mine—could."

"There are so many questions; I don't even know where to start," Prez grumbles. "Was this guy for real? Did you go with her? Was there any change? What was his name? Did you report it to the Society?"

Seer shakes her head, looking even more rueful. "I figured *she* was a fraud, so I didn't write it up. You know celebrities—always trying some hoaxster garbage and it was this hot rock star who told her so… I noticed nothing worth mentioning. She didn't have another fit, but they come and go. Her blackouts were unpredictable until she came here. Now they seem triggered by stress."

"Jaysus, woman! Didn't it occur to you this might be important? What if this chit was an empath or a witch or some version of a mind-bender? I can think of a dozen beings that would take joy in spreading chaos by fucking with an unemerged supe's head!"

Doyle's right. As much as I hate to admit it, it's entirely possible that part of why her emergence is blocked is because of this mystery hypnotist.

"Seer, do you have any idea who this woman was? Her name, or maybe who recommended her? It seems extremely coincidental that

Tilly has a block created by some major magic no one recognizes and she had a private visit with some con artist a couple years ago." I frown, considering the possibilities Doyle tossed out a moment ago.

The Guardian scratches her head, pondering for a second. "Dionysus, help me. We were partying so much with so many feckin' celebs back then… I might have to pull out some photo albums from storage and try to jog my memories. I know it was an embassy party because we wore the naked swoosh dresses that night."

"The… what?" Benjy almost chokes, and I have to cover a laugh.

"They did it up like fashion as an art—a Met gala rip-off theme. I designed these bloody *hot* dresses that—with a wee bit of magical help—were basically metallic swirls that crawled over the important bits, and not much else. Being as my girl is curvaceous and not a stick like me, she drew a *lot* of attention, hence the rock star."

The growl escapes before I can stop it, and everyone laughs. I know it was years ago and I have no right, but my imagination is running wild. Jolene running around encased in some mystical metal goddess garb is sexy as fuck. "I have a feeling poking through your albums is going to make all of us crazy."

She snorts, shaking the wild braids around her head. "You have *no* idea, doggy. Peanut's secrets aren't as world shattering as ours, but she spent five years as part of the glitterati in ways none of you are ready for. It's how she healed after that fuckwit destroyed every ounce of confidence she had left after you and your friends stomped her in high school."

"Then it sounds like we need to make a trip to your place to find these albums before we go home," Doyle says. "To the dragon's den, doggy!"

I suck in a calming breath, trying not to let my temper get the best of me. The question has to be asked, though I'm fairly certain I know the answer—and I *hate* it. "Where are we going after we pick them up? I assume we're not welcome in our current abode."

"Definitely not. She won't even look at us, much less allow us to live there right now," Wolfie murmurs sadly.

Prez finally loses his cool. "I *knew* we should have talked about this sooner. Our place is being renovated for the new offices already."

Grimacing, I nod. "Same. Repairs and upgrades for the sale. Fucking elf-infested at the moment."

"Christ on a cracker, you're all pathetic. Since the pixie has a place to go, you eejits can come to mine. I'm not happy about it, though."

I'll be damned. The prickly asshole didn't even give us hell.

"Then it's settled. We get Saoirse's old books and take them to whatever this nut job calls a home. Maybe if we can understand what happened between the Catastrophe and now, we can figure out how to fix the mess we made."

Nᴏɴᴇ ᴏꜰ ᴜs ᴇxᴘᴇᴄᴛᴇᴅ ᴛʜɪs——ɪᴛ's ꜰᴜᴄᴋɪɴɢ sᴜʀʀᴇᴀʟ.

We stopped at Saoirse's house to pick up ten boxes of shit she swears may have insight into their time in Europe first. Then we headed for Doyle's house with an eerie quiet falling over us. I'm not sure if it's because of the weight of what's happened hit or because we don't have the slightest inkling of how to fix the mess without making it worse. That all changed when we pulled up to a normal-looking Southern house just outside the end of town, opposite from where everyone else lives.

Doyle rolled out of the car and whistled, calling the spooky raven he calls Odie, and turned to us as if he was going to say something. Instead, he grinned and muttered, "Fuck it."

It seemed like his subsequent departure was our cue to move, so we did.

I almost ran into the idiot as he stood in front of his door, looking at it but not touching the knob. He ignored my grumbling protests until the rest of the crew followed, and then waved his hand in an intricate pattern in the air.

That's when a goddamned portal opened instead of a door.

When we stepped through it, we were in the middle of a Classical Greek temple style entryway full of columns and marble. His bird took off to sit on an ornate golden perch above the arch in front of us, squawking like it was auditioning for a fucking Poe poem. No one knew what to say——every single mouth was dangling open.

Finally, I grabbed the dipshit by the shirt and let the hound out a little. "*What. The Fuck. Is. This?*"

"It's my home, you furry arsehole. I'll thank you for not assaulting me since I'm being so kindly by letting you stay here."

Words escape me, but luckily, the Irish lass untangles her tongue. "You feckin' bastard! This… You live in a Bloody Mary Poppins portal!"

Doyle smirks. "Aye."

"What's a Mary Poppins portal?" Wolfie steps around Prez, gravitating to my side, and I immediately feel the calm rush over us both.

"It's not real. It's some sort of glamor. These don't exist," Prez mutters. "I mean, not unless…"

The red-headed jackass rolls his eyes, waiting for us to get on the same page.

"Unless he's a son of a whoring *deity*!" Seer shouts as she stomps over to him. She pokes him in the chest with her finger, a ripple of energy filling the air as armor and scales cover her body. It riled both of her sides, and she's ready to pull the sword from the scabbard at her waist when I finally put the pieces together.

"Stop." Jolene's best friend whirls on me, glaring at me with the slitted eyes and golden glow of her people. "He's not a deity."

"*Explain the bloody temple then, Edgar!*"

I ruffle Wolfie's hair when he presses closer and then shrugs. "At least, not fully. He's a dirty hybrid, like most of us. Prez excluded, of course."

Doyle claps, his eyes full of merriment. "Very good, Judge! Although, much like young Wolfgang, I don't have a clue who dear old dad is. My mum is disinterested in me on a good day and despises me on others. Withholding the info seems to be a thing for powerful mythical women, I suppose."

Wolfie flushes bright red and curls his head at the mention of his mother. I don't know much about the situation, but Prez looks murderous at the mere mention, so she must be worse than mine.

That's saying something.

Before any of us can blink, Seer puts her blade to Doyle's throat and hisses. "*Which. One?*"

I'll give him credit; he doesn't even blink. But I suppose being immortal makes threats a bit blasé. Lifting one hand, he pushed the blade away with a sigh and shakes his head. "I can't tell you—or anyone. Even Nelia doesn't know. My mission here wasn't ordered by my mother and the letter of law unfortunately states I can't reveal my heritage unless you find out on your own. Hence, bringing you here started a dialogue."

"Games. All you ever do is play games," I growl.

"That's my nature, doggy. Some say it comes from my father, but fuck if I would know. I only know it's not from within our own house, so to speak, or I wouldn't be the big secret that I am."

Interesting. He's clearly partially Greek—and ancient as hell probably—but whomever his mother did the deed with isn't from their pantheon.

"You're telling us a Greek goddess played slap and tickle with another being that she shouldn't have, and you ended up a hybrid?" Presley frowns and pushes his glasses up, but I can tell he's intrigued.

"Aye. You lot thought the only abandoned lost ones were shifters, fairy, and the like?" Doyle snorts and then laughs. "Fuck, no. My kind—of all them, not just the olive lovers—mess about like fools, too. Many of them broke ancient accords in doing so and I'm likely not the only mixed breed demi out there. But it's not like there's a club or handshake, so don't ask if I know any of them."

"It makes sense that any high level being caught coloring outside of the lines before the Society came about would cast the proof out. I'm sure that's what my mother and father did, though obviously more recently," Wolfie says softly.

Aw, fuck. I can feel the sadness radiating from him.

Leaning down, I press a kiss to the top of his head and wrap an arm around him. Prez smirks at me and I blink, unsure of why I felt I had to comfort him that way. It must be the mating thing—that's a whole other ball of wax we haven't had time to deal with properly. I glare at him before looking at the demigod in front of us.

"You know, this is going to be the hardest part for her."

His laugh is mocking. "No, she'll have others who will be more difficult to grasp; I promise."

"Right now, we need to figure out how to apologize and make her understand the limitations we have, not speculate on potential mates," Saoirse snaps. Sheathing her sword, she backs away from the idiot and her shift disappears like shimmering water. "Let's get to work, you eejits."

She's got a point. I don't plan on staying in this weird ass marble mausoleum for very long.

I Hate Boys

Jolene

"What the *fuck* were they all thinking?!"

I've been pacing a hole in the floor of my living room, tossing meatballs to the cats and dogs while Isis tries in vain to squeeze my panic into submission. The animals can sense my mood—none of them have misbehaved even a whit. Fury took off to hunt the minute we hit the driveway, and I stumbled into my house without a backward glance at Julia and her merry men. I simply *cannot* wrap my head around the fact that every single person I trusted—even Seer—has been lying to me from the beginning.

I had one fucking friend after Trevor—one.

Tears of both rage and pain leak from my eyes as I stomp around, yelling to the gods about the course of my life like a lunatic. I don't understand why I let any of them in when I *knew* caring about people *always* leads to heartbreak.

Seeing Trevor didn't hurt me like I thought it would—no, he and Antigone betrayed me long ago. The damage their betrayal did, however, *that* is ripping my chest apart. Antigone caused one of the worst traumas in my life—the Catastrophe—and for her encore, she destroyed what little I'd done at State U to rebuild myself. The most grating part of the situation is she *enjoyed* decimating my self-esteem and making me spiral out of control.

I don't know what I did to her in high school besides being her friend, but clearly, she wasn't the person I thought she was.

But her coup de grâce at college was pure evil, and I've never figured out if it was her own plan or if Sherilynn put her up to it. The allure of popularity and wealth certainly charmed my geeky friend; I don't know if it corrupted her entirely. That doesn't matter, though. Whatever goodness she offered died when she systematically pursued, fucked, and stole my fiancé for sport.

Now she's back with that wet napkin in tow, gloating like a true mean girl on her throne.

Adding her to the original group of snarky witches would have been bad enough. But I'm alone again—drifting on a sea of betrayal and lies from the people I was falling for and my best friend. I don't have a support system in place and I have no idea how I'm going to go to work tomorrow, much less walk around town.

How can I face all the people lurking in the background waiting for me to fail?

"What am I going to do, guys?"

Kali and Hecate put their heads on their paws, letting out mournful doggy noises. I turn to Jekyll and Hyde, who sit up tall, their carriage haughty as they *'mow'* in response.

"Strut in like I own the place and ignore the women trying to bring me down?"

The affirmative sound from my cats tells me I understood.

Now I just have to figure out how to do *that.*

WALKING INTO THE SCHOOL THE NEXT DAY IS ONE OF THE HARDEST things I've had to do in a long time. I feel the eyes on me as I stride to the animal enclosure and even more on me as I push the front doors open with my head held high. I considered dressing up to bolster my confidence, but I nixed that idea fairly quickly.

I am who I have always been and I don't need to do anything to impress these closed minded assholes.

A warm tug inside of me tells me Teddy is nearby, but I keep moving towards my classroom without meeting any of the gazes of lookie-loos. They won't get me to break down or lash out today; I am prepared to weather whatever storms appear with grace and firm boundaries. No student or staff member is going to get the satisfaction of seeing the emotions roiling inside of me. None of them deserve it.

I'm almost to my studio when something flashes in front of my eyes. Stopping to put my hand on the wall, I steady myself enough to walk the ten feet I have left and slip inside. Closing the door quickly, I lean back against it as another wave of fire runs through me. It feels like it's seeking something and when I refuse to move, the flashes of memory spark behind my closed lids.

The smell of the night and ash. Bright moonlight and burning fire. Heat and cool breezes. Branches and brush touching me.

Muscles flexing as I run and run until I pause to let out a long, low sound that echoes off the hills. I hear birds screech and answering howls. Furry companions rub against me.

Every sense feels sharper and the smells… I can smell everything. There are several enticing scents I want so badly to follow until I find them, but my mind and my instinct are at war.

Frustration and anger flood me, making the fires burn hotter and higher around me.

Am I at a campfire? Is this a memory from my childhood?

It can't be. Nothing about how the world looks or feels is familiar—it's all so focused. Nothing has ever looked like this, especially at night.

The angry ball in the pit of my stomach loses patience and I take off into the darkness, heading for the forest. My soul is aching and part of me is fighting against my brain, trying to push me toward the scents that call to me, but I don't care.

Howling into the starry sky, I focus on the satisfaction of running free and being one with nature.

Suddenly, I snap out of it, gasping for breath as I look around the room. There's only an empty art studio and a soft knocking behind me. Putting my hand on my chest, I whirl around, sniffing the air as if I can smell what's coming. Of course, I can't, and I shake my head to clear it. I've never had waking dreams like that before now and it scares the living *shit* out of me.

Goddamn it, this shit has to happen when I have no one *to talk to or lean on.*

"Jolene? Jolene, are you in there? Is everything okay?"

Blinking, I have to stop and place the voice before I realize that it's Hugo. He has an odd habit of showing up at exactly the right moment and I don't know how he does it. "Uh, yeah. I was… uh, hold on. I'll open the door."

I scrub my shaking hands over my face, trying to gather myself, and when I feel like I can look somewhat normal, I open the door with a forced smile.

He tilts his head at me, studying my expression for a moment. "You don't seem okay. In fact, you look like you've seen a ghost. This place isn't haunted, to my knowledge, so what made you look so stricken?"

How do I answer that?

"I saw a mouse," I blurt out. "It scared me."

His brows furrow and his face goes from concerned to suspicious in a blink. "A mouse? Doesn't your bird eat stuff like that? You don't seem like the type to be worried about creepy crawlies."

Glaring at him briefly, I turn on my heel and head to my desk to organize my papers for the day. "It caught me off guard. Why were you creeping around my classroom? Come to ask about my humiliation in person rather than stare at me all day?"

"No," he says as he shuts the door behind him. "I actually came to see how you are. I know you were in the hospital for quite a while and now that you're back, I wanted to check on you."

Okay, that's a little sweet, especially coming from someone who looks so serious all the time.

"I'm coping." I shrug and look out the window. "That incident brought back some rather ugly wounds from the past that I thought I had healed. And it also shined a light on things that were unacceptable in my life recently, so it's a lot to process. Thank you for checking on me, though. No one else has."

Admitting that is actually the hardest part. I sent my friend and the guys away, but not even Niecy has been by the house to see how I'm doing.

He gives me a tiny smile. "That might have been Mayor Nelia's doing. After your entourage left for the hospital with you, she got up on stage and read the entire room the riot act. She said she wouldn't stand for this type of rude, childish behavior and we will not tolerate it at events in her town. Then she sent Antigone, the guy, and all the Harleys packing. There was also a mention of not bum rushing your house when you returned home because you would need space to process such a flagrant violation of decorum and boundaries."

My hand flies to my mouth, and I choke back a gasp. I assumed people were doing the old 'shun the embarrassment' thing from my youth, but Nelia has warned off even the people who might have supported me so I'd have time to sort myself out. I'm not sure if I'm grateful or aggravated that she didn't think I could handle the confrontation—but I know she meant well. Outside of the weird dreams that are now coming when I'm awake, space to breathe has been good for me.

"Oh. I suppose I can't be mad at the people who didn't come to check, then." I give him a sheepish look. "But you're in violation of her decree right now, aren't you?"

"I am. But I have a sixth sense for when I might be needed, and Mayor Nelia will understand." His eyes sweep over the projects in various stages of completion. "You have your students doing an impressionist unit?"

Beaming, I nod. "Monet is a personal favorite, though Dégas is a close second. When I'd visit Paris, I'd spend hours sketching at the *Musee D'orsay* or in his garden at Giverny. Pastels and watercolors, of course, but I love the emotion in them. And I can relate to things that look beautiful from far away and are a big mess up close."

Hugo laughs and the sound warms the ice in my chest a bit. His eyes twinkle as he looks at the canvasses again, studying them closely until he approaches one in the corner. "This. You did this one as an example."

"Good eye, Mr. MacAuley." I say as I join him in front of my large waterlily. "The Waterlilies are my favorites, though I'm surprised you picked it versus a couple of other students' versions."

"Your energy radiates from it." He steps closer and touches the edge of the canvas carefully. "There's sadness and loss, but also this infinite joy and yearning to be seen. It comes across in how you paint."

I arch a brow. "Uh, huh. You get all of that from a flower?"

Of course, I'm testing him. Good art always grabs you by the ovaries and tugs; I would accept no less from myself. But I want to hear more from him.

"I do. The brushstrokes, the colors, and the vibrancy… they all speak to the emotions you were feeling when you were creating it. It may be a flower on the canvas, but it's your heart in my senses," he replies as he turns to look at me.

His face is so earnest and guileless that my heart leaps and I *almost* breach the distance between us to kiss him. But before I do, a voice in my head whispers to me—it says I have other issues to clear up before I make decisions like this again. It would be unfair to cast them out for their mistakes and start something with Hugo, especially because I don't know he if he *also* knows this big stupid secret. So I back away, giving him a sad smile before I go back to my desk. "Thank you. I'm always appreciative when people compliment my art in such a lovely manner."

"Anytime, Jolene. If you need me, all you have to do is call." Hugo waves and heads for the door without another word. Disappointment is evident on his face, but I don't address it.

I've got enough men frowning at me at the moment; one more might send me off the deep end.

Numb

Presley

We've been stuck at Doyle's ostentatious abode for days and it feels like the only thing we've learned from going through Seer's boxes is that our girl was wild as fuck in Europe. Photos of the two of them at movie festivals, raves, galas, state dinners, and even a few in castles show a progression from an unsure graduate to a confident, take-no-prisoners type of woman. Seer really helped her heal and grow into the person she wanted to be, but along the way, they definitely made the most of Jolene's connections.

The judge looked like he was going to burst from his loungewear every time we hit snaps of them with guys; unfortunately, there were a *lot*. Girls, too, but that seemed to set him off less. Typical Southern jock upbringing has him frothing about random dudes when I'd bet the ranch Jolene was far more attached to women. But to his credit, the grumpy oaf is trying because Wolfie has snuggled him out of a fit every time. Hell, he even let me flank the other side of him and that's definitely progress. I'm actually amused as hell as I wait for him to figure out he's falling like a stone for my darling boy. The mating should have told him, but sweet Athena, he's dim with emotions.

What we *haven't found* are the pictures Seer mentioned of the rockstar Jolene cavorted around Italy with for a bit. That's the person who recommended the hypnotist and we need that link to figure out if it ties to the strength of her emergence spell. Clearly, the debacle at the ball shows she can shift into a hellhound form—whether she got that from Edgar or her true parents, we don't know. Since she still doesn't have a damned clue about our world, her spell is weakening, but not gone. She must have other sides like Wolfie and Edgar, but Seer says even her handlers don't know where Jolene appeared from.

That's suspicious, right? Usually, intakes at the enclaves have some information on species or parentage. They have ways of trying to find it out, don't they?

"Prez, pass me that album from Germany 2018," Edgar mutters as he sips his bourbon. "I'm finished with Spain 2017."

Seer grins broadly. "That's the year we ran with the bloody bulls. There were these triplets who—"

The glare Boone gives her forces me to smother a chuckle. Perhaps I spoke too soon about his irrational jealousy of the past. "You were so close to the enclave when you were in Tokyo in 2016. Did you find time off on your own to visit? My mentor still lives in the area despite being retired."

"No. Peanut and I were there for a fashion show and some big gaming thing she wanted to see. It was only a couple months after we met and she was still making a name for herself as a corporate consultant. We partied a lot, but we also took a fuck ton of meetings. Drove me batty because I don't speak Japanese, nor do I have the patience for sitting there and looking all *waifu* and agreeable."

Wolfie sits up, waving his album before I can reply. "I found pictures at a knighting ceremony. Sugarplum is standing with some guys who look like rock stars—or criminals, I can't decide which."

All four of us crowd around the book, looking at the pages as Wolfie points at the people. I tilt my head as I look, sighing. "I'm useless. I don't follow the big names, but I assume at least some of these people are famous because they're at a bloody royal family event."

"You think, Hamilton?" Doyle rolls his eyes. "This idiot offed himself two years ago. If it was him, we're shit out of luck. However, the other eight people are still kicking. Some of them are even still touring because this was pretty early in their careers." We all stare at him and he shrugs. "I like modern music. Much better than half the shit I've seen over the centuries in terms of being accessible."

"Okay. So Doyle may be a Swiftie and we think we have eight dudes to look into. We're going to have to put faces to these names, you know," Wolfie says as he leans back against Edgar's side.

"I know who they are!" Doyle stands and runs his hands through his hair. "All of you need to take me more seriously. I know I play about and enjoy the products of chaos, but I'm a good bit older than half of this town put together."

Seer rolls to her feet and sets the albums we finished aside. "Look, that might be the picture, but we need to meet again tomorrow night to finish the rest of these. We met over eight rock stars in the four years we flitted around the globe. There might be another handful of morons to look into before we're done. Since none of you have approached our girl yet, that means we have plenty of time to work on this."

My eyes narrow and I look at the valkyrie as she issues commands. "Would you like to tell us what happened when you spoke to her?"

"Oh, fine. I haven't, either. What the feck am I supposed to say? 'Sorry I lied about our totally *not* random meeting in Europe because they assigned me to you' and follow it up with why I can't explain about being assigned?" She digs her hands into her wildly streaked hair and groans. "I have *no idea* what to tell her, so I've avoided anywhere I think she'll show."

Edgar sighs and sits his glass down, leaning his forearms on his knees as he looks at all of us. "It's time for us to discuss our secrets, folks. The leprechaun over there might not give specifics, but we need to get used to admitting things we've kept secret for whatever reason before we approach my *drugar*. If we can't do that, we'll never be able to tell her the things we can actually share, much less what we can't."

I hate when that asshole is right.

"I'll start. Obviously, as the town physician, I'm a caladrius. My people are secretive and tight-knit because otherwise we become the targets of bounty hunters. When the Society places us in enclaves like the Hollow, we are safe because of the amount of supes in town who can help protect us. The entire population of caladrii live in a hidden village that no outsiders may know about or visit. Parents send their children to schools and mentors recommended by the snakes until they go to medical school. For our own protection, we are a pipeline for enclave doctors and nothing else."

Even my darling boy blinks at me when I finish. Clearly, no one talks about how unsafe it is to be my species and that we don't have options outside of being healers under the protection of bigger supes. Our innate healing and therapeutic abilities make us far too appealing to trophy hunters and those who would want to lock us up for their own gain.

"Your people don't do *anything* else? Like they go to school, grow up, become doctors, heal, and retire without going anywhere but home and their assigned enclaves?" Seer asks, her brow furrowing.

"Correct." I shrug. "We're made for this, truthfully, and being able to take care of those who need us is fulfilling. But usually, we are required to come home to… propagate the species rather than have actual relationships. It's mostly arranged by our parents. Luckily, mine have passed on, so I'm not under pressure yet."

Wolfie lets out an indignant gasp, climbing onto Edgar's lap so he can settle into both of us. "Fuck that. It's not happening."

I open my mouth to speak, but feel the hound next to me wind his other arm around my waist as he growls darkly, "It's not an option, pup. The doc is ours, and no bullshit tradition will force him to act like a breeding stud."

Well, I'll be a son of a beer swilling frat boy. There's hope for the judge yet.

"If anyone cares, despite my heritage, I'm not okay with that shit, either. There are plenty of ways to keep your species going without forcing people to take part. Fucking hell, Doc, it's 2022 and your people are all medical personnel!" Doyle runs his hands through his hair in aggravation and he glares. "This is shit that makes it impossible to get all the supes to come together—rare groups like yours are clinging to ancient bullshit that the rest of us can't abide."

"On a lighter note, I don't know any of my people," Seer interjects. "Valkyries and veela are both fairly solitary, but I've also grown up with adoptive parents who are high in the Society. I never questioned being adopted, nor was any of their lifestyle hidden from me. So I didn't feel the need to look for others or my bio donors. We are prone to bad tempers, though. I've always had one."

Doyle arches his brow. "That could just be *you*, little rich supe. Though, the valkyries I've met over time have been pretty aggressive. Every single one is a badass, metal undies wearing Domme—at least the ones I knew."

"Can we focus?" Edgar leans his forehead against the top of Wolfie's head as he sucks in a slow breath. "You all know about the hound. That was the first side that appeared when I was about eight or nine. Once I was a preteen, the lust fog started and Bane deduced the incubus. Dual sides aren't uncommon anymore, but when I didn't emerge after that, we waited. The Quetzalcoatl appeared after a severe loss my freshman year of high school. Luckily, it was on the way home and I was riding with two older teammates, not on the bus. Their parents summarily shipped them off to some boarding school, but I suspect Andromeda bribed them to do so. No one but her has ever known about my third side—not even my parents."

Tilting my head, I pull back and give him a serious look. "How did you hide such a rare and temperamental side? You had to have struggled."

"I still struggle. Part of my risk-taking shit has always been about giving as much serotonin and adrenaline to my three sides as possible to keep them satisfied." He sighs and runs his other hand through Wolfie's hair. "The bird came out first with Tilly. It's always liked her. I'm just lucky it was in private."

"Hecate in a handcart, we've all got enough hidden shit to float Charon's boat," Doyle mutters. "You know I can't say more than I have until you figure it out for yourselves. Real mother unnamed on high and father likely as high, but also unnamed. Older than anything in most of this country. Not Irish. I simply like this persona."

Seer rolls her eyes. "Helpful as always."

"I'm probably dark Fae. My adoptive mother is in the hospital and has been since my dad died. My actual mother is awful and the only one of her kind. She won't tell me who my dad is, but it's obvious that's where the Fae comes from," Wolfie says softly.

"His mother is an absolute bitch," I add. "She's known for her frigid demeanor, but she treats him like a chess piece."

"Yes," the vet murmurs. "I found her when I was young and I've regretted it ever since."

Edgar looks at each of us. "Is this everything we can share? Because if so, then our next step is to each figure out how we're going to talk to my *drugar*. We also need to get more information on the last lead we had in her parents' death—that's one of her biggest stumbling blocks and if we can help her solve her mysteries, she'll have less to worry about. All we can do until she forgives us is try to ease her burdens from afar."

"What about MacAuley and Benjy?" I ask. "Should we talk to them as well? Haggerty thinks they're joining the boy band, eventually."

"I'll talk to Benjy. You find MacAuley at lunchtime tomorrow, Prez. Doyle, find time to visit Hazel. She always knows more than she's letting on."

"What about me?" Seer rises to her feet and stretches, giving Boone a curious look. "What's my assignment, Coach?"

His lips curve up as he replies, "You get to handle the Society angle. Talk to Bane, your handlers, Julia… anyone you can find to track this deputy crap down. We all have to work during the day and you don't."

"I'm on it." She turns to head for the door, glancing back at us to add. "Be good, boys."

I roll my eyes and stand, offering a hand to Wolfie. "If we must."

"You must," Edgar mutters.

Yes, sir.

Fight Song

Jolene

Every day for the rest of the week, I have to endure the stares every time I come into town. It doesn't matter if it's at work or after lessons… people watch me like they think I will break down right in front of them. I'm sure some are rooting for it since I dared to fight back against the cruel prank the Mean Moms of Whistler's Hollow set up, but I refuse to give them the satisfaction. I make sure I'm groomed, caffeinated, put together, and flanked by threatening animals no matter where I am.

In a small town, any chink in your armor is a weakness to exploit, even something as small as a messy ponytail at the store.

To their credit, the students haven't misbehaved any more than normal. The jocks stuck in the low level art class for humanities are still painting flicking dipshits and the AP students are working like Trojans to get portfolios done to submit to shows in the city. My private students are quiet or as standoffish as normal—a fact that I'm grateful for. When I was their age, so many of the adults talked freely in front of their kids that every conflict made its way to the schools. That's how the Nip/Tucks ended up pulling the Catastrophe stunt that led to my big public humiliation.

I honestly don't have the spoons to dance around those kinds of topics with kids without losing my temper. Sherilynn and her friends brought Antigone back because I got them in trouble after the newspaper incident. It was a petty revenge enacted by petty women who have nothing better to do than tear other people down. Unfortunately, it's not only a 'small town boredom' reaction. When I taught in the inner city and even when I was a fixture in boardrooms, I watched bullies look for targets and systematically destroy them for the fun of it.

Niecy used to tell me that 'People who play in filth, stay in filth.'

It took a lot of therapy and years for me to realize she meant some people enjoy being nasty because it makes them happy. Whether it's making themselves feel better or because they're broken is inconsequential. Their joy comes from other people's pain and they won't stop until they've completely obliterated the person they're focused on. They surround themselves with toadies and 'yes men' who adore everything about them while ignoring the red flags. That's why there's always a pack… they have to have an audience.

We're all too old for this shit, and I will not be part of the abuse cycle.

That's why I'm pulling to the parking lot of Atwater's getting groceries rather than having them delivered. It's been over two weeks since that damned Halloween party and I'm tired of hiding. My phone rings as I slide out of the Impala and I click the button on my Airpods to answer. "What?"

"Oooh, touchy, Jo-Jo."

I roll my eyes and sigh as the cats jump out of the car first. "Jackson, how many times do I have to tell you—"

"I know; I know. Don't call you Jo-Jo. But I *love* getting under your skin, so it's never going to stop."

"Did you call me for a reason or just to annoy me? I'm unloading pets so I can go to the store," I growl in response.

My old friend laughs and I can hear a faint echo of another chuckle. "Eli and I have been working on the leads your men sent us. It surprised me to hear from Boone because the word is, you gave them all the heave-ho."

Jesus Christ in a tweed suit. The gossip about my sex life made it to another fucking city??!!

"Jackson, I refuse to discuss my sex life with you while I'm standing in Atwater's parking lot. Get to the point."

Kali and Hecate bark loudly and the cats make a low '*mrowr*' sound that catches my attention. I look over and see Zelda Grant gaping at me next to her car. I'm about to tell her what she can stick in her giant piehole when Eury swoops out of the sky and grabs at her hair. The harpy eagle makes a sharp turn upwards and when I look back at the nasty woman who called me a whore on my first week in town, she's wearing a wig cap over gray hair.

Holy fuck, my bird just snatched the wig right off of her head.

This will not end well.

"Monster! Thief! *Unruly hooligans!*" Zelda shrieks as she tries to wave her hands and cover her head at the same time.

I cover my mouth with my hand before my laughter tumbles out of my mouth. If Eury had swiped something that she wore for any reason besides vanity, I'd be chagrined, but it's obvious old Z just didn't want anyone to know she'd gone gray. The dogs and cats are jumping around, clearly hoping Eury will allow them to play too, and I don't even know how to handle this without making it worse.

"Jo-Jo? Where'd you go? What's that yelling?"

I have to close my eyes for a minute so I can gather myself to respond as Jackson keeps babbling in my ear. When I catch my breath, I take my hand off my lips and gasp, "Zelda. Wig. My eagle. Have to call you back."

He's still yelling when I click the phone off. Eury notices me paying attention again and decides that's her cue to ascend higher into the air to fly away from the store—with the wig still clutched in her claws. Zelda continues squawking and pointing at me, but I don't know what to do. The bird has taken off and I can't very well do some weird *Game of Thrones* raven thing to get her back.

Looking down at Kali and Jekyll, I mutter, "Guess she'll have to stay here and look like a fool. Nothing we can do, right?" My answer is a resounding set of barks and *mows*, so I pull my reusable totes out of the trunk and give Zelda a wave as I head for the door.

Man, karma is a straight up bitch when she wants to be.

Jekyll and Hyde bound into the store first, with Kali and Hecate behind me. Since I left the hospital, the animals have formed a circle of protection around me everywhere we go. Eury takes the air and Isis now curls around my torso and left leg in a familiar pattern at all times unless we're at home. It's odd that Teddy's dogs refuse to go see him, but since he's a stubborn asshole who hasn't stopped watching since I got to town, I'm not surprised his pets are just as fucking bull-headed. Luckily, the dogs didn't lie to me, so I'm happy to let them snuggle up in his spot at night.

"Jolene! It's so good to *see* you!"

Ten. Fucking. Seconds.

Craning my neck, I look to see who is foolish enough to be calling me from across the grocery store before I even get completely inside. The waving woman is Mina Cantwell and I'll be *damned* if the woman looks a day above forty. I walk over towards where she's molesting oranges as she selects them, trying not to look like a moron. Mina is Jamie and Fidelia's mother… she can't be a day under sixty and yet she looks fresh as a daisy. When I used to ride at the farm as a kid, she always brought out flowery herbal tea and deliciously citrusy biscuits that made my entire body tingle with happiness.

It was a bit like magic, how she used to brighten even the stormiest day with her presence.

"Hello, Mina. It's been a dog's age," I say with a smile. The animals study her warily and I shake my head at them. Mina isn't a danger; she's as threatening as a Kleenex.

Before I know it, I'm engulfed in a warm hug and my body stiffens. I've never been big on people touching me without warning, and after the newest disaster, I'm even more withdrawn. Isis wiggles her head out from under my shirt, letting out a hiss until Mina pulls away. Her lips split and she lets out a tinkling laugh that floats through air like sleigh bells.

"Oh, what an interesting accessory you're sporting, dear. You seem to have a mini army of protectors. I don't blame you after that shameful display at fall event." Her expression changes to one of sympathy when I flinch. "Don't worry, honey. Poor breeding *always* shows itself when given the chance. I fear the harvest from those your age was a bad crop altogether for this town. So many weeds in the garden and no one ever bothered to trim them—that's what I told your father."

My brow furrows and I pick up a few oranges of my own for the house. "Mina, I didn't know you were friends with my father."

"Not friends, really. But Jamie took an interest in you and you remember how rigid his father was back then. We had little get togethers with him and your mother every once in a while after you started coming around so often. I think Anderson was afraid Jamie would get sweet on you and since there's a four-year gap in your ages…"

What.

"Mina, are you telling me you and my parents met to make sure Jamie and I weren't dating?" I rub my temples, trying not to lose my temper at the woman who was kind when others were not. I was never interested in Jamie that way, but who the hell were any of them to monitor us like the mares on the farm?

"Oh, no, dear. Your mother and Anderson were quite the schemers. They thought they could push you together. Jamie's heritage and name with your wildcard possibilities seemed like *such* a good recipe for the future. You were so good with the horses and so smart. When you left for State U, we were sure you'd come back for your destiny. Your parents promised."

The bag of oranges I'm holding drops to the floor and my vision goes fuzzy for a second as I try to process that. Snippets of an old memory echo in my head, making me freeze in place.

"Jolene, you can't just flit off wherever you want when you graduate. You have responsibilities!"

"Eloise, she's an adult. We can't force her to come back because we made a promise."

"No one asked for your opinion, Andrew! Do you know what this will cost me? It will set back my ascension to the Council by years!"

With a soft gasp, I snap out of it, looking at Jamie's mom in shock. One thing my brain wiped out was about this weird arranged marriage our parents had in their heads. All I can think of to say is, "Did Jamie know?"

The petite blonde woman shakes her head. "Definitely not, honey. We were all committed to allowing you two to find the right path on your own. We didn't tell either of you on purpose."

Oh, how sweet of you all—not.

"It was nice chatting with you, Mina, but I need to get moving along. I'll call on you for tea sometime?"

She doesn't need to know I have absolutely no intention of doing that. I'm being as genteel as people would expect because I can't afford to make more enemies at the moment. Every time I think I've got my hands around the bullshit going on here, someone throws a curveball at me and I'm getting pretty tired of it. Mina finally nods and I bend to pick up my oranges, collecting them before I go back to the front of the store to get a cart.

It takes everything in me to roll that fucker to a corner near the restrooms in the back where people can't see me, so I can freak out in private.

Not only were my parents distant and disconnected, they were planning to fob me off as some kind of political power move?

And what did she mean by Jamie's heritage and my wildcard possibilities?

Why the hell *is everything in this town a goddamned riddle?*

I lean back against the wall near the ladies' room door, sliding down until I'm sitting on the floor with my forehead on my knees. It's too much, all at once, and I don't know how I'm going to handle it by myself.

I need to get out of here and feel something real.

Rolling to my feet, I ditch the bag of oranges on a shelf, leading my animals out the door without a single purchase. I know where I'm going before I even get in the car—I'm going to the farm to work all of this out of the system as I fly over the bluegrass on the back of one of the most beautiful horses I've ever seen.

It's time to fly.

The energy in the air changes abruptly, and I stop talking to Eliot about the pause in Medhi's training.

"She's here," I murmur as my eyes close. Everything around us has become charged; there's such *power* filling the atmosphere that I sense it even though she's far from the main building. Confused looks greet me when I open my eyes. Isra shifts, her hand instinctively reaching for whichever concealed weapon she's chosen, but I shake my head. An excited smile graces my lips as I turn to Fazal. "Go outside and bring her to me."

His speedy exit makes my Southern business partner scratch his head. "Amiri, don't leave me hanging like a lost ball in the high weeds. Who's here, and why did you send Fazal after her?"

"The lost one from the city—I did not find out her name until I researched the trainer I wanted for Medhi. Your people's need to gossip is both useful and perturbing, though you know that. Miss Whitley has arrived, and I am eager to speak with her about her plan." Settling back in my chair, I steeple my fingers as I contemplate the visions in smoke when I had her on stage.

Cantwell pales and looks nervous. "She might not be in the best of mindsets to discuss that right now. As I mentioned, there was a problem a couple of weeks ago, and she's been recovering after a stay in the hospital."

Before I can dismiss his concerns, Fazal slips into the room with a look of shame on his face. "I apologize, Your Highness. She… refused to accompany me to visit."

I frown, noting his intense discomfort. "What did she say *exactly*, Fazal?"

My lifelong valet pales and shakes his head. "I do not think—"

Isra pushes off the wall, approaching him like a ninja in her all black suit and flashing silver blade. "The sheik did not ask for your opinion, Fazal. Know your place."

Waving my hand, I gesture for Isra to back off. She knows better than to throw my family's titles around to demand people bend to my will. I can make them bend to my will on my own and without making a spectacle. "Fazal, repeat what she said. I am unconcerned that it is not to your liking."

Though I sense it will be amusing…

"Miss Whitley said 'if that rich asshole wants to speak to me, he can get off his ass, mount up, and find me. I have a horse to exercise.' Then she headed for the stable as if on a mission."

"Sweet baby Jesus, Jolene," Eliot mutters. His hand scrubs over his face and he looks at me apologetically. "My apologies, Amiri. She's had a rough go of it lately."

Biting back a laugh, I shake my head at him. "No need, Cantwell. My *muharibi aleaziz*[1] would not be herself if she wasn't fighting the world."

"Your…" He frowns and looks at me curiously. "I didn't think you'd met."

"Ah, but we have. I was graciously allowed to perform at *Howl* when I first arrived in the country and she was present in the audience with her Guardians." His eyes widen and I shrug, as if it is of no consequence. "I called her on stage to receive the gifts of my people. I feel like I know her very well, though she does not know it."

"Shit. What were they *thinking?* Taking her to *Howl?*" Once he processes that, Eliot turns back to me with a serious expression. "There are things you should know about her before you decide to chase her."

Arching a brow, I wait.

"It's clear you know she's unemerged, but rumor has it she has mates —several and the possibility of more to come. I've known her since we were kids and our parents were close at one point. She's had a lot of emotional trauma in the past. Some of that recently came back, so if you're simply looking for an interesting notch on your bedpost, look elsewhere."

Alqaraf almuqadas.[2] *That was a brave statement.*

"I admire your honesty and your defense of your friend, Eliot. But I assure you, I do not have ill intentions. What I see in the smoke is quite accurate, and I know that the threads of our fate are inter-twined. I will not hurt her; that I guarantee." I give him a sharp nod as I stand, looking over at Fazal. "Fetch my riding clothes and I will change. It seems I have a runaway woman to locate."

"Why do I think this is a bad idea?"

"Because his Majesty should *not* be chasing after some common woman like a lovesick teenager?"

Whipping around, I lose control of my anger for a moment as my guard forgets to mind her tongue. Tendrils of dark magic spiral out from my palm as I hold my hand up for her to stop and they wrap around her neck like ropes. Her face reddens almost immediately and the lights flicker above us. My temper is well known in my home, but rarely do I allow people in the new world to witness this.

But Isra will learn to respect the woman who is meant for me or she will suffer the consequences.

The lower *djinn* dangles as I raise my arm, lifting her towards the ceiling while she sputters and gasps for air. "Disrespect will not be tolerated, Isra. Practice what you preach."

She struggles, phasing in and out of her humanoid form for a moment as the impact of my powers on her causes her to weaken. After a few long moments, she ceases to fight me and I lower her to the ground. Her voice is raspy as she dips her head and says, "My deepest regrets, *sahib alsumui*.[3] It will not happen again."

The rage filling me subsides as she submits and my magic releases the grip on her neck. "Do not forget again, Isra."

Fazal is the peacemaker because he clears his throat and gestures for the door. "This way, Amiri. We will make use of the same room we did on our previous trip here. I will ask the staff to prepare your other horse while you dress for the ride."

"Excellent." I look over at Cantwell with a narrowed expression. "Non-disclosure, my friend. I do not allow most people to witness the extent of my powers and though this is certainly not the limit, I'd prefer you never to speak of this."

I don't wait for his answer as I stride out of the room, following Fazal eagerly.

Regardless of her mood, I am quite excited to see Jolene again. It feels fortuitous that she stormed in when she did, and I do not question the whims of the universe when they present themselves.

MALIK THUNDERS ACROSS THE FIELD, TAKING HIS HEAD AS I USE MY magic to follow the trail of my errant prey. I'd be lying if I said I'm not enjoying my hunt—I may not be one of the animalistic species of supe, but predatory instincts come easily to my people. Eons of searching the deserts for those who have desires they cannot fulfill to feed our power runs through my veins. The *djinn* may not have the population density of more common species like wolves or witches, but those who remain keep our ancient traditions intact.

It would amaze both humans and supernatural beings alike to find out how many successes and failures in history have been at the hands of wishes we've granted.

Our own ethos demands we keep living records of what we have granted so as not to cross another's source. Since we draw power from the beings who request our services until they meet their end, it is imperative none of us shift the balance by contaminating the reality created by each individual wish. It's extremely complex and takes an enormous amount of communication—arguments about what qualifies as upsetting balance can only be solved by viewing other realities together. For ancient *djinn* like me, this is not a painful process, but the younger ones like Isra struggle with it mightily.

However, I did not have to alter reality when I delved into my *muharibi aleaziz*[4]'s mind. Her destiny has been written in the stars for much longer than she was a twinkle in the eye of her parents. I only helped by removing the mental restraints she'd put on herself during her unhappy past. The family she coveted so strenuously was a foregone conclusion if she simply allowed it to form. Unfortunately, some devious little brats in this town have thrown a knot in the threads of Fate, and I am honor bound to help her untangle them.

For her own good and that of the world in the future.

When I reach the crest of a higher hill, I tilt my head to look into the waning light. It is dusk and finding her in the dark will be more of a challenge, but I can do it. The more pertinent question is how skilled she is at riding in the dark. That is unknown and given the value of the horse she's mounted on, I need to pick up my pace. "*Asrae ya milaki*[5]!"

The wind blows my hair out of the loose ponytail I had it in as Malik gallops over the terrain. There's an old swing in a tree at the edge of the horizon, and I feel a wave of sorrowful energy radiating from it. Jolene is hiding in that far corner with Medhi picking at grass along the fence line. The gold from my mare's coat picks up the light when we get closer, and I tug the reins to slow our progress. Crashing in like an invading horde will not endear me to the woman I hope to soothe.

She doesn't look up as we approach, though I suspect she can hear the beat of Malik's hooves. I can't tell if she's surprised that I accepted her challenge or if she's irritated that I'm intruding on her private moment. Regardless, I slide out of the saddle in a practiced motion, even though my horse hasn't stopped yet. I land on my feet gracefully and prowl over to where she's hunched over. The sound of soft sobs stops me for a moment, but only briefly.

She needs me.

"Jolene…" I wait for her to acknowledge me, but she continues sniffling into her palms silently. "I am certain you meant for your challenge to be ignored when you instructed Fazal to tell me. You will find that I am not one to back down so easily."

Her head lifts, and she squints at me with tear-reddened eyes. "You… *You* are the prince who owns Medhi? *You?*"

Ah, so she recognizes me without all the stage glamor.

"Indeed, little one. I did not know when I met you at *Howl* that you were the new trainer Eliot bragged about—that I can assure you. But I will admit to researching you afterward; it was purely a business decision at first."

Her eyes close, and she tips her head up to the sky. "At first. Hera, help me if this is another one. I don't have the spoons for this!"

I can't help but laugh at her cry to the heavens. As if our capacity to cope with the whims of the Universe means anything to the women who weave the threads; it's adorable that she's been raised so completely ignorant of our world. It feels blissfully naïve, but I know it's a lack of comprehension about the true nature of life.

"I don't believe any of us can convince the gods of our preferences by yelling at the clouds. Though it may be therapeutic, I'm sure." I give her a small smile, walking a little closer. "You may continue if you wish. I will send the horses afield so they do not get spooked."

"Really? You don't mind?" she asks in a tiny voice. "It might be loud."

"Really," I reply. Winking at her, I stride over to Malik and Medhi, murmuring low in my native language. They toss their manes and trot away from us at a relaxed pace. "See? Let loose, *muharibi aleaziz.* Do what you must and unburden yourself."

Jolene rises from the swing, looking up to the slowly setting sun and shakes her fists. "*I do not. Have. Enough. Strength. To take all of this. At once!*"

Crossing my arms over my chest, I watch her quietly. I disagree with her assessment, but she does not need me to correct her, only to allow her to vent the riotous emotions inside of her. The human part of her is so overwhelmed with the events transpiring that it's impossible to see a road forward. I would love to help her see there are other paths, but I've found that simply allowing people to realize on their own is more empowering.

So I stay silent.

"It took me years… years! I had to hit the bottom and be scraped out by Jackson before I could start the healing process. Afterwards, I was alone for almost a decade before I allowed a friend in. And look what it got me!"

Her rage and sadness are heavy in the air as she drops to her knees on the ground and starts sobbing again. My heart aches for the woman I believe is meant for me. Though she may not have had a life that everyone would consider difficult, the doubt and shame created in her childhood impacted her indelibly. Trust is a thing to fear and every time someone breaches it, the voices in her head remind her they were right.

I have known many who are damaged like this; it is not an easy belief to overcome.

"And the guys…" Those words are followed by a crack in her voice and another shivering sob. "I let it happen so quickly. It felt right, and I allowed them to become integral to my life. Why did I do that? *I know better!"*

Approaching slowly, I offer my hand to her. She looks up at me suspiciously and I try to convey my sympathy with my gaze. It is not time for words yet, but I can sense what she needs. When she finally takes it and rises, I envelop her in my arms. She struggles a little at first, but I don't let go. I'm not a small being and I've been told many times that my embrace creates a feeling of warm safety.

"I barely know you," Jolene murmurs. "I don't know why you're being so nice. And it worries me because I barely knew most of *them.* That hasn't worked out so far."

I look down at her, waiting until she tips her head to meet my eyes. "You are hurting right now—rightfully so—but I believe your assessment is not accurate. It is too raw for you to see clearly what the addition of your friend and men have heralded positive changes."

She snorts. "A house full of shit that isn't mine and people who are hiding things from me like I'm a child. That's not positive."

Tapping her nose, I shake my head. "Try again and hold the rancor, *muharibi aleaziz*. What good things have come into your life along with them?"

"Well…" She sighs and closes her eyes as if thinking about is causing her pain. "Seer and I had such amazing adventures in Europe. I'd never had someone who was so close to me before. She's like a sister."

"Mmmm. What else?"

"When Wolfie asked me out, it was the first time I felt… this spark. Like I knew he was more than the casual flings from my time overseas. I felt it with Teddy the first night and Prez when he showed up for Eury's arrival. Something about them made me feel complete." Her eyes open and she frowns. "Why am I telling you this? Are you a sorcerer?"

I throw my head back and laugh at her suspicious question. She has no idea how close she is, but that is not why she is opening up to me. I'm not using my power on her; she's reacting to the bond connection I feel. Jolene doesn't know it yet, but that's part of what she's describing from when she met the others.

"No, I am not. Many have complimented my listening skills, though. It comes with age, I believe."

She squints at me. "You're not *that* much older than me."

If only you knew…

But I grin instead. "I don't know how old you are and my mother would take a cane to me if I asked a lady how old she was. I cannot answer that in good faith."

Rolling her eyes, she snorts. "Age is a man-made construct used to make women feel a need to propagate the species. I'm thirty-four and I don't give a shit who asks."

How delightful she is when she's fighting me. I like it.

"Then I shall reply that, alas, I have a few years on you. I am thirty-nine."

That's shaving off a thousand years, but who's counting?

"See?" Jolene smacks my chest. "You don't get to pull the sage wisdom act when you only have five years on me. I won't allow it."

"Your wish is my command," I reply. The irony of that phrase isn't lost on me, but the change in her demeanor is so enchanting that I can't help but tease back. Her eyes have dried and some of the hopelessness is gone from her face. That's what I wanted.

"Ugh. No, thank you. I never want someone to give in to me just to win my favor. Fight me if you want; I prefer it."

No shit.

"You are not ready for my version of fighting, Jolene. But you will be and when you are, we will dance together." I lean down and place a gentle kiss on her lips. "For now, you have other bridges to cross and mend. I am happy to be your sounding board anytime."

She's quiet and I think perhaps I've offended her, but she finally nods. "You're right. I need to make peace with the mistakes I made and the ones those I care about made. At least enough to come to decisions that aren't rooted in my past trauma."

"Ah. Therapy, I assume?"

"Oh, so many hours. Enough to know when I'm self-sabotaging and that's definitely now."

I smile and jerk my head at the swing. "Perhaps we can avoid that by chatting? I'll push and you can answer whatever you feel comfortable with. It will be an excellent distraction."

Pulling back, she tucks her hair behind her ears and nods. "I'd like that."

"Excellent." I walk over and wait for her to settle before I give the old rope swing a shove. "It is wise to remember that sometimes, in order to be mended correctly, things have to be re-broken. Your doctor would agree."

"Stalker," she grumbles. "That info isn't online for research."

"I may have had Isra do a little checking around. Call it precautionary. I *am* a prince. People seek to take advantage of that."

"Whatever you say, Your Highness."

Now, when she says it, I like it. Who knew?

Blow

Jolene

The time I spent with Dhameer left me feeling more at peace than I have since the Halloween disaster. His gentle yet firm way of addressing the problem could have felt condescending, but… I felt like he was trying to take care of me. He's right—I need to sort out my mess before I do anything else. That's the same thought I had with the enigmatic Hugo earlier.

Looking over at my cats sitting shotgun, I sigh. "Am I wearing some sort of pheromone? I'm no blushing virgin, but why in the name of Aphrodite are so many hot dudes rushing to my aid lately? I feel like I'm wearing a 'princess in distress' placard."

"*Mow!*" Jekyll replies. Hyde adds nothing, but the dog in the back let out a low mournful sound.

Worried about whether I'll give their Master an Irish goodbye, I suppose.

"I'm not saying I'm abandoning Teddy or Wolfie or any of them, guys. I have shit to work out, sure, but there's this weird draw to Hugo and Benjy… and now the sheik. Does the universe want me to stock my own bunny mansion? As if the women in this town don't hate me enough…"

I can't seem to wrap my head around the whole situation, so I turn up my playlist, singing along as we speed towards Main Street. There's no hope of me cooking anything now. I'll have to pick up some pies at Derby Pies. I'd go to the diner, but something tells me old Hazel would see right through me and I don't know if I'm ready for that much wisdom in one day.

Pulling into an open spot down at the end of the block, I note how busy the restaurant and Speakeasy are. There's many people going in and out, which means I need to be careful with my animals. I open the door and they jump out, flanking me as usual. A screech in the air tells me Eury is circling, so I know I have another ally in this snake pit, but I can't allow any of them to get us in trouble.

"You guys need to stay outside. *Do not* get involved if anything goes wrong. There are too many people around and we all know some citizens here are looking to have you locked up. Isis is with me and I can handle getting some pizza for us. Got it?"

The dogs bark first, looking angrier than my servals. Teddy definitely ordered them to protect me—the tension in their bodies speaks volumes about their dislike of my command. Hyde steps in front of the others, taking point as they follow behind me. She's the first to jump onto an empty bench close to the doors to the restaurant. I pause, waiting for Jekyll, Kali, and Hecate to join her. Once they do, I blow them a kiss and walk the final few steps to the crowded entryway.

"What are *you* doing here?"

For the love of Jimmy Choos… of course, *Sherilynn is here instead of Benjy.*

Ignoring the screech, I walk up to the counter and smile at the teen working. "One extra large Animal Kingdom Meat Lovers, a dozen meatballs, two garlic cheesy breads, and a small vanilla Coke to go."

The girl's eyes dart back and forth, then she sighs as if she's in pain. "Are you sure you don't want to try… our new Pineapple Under the Sea special?"

I snort so hard it actually hurts for a second. "Uh… no. First, pineapple doesn't belong on pizza and second, that sounds like it's some weird combo of pineapple and tuna which… is beyond unappealing. I'll stick with my relatively sane order, thanks."

Her lips quirk for a moment and I realize the employees must be required to suggest this rancid sounding new menu item. And if they're being forced to do something so stupid, the creator of this ridiculous hodgepodge of pop culture reference and cringe, it's probably Sherilynn's brain child. I flash her a sympathetic look—I can't be the first person to tell her I wouldn't feed that garbage to a hog.

"It'll be about ten minutes, ma'am. We're pretty busy tonight. The 'Cats are playing."

Nodding, I point at a corner near the door. "I'll wait over there."

"What name should I call when it's ready?"

"You could write *loser* on it and she'll come running," Sherilynn cuts in as she walks up. "Make it snappy so the trash doesn't stink up my restaurant, Beth."

I close my eyes, counting in my head to keep my cool. No matter how many times I let the bullshit go, this chick just keeps coming. Even after the debacle at the Ball and the mayor's supposed decree, she still won't leave me alone. I don't know if it's stupidity or what, but I cannot continue to allow this woman and her groupies to abuse me in public. They can call me bitchy or crazy or whatever they want, but this fuckery ends tonight.

"Sherilynn, I have to confess something."

"We know you're a washed up tramp, Whitley. It's unfortunate that so many fine gentlemen have rolled around in the mud with a low-class pig, but men aren't known for being discerning when they want to fuck."

The room goes quiet as heads turn our way and I have to suck in a slow, deep breath again. I cannot lose my shit like I did a few weeks ago. Whatever happened, I ended up in a hospital for a week, and Sherilynn isn't worth my mental or physical health.

"Sherilynn Foster," I say, emphasizing her maiden name because of the divorce. It's petty, but the look on her face says my bar hit. I need her to shut up long enough for me to say my piece. "I confess to being confounded. After the mess in high school, I left with no intention of coming back. In fact, before I arrived home, I hadn't thought of you in *years*. I was out in the real world, creating my success and living my life to the fullest."

"Clearly, *that* didn't work out for you. You came crawling back."

"When I returned, I had no intention of dredging up childish bull-shit. But there you were, still here and being followed around by a mindless bunch of twats who believe every ounce of tripe that escapes your mouth. Still, I didn't engage with you until you sought me out."

She starts to reply, but I shake my head, holding up a hand. "It begs the question, Sherilynn… How unhappy and pathetic is your life that you only derive pleasure from tearing others down? I want nothing to do with you, your minions, or your inferiority complex. I'm tired of you running around spreading gossip, lies, and hateful shit about me and anyone else who sees you for who you really are. You may present a pretty picture to the masses, but you're rotten to the core."

"Oh, Jolene. Do you really think the *Catastrophe* can order me around? My parents are part of the founding families! I'll have you blackballed in every social arena before you get home tonight. You'll be ruined." The bottle blond runs a hand over the carefully coiffed updo she's sporting and sniffs at me imperiously.

Seriously? She thinks I'm afraid of her?

Fuck. This.

"Go ahead. Tell everyone far and wide all the nasty things you think about me, Sherilynn. You can call me a pig in public and say I'm a talentless loser. Knock yourself out." I walk closer to her, my gaze narrowed as I look into her eyes. "But know this: if you want to make me the villain in your story, be prepared for me to wrap that shit around me like a warm winter coat. When I was younger, I let you get away with your abuse, but I won't now. I will dig up every skele-ton, every body, every single speck of dirt you've buried and make sure it goes so viral that you won't be able to step into a Waffle House without the whole joint pointing and whispering. Do you really want me to expose all the backstabbing nastiness you're capable of?"

"You've got nothing, Whitley. I have hard evidence that you're trash and my name means something—you're a failed loser living in your parents' house." Her sneer is ugly, but it matches the narcissism in her words.

"I'm giving you one last chance. Back off, leave me alone, and keep your toxic bullshit away from me and mine. If you don't, I won't be kind and I won't back down. Actions have consequences and if anyone is going to be held to account, it's you. Think carefully about the things you've said and done in the past. How many of your *fans* will stick around when they find out who you really are?"

Her brow furrows, and I smile slowly. I have her now. She doesn't know what I'm referring to and she can't ask without revealing whatever evil shit she's done. I'll make certain Jackson and Eli do a deep dive into her social media and phone records. I have a feeling there's some socially unacceptable things she's said lurking within easy reach of my hacker friends.

"Um… your pizza… is ready," the girl at the counter squeaks as she tries not to draw Sherilynn's attention.

I walk over and take my food, feeling Isis squeezing me under my clothes. That's the best compliment I could receive, and it makes me glad I kept the other animals outside. They would not have dealt well with Queen Bratwurst's outburst. "I'm going to take my food home now. I suggest you seek some therapy for your issues, Sherilynn. I know you're still smarting because your Oxford scholar sister makes you look dumber than a kumquat, but the rest of the world doesn't have to suffer because your daddy loved her more."

Turning on my heel, I stride out of the silent room with a smug smile on my lips. I know I played dirty, but I've been the bigger person since we were teens. She wasn't going to stop coming at me and though I've never understood why I live rent free in her head, I'm tired of her and her flying monkeys. I have bigger concerns than her self-centered sociopathy and I'm not wasting anymore of my energy fighting a battle of wits with an unarmed amputee.

Jekyll wanders up to me as I exit, letting out a questioning, "*Mrrp?*"

"Don't worry about it, buddy. I had to show an emotional terrorist how we deal with their kind." I pause for a moment and grumble under my breath, "And I didn't do it with a weapon, so everyone should be proud of me."

ONCE I GOT HOME, I GOT ALL THE FOOD READY AND SPREAD OUT MY research in the living room.

I'm stretched out on the giant beanbag on the floor, looking at files and the various emails Jackson has sent since our talk. Eury is perched on my mother's buffet table—which would *horrify* her—and the dogs and cats are lounging on various furniture. I have the Firebird suite on the wireless speakers Prez set up and though remembering the hijinks of four men trying to outdo one another while they installed all of this high-tech equipment all over the house.

All I have to do is call for one of the robot women and my house will practically live my life for me.

Frowning, I rub my chest as an ache starts up. Since I left the hospital, I've had a lot of random aches and pains, ranging from dull throbs to odd pain in my joints when I wake up. I probably should contact a doctor, but in this town, that means Prez and I'm not ready for that yet. One drawback of living in a small town like this is that you can't avoid anyone for very long; there's simply too much crossover in day-to-day lives. Sighing in annoyance, I wiggle my way over to the TV stand where I left the ibuprofen yesterday.

I swallow them dry and scoot back to my research. While I was driving home, there was a niggling sensation in my head that I missed something that was said. I don't know if it was when I talked with Dhameer or Hugo or even someone random. There's just a bit I'm missing, and it ties to the stuff in my files. I've read the reports and supplemental information about the mysterious disappearing cop over and over, but I can't figure out why it bothers me so much.

It's so strange that someone with those means would get hired for something completely out of their skill set and be able to move with no issues.

Based on my experience, moving to Europe was a process that I had to endure for the entire last semester I taught in the city. Passports, visas, selling extraneous items, long-term storage for others, canceling leases and services… It was a nightmare of red tape and paperwork. How could this dude manage it within a month for an entire family? He had to have majorly powerful help to get all of this pushed through so quickly. There's virtually no trail left after he skedaddled overseas.

I can't run around asking people about this guy without raising eyebrows if there's some sort of conspiracy going on. The only way I'll find out any *actual* information is to get it from the horse's mouth.

I have to go to Istanbul and pump this dude for information myself. It's the only way I'll be able to put this line of inquiry to rest.

Honestly, time away from all this bullshit would be good for me.

WHFS takes the month of December off for the winter holidays, so I'll have time to really dig deep. I can't leave the country with some dipshit stalking me and no one to watch my back, though. I have to take the animals and *that* will require a great deal of favors unless…

Jackson.

Grinning to myself, I text my old friend about my plans. His family owns several private jets and arriving on a plane owned by the Thorns will provide me with almost no security or customs issues, even with two cats, a bird, a snake, and two dogs. The ultra-rich are allowed to do *so* many things normal people would gasp in shock over. Luckily, I have a valid passport and a folder full of vet records Wolfie provided me when he examined all of my menagerie. All I need to do is guilt my old friend into allowing me to whisk myself away to a foreign country on one of his jets for a month long clue hunt.

Shouldn't be hard, right?

I wait for his answer, tapping the pen cap against my teeth. No, it won't be hard to convince Jackson. What will be hard is what happens when the guys figure out I took off for parts unknown, telling no one.

That feels like it'll earn me a punishment someday.

Oh, well.

The Monster

Wolfgang

The sound of Eminem blasting at full volume jerks me out of sleep like a tornado alarm. Blinking blearily, I look around the room for the source of the sound. My eyes finally land on the smartphone vibrating on the dresser. I'm not fully awake, but the case appears to be shiny and black, so it's definitely Teddy's. Of course, unless the Irishman got ahold of either my or Prez's phones, it'd have to be his because neither of us even keeps our ringtones on, for fuck's sake.

It's the minor differences that remind of the age gaps in our family.

I scoot out from under the heavy arm holding me to the judge's warm body. Prez's spot is still warm, but he's obviously left for the office already. Late November is a busy season because of colds and flu, so his schedule is full just about every day. I know that's helping him not to focus on our separation from Jolene, but I miss waking up with him just the same.

My feet hit the floor and I marvel again at the crazy power it has to require for Doyle to keep this place the way he does. He shrugs it off. But having a marble temple decorated and furnished to the nines that stays both warm and cool at the same time is beyond my comprehension most days. I pick up the phone and scurry back to the nest of blankets, poking Teddy's side as I hold the phone up.

"It's for you," I say softly when his eyes open.

"Hell, baby, you could have answered it. It can't be anything *that* important early on Saturday morning," he mumbles as he takes it. "That's not a work tone, anyway."

Ducking my head at his casual use of 'baby', I settle behind him as he flicks the screen open to answer. I'm still getting used to having a man like Edgar Boone claiming me as his. Presley is so easygoing and fluid; being topped by my laid-back doctor is like a warm, comfy blanket. A sexy one, mind you, but it's so different from the vibe with Teddy. Everything from his broad, tall, muscled quarterback body to his alpha male demeanor is a direct contrast to Prez's style. Teddy engulfs me from head to toe and while he's still figuring out how to navigate how he feels about me, I know without a doubt he'd rip someone's throat out for upsetting me.

It's hot as fuck and I have no idea how to handle him without getting ridiculously deep in sub space.

But he likes it and Prez enjoys playing the softer Dom in opposition. Thinking about the two of them together makes my dick throb, and I close my eyes. A low chuckle rumbles out of Teddy's chest, and he looks over his shoulder at me with a smirk. Apparently, I've been so lost in my thoughts that I missed whoever he's having a conversation with.

He pushes the speaker button and I hear Jackson Thorn talking about reserving a private jet. Before I can suss out what this has to do with us, Teddy hits the mute button. His eyes are ringed with fire as he ignores the babbling lawyer to roll over. His big hand reaches for my cock, running his fingers over the rungs of my ladder slowly. He knows that drives me crazy and I whimper.

"Teddy…"

"Mmmm, I don't think so. We're in the bedroom," he chides as his fingers squeeze the head of my cock gently.

"Fuck."

"If you're a good boy, yes. Now try again." His hand cups my balls, rolling them in a way that makes my hips arch up.

"Y-yes…. Daddy," I pant. I lift my hand to touch him, but he shakes his head. "Please."

"Oh, I love when you beg and we have time. Thorn will talk until he passes out if I let him." His hand releases me and he picks up the phone, placing it on the pillow. Then he pushes me onto my back, leaning in to nip at the mark he left on the juncture of my neck and shoulder. His teeth make me cry out, but I know the rules, so I don't arch up to press against him.

I have to get permission first.

"*Such* a good boy this morning, my little Wolfie." He rolls back over, reaching into the drawer in the nightstand. "Let's see how long that lasts."

When he pulls out the vibrating cock ring, my eyes widen. Presley has been giving him tips for sure. He knows how much that particular toy affects me. "Shit."

His grin widens, and he grabs the lube before using it to help slide the silicone down my shaft until the vibrating piece is resting against my balls. I suck in a breath and his mouth covers mine to kiss me hungrily. When he pulls back, he puts his fingers to his lips and unmutes the call. "I'm glad you called me to tell us, Thorn."

Jackson starts talking again—something about a trip to Istanbul—but I'm not paying attention because Teddy goes back to the drawer. He comes back with a set of nipple clamps and it takes everything in me to keep still, like I'm supposed to. Applying them one at a time, his eyes darken as he watches me fight not to squirm or make a noise. I bite my lip hard enough to draw blood and he dips his head to lick the droplets away. A low growl echoes through the room, and I give him a satisfied smirk.

I know how to push his buttons, too.

"Someone's asking for it," he growls. Teddy reaches up and grabs the phone, barking into it. "Thorn, I'll call you back about the arrangement later. I have something pressing to attend to."

That said, he flings the phone across the room and I can feel the hound beneath his skin pushing to break free. Teddy's sides are stronger than mine or Prez's; when even one of them is close to the surface, you can feel the energy crawling all over you. He slides down my body, hands gliding over my skin until his face is hovering over the head of my dick. Sharp pains at my hips make me gasp and he looks up with a feral grin.

"Holy fuck, daddy… are you… that's…"

"Mmmm, yep." His mouth closes over the tip and his tongue swirls over my slit. "I told you to be good."

I have to clench my abs and thigh muscles hard not to move as his hot mouth works over me at the same time as the vibration from the ring. "But… but… I am…"

A gentle nip almost does me in, and he lifts his head when I stay still. "I know. And you're going to *love* what's coming… besides us, I mean."

"There's more?" My eyes widen as the sting at my hips sizzles through me, putting me on that fine line between pain and pleasure. "Show me, daddy."

Teddy's eyes flash with the fire again, and I feel the air fill with his fog. It makes my dick weep and my struggle not to move even worse. He's definitely playing dirty, letting the incubus out to play as well, but that I'm used to by now. "Are you ready, baby? You sure you're ready? Daddy's gonna be rough."

Yes, please.

I nod, panting, as he digs into my hips a bit more. "I want it. Please."

My words make him lunge forward, grabbing the lube with a dark smile that promises I'm going to enjoy whatever he has planned. He lets go of me, rolling to the side as he opens the bottle. "Lift and spread."

Obeying automatically, I close my eyes and breathe deeply. His fingers probe my hole, pushing the lube he warmed in his palm in with a slow sawing motion. The stretch makes me moan and before I can beg him to give me more; he bites the inside of my thigh with sharp teeth. It makes my entire body tremble, and I look down at him pleadingly.

"Did it hurt, baby? Or did it feel good?" His voice is darker, more raspy and gravelly than normal.

"Good," I whimper. "But I need…"

"Oh, I know what you need, pup." His fingers slip out of me and he replaces them with the head of his cock, sinking into me inch by inch. "And you're going to get it."

"Can I move?" I have to give in and ask because I want nothing more than to pull him deeper inside of me. The vibration from the ring and the sharp stings and bites are going to make me lose my grip on the orgasm building in my balls.

His laugh is more of a bark and he thrusts forward, filling me completely. "I insist, actually. Wrap around me and move with me, Wolfie."

Winging my thanks to all the gods in the sky, I rock my hips into his hips as he thrusts in and out. His cock is thick and long, stretching me in the best of ways as the head bumps the sensitive spot over and over. His hands grasp my thighs again and that sting of pain comes back, making me shiver.

"I need… take it off… please…"

He keeps pumping into me, hips slapping against my ass as I writhe under him. "You're strangling my dick, baby. It's driving you crazy, isn't it? Being split in half while that vibrates and keeps you from coming too soon?"

"Yessssssss," I hiss. "And your claws. I didn't know you could do that."

"I've never been with one of our kind. I've never felt comfortable letting the hound go with… except you and my *drugar*."

"Fangs?"

His answer is a smile full of sharp points, and I throw my head back. "Daddy, please take the ring off. I want to come with you. I feel you getting close."

Leaning down, he slides the ring off slowly and puts his lips against my ear. "Good boy. Show me how pretty you are when you let your powers loose while you come with me."

Oh, shit. He wants me to….

Magic fills the air as I let the sparkling Fae loose, wings and all, looking up at him as he continues to slam into me. "Yes, daddy."

His eyes roam over me, glowing with the power of his hellhound and the incubus. "I know I claimed you, Wolfgang. I made my mark to protect you."

"I love it."

Our breaths are harsh as we move together and he leans down, putting his weight on his elbows. "I'm going to do something else. Something I've only done with our girl, but it seals the bond completely. Do you want that, baby?"

His question has more implication than it sounds like. He's really asking if I love him and I'm not surprised to realize that I do. We haven't had time to analyze any of this with all the chaos, but I think deep down, I knew. "Yes."

The snarl that escapes him precedes his hips, snapping harder and faster. I feel the emotions surrounding us increase, heading towards a crescendo that makes my heart thump like a bass drum. Suddenly, his cock pushes deeper and I feel it—his dick swells, pressing against my g-spot hard as it stretches me even more. Throwing his head back, he roars and fills me with hot come.

Was that a…

Just the thought of it makes my orgasm break free and I gasp as it rips through my body. My wings flutter against the sheets, throwing sparkles and dust into the air. I know it's going to make us loopy as fuck when we come down, but I can't help it. "Daddy…"

His voice is barely a whisper against the bite mark. "I love you, too."

That makes my ass clench, drawing a groan out of him, and I shudder as we come down. Fangs scrape over his mark just enough to create a trickle and I can feel his rough tongue lapping at the blood. My limbs are trembling and when his dick finally returns to normal, he slips out of me, gathering me into his arms. I wrap my arms around him, leaning my cheek against the top of his head as he suckles.

"Prez is gonna want to hear all about this," I murmur with a smile.

"Don't worry. He'll see. That ancient fucker has cameras everywhere in this weird ass museum," Teddy chuckles against my neck. "We can watch it together tonight. I'll enjoy his reaction. You might get spankings."

I groan softly. "You're assuming I'll be able to walk by then."

"If not, I'll carry you. Don't worry."

I could get used to that….

One Woman Army

Making the plan last night helped immensely. I didn't have the weird dreams about running through forests or odd magical gardens, so when I got up, I actually felt rested. That alone is a win, and it's helped me focus on getting a list together for travel. Packing my clothes and shit isn't hard; I moved around at the drop of a hat for years, but now I have companions and a bunch of other considerations.

Is this what people with kids feel like? If so, I know why they look tired all the damn time.

Jackson fought me a little when I presented the idea, but I expected that. I have some weirdo hiding in my bushes and a bunch of nasty bitches wasting their time trying to destroy me, so going out on my own sounds like an ill-advised plan. But since he and I are pulling enough strings to get my protectors allowed entry alongside me, it changes the landscape. With the wild cats, big dogs, python and giant eagle, I have enough distractions to allow me to run if necessary.

Not that I would.

I'm well trained in hand-to-hand combat and I'll be taking at least ten weapons to hide on my person. Whether he agrees or not, I'm not a damsel that needs saving. The fucking FBI trained me before they gave me the heave-ho, and I had plenty of experience with weapons and fight training in Europe. Just because he remembers the pathetic girl curled up in her dorm room listening to Jewel doesn't mean it's who I am today.

Shaking my head, I poke my head out the back door and whistle for my crew. They come bounding up and I put my sunglasses on before checking to see if Eury is flying overhead. Once I confirm she's on board, I step outside and click the key fob to set the locks and alarm. We walk to the driveway, hopping into my car in a practiced order, and I peel out.

Time for yet another iffy journey into the belly of the beast that is this gossipy town.

"Peanut!"

Oh, shit.

I turn towards the voice I'd know anywhere with a wide-eyed expression. Saoirse is waving her hands at me from across the store like a madwoman. I have seen little of my exiled family since I came home and I've been grateful that they are at least pretending to give me the space I demanded. I know I've felt Teddy's eyes at school occasionally, but he's stayed out of sight and kept his distance. Wolfie has made certain I don't see him at the farm. Even Doyle has behaved well enough that I haven't glimpsed his trademark fiery red hair.

But now Seer is here, and it's in public, so I have to be very cautious of how much information I give the wagging tongues about our rift. People will flock to get in the middle of the fight, especially if they think they can worm their way in between me and the guys. I'm not ready to decide like that yet and I don't need a herd of grasping debutantes making it even harder to work through.

So I walk down the main aisle of Atwater's with my head held high so the surreptitious glances don't see a chink in my armor. I know the animals are following me like a tribal leader and Isis gives me a fortifying squeeze from the inside of my jacket. I don't bring Eury inside of spaces like this, but I have the feeling she'd figure out how to get in if I needed her. Over the past few weeks, I realize my pets are purposefully surrounding me like a small army of fur, feathers, and scales to help me stay in balance as I process all the emotions rioting through me.

I'm grateful for it, to be honest.

I'd grown used to my found family during the short time we were assembled and without my companions, I am not sure I'd be doing as well as I am.

Once I get close enough to speak at a normal volume, I look at my bestie. She's as colorful as always, but there are dark circles under her eyes. Her face is pale and despite the makeup and accessories, she doesn't look as happy or full of sunshine as she normally does. I assume she's been staying with Julia and her men, which makes me wonder where the guys are. Some of them were in the middle of renovations to sell their places and for a tiny moment, I feel guilty.

That stops when a pang of betrayal echoes in my chest. I have a right to be angry with all of them and they are simply facing the consequences of their actions. With that thought, I give Seer a cool look. "Good morning, Saoirse. I didn't think I'd find many people here this early."

"I'm glad we ran into each other. Maybe we could grab a coffee at the diner and talk? I've been meaning to—"

"I'm very busy this morning. After I get what I need here, I need to drop it off and head out of town to the bigger stores for other things. I won't be able to do that, unfortunately." I give her a tight smile, hoping she understands I don't want to delve deeper into this conversation in this setting.

"But we need to talk, Peanut. It's been almost a month and—"

"Saoirse, I'm really glad we caught up," I say loudly enough for prying ears to hear. "We'll set something up later this week, okay?"

Her face falls, but she nods when she understands. I feel like a total bitch, but she should know this isn't the time or venue to discuss private things in the Hollow. There are too many people hoping to see me fail or looking to gather information to hurt me. Even something as innocuous as a fight with my best friend is fodder for their machinations and I don't have the spoons to deal with anymore bullshit right now.

"Looks like you're losing *all* of your allies, Jolene. Tsk, tsk."

My eyes get round as the grating tone of the woman who simply *cannot* stop digging her own grave hits my ears. I do not understand why Sherilynn Foster is incapable of understanding that I want nothing to do with her or this petty spat she keeps trying to propagate, but it's truly pathetic. Like Ursula in the *Little Mermaid* voice 'Pathetic'. I have set my boundaries over and over, both politely and in firm warnings, but she is so obsessed with making me her enemy that she refuses to let go.

It's going to ruin her reputation because I am only responding when she purposely provokes me. Her malevolent, toxic behavior will become obvious eventually and she will be the author of her own destruction.

I turn to look at the woman who has perfected an outward appearance of being a friendly, community focused citizen. It's no coincidence that she only personally attacks me in nearly empty grocery stores, closed door conferences, or the safety of her echo chamber at the restaurant. In public, she and her trolls send someone else like Antigone to do their dirty work. It's because they're all cowards and they want to maintain the 'welcoming committee' image they've crafted when others are watching.

Too bad I won't break like they want me to. Bigger monsters than them have tried and failed… even with sharper weapons.

"Sherilynn, I—" I'm cut off before I can finish my scathing retort by a flash of rainbow hair and colorful clothes.

Saoirse stands in front of the rail thin bobblehead, her expression full of fury. She's actually smaller than Sherilynn naturally, but the four-inch combat boots' heels bring her eye to eye with Princess Prada. They're like opposite ends of the spectrum: beige Burberry plaid and muted tones to a wild, punky rainbow raver. My bestie raises her hand and pokes the queen bee in the chest with one finger before she speaks.

"You, missus, need to Back. The Fuck. Off. Of. My Girl." Sherilynn looks like she's going to respond, but Seer stops her with another poke.

"I know your people, Foster. I've combed the files and I'm fully aware of what power you *think* you have and what you *actually* have. You may have gathered a cadre of low level hangers-on who are filling your head with delusions of grandeur, but that doesn't make their claims true. You are a self-centered, narcissistic, abusive bully that moves from target to target, pumping your undeserved ego for everything they can give you before you toss them aside for an alternative source. You don't have any power or skill of your own—you suck everyone around you dry, using them until they have nothing left to offer. That's why you have to take your frustrations from life out on others, even if they don't deserve it."

"You're crazy, O' Flanagan. You and that talentless hack you are friends with… you're both the bullies. You're telling everyone lies and making me and everyone who loves this town look bad by slandering us!" Sherilynn's head tilts as she makes that annoying smirk she thinks is cute. "Both of you need therapy and a life so quit being so awful to the people who make this place great."

I arch a brow as she continues to spout a bunch of nonsense full of psychiatric buzzwords and online catch phrases. *Does she think this makes her look more credible? Jesus Christ on melba toast, she sounds like some dipshit on social media waving their ass about shit they have no training in.* This will only make me look better if this devolves further than it already has. I mean, nothing on camera or in writing ever goes away. I guarantee Atwater's has cameras.

"Look, you fruitcake. Every time you approach Jolene like this, you show how incredibly unstable you are. One time, you got spanked by the Council. Since then, you've been coming at her like a stalker off their meds. I get that no one ever has ever called you out on your bullshit successfully because you dirty them up as much as possible so they can't fight back. That won't work this time. So take my advice and back off before one or both of us shows the world what lurks beneath the surface of that Facebook perfect facade. You won't like it when we do."

Something inside of me clicks and I let out a slow breath. It's not the right moment, but I think Seer just gave me an apology that triggered my forgiveness without even saying it out loud.

Damn it.

Movement behind Sherilynn catches my eyes and I see Benjy coming up behind her. I don't know if someone called him or this is fate, but he walks up to the group with a disapproving expression. "Ladies. This is not the place to have a street fight. It would mightily displease Nelia and the Council. I feel the tension in the air and just look at your animals, Jolene."

I blink, looking over my shoulder to see Jekyll, Hyde, Kali, and Hecate standing at the ready with pinned back ears and snarls. They're poised to fight if I give the okay and that would only get all of us in trouble. Sighing, I nod at Benjy and Seer. "He's right. This isn't fair to anyone here nor the Atwater's starting a brawl in their store. Seer, you and I will gather the rest of my stuff and leave. Sherilynn… I say this with the *utmost* disrespect. *Go. Fuck. Yourself.* If you don't stop coming at me, I *will* start caring about destroying you. I don't at the moment, but keep pushing me, and I will start caring."

Seer smirks at her. "You should see what happened to the last person she cared about destroying. It got us kicked out of Thailand. Several intelligence agencies had to cover our exit. It was epic in ways I *still* can't describe. You won't survive it; I guarantee. Your gremlins will flee, your support will vanish, and just like every other 'project' you've tried, you'll find yourself failed and alone."

Benjy gives her a look. "Enough." Turning to me, he pauses before he adds, "A friend as good as her isn't something to toss aside because of a disagreement. You should talk."

I give him a stern look and he shrugs, then takes Sherilynn's arm to lead her away as she complains loudly. That's the second time he's rescued me without asking for anything in return and I'm going to have to have a nice long talk with him, too, I think.

Christ, my life is complicated. I miss being footloose and fancy free.

No, I don't.

Fuck.

Scars to Your Beautiful

Saoirse

I *should buy the bootlegger a bloody bottle.*

Even with my heartfelt defense, I probably wouldn't have talked Peanut into hearing me out today. His intervention not only cleared that bint out of our airspace, but it forced my girl to allow me access to her as she shopped. Her animals are observing us, and I know they'd get in between us if I upset her. But that's not what I want.

What I want is to explain myself—not to excuse my behavior, but to help her understand my motivations.

"Look…" I pause as I gather my words. "I'm sorry for hurting you. I'm aware you have trust issues for a multitude of reasons from your past, and this cut you to the core. For that, I truly am regretful."

She looks at me with dark eyes, her face creased in a frown. "If you know all of that, it makes it worse, doesn't it?"

"Maybe?" I sigh as I pluck one item on the lists she's holding off the shelf and put it in my trolley. "I don't expect you to forgive my actions right now. I only want to explain what I can and hope we can build a new foundation together. Maybe you'll be able to forgive me later on and if so, we can repair the damage."

Jolene tosses another item into the basket. "You seem to believe that I'm incapable of understanding the explanation Julia gave me. I got it, but that doesn't mean I accept its premise. My best friend and lovers all know some huge secret about me I'm not allowed to know, and they developed relationships with me despite being aware of it. It poisons everything; I feel like everyone I've ever trusted is lying to me. The reason is irrelevant—you're all complicit."

"That's why I want to tell you what I *can* say so we can start... not fresh, but from a more honest place." I stop in front of the travel size display and my brows furrow. "Why are you buying this stuff? Are you going somewhere?"

"I don't believe it's any of your business at the moment," she sniffs. "If you have things to say, do it before we're done or don't do it at all."

Pinching the bridge of my nose, I try to wrangle words in a way that won't get me in trouble, but is also palatable for this public venue. The last thing I need is to get called in front of the damned Council. "We didn't meet by accident all those years ago. They sent me—for reasons you know I can't divulge—and that began the duration of my assignment. However, after spending time with you for a couple of weeks, I started thinking of you less as a project and more as my friend. That emotion grew quickly, and it didn't take long for me to be as devoted to you as my friend as I was to my work. I would have moved back to the States with you, but they ordered me not to."

She whirls around and glares at me. "You told me you had jobs lined up and would visit when you could—but you never did. Was that part of your 'orders', too?"

I nod. "Yes. There was a temporary person who watched when you came home. It's mostly for your safety and you're not the only person who has this type of... detail. I can't explain why or who commands it. But that person should have discouraged you from the path you chose and did not. No one knows why, but they've fallen off the grid since you got rejected and came here."

"What? The other person just disappeared?"

"Yes. There are people looking for them, but it's not been fruitful. That's part of why Julia and the guys traveled to Salem before Halloween. They asked me to join because I have specific skills that assist with tracking people who don't want to be found." Scratching the back of my neck, I ponder for a second and add, "We came back because a lead headed this way and it seemed to be dangerous. I don't know if that situation had anything to do with the fracas at the ball, I swear."

"Did they all know this? All of your shit? The reason for the trip?" Her expression turns unsure and my heart aches for my friend. She clearly loves those men dearly and after my weeks working on the mystery with them, I know they adore her.

"Some of it, not all. I made sure they knew when I'd be gone so they could help keep you safe while we were out of state. Each of them was aware of various amounts of the information based on their ties. We've been sharing more information now because everyone is worried about the creeper, the drugging, and a general unrest that seems to follow you."

Stomping her foot, she growls. "I'll just bet Teddy is neck fucking deep in all of this. His daddy is tied to everything in the fucking universe and the others are less encumbered by glorious purpose because of birth."

Oh, boy, is she wrong about that. Wait till she figures out my fellow fake Irishman.

"Edgar knows a lot. He's pretty ingrained in this shit because of heritage, but the others have their own purposes and duties. Jolene, you must understand that we *will* include you when the time is right. Right now, I honestly believe your lack of knowledge is safer than you realize. There's definitely someone or multiple someones putting pressure on you. Whether it's forcing you into the light or to harm is unclear, even to people who normally know everything. You *not* knowing yet is good—for now."

I walk closer, laying my hand on her arm. "We petitioned to give you more info once the guys started getting close to you, but they denied it. It's not the way things have been done and the people deciding do it for a much larger group than the amount of people living in the Hollow. The needs of the many and all that."

"Bullshit. I've been in many a hallowed hall of old money and influence. Those kinds of people decide based on what benefits *them* the most—never the masses." Jolene crosses her arms over her chest, glaring at me indignantly. "You know that as well as me. We were in those rooms and events *together*. We listened to the elites laugh about the 'little people' and 'peons' while they ate two thousand dollars an ounce of illegally imported caviar, Seer."

She's not wrong.

"I know, Peanut. Trust me, I know. And this… is not that. At least, not most of it. There are definitely *some* assholes like that involved, but the major players are fairly varied and more interested in protecting their people than making money or having influence. I can't explain how I know, but when we can show you, you will understand. I promise."

One cat lets out an irritated sound when she buries her face in her palms and moans in aggravation. When she raises her head, I can see how tired she is. I didn't notice before because I was focused on getting her to listen and then Sherilynn. But Jolene looks bloody exhausted, even if she's not acting like it. I lift my hand and pull back to give her some space. Her smile is grateful for a fleeting second, and it occurs to me she *must* be starting to absorb some of the guys' powers through the mating bonds.

That means pieces of them are in line with her own mysterious heritage.

"I'm being difficult because I'm hurt and I'm tired," she finally says. "I haven't been sleeping well. I don't know why; I slept fine on my own for years before those clowns came busting in."

Chuckling softly, I give her a knowing smile. "It's easy to get used to comfort and support, Peanut. But you need to sleep. Is anything else bothering you? Physically, I mean?"

My question is both out of concern and curiosity. If she's displaying physical quirks beyond what Prez knows about from the night Teddy mated with her, they need to know. A partially emerged, unaware shifter or supe is dangerous to themselves and others. I don't want some dickwad to send a hunting party after her out of spite.

"Yeah. I have weird fucking dreams—sometimes during the day— and I can only remember pieces of them. My body aches like my joints are on fire when I wake up and I've doubled the yoga trying to get it calmed down, but it's not working. I even added a shit ton of herbal stuff to my milkshakes and stuff to ward some of it off. But last night was the first night I slept well in weeks." She looks around for a moment, then pulls her sleeves up, showing me scratched up forearms. "I have this kind of shit everywhere. I'm thinking I'm scratching in my sleep. It must be the anxiety."

Uh, nope. She's shifting after she sleeps and the magic of the town, plus her binding, is keeping her from remembering everything.

"I think you need to visit Prez, Peanut. He might give you something to help you sleep. You can't run like that forever." I pause for a moment before I continue. "You could be... sleepwalking. That's dangerous. What if you fall down the stairs and no one's there? I mean, sure the animals, but by the time they found someone, you could die of a damn brain bleed."

Her skin pales and I know I made my point well. "Shit, Seer, I didn't think about that. I figured it was because of the stress and once I wrapped my head around everything, it would stop. It didn't seem like a big deal."

"It is," I say firmly. "See the doc. It's time you allowed the others to say their piece like I have—even if Benjy had to force it."

Her eyes narrow. "I'll consider it. Don't push me. We're not better yet just because we had this conversation, Saoirse. It's a start, but we still have work to do before I'm comfortable letting you tell me what to do."

I snort. "You're *never* comfortable with people telling you what to do."

That gets a soft laugh, and her expression softens. "Are they taking care of Wolfie and each other? Tell me they're okay."

She hates she feels like she has to ask, I can tell. But she wants to know.

"Yes, your darling boy is being looked after. Between the doc and the judge, he's being coddled to death. But like them, he misses you. They all do, even that assface Irishman."

"Good," she whispers. "I can't face them yet, but I don't want them to be alone."

"You're alone," I retort. "Why is that different?"

Her lips curve up. "Only sort of. I have the animals to keep me company and watch over me, plus other people have poked their heads in."

"Ah-ha. Besides Benjy, the white knight, I assume you've seen the history teacher and the prince, mm?"

Her eyes widen. "How did you know?"

I shrug. "I just do. Don't worry—that's not an issue. The guys won't be upset."

"Good goddess, Seer. How many dudes do they think I can handle? I am *not* adding any other people to my house. It's already a fucking zoo when everyone is in residence."

"Keep telling yourself that, Peanut. You've always been good at tragically lying to yourself." I smirk, then wink at her playfully. "I think you won't be given anything you can't handle—eventually."

Jolene takes in a deep breath and then grabs a few bottles out of the travel bins. "I am *not* caffeinated enough for this shit. Can we finish this list and grab some coffee on the way to my next errand? I'll let you come if you keep behaving."

The smile on my face is so big it feels like it might crack it. "Aye, Peanut. I'll come along for the ride. And coffee sounds like heaven in a cup."

"Let's go, guys," Jolene says as she jerks her head at the animals. "We've got shit to do."

EVERYTHING SUC

Jolene

The errands and coffee turned into an all day adventure as I purchased the things I'd need for a month-long trip overseas. I was careful to omit items that might give away my intentions because I have at least a week before school is out. The things I want that would tip Seer off can be ordered online and until I feel comfortable with other people knowing where I'm headed, I'll sacrifice a convenience for secrecy.

Truth be told, having Seer spend the night while we talked and reminisced about our past helped a lot. I wasn't looking forward to wondering if I'd get a good night's rest when she left. Since she stayed, we might have been up late, but I didn't have confusing dreams or wake up aching. She helped me clean up our mess in the kitchen from cooking dinner and breakfast, then hugged me and left. It surprised me she didn't extend her stay more, but maybe she listened when I said I need time to work through all of my emotions.

I don't know that the guys will be as patient, especially once they find out I've spoken with Seer.

I pop my Airpods in and grab my mat. During the re-model, Teddy insisted we extend the back porch and build an enclosed living area with all the creature comforts for the winter. I thought it was silly and extravagant, but now that it's November and I can set my yoga stuff up outside but not in the cold, I may have changed my opinion. The damn thing even has an electric fireplace and I can let the morning light in by raising the shades.

It figures that asshole would design me the perfect space to meditate and by the time I figure it out, he's made me kick him out.

Jekyll and Hyde perch on the couch, standing at the ready as I turn on the fire and scents. Kali and Hecate hop onto the chairs while Isis and Eury find their own spots. My audience all waits for me to begin, and I chuckle. "I'm going to call Jackson and iron out the details. He was a little blasé when we spoke the other night. I need to make sure he's got everything settled."

"*Mrrp,*" Hyde responds. Barks echo her sentiment, so I know they'll all behave.

Positioning myself on the mat, I reach up and tap the earphone. "Call Jackson." Once the line rings, I forward fall, holding the stretch while I wait for my party loving friend to answer.

"*Hola!* Jackson's Party Line, how may I direct your call?"

Frowning as I wrap my arms around my legs, I snap, "Who is this? Jackson, if you're cheating on Eli, I'll chop your balls off and stuff them somewhere uncomfortable."

"Ooooooo! You *must* be the spicy Jo-Jo. I appreciate the sentiment, but alas, I *am* Eli, and I enjoy his balls where they are currently."

Christ on a unicycle.

I make my way to the floor, lying on the ground as I feel myself connect to my body and the earth. "That's comforting. Can I talk to Jackson, please?"

"You're breathing funny. Either you're exercising or doing something naughty while you're on this call, and I'm definitely hoping for the latter. I'll put this on speaker because Jackson is a little tied up."

"I can call back if you're—"

"Jo-Jo, he's being a shithead. I'm kneading bread dough, not tied up on a St. Andrew," my friend finally calls out.

He's… making bread? I'm much more inclined to believe the silver spoon-fed lawyer is on the aforementioned cross, honestly. "I'm weirded out by that, Jax. You burned water in college."

A deep, knowing sigh echoes over the line. "I will *never* live that down. Yes, Eli has me 'broadening my horizons', which I think is code for living like a normie. So today, we're making bread although we can order, buy, or jet plane to gourmet bread that is *pre-made* by five star chefs. It's quite the *experience*."

I release my foot and muffle my giggle at his ridiculous elitism. Jax isn't really as superficial as he pretends, but he's definitely not someone who's fully in touch with reality. "Eli, I commend your effort and patience. He's useless at everything that doesn't involve partying, shopping, the law, and sex."

"Truer words," the hacker replies. "So, for what do we owe the honor of your call this bright and early?"

"I spoke to him the other night about taking a month-long trip to Istanbul. He said he'd arrange for me to borrow one of the Thorn family jets so I can skirt the hassles at customs about my companions and weapons." I pause for a moment, rolling my eyes at myself. "I sound like some cheesy spy in a movie, but that is the reason."

"We settled that, Jo-Jo. You didn't need to call about it!" Jax yells. "Man, I'm giving my hands a hell of work out here. Poor Eli's sex life is gonna suffer when my fingers won't move for days."

I groan as I push up into a sea lion pose, stretching my lower back. "Gross, Jax. Don't be a perv. I wanted to make sure it would be okay if I maybe—not for sure—added a guest."

"Whiiiiich onnnnne?" he sing-songs. "One of those hunks found his way in the back door… maybe literally."

Eli snorts. "Only if he was lucky, I'm sure."

Hecate save me. I might kill them if they don't stop being so vomit-inducingly cute.

"No back door action here besides me coming out to the porch to do yoga and call you dipshits. But I started a dialogue with Seer and I haven't asked her because I don't want anyone to know, but—"

The snickers on the other end of the line confuse me. Is it funny that I might make up with my best friend? I can never figure out what the hell is going on in Jackson's mind since he and Eli became an item.

"What's so funny?"

"Oh, nothing, Jo-Jo. I'm sure one more person won't be a problem. The plane is pretty big, even with your furry cargo along. I'm sending the larger one because it gets used less. No one will notice it's gone."

Uh...

"Jackson, you *are* informing whoever the hell you need to that it's going to be in use, right?"

"Of course!" I hear a smack that says he's still working on the bread—probably not well. "But I'm going to have the accountants tuck that expense somewhere beneficial to me and I don't want people looking at its destinations too closely."

Great. Now I'm part of his tax scam. Good thing he's my lawyer.

"Okay. Are you working up an info packet with Eli? I'll need everything you can find on the cop, the embassy, and the area we're traveling in. I want to study it all on the long ass plane flight. I plan to be completely ready when I walk onto the tarmac." I lean over and fold my body in half, holding onto my feet. "The more prepared I am, the faster I can accomplish what I came to do. Then I can come home and you won't be worried."

"Fine! Eli will get it all ready and send along the files digitally and by courier in hard copy. But you promise you will not take chances while you're over there. Even if you bring those zoo refugees and your girl, I'm still not convinced it's safe."

"I promise, Jax. I'll stay in touch daily and I'll be careful. It's not my first time overseas or my first time in Constantinople."

"It's Istanbul, not Constantinople," he replies automatically.

I laugh at our nerdiness and reply, "Then I'll be waiting in Istanbul."

Once I finished my morning meditation and the conversation with Jax, I showered and threw on my painting clothes. I had to be at my studio so Brittania and a few other older students could work on their projects. Since we didn't have school on the Wednesday before Thanksgiving, I volunteered to let them work on their shit while I started the cleanup for the winter break. I'd have to do this much more quickly at the school, but in my space, I can get the place ready for an extended absence.

Luckily for me, the teens were all way too focused on their pieces for exams to be jerks to me. I could get unused spaces straightened, the front gallery ready for another show in mid-January, and answer emails while they worked. When the last kid finally finished cleaning up their spot, I called the pack from the back and closed up. I'll have to do one more run-through before I leave and put a sign in the window, but the first two weeks of Winter Break in the Hollow usually consisted of the rich kids leaving to ski before Christmas and the not rich kids working.

I won't be missed.

The last thing on my list for the day is to file some paperwork with the mayor's office about the closure for the month and I'll be free to head home and veg. I'm thinking I should watch British comedies tonight, and if I order early enough, I can get DoorDash to deliver Chinese from one town over. I've earned a break from all the prep and chaos swirling around me as I go about my week, I think.

It's too cold to walk down to the office, so I load up my crew and drive the short distance to park in front of Town Hall. I buried Isis under my coat, sucking up all of my warmth, and the others are sporting matching sherpa lined fighter pilot jackets I ordered on the 'Zon. I'm sure Teddy has never outfitted his King Danes in anything but their spiky collars, but I refuse to let the wiry-haired guard dogs shiver as the weather gets colder. Plus, I kind of like the look of striding in with an army of leather jacket wearing protectors. It's *trés* West Side Story and if he doesn't like it, he can have a quarter to call someone who gives a fuck.

I walk into the main atrium, looking around for the odious toad who runs the desk. When he appears from behind a curtain, I damn near lose my shit. "Afternoon, Aldous. Were you getting ready to ask who dares approach the great and powerful Oz?"

His glare makes my heart sing. "You should know better than to insult the person who controls access to the building, Miss Whitley. I'll have you know that absolutely no one is available today and you've wasted your time."

Rolling my eyes, I unzip my jacket slightly to allow Isis to peek out. Her low hiss makes him jump, and he leans down to pick up two of the ugliest Sphynx cats I've ever seen. "Jesus Christ in pickle brine! Where did you catch two Gollums with tails?"

"Do *not* say such things about Poe and Parker! They have delicate sensibilities!"

Give me a break.

"I need to see the Mayor. I'm sure she has time for me. It will only take a moment, Aldous." I tilt my head and give him the patented, bitchily polite Southern smile. "I doubt you want my overprotective gang of beasts around your precious…" I have to stop because my own unintentional pun cracks me up and I cover my mouth to keep from snorting.

"I never! You are the rudest little tra—"

A voice echoes in the wood paneled room, cutting him off. "Aldous, I hope to Hades you aren't going to finish that sentence the way I think you are."

My eyes widen and I look up at the staircase to the upper level to see Doyle smirking down at us.

Fuck, fuck, fuckitty, fuck, fuck….

"I don't take orders from you, Haggerty. I'm only beholden to the May—"

Aldous' face turns red, and he chokes, his whole body shaking as he tries to breathe. The red-haired man descends the stairs slowly, his expression bland as he holds a hand to his ear. "I'm sorry, Long-worth, I don't believe I can hear you. Do you need some water?"

The malevolent little Oompa Loompa glares at us and continues, trying to catch his breath. His cats hiss and jump from his arms, abandoning him to curl up in a bed near the curtain. When he turns purple, I look at the gleeful man I didn't intend to see today with concern.

"I hate this motherfucker, but maybe we should do the Heimlich. If he dies in front of me, I'll have to feel guilty."

"Oh, fine." Doyle sighs and walks over to the water pitcher on the sideboard.

The blockage seems to clear up immediately and Aldous takes the glass my lover offers with a murderous look in his eyes. "I'll get you for that, you nasty man."

Again, I'm reminded of the *Wizard of Oz* and I almost lose it. "Doyle, is Nelia up stairs? I need to speak with her."

"Aye, love. You go on up with your beasties and I'll stay here to help our struggling friend."

That doesn't sound sinister at all.

I decide I hate Aldous just enough to ignore my bad feeling. "Thanks. Come on, guys. We have to get this done before we can go home and relax."

Doyle waves as I turn on my heel and head upstairs, but I can feel his eyes on me the entire way.

Something tells me he will not stay away for much longer.

Love The
Way You Lie

Doyle

The people in this town are infuriating, but my auntie won't allow me to deal with them in a manner befitting my bloodline. So I let that weasley little shite off with a warning that would have turned his hair white if it wasn't already. I've never liked his smarmy, entitled attitude, but I draw the fucking line at him calling my woman a tramp to her face.

It should have earned him a punishment equivalent to having his liver eaten daily only to regrow, but my hands are tied.

However, I sent Odie up to listen in at the Mayor's door while I took out the trash, and what he found out set me on the path I'm taking now. My raven is accustomed to sneaking around and staying out of sight—something that comes in very handy in this town. Most people don't even realize he's a companion, much less that he belongs to me. It's useful in more ways than I can count, as is the fact that he can show me what he sees when I send him out to spy.

Yes, yes. I'm aware some gits stole the old ways for a hit TV show. I'd like to smite Hollywood, too, but again… auntie says 'no'.

I walk behind the column, waiting for Aldous to disappear into his cubby hole again and then disappear. I'm also not supposed to use portal jumps to travel here, but I can only follow so many rules before I want to test my immortality. It's bad enough that I'm stuck in

Hicksville, USA, with these rich first and second gen supes who think money makes them untouchable, but limiting the use of my powers makes it so much worse.

Appearing on my front porch, I yank the door open and stalk inside. "Oh, LUCYYYYY, I'm HOOOMME!"

Wolfgang's head pops over the upper railing, and it occurs to me that Prez calls him that. He probably thought I meant for just him to come running, but I want these assholes to get down here. It's time for a family meeting.

"Oi! Boone, Hamilton! You, too. Family meeting or some shit," I yell as I walk into the lounging room. It's not a living room—all rooms are bloody living rooms if it's not a goddamned funeral home. I'll fight people on that because I'm old enough to remember when words weren't ridiculous. Pouring myself a Jameson, I realize I'll need to calm my ire before I set the alpha dog and his pups off with my bristly attitude.

When they finally file in, I plop onto one of the huge lounges, moving all the materials we've been using to research aside. "We need to talk."

"I gathered that, given your bellowing," Boone replies as he walks over and pours his bourbon. He looks at the other two and when they nod, he procures two more.

What a soft Dom that git is. He's taking care of them like he's claimed them both.

I pause my thoughts before they derail by shaking my head. It wouldn't be the first time I lost focus because I found something to poke at; I live for causing chaos and I haven't done nearly enough of it today. "Right before I left, our girl came in to talk to Nelia. I used Odie to listen in because I was busy taking care of an insect that needed to be squashed. But what he heard is important."

"What did he hear?" Wolfie asks as he accepts the drink from Edgar. The judge drops down next to him and he curls in between the two of them like a cat.

I'm feeling left out, and that irritates the shit out of me.

"I'm getting there. He showed me their conversation, and it sounds like she's planning to take off somewhere for the month you gits are off school. She didn't say *where* she's going, but it sounds like she intends to go without telling us."

Boone chuckles, looking at the vet with a smirk. "I know where she's going."

Prez and I both look at him in surprise. I run my hand through my hair and pace, trying not to take my frustration out on them. I hate not being in control. "Did a cat get your tongue or are you going to tell the rest of the class?"

"You just got home, Haggerty. Chill. I was going to call this meeting, too." Edgar stretches his legs out on the ottoman and stacks his hand behind his head. "Jackson called this morning. Tilly asked him to borrow one of his jets so she can go overseas with the pets."

"*Where* overseas?" Presley asks. He sips the bourbon calmly, but I can tell he's not happy.

"Istanbul," Wolfie supplies. "She's obviously going to look for that cop."

My temper flares and a burst of magic flares over me. "What?!"

"Calm down, Hades," Edgar says with a smirk. "Cool your godly bullshit. I took care of it."

"How?"

He grins at Presley and ruffles Wolfie's hair. "The same way I always do. With wit, charm, and a little pressure applied in the right places. Thorn will let us hop along over on his plane with her, but we have to go convince her to let us come."

Squinting, I look at the lounging alphahole like he's either simple or idiotic. "She barely spoke to me today. Exactly how do you plan on convincing her to allow us to escort her on a trip she's purposely kept secret from us?"

Boone just smirks and the other two look at one another before they say, "Wit, charm, and a little pressure applied in the right places."

"Gag me with a spoon, Doubledick Twins." I shake my head and let the magic coursing over recede. "That's not going to work."

"Care to place a wager on it, Haggerty?" The dark-haired judge is in his element now. Gambling is his third favorite vice, and he definitely knows how to play the odds.

But I know entropy like it's part of my DNA.

"Fine, I'll play along. But when she throws us out on our arses, you all have to post a video extolling my virtues on social media."

"Agreed," he grins. "But if you lose, deal with the animal clean-up for the entire trip."

I nod and jerk my head at the door. "Let's ride, fuckers. I can't wait to see Edgar discussing how magnificent my cock is on TikTok."

"You wish," is all he says as he struts towards the front door.

Huh. Maybe. We'll see Teddy Bear.

WHEN WE ARRIVE AT MY TíOGAIR'S HOUSE, I'M ABOUT AS HYPER AS I can be without being destructive. It hurt a little to see her and have her look through me, but we all knew she was going to be angry. Normally, I would have stormed the gates and ignored the wishes of the person keeping me from what I want, but with Jolene… I don't want to fuck this up.

I've never felt like that before—not once in all the millennia I've been kicking around this spinning ball.

"I hope your fecking plan works," I grumble as we tumble out of the car. "Because I'm in no mood to get kicked to the curb."

"You need to calm down," Presley says quietly. "It's obvious that you're on the edge. That won't help anything. Take a couple of breaths and get it together."

My eyes narrow, but I nod sharply. He's not wrong and if it had been Boone who said it, I would have punched him. Luckily, the birdman and the Fae are the more placid of the four of us. "I'm trying. If I'd know we were going to do this, I might have burned some of this shit off, but you kept it to *yourself.*"

Edgar stops, rubbing the back of his neck. "Shit. I probably should have texted, but I didn't want to interrupt people since both of you had busy days. I wasn't actually hiding anything."

Again, Presley and I look at each other in shock.

Wolfie looks up at the judge and squeezes his hand. "That was good."

I'll be damned. The subbie is taming the big bad hellhound. Will wonders never cease?

"I appreciate that, Edgar, but personally, Jolene is always worth an interruption." The doc pushes up his glasses and looks at me. I nod in agreement and he continues. "Keep us all in the loop. Because if Doyle is right and there are more who will join, we will *have* to communicate."

"Bugger, don't remind me," I groan. "Four is hard enough at the bloody moment. Seven is going to be a feckin' nightmare."

"Uh, guys?" We look at Wolfie as he points at the front door. "We've been spotted."

I swear, it's like I hear the fucking death knell in my ears as we all trudge up the driveway to the porch.

"I don't recall extending an invite," my Tíogair says as we filter in and find seats among the various companions lounging on her furniture.

Looking around, I see she ordered Chinese and has been indulging in several flavors of milkshakes while she watched comfort movies. The scattered pillows and blankets tell me she's not sleeping in her room and, for a moment, guilt races through me. It's not an emotion I've felt often in my many years and I ponder the changes in me since I met the raven haired woman who's still grumbling at us. I didn't think it was possible to change beings as old and set in our ways as me, but here she is, barely a few decades old and dressing me down like a kid.

I'll be a two headed goat.

"Tilly," Edgar says, finally cutting off the flow of her irritable babbling. "We didn't come to make trouble, but there's no way in hell we can let you go overseas by yourself with all the shit that's happened."

Her eyes blaze and I grin as I see the hound he tries so hard to suppress flare up in our girl as easily as breathing. Jolene is going to be an absolutely stunning force of nature when her powers all emerge. She won't hesitate for a second to turn someone to ash if they make her angry—I can hardly wait. "*Let me?!!*"

I suck a slow breath in through my teeth and look at the docs with a smirk. The chaos is about to begin and it's making my blood hum. *This* is why I made the bet with dog breath; I knew he'd come on so strongly that our girl would lose her mind. Amping up the tempers in the room is *bound* to make for fun and games—something I didn't get nearly enough of today to feed my hunger.

None of them understands how much I thrive off of the energy that unpredictable mania gives off.

"I don't think he meant—" Wolfie starts, but her cutting glare cuts him off. He ducks his head, cheeks flushing as he shuts his mouth.

"It's not *safe*," Boone huffs as he looks at the three of us for support. "Hell, running around in other countries alone isn't safe for most humans, but definitely not for someone with a propensity for stumbling into trouble. Don't get me started on the stalker we haven't identified yet."

Presley pauses for a moment, then finds his spine. "It worries me, too, Magpie."

She puts her hands on her hips, the fury in her aura swirling around her like a whirlwind. They can't see it, but I can, and it's magnificent. "Tíogair, no one is saying you can't take care of yourself, per se…"

Sue me, I'm fomenting the delicious dissent because I know where it's going.

"Per se???!!" she practically screeches. Her cats jump up, hair standing on end, and the snake on the floor slithers towards her like a homing missile.

Wolfie tries again, rising to his feet as he holds a hand out. "Sugarplum…"

"Don't. Patronize. Me. Wolfie."

I grin as that fire in her eyes flames up again, and the air thickens. Looking over at Edgar, I can see the ripples of his supe sides pushing at him. His jaw is set, fists are clenched, and his entire body is tense. A glance at Hamilton tells me he's having trouble as well. All is on schedule—the more Jolene's supernatural sides demand to be set loose, the more her mates and future mates will feel the burn to allow theirs to emerge as well. She might not remember a second of it tomorrow, but the effects of this will help us all move on.

Jolene walks away from the vet, striding over to our resident hellhound and bending to get in his face. I almost clap my hands in glee; this is perfect. "You four lost the right to have a say in where I go or what I do when you spent months *lying to me.*"

Edgar's hand shoots out, grabbing her shirt and hauling her onto his lap in a straddle. His other buries in her hair, wrapping it around his fist to pull her face back so he's looking up at her. "Not by *choice.* After our past, I would never do anything to hurt you again by *choice.* All I want to do now is protect what is *mine.*"

"I don't belong to anyone," Jolene spits back.

The scent of everyone's arousal fills the air, and I observe carefully. There will be a precise moment when I can allow my magic to spill, and that will be the tipping point. I have to do it at exactly the right moment, though, or it won't work.

Patience isn't my strong suit, so it's killing me.

"We all belong to someone, Sugarplum," Wolfie says as he approaches. He looks down at her as Boone holds her hair tightly, his expression serious. "There are three types of family: those you're born to, those you give birth to, and those you accept into your heart when you find them. The last one is us—you found all of us and now we're a family."

Her expression softens for a moment as she looks up at the Fae and I know the moment I'm waiting for is getting close. "Goddamnit, Wolfie…"

The growly hound she's perched on takes that opening, burying his face in her neck and nipping at it before he lifts his head again. "You're mine. He's mine. These idiots are mine."

There's the full on doggy, but I'm waiting for contestant number two.

The doc stands up, heading over to wrap his arms around Wolfgang as he looks down at our girl as well. "As poetic as that was, you're all mine, too. Don't you feel the same?"

She wants to keep fighting because her human side says there needs to be more words, more groveling, and more begging for forgiveness. But the truth is, forgiveness isn't supposed to be about demanding subjugation in exchange for approval. Sometimes, it's about accepting when people admit their mistakes and setting boundaries for the future. Maturity is knowing how to allow others grace when they fuck up without expecting people you love to prostrate themselves for failing.

I'm interested to see what my Tíogair chooses.

"I owe all of you an apology as well."

That garners a chorus of denials from the three men surrounding her, but I stay quiet. I want to hear what she has to say.

Jolene rolls her eyes up to look at the docs, then back down to Edgar, and over to me briefly. "I lashed out because it hurt me. My trauma from Trevor and the betrayal in the present collided to trigger the shit out of a wound I thought was long healed. I should have allowed you to explain, not sent you all packing without a word. It was unfair and I'm sorry for it."

Boone blinks, looking at Prez and Wolfie. They seem equally confused by the situation, and I sigh heavily. You'd think being one of the Greeks, I'd have the most dysfunctional family, but obviously, I don't. None of them know how to take someone taking account-ability for their actions like a fucking adult.

"I accept your apology, Tíogair," I reply as I tilt my head. "I'm not ashamed that I could not be totally honest with you, but I am quite regretful that it hurt you. That I won't be able to give you everything you want despite this lovely conversation irks me as well. I'm displeased, but my hands are tied—not in a good way, either."

Someone had to address the elephant in the room.

"Don't be an ass, Haggerty," Edgar growls as he shifts under her. The movement pulls a groan from Jolene and his lips curve up. "Otherwise this won't end with nudity."

"Oh, I'm not worried about that." Our girl didn't protest at his remark and *this* is the opening I was waiting for. "Not when she's practically dripping for us over there."

Her head whips to the side to give me a dirty look, making Edgar's hold on her pulled harder. The sensation makes her gasp softly and the chain reaction starts. Presley hauls the vet against him and kisses him hard. The snarling judge tugs her back to kiss her roughly, and I stack my heads behind my head in satisfaction. All I have to do now is give the darker parts of my makeshift family a wee nudge and this will be grand.

"*Apeleftheróste ti nýchta mésa…*[1]"

As soon as the words leave my mouth, the darkness descends like a familiar blanket.

It's about to get very interesting in this house.

I Wanna Be Your Slave

Jolene

There's no time to question what the hell Doyle just said because Teddy yanks me forward by the hair and kisses me like he's trying to swallow me whole. A jolt of energy sparks over my skin and it sets me on fire from head to toe. Wriggling my hips over the very noticeable erection I'm perched over, my mouth clashes violently with his as lips, teeth, and tongues battle for dominance. My fingers dig into his shoulders and my back arches, making the sting on my scalp intensify.

Holy Aphrodite in a brothel. I think I almost came just now.

Shivers run through me as I lament the impending death of the lingerie I'm wearing. There's no way any of it making it out intact, not with the sounds Teddy is making and the scent of my boys' arousal behind me. I vaguely hear tearing and zippers, then a dark moan of pleasure. Wolfie is definitely on his knees; I know what it sounds like when Prez is getting head and he's making those lovely little chirps and gasps. When Teddy tugs my head back, his eyes are almost black and his expression is hungrier than I've seen. It's like whatever the fuck Doyle muttered unleashed something in him and it's ready to feast.

His hands frame my hips, lifting me up to sit me on the couch facing the back of it. "Put your hands on the back and your ass in the air, *drugar.*"

I don't always take orders, but fuck, he's hot right now.

I place my hands on the back cushions, holding on them as I position myself as instructed. Looking over my shoulder, I see Presley with his hands buried in Wolfie's hair, guiding his head as he sucks him off like a pro. That makes my pussy throb—the sight of them is always hot, but the adoration my little vet has gleaming in his eyes as he looks up at the doc is breathtaking. A sharp slap on my ass brings me back to focus, and I see Teddy standing behind me with that wicked look on his face.

"Good girls get to watch. You haven't earned it yet, Tilly. Turn around."

Fuck. Me…. please.

Shades of the first night I was home and he damn near destroyed me flash before my eyes, so I do as I'm told eagerly. Doyle suddenly appears in front of me, his cock out in his hand as he strokes it roughly. His smile is just as dark and delicious as my ex-bully's and I realize I'm about to have a *very* rough ride.

"Open those pretty lips, Tíogair. I'm going to watch him fuck you senseless while you suck me off. If you're good, we might even let Hamilton and the pup join in when they're done. Do you want that? Do you want to be completely filled?"

My eyes widen as another burst of energy pushes against my skin, making me even wetter. I don't know how they're doing this, but I'm gonna leave a spot on this couch for sure. "Yessss…"

"Then open your mouth, Tilly," Teddy says. He doesn't wait for me to respond. He simply reaches down and rips the crotch out of my silky PJ pants with one yank.

As if this couldn't get any fucking hotter.

I open my mouth, darting my tongue out to lick the moisture on the tip of Doyle's cock. He grunts and tugs on my hair roughly, making me wiggle my ass in the air. Being exposed while my cunt is dripping with arousal and the room is filled with lovely moans is making me clench inside. I need something and for now, this is what I'm getting, so I wrap my lips around him. Swallowing him down as far as I can immediately, I revel in the sound he makes as my tongue teases over the vein on the underside. I rub against it slowly, breathing in his scent as I slide back and bob over his dick.

"That's my girl," Teddy murmurs. "Keep taking him while I get you ready."

There's no mistaking what the means because I'm soaked, so he's definitely planning on fucking my ass. My lower body pulses again as I moan around Doyle. I'm not sure what's going to happen after tonight, but for the moment, all I can think or feel is this connection we all have. The desire is so thick that it's choking me almost as much as Lucky's cock, and I have no idea how I'm going to walk tomorrow.

Cool gel makes me gasp and I feel fingers working in and out of my ass slowly, scissoring as they stretch me. This is not my first time— thank fuck—but it's been a little while. I push back into his digits and Doyle thrust into my mouth at the same time. He brushes the back of my throat, but I breathe through it as tears fall from my eyes. When the fingers slip away, I look up at my Irish firebrand and for a second, I see a flash in his eyes I haven't seen before. He lets out a soft huff, pausing his thrusts as he stares at me.

"There she is," he whispers. His eyes tear away from mine to look behind me. "She's ready, Boone. Do it now and don't hold back. Take what you need."

Teddy's cock slams into me almost immediately and I cry out, the sound vibrating over Doyle's dick as it pushes further into my throat. It feels like I'm being split open as the dominant behind me stops when he's fully seated inside of me. His voice is raspy when he replies. "Hamilton, let the pup wiggle under her. I want to feel him push against me while we fuck our woman. He can keep sucking you once he's in position."

Oh. My. Goddess.

I close my eyes, letting them run the show completely. My teeth graze over Doyle when I feel Wolfie slide under me with more ease than I would have expected. Within seconds, the feel of his ladder sliding inside me damn near sends me over the edge. I've been holding on as the boys took control, but something about this room on this night is making me crazy. I'm going to come soon and I won't be able to stop it.

Another groan tells me my little Wolfie has Presley taken care of next to us. I run my teeth over Doyle's shaft lightly, loving how his hips buck in response. All of them surrounding makes my chest ache and I almost get teary-eyed for a very different reason. Humming softly, I push my hips down and back, reveling in the stretch. If Doyle wasn't fucking my mouth, I'd tell them how good this feels, but I can't, so instead, I let go of our problems to live in the moment.

"There we go, pup. Fuck, I love feeling you push me against while we do this. Suck on Presley's cock so daddy can watch." Another burst of arousal that makes me clench around them and suck hard on Doyle follows his words.

Shit. I was sure I didn't think the daddy thing was sexy, but day-yum when he says it to Wolfie….

Every inch of my body trembles at his words and the orgasm crashes into me before I know it. Squeezing both of them as the pleasure crawls over my skin, I have to consciously hold Doyle deep in my mouth as the muffled sounds escape me. Teddy's fingers dig into my hips hard, bruising my skin as he leans down and puts his nose next to my ear. I can vaguely hear some foreign words and then yet another orgasm slams into me. His lips land on a spot on my neck, and the oddest sensation takes over.

"Fuck, Boone, you might have triggered one…"

Doyle's voice sounds awfully far away for someone who has their dick in my mouth. The crawling under my skin gets more intense and I rock back into Teddy, then forward into Wolfie, spearing myself on them as I blindly work my mouth over the shaft in it. It feels like I'm chasing *their* climaxes now and though my vision is getting foggy,. I keep moving until I hear each of them make the telltale sound that signals the crest has hit them.

Pulling my head back, I swallow the evidence with a drowsy smile, squinting my eyes as I try to focus on the shadowy figure that is my fiery lover. "That wassss hottttt…"

It's all I can manage at the moment, but I feel the guys withdraw, and powerful arms lifting me up from the couch.

"You lose, Haggerty. Clean the fucking couch."

Even when we're not fucking, Teddy's an alpha asshole.

My eyes close and I let them take me wherever they want. I'm so lazy and buzzing with pleasurable sensations that I don't have it in me to fight. Just for tonight, I'm letting them be in charge while I rest for a bit…

MY EYES FEEL GRITTY WHEN I OPEN THEM AND I HAVE BLINK THEM several times to see the room.

I try to move, and every single muscle in my body screams. It feels like someone tore me limb from limb and reassembled me—poorly. Tilting my head a little, I squint at the new view of the room, noting that it's completely trashed.

What the shit? I know they fucked the bitch out of me, but what fresh hell is this?

The fuzziness in my brain frustrates me and I loll my head to the other side, wincing as my neck protests. I know for sure I've never in my life had sex so gymnastic that I can't even turn my fucking head in the morning. These assholes have some explaining to do. Both me and my fucking living room are *destroyed,* and I can't seem to remember how it happened.

"Don't worry, sugarplum." His mumble comes from my left armpit and I carefully arrange myself so I can look down at Wolfie.

"Easy for you to say," I croak weakly.

A rumbling chuckle vibrates under my cheek and I realize Wolfie is curled up between Teddy and I. That means the body behind me is likely Doyle and Prez must be the one with his head on my stomach.

That's why it's hot as fuck in here. Too many bodies cocooning me.

"Gonna need air. You fuckers are roasting me." My eyes close and I smile a little, feeling better now that I can snipe at them a little.

Doyle leans over and presses a kiss to my temple. "Says the chit who *insisted* we make a nest on the floor to sleep on."

I did? Why the fuck wouldn't I want to go upstairs?

"Leave her be," Presley chides as he yawns against my skin. "She'll need to eat. We all do. Last night consumed a lot of energy."

"Thank you, Doctor McNuggies. Your clinical opinion is noted," I grumble. How do they know what happened and I'm drawing a fucking blank… as *always*.

"You haven't called me that in a while, Magpie. I enjoy hearing your sass."

"You're gonna love when I let you dipshits have it for whatever the fuck went on in this room. All I can see is broken shit and torn up shit and it smells like a French cathouse in here. Ugh…"

They all laugh and I sigh deeply. Men will always preen at evidence of their sexual prowess, even if it gets them kicked in the balls. Which, to be honest, is looking like a distinct possibility if their smugness isn't dialed down a notch by the time I can move again.

"Pup, you and the other doc start breakfast. We have to feed this woman before she'll be capable of kicking our asses the way she wants to." Teddy rolls to the side and tugs me free of the pile. I glare at him because even that hurts like a bitch, but it's nothing compared to the sound I make when he bends down and hefts me up. Throwing me over his shoulder with my bare ass pointed at the group, he gives it a slap. "C'mon you lazy shits. Time to take care of our girl."

My mouth drops open and I protest, especially because now my ass is *cold*, but he rubs his hand over the spot soothingly and all the angry words disappear.

Fucking sex wizards, that's what they are.

"I'm not eating at the table naked!" I grumble against his back.

"Of course not. We're sitting at the counter," Doyle says cheerily.

"Find her robe, Haggerty. While you're at it, find us all pants. No one needs to eat naked unless they're at a hippie commune."

"Fine. But I already paid my debt!"

I raise my hand to pinch the bridge of my nose. If I had any idea what was going on, I'm sure I'd be much more irritated. As it is, I'm watching hot guys parade around my kitchen, flashing their biteable asses at me.

Maybe knowing what's going on is overrated.

TROUBLEMAKER

PRESLEY

Lucy is a fantastic chef and I'm little more than his line cook, but he whips up all of our girl's favorites with ease. Waffles, scrambled eggs, bacon, sausage links, and a pitcher of milkshakes that smell fruity and flowery at the same time grace the counter. Doyle found everything we needed to cover the important parts, though every time Magpie stops talking mid-sentence to watch one of our asses in the boxer briefs, I have to cover my mouth. She won't like the teasing, but I can tell she likes the view.

"More eggs, please," she says, wiping her mouth on the fancy napkins Lucy picked out of her drawers.

I grin, taking her plate and heaping more protein on it, including more bacon. Boone has her settled firmly on his lap and she's not moving anytime soon. He kept her hanging with her ass in the air until we sat down and no amount of wiggling deterred him. I know why, of course. Jolene can't see it because of the binding, but his eyes are still pitch black and he's still feeding off the sexual energy coming for her as she ogles us.

I wasn't the town doc when he emerged, but whoever was should be whacked over the head with a SMDM 2022.

No caladrius alive would have allowed him to emerge with two sides, but never learn to control one of them. That's not even addressing how he hid a *third side*, but I plan on having a talk with Andromeda Bane when she's back from her latest trip to Salem. I know the last doc here wasn't one of my kind—he was a centaur because there wasn't an available caladrii when the doctor before him finally passed away. That doesn't excuse not keeping up with the yearly version of the *Supernatural & Magical Diagnostic Manual*. Taking care of emerging supes is our primary role in the enclaves, and that idiot clearly failed on multiple accounts.

"You can have as much as you want, Magpie. We wore you out last night; it's probably still *draining your energy*," I say carefully. My eyes meet Edgar's and his face flushes a light pink. He'll never admit out loud that he's going to have to learn to control the incubus as well as he does the hound and the Quetzalcoatl. Though, I kind of wonder if he knows how to control the bird now, too.

Great. I've helped Lucy learn his mother's side and now I have to help Jolene and Edgar with their beasts.

"He's right, Tilly. We love watching you refill the tank after we… filled your tank." He smirks, but I see the glimmer of recognition in his eyes.

"Don't be gross, Teddy." Jolene leans back and rubs her nose on his jawline. "It's unbecoming."

"I'll be coming soon en—"

"No." Lucy points a piece of bacon at Doyle. "Bad."

Our girl giggles, and the sound makes my heart jump. I've missed her so much—we all have—and being here for the breakfast routine is familiar and comforting. "He's right. No jizz jokes at the table, please. We don't even have pineapple."

Doyle roars in laughter, rocking back on the legs of his chair. "Nice one, love. These idjits have no sense of humor. It'll be nice to be back with someone who does."

Her brow arches and she gives him a pointed look, then turns to pin each of us as well. "Last night, at least what I can remember of it, was amazing. I hurt, but it's a good ache and I'm enjoying breakfast. But you're not totally forgiven, and no one is coming home yet. I need to rebuild the trust we had before I can commit to that."

Edgar tightens his arms around her, frowning darkly. That's the hound, not the incubi, and I give him a warning look. "You're all mine."

"Yes, cave-Teddy, but I need—"

"No," he growls low. "No more separation."

Uh-oh. Lucy and Magpie got him to let the dark sides out and now he's even more of a possessive dickhole.

"Sugarplum, maybe we can sort this out after the trip." I grin as my peacemaker looks at the two of them with his patented, adorable smile. "Surely you can invite us to come along now? At least we'll know you're safe and it will make the sleuthing easier with more people."

Her brow furrows, and she thinks about it for a long moment. I watch Doyle and Edgar stare intently while Lucy just smiles prettily. At least one of us knows how to get our girl on his side. The frowning twins are going to piss her off—she's never going to let them tell her what to do when we're not in the bedroom. Personally, I like both of the facets of her personality, but then, I'm as much a switch as she is.

"Okay," she sighs. "You can all come. But you have to give me space when I need it. *And* you have to remember that they have trained me in weapons, combat, martial arts, and a slew of other things. I *can* take care of myself and did for years. Sure, I had Seer with me and I guess she was… watching me to help keep me safe or something? But even she would tell you I saved her ass just as much as she saved mine."

It looks like Boone is going to argue, so I jump in. "We understand. And I remember you hitting those damn cans from that distance in the backyard. Edgar wasn't here, but I don't know a lot of women who can hit all twenty-four targets with a Macmillan, like you did."

"I'm sorry, she what?"

Jolene's laugh is dark as she turns to look at him. "You, Teddy bear, haven't seen me shoot *or* fight. All you want to do is knuckle drag and beat your chest."

The change in the atmosphere is palpable, and I wink at Lucy. He did a good job of getting her to agree to us joining her, and I could calm the volatile judge down. So far, this morning is a win. If I can figure out how to get a message to Saoirse so she fills in the other 'candidates' in our supernatural bachelorette, we'll be on track.

"Haggerty, can you work on gathering paperwork for us to travel?"

Oh, that's a good question.

"I'm sure I can get us cleared. We'll all need physicals before we go, though, including you, Tíogair."

The Irishman looks at me, then darts his eyes to Jolene. I frown. *Why is he giving me that look?* Physicals aren't required by the Society or USCIS, so I have no idea why he's trying to act like it's necessary. "Uh, well. I'm sure I can fit everyone in tomorrow morning since the office is supposed to be closed over the holiday weekend…"

"Grand. It's settled then." He looks over at our girl, noting she's wolfed down her second portion and smile. "Boone, since you won, why don't you and our girl get showered while we clean up the kitchen?"

"Hey! I cooked and the rules are—"

I shake my head at Lucy. Doyle didn't lose a bet about house cleaning and he wouldn't take anything on willingly. He's got a reason for specifically asking the two of us to stay behind and I bet it is his 'physicals' charade. "It's okay, baby. Let Edgar take her up to get squeaky and when they come back, we can start ordering stuff for the trip."

His nose wrinkles, but I think he finally understands because he rises, pouring Jolene another milkshake. "Take this one to go, sugarplum."

"I swear this tastes like actual fucking spring, Wolfie. I don't know how you did it." His cheeks flush adorably and she laughs softly. "I love when you do that."

"It's the praise, you know," Doyle says with a smirk. "He responds to it. Tell him how good he is and you get a pink puddle of goo."

Edgar grins as he leans in and whispers something in Magpie's ear and suddenly, her cheeks turn pink as well. "Would you look at that? It works on Tilly, too."

Such a showoff, but you can't fault his methods.

"Go, you brute," I say, waving at him dismissively. "She needs a bath more than a shower. I can sense her aches and pains. Keep her company for a nice long soak and we'll deal with the downstairs."

"Are you su—oooh, Teddy!"

The yelp of surprise as she's slung over his shoulder and hefted off yet again makes us all smile.

He's going to get his ass kicked one day.

ONCE THEY'RE GONE, WE CLEAR THE TABLE AND I WATCH DOYLE AS he paces. Finally, I can't stand it anymore. "Doyle, why did you want to get us alone? Are you going to share with the class?"

"Buckle up, docs. I'm not sure if I'm right or what the feck all this means. Even for me, we're in uncharted waters. By Hephaestus' beard, I don't know if they have ever charted it."

Dramatic prat.

"Calm down and talk to us," Wolfie says as he stacks plates along his arm and takes them to the sink. "I assume it will not kill anyone or you wouldn't have sent them up to play in bubbles."

His lips curve up. "You know, I like it when you're a wee bit saucy, Fletcher. It's fun."

I roll my eyes and sigh. "Yes, it is. Now spill it for fuck's sake."

Doyle plops back into his chair and leans back precariously. "See, I've been curious. It seems like our girl is mating with all our bloody parts, which is rare enough. It requires some sort of… compatibility on her end with various things, as far as I know. And we don't have a ruddy clue what her lineage is."

"Uh-huh," I say, wiping the table while I think about it. "What significance are you attaching to that?"

"So far, you say she mated with the Fae and Boone's hound. I *know* she got the incubi last night and I'm damn sure she activated my mother's side before. Maybe that binding we're trying to investigate won't be released until *all* the mating's done. I mean, I don't know if her supe sides have to be reciprocated and emerged or if it's all of our shit, but it seems like every time one of us seals a mark, she seems to see a little bit more than she did the last time."

I frown. "And she gains shit she doesn't realize she has. Like the shifting after Edgar and the calling of animals near Wolfie, and…"

He smirks. "Oh, she definitely has serpentine eyes before she was out the first time last night and the *second* time, I think she was emitting as much buzz as the judge."

"That's dangerous as hell," Wolfie says. "I mean, she doesn't know any of this exists and she still can't see any of it happening. She has no idea she's wielding her companions like weapons or running through the woods at night."

We both whip our heads around and look at him in shock. He shrugs. "It's a rumor I heard. A new, big black dog in the woods at night with a pack. People haven't connected to Teddy or her or even come close enough to realize the pack isn't all dogs. I've been guiding people towards believing Kali or Hecate are out for a stretch."

Wiping my hands over my face, I groan. "Fuck, Lucy. We needed to know that. I mean, that's why she's not sleeping. If she's shifting and running all night and doesn't remember, no wonder she looked zombified this week."

He loads the dishes in the dishwasher and shrugs. "If I thought she was in trouble, I would have. We all know she's going to do better if she gets her subconscious used to this before she emerges. None of us were locked down or watched over so closely when I was pre-emergence."

"Love," I say softly. "Your mother… I mean, Aurelia was…"

"I know she was losing her marbles. I had to have her put in the home before I was sixteen. But I mean, even the other kids my age weren't monitored that closely. Supes need to find their way," he replies. "Shifting or playing with their magic on their own is part of that."

Fuck. That old doctor let these kids just run around figuring shit out on their own.

"That codger who worked here really did screw up three generations of hybrids before I got here. Didn't he?" I mutter.

Lucy laughs. "Hell, you should have seen how the hybrids, even five years older than Teddy and sugarplum, behaved. They were wild as shit and when they left, many rumors flew. Few ever came back."

"I can't imagine why," Doyle snorts. "Being allowed to free hand magic and shifting and fuck knows what else probably has them out doing ridiculously unethical shit in the real world. They weren't given boundaries and I suspect you'd find none of them even understand what they mean."

"Maybe." Wolfie takes the rest of the dishes we brought over off the counter. "Thorn is one of them."

Well, that explains a hell of a lot.

Human

Jolene

It took some convincing, but I got the boys to go back to whence they came that night. I spent most of the day with them, including the invigorating soak in my tub, while Teddy read to me. But I just couldn't allow things to slip back into place completely yet. I'm not *angry*, but I'm not healed enough to jump in with both feet.

I met them at Prez's office the next morning and let him run a full court press on me and I let Wolfie cook us all a lovely yet non-traditional Thanksgiving dinner that evening. All I can do is give them as much as I'm comfortable with and, for the moment, that's my body and my time. My heart isn't there yet—not that I harbor any illusions about how I truly feel about all of them. I can't think about it yet, much less admit it out loud, and that's not fair to them. I want it to be solid when they come back to the home we're building.

Christ in a cartoon. Listen to me. This is why I can't let them stay in the house.

Monday came faster than I would have preferred, but it's also a few days closer to leaving for the trip. I filled Saturday and Sunday with trips to the Wally World in the next town, suitcases, and Wolfie mainlining caffeine as he worked to get us all organized and packed. I can do it myself, but despite his frenzied behavior, he seemed to enjoy himself.

Perhaps growing up with a mother whose mind was so disorderly made him crave order and stability outside of his home. It would explain the joy he feels when submitting, too. I sigh, feeling bad for whining about my disinterested parents when my guys have definitely had it worse. Teddy's mom is a nightmare and I'm sure his dad was heavy with the fists after a few bourbons. Wolfie and Doyle both have moms who don't care and mystery dads—even Wolfie's adoptive mom got sent to a mental health facility. Presley doesn't know his parents well because they sent him to boarding schools young.

I'm definitely not as fucked in the parents department as any of the guys.

I close up my classroom, checking that everything is off and all of my drawers are secured. Students won't rotate into my room again before Winter Break starts, and this is the last time I'll be here before I leave. When I'm sure I've got everything done, I pick up my bag and head out. I need to pick up the animals from the daytime companion area and head home. There are a few more touches I need to put on my things, especially regarding the pets, and I want to look over the lists I made for Niecy one more time.

Niecy and Gene will come over while we're away, making sure no one breaks in and the mail gets tucked away. I know she'll probably give herself some sort of cleaning project as well, so I made a mental note to buy them something nice while we're gone. Those two were always good to me when I was younger and they're still helping me now. I don't know what I would have done without seeing that first friendly face when I got home a few months ago.

Has it really only been a couple of months?

I shake my head, marveling at how much shit can go on in such a short time. So many small things have turned into bigger problems— like the weirdo in the bushes or fucking Sherilynn—and things I worried about earlier don't seem important. I'm not worried about Julia and her crew anymore; the conversation after I woke took care of that. Hell, I even asked her to monitor the place besides Niecy when she gets back from Salem. She's brusque and I need to get to know her better, but my initial knee-jerk reaction was fear of losing my only friend.

Little did I know my friend would almost do that to herself…

But Seer and I are on a good path right now and if she continues to be as honest with me as she can, we'll get back to where we were. I'm not going to hold what she did over her head like a sword of Damocles; that will only perpetuate the issue. We're starting fresh and I intend to do the same with the guys. I probably need to express it better out loud now that we're not crazy with lust and pent up sexual tension, but I believe we're going to get past this.

I'm so much healthier mentally than I was when I dated Trevor; I had no idea how co-dependent he kept me until now.

My life in Whistler's Hollow differs completely from what I imagined for myself when I was packing up in Richmond or even when I moved home from Europe. I'm not upset about that in the slightest. I wouldn't have expected to meet someone, much less several people, that I let into my heart, nor would I have thought I'd be happy teaching snooty rich kids and having small gallery shows. It's like I've found the key to why people come back to this ridiculous little town full of vipers and harpies… There's a sense of family and even comfort in the familiar and predictability of life.

Even when it's petty bullshit.

Shaking my head in astonishment, I put a few extra lingerie sets into the suitcase. They don't weigh a thing, but I'm pretty sure the boys will destroy every pair I put on. I'll still end up having to buy replacements—no, *they* will end up replacing them—but at least I have a good stash for the first week. A smile crosses my lips as I remember how shocked I was at the perfectly cleaned downstairs gleaming at me when I finally got out of the bath the other day. I'm sure Wolfie was the ringleader of that sideshow, but my house was put back together and I didn't have to lift a finger.

It was both sweet and an immense relief. The first thing I thought was 'I could get used to this', but I knew I couldn't say it out loud. At least, not until I'm ready for them to come home full time. It wouldn't be fair and if nothing else, I'm an extremely fair person. I accept my flaws and admit my mistakes readily; I only expect others to do the same. My standards don't always jibe with others'—especially raging narcissists like Antigone and Sherilynn—but I apply them just as rigorously to myself as I do everyone else.

That's why I admitted I jumped the gun by sending them away.

Looking over at the cats, I sigh. "Should I just let them come home, anyway? If I was wrong to send them away, keeping them away is bad, too, right?"

"*Mrrrp*," Jekyll says before returning to cleaning himself.

"Some help you are," I mutter. "Hyde? Do you have an opinion? Isis?"

The python squeezes me tightly, and I have no idea what that means. Snakes are so much harder to judge than my expressive servals or Teddy's dogs. Hyde stands and stretches, moving each of her limbs before walking up to me. She looks up at me with huge eyes before tilting her head at the closet and letting out a mournful *'mow'*. "*That* wasn't subtle. I get it, girl. You miss Wolfie. He spoiled the hell out of you two, even if Jekyll pretends he doesn't give a shit."

What am I going to do?

Closing the suitcase, I jerk my head at my companions and head out the door of my bedroom. I haven't slept there since I got home from the hospital and that's getting old, too. I can't seem to get comfortable in some parts of the renovated house since then and it's contributing to my edginess. Everything is a bloody mess, and it's always lurking in the back of my mind. The night they stayed was the first one in weeks where I'm fairly certain I got proper sleep—not a lot, but enough to be noticeable.

"You need to decide, Jolene," I grumble to myself as I head down the staircase. "Do you need space or support? Can you stand by your own thoughts or will you let fear cost you something amazing?"

I've never been one to back down from hard work or a challenge. After Jackson found me that morning during my undergrad, I clawed my way back to normal with bloodied fingertips. I did the work in therapy that helped me focus on school and pursue my Masters. I took the position in the school in the city to pay off the loans and worked on my PhD online. When the environment became too toxic, I made the choice to leave, even though it broke my heart to know my students wouldn't have an art teacher anymore. And I made it on my own in Europe, building a reputation from the bottom up. I even let Saoirse in when we met, despite the bills I racked up in overseas calls to my shrink when I worried I'd be trapped in the same situation as high school.

None of that would have happened if I'd let fear rule me.

Descending the stairs to my bunker in the basement, I gather all the unpleasant emotions inside and let them flow through me. I open the cabinet with the smallest weapons, picking which ones I want to take along and methodically checking them as I think. Cleaning and maintaining my weapons is more of an automated process than anything else I've done today, and it allows me to really consider all of my options. By the time I get to the last pieces, I land on a solution that I can live with.

While we're away, the guys can stay with me in the small house I rented. We can live together like we did before the enormous blow up and if it's stable and comfortable, when we come home, so can they. I know it's not the same as being here, where there are innumerable pressures and expectations, but it will give me a foundation to build on again. I won't be dealing with a hundred other things and I won't be reminded of being hurt and humiliated in public in a foreign city, especially since I don't have any questionable experiences in Istanbul.

It might just be genius and I'm glad I worked this out the way I did. I needed to get my brain to split focus so I could see a bigger picture than my hurt was allowing me to see. They're supposed to stay home and pack wherever they're staying—goddess, I'm an ass because I didn't even ask *where* that was—so I can call and let them know what the housing arrangements will be when we get to our destination. That should cheer the boys up and it will make me feel like less of a fucking hypocrite.

Way to adult like a fucking boss, Jolene. You're killing it today.

Clicking the slide of the .44, I sigh in relief. It'll be great when I have people who can give me encouragement rather than talking to animals like they understand and giving myself cheesy ass 'girl queen pussy boss' speeches in my mind. I'd like to *not* feel like a giant tool when I'm trying to amp myself up for a while. I may have survived on my own while I was healing, but I'm not the bitch anymore.

I want it all, and I'm going to work my ass off to get it.

SHE'S MY KINDA C...

EDGAR

The pup convinced Tilly to let us come along and that alone earns him something special.

I'll have to ponder that a bit because fuck if I have any experience with this. Honestly, I don't have experience with *half* the shit I'm apparently into and all of it is a little overwhelming. I'm terrified I'll fuck something up—not that I haven't already—but Hamilton swears I'm doing fine. I have to take his word for it; it's not like I'm going to ask that hyperactive leprechaun *anything* and our girl is still figuring out her own emotions.

So I'm browsing websites I *never* thought I'd be looking at on my phone as I sit at the bar in the Speakeasy.

This town is fucking weird and everything that happens here boggles the mind.

"What are you glaring so intently at your phone—oh," my oldest friend says when he peeks over my shoulder. "I have to give you credit, man. You don't do anything by halves, even if people are going to give you shit about it."

I snort. "Not since high school, no. I'm lucky Jolene even speaks to me, much less…" I wink at him and shrug. "Because I find myself with the astoundingly good luck to have found a family that is light years better than the one I grew up in. I'm not willing to let judgmental fuckwits ruin it."

"That's why you're openly surfing gay bondage shops in the middle of my bar?"

"Yep." I raise my glass of bourbon in a mock salute. "Because I do not give a randy red fuck what anyone thinks about me or the people I care about."

Huh. I mean that. How… freeing.

Benjy claps me on the shoulder, grinning broadly. "Dude, that's fucking amazing. I know everyone thinks you thumb your nose at shit because of the bookie thing, but I know that's your business sense. The Senator sends more business your way than he does censure with that. Deciding to find happiness instead of doing that playboy fuck around shit… this is you breaking free."

I nod, tilting my head as I look at my old friend. "Leaving Sherilynn is your version of that, you know. You've been miserable since *high school*, man."

His face falls for a moment, but he finally rounds the bar, leaning over it as he replies. "Yeah, it was. I mean, sure, the whole 'finding a mate' thing helped me cut the cord, but you're right. I let both of our parents push us into a union that was never what I wanted. Hell, I don't even think it was what Sherilynn wanted. And we let them push us to adopt the kids—who my ex trained to hate me from the minute they arrived."

I wince. It couldn't have been easy to live in a house populated by people who treated you like a furnishing rather than a person for these years. "Yeah, I heard from another professor that they're all being twats about the divorce—loud ones, at that."

"Fuck, I know. Do you know how many times Bobbi Jo has called me about the shit they're saying at school? All I can tell her is Sherilynn has custody and I'm not able to help her. Then I get to hear the bull-shit they're spouting and I have to defend myself to a principal. Some of it is outrageous—I haven't lived there since the papers were served."

"You need some time away from this garbage and I know just the fix. It might take a little finagling, but what's being a senator's kid for, if not occasionally recklessly abusing my connections?" I toss back the rest of my Blanton's and push to my feet. "Do you have coverage here if we take a brief trip?"

"I'm gonna say the same thing I used to say when you got that look when we were teens, Boone. If this gets me arrested, I'll dime you out for a pack of smokes."

Smothering my laugh with my hand, I tip my head at the door. "And I'll reply the same: you don't smoke and you'd do better offering your body for trade."

"Christ, that hits different now," he mutters as he grabs his coat. "But I'm in. Let's go on an adventure."

"Atta boy," I reply with a smirk.

When we pull into Tilly's driveway, Benjy turns to me and arches a brow. "I thought you're all on the outs with her. What kind of adventure is this?"

I chuckle and shrug. "We're working it out. And luckily for me, the bird and the pup are *much* better at holding their tongues than I am. Hell, even fucking Doyle was even-tempered for the first part of the night."

"First part?"

Grinning, I shake my head. "You're not ready for that part yet, buddy. Suffice it to say that no one ever told me what happens when you let the monsters loose with your mate, but it's the hottest shit on earth."

He sucks in a slow breath, then looks out the window. "Didn't think I'd ever have the chance to know what that's like."

"I know, but you might now. You're not tainted by the betrayal thing because you weren't on the radar until Halloween. That gives you a chance to build shit as honestly as possible from the start. Let go of your regrets about your ex and get to know our girl for who she is now. I promise; you won't regret it."

Benjy turns back to me and shakes his head. "Who would have thought hound dog Boone would not only get mated to two people, but be giving *me* love advice? The world is topsy-turvy, I fucking swear."

"Shut up and get out of my car, Foster. We've got wheedling to do."

I'm definitely projecting a lot more confidence than I have in this situation, but I figure if I can get Benjy to buy in, we can do this. Tilly wasn't nearly as angry after the big growly fuck fest, and she was acquiescent when I took her upstairs for the bath. The rest of the weekend went well, even if we had to go home and come back the next day.

She's not going to blow her top when I show up without calling. Right?

"Once more into the breach," I mutter to myself.

"What?"

"Nothing." I wink at my friend and raise my hand to knock on the door. Before my fist strikes the wood, the door is flung wide and the sound of a hammer cocking fills the air.

I might have been wrong about that earlier statement.

"Teddy! What the unholy *fuck* are you doing sneaking around my house at night? I could have shot you in the face, you fool!"

Benjy looks between us and sighs. "Working on it, huh?"

The way she clears the chamber and latches the safety before tucking her bulldog into a pocket on the side of her yoga pants is hot as hell, but I wave my hand dismissively to calm my friend. "Yes. I don't know why my *drugar* is wielding a hand cannon like a maniac, but it's not because I'm unwelcome on the porch. Right, Tilly?"

My answer is an eye roll and a whistle that calls off the animals perched on the stairs behind her. I wait for her to speak and she huffs, "Yes. There were weird noises outside again, and I was out there trying to shoot that pervert in the ass. That's why I was prepared when I opened the door. The noises seemed to lead me back into the house and toward the front yard."

"You were crawling around outside trying to find the stalker?" Suddenly, the tactical yoga pants—who knew they made those—and the rest of her attire makes sense. She's got her hair pulled up high through a stocking cap and a long-sleeved black top on with them and some kind of low-profile shoes. I squint at her in disbelief, vainly hoping to control my temper before I explode.

"That seems a little dangerous, Jolene," Benjy says hesitantly. "Why didn't you call someone?"

Her gazes narrows as she looks at us. "I'm going to tell you apes *one more time*. I can defend myself without having to be rescued!"

"I'm not saying you aren't, *drugar*! But even law enforcement and feds don't go off without their partners except in movies!"

The porch goes silent for a moment and I'm certain we're getting tossed into the night or maybe even shot in the ass on our way out. But she thinks about my flip comment for a long moment and, miraculously, she nods. "Okay. *That* makes sense. You're not saying I need to be rescued, only that I need someone watching my six."

Letting out a breath, I smile fondly as all my anger melts away. "Yes. That's exactly what I'm trying to say."

"Noted." The door opens further, and she holds a hand out. "Come in, gentleman. Now that we've sorted out our miscommunication, I'd be rude not to offer you a seat and a drink."

There's that Southern woman poking her head out.

"A Blanton's would be delightful, love," I murmur as we walk in and head for the living room.

"Benjy?" she calls over her shoulder as she pads towards the kitchen with her ponytail and her ass bouncing.

"Uh, bourbon's good."

"Back in a tick," Tilly says as she disappears into the other room.

My friend looks at me with a surprised expression. "Is she wearing yoga pants with a holster?"

"Apparently so." I shake my head, watching the doorway until she comes back with a tray full of glasses, ice, a bottle, and just like the first night, a small plate of charcuterie snacks. "And now she's serving us fancy meats. We really fucked up in high school, man."

"No shit," my girl says as she sits the tray down. "Good to hear you say it, though. Have a sip and tell me why you're at my door without an invitation late at night again, Edgar Boone."

The memory of her saying that the first time makes me smile and I pour Benjy and me a drink before I reply. "I'd like to request an amendment to our agreement from last week."

"Oooh. Procedural Teddy. This is the part of you that was raised by the Senator." She leans back in her chair and gives me a playful expression. "Present your amendment, Your Honor. Legislature is in session."

"Can I interject to say that it's weird how much flirting is going on when you're pretending to be lawmakers?" Benjy mutters.

"No," Tilly and I say in unison.

"Seems unfair, but okay."

"The chair recognizes the gentleman from Whistler's Hollow. Speak and be heard."

The gentleman thinks the chair enjoys being bent over this couch and that alone is going to get this amendment passed.

"Allow me to start at the beginning."

"Good thing I brought the bottle. You're going to be as full of hot air as your father." She looks at Benjy and winks. "Get comfy. We're going to be here a while."

FREAKS

JOLENE

Is being dick-drunk a real thing? Because I think I'm suffering from it.

Not only did I agree to allow Benjy to join us on the damn trip, but I let Doyle arrange for transportation to the airport. Much to my chagrin, that turned out to be an envoy of huge SUVs in a long ass motorcade that makes me feel like I'm riding along with a diplomat. Wolfie borrowed a cage for Eury from a friend who works at the zoo and she's currently hating life on one of the other cars. The rest of them can be free in the cabin, but he insisted my girl won't be able to stay comfortable unless she's in a nice, dark hold where he can go down and occasionally check on her.

I can't say I envy Presley and Wolfie their spot in that vehicle, but I'm also stuck with Teddy and Doyle sniping at one another. Benjy is riding with Seer and the luggage in the last car and if that doesn't make me feel like the Queen of Rich Assholes, nothing will. We could have done this a hundred less flashy ways, but they all seem determined to make me self-conscious.

Of course, I am the girl who called her friend to 'borrow' a plane, so I should probably shut up.

By the time we get to the tarmac, the boys have argued about sports, booze, cards, music, and the best way to collect on an unpaid debt. Spoiler alert: none of their methods are legal and I cannot believe that three months ago I was applying to the FBI and today I'm riding in a car with white-collar criminals to jet to a foreign country and hunt down a crooked cop. It's surreal, and I didn't even mention the whole 'cadre of boyfriends' part.

The guys hop out of the car, immediately helping the baggage handlers with Eury and the stowed luggage. It makes me feel a little better as I roll my small carry on towards the stairs with Jekyll and Hyde in tow. The dogs follow Teddy happily and for a second, I feel guilty that they were away from him for so long. Watching them renews my dedication to using this trip to repair the pieces that broke so everyone can come home. Not only do I want that, but our shared 'kids' want it, too.

When I step inside of the plane, I blink for a second. I shouldn't be surprised given how big Thorn Enterprises has gotten, but this is a swank ass plane. There's an open floor plan with a couch and chairs, a full bar, a hallway that I assume leads to a bedroom and bathroom, plus a workspace. The flight is over eleven hours and we'll have a brief stop at JFK for fueling; this setup will make that *much* easier. We left at the ass crack of dawn for a reason, of course. We should arrive in time to order dinner and collapse, then get up in the morning to go shopping for the shit we'll need while we're living in the villa.

I'd rather go straight to the embassy, but we couldn't get an appointment until two days after we arrived. Edgar said it was better that way because it gave us time to prepare and snoop around before we go through official channels. His reasoning was sound, so I didn't reach out to my contacts to push it. I'd rather be seen as clueless Americans than have the staff there on guard because someone influential requested special treatment. It would make it harder for the guys to sneak around.

"Not gonna lie, Jolene. This is baller," Benjy says as he comes in. "Thorn outdid himself."

I give him a gentle smile. Since he saved me twice on Halloween, I've noticed that he's a stark contrast to the rest of the guys. He's not completely gooey in the center like Wolfie, but he's also not as hard as Doyle or Teddy. Benjy falls into that mythical 'big guy with a heart of gold' archetype and I'm glad I let Teddy sweet talk me into allowing him to join us. His placid nature will help me balance out all the testosterone, I think.

"He did. I've not seen this one before, but I have been on ones like it with clients. This is like the one Seer and I took to—"

"Thailand!" My bestie comes bounding in with a broad grin. "Holy feck, that was a trip and a half. We barely got out of that country with our asses intact and I'd do it again in a heartbeat."

The rest of the guys filter in and arch their brows at me. I shake my head with a grin. "You have your high clearance secrets and I have mine. When you're able to tell me *everything*, I'll tell you about Thailand. Until then, you'll have to suffer."

"Doesn't seem fair," Teddy grumbles as he stalks in. Kali and Hecate make a beeline for the corner where my cats are curled up as he heads over to me, picks me up, and carries me to the couch in a fireman's hold. When he sits down, he positions me on his lap with a grin. "This will help, though."

I thump him in the chest hard. "You don't get to pick me up and move me, you big ape! Do it when we're not on a plane and I'll flip your ass on the ground."

"Uh, sugarplum?" Wolfie says as he comes over to join us. "I don't think that's much of a punishment."

Doyle nods. "I would have said you were threatening me with a good time, Tíogair."

Rubbing my hand over my face, I look at Benjy and Presley pleadingly. "Can you guys help me get these dipshits under control? I'll owe you."

That seems to get every male in the room to perk up.

"Wagers?" Doyle and Teddy say simultaneously.

"*No!*" I shout. "No bets on the plane. No fighting on the plane. No male bullshit on the plane."

"But there *is* a snake on the plan," Benjy points out.

That stops us all in our tracks, and we look at each other before bursting out laughing.

Okay, this might not be terrible.

"Can I get you gentleman anything?"

My eyes narrow as the flight attendant makes googly eyes at my men. She introduced herself as Coco before we took off and if that didn't indicate a problem, I would have figured it out after she primped once she saw the passengers. She's been in and out more often than is necessary and I wrote it off as nervousness at first. We have wild animals and odd shit going on, so I figured maybe she was just being overly cautious. But after the first six 'check-ins' during the hour and a half long flight to JFK, I wondered why Miss Messy Bun kept coming back here. Now that she's standing here with wide eyes and perfectly applied red lipstick, I'm certain I'm not imagining things.

Gross.

I doubt Jackson has any interest in her—he swings solidly towards men or gender fluid folks—but that doesn't mean the staff aren't hired with his clients in mind. And he's *definitely* the lawyer who would hire 'models' to work his various homes and luxury vehicles to keep his clientele happy. If this chick doesn't back off, I'll have to make it abundantly clear this isn't one of *those* trips or Jax will have to do an emergency replacement in NYC.

I won't be able to hold my temper for another nine plus hours to Istanbul; that's for sure.

Teddy doesn't pay attention to her. He's reading a research file from Eli with one hand and running his hand through both mine and Wolfie's hair. We're lying with our heads next to each but facing opposite directions as we work through our own documents. Presley looks up at her blankly from the far end of the couch, but he says nothing. Finally, Doyle spins around in his chair with a charming smile that means he's about to cause trouble.

"I'm sure the judge would love a bourbon, dear. Wouldn't you, Edgar?"

The man in question stops reading and looks up, realizing he's being rude, and turns on the Southern charm. "Why, sure, darlin'. I'd love one. Anyone else?"

Miss Fluttery Lashes simpers a little—I fucking swear she does—and puts a hand on her chest. "I'd be *delighted* to get your drink, Your Honor. We weren't told we'd have such *high-ranking* guests on this trip. I would have made sure everything was exactly how you needed it."

"Unlike us mere mortals who don't qualify for special treatment on a private jet?" I mutter under my breath. "Fucking spare me."

I can hear Wolfie snickering and I reach over my face to put my hand over his face playfully. That little shit knows why I'm irritable and he's pretending it's funny. I bet if this was some eight packed dipshit with a white smile and bleached surfer hair, he wouldn't be so cavalier.

"Run along and bring the bourbon and a bottle of Irish whiskey, love. Don't forget the glasses and ice," Doyle says with a wink.

That motherfucker made his accent more noticeable on purpose; I know it.

"Oh, what a lovely Irish brogue!" Messy Bun says as she wiggles her way to the galley.

I repeat her words in a mocking, high-pitched voice as I continue reading my papers. This time, Presley snorts. Between him and Wolfie, I've got vengeance planned later on, but that will have to wait until the perfect moment. I'll teach them to make fun of my weirdly possessive feelings that I have no idea how to handle. Mark my words, I'll show them.

My spitefulness increases tenfold when I'm trying to figure out how to process emotions. It's a flaw and I know it.

"Something wrong, Tíogair?"

"Not at all." I don't look over, continuing to read as I ignore his bullshit.

The perky hostess comes back with a fancy cart and makes a big show of setting everything out on the small coffee table in front of the couch. She aims her ass at us as she pulls conveniently placed items on the bottom of it and then at the others as she pulls out more napkins and coasters. There's no way in hell that kind of drawn out shit is needed for two bottles of booze and ice, so my temper heads towards a boil.

"Tilly." I look up over my head at the reproving look Teddy's giving me. "There's no reason to get salty."

I snort and go back to my file. He sighs, but I can *feel* the smile on his handsome face. My idiotic jealousy is making these fools preen like peacocks and I can't stop myself. His fingers tip my chin up to look at me again, and I glare at him. His lips curl up and he chuckles softly as he looks down at me. Finally, he pushes my hair behind my ears and waves his hand at something, but I'm too busy looking into his eyes to pay much attention.

The clatter of the cart leaving the area breaks the stare and I look out at the rest of the room. Teddy taps my shoulder so I'll sit up, then he does the same to Wolfie. "*Drugar*, we're going to relax in the bedroom until we get to New York. I'll even read to you, so you get a little sleep."

"Uh, no, we're not. I doubt anyone here *isn't* a member of the Mile High club and it's too damn early for that shit." I cross my arms over my chest and he bursts out laughing.

"You look tired. If it will make you feel safer, I'll come," Benjy says softly. "I've been told I make a good pillow."

Blinking, I look over at Teddy, and he nods. My eyes skitter over the others, but they're all busy looking at their shit or drinking the booze that just arrived.

Well, shit. I guess Benjy's now considered part of the family.

Take Me to Church

Benjy

Edgar wasn't wrong.

We took turns reading to Jolene from some smutty book about a school full of horny shifter predators and she was out like a light. It cracked me up that she's reading about something that exists—exaggerated as that shit was—as fictional entertainment. The authors don't get everything right, of course. For one, teenage me would have *loved* if shit like that went on in school and professors may *not* fuck each other or students all over the place.

But our girl listened raptly, curled between the two of us as we passed her Kindle back and forth. Her eyes fluttered shut after a few chapters, but we kept reading to make sure she stayed asleep.

Not at all for research or anything.

After a while, I look over at my old friend. "Is this the shit you all get up when you go home?"

He chuckles and shrugs. "To be honest, I'd done a *lot* of shit before she came home and upended my life, but none of it is as wild as being part of her family. But I don't regret it for a second, dude. I figured out shit I didn't know about myself and changed things I realized didn't fit anymore. It's a rollercoaster of surprises and new things."

Running my hand over her hair gently, I look down at the girl I tried to save in high school. She's definitely become a woman worth fighting for and despite my divorce, it *will* be a fight once Sherilynn figures out I'm with them. "I get that. And I'm curious as hell, to tell the truth."

"You're worried about your ex-harpy escalating." It's not a question; Edgar knows she'll be a nightmare. He's the one who helped push my divorce through despite her asshole father hiring some big city lawyer who tried to tie it up in red tape. "Don't. Despite what I say, I know Tilly can take care of herself. She'll cut old Sheri to ribbons if she comes for someone she cares about."

I frown. "I don't think we have that kind of relationship yet, Boone."

His laugh is soft. "It doesn't matter. If you're part of the people she considers hers, she'll go to the mat for you. I guarantee it."

"Her friend has been sleeping like a corpse since she curled up in the big chair. That's kind of weird, right?"

"Yeah, Seer is odd. But those two are thick as thieves—or were before the incident—and now that they're back in sync, where Tilly goes, so does the rainbow wild child."

I consider that for a moment. Sherilynn had a clatch of women who followed her like adoring fans, but she never trusted any of them. She was always sure Ophelia or Reese or Jillian or Amy would betray her or try to wrest control of their various committees. They treated me with as much disdain as she did, even though we all hung out together as kids. I never understood it, but then I understood little about my ex-wife.

"It's so interesting how all of you seem to fit together, even though you're so different. And no one seems even a little concerned that I'm back here with the two of you." I rub my hand over my face and sigh. "It's completely unlike how the rest of the people in town act."

"Don't you want to be here?"

Jolene's voice startles me and Edgar laughs. "She can be a light sleeper when she's misbehaving."

"Shut up, Teddy," she grumbles. Shifting so she can look up at me, the dark-haired beauty slides a hand up my neck to my cheek. "You don't have to be here if you're not comfortable, Benjy. I won't get upset."

Damn, she's a kind person.

"No, I want to be here. On the plane and in here, I mean. I just don't want to contribute to you getting hurt again," I murmur.

My entire body seizes when she wriggles even closer to me, stroking a thumb over my jawbone. "That's good. Because I think I'd like you to kiss me."

Edgar leans down and murmurs something in her ear that makes her flush an adorable pink, but she slides a leg over mine. "Our girl wants you to kiss her, Foster. Don't keep her waiting or I'll be very cross."

I put my hands on either side of her face, pulling her closer until our lips meet. The minute the kiss deepens, electricity rockets through me and the animal inside of me wakes up for the first time in years. He's been quiet for so long I almost don't recognize it, but as I twirl my tongue around Jolene's, the dormant primal nature inside of me unfurls. When I pull back, a soft grunt escapes my lips and my eyes widen. I look over her head at my friend, concerned I won't have the slightest clue how to control myself.

And the fucker laughs. This must be what he means by wild.

"Excellent," Boone says before he turns her head and kisses her hard. Jolene arches her back, pushing back into him with a moan.

That's when my cock joins the fray, thickening in my sweats like I just flipped through my first *Playboy*. The leg resting on mine wraps around my hip tighter, urging me to scoot closer. I can't help myself; I press against her until the three of us are entwined. Her hips grind against me and I lean down to sink my teeth into her shoulder.

"Hot damn. I *knew* you didn't want to sleep," Jolene says when she breaks the kiss. "You boys are up to no good."

"Tilly, we have thirty-five minutes before we touch down in New York. I think we can make you come at *least* five times before then. What do you think, Benjy?"

I freeze for a moment. It's not the time to tell them I've never slept with anyone but my ex, but the needy look on Jolene's face tells me she won't care. Sliding my hand down her side, I pull down her yoga pants and cup the bare heat inside. "I think five is a good start."

"Well, boys. I'd say you need to get to work then," she breathes.

Arching a brow, I run my finger along her slit, teasing her. "As you wish, Princess."

She likes that because she bucks into my palm. Grinding it against her mound, I dip my head and suckle along the line of her neck. Edgar's hands move to the hem of her sweatshirt and when he pulls it up, I move back for a second so he can remove it. Almost at the same time, I discover Jolene has pretty jeweled nipples and a matching piercing down below. Making a strangled sound, I look at my friend and he grins broadly.

"Our girl is bejeweled and beautiful from head to toe. You'll love playing with them." His big hands cup her tits, holding them up for me to inspect.

I can't help myself, so I lean down, taking one into my mouth as I slip two fingers inside of her. The sound she makes almost undoes me. Flicking my tongue over her shield, I pump the digits in and out of her slowly. She's soaked and moving with me as I add another finger and place my thumb on her clit. A few soft brushes later and Jolene yanks my head up to look at me with fierce green eyes.

"I lied. I don't want you two to make me come five times."

"You don't?" Edgar murmurs as he bites a mark on her neck. The way she squeals tells me it must be his and I know that means she can't see it, but she can feel when he touches it. "Are you sure?"

I brush over her clit again and pump my fingers in and out slowly. "It feels like you do, baby."

"No, noooo…" Her head falls back onto Boone's shoulder when I flick her again. "I want you both to fuck me."

That gets my attention.

"*Drugar*, I didn't bring the bag in here because I thought you were going to sleep," Edgar whispers against her ear. "I don't have lube."

Her eyes are closed, but her smile is wicked. "We don't need lube. Stretch me together."

Holy. Fucking. Shit.

"I *like* it, Tilly. You're a bad girl this morning. Are you gonna scream loud enough to make everyone jealous?"

"Mmm. Fuck me right and I'm sure I will, big man."

They gods made these two for one another and I don't have a clue why I get to play along except that dark, growly feeling that's settled in my gut. It's the one that told me she was my mate and it's the one that wants me to jump into this shit with two feet.

"Get naked." The words surprise me when they come out of my mouth, but as soon as I remove my hand, she wriggles out of the pants like a contortionist. I nod at Edgar and he pulls back to deal with his clothes while I stare at our girl. "Take mine off now, Princess."

She gives me a minxy smile, hands slipping to my waistband and pulling my tee shirt up over my head. When it's tossed aside, she tugs my sweats down, freeing my cock. "Commando. That's my favorite kind of underwear."

"Which is to say none," Edgar says as he watches her finish ridding me of my sweats. "But we're agreed on that."

"Now for the fun part," Jolene says as she slides her thigh up onto my hip. "Benjy, you'll go first. Fuck me until I come hard. Then we'll take it further."

"Yes, ma'am." I reach down, positioning the head at her entrance before I grab her hips and slam my dick home inside of her. My eyes roll back when the tight, wet heat of her pussy grips me and the simian inside of me beats its chest. I feel it pushing me against my skin and I rock my hips, sliding in and out of the woman who's changed my life.

"Good job, *drugar*. Take his cock. Squeeze him. Feel how good it is when he fucks you. I want you to be so wet when we both slide in that it only takes a little before you coat us with come."

Who the hell knew Edgar has a mouth like that? It's making me hot, for fuck's sake.

"Teddy," she whines when her back arches and I trail my lips down her chest. "I want that. I need both of your dicks stretching me while you do that biting thing."

If I weren't being strangled by the sweetest cunt I've ever felt, I would question the 'biting' thing, but I feel these guys are letting their supe sides out with her. I slip my hand between us and pinch her clit to get her attention. "Princess, focus."

Jolene groans, her hips rocking up to meet my thrusts eagerly, and I keep stroking the spot that makes her clench around me until I feel her shiver. When her orgasm hits, I have to fight hard not to come at the same time. By the time she finishes riding it out, I'm getting my teeth.

That's when I feel Boone push inside along with me.

"Motherfucker," I snarl as my eyes fly wide.

He grins like a cat that got the cream. "Oh, not yet, but I'm not averse to filling our girl until she's got one of our babies in her."

"Absolutely not, you dickhead," Jolene pants. "Now shut up and fuck me before I kick you both out."

I chuckle softly, moving my hips in opposition to Edgar's. "Again, as you wish, Princess."

"Suck up."

Woman on a Miss

Jolene

When I wake up, I'm surrounded by the hottest pile of bodies in the Universe. Being cuddled in a puppy pile is an emotionally satisfying sensation, but the physical reality is feeling like you're wrapped in a hundred blankets at once. The lady bits find it sexy and my heart gets squishy, but my bladder says it's time to escape before we end up exploring a kink I'm not interested in.

I shift a little, wiggling out from under Benjy and Teddy's arms, only to discover I can't slide downward because Prez and Wolfie are firmly wrapped around my lower half. I assume Doyle is here somewhere, too, because there's no way he'd let himself be left out. Poor Seer must be snoozing in the cabin like an animal au pair.

My sympathy only lasts for a moment; I *really* gotta pee.

"You jokers need to move," I finally say.

"No." Teddy doesn't even open his eyes to deny my request.

Bastard.

"That wasn't a request."

"Princess, we're comfy. You slept through the pit stop, and we're probably over the Atlantic somewhere. If we sleep now, the jet lag won't be so bad."

He's not wrong, but that's not why I want them to let me up.

Wolfie rubs his cheek against my belly and mumbles, "He's right, sugarplum."

Oh, for crap's sake.

"Guys, I appreciate you reminding me of things I definitely know from years of international travel, but I need to pee. Unless you want to lie in a wet spot, y'all need to move."

They move like lightning, tripping over one another in their scramble to let me get up. My giggles don't stop until I close the bathroom door, leaving them bitching in my wake. Men are predictable and even in a group, they behave how you'd expect.

Once I finish my business, I step into the shower. True to form, there are already fancy schmancy toiletries waiting, so I take my time washing away the sweat and sex smell. I roll my eyes as I notice the bruises and hallmarks of the rowdy play that's characterized the return of my men to my bed.

Their fear of losing me seems to have manifested in some overly possessive cave dude shit, but nothing that's so annoying that I have to put my foot down. I finish washing the shampoo out of my hair, breathing the scent of lavender and rose hips in with a smile. At least I'll smell nice when I deplane, even if I'll desperately crave a change of clothes.

I dry off and hang the towels before standing in front of the mirror to put my hair back up in a ponytail. Something catches my eye and I squint at the mirror with a frown. My reflection looks normal, but it feels like what I'm seeing isn't right. Tilting my head back and forth, I turn around, looking at my body. I can't shake the niggling feeling, no matter how closely I look. Everything *appears* to be fine—piercings, tatts, a few little marks from sexy times, my frustrating softness in certain places—but my brain keeps telling me I'm missing things.

I haven't been this paranoid since Seer and I ate those magic cookies at the Beltane Fire Festival.

"Why does my reflection feel wrong?" I mutter. "How can it feel wrong?"

The lights flicker briefly, plunging me into darkness. I barely catch it, but a ring of fire flashes in my eyes, followed by a slit, then a sparkle, and suddenly, the lights come back on.

What in actual goddamned fuck *was that?!*

Wrapping myself in the last towel, I stride out into the bedroom, ready to demand they tell me if I ate some funky mushrooms or someone burned one while I was sleeping. The guys have exited the room and my clothes are laid out on the freshly made bed as if waiting for me. I tug them on quickly and stomp into the cabin, determined to find out why I'm hallucinating.

"Sugarplum!" Wolfie says with a bright smile. "I helped get breakfast ready. Now that you smell all flowery and sweet, you can have a seat and eat with us."

His enthusiasm deflates my irritation immediately and I accept the plate he hands me gratefully. "You are my favorite today, baby. Bacon and eggs and waffles always soothe the beast."

"Oi!" Doyle grumbles. "I made the mimosas."

"Thank you, grumpy pants." I wink at him as I pad over to sit on the couch next to Teddy. He's not asking for favor; no, he's smiling indulgently at our antics. "So who wants to tell me what weird shit went on that I'm having acid flashbacks this morning?"

Seer spins around in her chair, her mouth open. "Acid flashbacks? All of you idiots just got a *hell* of a lot cooler."

I roll my eyes. "Not the point, Seer."

"I think it is."

Benjy chuckles and takes the chair next to hers, pulling the tray up to sit his plate down. "No one did any party favors, Princess. All sex, no candy."

"Which *they* did not invite us to," Doyle grumbles as uses his foot to spin his chair in fast circles. "Party foul is more like it."

"There is no way we would have all fit in there for that," Presley counters. "We had to pile up like a football huddle to snooze together."

"Fine," the Irishman replies with a pout. "But I call dibs on the next round."

I pick up the knife from the table and point it at him. "First, he's right. Second, I am *not* 'shotgun' or a carnival ride. You act like you need a fucking Fast Pass to my pants again and I'm kicking you out of the damn theme park."

That makes everyone laugh, and I huff as I wolf down the waffle. When they finally stop snickering like teenagers, I take a sip of my mimosa and continue. "No drugs, then? Interesting."

"What did you see, Sugarplum? Was it bad?" Wolfie looks at me with concern as he walks over with the next two plates in his hand. He hands them to Prez and Teddy, then goes to get his before he takes the seat next to me.

"I don't *think* it was bad. I mean, I don't know. The lights in the bathroom went off for a minute and I was looking in the mirror. My eyes sort of changed—like I'd used a couple pairs of SFX contacts in rapid succession. And before they went off, I kept feeling like something was wrong with my reflection, but everything looked normal."

Teddy sits up straighter, his eyes darting to the others before he finally turns to face me. "What did your eyes look like in this weird little fever dream, Tilly?"

"Pretty cool, actually. There was a ring of fire, then sort of slit like a snake, and then this icy sparkly ring." I shrug and bite off a piece of bacon, chewing before I add, "They all looked good. I'll have to consider something like that for Halloween next year."

Doyle chokes on his drink, covering his mouth with a napkin as fast as he can. Prez whacks him on the back with an eye roll and Benjy howls with laughter. Only Teddy and Wolfie seem to be unamused. They're doing this 'conversation without talking' thing with their eyes and when I look at Seer, she's frowning.

Why is everyone being weird about this? Do they think I have a brain tumor or something?

"Uh, you guys don't think I had a stroke, right?"

Presley smiles, waving his hand. "Absolutely not. You probably had a drop in blood pressure that made your eyes play tricks on you. I'll monitor you to make sure, Magpie, but nothing you said seems like we should worry."

"Then why is everyone being so fucking weird suddenly?"

"I don't know how you can tell," Seer mutters. "These nimrods are always weird."

"You're one to talk, O'Flanagan!" Teddy shoots back with a smirk.

Point well taken; we're all odd.

"Fine. I didn't have a stroke, and we're strange. Let's talk through the plans for when we land." I say as I finish my food. "As long as we're on course, we should hit Istanbul at four am because it's GMT plus three. We'll head straight to the rental and get our shit inside, feed the animals, and sleep for a couple of hours, right?"

"Right," Teddy says. He stands, taking both of our plates to the cart, and I cringe.

Coco will be here to collect that shit eventually and despite knowing my guys have shown where their loyalty lies, I'm not keen on seeing that chick again. I don't like feeling like I'm in competition with her because normally, I wouldn't even notice her bullshit. But the recent incidents with Trevor and Sherilynn have dealt my confidence a blow, so she's hit buttons I'm not proud of having. Most of the time, I could give a fuck less whether some woman was waving her ass around in front of me. Unfortunately, right now is not the time and I am not the one.

I'm far too volatile emotionally to handle a self-centered bint practically begging me to crush her like a grape.

Seer must see my frustration because she winks at me. "No worries, Peanut. That chippy has been dealt with."

This *is what genuine friends are for. Preventing you from strangling the people who are determined to bait you at every turn.*

"Thanks," I mumble. "That helps a lot."

The guys look at us both in confusion and my bestie shrugs. "It's a girl thing, gents. No ding dongs needed. Carry on."

"Christ, it makes me shrivel up when she talks about that," Teddy says as he returns to his seat. "Balls go right up into my fucking body, no lie."

"If you hurt my girl, I'll make sure that's never a problem again, doggy. Cross me heart and swear on a bottle of mead."

I give Seer a look and lean against the man cringing next to me. "He knows better now. We've had a chat about boundaries, haven't we, boys?"

"Yes, yes. Be good. Tell the truth. Don't hide shit if we can help it. All the Boy Scout stuff," Doyle says as he pours himself a whiskey. "Domesticated, the lot of us."

"Fuck, I hope not," I snort. "I like you all a little wild. Just cut out the bullshit. Otherwise, I like you all for who you are, the way you are now."

That seems to brighten the mood, and Presley pulls out his tablet, waving it. "On that note, should we call Thorn before it gets too late?"

"Definitely. I want to know what he and Eli have to add before we set foot on foreign soil. They're supposed to be working on something we can download to help get access to the embassy files. That should unlock more info on our disappearing crooked cop."

Wolfie clears the rest of the plates while we all get comfy around the couch. Once he's done, Prez sets up the call as we peer into the screen like a bunch of Boomers trying to Skype their grandkids. It rings for a few moments and I frown. Damn, that party going fool. He's supposed to be waiting for this chat and it's not even two pm our time. He can't still be asleep from the night before.

"Hellloooo, weary travelers!" Jax says as he finally comes on screen. He looks a little worse for wear and I note Eli is lurking in the background rather than being front and center.

That's unusual; they seemed to be going pretty strong the last time we spoke. Fidelity isn't Jax's strong suit, but this time, I thought he might actually have landed a good one. "Jax, you look like shit. What's going on?"

His scowl darkens, and he looks over his shoulder briefly before coming back to us. "A little domestic dispute. *Someone* whose name I won't *mention* has a big, dumb, bearded ex who can't seem to understand that having a big dick doesn't mean you're not a fucking asshole."

"I *told* you he doesn't even know how to use it!" Eli shoots back.

"*That* is not comforting! You dated Nox for two years despite his rancid, two-dimensional personality and inability to fuck well. What does that say about your ability to ignore giant red flags in the people you date? What's wrong with me?"

I blink for a second, then grin, knowing exactly how to get Jackson to pull his head out of his perfectly shaped ass. "Jax, you're a spoiled, obscenely rich brat who spent a decade fucking around worldwide until your evil, abusive father died and left you with the keys to his kingdom. You have trouble with fidelity, addiction, elitism, and the attention span of gnat. However, despite those things, this adorable sweet dude seems to like you and is trying to make a go of it with you. Perhaps his ability to let go of people's flaws is actually a good thing?"

My words stop the pouting lawyer in his tracks. He squints into the camera, giving me a look I saw a *lot* after he found me holed up in grief in college. "Jo-Jo, you know you're the only person in existence I will allow to say that shit without looking up a hitman, right?"

"Yup," I reply. "But you'd do the same for me. Luckily, this time I figured it out on my own, so you don't have to use armchair Psych 101 on me."

He sighs. "Thank fuck. I only have so much repertoire in that arena before I have to make it up. Trust me, there are enough idiots out there listening to idiotic catch phrases from TikTok as if they're actual mental health advice. You don't need me to be one of them."

"I really don't." I chuckle softly and shake my head. "Can you imagine being that uneducated and condescending that you think telling someone to touch grass is a viable response? People that narcissistic *kill* me—they *never* see reality beyond their delusions of grandeur. And I say that as someone with degrees to back it up."

Doyle pushes into frame. "Not to break up your little Hallmark moment, but what did you and the hacker find, mate? I assume you didn't spend *all* of this time arguing about some roided out loser."

"Ah, yes. Thank you," Jax says. "Eli created a worm he's pushing to the devices we gave you for the college snooping trip. You should be able to sneak it into the Wi-Fi or through Bluetooth into some device in the building if you work in tandem. The second part of the scheme involves someone making a distraction and someone else using the other piece of software to disrupt their firewalls. Same phones, of course."

I frown. "So we'll have to split the party up in order to get some of us on our own and some of sucking up the attention of the staff and security?"

"Correct, Jo-Jo. You'll need to work as a team and stay in contact. I believe your bestie can procure some earwigs once you get to Turkey, right?"

"Aye, I can," Seer calls out. "I'll start hitting my contacts for a few things, and when we land, I'll peel off to go get them."

"Excellent. Then everyone, make sure you connect to Wi-Fi on those spare phones once you get on the ground, and let me know if you need help to get it all loaded up. Eli and I are going to have a chat, thanks to Jo-Jo."

I grin and wiggle my fingers at him. "Be good or be good at it, Jax."

"You, too, Jo-Jo. Over and out."

The feed clicks off and I look at the guys. "Okay, now it's time to talk brass tacks before we land."

Fuqboi

Doyle

Human travel methods are exhausting. They've done well in inventing faster shit over the years, but sitting in this rocket fuel propelled tin can for hours when we could have used hundreds of faster magical transports is killing me. I know supes like Boone and the others who are used to moving like they aren't what they don't notice, but being a demi-god with no ties, I hop portals more often than not. I'm sure Julia and her lot fly more often than they get in cars or planes for the same reason.

Until my Tíogair fully emerges, though, I'm stuck in the slow moving human vehicles when we move in groups.

The boredom is interminable, but I'm happy that she capitulated, so I'll suffer in silence.

"She's asleep again," Hamilton says. He's smiling as looks down at Jolene as she lays with her head in his lap and her feet in Boone's. "I bet she's slept more today than she has in a while. Especially given those rumors about the new dog in the woods."

"Stubborn as a mule, as always," Edgar adds ruefully. "She was so mad she didn't want to ask you about whatever symptoms she was having— whether they have to do with mating her emergence."

I think about that for a moment, concluding they're probably right. However, if she's been accessing any of her powers, it will have been noticed by more than the townspeople of Whistler's Hollow. Higher ups in the Society or even some of our relatives have to know about it. For someone like Presley, it wouldn't matter if his mentor or people at the caladrius enclave found out. But for folks like me or Wolfgang? That could be extremely dangerous. We have far too many unknowns in our bloodlines and fucking with our mate might get our relatives' motors running.

"We haven't considered another potential issue," I interrupt. "While Boone and Foster's families or exes are basic, terrestrial threats that we can handle if need be… Wolfgang and I have a more complicated lineage. Our birth mothers enjoy torturing us and ignoring us, plus not knowing who our fathers are allowed for more chicanery. Many beings could decide to take an interest in us because of our raven haired unicorn."

"Son of a bitch," Edgar mutters as he runs a hand through his hair. "You're right. Most mate groups are 3 or less *at most* unless you count some of the pack animals. Even then, that's single species groups, not a mix of hybrids like us. As word gets around about Jolene, it will also spread that she's essentially powerless at the moment. It will paint a huge target on her back—and not just with our families."

Well, fuck. That's even worse than what I was imagining.

"Can we try to head some of it off? I'm sure Bane and Nelia will help with the Society," Presley says as he scratches his chin. "Seer and Julia can work on getting the Guardians to keep their eyes peeled for movements in the hunters, traffickers, and bad seeds."

"We can," Seer says with a nod. "And I might know a few ne'er-do-wells on the human side who owe me a favor. They can help put out a ban on humans being sent for her. I'm pretty sure I have the connections, but don't forget to ask Nelia. Some of her wildcards from the trial might have influence in other countries."

Closing my eyes, I press my hands together in a prayer pose against my lips as I think. This is good, but I think we need to be more proactive. I can slip home to the Mount and talk to my auntie anytime, but the actual question mark lies with our adorable submissive. He's not talking right now and I'm sure it's because he knows he can't control what his shitty mother does. We need him to steel his spine and help us protect our girl. "Wolfie, mate, I think you know what I'm going to say."

His eyes widen. "We can't."

"We can and we should," I counter.

He shakes his head and buries his face against the judge, who pulls him closer as he glares at me. "What the hell are you suggesting, Doyle?"

"I think we need to visit his mother—in person. Obviously, we'll have to stop by somewhere she feels comfortable after we handle our business in Turkey. But we should find the time to start negotiations after we land. I'm sure it will take a little time to get Tíogair to agree and longer to get his mother to do the same. But if we're in range of her lair, so to speak, we should see what she knows. If only to protect ourselves, we need to do it."

Wolfie lifts his head and gives me a pleading look. "You don't know what she's like, Doyle. She's so cunning and so calculating—if we take Sugarplum there, she'll spill the beans and everything will be fucked up."

"Oh, no she won't," I smirk. "If there's one thing I'm very good at, it's convincing people to do what I want without them knowing what my true goal is. I do it for amusement daily; she won't be able to resist when my intent is to trap her."

"Maybe. But she also knows how to hurt me. She'll spend the other half of her time hoping to drive a wedge in between us or picking at scabs until we have issues. I don't know why she's like this—it's not how her kind is supposed to be, but… I've always wondered if my father's absence made her lose it." The vet presses his face to Edgar again, and it's clear he will need an enormous amount of support to get through this.

But it's necessary. If his icy-hearted bio mother believes his birth drove the one person she cared about away, she'd be delighted to harm his lovers.

"Don't worry, pup. None of us will let her hurt you. Right?" Boone looks at all of us, waiting for us to respond.

"I've been waiting to smack some sense into that bitch for *years*."

I grin at the doc's vehemence and nod. "Absolutely. I'm not allowed to unleash on people very often in the Hollow. I could use some *real* fun—like having a super power fight with the winter witch. That sounds like a great time."

Benjy holds his hand up, giving us all a surprised look. "Uh, I know I'm not dialed all the way in but… Wolfie's mom is the Cailleach?"

"Ding ding, the gorilla's got it," I say as I put my finger on my nose. "And if you think that's impressive, someday I'll have a surprise for you."

"Fuck, I don't even want to *know* who they hell spawned you, Haggerty. The thought terrifies me," he replies. "But I'd be lying if I wasn't a little intimidated by what shit we may get up to on this seemingly innocuous trip Edgar invited me on."

His answer is just a shrug and a grin—classic Boone.

"I didn't think of adding destinations until now. But it occurred to me we agree that our woman is special—not just because we love her or she's unique, but because there's something hinky about her binding and mating. That won't escape people outside of our circle for much longer because she's attracting mates and companions like bees to honey." I sigh and pour myself another Jameson as I ponder it. "We have to figure out where the unknown dangers are before they come at us."

Seer folds herself into a pretzel in her big chair. "Mystery stalker is not unknown, but human surveillance and methods are failing. We should tap a magick user to see if the threat is supernatural. A couple of sigil traps around the house and yard should do it. I'll get Julia to start that process."

"That will help. I'll try to work a visit to my ridiculous relatives when it won't be noticed. My Auntie can be helpful when she's in the mood and I might visit a few others while I'm there. I don't know about my mother, though. That will require much more thought and some probing before I try to tackle her. She's… mercurial and cruel on good days, unlike her mythical reputation."

Edgar arches a brow at me. "Was that a clue? We should consider Greeks who aren't known for being mean by reputation?"

"You know I can't tell you," I sing-song. "But you're all clever; you'll get there, eventually."

"Greeks?"

Poor Foster—he really joined late, and he's been so sheltered in that town. His ball-busting wife kept him out of the Society meetings and he doesn't have a clue.

"Yes, Benjamin. Try to keep up," I say with a wink. "I'm forbidden from giving you many clues, so you'll have to work with a partner to catch up with the class."

"If we have to, we can arrange a visit with her," Wolfie finally whispers. "But everyone needs to understand that every word that comes out of your mouth can and will be used as a weapon. Even the negotiation about the meeting will be fodder for her to gather information she'll use later on to hurt you."

"You don't have to talk to her until we all do," Seer says firmly. "I can get word to her through my adoptive parents. They're big enough in that part of the world to make sure she shows up for a summoning."

"Perfect. So when we land, we'll split off to either get to the house or get equipment. Saoirse is in charge of the shit Jackson asked for and contacting Julia and her parents. Wolfgang and Hamilton can get the animals settled. I'll think you'll find a stowaway will magically appear in the cage with Euryale, but don't make a big deal of it."

"You cloaked Odie so he could run around and be your eyes, didn't you?"

I wink at Presley. "Aye. Secret weapons are never more useful than when they're actually secret."

"We've got our itinerary, then. Now everyone should shut up and make like Tilly. The time zones we've crossed are going to hit us and we need to be hyper aware since we have no idea if anyone is tracking us. Get some sleep—even I'm going to catch a few more z's."

I roll my eyes and give Boone a salute. If he wants to pretend to be in charge, I'll let him.

For now.

THE LANDING AND OUR TRIP TO THE HOUSE JOLENE RENTED WERE uneventful. With all of us working together, we wrangled the animals and the baggage with ease. Jackson's contacts came through—all the weapons and paper we didn't want examined were locked in diplomatic pouches and sealed boxes, so customs couldn't open them. It was the perfect plan and I'm surprised the git thought of it. I was worried I might have to do some difficult to explain magic to achieve our goals, but what do you know?

Sometimes even the squirreliest supes come through.

We pull into the gated community by the sea and I watch the scenery go by. Apparently, a British company started building this before that pesky virus ran rampant across the globe. It's near the Ottoman Palace and there's a five-star hotel, amenities, and a bunch of apartments and villas. I assume we're staying in a villa owned by one of Thorn's friends because I'm fairly certain nothing in this area goes for under three million. Boone could probably afford one and obviously I could, but our girl lives pretty normally. I doubt she's paying the premium that goes with this sort of place.

The car stops in a driveway and Jolene turns to look at us excitedly. "Isn't it beautiful?"

"Hell yes, it is," I grin as I look back at her. She's in the back seat with Boone again. He really is an overprotective pain in my ass. "Let's go look around."

She claps her hands, kisses him on the cheek, and throws her door open. Giving him a smirk, I follow suit, chasing her up the path to the multi-story villa with a lovely porch. We open the door with the code she gets off of her phone and walk inside to gape at the interior like rubes.

Inside, there are high ceilings with exposed wooden beams in the brick building. The first room is an open floor plan living and dining room furnished with huge spacious furniture and obsequious fixtures. I walk over to the mantle where there's an unnecessarily large television mounted on the wall, looking at the photos there. A snort escapes me before I can stop it and by the time my Tíogair comes back from looking at the kitchen, I'm dying of laughter.

"What's so funny, Doyle?"

"Yeah, what's got you going, Haggerty?" Presley asks as he guides the dogs and cats in first, lugging their supplies on his back.

I shake my head, trying to stop the amusement from making me howl. "Who did you rent this from?"

Jolene's nose wrinkles and she sighs. "The caretaker is an old friend of Jackson's."

That didn't answer my question, but I'll let it go for now.

"Well, we have located the most idiotic caretaker in all of Europe— that is, unless it's the owner. Walk around the lounging areas and have a look at these pictures."

She frowns, walking over to a set of frames on a low bookshelf, then gasps. "Holy shit. Does this guy have a douche-stache?"

"Yep," I say as I hold up an 8x10 of said guy pretending to whack off the statue of David in Rome. "And apparently, he's also about thirteen years old emotionally."

"He's like a walking, talking 'that's what she said' joke," Wolfie says when he holds up one of the olive skinned perv pretending to hump the lions outside of the Tower of London.

Tíogair shakes her head, looking at a few more of the ridiculous poses immortalized in the frames around the room. "I can't believe anyone wants to have anything to do with this moron. He looks like a graduate of one of those 'pickup artist' classes; only a shut-in with no experience in the real world would let a joker like this be in their bed. I wish Seer didn't have to go grab our equipment; she and I used to eat these morons for breakfast in clubs."

"You did, huh?" Edgar comes in and wraps his arms around her from behind, growling into her neck.

She rolls her eyes. "Yes, we did. There was a time when I was confident in myself and didn't worry about a bunch of judgmental fuckwits or creepy stalkers. I'd like to get back there as soon as possible, if you please."

Putting down the pictures, I walk over and take her hand, looking at her seriously. "We all promise that time is coming, Tíogair. Once we figure out what happened to your parents and why you were given the heave-ho, we can take trips like this anytime we want and not do detective work. Got it?"

Jolene's face lights up and she beams. "Got it."

"Good. Now let's finish getting settled so we can head out for the day."

PRINCE CHARMING

JOLENE

"I'm sorry, madame. We simply cannot allow guests to visit the ambassador today."

Pulling off my sunglasses, I stare at the bespectacled man at the front desk. Both Jackson and I triple verified our appointment this afternoon and I have no idea why suddenly we're being denied entrance. "Look..." I peer at his name tag since whatever he said earlier made no impression on me. "... Bennie. We've come a long way and I have confirmation that we had an appointment. What's the problem suddenly?"

He re-stacks his papers fussily, looking at me in annoyance. "I don't know what to say, ma'am. My instructions are to turn visitors away. You'll have to reschedule."

I'm ready to protest again when Teddy steps up. He gives the academic a charming smile, showing all of his impossibly white teeth. "My father is Senator Boone. He also assured me we could speak with His Excellency and tour the building while we're here on vacation. Perhaps there's someone you could call and check before I have to call him?"

The staffer rolls his eyes and sighs. "Fine. I'll call my superior and ask. But I doubt it will make a difference. We have children of legislators and statesmen all the time. It's not a special occasion."

Jesus, this guy is really full of himself for someone with the charisma of mashed potatoes.

I turn around as he picks up the desk phone and makes his call, irritated by the snooty tone he's taking as he talks to the person on the other end of the line. Wolfie walks over and takes my hand, giving me a smile that melts the ice forming in my veins slightly. His sunshine is always a good balm for the grumpy dominance of some of our group—including me.

"He's coming down to speak with you."

Doyle snorts and leans against the door frame. "How gracious of him. I suppose we'll wait in the entrance like idiots until *he* arrives, then?"

"That would be correct, sir." Bennie goes back to clicking away on his computer and I get the distinct feeling we've been dismissed as far as he's concerned.

I'd like to punch this little shit in the nose, but since we're guests, I suppose I should behave.

Teddy grins at me as I flex my free hand. "That won't help, Tilly. But it's sexy when you lose your shit, so I hate having to tell you not to do it."

His teasing helps a little, but I've noticed my temper simmers much closer to the surface than it used to. I don't know if it's because I was recently traumatized or because I'm getting comfortable in my new home and I feel like I can truly be me again. The behavior of the people in town has allowed me to cast off a lot of the polite, Southern exterior because I have every reason to be angry; when I first arrived, I didn't have the luxury. But when I think about it, I still feel like something in my gut is pushing me—it wants me to exact vengeance on people who wrong me or those I care about.

Am I losing my mind? Paired with the weird dreams and that flashback in the plane restroom, I'm not so sure.

"Excuse me!"

The voice pulls me out of my reverie and I turn back to face the desk where Bennie is smirking at us. Behind him, a tall, impeccably dressed muscle man is practically eye fucking my entire group. I arch a brow, giving the newcomer a bored expression when I respond. "Yes?"

"I'm Ozzie and I am the ambassador's executive assistant." His creepy grin widens and his eyes sweep over me in a way that makes my skin crawl. "Bennie called and asked me to dialogue with you."

This will not end well; I can feel it in my bones.

"Dialogue?" Doyle snorts derisively and rolls his eyes. "Mate, we have an appointment and we have confirmed it through multiple parties. Your door monkey here is refusing to allow us entry. Do your job and make it happen."

"Oh, sweetie, your accent is adorable, but I'm afraid that it won't change my answer. His Excellency is unavailable today." The blond angel faced pervert flashes his own pearly whites as he rakes his gaze over me and Wolfie. "I, however, am totally open to whatever this… is. I can give you my number."

Teddy pushes his way through the group with a snarl of anger, stepping in front of all of us before he speaks. "I suggest you allow us to keep our appointment and back off the cheesy player shit. Just because you work overseas doesn't mean my father and his friends won't pull your State Department clearance so fast your frosty tips will spin."

Fury fills my veins as the lampoon of a guy continues to lick his lips and stare at us. I have no idea how anyone finds this attractive, but I'm sure he'd get along with the douchecanoe who takes care of our villa. Is this normal behavior for guys over here or did we hit the asswipe lottery? Benjy pushes around me, joining Edgar in the barricade he's formed in front of us.

Great. Now the testosterone in this small waiting area is so thick I can't breathe.

"We may have to come back, Magpie," Presley whispers in my ear. "The big guns are going to lose their tempers and we'll get booted for good."

I sigh, rubbing my temples as they continue to argue with the two-dimensional dipshit at the desk. Nothing I do is ever easy since that day when Agent Grant sent me packing—it's like there's a force actively fighting me and I'm so fucking tired of it.

"Masa' alkhayr ya sayid.[1]*"*

The deep, musical baritone is familiar and I turn around in surprise. Standing behind us with a cadre of employees is Dhameer. He's dressed in a sharp suit, but has a *kaffiyeh* and *agal* on. He didn't wear the headdress in the States, but that might have been because he didn't want everyone to recognize him. Today, he definitely wants these jokers to know who he is.

The question is, how did he get here and why the hell did he come?

But I can't ask that at the moment because the two men at the desk are frantically making hushed phone calls and the handsome horse-owning sheik is winking at me playfully. "Dhameer…"

He holds a hand up and shakes his head. "Later, *muharibi aleaziz.* We must negotiate with these gentlemen now."

"Your Highness, there is no negotiation with clowns," the suit-wearing woman next to him practically hisses. "Denial would be an affront to your family."

Ozzie goes pale, and he moves away from the counter to continue his whispered conversation with whomever he's informing about the Prince's arrival.

I squint at the small crowd of people behind the sheik and my eyes go wide when I realize Hugo is among them, just hiding under a *keffiyeh* with the rest of his staff. It makes me extremely suspicious and I turn a calculating gaze at the smiling prince as he patiently waits for the embassy staff to get their shit together.

When you have that much power, you don't have to do much beyond showing up to get people to bend the knee, I guess.

Finally, Ozzie and Bennie have a conversation and they come back to the group, all smiles. The perv isn't smirking anymore and his minion is quiet. "We are happy to receive you and your friends, Prince Dhameer Mirza Al Sharqi. The ambassador is, unfortunately, still detained, but I will take you on a tour personally. You honor us with your visit."

Dhameer gives the nasty fucker a brilliant smile. "Most excellent! Since we are many and you are few, we shall break up, don't you think? I should like a tour of the downstairs and the gardens first with my entourage and Miss Whitley. Perhaps your assistant could take the others upstairs to view the galleries and other architecture?"

"It's good to be the king," Teddy mutters.

"Shut up. He's getting us in *and* he gave you all a reason to be in the less trafficked areas. Do what Jax said and by the time we meet up, Eli will have a way into their system," I hiss softly.

"Can't look at a gift horse and all," Wolfie adds. "Besides, Sugarplum will have him and that extremely dangerous looking chick along to keep her safe."

"Agreed." Doyle looks at the prince with a grin. "We should get used to royal grandstanding, if you ask me."

What the fuck does that mean? I can not *with this many men surrounding me. I miss Seer already.*

"Fine, but I still don't like it. He's far too pleased with himself for saving our bacon. Maybe he set this up so he could save the day. He has the pull to do it," Teddy grumbles.

"No way, Edgar. That blond guy looked like he shit his pants when the prince arrived." Prez shakes his head. "I think someone else sent backup for us and we're lucky they did."

"Alright. But keep your eyes open and don't stray from his side, Tilly. We have no idea who we can trust except each other right now." Teddy leans down and kisses my forehead before he walks over to where the nervous-looking desk jockey is standing.

Truer words, Teddy bear. Truer words.

"How are your friends doing with their subterfuge?" Dhameer whispers as he leans in.

So far, we've gone through a slew of rooms that have some minor historical significance and a lot of artifacts that our reluctant guide clearly knows the bare minimum about. The contingent stays behind us, including Hugo, so I haven't been able to talk to him just yet.

"I don't know. They've got all the signals blocked in here so they can do what is needed, so I can't text. And Seer didn't make it back in time with the earwigs, so… I'm feeling blind, if I'm honest. That's not even mentioning that you showed up out of nowhere." I give him a pointed look after checking to make certain the prince's staff have Ozzie distracted for a moment.

He laughs softly, looking down at me with twinkling eyes. "Yes, I am well known for appearing when people need me. I daresay it's my trademark."

"I'm no damsel in distress you need to save, Dhameer."

His hands land on my shoulders, and his eyes delve into mine. "I am aware of that, *muharibi aleaziz*. However, I'd be lying if I said I am not enjoying being able to rescue you this one time."

I step out of the view of the babbling staffer, using his large body to block. Rubbing my temples, I sigh. "And I appreciate it. It must have been expensive and time-consuming to come here just in case we failed to get into the embassy."

"Oh, no, Jolene! I never rush into things without a backup plan. I am attending an auction tomorrow. I hope to add a few more studs to my stable; perhaps even one for Medhi one day. So all would not be lost had you not needed me."

My eyes widen, and I give him a shy smile. "A thoroughbred auction? Here?"

"Yes. Would you like to accompany me? It's quite an affair. The last time I attended one in Turkey was when I found your favorite horse and was convinced to let go of one I could not tame."

I ponder that for a moment, but I know the guys would rather I go horse shopping with the prince than skulking around the cop's house. I hate giving them the satisfaction, but I also really want to see the auction. I wrestle with it for a moment or two before I nod. "I would love to come. I think my companions have a task they want to deal with, and I'm sure I can get away to come with you."

"Excellent," he booms. The others look at us, pausing their conversations. Dhameer waves his hand and everyone goes back to doing what they were before he spoke. "I will send you everything you need to come along. MacAuley can help your men achieve whatever goal they have, and by the time they finish, we will return from the auction."

I smile shyly, taking the hand he offers me. "And here you are again, trying to make me soft on you. I see what you're doing, Your Highness."

His brow furrows, and he shakes his head. "No, *muharibi aleaziz*. You never need to address me in that way. You may call me Amiri—all of my most intimate relationships do."

That answers the question of why Doyle said they should all get used to having royalty about—the prince plans to stick around.

Smooth Criminal

Hugo

I'll admit, I was a little intimidated when Mayor Nelia called me into her office a few days ago. She's been contacting me more since Jolene came to town and I have to be very careful what and how I answer when she does, lest I betray my first fealty to our temple. But this time, she wasn't alone. The prince who was training his horses at Cantwell's farm was there, smiling broadly when I arrived. It's a topic that's been whispered about in the break room at school and all over town, but few have actually encountered him.

He seemed almost normal, though the air of power around him was electric.

Nelia did not mention we would have company, and I knew by the look on her face that I was about to be conscripted for something. The Mayor is not subtle when she wants you to do her a favor and though I've been on the receiving end of that look more lately, I couldn't imagine why a Royal was involved until she revealed his secret…

"Hugo, I'm so glad you could make time for this meeting. I'd like you to meet Prince Dhameer, Mirza Al Sharqi." She gestured for me to have a seat and I did, though I was still puzzled.

"It is an honor to meet one of your kind, Mr. MacAuley, especially one as rare as yourself."

That made me panic. I'm not supposed to allow people knowledge of my purpose in town, nor am I to reveal what I am.

"Don't worry, Hugo. They gave me permission to share your secret with the prince and his with you. You are both needed to assist a mutual interest and the Society, as well as your patron, has granted us the ability to speak freely."

Nelia gives me a reassuring smile, but I am still nervous.
After all, knowledge of my existence has been strictly guarded. I am not the only one of my kind by far, but I am an anomaly by gender.

"I knew one of your kind many, many years ago. She is of very high importance in your temple now, thanks to my intervention all those centuries ago. But back then, crossover between species was taboo and now we work together to help protect all supes through the Society. It is not a system without flaws, but it is an improve-ment, to be certain."

I blinked at the prince. There could not be many who realized such a public figure was not human. Was that true of most of his family or only him? I didn't sense his presence when he arrived in town, but perhaps if he was as old as he said, he mastered cloaking himself.

"Nelia, I must admit to being confused. What conceivable use could you have for me that involves a prince?"

She laughed and shook her head. "It is not solely about Amiri. You are both required to ensure someone else can find what they need and you are both uniquely qualified for the task."

That surprised me. "What task involves two such vastly different people?"

"You are asking the wrong question, young MacAuley. The one you should ask is who *are we uniquely qualified to assist and why." The prince grins again, holding up his hand before I answer. "I am obviously not the image I project—I am one of you. And like you, I have recently come upon something I did not expect to find in my thousands of years on this planet: a mate."*

What? I don't have a—oh.

"Much like you, Hugo, there are few of Amiri's kind left. That is because they have strictly monitored their breeding over millennia because of their immense powers and capability to change the course of history, much like your people." Nelia pauses and considers for a moment before continuing. "But we all know someone special has arrived and, with her, possibilities that have never been imagined." Jolene. She was talking about Jolene and mates.

"Jolene has mates already and—"

"Her pack, so to speak, is not complete until we join, Hugo. I have seen it in the whispers of smoke and they are never wrong. You must have had visions," the prince says as he studies me. "Things that are clouding your thoughts unlike any others before."

How did he know that?

"Smoke?" I reply carefully. "What does that mean?"

"I perform at Howl when I am in town. She was there the first night I arrived in the area and I had a feeling she was significant. I called her up from the audience to grant her a boon—something I am not supposed to do without contracts, but I enjoy doing occasionally to help troubled souls." He shrugs, his eyes dancing. "I am ancient enough that no one can stop me, not even the Society, so they look the other way when I step out of line."

Granted, her a boon. Was he a—

"A djinn, yes. As the Mayor said, we are very slim in numbers and highly moni-tored. I have survived by playing by the rules—mostly—and providing those I am asked to with favors. It is not a sordid arrangement, for I have the freedom to decline should the smoke tell me something is not the will of the universe. But your Fates and I are not on good terms, as you can imagine."

I would have thought not. Those women were infinitely more terrifying than my patron, and they answered to no one.

"Over the long years, they periodically attempt to redirect my booms or use someone to remove me from the board, but we are evenly matched strategy-wise. I've escaped their machinations more times than I can count—the most recent time led

me to the horse that brought me to your town. I am still unsure of the motives behind that incident, but it gave me my greatest desire: a mate."

The Mayor shook her head. "I doubt finding a mate is a trick of the Fates to eliminate you, Amiri."

She clearly didn't know them like the two of us. They were absolutely devious enough to have wrapped a weapon as a gift.

"Regardless, I am here and we are needed. Nelia has asked me to transport us to Istanbul to follow our future family and ensure their current mission is success-ful." The prince's expression turned troubled as he added, "There seems to be unknown forces gathering in many places and their intent is unclear—that you know after your bout with the witches. Our mate may be the nexus of the unrest given her special circumstances."

I didn't know how to take any of this. It was all too much.

But after a long conversation, they convinced me to come with the prince as part of his entourage. In the end, they were right; Jolene needed us at the embassy. Now, I've been sent to help Edgar and the rest of her family with locating a cop who they believed to be part of a cover-up surrounding her parents' death. I'm not completely sure how that will help Jolene, other than give her closure, but I'm willing to be part of anything that helps her find peace.

"MacAuley? Hey, MacAuley!"

The shout gets my attention and I leave the questions in my head as Presley approaches with Wolfgang. "Yes?"

"Let's get moving. Eli just texted the coordinates, and the guys were waiting in the SUV. We have to get this done before Magpie gets back from the horse show with the sheik. None of us want her anywhere near a potential killer," he says as he jerks his head at the doors to the lobby of the hotel I'm staying in.

"Got it." I roll to my feet, sitting the paper I was holding on the table. I didn't get to read much; only that some rockstar went missing briefly after a bar fight in Paris and was found intact. Humans have so little care about their mortality that it's shocking, but I guess rich humans are as bad as rich supes.

I say as I climb into a hundred thousand dollar armored SUV provided by the ancient prince I'm staying with.

The irony isn't lost on me,

"THIS PLACE IS AS SWANK AS THE ONE WE'RE STAYING," BENJY remarks. "How in the hell does an ex-rookie cop who works low-level security for an embassy afford a place like this?"

"Exactly," Edgar replies. "This is a gated community in the capital city, near the seaside. When I looked up what the villa we're renting goes for on purchase, it *started* at two point two mil. Jolene has friends in high places, like Thorn, so it doesn't shock me we're in such a nice home. This guy, however, should live downtown in a walkup."

I'm about to reply when it hits me like a piano dropped from the top of a building. My eyes go completely white and my body tenses as the vision rockets through me like a jolt of lightning. There are a lot of unclear images and symbols I can't place, but when I finally come out of it, they're all looking at me in fear. It's not unusual for people who haven't witnessed the onslaught that is a hallmark of my gift; it resembles a seizure, so it scares people.

"Sorry," I pant. "I didn't feel it coming. I couldn't warn you."

"Are they... Are they always like that?" Wolfie says softly. "If so, I'm sorry. It must have been terrifying when they first manifested."

I shrug. "Sometimes. Occasionally, it's worse and for much longer. I've lost days before. Luckily for me, I grew up in a place where it's commonplace and my gift was expected. They prepared me when I came of age."

Edgar arches a brow. "I'll bite. What age is that for... whatever kind of seer you are?"

"Five." I give him a tight smile, ignoring the looks of horror on their faces. "Again, everyone in my original home has them. We, much like Hamilton's people, know what our powers will look like and are trained from the moment we can walk and talk to prepare for them."

Benjy is the only one brave enough to speak. "That's a rough childhood, man. You're a strong dude for surviving it without losing your marbles."

"Not really," the Irishman says as he smirks at me. I knew he'd toss in his opinion soon enough; he's from the same side of the world as me and he definitely knows exactly what I am because of his own relatives. "Hugo is one of hundreds of his kind and they all accept their visions young. It's not a shock, and it doesn't hurt him in the slightest. It merely *looks* painful and jarring. I'm well acquainted with his people."

I nod, giving them all a reassuring look. "He's right. It's dramatic on the surface, but it doesn't cause me pain. It is frustrating to sort out what I'm allowed to share and what I must guard the knowledge for fear of altering the threads of the tapestry, but otherwise, I am fine."

Presley leans in, touching my neck to feel my pulse briefly. When he pulls away, he sighs. "He's telling the truth. His heart rate isn't even elevated."

"So what can you tell us?" Edgar asks, as he points to the house behind the iron bars. "I assume your visions come when they are needed."

"Yes, they do." I look at the house and think for a moment. "Someone will need to bend the bars. We must go inside. It is imperative that we learn what this place is hiding. We will need to be in true forms to go in; it may be dangerous. That's all I can say."

Doyle claps his hands in glee. "Everyone has to get naked! I *love* it!"

"Naked?" Benjy says, his expression confused. "We're breaking into a house without clothes?"

Edgar claps his hand on his shoulder, laughing softly. "No, dude. We all have to shift before we go in. Naked as in… let the ape escape, buddy."

My eyes widen. I didn't realize how little I knew about these guys until it became clear I was going to see supe sides I didn't know about.. Of course, I'd seen Wolfgang's gorgeous Fae wings and Hamilton's feathered caladrius at the trial, but the others didn't show me anything. I'm a loner most of the time and I don't go to things where supes might let it all hang loose. The night of the Halloween ball, I went along with Saoirse, Bane, and her friends. That was the most uncloaked supe shit I'd seen in town since I got here, even with the trial.

Now I'm going to be part of their secrets, just like Amiri.

"Let's get it done, boys," Doyle says as he flings his door open.

The others follow and I watch in wonder as Judge Edgar Boone shifts into a giant hellhound. It has to be his dominant form because he does it within the blink of an eye and without so much as a growl of pain. Presley unfurls his beautiful white wings, choosing only a half-shift, and Wolfie's shimmering skin and Fae features appear in a shower of glitter. I'm not sure what his wing dust does, but I'm not getting near enough to find out. A loud grunt catches my attention and when I look over, a gorilla four times the size of a normal one is looking at me through the sunglasses belonging to Benjy. His grin makes me think of that comic book villain, Grodd, and I walk over to look up at him.

"Goddamn, you and Boone are huge when you shift," I mutter.

"Just wait," Presley says with a chuckle. "I'm pretty sure that Irish fucker is waiting to enter like the drama queen he is."

I turn, and a burst of radiant energy flashes in front of my eyes, blinding me. When they finally adjust, an eight foot tall version of our companion is smirking at me through the telltale haze that surrounds a demi-god when they ditch their human form. The surrounding aura is golden, which tells me he's got Greek lineage, but the swirls of black and emerald surprise me. It can mean several things, and I'm fairly certain no one has ever shared those with him. If he knew what his aura said about him, I believe he'd be twice as obnoxious as he is now.

"Behold my true form, MacAuley," he preens.

Spare me, dude. I've seen plenty of full-blooded gods and even more of their mixed-race children.

"I'm not impressed. Quit swinging your magical dick around so we can figure out what's in this damn house."

Hound Edgar makes a sound of approval and, I swear, his giant fangs form a canine grin. With a brief howl, he takes off towards the back edge of the property with flames in his wake. I look at the rest of them and we all follow behind, stepping around the fires he left in his wake as he ran. When we catch up, he's sniffing around a tree several yards from a back gate. His eyes swing to Benjy, who immediately climbs the tall oak and drops over the wall with ease. A few moments later, the sound of breaking metal fills the air and the gate swings open.

"I could have done that without breaking shit," Doyle grumbles.

"Why didn't you?" I ask with a grin. He doesn't answer and I follow the winged docs as they enter the yard behind the huge flaming dog.

The son of an uncaring goddess doesn't like being questioned, I suppose.

Doyle snorts at me as he makes the locked French doors in front of us disappear by looking at them. "I save my parlor tricks for when they're more striking."

Of course he does.

The smell hits me as soon as we walk in—the copper tang of blood and the unmistakable scent of bodily gasses that escape during decomposition. Edgar rears back, letting out a howl of indignance and I don't blame him. Dogs, even hellhounds, have noses a hundred million times more sensitive than humans, even those of us with supernatural powers. If this is killing me, it has to be making him sick.

"Boone is going to struggle with this because of his canine instincts. I'm used to the smell because of my training, and so is Wolfie. We can leave the rest of you out here," Presley says.

A growl of disagreement echoes in the kitchen, and I shake my head. "As bad as it may be, I believe we all should stay together, and clearly Edgar does as well."

Benjy grunts his approval and Doyle shrugs at me. "I've been on many a battlefield over the years. My uncle's realm doesn't bother me. Let's go figure out what the hell happened here."

"I'm suddenly thrilled your royal friend invited Sugarplum to the horse show," Wolfie says softly.

I nod as we head through the dining room to another room, and the smell gets worse. "Agreed."

The sight that greets us there is one straight out of a crime TV show. There's blood everywhere—and the body of a middle-aged guy that appears to have been tortured for information via having his skin peeled off. It's disgusting, barbarous, and still not the worst thing I've ever seen—live or in a vision.

A shimmer catches the corner of my eye and I look to see Boone back in his humanoid form. He has fiery eyes, black hands and claws and sulfur is coming off him in waves, but the dog is no more.

"Motherfucker. This guy has a wife and kids," he says as he walks closer to examine the mess. "Haggerty, you check upstairs with Hamilton. I suspect there's nothing good up there, either."

"How do you know, Teddy?" Wolfie asks. I'm wondering as well, so I nod.

"You were all focused on the smell of death, but I smelled rotten food as we walked through the dining room. There was breakfast on the table for five people that had blood on it," he sighs with a sigh. "That's not a good sign."

Holy Hades. He thinks they're going to find dead kids upstairs. That's why he sent those two.

"I'm going to call the Mayor, Edgar. She wanted to know what we found and I think this qualifies as something that will require a clean-up team before humans find it." He nods and I walk back out through the dining room, noting he was right about the food.

Something tells me we've stumbled onto more than they bargained for with this trip.

But how does it relate to Jolene?

Rich Girl

Jolene

The box that was delivered to our house this morning contained every single item of clothing I'm wearing. I'm not certain how he managed to get all of this on short notice and perfectly my size, but I suppose being a freaking prince has its benefits.

Adjusting my special shades, I look around the sales arena curiously. It's fairly small for *Arqana* and the event is late in the season. I wipe my hands on the understated couture jeans, noting the amount of expensive clothing and accessories on the people who are filing in. The black blouse and natty black straw fedora Amiri sent are sleek and sophisticated while kickass, block-heeled lambskin boots mold over my calves until they hit my knees. It makes me look like I fit right in with this crowd—outside of my non-surgically altered curves. He has my arm tucked in his, and despite wearing more casual attire, the kaffiyeh tells everyone he's someone to be deferred to.

I've had more people bow their heads to me today than ever before in my life.

"Amiri, people are staring holes in my back. Is this what it's like to be you all the time?" I whisper when we pause to look at an animal.

His smile is genuine as he nods. "If I identify myself. It's why I don't wear the traditional garb when I am not representing the family—or at least, when I am expected to by virtue of where I am."

I shake my head as I wrap my arms around myself. "It's creepy as hell. I can feel the emotions zipping around me; it's everything from jealousy to fear to hatred. I've been in the spotlight plenty of times, but *this* is a whole different level of weirdness."

"Very true, *muharibi aleaziz*. I suppose over the years I have grown accustomed to it and it no longer bothers me. But for someone who has not experienced it as part of their everyday life, it would be very jarring," he muses. His hand comes up to tuck a hair behind my ear and he looks at me seriously. "If it is too much, I can have Isra lay my bids and we will leave."

"No, no. I've wanted to come to one of these for a long time. I won't let the same kind of people who whisper about me at home drive me away here, too. Even if these people make those people look like paupers." I wink at him and he lets out a bellowing laugh. There are a few flashes around the room and I sigh. Those pictures are either going in a paparazzi rag or online; I can feel it.

Dhameer leans forward and whispers near my ear. "Don't worry. Isra will take care of the amateur journalists. She is *very* convincing and we will not appear anywhere we do not wish to."

Sounds a little scary, but I suppose it comes with the territory.

"And how does your fierce protectoress feel about me?" I ask curiously.

"Ah, well. Isra does not like new people. It took her many years to get used to Fazal. But she will come around eventually. Her level of suspicion is part of what keeps me alive, so I allow her to run my security as she sees fit. However, she does not get a vote when it comes to people I choose to care about."

My cheeks flush and I grab his hand, tugging him away from the fence to walk towards another horse. I knew he wouldn't be bidding on the one we were next to, but we can't speak freely when we're moving in a crowd. There are far too many people looking to get dirt on the prince. "Don't be mushy."

"Ah, but I enjoy the response, *muharibi aleaziz*. You are very strong and capable, but when you soften, it is a thing of beauty."

"Don't be cheesy," I say as we stop at the next stall. The horse is a beautiful thoroughbred with a long neck and powerful hindquarters

—this one could be a possibility. Dhameer picks up one of the cards, perusing the information quietly. When he's done, he holds it up and Isra appears out of nowhere to take it from him with a nod.

He sees my surprised expression and shrugs. "She is always watching and her training allows her to move with stealth and speed. It is very unusual to look for her and not find her within seconds."

"Isn't that a bit weird? I mean, it doesn't leave a lot of room for private moments."

"Would you like to have a private moment? I believe Isra will be occupied for another three to five minutes, though if I called that would change," he teases.

I roll my eyes at him as we head to another animal's stall. "That's not what I meant and you know it."

The prince gasps softly and I whirl around, looking for what caused him to sound alarmed. "*Reine Panthère*[1]…"

Frowning, I follow his gaze to a tall, redhead dressed in black from head to toe. Her leather pants and boots are even more expensive than mine and she's wearing a slinky silk top that clings to every one of her curves. Her long red curls hit her thighs as she stalks in front of the horse we were about to look at. Large old Hollywood-style sunglasses cover her eyes and there's something very familiar about her that I can't place. She definitely has the show stopping charisma down pat, though.

"Who is that?" I ask. When my companion doesn't answer, I shake his shoulder. "Amiri, who is that woman?"

His face is pale as he turns to me. "That is the Panther Queen. She is well known among a certain element of people, though she's a fairly new addition to her employer's stable. I know this because I had Isra do extensive research on her after she decided to strike a bargain with me rather than kill me at a show like last year."

"I'm sorry…what?" I blink at him, feeling panic rise in my chest. A hot sensation starts in my chest and crawls through my veins as I look over at the woman who might be a threat.

He shakes his head. "Do not get upset, Jolene. She wasn't here for me and I was able to bargain with her for an animal I was already contemplating selling. It was very amicable at the end, though, at first I was not certain it would end well."

His ability to shrug this off, despite the obvious physical reaction he's exhibiting, makes me think there's more to the story, but I don't think I'll get it out of him now.

"Your Highness!"

Oh, shit.

The redhead practically oozes her way over to us with an excited wave. I have to rub my eyes when she approaches because I'm certain she's being followed by a tiger with a coal black ferret riding on its back. But that can't be right, can it? We're not in the Hollow; no one would allow a woman to be walking through a horse show with a goddamned white tiger, right?

"Jolene, it is my turn to ask if *you* are okay?" Dhameer murmurs before he holds his hands out to the woman. She darts in and does the air kiss thing with him, but he doesn't say a word about the wild animal.

Maybe I am losing my fucking mind. Maybe I have a tumor.

"Who is this lovely creature you've brought along?" she says with a smile that is half beautiful and half feral.

"Pardon me, *Reine Panthère*. This is my date, Miss Jolene Athena Whitley of Kentucky," the prince says formally.

"Oh my," she says. Her hand goes up to her glasses and she takes them off, studying me with sapphire eyes that seem to see right through me. A delicate sniff of the air makes her lips curve up slowly. "She is a special find, Your Highness. Quite fitting for you, I think. I am glad we were able to come to terms last year. Something about your date tells me I won't regret it."

My eyes narrow as she talks about me as if I'm not even here. "It's nice to meet you as well, Panther Queen. Have you ever been to the States? Something about you feels very familiar…"

"I bet it does, darling." Her wink is playful and I swear to shit, she looks over at the tiger I'm certain no one but me can see with a smirk. "However, I don't think today is the day we will discuss that. I'm on a deadline, you see. I have a job and if I'm not quick about it,

I won't make it home before my husband. He's such a bear when we're late to dinner with our spouses. It's a total bloodbath."

Dhameer arches a brow, but I ignore it. This woman doesn't feel like a threat but I can't seem to get my body to stop sending fight or flight signals to my brain. I'm flushed and I can't figure out why, nor can I understand why I'm having a hallucination involving jungle cats at a horse show.

"It was delightful to see you again, *Reine Panthère*," the prince says as he lifts her hand to kiss it. "Please reach out to my staff should you want to contact me about your horse."

Her grin is absolutely wicked as she flips her hair over her shoulder. "Oh, that won't be necessary. Hippolyta is doing very well in my stable. She terrorizes the staff and my family, but we are perfectly matched as horse and rider."

"Excellent," he says. I can see the surprise on his features, and it makes the woman laugh more.

Her eyes flash at me as she nods and for a moment, the memory of the airplane bathroom and my weird vision of my eyes changing in the mirror. "Enjoy the show, Jolene. I'm certain we will see one another again."

I wave as she turns to go, unsure of what to say to that. Our meeting today was by chance and despite the intense sensation of familiarity, I highly doubt our paths will cross again as she suggested. A tap on my arm brings me out of my thoughts and I give the prince a sheepish look. "I'm sorry. I just… I have the oddest feeling that I know her and I can't place where we might have met. It could have been in a million places during my time with Seer, so it's going to drive me crazy."

"Perhaps it will come to you when you are not so focused on it. Come, let's go find the refreshments area. You're flushed and I would be remiss if I didn't get you some water." Dhameer takes my arms and tucks it in his again, guiding me away from the viewing stables.

"You know, for a prince, you're very approachable," I say as we stroll through the arena towards the door. "I know the people here are all in your sphere, but I saw you with Jamie at the farm. You like him and you don't act like he's your staff. Even at the embassy yesterday, you threw your weight about with those assholes, but you didn't act like my… boyfriends… were any less important than you."

"I have learned that wealth and fame do not make a person good. In fact, many times, it's the opposite. The constant fulfillment of your desires with little effort tends to make good people turn demanding and shrill. Even those who are not obscenely wealthy or successful are misled by the siren's call of their egos. It can ruin friendships, destroy marriages, and decimate the people around them when they start believing the pretty words whispered in their ears."

Sighing, I think about his words for a moment. Whistler's Hollow has families with a great deal of generational inheritances and it definitely causes a divide in those who and those who have not. The children of the founding families are afforded a status and grace others are not, further pushing the gap between the two sides apart. It's why shrews like Sherilynn and Amy and their ilk felt perfectly fine humiliating someone at an event where most of the town was in attendance. They believe that because they have an elevated status in our community, they can get away with anything. Unfortunately, history has proven them correct over and over again, so the cycle repeats *ad nauseum*.

"I agree. At home, I'm struggling against a group of women who haven't taken the time to reflect on what behaving the same way they did in high school says about them." I stop and he follows suit. His hand comes up to cup my face as I continue. "It took a long time for me to heal from the scars of my youth and when I came home, I would have been happy to be quietly civil instead of reliving the past. But from the second I arrived, these women picked up their campaign of terror like I'd never left. It's disheartening to see the good people around us sit back and watch."

His thumb brushes over my cheek bone and he leans in to brush a light kiss on my lips before pulling back. "I'm sure you know this, *muharibi aleaziz*, but we are all victims of our past. All of the bad and good that happens helps to forge the core within us and teach us how to navigate the world more successfully. The women you speak of may be finding joy in trying to hurt you again, but where they have not evolved, you have. Your strength was fired in the flames of their abuse, so whereas they are still the bullies they have been, you grew into a smart, funny, capable woman."

I lean into his hand and give him a rueful smile. "Are you getting ready to tell me they're just jealous of me? They want to shine as brightly as me, so they work to dim my light? Because it's sweet, but I'm definitely too old to fall for that old chestnut."

"Ah, Jolene. I do not know enough about them or their lives to make that assumption. What I do know is that you have traveled the world, met with princes and CEOs, been a teacher, interviewed to be a profiler… and even when you were kicked in the teeth, you moved home and picked up your pieces without missing a beat. That kind of resilience and confidence in yourself is enviable to those who secretly doubt themselves."

Put that way, I could see how my presence, especially after the guys attached themselves to me, might be a threat to their self-assigned queen bee status.

"They're afraid this time around I could take their crowns?" I squint up at him, trying to wrap my head around that seemingly impossible theory.

"Yes," he says. "They know they have limited appeal and if you are given the opportunity, you will eclipse them without trying. Your Edgar and Benjamin are walking, talking proof of your ability to win without even playing their games. Their fear is not unwarranted; I wholeheartedly believe once the larger populace sees who you really are, there won't be a comparison. Their power will be gone in the blink of an eye."

"Thank you," I whisper. "I don't know if I believe you, but thank you for being honest about your feelings. The guys defend me and I know it's because they care, but I'm not sure they understand why I can't seem to ignore the pokes and prodding."

Dhameer steps back, offering me his arm again. "It is because you are a born warrior, Jolene Whitley. One day, you will show everyone the ferocity I see in you and when that happens, there will no longer be doubt."

Be still my fucking heart, Prince Charming.

OUTSIDER

BENJY

I t's terrifying how matter-of-factly the rest of the guys are going about searching a murder scene. Sure, MacAuley peaced out to call Nelia, but once he was gone, Presley and Doyle trooped upstairs like Edgar commanded. Wolfgang surprised me by walking around the room snapping pictures without being told and my oldest friend made a beeline for the body, crouching next to it with his own phone.

"Uh, what… What should I do?" I ask, rubbing my hand over the back of my head as I watch the surreal scene in front of me.

"Check the doors. Well, the ones Doyle didn't fucking disappear so he could show off. See if they show signs of forced entry," Edgar says distractedly.

Does he expect me to have CSI experience or…?

"Teddy, you know he didn't do the training. He wasn't shipped off because he's not active."

I frown at the vet, watching him continue to snap photos as he makes his way around the room. "Training? What training?"

"Shit. Those morons sent his idiot ex to that. She fell in a kiddie pool full of sewage and stormed off. I remember now." Edgar rises to his full height, giving me a sheepish look. "Sorry, man. Your ex really cut you out of everything and left you running the store—literally."

"She did? Like what?" I cross my arms over my chest, feeling angry at myself all over again for staying married to a woman I didn't love for as long as I did.

"Society stuff, man. She was the rep from your family so she went to all of the meetings, trainings, and active agent shit. If it makes you feel better, she sucked ass at almost all of it and some of the places we went refused to allow her to stay after the first day." My friend tilts his head. "Where the hell did she tell you she was going when we did all of the out of town jaunts?"

My head falls back on my shoulders and I look up at the ceiling, closing my eyes. "Spa getaways with the girls. Goddamn it. That woman controlled every damn thing in our lives so tightly that I missed everything."

"You're free now," Wolfie says as he turns to look at me. His expression is sympathetic yet hopeful and I arch a brow at Boone.

"Yes, he's always this way," the judge says with a smirk. "It's both infuriating and endearing at the same time. And completely impossible to say no to."

The fae blushes under his blue tinted skin. "Stop it, Teddy. We don't have time and it's gross in here. And I'm not being sunshiny—I really mean it, Benjy. You're free now and you can do whatever you want. Sugarplum will support you and so will we."

"That's true. We all went to the stupid shit you missed, so we'll teach you as we go along. Tilly would love to work with you on martial arts or shooting. Just ask her." Edgar chuckles and shrugs. "For now, go check out the locks on the front door. Look for scratches like someone tried to pick it or splinters in the frame like a crowbar opened it."

This is not what I imagined when Edgar told me I should come on a trip overseas with them, but when in Turkey, I suppose.

"Got it," I say with a lot more confidence than I feel. I'd Google a video, but the guy with the cell net device is upstairs doing…things I don't want to imagine. At least they didn't ask me to go hunt down tiny bodies.

And that is a sentence I just said in my head—great.

"You know, I think she's warming back up to us," Wolfie says randomly. "Look at how easily we all fit into the house. She didn't even complain about everyone piling in on the plane until she had to pee."

"There's still distance emotionally, though. I don't like it," Boone growls. "I want it gone."

Kneeling by the door to do as they asked, I call over my shoulder. "Have you actually addressed the past with her? Like besides just telling her how she became the Catastrophe? You may have been honest as much as possible about our secrets, but have you truly worked through what you did *before* that?"

"Shit."

That would be a 'no'.

"Do you really think she needs to hear me lay out how badly I felt afterward? After all of these years?" He comes up behind me, his brow creased in concern.

"Uh, yeah, dude. I think she does. I can come with you if you think you're going to fuck it up as usual."

He nods, then points at the loose strike plate. "Definitely forced entry, but they knew what they were doing. I wouldn't have caught it if we weren't looking closely. This wasn't random; I think someone took this guy out."

Footsteps sound on the stairs and I see a much paler Hamilton and Doyle descending them with solemn expressions. They shake their heads when we look at them and I swallow hard. That means they found the rest of the family and by the look of them, it wasn't pretty.

"Jesus fuck," I mutter. "What the fuck did this asshole do that got his kids slaughtered?"

"I don't know," Edgar says tiredly. "What I do know is that we *cannot* tell Tilly what we found. We have to say he was gone. This is part of the necessary lies until she's ready to defend herself."

Wolfie walks over and wraps around Presley. The taller doc relaxes immediately, his wings coming around them both.

Doyle looks over at us with mischief in his eyes. "No one wants to comfort the demi-god, eh? I see how you all are. Speaking of Greeks, where's the spook?"

"Spook?" I ask in confusion.

"MacAuley. Is he still listening to our fine Mayoress chew him out for breaking into a crime scene?"

"I think so. I don't envy him that, though you and Hamilton got the short end of the stick," I add with a shudder.

The red haired supe looks at his hands and shrugs. "It's not the first time I've seen shit like that and likely won't be the last. Humans are constantly coming up with better ways and flimsier reasons to kill one another. I gave up trying to understand it centuries ago."

Ouch. It's easy to forget how old he is until he says shit like that.

"Are we done here?" Presley asks from under his wings. "I'd like to get the hell away from this massacre and have a few dozen drinks to forget."

"We are," Edgar replies as he looks around. "When we get back to the house, we'll check on the animals and wait for my *drugar* to get home. Benjy and I are going to take her out tonight. If I can be honest about high school, maybe we can get her to open up about the Trevor shit."

"And what the hell are we supposed to do while you two wine and dine our woman?" Doyle asks indignantly.

Wolfie sighs and comes out from under the doc's wing shelter. "We can get Seer to help us do a summoning for my mother. We should get it over with before anything else terrible happens. If we do it while they're out, I can avoid her seeing Sugarplum."

"Good thinking, pup," Edgar says as he pulls him close and drops a kiss on his head. "I'm proud of you."

The Fae blushes so hard his blue skin almost looks purple and I chuckle.

Yeah, it's not hard to get why everyone is soft on the vet.

"Let's get the hell out of here," I grumble as I turn to walk to the front door. "We're all going to smell like death if we stay here and the lover boy over there has a date with our woman tonight."

"TELL ME AGAIN WHY WE STOPPED HERE ON OUR WAY HOME."

Wolfie smiles patiently. "When I texted Saoirse, she asked me to look up a place where we could get supplies for the bullshit with my mom. It seemed unlikely that the joker who watches our rental would have what we needed in the house."

I roll my eyes as I think about the pictures of him dressed in frat boy style costumes and making prepubescent Insta shots in public places that are strewn about the house like badges of honor. "Yeah, that makes sense. That dude seems like the guys we were in the frat with in college—emotionally stunted, insecure, and dying for attention for all the wrong shit. Sadly, much like him, those dudes are probably *still* doing that well into their thirties despite being lawyers, doctors, stock brokers, and military men. His name is probably Vann or Chad or something."

Edgar laughs as he whips the SUV into a tight spot on the street like a pro. "Do you remember that one dark haired guy with the angel wing tattoo on his back? His dad was from that big metal band and he acted like he was related to the king of Hell? His lineage got him in, but he stuck out like a sore thumb even in a frat full of rich assholes like us. What was his name… Slade? No, Razor. No… shit, Benjy."

"Mage. The dude called himself Mage, man. He really leaned into the whole 'my dad says he's Satanic' thing. It was comical in a place so strait laced and preppy as State U. He was from Bay City, I think. Supes are *weird* out west." I laugh as I think about him running around being broody and alternative, thinking that would attract the elite women who attended our college. "I guarantee he didn't get laid once all four years. He was about as dark as a mocha latte."

Presley's eyes widen and he snaps his fingers. "That guy is an archivist up in Salem. I only recognize it because I requested all those files from other enclaves when our girl came to town. I was trying to find out where she'd been left as a baby before the Whitleys adopted her and his response email was in a four beat iambic verse like a Poe poem. I laughed so hard I spit my salad out."

"I remember that!" Wolfie chimes in. "We made fun of it for days."

"Yeah, he was a complete tool," Edgar says. "Some of the founders in other enclaves make ours look *way* less wacky."

"Now that we strolled down memory lane, we should get this crap and get home," Doyle says, his voice full of boredom. "Some of us didn't join fake Greek party clubs for social cache."

"It's not our fault you're older than most developed nations, Haggerty," my old friend says. "It probably chaps your ass that one of your relatives is the god everyone worships at parties."

He opens his door, grinning. "I'm rather fond of the old drunk, actually. He's a shitty poker player and I kick his ass in the deity tourney every decade." We all look at him, trying to imagine playing in a poker tournament full of various gods and demi-gods. He shrugs and exits the car. "Let's go, dickwads."

That gets everyone moving and we follow suit, walking to the small, cramped entryway of the store. The sign says '*Destiny*' and it's slicker than the surrounding shops. The walls are shelves bursting with magical books, items, and various spell ingredients. I sniff the air, trying to identify the scent wafting around us.

"It's a mixture of jasmine, vetiver, clove, and patchouli," the Irishman says under his breath. "It's supposed to attract money, which I suppose makes sense in a store. But it means the owner isn't completely full of shit. Maybe."

"Maybe is right. There's stuff that feels real and things that are complete tourist traps," Wolfie remarks as he holds up a Tarot deck featuring characters from a TV show. "This kind of stuff is to get sales from tourists. I have a feeling we need to go deeper to get to the things we'll want."

"How do you know?" I arch a brow at him, curious since he doesn't seem like the type.

"Aurelia and my adoptive father were both agents up until…everything changed. He was Fae—Daybreak Court—and she was a witch with the gift. I grew up with all the ceremonies and knowledge they could give me. Now I wonder if it's because they knew my real mother would find me one day and they wanted me to be prepared."

Edgar looks over his shoulder as he leads us through the winding rows and shelves. "She won't hurt you, pup. You can do this and you'll have plenty of people to keep her in line tonight."

"I trust you all. But we have to find the true stock—the things supes use for their magical working or my mother won't respond. She's a snob as well as a sociopath."

"What a combo," I mutter and the others nod.

As we make our way deep into the seemingly never ending store, we find a spiral staircase that leads downward. The vet nods his approval, letting us know this is where we want to go. Before any of us can start our descent, a loud, baritone voice echoes out of the stairway.

"Nothing you have here is powerful enough for a witch such as me. I am one with nature, a child of the forest, and people seek out my brews from all over the world!"

"Uh-oh," Wolfie groans. "That doesn't sound good. Should we come back?"

"Negative," Boone says. "We don't have time to double back before Tilly is due home. We'll have to navigate around this nutter, get what we need, and get out."

Great. I cannot wait to meet the person behind that self-important ranting.

One by one we trudge down the narrow staircase, spilling into the huge underground warehouse. This time, I can actually *feel* the buzz of power coming from every direction. Scents mix and float by on gentle breezes as if to draw me in the direction of the emotions they evoke.

Candles and dim lamps are randomly scattered throughout the room, placed to highlight small signs that mark the locations of different items and ingredients. A tall case behind the counter gives off a scary vibe and I'd bet Cantwell's farm that nothing in there is fake tourist crap. I don't even want to know what is kept in there, honestly.

"Do you see the men with me? They are powerful allies who recognize my dark power. You need to heed my words, shopkeeper, or you will regret it!"

Our group approaches the counter carefully, letting Wolfgang take the lead. The woman who is shouting like a lunatic is short and angry looking, but nothing like I would have imagined based on her claims. She's got several dudes with her, but they seem to be standing off to the side while she throws her hissy fit. By the looks on their faces, they're used to it and choose not to get involved. I don't blame them; I wouldn't want to be part of this nonsense, either.

"Excuse me? Can you point me toward the fresh herbs?" The vet charges in with more confidence than I would have expected, but then, this is a world he's comfortable with. Maybe chicks like this haunt occult shops acting like fools everywhere. I sure as hell wouldn't know.

The shopkeeper comes out of the shadows where she'd been quietly allowing the other customer to wear herself out. When she's visible, Edgar turns to look at the rest of the group in shock, cutting his eyes at her pointedly. I frown, not sure what he's getting at. She's tall and powerful looking, dressed in some sort of metal armor like get up that feels more fitting for a geek con than a magic shop. An enormous black wolf is standing by her side glaring at us.

"Oh, shit," Wolfie mutters. "It's the wildcard woman."

Her laugh is deep and rich as she nods at him, completely ignoring the other customer as she continues to stomp around in her yoga pants and combat boots bitching. "It is me, young Fletcher. This is my shop and it is always there for those who are in need. Hand me your list and *Destiny* will find what you need."

This is weird as hell and I'm a gorilla shifter who lives in a town full of supernaturals who hide in plain sight.

"Thank you," he says simply. "But the list was sent digitally. Do you have a pen and paper?"

She nods, producing a piece of parchment, a peacock feather, and an ink well. "Write it down and it will appear. I will charge it to my sister."

"Your… what?" I sputter.

The woman smiles and I can see the magic of whatever she is in her eyes. "My sister. She's much older, of course, but we discovered one another when she arrived in your town to take over. Nelia and I share the same biological mother. That's why she came to Whistler's Hollow in the first place—to find me."

We all gape at one another, unable to figure out what to say. This woman is intimidating as hell and according to her, she's related to our Mayor and from our hometown. Silence falls over us as we try to process all of that information.

"This seems like a lovely reunion, but I was here first." Heads swivel to look at the shrewish witch as she glares at both us and the shopkeeper. "Since I am the more well known magic wielder, I demand you pay attention to me and offer the respect I deserve!"

Even I know that was a mistake.

A flash of black fur, blue eyes, and sharp white teeth leaps over the counter in a blur of motion. The wolf is standing on the chest of the obnoxious twat, snapping its jaws in her face menacingly. She shrieks in fear, looking at the people standing behind her, but they don't move. The shopkeeper drifts out from behind the counter gracefully, looking down at the prone witch with a feral smile.

"You've angered Argus and most beings that do so do not survive to tell the tale. Your hubris will be your undoing; I can feel it in your aura, witch. The Fates have conspired to continually toss the apple in your path and you will forever pick it up. It is your curse and why you act in this way." Her head tilts as she waves her hand over the woman's face briefly. "However, since I find your squawking pathetic and beneath me, I will ask him to let you live if you simply take your minions and never return. You will cease your prattling about things you have no concept of."

The woman nods, looking as though she might have just pissed her waffle printed pants. Argus steps off of her, tosses his head and howls into the air. That signals the men and they grab the witch, dragging her towards the stairs without another word. Our hostess smiles wickedly as she watches, then turns back to us.

"Now, allow me to help you collect what you need to summon the Cailleach, young Fae."

Okay, now this woman is even scarier.

Sorry Not Sorry

When we pull up to the villa, Dhameer insists on escorting me to the door and saying hello to the guys. His 'ye olde' gentleman stuff is cute, so I let him get away with it. It's hard to imagine the rest of the guys behaving so formally and not cracking me up, but with him, I find it more endearing than silly. I punch the code in, leading the prince into the foyer with a smile. He looks around, his expression approving as he takes in the decor. The sound of laughter is coming from the sitting room, so I take his hand and drag him towards the noise.

"I'm home, you reprobates!" I call. "Say hello to the prince."

A chorus of muttered greetings are the response and I roll my eyes when I figure out they're all piled on the couches playing Mario Kart on the big screen. They've got beers and snacks littering the formerly pristine table, making the room look more like a frat house than an elegant villa.

"Clearly, I've been missed."

Dhameer grins and holds up my hand, kissing it. "Obviously. However, since Hugo is not here, I assume he is awaiting me at my suite. We have some business to attend to this evening, so I will leave you in the capable hands of your entourage."

I roll my eyes. "That, Amiri, is very subjective."

"Oi!" Doyle shouts. "I'm extremely capable. In fact, I'm capable of kicking Boone's ass and I'm doing it *right now.*"

All it takes are sports or video games and every single man in existence becomes a teenager again, I fucking swear.

The prince leaves and I walk over, flopping down on the couch beside Presley. He tugs me to his side and looks at me. "Did you have a good time, Magpie?"

"I did, actually. What did you guys find when you went to the address Eli gave us?"

Teddy snorts as he works the controller with expert precision. "The guy was gone. We couldn't question him or his family. Did a sweep of the place, but didn't find any useful information, but we sent all the pics and shit to be analyzed. We might have missed something; who knows?"

I sigh, frustrated that every lead seems to dead end in nothing. "What else can we do? Now I feel like we came here for nothing."

"For tonight, Edgar and I are going to take you to dinner, Princess. You looked happy when you came in and I think the distraction did you good." Benjy looks at me over his shoulder quickly, then looks back at the race where he's trying to maneuver his Donkey Kong around Doyle's Waluigi.

"Just us?" I echo. "Are the rest of you okay with that?"

The last thing I need is a bunch of macho internal jealousy stuff flaring up.

"Of course we are, sugarplum," Wolfie says quickly. "We had to do a lot of shit to search that place from stem to stern and I'm perfectly fine with lounging at home with take out. Besides, we have all month away from home; we can all take you on dates if we want."

Presley nods in agreement. "What he said."

"Doyle?"

"Peace in the Middle East, Tíogair. Except for in this feckin' game, of course." His eyes tear away from the screen and he gives me a playful wink before he turns back.

Did they all get high or something? This is weird as hell.

"Oooookay. Well, if that's how you all feel, I'm going to go upstairs, shower, and relax while I get ready. It was fairly hot and dusty at the arena, so I need to freshen up before we go anywhere nice." A scent catches my nose and I frown when I recognize it—but that can't be, so I shake my head. "Someone here should hit one of the other bathrooms, too, especially if you're going out with me. It smells like decomp in here for some reason."

Silence is the response so I shrug and head upstairs.

Men are so goddamned bizarre.

THE BATH WAS LUXURIOUS AND EXACTLY WHAT I NEEDED.

I read while I soaked, got everything squeaky and soft, and finally got a text from my errant best friend. I tried not to worry about her when she didn't make it to the house in time to go to the embassy and when she didn't show up last night, I struggled not to set off alarm bells. But long before she landed in my hometown, Seer would disappear for days and I never felt the need to track her down. The paranoia from the bullying and the weirdo watching me have made me act like a schoolmarm and I have to let my friend and lovers do shit without panicking when they're out of touch.

Don't be a controlling asswad, Jolene. Saoirse can definitely take care of herself and whatever she got caught up in with this contact is probably important. She's not abandoning you and she's not tied up in some creep's basement.

But now I have to put myself together for a night out on the town with Teddy and Benjy without my personal 'girly shit' coordinator. I wrinkle my nose, plodding over to the closet where Wolfie insisted on hanging my clothes. I swiped a few of the expensive designer things in my mother's closet to bring in case we had to attend something a little dressier just in case. Thank fuck my compulsive packing gene made me do it or I'd have to wear jeans to a nice restaurant.

Studying the three outfits, I finally pick the *Balenciaga* cocktail dress. The brilliant emerald cocktail dress has a strapless sweetheart neckline that dips almost to the bottom of my ribs and a skirt that sits just above my knees. The real showstopper is the back—it stops right above my ass and there's a deep slit in the skirt. Normally, I wouldn't wear something that clings this tightly, but…

I refuse to worry about what anyone thinks of me anymore. There are people who care about me who don't give a shit if I'm not airbrush perfect head to toe, so fuck the expectations of small minded idiots.

Twisting my lips, I pace back forth around the room as I think. The real question is: am I brave enough to back that sentiment up? I don't mind wearing a strapless bra, but I'd like to enjoy dinner. I won't if I squeeze myself in shapewear to make smooth lines in that dress. Waffling over it for a moment, I wiggle into the wizardry that is my bra and panties.

You know what? Fuck it. I'm not doing it. Let them stare.

With that decided, I leave the dress on the bed and walk to the bathroom to start the hair and make up thing. I'm not going to ask Wolfie to help—though he'd probably love to—because I'm going to go as Jolene (mostly) au naturel. If the boys don't like it, they can find someone else to play with. Feeling free, I set my phone to play a 'going out' playlist and sing along as I wait for the curling iron to heat up.

A few minutes later, I'm dancing around as I squeeze and release the fat curls when a voice startles me.

"Sugarplum? Is everything okay up here?"

I almost drop the hot iron as I shriek. "Hecate in a handbasket, Wolfie, you scared the *shit* out of me!"

His expression is sheepish as he walks in, barefoot and rumpled. "Sorry about that. You were just… uh. It sounded like…"

"Like someone strangled a cat, right? And Jekyll and Hyde are downstairs with the others, so you thought maybe I was being attacked?" I give him a wry smile as I flick the last curl out of the iron's grip.

"Maybe?"

"I can't sing. Everyone thinks I don't know, so they pretend they don't notice. But I'm not deaf or profoundly stupid—I realize I sound like dying water buffalo, but I love doing it. So I do it anyway and people seem to play along." The significance of that philosophy hits me and I cover my mouth.

Wolfie smirks. "Did you figure something out just now?"

"Shut up, smarty pants. Christ, if my therapist could hear this. That woman barely finished our time together with all her hair on her head and *now* I figure this shit out." Stomping over to the sink, I slip the soft headband up my neck to gingerly push the untouched curls back so I can do my face.

"And what is it?" he asks as he walks over and starts picking through the neatly packed pouches of various shit Seer thought I might need.

"I should have been—should *be*—living life with the same philosophy as I take with my shitty singing voice. It's not perfect and occasionally really bad, but I do it anyway no matter how many people think I suck. Because it's for me, not them, and they can suck a giraffe dick if they don't like it."

"Bingo!" he says, bopping me on the nose with a big powder brush. "Give the lady a kewpie doll."

"Alright, alright," I grumble. "No need to be sarcastic."

"Since you had such a momentous discovery, I think I can reward you by helping you with this." He gestures at the makeup on the sink with a knowing look.

"Aren't I supposed to be the one rewarding you?"

"Po-tay-to, Po-tah-to," he shrugs. "You probably just didn't want to admit you needed help anyway, right?"

My answer is a glare and he winks at me. If this was anyone but Wolfie, I'd give them an elbow to the sternum, but he truly isn't making fun of me. "Fine. Do something pretty but no fancy stuff. I decided I'm going sort of natural tonight. No lashes, no contouring, no Spanx. Just me."

"Good for you, sugarplum. I don't know why you've even bothered. None of us even want you to wear underwear, much less that boned shit." He pauses as he picks up a sponge. "Okay, Teddy loves to rip the fancy lace, but I think it's more like an ingrained dominant thing more than a fetish."

"Wolfie, have I told you how much I missed you?" I open my eyes and reach up to ruffle his hair. "Out of everyone, your feet are so firmly planted on the ground. You take care of all of us without being asked and you have this eerie sixth sense for when people need you. It's really lovely."

His cheeks flush and he wrinkles his nose. "I'm supposed to put blush on you, Sugarplum. You've got everything backwards today."

"Mmmm, well, I'm happy to be backwards with you. Hell, I'd be happy to be upside down with you again, but that will have to wait until later." I bob my brows at him and he laughs as he picks up a shadow palette.

"Yes, it will. Now, hold still so I can finish you up so the boys downstairs don't get too squirrely. I think Teddy and Benjy are a wee bit excited, so I don't want to keep them waiting because we were flirting."

"Oh, that wasn't flirting. It has been a while since we've played if you think that was flirting, darling boy."

"You can teach me a lesson later." He bops me with a powder puff. "Now, hold still."

Season of the Wi

Wolfgang

"I hope they have a good time," I say as we hustle to the door of the innocuous building located in a back alley.

Doyle knocks on the door rapidly in a familiar rhythmic pattern and a hole opens in the center eye of the carving on the heavy wood. They don't say a word, simply staring at us with monocular suspicion. The Irishman sighs and places his finger on the fingerprint scanner panel that opens on the right side of the door, then says, "*Diatírisi, prostasía, yperáspisi… o kýklos den teleiónei.*[1]"

The voice behind the door is raspy as it replies, "*I epivíosi enós eínai aioniótita gia ólous*[2]."

"Are we done with the ridiculous cloak and dagger shite?" He pushes on the door. "It's hot as hell here even in the evening."

An affronted sniff is his answer, but the door opens slowly. We follow him inside and I peer around in curiosity. I'm sure Doyle and Presley have been in plenty of Society safe houses in other countries, but I know I haven't. The atrium is a dark, cherry wood paneled room that looks a lot like one of the waiting rooms in our Society meeting hall and I wonder if they design them all as similarly as possible to make people feel comfortable. There's a bar full of crystal glasses and decanters, big leather chairs, and a large stand like a hostess would stand it in the front of a restaurant.

"What is your purpose?" A short, gnarled woman steps out from behind the lecturn, eyeing us with the same glare that was visible in the peephole.

Holy shit, it's a Muma Pădurii!

I look at her with wide eyes, knowing what her kind are famous for. It seems odd the Society would place one of her kind in a safe house, but I suppose they place the children in enclaves and adults come to the safe houses. There wouldn't be temptation if her food source never comes through the doors.

Prez whispers in my ear, "Why do you look terrified?"

The old witch cackles and points at him. "It's rude to whisper, young man. Your friend is scared of me because I am a supernatural legend from which many fairy tales sprang. They're all nonsense, of course. Not *all* fairy tales—those are usually based on a supe who has achieved legendary status in the human world and therefore, immortality—but the ones about *my people* aren't true. Humans fear what is different and that sometimes passes on to supes in less... educated areas of the world."

"*Hansel and Gretel* is about your kind," I grumble. "I figured it was one of the real ones."

A newspaper flies off one of the tables, rolls itself up, and bops me on the head. "You aren't very bright for a Dark Fae, boy. Only trolls eat children."

In a flash, Doyle is standing in front of the woman with absolutely no regard for whatever other powers she might have. "Do. Not. Strike. Him. Old Woman."

The shiver that runs through me is ill-timed, but I can't help that possessive Dom shit is hot, even when it's this asshole.

She lets out another crazy laugh, slapping her thigh as she looks at us in amusement. "Oh, to be young and stupid again. Imagine thinking it's a good idea to threaten a thousand year old magic weaver. Such grandiose gestures men make when they are full of baby juice and bravado."

"Ew," Presley says.

Agreed.

"How do you know what we are, crone?" Doyle finally breaks the standoff. "These places are supposed to be magic-free unless members use specific rooms for rituals or casting."

"Do not question my methods, son of…" She pauses again and I roll my eyes. "…oh, you don't know! Far be it for me to spoil the surprise, exiled demi-god. To answer your rude statement, I am the keeper of this house and it's my job to identify, catalog, and record the supernaturals who come through my doors. Do you not have a keeper in your Society hall?"

I frown and shake my head. "Not to my knowledge. Do we have one, Doyle?"

"Yes, we have one, but ours hides in plain sight and doesn't sass the members." He gives the woman an assessing look as if he's considering how he can shake the name of his father out of her before we leave.

Fuck, I hope someone dispels that plan so we don't get turned into fucking newts or something.

I look at him in shock. "We do?"

"All the halls have keepers. You idiots in the Hollow don't travel anywhere, do you?" The demi-god gives us a disgusted look. "Ours is Zareb. His eyes see all and because he has a special relationship with Nelia and her mates, they are able to use what he sees and smells to form our records. Prior to Nelia's arrival, it was a gargoyle, but that guy is retired in the Carpathians by now."

"See? There are beings with my position everywhere and we keep our homes safe in different ways. I'll bet that lion wouldn't hesitate to eat one of you fools if you stepped out of line." The Muma totters over to her lectern again, opening a large book and waving her finger at the quill next to it. "Now, let's see here… it's December second, year two thousand and twenty-two at nineteen hundred hours local time. I am Irina, keeper of the safe house and I make these entries of my own free will."

Glitter fills the air as the notations from her guest book appear in front of us as if to verify what she's recording.

The following supernaturals have been granted entry:

Wolfgang Lucien Fletcher- dark Fae, son of Cailleach, father unknown, hybrid
Presley Hemingway Hamilton- caladrius of Whistler's Hollow
*Doyle Aloysius Haggerty- demi-god, son of *** goddess and *** god, hybrid*
deity
*Hugo MacAuley- oracle of *** goddess*
Dhameer Mirza Al Sharqi- djinn

"What? MacAuley and the prince are here?" Prez looks around as he scratches his head. "Where did they come from?"

The men in question step out from behind the partition that blocks the rest of the hall looking equally frustrated. The Muma must have driven them as crazy as she is us and they elected to wait until she finished her rant to poke their heads out.

"I feel like we're focused on the wrong thing," my lover rumbles. "Anyone else notice this nutter made sure to bleep out information we aren't allowed to have even in her magic book?"

"Of course I did! I've been doing this longer than *most* of you have been alive. I never betray the gods when they make rules. I cannot reveal what is not known to you anymore than your friends can, healer." Irina looks affronted again, and she slams the book shut.

We're never getting out of here if someone doesn't calm her down.

"Ma'am, no one is saying you are not an excellent keeper. We're eager to get to the summoning room so we can finish an unpleasant task. I'm afraid it has put all of us on edge."

She cackles and points at me. "Your mother will not be pleased to be called to a group chat, young Fae. Be wary of her words and mind what any of you reveal."

Is this woman a fortune teller, too?

"Mumas can hear thoughts," Hugo says. "You're all broadcasting everything she's pretending to reveal."

"Stay out of my head, witch." Doyle's skin starts to glow and I move back, hoping he's not going to lose his shit with this irascible old biddy.

"Come, friends. Irina will allow you entry and cease being rude since you have been recorded. Isn't that right, keeper?" The prince gives the witch a look that practically dares her to argue and for once, she shrinks back.

She's not more powerful than a djinn—good to know.

"Go, go. I prefer the quiet when my waiting room isn't clogged with horny men anyway."

"Ugh, gross," I mutter as we all walk behind the royal supe and into the main hallway. "Why does she keep talking about sex?"

Hugo looks over his shoulder, grinning smugly. "Mumas are extremely blunt and highly oversexed. Legends get so much wrong when the people telling them have an agenda. They don't eat children, you see. They turn boys into men."

That gets a resounding groan of disgust from the entire group and we all stay quiet as we make our way to the summoning chambers.

There's nothing any of us can say to make that less offensive.

"*Nochdadh, Mathair, Cailleach, Bana-bhuidseach a' gheamhraidh…*³"

Presley looks at me nervously, his hand squeezing mine tightly. This isn't the first time he's met my biological mother and he knows what contacting her costs me. Every single word, every expression, and every tiny twitch is cataloged by her sharp gaze and stored for future use against me. When Aurelia first started to lose it, I thought maybe my real mother was involved because it would amuse her to take something else away from me.

But it wasn't true; something else made my adoptive mother have a break with reality, and it could have to do with Jolene's parents' death.

"Who dares to…ah, my son!"

I swallow hard as I look up at the crown of antlers on her head first, then at her icy visage. She changes her looks with her moods, but today she appears to be not much older than me. Her hair is violet, hanging in a long braid over one shoulder, and she's wearing ice blue and white adorned with snowflakes and ivy. Her rosy lips curve into what she believes to be a friendly smile, but it's easy to see the malevolence behind it.

"Good evening, mother."

Her brow arches as she looks over the group, studying each of them before she speaks again. "You've brought friends. How lovely! I was certain you would never have any beyond your lowly healer."

The hand in mine squeezes and I can feel Prez's temper sparking. My natural empathy makes it easy for me to read a room and the tension in this one is building slowly. I can only hope everyone manages to stay calm—you cannot negotiate with an emotional terrorist like my mother. She will find every one of our fears and spit them back at us just because she can.

"Veiled One, we have come to parlay!"

Blinking, I look over at Doyle. Quoting movie lines at her rather than actually talking is… an interesting plan, I suppose.

My mother's porcelain features pinch for a moment, but they relax into that suspicious smile again quickly. "I accept your request, demigod. What knowledge do you seek and what do you offer in trade?"

Oh, no. Trading her information is never a good idea.

"We seek an audience with you in person to discuss our terms. Such delicate negotiation cannot be done through astral channels. Far too many supernaturals have the ability to access the planes," Dhameer interjects.

My eyes widen and I shake my head. That's even worse. If we visit her in person, I won't be able to avoid my sugarplum coming with us.

"Have you all lost your minds?" I hiss.

"Wolfgang, darling. Don't be so dramatic. Your new friends wish to pay me tribute in person. I've not met a djinn in person before and the rest of them—even your poor, not fated boyfriend— interest me as well."

This time, I squeeze Presley's hand, knowing the barb about our mating hit him square in the heart. She doesn't know what's happened since last we spoke and she's clearly too distracted to use her power to pick at my shields. "Mother, I don't think we can—"

"Nonsense. Djinn, I accept your invitation. You will meet me at *Tiagh na Bodach* in four days hence. Do not be late; the Cailleach waits for no man… even her son."

A loud clap echoes in the room and she disappears in a cloud of snow.

"So… that was my mother," I say as I rub my hand over the back of my head.

"She's a peach," Prez drawls as he pulls me into a tight hug. "Don't let her bullshit get to you."

Dhameer clears his throat. "I understand you may not see the wisdom in meeting her in person, but trust me. I was able to read her face like a book. She would not have given us any information that someone could trace back to her with magic. The astral realm is as traceable as the internet if you find the right…hacker, so to speak."

Doyle frowns, responding before I can protest. "Which means the bitch knows something good and doesn't want it to splash back on her if it gets out."

"Exactly." The prince looks over at Hugo, tilting his head. "We have done our part for this evening. If we are lucky, perhaps this will jar out seer's visions. I will contact you if it does."

"Okay, but you don't have—"

Prez's words are cut by both Hugo and Dhameer disappearing in a puff of purple sparkling smoke, leaving all of us gaping.

"Could people *stop* fucking beaming out like Scotty?" I throw my hands up in the air in frustration, finally losing my patience. "I've seen more spooky shit today than a fucking Winchester."

"And I suspect there's more to come." Doyle grimaces at us as he stares at the spot where my mother was. "Especially once we're in Scotland."

"Who's going to tell Magpie?"

The chorus of 'not it' echoes in the chamber and we all look at one another. Finally, Doyle grins like a loon and says, "Boone can do it. After all, I'm on shit duty because of him."

This should be interesting…

Monsters

Edgar

Tilly looked radiant when the pup sent her down.

I don't often regret things, but our past will haunt me until the day I die.

Benjy and I took her to a five star restaurant in one of the fancier hotels in town. Together, we drank and tried way more food than we could ever eat. My *dragon* was in high spirits—I don't know what he said to her while they were upstairs, but she smiled in a way I haven't seen since we were kids. It's how she smiled… before.

But as the meal ended and we were all full to the brim with good food and company, I knew the time was coming to have the talk we brought her out to have. I hated to wipe that look off of her face, but I also know that in order for us to keep moving forward, we have to knock this out of the equation.

So now we're walking along the sea in the community where the villa is located, surrounded by the gentle noise of the waves and the light of stars. Benjy keeps looking at me, waiting for me to start the dialogue, but I haven't been able to get my tongue unstuck. As beautiful as she looked at the restaurant, she's even more gorgeous walking with bare feet on the sand, her hair unbound, and her heels slung over her shoulder. The moonlight highlights her curves and the twinkle in her eyes as she kicks the water with her toes.

"She walks in beauty, like the night, of cloudless climes and starry skies, and all the best of dark and bright, meet in her aspect and her eyes.[1]*"*

Jolene turns and looks over her shoulder at me with a crooked smile. "Edgar Olivier Boone! Who knew you paid attention in senior English?"

Benjy snorts and shakes his head. "He didn't. Dylan tutored him at my house on the weekends."

"Ah, that makes sense. Sherilynn's nerdy book-loving younger brother kept you eligible for football seasons," she says with a soft chuckle.

"Hey!" I frown. "Dylan only helped me with the boring shit. I was smart enough to pass the bar on my own and make law review, Missy. He wasn't there to hold my hand then."

"Boring shit is awful snarky for a guy who just quoted Byron off the cuff," she sing-songs.

My friend walks up to our girl and picks her up by the waist, stopping her in her tracks. "You're a smarty pants, Princess."

Tilly pretends to kick and fight a little, but she puts her hands on his shoulders to balance as he lifts her higher. "Benjy! If you drop me, I'm going to gut you like a Cumberland bass!"

He looks over at me and I rake my hand through my hair. "Okay, put her down, B."

"My hero!" she says when her feet hit the ground. Tilly throws her arms around me when I get close enough, holding on tightly.

"Maybe not for long," I say as I lift her arms from around my neck. "I want to talk about high school."

Her brows furrow and she steps back, looking from Benjy to me in confusion. "High school? Why? I mean, we talked on Halloween for a bit."

Dropping onto the sand, I wait for her and Benjy to join me before I reply. "I'm worried that if we don't settle the old scores now while we're building the foundation, it might come back to bite us in the ass later."

"We screwed up, Princess. I mean, less me than that jackass, but we were total douches even before the Cotillion."

Jolene gives him a wry look. "Duh. Everything changed the minute we all stepped into the building at WHFS from the Formative School. It was like some sort of magical spell blanketed the building and the gulf between the cool and not cool opened up like a chasm."

"More like we all got the same 'representing the family name' speech from our parents the night before," Teddy sighs. "I know the Senator and old Mags weren't in the least bit subtle with mine."

Benjy nods. "Vlad and Flan were pretty specific, too. They made sure I knew I was supposed to follow Edgar's lead and I was expected to date one of the girls. Sherilynn was mentioned by name; hell, for all I know they arranged it with Zelda and Oscar from birth."

"Oh!"

I arch my brow and look at Tilly as she holds her finger up, her face screwed into an angry expression. "What is *that*?"

"You will never believe what I found out while you guys were in exile. My parents… well, probably my mother more than my dad… tried to arrange a marriage for me and Jamie!" Her indignation shines through the declaration and she stomps her foot on the sand.

What in the actual hell? First Benjy, now Tilly? Were all the parents playing some sort of Victorian matchmaker when we were kids?

"Cantwell is like… four years older than you." My friend looks perturbed by that, but Jolene just snorts at him.

"Benjamin Foster, age is a human construct. Don't be a dick."

I lean in and whisper dramatically, "She says that because she's more than a decade older than the pup."

A hard smack is my thanks. "Shut it, Boone. You're the same age as me, last I recall. We can rob the cradles together."

Tilting my head, I study her with adoring eyes. I would have never expected to be where I am, with who I am, before she came storming back to our town. I owe all of the happiness I've felt since then to her. "You realize that in kindergarten I asked you to marry me, right?"

Benjy's eyes fly wide and I wink at him.

"Teddy, you'd better not even *think* about it!" Jolene scolds.

I laugh, enjoying both of their reactions immensely. "I'm not. I'm just telling you I was smarter at five than I was at eighteen and I'm smarter now than either of those dummies. I want you to know I'm in this for the long haul and I can admit when I was a super douche."

"Fucking hell, Teddy," she grumbles as she holds her hand to her chest. "Don't scare me like that again. We've been dating for like a couple months and three weeks of that, I kicked all of you out. You're *still* living with… someone. I refuse to explain to people that I not only slept with you the first night I was home without making you apologize, but then I found out you all lied to and I accepted a proposal! It's too ridiculous for fiction, even."

I grin and shrug. "Oh, I'd ask you if I thought you were ready to admit how much you can't live without me."

"How exactly would that work, even? I mean, with her and the vet… and the fake Irishman and me and the doc and now…a prince and a teacher?" Benjy scratches his head as if trying to fit Legos together in his mind.

"The Council will have ways. We would not be the only polyamorous group in town, remember. The others aren't very public, but they exist," I say as I look at our girl.

"Stop it! I can't hear you! La la la la la la la…" Her fingers are in her ears as she sings to herself in a key I swear I can only hear because of the canine part of me.

"Tilly?"

She stops and looks at me. "What?"

"Shut up and kiss me."

Bad Dreams

Jolene

"*She still has shown no signs of emerging, Andrew.*"

I peeked through the crack in the doorway, hoping to understand why my mother was so mad when I got home. She'd been gone for two weeks and I came home excited to see if she brought me something from her work trip. Instead, she slammed around the kitchen during dinner and sent me to my room as soon as I asked how recruiting went for the college. I know most girls my age fight with their mothers all the time, but I tried hard to please mine.

After all, I know she's disappointed that I don't look as glamorous as the other girls in my class. She's never said it to me, of course, but when we go shopping for school clothes or dresses for the debutante balls, I've seen her gazing wistfully at the girls who could pick armfuls of gowns off the racks. Every time we've found something for me, she has to take it home and ask Niecy to take it in because we bought sizes from the plus size department so the dress would fit.

Without Niecy's skills, I would have been left to ill-fitting things or having my gowns handmade.

So I tried not to do anything else to let her down. My grades have always been perfect, and I worked hard at dance, so I'd shine in the deb classes. My art got selected for several shows at the college and in galleries in the city. But nothing ever made her happy.

Today, I didn't even have time to say 'hello' before she fell into one of her snits.

"Eloise, give it time. We don't know what she is and you know different species emerge at varying intervals."

My mother scoffed, slamming a glass on the counter. The smell of gin was never a good sign in our house. She's not an alcoholic—I looked it up—but she wasn't a friendly drinker, either. "Don't lecture me on biology you will never understand. You're not one of us."

"Why do you always throw that in my face, Eloise? It never mattered until Jolene came into our lives."

"It matters because they gave us a defective one! It's humiliating—everyone is smirking at me, I know it," my mother complained in a bitter voice. "Especially the wealthy members. They know I've got a dud and I can see it in their eyes when I have to stand in front of them and give reports on my missions."

My dad sighs and I imagined him taking off his glasses to pinch the bridge of his nose. "You're her mother. I'm her dad. We're supposed to love her no matter what."

"What if I don't agree with that? They promised me a ticket out of mediocrity when we took her in and I'm not getting a return on my investment. I have a right to be angry." Her heels clicked on the floor as she walked across the room, and I scrambled into the shadows of the hallway. "If she doesn't come through, Andrew, we're cutting her loose after high school. She can make it on her own."

I wake up in a pool of sweat, looking around the room in confusion. The dream was so vivid, but that scene wasn't familiar. I don't know if my mind is filling in gaps to make me think I'm remembering more of my childhood or if that really happened. If it did, what in the hell was my mom talking about? It seemed like she was saying I wasn't their biological child. But nothing I've ever found in their house or documents after they passed indicated I was adopted.

My brain has to be mush from all the sex; that's it. Teddy and Benjy fucked me so well that my brain isn't making up fantasies—it's creating nightmares instead.

That makes little sense, even in my groggy state, but I shake my head and rub my hand over my face. All this tells me is that I definitely have to find out where the hell that cop went and Eli needs to dive deeper into my parents' lives. If I was adopted, there's a paper trail somewhere, no matter how hard anyone tried to bury it. And I'd be lying if I didn't admit to myself that it would explain a lot about my childhood and teen years—especially the distance my parents kept from me after I graduated.

"Sugarplum, are you awake?"

I look up to see Wolfie peering down at me. He's holding his hand out and I take it, letting him help me up from the low bed. "I am now. Do I smell breakfast?"

He beams and nods. "You do. I was coming to get you, honestly. Everyone is downstairs waiting."

"Everyone?" I run a hand through my tangled waves, wondering if it's just my guys or if we have extras in the house.

"Well, Doyle and Teddy and Prez and Benjy and me. Teddy said we needed to make sure you eat well because they wore you out last night."

Blushing, I grumble, "I hope they didn't brag like idiots."

He blinks. "Of course not. But they told us all about your outing."

"That doesn't bother you?" I ask curiously.

"Not at all, sugarplum. We all care about you and want to see you happy. Our family only works if we can share like adults—even our grumpy, alpha dogs know that. They might bluster and snarl, but they wouldn't begrudge you a date or time alone with any of us."

I smile in relief. "Good. I'd hate to be hurting anyone's feelings."

"Nope. I spent time with Prez, which was wonderful, and we even hung out with Doyle before we went to bed. Not a bruised ego in sight, sugarplum."

Wolfie leads me down the hall and down to the kitchen. The others are waiting with smiles on their faces and an enormous plate of food that smells like heaven. I inhale as I sit down, and my stomach makes a rumbling noise. That makes Teddy snort and reach over to tug a strand of hair.

"Eat, Tilly. We've got something to run by you, and I'm very familiar with what happens when we don't feed the beast before we pose questions."

My eyes narrow and I point my fork at him menacingly. "You get stabbed, is what happens."

"Exactly," Prez says as he passes me another mimosa. "So fill your belly and then we'll talk."

If I wasn't so damned hungry. I'd take issue with that.

"SO THIS DUDE AT THE TABLE NEXT TO US WAS *RIDICULOUS*," I SAY AS I stuff another bite of eggs in.

Teddy groans and puts his hand over his eyes. "Fuck, I'd almost forgotten about that."

"*How?*" I ask once I swallow. "I mean, even listening to him degrade that guy in public was embarrassing. It was like the male version of a Karen."

"He was definitely a grade-A dipshit." Benjy reaches for the fruit bowl and heaps some on his plate. "I'm not very experienced in that… arena… but I could tell he was pretending to know what he was talking about."

"Christ on a trampoline, he was talking to his sub like a bad porno!" I giggle as I puff my chest up and do an impression of the self-important douche. "*If you're a good boy, you'll get my dick when we get home. Don't speak when you're not spoken to, boy. Daddy wants to reward you, but you're being so baddddd.*"

The whole table snickers, and Teddy shakes his head. "It was painful, pup. I almost had to get up and ask the waiter to move us. The poor guy he was 'disciplining' was trying hard to comply with all his bizarre directions, but it kept getting closer and closer to infantilization and you could tell it wasn't comfortable."

Benjy peels his banana and wags it at us. "Supposedly, his dick would taste better than any dessert on the menu."

I choke on my drink, almost spitting it out. "I'm going with no fucking way on that. Their tiramisu was to die for. None of you have dicks that sweet—don't even ask."

My declaration gets another round of laughter, and finally Presley looks at me seriously. "I know this is off-topic, but we can come back to how our dicks taste after we talk about where we go next."

"Like… as couples?"

"No, Tilly. I think I made *that* very clear last night," Teddy says with a wink.

Scooting to the edge of my chair, I stretch my leg until I can kick him hard in the shin. "Enough of that. It's too early for that shit."

"Oooh, tell us," Doyle says as he leans forward on his forearms. "I want to know."

That motherfucker just wants to cause chaos, and he's not getting it right now.

"Stow it, Haggerty," Presley says as he pushes his glasses up. "Magpie, we think we need to go to Scotland. Saoirse has been in contact and she's working something pretty hush-hush, but she said we need to meet her there."

I frown, irritated that my bestie is contacting them and hasn't said much to me at all since she yeeted herself off the face of the earth. "What kind of contact?"

"We don't know," Teddy says, his gaze cutting over to the others. "It could be dangerous, but since the trail is cold here and we have plenty of time, I messaged Thorn about gassing up the plane."

"This isn't a discussion; it's a foregone conclusion," I reply coolly. "You're telling me we need to get packed."

"Well…"

"Don't well me, Presley. I know a con when I see one." Tossing back the last of my drink, I push my plate away. "When do we leave for Scotland?"

"In three hours," Wolfie says softly. "If you get your stuff ready, I'll get the guys to help me clean up and get the animals together."

I blink, groaning under my breath. "We *just* got Eury to quit shitting everywhere because she was mad about the cargo hold!"

Doyle gives me a sour look. "Don't remind, Tíogair."

"That's what happens when you lose bets." Teddy gives him a smug look and I roll my eyes.

I'm not even going there.

"Fine. I'll go pack up and you guys do all of this… stuff." I pause for a moment, frowning. "Are Hugo and Amiri following along?"

"We've contacted MacAuley. He says the prince is finishing up some business here and they'll join us when they can."

I smile at Prez, appreciating his thoughtfulness. He's a good organizer, even if Wolfie does the more physical parts of that job. "Good. I wouldn't want anyone to think we left them out, since it seems like I have to travel with an entire entourage now."

"How long is the flight again?" Doyle asks as he clears the table.

"A little under four and a half hours to Inverness for the flight, but we'll have a long car ride to the Highlands after."

I look at them both. "We're going to the Highlands? By car? With a fuck ton of animals?"

Teddy chuckles softly. "We'll let Eury fly during the car ride and the others will be fine if we give them space to lie down."

"You'd better add some time to whatever calculation you made for pit stops. I'm not riding for hours in a car with yowling dogs and cats who have to pee," I grumble. "And if we run into ghosts, I'm skinning all of you. A stalker is bad enough."

They look at one another and then at me. Benjy finally takes the hit when he asks, "You believe in ghosts?"

"I believe in anything I haven't seen proven false. And some places Seer and I went had eerie fucking vibes. Leave me alone."

"Don't worry, Tilly," Teddy says with a smile. "I ain't afraid of no ghost."

I rise to my feet, smacking him in the back of the head, and make my exit on that high note.

At least they didn't ask me if I believe in vampires, too.

High

Presley

We got everything closed up and went to the airport on time—which was a miracle. Between the traffic in town and the locals on the tarmac getting wigged out over the animals, it was a fairly close call. But now that we're in the air, everyone is engrossed in their own shit, and it leaves me to fret over the details.

For instance, taking Magpie to meet Lucy's mother.

I know I told him not to worry; that's my job. But knowing his mother like I do and seeing how she behaved when we summoned her, I'm worried that she'll break the rules just to hurt him. The Cailleach certainly knows she cannot reveal the existence of our world to a non-emerged supe, but she can be less than subtle and point our girl in a direction she might not have headed on her own. If she snoops before it's time, all hell will break loose. Her *not* knowing is protecting her right now, even from pests as small as Sherilynn's crew.

There's also the fact that Lucy has mated with Edgar and your bond isn't fully completed. She's going to figure it out.

I sigh and lean my head back against the pillows on the bed. Taking my glasses off so I can rest my eyes, I consider what kind of manipulation his mother could achieve with that knowledge. It's neither of our faults that Reiki is being stubborn—my caladrius simply refuses to do his part until the moment is right. What the fuck *that* is, I can't imagine. He's just resistant to doing it before he's ready.

"What's wrong, love?"

Squinting at the doorway, I roll to my side. I know it's Lucy, but I can't see a damned thing. I should have gotten LASIK or an oculus spell years ago, but I was too stubborn to admit I needed it. Now I'm regretting that prideful decision. I hate wondering if I'll miss something because I need specs when I hop out of bed. At least I don't have that problem when I'm fully shifted, but I do that so rarely it almost doesn't count.

"I'm worried about so many things." He walks over and sits next to me, pulling my head into his lap and combing his fingers through my hair. "Your mother, of course. I know we can handle her, but I don't want her scarring you more. And I know Magpie can hold her own, but I also don't want her finding out about our world through some bullshit trickery."

"All valid concerns and things we've discussed. What else?" he murmurs as his fingers travel over my scalp soothingly.

"Your dad. Obviously the Muma had an idea and we're so close to that part of the world. There will be a gate near your mother's chosen spot." I lift my head and look up at his fuzzy visage. "I think we should go into it and see if we can get intel on your dad."

The shift in the room is immediate, and I know he's holding his breath. When he lets it out, Lucy's voice is soft. "Why?"

"Because it bothers you, and perhaps he didn't abandon you. We both know your mother would relish hiding you from him and telling you he didn't want you. It would hurt everyone involved and she'd get her rocks off on manipulating people. Doyle's mother seems exactly the same."

"How in the hell will we manage getting sugarplum in and out of the Faerie without giving up the ghost?" He chuckles softly. "Fae are the most gossipy of all the fair folk."

"True. But maybe Seer can find us something to help keep her from seeing anything for what it is. I mean, the binding alone will cloud her vision. She won't see any of it for what it really is," I muse. "Have you seen any signs that it's loosening?"

Lucy thinks about it for a moment. "Outside of the hound and the dreams, no. As far as I know, she's blissfully unaware."

"Good. Then I think we might swing this." I smile up at him, even though I can't see him clearly. "I think it's important for you to try while we're here."

"I can't wait to hear what Teddy's going to say," he says wryly. "I have a feeling it'll be colorful."

"That's a future Lucy/Presley problem. Why don't you come lie down and we'll figure that out after a nap?"

"Sounds like a perfect plan."

THE BED DIPS AND I OPEN MY EYES, LETTING THEM ADJUST TO THE darkness slowly.

"Shh. I don't want to wake Wolfie up," Magpie says in a low whisper.

The body next to me shifts and I feel his face run over my chest. "Too late, sugarplum."

She crawls up and wiggles her way into our embrace. The feel of her snuggled in with Lucy and me makes me smile broadly. I love that she's comfortable coming in to be with us and that it feels like she's meant to be there. Her hair spills over my bicep as she presses her warm skin to mine and I feel Lucy move again. Before I can ask what he's doing, his warm mouth is trailing down my stomach, pressing kisses as he goes.

"Oooh! Someone's being naughty," Jolene sing-songs. I can almost *feel* her grin as she leans down and bites my arm.

Shit.

Her teeth combined with his mouth wake my dick up and I have to move to relieve some pressure. "I'd say more than one person is being naughty."

"Perhaps," she murmurs as she nips her way up my arm to my shoulder. When she reaches the juncture of my neck, the air in the room gets thicker and heat flares over her skin.

Uh-oh. I think one of her sides is waking up and I'm not sure how that's going to go in an airplane bedroom.

"Lucy, you may need to cool our girl down a little," I whisper.

She shakes her head, biting a little more firmly. Before she licks the spot. "No, I like it hot."

Unable to argue with that, I bury my fingers in her hair as her mouth moves over my neck and my darling boy pulls down my sweats. His mouth is warm when he takes my dick into it, but not as hot as Jolene is getting. My eyes close as Lucy suckles the tip, his tongue flicking over the sensitive underside while his hand cups my balls. The fiery woman in my arms bites me again, and this time, I feel the skin break. She laps at the trickles coming out of the wound as he does the same to the pre-cum and I moan. Both of them following one another is almost too much… and not enough at the same time.

For the first time, I feel the bird inside of me stretch out and allow his power to fill my veins when I'm not healing a patient. The faint echo of a screech in my mind makes me shudder. I'm not sure what is going to happen, but I know I don't want it to be when I'm not inside of the people I love.

"Stop," I murmur softly.

"But you taste good," Lucy mumbles.

"Agreed." Jolene's voice is dark and growly—a hallmark of the hound inside of her that seems to break free a bit more day by day. "Tassssssty."

Was that a hiss?

I blink as my mind whirls, trying to figure out what creature she might be manifest that hisses, but the insistent push of Reiki inside of me destroys my focus. "I want… I want to fuck someone. Now. I need to."

"Maybe we'll make *you* wait this time."

Lucy chuckles against my skin, and my hips buck with the vibration. "Can we?"

"No!" I reach down and yank Magpie up, smashing my lips against hers. The kiss is violent, a battle of tongues and teeth, and when she breaks away, I know I can't wait. "Not now. Magpie, get on my dick and Lucy, I want you in my mouth."

"Well, if you insist," she says. Her hands land on my shoulders and she slithers up my body, her skin like fire against mine. Her thighs bracket mine when she sits up and within seconds, she sinks down onto me, hard and fast.

Her moan is like music to my ears.

Lucy rises to his knees, scooting up to the top of the bed. His cock is hard, and the steel is cool when I tug him closer and swallow him down. He groans and holds onto my head, pulling me closer and shoving his dick farther into my throat. He knows I have very little gag reflex, so his hips rock and push deeper with every thrust.

"Prez, I'm going to ride you until we all collapse."

I can't answer, but I hum around my boy and he fucks my mouth. The intensity only increases when Magpie lifts and drops, moving her hips in patterns on top of me as her inner muscles squeeze me hard. The heat coming from her is making the air more and more oppressive as she rocks over me. Every muscle in my body is tense when Reiki pushes more magic out; the sensation is incredible and I rake my teeth over Lucy. His shiver makes me do it again, but this time, I feel the delicate skin break.

The second the blood hits my tongue, combined with his fluids, I know we're in trouble. My skin prickles with the feathers as they poke through slowly—not how I usually shift at all. I pull back, popping Lucy out of my mouth so I can speak. He'll have to use his magic to keep Jolene from seeing what's about to happen.

"Dust, baby. We need the dust. Reiki's coming."

"Holy fuck," he whispers.

Magpie rakes her fingers over my chest as she pants. "Who's Reiki?"

"Now," I growl at Lucy.

As soon as he lets the Fae out, everything goes sideways. I knew when I asked that he wouldn't be able to control it in this small space and it would hit me, too. We've been together long enough that it doesn't affect me like it will Jolene, but it definitely still packs a punch. "There we go."

"Woooo! Who spiked the punch?" Magpie says as she keeps riding me. "I feel like I'm back in Germany, but better. Damn, I love a good dick and a double-stack."

I blink for a second, then laugh as I look over at my boy. "Well, you made her high and apparently, that makes her horny, so that's a win."

"Less talk, more fucking!" she calls out.

Lucy shrugs, moving back into place, and I hum in satisfaction as his dick slips between my lips again. "Whatever my sugarplum wants, she gets."

Satisfied that I've covered for what I assume is going to happen, I work my lips and teeth over Lucy as I buck my hips up to meet her movements. The circle of pleasure is complete as we all pant and grind and rock together until my wings pop free. Closing my eyes, I let go of everything as my caladrius finally decides to completely take over.

"Prez, I'm going to—"

"Meeee tooooo."

I reach up and tug Jolene down, giving her access to the spot on my neck she bit before. The moment I feel fangs sink in, I let go of my orgasm. My cock kicks inside of her, spilling my seed as she suckles at my neck and I swallow Lucy's come. Her walls clench hard, strangling me as her climax ripples through her and claws sink into my chest.

A vision flashes behind my eyes, showing me spirals of magic and fire and glitter twining together like vines climbing up into the air. Wings like mine sparkle at the bottom of the swirls, then catch on fire, flexing as they burn.

I have no idea what it means, but it's definitely important.

Jolene finally stops moving, her cheek resting on me as she shudders and pants her way through the aftershocks. Lucy pulls back, taking himself out of my mouth before rearranging himself to press against my side. Hot and cold bodies surround me as we come back to earth together. I slide my hand up Jolene's hip to her back and she whimpers. I frown, using my other hand to do the same to Lucy. His answer is a groan of pain.

Something tells me I'm going to be in trouble when we all get up.

Oh, Reiki, what have you done?

WITCHY WOMAN

JOLENE

I was strangely sore when Teddy came to wake me up because the plane was landing. Prez and Wolfie were already up and about, gathering their stuff, so I freshened up in the bathroom. I had another one of those weird flashes, but this time, I didn't tell anyone. It occurred to me it's been years since I traveled across time zones and stayed up late every night getting railed until I passed out, so maybe the passage of time has simply caught up with me.

Who wants to admit that in front of their Energizer bunny boyfriends? Not me, that's for sure.

So I stumbled down the stairs to the SUV blearily and curled up next to Teddy in the back seat with a yawn. Hyde joined us this time because Presley wanted one of my cats to come with us and the other to stay with Doyle and Wolfie in the second car. Since Seer isn't here and Eury is flying above us happily, we are crammed into two instead of three. We have to hoof it back to the airport to fly out anyway and that meant we could leave the big ass cage, so it worked out well enough.

"Are you doing okay, Magpie?" Presley asks as we turn onto the road behind the other car.

I frown, stretching a little and tilting my head. "You've asked me that ten times since I came out of the bathroom, Prez. Do I look that bad?"

He grumbles under his breath as the other seems to speed up quickly once we're on the highway, then shakes his head at me. "Not at all."

"I think you've been tired more often than usual and he's just checking in. Right, Hamilton?" Teddy runs his fingers through my hair as I lean against him and I sigh in pleasure.

I also love being stroked like a lazy kitten, apparently. I'm learning new shit about myself every day.

"Probably the time changes and all the bustling around," I mumble. If I parrot my own thoughts back at them, it makes them true, right? I fucking hope so because I have enough problems with the stupid ass blackouts. I don't need another health issue to randomly crop up and make even my small town life impossible.

"I'm sure the sexy times aren't helping," Presley says as he smirks into the rearview mirror. "You're definitely keeping us all on our toes."

My face turns bright red and I give in to the urge to bury it against Teddy's arm. I'm not shy about how much I enjoy getting laid, but these guys make me act like such a girl. I think I love it and I hate it at the same time. "Shut up. Wolfie started it last night."

"Ah, love, but you most certainly helped finish it."

A rumble of laughter vibrates in Teddy's chest, and I thump his abs. "Don't laugh, buster. You and Benjy haven't been any less frisky. If y'all keep this pace up, I'll be walking funny for the rest of life."

"That seems like a worthy goal," the judge says as he notes me peeping up at him. "I'll put it on my planner."

My eyes widen comically. "Don't you dare! Other people see your fucking calendar, Teddy."

Shrugging, he pulls his phone out and starts flicking through the screens. "I think the phrase is 'let's give them something to talk about', isn't it?"

Presley snickers and I sit up, grabbing for the phone. Teddy keeps moving it, his powerful hands keeping a tight grip as he clicks over the screen. His grin is wicked when he finally stops to click the screen off. I growl low, eyes narrowed as I look at him.

"What did you do?"

"I put a daily reminder to make your thighs wobble until you can't walk—with no end date."

By the horns of Hel, I'm going to murder this asshole.

"Teddy, everyone in the goddamned courthouse can look at your schedule!"

"Yep. It occurred to me that people at home are going to talk whether or not we want them to; I might as well amuse myself if they're going to poke their noses into our business. I'll think of more fun stuff to horrify them as we travel."

Rubbing my palm over my face, I imagine the stares we'll get when we get home. Sherilynn and her cronies have enough ammunition— this will only give them another thing to crow about. "You know this is going to cause problems."

"Ah, but it's *my* shot across the bow. The more we push back at their judgmental fuckery, the less effective their barbs are, Tilly. I'm not ashamed of you or the rest of our family. Letting them know that's not a pressure point actually takes weapons away."

I blink, thinking about that for a second. He's right. If they want to come at me by trying to humiliate me in public, telling them my life is nothing to be ashamed of will take all the starch out of their bloomers. "That's an excellent strategy, actually. Throw their barely concealed jealousy in their faces."

"Exactly." His chest puffs out, and I put my hand on it as I look at him.

"Thank you. I needed that, baby." Stretching up, I kiss his cheek.

"Aw! Innit that cute." Presley teases from the front and I make a face.

"The only reason I'm not smacking you is because you're driving. Don't think I'm not keeping count, though."

Teddy rubs his cheek against my head. "That's my girl. Keep him on his toes."

"PRESLEY?"

"Yes, Magpie?"

I look out the window at the craggy glen, studying the mostly barren hills curiously. "This is really far out to be meeting a contact. I've only seen a couple of structures as we passed by. Who are we meeting again?"

The silence is heavy in the car for a moment before he sighs. "We're going to see Lucy's real mother. She's… not one for civilization. She lives a bit like a hermit, and this is the only place she would meet us."

Blinking, I feel my chest tighten and my entire body freeze. I don't have the best luck with meeting the mothers of men I've dated. Teddy's mother was a nightmare of Lucille Bluth proportions and the last matriarch I met before that was *many* years ago. To say the relationship was strained would be severely underestimating it— Trevor's mom looked at me like I was sent by Satan and raised by wolves. She wasn't any wealthier than my parents—unlike the Boones—but she had airs to climb the ladder.

Marrying me would not get her there, and she made sure I knew what she thought of all my 'faults' as often as possible.

Seeing Trevor with Antigone at the ball was a shock for many reasons, one of which was that her family's status was only marginally better than this. I can't imagine how she got his snooty mother to allow them to tie the knot, but I assume it was through treachery and sneaky shit. That seems to be the oeuvre she picked for herself.

"What's… What's his real mother like?" I ask. My hands fold together and I squeeze them, trying vainly to control the anxiety rising within me.

"Relax, Tilly. She's not like Mags, though she's definitely not one to trifle with. At least, that's what I hear. Right, Prez?"

It's quiet again as the doc turns onto a dirt road and the terrain gets bumpier. "Well, she's not without her challenges. She won't dislike you because of shit like money or a family name. She'll analyze every word out of your mouth for a weakness so she can find a place to stick a knife. But it's not about you—her goal is to hurt or upset Lucy."

I feel anger well up inside of me, touching that place that seems to be a hair trigger for me lately. "Why? Why is she actively looking to hurt her son? Wasn't giving him up to strangers enough for her?"

"Nothing is enough for her. She feeds on emotions and she enjoys strife more than joy. I'd prefer he have no contact with her at all, but once she found him as a kid, that became impossible. Her reach is too vast and battling her isn't worth the struggle. He keeps her at arm's length by occasionally speaking with her, but it definitely wears on him. You need to be very cautious about what you share with her —even if it's only about you."

The warmth of Teddy's body helps me center as bit as he tugs me closer and wraps me up in his embrace. "I'll do everything I can to protect both of you, *drugar*. We don't know what information she has, but since she seems to think we will bargain with her for it, we had to come."

"Okay. So treat her as if she's made of C-4 and I'm walking across a tightrope in a room full of gas and matches. Got it." I exhale slowly as the fire inside of me calms to a cool, detached sensation full of suspicion. "I can do that. I assume she'll be more interested in striking out at you and I, Prez, because Wolfie won't have mentioned Teddy."

"That's true. He plays his hand very close to the vest to keep from piquing her interest. The less she knows, the more likely she is to stay away and not meddle."

"Good. That gives me an edge. I can honestly say I know things she does not, which will make her defensive and possibly throw off her game." I tap my fingers against my lips, imagining the possibilities in a three-dimensional strategy. Since this woman is not part of my rocky past, it's much easier to separate myself from the emotion of the situation and start plotting moves. It's a skill I was paid highly for at one time and now I need to use it to protect the people I care about.

I'm not gullible enough to believe she won't aim for the jugular with Doctor McNuggies, too.

Women like that play dirty because they play to win. Luckily for my boys, so do I. I'll stay back for as long as I can so I can assess her just as she's studying us and when the time to strike presents itself, I'll circle back for the kill. I want her information—assuming it's useful —but I also refuse to allow one more self-centered bitch to manipulate us.

"What's her name?"

That seems to give Prez pause. "Uh…"

"Obviously, it's not Mrs. Fletcher; that's Aurelia."

"The pup told me she likes to play games. We'll have to see what she tells us when she arrives. He warned me she could show up looking like anything from an old woman to a forest goddess to a socialite. What she wants to be called will depend on what 'skin' she wears, I think."

I think about that for a moment, nodding slowly at Teddy. "She likes to throw him and anyone who comes with him for a loop by subverting expectations. Interesting. It sounds like the only reason she wants him to stay in contact at all is to keep him dancing to her tune. She doesn't actually give a shit what he's doing… or whom."

"That's it on the nose, Magpie."

The car stops by the side of the road. Eury swoops down and perches on the luggage rack on the front car as Wolfie unloads the dogs and Jekyll. He looks worried and I hate seeing him without his usual sunshine demeanor. It makes me angry, but I channel the fury into the cold, calculating part of me that is eager to have a fight with someone I can actually lash out at without getting in trouble.

At least, I think I can.

Madness

Saoirse

I've avoided contacting Peanut more than necessary because when I stopped by the Society safe house that morning in Istanbul, I received a message from Julia. She and her men have been trying to quell the bad coven problem in Salem since before Halloween, but every time they think they have a handle on it, a new group of bad seeds takes root. I had to meet with a couple of high-ranking officials on the Guardian allocation team, and that wasn't even something I could share with her men. The training and allocation of Guardians, especially ones that have not been assigned lost ones to mind, is highly secretive. The representatives of the major magic lines were called in to discuss the problem and whenever you get a high-ranking witch, mage, wizard, and warlock in the same room, it's chaos. Unfortunately, my big wigs needed to find out why those eejits weren't minding their stores, so to speak.

It's uncommon for the non-creature based magic wielders to have need of Guardians—they dislike mixing of the species even more than deities and rare species. I believe it's the humans in their lines because it seems like a bloody good idea to mix a Fae with a witch or a mage with a dragon if my goal is to get more power within the community. But bias against those who are different is a blight even among supe types.

Could be the reason no one's fought a territory war on a global scale since the 1940s, though, so maybe it has a purpose more positive than I know.

I snored my way through all their pompous meetings—of course, my ruddy parents were there—and finally, I got free. Since I was stuck in the building with only that psycho Muma for company, I slipped into one of the offices and did a little insider recon on the Society's records. I could get into Whistler's Hollow's server and even into some of the agent profiles and reports, but I ran into a wall when I got to the timeframe when Jolene's parents died. There were so many password protected files and firewalls that I knew I was going to get caught if I even attempted it.

By the time I closed everything up, it was time for the meeting to be over, so I checked in with my bosses and got the hell out of there before I got held up again. I thought I'd be able to go back to the villa and meet up with the group, but my phone rang the second I got into the cab.

You don't screen calls from Andromeda Bane, but I wish I had.

The favor she asked of me led me to Greece, and that meant I definitely would not make it back in time to go to Scotland with Peanut. So while she's gearing up to meet Wolfgang's mother, I'm running around Athens gathering items for an equally tenuous appointment. I would have declined this shit-tastic mission outright if it hadn't been Andromeda asking. Dealing with the women I'm visiting is well above my paygrade and it's not even to help someone I care about.

No, it's to get a clearer view on another lost one's path because Bane says there's trouble brewing across the country in Bay City. Some unassigned Guardians are about to get tangled in a big way, and she wants to see if we can head it off at the pass. Their future charges are supposedly *very important*—though where that info came from, I haven't the foggiest clue.

But everyone knows asking the sodding Fates for a favor is ill-advised.

Apparently, if you don't have an appointment in their books, you have to show up with special tributes for each of them. Mind, appointments are made *centuries* ahead, so you can imagine their constantly getting emergency tributes to hear questions. And they rarely answer of the damn questions, so this is doubly stupid. The

Society board would be better off getting a fucking Ouija board than trying to pry info of these women.

But here I am anyway, running around Athens in search of their freaking presents.

I look at the market, trying to figure out if a section of it might have the necessary items. I found Clotho's favorite candy; I have a fancy Ring light for Lachesis, and now I have to find this list of shit for Atropos. I don't know what the hell she wants with these herbs, but I'm tiring of running errands for people who have their own staff. A sign down the street a little more has a symbol on it that makes me think it's a shop for practitioners, so I rush down it.

The faster I get this shit, the faster I can get this meeting over with before I stick my fat foot in my mouth and end up as a newt.

THE UBER DROPS ME OFF AT A FANCY VILLA ON THE CHI-CHI SIDE OF Athens. I sort of expected a long ride out of town to a weird cave in the mountains, but I guess the weavers of destiny have gone Insta friendly. They demanded a ring light as a tribute, after all.

"Alright, Saoirse. You can walk up here, give them your shit, and ask *without* losing your temper if they act like shitehawks. If you do all that bloody yoga breathing Julia has been teaching you, the valkyrie side will chill out so you don't get woven into an earthquake or something."

My little pep talk with myself is a necessary evil. I'm almost physically allergic to snotty women and Peanut would testify that I'll jump into a fight I can't win to teach someone a lesson. My powers aren't anything to waggle your finger at, but they aren't on par with immortal demi-goddesses who hold the strands of destiny in their fingers.

Though, they weren't strong enough to take on that fucking ice elemental/yeti hybrid in Moscow, but I dove in headfirst, regardless.

This is why Peanut and I made such a good team for all those years. We're good at being triggered by different things and even though she doesn't know my big secret, she's always helped me stay on the straight and narrow——-mostly.

Putting my curiosity about how she's doing aside, I heft my bags of bribes and head up to the immense door. There's a large knocker on it in the shape of an infinity symbol and I pick it up, giving the oak a good whack. The sound echoes around me, but nothing moves. Not a sound from inside and no sign of anyone coming to allow me entrance. My eyes narrow as I lift the shiny knocker and give the door another few hard knocks. It's annoying as hell to wait like this. Andromeda assured me they were expecting me during this time span.

After a few minutes of waiting with no answer, I give up on the knocker and try the handle. It opens and I blink. *Okay, then.* When I step inside, I realize the damn thing is yet *another* Mary Poppins portal —that must be a favorite trick of the Greeks. The inside of the house is a massive cave with only low burning torches placed every couple of feet, so I can't see much beyond what is right in front of me.

Freya, save me from dramatic ass supes who want everyone to see how great their damn power is.

I heft the bags of gifts and make my way down the tunnel, looking at the walls, floor, and ceiling suspiciously. I wouldn't put it past the Fates to have booby traps or puzzles embedded to keep people from getting in if they aren't 'worthy.' When I get to another smaller door with a peephole, I sigh. If a crazy old coot asks me what my name and my quest are, I'm out of here. Bane can deal with these nutters herself.

Lifting my hand, I give the door a rap with my knuckles, praying this is the end of this nonsense. The entire building rumbles around me and my eyes fly wide as the wall in front of me moves, revealing an open cavern with stairs leading deep down below the level I'm on. It takes every ounce of control I have not to scream, but I head down into the blackness carefully. The trip takes me so far below the house I wonder if this is heading towards the center of the earth, but finally, I reach the end.

Three women are standing in front of a cauldron, watching it simmer. The room illuminates as I step towards them and I look up to see a tapestry covering the cave walls from the bottom to the top of the stairs. It covers every inch of the stone for three hundred and sixty degrees and the details work on it is so tiny that I cannot make things out from this distance.

This is a history of the world and the key to the future is hanging like a poster in a college kid's dorm room.

"Greetings, Saoirse Viola O'Flanagan, daughter of Odin and a keeper of lakes."

I do an awkward curtsy, unsure of what else I'm supposed to do otherwise. "Hello, great and powerful Fates."

That gets a chorus of laughter and the tallest one steps away from the cauldron. "Do you have the tributes? The boil is almost ready and I need my ingredients."

Guess that's Atropos.

"I do," I say as I walk forward and sit the three bags on the ground next to their pot and back away carefully.

"Sisters, someone has been spreading rumors again. Look how scared she is of us! This is a Guardian, one whose ferocity they hone to protect the young, and she shrinks from us as if we're going to put her in our pot for dinner!" The short, round woman shakes her head and walks over to pick up the bag with the candy with a bright smile. "Excellent, young Guardian!"

"Well, Attie did that weird, mysterious greeting thing again. I keep telling you it wigs people out," the final Fate shakes her head, sending crazy red curls flying. She's definitely Lachesis; I can tell by how fancy her makeup is. She's the one who asked for a new Ring light.

"Thank you?" I reply to the sentiment from Clotho, giving them a tight smile. I don't care how down to earth they seem; it seems prudent to be cautious, anyway.

"Our requests seem ridiculous, I know. But we have to do this to test people—otherwise we have schedules full of cancellations and it's a giant waste of time. We have plenty, of course, but no one likes to feel as though they've been taken advantage of. So even though we want for nothing, we find various things to require so we know people who come for 'emergencies' are serious."

Actually, that's pretty reasonable.

"And my light *just* broke and I have a *Live* performance tonight. I can't read cards for my fans if I don't have proper lighting. I'd look ghastly," Lachesis says with a shrug. "Andromeda's call came at the perfect time. Plus, Attie's been wanting to try this new mask recipe and her requests were the things we were short on."

"Oh, well, I'm glad I could help." I wait for them to flit around with their bounty for a moment before I ask, "Are you ready for the question, or should I wait?"

Clotho snorts as she waddles around the simmering iron pot. "We know what your question is. We are the Fates, dear."

I squint at her. "You know it before I ask?"

"Oh, the field right before the door has a spell in it, dear. We know what question you are supposed to ask for the grumpy banshee, as well as what question you would like to ask for your friend. Nothing can be hidden from the threads of Fate once you walk through them," Atropos says as she stirs her mixture. "They hang over the doorway like a spider's web."

I knew there were feckin' booby traps!

"That's very clever." I pretend to think about it for a moment as I look around suspiciously. "What should I tell Andromeda about the problems in Bay City?"

The sisters gather around the cauldron, standing behind the steam, and an eyeball appears in the air in front of them, spinning and shining like it's the Snitch in the wizard movies. They speak as one creepily monotone voice when they answer. "Tell the banshee there is one there who will rise to the top. She will be the one who is in the center of the chaos and from her rise, there will be both blood, vengeance, and eventually peace. The turmoil in the home of the Trials will also fall when another comes to light."

"Cryptic," I mutter.

"Our answers are not meant to be horoscopes, shield maiden. They require interpretation, and every thread contributes to the ultimate solution. We cannot tell you what the picture will look like until the strands form pictures." Lachesis tilts her head at the tapestries with a shrug. "We are keepers of destiny and we follow what the universe weaves."

"However," Clotho adds. "We *can* tell you that you are not meant to join your friends in Scotland. You must travel to Prague. Answers you have been seeking are there—a powerful woman, a new face, and a shadow from a time long past will help guide you."

Making travel plans based on the Greek equivalent of a fortune cookie doesn't make me happy, but what voice do I have?

"Thank you. I will head there at once."

"Be cautious. You may find more enemies than friends as you search for the answers you seek. Your charge is not safe, even in places she should be. We cannot see what forces are seeking her as she seeks her truth."

I nod at Atropos, and the eyeball stops spinning, disappearing in a trail of sparkles. I think that means they're done with me. "Enjoy your tributes, ladies. I will take my leave."

"Do not trust the ones who look alike!" they call out as I turn to go.

Twins? Is that what they mean?

Jaysus, I hate riddles. Bane owes me a hell of a lot more than a favor for this bullshit.

Dark Lady

Jolene

The guys lead me to a weird-looking pile of rocks shaped like a fireplace. There are piles of rocks around the small structure with random items on them. Everything from bowls of fruit to bouquets of flowers to vials of liquid is sitting around it like they've been purposely left. The last time I saw stuff like this was when Seer and I visited Stonehenge on a pagan holiday. The locals must use this for offerings, but to whom, I don't have a clue.

Wolfie comes up to me, lacing our fingers together and lifting my hand to his lips. "I have to keep my distance from you while we talk to her. Don't be upset."

I smile softly, stopping to respond. "I won't be, but thank you for telling me. Teddy and Prez made it very clear what kind of woman your bio mom is. I'll be careful."

Doyle approaches, arching a brow. "Whatever they told you, multiply it by a million. She's a right bint."

"What he said," Wolfie nods.

Super bitch—got it.

"I can handle it, even if she attacks us." The cold, slithering sensation in my gut comes back, spreading through my limbs like ice. "I know what to do."

"Come on, guys. Let's get this over with," Presley says as he walks past with the animals at his heels. "I don't want to be here any longer than we have to."

Teddy and Benjy catch up with us, each of them carrying a bag. Wolfie looks relieved, so I arch a brow at them, but they only shrug.

Fine, keep your secrets, jackasses.

I walk over to a big flat rock, sitting down with Jekyll and Hyde on either side of me. "When is she going to get here?"

"When the sun sets," Presley says as he drops onto another stone. "So, now, we wait."

AFTER A FEW HOURS, I GET UP, STRETCHING MY LEGS AND BACK. I'M not sure what the hell the guys expect, but I'm tired of sitting on my ass. Wolfie's mom is inconsiderate and I don't care if she shows up while I'm taking a walk. I was on a plane getting my guts rearranged, then riding in a car, and now plopped in a field like I'm waiting for a UFO to beam us up. My ass is sore, my muscles are cramped and I'm getting hungry, to be honest.

If her goal was to piss us off, it's working.

"This shit better be good or I'm going to—"

"You're going to what, my dear?"

Whipping around, I drop into a defensive pose as the voice comes from nowhere. "Who are you? Fuck that. *Where* are you?"

A woman walks out of a mist like she's straight off the pages of a Victorian ghost story. She has long raven hair in loose waves, pale skin, and bright red lips. Her dress is made of lacy white material and she appears to be about forty—only a few years older than me. The smile on her face is cunning and her gaze is sharp as she looks at me.

"I'm pretty sure I spoke English. Who are you?" I repeat. My fists are up and the icy knot in my gut crawls farther up into my chest, spreading through me slowly like it's unfurling.

Her laugh is like breaking glass—cutting, hard, and pointed. "I am Wolfgang's mother, of course. You may call me… Callie."

I don't move; I simply look over my shoulder and call out. "She's here!"

That causes a minor commotion as Teddy, the dogs, and the rest of my crew come over to the small copse of trees I'm standing beneath. Once they all spread out in a semicircle, I finally drop out of position. The heavy aura of distrust in the air makes my skin crawl, but I refuse to let this woman know she's creeping me out. I step back, letting the cats and dogs surround me.

"Your bird is quite magnificent," she says as she looks up. "You have quite a few companions."

I nod. "I do."

"So unusual. But I admire your dedication to your animals. My son has always been an animal lover."

Wolfie sighs loudly and walks up to her. "I have, but you don't actually know that. You didn't show until well after I was in middle school. This charade is silly."

Callie pouts, tapping matching red nails against her chin. "There's no need to take such a tone. I'm merely pointing out that you've always been soft-hearted with… strays."

Presley makes a disgusted sound and joins him, his body full of tension. He's never this irritable; Wolfie's mother gets under his laid-back exterior in a way I haven't witnessed yet. "You agreed to negotiate. What do you want for your information?"

That gets her attention and the glee that flashes over her features isn't lost on me. Her jab was aimed at Presley, though I can't figure out why. He doesn't have a pedigree like Teddy or Benjy, but he's a doctor. I don't think her problem is with him being male, so it's not bigotry. But the idea of forcing us to give her something she wants is more important, so she lets go of her need to poke at the doctor.

"I have very useful things I could tell you. Things about the past, things about your home, even things about this fiery woman you brought along despite her ignorance. What are you willing to pay for my knowledge, I wonder? Will the price be too high?" She holds her hand up, and a crow appears out of nowhere, landing on her finger and cawing loudly.

"Jesus Christ," Teddy says as he folds his arms over his chest. "Is this a Bond movie? Tell us what you want. We all know you have something specific in mind and nothing else will do. So give it up or we can climb in the car and leave."

Wolfie's mother glides over to him, sniffing delicately before her face breaks into a smirk. "Oh, how delightful! Darling, you didn't tell me you'd landed another one. And *this one* is so much more… powerful."

The tension around us ratchets up immediately, and I put my hand on Kali's head so she stays in place. "I believe he said you need to put up or shut up, Callie."

That got her attention.

"Yes, he did. This one truly believes he's in charge, but despite whatever silly bedroom games you all play, it isn't the case." Her gaze falls on me and that evil grin comes back. "The one with all the power here is you, my dear. Everyone from the monkey in the middle to the fatherless Irishman gravitates to your every word. They are so concerned with keeping you from the truth that they gave away the game long before I arrived."

Playing on our weaknesses, just like Prez warned.

"I don't see how our dynamic is any of your business." I cross my arms over my chest, fixing my expression into one of boredom. "I think you're just enjoying stringing your son along. You know nothing, and we're wasting our time."

She laughs softly. "Taunting me won't work, child."

"Baiting me won't, either."

Callie arches her brow as the animals around me let out unhappy sounds and she shrugs. "No, I suppose it won't. You are stronger than Wolfgang's previous lover—the good doctor is much easier to read. There's something… reptilian about the manner you're handling this. It's as if you have something deep inside of you, lending its strengths to the weaknesses of other parts of you."

I frown, but before I can respond, Teddy stomps over to her. "You tread very close to the line, witch. There will be consequences, even for you, if you continue on this path."

"He's right, mother," Wolfie adds softly. "Before you do something you cannot take back, tell us what you know and we will pay a reasonable price for it."

"*Reasonable*," Benjy echoes. "That's the key here."

Sliding my gaze to Doyle, I marvel at how quiet he is. His temper is as fiery as his heritage, and I'm surprised he's not the one threatening this awful woman. "What do you know, and what do you want for it?"

"Since I'm growing bored with this game, I will accept a truth from all of you... a deep, dark one that you do not want anyone to know. And of course, you will be honor bound to keep my involvement in this affair a secret. I do not have a reputation for being helpful, especially at such a small cost." Her eyes sparkle with excitement and she tilts her head. "Go on. One of you begins before I change my mind."

"I never loved my ex-wife, and they pushed me into marrying her." My eyes widen as I look at Benjy, but he's clearly ashamed of his admission.

"Perfect," Callie says, clapping her hands.

Teddy sighs. "I had a crush on Jolene in elementary school and my parents found out. They forbid me to interact with her because she wasn't suitable and that's why I couldn't intervene when the girls started going after her. Hell, based on my mother's bullshit, it may be *why* the girls went after her."

Yet another reason to despise old Mags.

"You treat your son like garbage and it pisses me off. My family was hands off, but they don't purposefully ditch their children because they broke rules and don't want to be held accountable." Presley's voice is harder than I've ever heard it, and I can tell he didn't want to tell Callie this, but he had to.

"Finally!" she cries as she looks at Wolfie. "Your lover grew a pair. I wondered how good your sex life could be when he didn't have the balls to confront me."

"Gross," I mutter.

Her gaze whips to me. "Criticism is reserved for those who have the courage to face their truth, Miss Whitley."

That odd feeling of something crawling through me, unwrapping itself from the bottom of my gut and working its way through my body returns, but this time, I let it have free rein. Blinking, I peer over at the nasty woman staring at me, so self-satisfied in her faux wisdom. She can't force me to fear or respect her—it's driving her crazy. I roll my neck on my shoulders, letting the liquid sensation in my bones calm me. "I will take my turn when I am ready."

"You claim to know about my father, much like you do about his," Doyle points at Wolfie with a grimace. "Your games mirror those of my own mother and I'd like to show you what little power you truly have, but I cannot. The rules of engagement are set and I cannot subvert them."

That makes Callie happy again because she walks up to him, whispering something in his ear that makes his face go red. It looks like he might hit her, but a deep breath and a muttered response I can't hear seems to keep him from doing so. She turns back, looking at Wolfie and I. "One or the other. I'm owed two more payments."

Wolfie lifts his gaze from the ground, pinning her with his eyes. "I only stay in contact with you to prevent you from meddling in the lives of those I care about in retribution. I feel nothing for you, and even the hope that you might reveal the identity of my father isn't enough to force me to visit you anymore."

"Ouch," she purrs. "I've trained you well, son. Your arrow was quite sharp."

"Leave him alone." I step forward, putting Wolfie behind me as shadows cloud my visions. I have to do this before I have one of my episodes—though I didn't feel this one coming until now. "I'll give you my truth. You give us ours, and we're done here."

"Agreed."

I wait until Teddy and the other guys come closer. I'll need them to catch me when I go down. Once they do, I close my eyes and gather every bit of strength I have inside of me. "I can't have children because of a procedure done when I was in my early teens. It's not genetic and people thought I had an appendectomy. My parents thought it was an appendectomy—I've been told. Some quack doctor in the city fixed the odd female problems I was having by doing an illegal and non-consensual surgery that resulted in sterility. I've never told anyone before—not Trevor, not Seer, and not any of you—because the therapist I saw afterward said that I had to move on and not reopen the wound every time the subject came up."

Every single person in the glen is silent, even the venomous bully we came to see. When she finally speaks, it's almost as if there's sadness in her voice. "I accept your payment."

"Then give us what we came for."

"The answers you seek are in the place the doctor has considered visiting. If you can navigate your way through that place without breaking any rules—theirs or the larger set—you may discover things about yourself you never knew. That is not just about you, Jolene, but your Irishman, my son, and even some who are not here to pay their prices."

Is she fucking kidding me? That wasn't worth one *of our secrets and* definitely *not mine.*

"You owe me more than that, Callie. But since I'm tired of your games, I'll accept it for now." I turn to the guys. "We're leaving. On the way back to the airport, I want to hear about this place we need to go. Wolfie and Prez, you're in my car this time."

"Good luck." Callie's tone is insincere, and she walks away from us into the night.

Why is everyone we meet so goddamned evil?

Secrets

Hugo

The prince has been off doing whatever he does for his family for days. I don't mind being at the hotel; I've gotten all my exams graded and gone out to explore the city a couple of times. But I wish he'd sent me with Jolene and the rest of the crew when they left for Scotland. Something felt off about it from the moment it was decided and I haven't been able to figure it out. I've tried meditating, projecting, and every other method I know to find the tiny thread of worry that's hanging on, but nothing seems to force a vision.

That is, until now.

The sensations that occasionally preface the onset of a premonition started while I was eating breakfast in a cafe nearby and now I'm trying like Hades to get back to the hotel before it hits. I don't have minders like the prince, and there's no one around to catch me if I go careening into a busy street. That's the drawback of my gifts and though I've been able to keep myself safe for a long time, I know the possibility of an accident is always there.

Especially when the symptoms are as strong as they are right this second.

Cutting into an alley, I put my back against the stone and close my eyes. I won't make it to my destination in time, so I need to pause and allow the vision to take over while I'm in a semi-safe place. But the shrinking field of sight doesn't come as I wait; instead, the pull of something completely different grabs me. In a blink, I know I've been summoned home—to my actual home.

My patron demands my presence.

I LOOK AROUND THE FAMILIAR TEMPLE, SCRATCHING MY HEAD AS I wait to be received. It's incredibly unusual for one of us to be called to the stand before our patron and even *more* uncommon for it not to be the High Priestess. I've only been in the goddess' presence a few times over the years and it was never alone.

What does she want with me?

"Hugo." The voice echoes in the room before she appears. Her faithful companion owl is with her, giving me a look as I'm filthy and should get smited.

Dropping to my knees, I lower my gaze as she approaches. "It is an honor to be summoned."

"Oh, please, rise and speak with me like a normal person. I tire of groveling." Her tone is full of amusement as she watches me roll to my feet.

"Yes, Wise One." She may have given me permission to stand, but she definitely did not tell me I could address her familiarly.

Her sigh is full of frustration. "You are attempting to be respectful, and I appreciate that. But this conversation will take much longer than necessary if you continue being so formal. I called you here because I need to speak with you about several things, including my nephew. It will be simpler if you call me Thea."

I don't even know how to respond to that.

"Yes, ma'am," I reply as I try to digest her words. "I will do everything I can to assist you."

"Good. I must be careful what things I tell you directly because there are many delicately woven strands being watched by the Fates. In fact, your Guardian friend has been to visit them recently, and it's why I called you here. She didn't go to them for information about the situation you are involved in, but they took a shine to her and revealed more than they should have. It's a constant, yet completely unmanageable problem for all of my family, even my blustering brothers."

I blink. It's well known that even Zeus cannot control the crones, but I've not been party to one deity trying to play catch up because they made a mess. "What can I do?"

The goddess sits back in her lounge chair, tapping her fingers against her lips. "Your friends and my errant nephew are about to embark on a trip to a dangerous land because of someone's big mouth. The Guardian is traveling to search for a shadowy figure that does not want to be found. The first group will cross to another realm, so I do not want you to join them. You and your ancient companion should seek the Guardian instead."

Frowning, I tilt my head. "But, my lady, wouldn't another realm be *more* dangerous, especially with a lost one who is not yet emerged?"

"It would if my nephew was not joining them. However, his power outweighs or is equivalent to most of the beings in this land. But your Guardian is looking for someone whose power is ancient and so immense that she needs help from you and the djinn, or something terrible could happen."

"This… being… is a threat?" I ask.

"No, but the ones protecting the secret are. And while I believe the secret will come out when the time is right, the one your Guardian seeks has spent millennia keeping themself hidden to wait for the prophecy to be fulfilled. You must convince her to stand down," the goddess says.

I have to stop Saoirse? My powers aren't offensive, so that must be why she wants me to get Dhameer to come along.

"You don't expect me to… harm Jolene's friend, right?"

Her laugh is musical. "Oh, merciful Olympus, no. I simply want you to impede her progress a bit and keep her from finding someone who does not wish to be found until the Fates have declared it so. Why they would contradict their own weaving, I don't know, but they get bored easily."

I nod, thinking about what she's said. "Is this person going to hurt my friends? Is that their primary goal?"

"No. That is not the destiny of your newfound family, Hugo. I cannot tell you what the threads hold, but I can assure you I am not sending you on a mission that will hurt them."

"Then tell me where we need to go and I will talk to the prince. If I can keep something bad from happening to any of my friends, I'll do it."

"You need to go to Prague…"

WHEN I REAPPEAR IN THE ALLEYWAY, I HAVE ENOUGH INFORMATION TO convince the prince to come to Prague with me. I don't know *why* the mystery person is there or why they're important, but my patron made sure I had enough to fend off the mouthy assistant and his guard. They weigh in far more than I would expect, but I suppose when you've been around as long as Dhameer has, you learn to keep loyal employees despite their glaring flaws.

At least then you don't have a revolving door of incompetence and disappointment.

I make my way back to the hotel, plotting out how I'm going to approach our abrupt about face. We'd planned to join the others in Scotland once the prince finished up with his bankers, but now we have to head in another direction. And I have to convince him *without* relaying that I got zapped to Olympus for a secret meeting with a goddess.

That shouldn't be hard at all.

RISE

JOLENE

The guys have been watching me like hawks since we got back from our trip to visit Wolfie's mother. I think they expect me to break down, but I let go of my emotional attachment to that part of the past a long time ago. It's something that happened and by the time I knew about it, there was nothing that could be done. That was my first time in therapy and I worked on it for a year before. I didn't get upset in the feminine aisle at the store. But after that, I had to accept reality and grieve.

You cannot undo what is permanent and there comes a time when you have to accept your fate.

That was a hard lesson to learn as a preteen and sessions with Andromeda helped. She picked up where the therapist left off and guided me through that and my mother's growing disappointment in me. Eventually, I had other things to worry about—like the popular kids' wrath.

"The more I learn about the world I grew up in, the less surprising it is that my brain has blacked out most of it," I murmur to Teddy.

"You struggled a lot more than anyone knew," he replies. "I don't know how you got such good grades and did all the shit you did without once letting anyone know what was going on."

I snort. "Oh, hell, Teddy. There are people who go through much worse than I did and keep it under wraps. No one beat me or starved me—I just had a lot of emotional garbage that fucked up my head enough to make my brain misfire all the time. And overcoming that is something people do every day."

"Tilly, that secret you shared is assault. It should have been prosecuted. You were harassed and bullied so badly in senior year that you had to go to home school. That should have been pursued. Your fiancé was a tool, and your parents were probably murdered. No one is asking you to compare your hardships to people with even worse issues. Trauma doesn't need to be qualified for it to affect you deeply."

"Someone's been reading my old textbooks," I say with a smile. "That's Psych 101, Teddy bear."

He tugs me onto his lap and squeezes me close. "I have to, Tilly. You've got a degree and none of us stands a chance with all of this adult shit, especially when you manage to constantly amaze us with your strength."

"Teddy, if you don't quit doing all of this shit to make yourself look good, I'm going to think I conked myself on the head four months ago and ended up in a coma fever dream full of romance novel dudes."

"Fuck, no, Magpie. Who would dream up an asshat like Haggerty on purpose?" Presley comes into our hotel room with Wolfie and carryout in tow. "Now, Lucy and I, on the other hand…"

"Oh, don't start this shit again," I say as I accept the bag with my food. "I am *not* ranking any of you—not by stamina, length, annoyance, muscles, smarts, humor… That is a hard 'no' from me. You're all different and I like that. There's… balance in your differences that I find comforting."

"Well said, Princess." Benjy grabs his food and flops on the couch. "Both diplomatic and honest."

"It would be more impressive if every time this shit came up, you fuckers didn't point at me as the sore thumb," Doyle bitches. "Because I allow all of you to live without doing something I would *not* regret, I'm the most amusing git in the room. Plus, I'm the least concerned with consequences."

Presley ponders for a moment. "He's right. If we had to send someone flying into a dangerous situation, I'd nominate him first."

Teddy's chest rumbles with laughter, and I bury my face against his shoulder. Their bickering doesn't bother me; in fact, it feels like the shit a family does. The sense of camaraderie between my guys makes it easier to accept that we all really can live together and be happy. When I stop snickering, I give Doyle a fond smile. "You can be the kamikaze psycho if it makes you happy. But I know you're more than that and so do they."

"Whatever," he grumbles and dives onto the other couch.

Uh-huh.

I open the container of delicious smelling, meaty stew and inhale before I look over at them. "So who's going to tell me where we're going and why no one told me you were considering adding a stop to our trip?"

"Once more into the breach," Doyle mutters before he looks at me. "The doc thought we should try to find the pup's dad in his hometown. We hadn't decided if it made sense to go, but since the bitch said we need to talk to people there…"

That story is full of holes, but they all seem to think I'm going to buy it.

"I don't even know where to start with this. Why are we trusting that woman? How does Wolfie know what town we need to visit? And how am I supposed to accept all of this wacky shit like that woman staging her entrance and exit with some sort of fog machine and weird effects, like she's a ghost on the moors?"

For a few long minutes, the room is completely quiet. They all look at me curiously, as if they're waiting for something to happen that doesn't.

"Hell, I told you she was crazy, Magpie. She must have hired a crew or something. Callie is rich, evil, and bored, so nothing she does surprises me. You heard what she said to all of us." Prez shrugs and gives me a sad look when my gaze cuts over to Wolfie.

"Fine. She's insane and willing to go to great lengths to fuck with Wolfie. How does that translate to following her leads?" I say as I pinch the bridge of my nose. I must be hungry because my head is hurting. While I wait for them to answer, I take a bite of the stew, groaning happily as the heat slides down into my stomach.

"We picked the right thing," Wolfie says as he grins at Prez. "I can tell by her sexy food sound."

"I do not have a 'sexy food sound'; take it back!"

They all look at one another and say in unison, "Yes, you do."

"Traitors," I hiss under my breath as I take another bite. "When I get finished, I'm going to punish all of you."

Teddy shakes his head. "No, you're going to eat and then take a nap, Tilly. We've been running since we got up yesterday morning. You slept a little on the plane after you played around with the docs, but since then you haven't gotten a wink."

He's not wrong. The headache might be a lack of sleep.

"Fine. I'll eat and take a nap. But when I wake, someone better have a better reason for us to go running off to Ireland because some mean old witch said to."

That doesn't get an answer, either, so I let them chew on it while I eat.

If they think I'm joking, they'll find out soon enough that I'm not.

I'M SURROUNDED BY GLITTERING TREES AND PLACID WATERS. THE AIR IS heavy with the scent of flowers and something sweet I can't identify, but I know I should follow it. Sniffing, I pad through the forest, watching carefully for threats. I'm not sure why I think I need to watch for things I can't see, but when I look up at the starry sky, laughter echoes off the hills.

Nothing about this place is familiar, yet I feel like I know where I'm going.

Coming to the edge of the dense copse of trees, I look out into the clearing in wonder. Crystalline waterfalls spill into an oasis surrounded by vibrant plants, and there's a small table set with a tea service.

That's the smell… It's an herbal tea steeping in the pot.

I rise from all fours, though my mind can't process why I would be crawling. My body aches for a moment as I stare at the set-up, waiting for the reason I've been drawn here to become clear.

A hooded figure emerges from behind the rocks of the waterfall, gliding through the water. It seems to allow the person to move through it without soaking them and I know I have to be dreaming again. But this dream isn't like the ones where I feel animalistic or the waking dreams I believe are memories. No, this dream feels as though I'm in a world apart from the one I live in and I'm here because they have summoned me.

One hand appears from under the robes and gestures for me to come closer and I do, despite the anxiety warring within me.

"I'm so happy you accepted my invitation," the person says. The voice isn't immediately identifiable as male or female, but the tone makes me believe it must be a woman. Men simply don't speak that way.

I tilt my head as I take the seat she's gesturing at. "I don't believe I had a choice."

"True. You would have heeded my call whether you wanted to or not, but you made a choice to follow the scent."

Looking down at myself, I note that I'm wearing the clothes I fell asleep in, but I'm covered in dirt and brush, just like I am when I wake up from the weird animal nightmares. "Why am I here?"

"So much like me," she murmurs. "You are not carbon copies, but you all possess the grit you need for the future. I am proud to see the world has not withered your thorns."

I give her a suspicious look. "That wasn't an answer."

"Also true! There are things I, too, cannot relay to you, Jolene, but I am not your enemy. I brought you here because you are about to undertake an important journey and it will require you to trust those around you implicitly. Like me, they are trapped by rules put in place many centuries ago to protect our kind. You are not yet at the place where you will understand, but it is imperative that you follow their lead."

"I swear to Christ, that weird drug from the club must have fucked up my brain somehow. All this bullshit with bizarre dreams and odd physical ailments cannot be normal."

"Your life was never meant to be ordinary, Jolene. However, it will take time for you to see the truth. What is important now is that you listen to what I tell you and follow my instructions exactly. Deviation could cause terrible consequences." She lifts the pot, pouring me a cup of tea before she continues. "That sounds rather distressing, but I must get you to understand."

I will not touch this crazy woman's drinks; I saw Alice in Wonderland and the Princess Bride. Who the hell knows what she put in it?

Instead, I give her a curious look. "What are your instructions? I can't agree to something if I don't know what it is. That's like signing a contract you don't read."

"Excellent! That suspicion will serve you well on your trip. Remember those words any time someone asks you a question, Jolene. The people you meet are very tricksy and they seek to trap people with their words."

"Again, you're dodging my question and I'm getting irritated. I'd much rather be dreaming about getting laid than solving riddles," I say with a sigh.

That earns me a throaty laugh. "Ah, yet again, the apple and the tree. Yes, I believe you would enjoy that more. But alas, this is urgent and you'll have to put off your spicy sexcapades until we are through."

This time, I don't even reply. I just look at her in annoyance.

"Fine, fine. I'll get to the point. Your family is taking you to a place to seek clues. There is a quirk of fate which deems that both a place they should not be taking you at this time, but it is also your destiny to go there. You are not ready for this, though the binding is loosening every day, so I must intervene to help them." She reaches into the pocket of her robes and pulls out a pair of rainbow cat eyed glasses. "These do not have a prescription, per se, but they will help your vision and your headaches. You must wear them anytime you open your eyes while you are there. If not, the consequences for your men could be dire."

Something inside of me pushes my hand out and I take them. When I put them on, the beautiful world around me turns into a grungy pub. We're not the only ones here, but everyone else seems to ignore our presence like we're ghosts.

"What the fuck?" I whisper.

"Indeed," she says solemnly. "An ancient friend who married someone he wasn't supposed to gave these to me. I have no need for them now because I have many pairs and I can spare one for you in order to keep you safe."

"Why would you do that?"

"Why does anyone do anything, Jolene? It is in my best interest to keep you safe and happily, I also want to do so. So I am here, breaking more laws than I can count, providing you with a tool to prevent you from making mistakes that will alter important events." She pauses, and it's eerie how empty the hood seems when she's not talking. "Do you agree with my terms?"

"This will help keep the people I love from getting hurt?"

"Nothing is fool-proof and your men have free will, but this will help keep you from being threatened by forces I have yet to identify while you are on this quest. That is as much as I can tell you now. There are no guarantees in life, and I would be lying if I gave you one."

"Okay. I'll do it."

"When you wake, they will be in your pocket. Keep them close and do not ask too many questions when your family explains where you are going. They will be clumsy and inept with their excuses because they do not want to lie, but also cannot tell the truth."

"Great. More lies."

"Only of necessity, Jolene. Now close your eyes and when you wake, remember only my words and your agreement."

"But I—"

I jerk awake when the alarm goes off on the bedside table. The guys are all draped in various places around the room because the bed was too small to fit everyone. They must have given me the bed, so I'd sleep rather than wiggle around until we got frisky.

"Sugarplum?" Wolfie says sleepily. "Was that the alarm?"

I nod, feeling oddly rested and groggy at the same time. When I roll over to turn the obnoxious noise off, something pokes me in the hip. I reach into the pocket of my yoga pants and pull out a pair of rainbow glasses, frowning at them for a moment, until I hear a voice in my mind.

"You must wear them anytime you open your eyes while you are there. If not, the consequences for your men could be dire."

I rub my hand over my face, trying to remember if we'd been drinking before I went to sleep. But if we had, these damn glasses wouldn't be in my pocket, would they? Someone has to be playing a prank on me—maybe it was Doyle. I turn to see if he's smirking, but he's still dead to the world in the big armchair.

Why is my life a cosmic joke? Dream glasses? I definitely have a tumor.

"It's not a tumor," Presley mumbles, and I realize I said that out loud. "The internet is ruining medicine."

My lips curve up and I wait for the others to slowly awaken as Wolfie gets up and starts packing things. There isn't much left besides the animals and a set of clothes for each of us, so I know he had everyone get ready while I was taking my weirdly prophetic nap. "Where are we going again?"

"Ireland," Doyle says. "To find the pup's da."

I frown, squinting at him suspiciously. "Wolfie's not Irish."

"Keep them close and do not ask too many questions when your family explains where you are going."

The voice in my head makes me want to cry in frustration, but I heed its words when Teddy comes over and kisses my forehead. "It's where his mother said to go, *drugar*."

"We think we'll find… clues… that will help us identify him. In… Dublin," Prez adds.

Benjy elbows him in the side and he grunts, turning to lean in and whisper something to him that makes them both laugh.

Nodding quietly, I pretend I'm going along with their charade.

After all, I don't think they meant for me to hear Presley say, "It's not like I can tell her we're going to Faerie."

I'm pretty sure they did not mean me to hear that.

Revealed in the Hollow

Off To See
The Wizard

JOLENE

The animals know something is off with me. Not only is Isis curled around me tightly as I lounge on the couch in Jackson's fancy plane, but Jekyll, Hyde, Kali, and Hecate have surrounded me from head to toe. The guys are watching the pile out of the corners of their eyes, but they've also been murmuring to one another intently when they think I've drifted off. Their low tones catch my ears better than I expect, and I've picked up bits of conversation I know I'm not meant to know about.

Such as they expect Wolfie's dad—if they find him—to be worse than his mother. Fat fucking chance of that.

My eyes are closed so I can continue to eavesdrop, but my mind is whirling with their words and the weird shit that the woman said in my dream. The goddamn glasses appearing like magic in my pocket were the kick in the ass I needed to start really looking at the shit going on in my life since I got home. Since I moved back to the Hollow, unexplainable crap has been crashing into me like a tidal wave. I've been so swept away in rebuilding and nursing the wounds that reopened when I got back that I brushed it off as paranoia.

Not anymore.

I knew growing up that our town was odd and a little sheltered. Hell, I knew my mother was weirdly standoffish and unsupportive when I stumbled. No one wants to admit their parents seem unimpressed with their very existence, so I set it aside to focus on my dad. He was always there and did what he could to mitigate the bullshit kids gave me. But he wasn't the force my mother was, and she never stepped in. I was too damaged to question it, even when that Dr. Frankenstein fucker escaped scot-free when he maimed me for life.

My brow furrows as I wonder whether or not he truly lied to my parents or if my mom somehow arranged that shit. She's not a Bond villain, so I doubt it, but how *did* that asshole not end up in jail? Who saved his ass from the justice he richly deserved? And why wasn't anyone nearly as mad as they should have been?

The past is so damn hazy in my mind still… it's hard to know what's real and what I've made up to fill in the gaps.

I thought after I left the Hollow, life would be so much better. I'd get away from my bullies, make something of myself, and go on to bigger and better things. In a way, I did—teaching, going to Europe, all my escapades with Seer—but none of it made facing this stupid little town easier when the time came. Seeing Trevor and Antigone on Halloween almost pushed me to destroy the happy life I was building.

Do we ever really heal from trauma to the core of our being?

"Have you guys noticed Magpie seems to be… noticing more? Like I catch this squint to her gaze that makes me wonder if what's binding her is getting thinner and thinner?"

My breath catches and I have to force it out slowly so they don't realize I'm not dozing. This is the thing I need to hear—whatever the hell it is, they aren't telling me because of some stupid oath. I don't know if tricking them into talking freely when I'm present is cheating, but fuck if I'm not going to try. As long as nothing weird happens while I do it, I'll know I haven't been caught.

In theory.

Teddy sighs and I imagine he's pinching the bridge of his nose like he does when he's frustrated. "I don't know, doc. There was definitely something up with her this morning, but she's putting on a good front. We've all seen hints she might have memories or flashbacks or something… But she obviously isn't ready to share it with us."

"I wish she would," Wolfie whispers. "I don't like feeling like Sugarplum is hurting. One or all of us could help her."

It's hard not to smile at his tone. My little Wolfie is the heart and soul of this jumbled family. No one scoffs at his words or even makes a snarky joke—not even Doyle. They know the vet is empathetic and always working to make peace between us.

A snort follows the silence as Doyle joins the conversation. "Aye, but you all know my Tíogair is stubborn as hell, though. She's still working on forgiving us and if she's seeing odd things she can't explain, we wouldn't be able to tell her what it was, anyway. Maybe that's why she's keeping it to herself."

Damn, that Irishman is clever. I can't fool him for a second.

"Guys, so much has changed for her in the past four months. I know I'm new, but… consider it for a minute." Benjy gathers his thoughts, and I'm surprised when they let him. "Jolene was told to kick rocks by the F.B.I. after they spent months training her. She had to come back here and I don't think she ever wanted to. There are animals appearing everywhere, guys up in her grill wanting to mate with her, women trying to fuck with her, and then she finds out everyone is lying to her, but they can't explain. Add to that the shit about her parents' death and normal Hollow shit? I mean, it's a fucking miracle the Princess hasn't had a breakdown."

"She might even think she *is* having one," Presley murmurs. "If she's waking with scratches and having weird visions and dreams, plus, none of us seem concerned… she might think her brain is shutting down."

I mean, he's not wrong. I've definitely considered that I might be off my goddamn rocker. The bruises, scratches, and other injuries have been weighing on my mind. Wolfie suggested I was sleepwalking, but paired with that wavy mirror incident on the way to Istanbul, my sanity was in question. But listening to them right now… they sound like they *expect* this kind of shit. If so, their adamant denial of me having a stroke or whatever makes sense.

But why? Why is this happening to me? Why now, and why aren't they shocked?

The memories that blink in and out lately feel *real*, and so do the dreams. Admitting that means I have to allow for out of the ordinary shit to be true, and that means I have to accept that the world might not be as black and white as it seems. More than that, I might be more than I seem, and so might everyone I know.

I'm not so cynical that I don't believe there might be more out there than people realize—everything from ghosts to aliens to vampires *could* be real. Just because I've never experienced any of that woo-woo shit doesn't make it completely bunk. But… whatever is going on here feels like it's life changing. Letting in the possibilities based on my experience in the past few months is bigger than putting up a Fox Mulder poster in college.

It means believing that there's a whole other world beyond the one I've been living in and I don't know if I can do that.

"We have to make sure she doesn't think she's going crazy, guys. Even the thought of it can really harm you," Wolfie whispers.

My heart aches for a moment because I know he's thinking about his adopted mom, Aurelia. The trail we followed to the crooked cop suggested her decline started right around the time my parents had their accident and her job at the police station made us suspicious. I bet he's been wondering if she saw or heard something she shouldn't have back then and the pressure caused her to have a mental break. I need to put Eli on another hunt—this one to see what happened to the one woman who didn't willingly hurt my darling boy.

"It's okay, Lucy. We won't let our Magpie suffer. Right, Boone?"

A grumpy grunt echoes in the cabin, and I realize Teddy must be brooding while they've been chatting. I think he's the most irritable about the constraints on him that are keeping him from cluing me in. Our past makes that difficult, especially since he's grown so much since the night he stood on my porch with a cocky grin. It would kill him to lose this and he's not willing to take the chance.

"I don't enjoy keeping her in the dark, nor do I wish to die for breaking the oath. Neither allows me to keep what's mine close and happy—a fact that irritates every single one of my sides to no end. Having three aggressive beings unable to do what they want is hard to manage on a good day. I'm worried what will happen when we have to deal with the fucking Fair Folk and their need for trickery."

Fair folk? They actually meant a real Faerie? Literally?

"I can help," Wolfie says softly. "I may not know who my father was, but I know how that half of my people work. Dark Fae are harder to predict, but if we are careful with our words, obey their rules, and avoid making any deals, we should be okay."

"Oh, is that all? I never would have thought it'd be so easy," Doyle says teasingly. "Especially when your kind exists to trick and trap the other supes and humans for sport."

Edgar's growl almost sounds inhuman this time. "Do not. Be. A. Dick. To Him. Haggerty."

"Oooooh. Touchy doggy." Doyle stills sounds amused as fuck and I can hear rumbling coming from Teddy's direction. "I wasn't being a purposeful dick, as much as being honest. His words are true, but the reality is much tougher. All the Fae will know we're there with someone who cannot be made aware of her surroundings. They'll use the oath to trap us."

"Shit," Teddy breathes in frustration. "You're right."

"How the hell do we avoid it, then?"

I smile as Benjy ignores the bickering to ask for the solution. He wasn't this peaceful in high school, but I find myself soothed by his no nonsense attitude now. He's not afraid to assert himself, but he's also not an aggressor like Doyle or Teddy.

"Honestly?" Wolfie pipes up. "We don't avoid their games as much as we have to play them better. That's really what I meant. Every word you say will be used against you, but you can also do the same with theirs. Following the rules can be as literal as you make it—because if they omit things, they aren't *in* the rules. That works both ways, of course, which is why I said don't make bargains, deals, bets, or any sort of agreement, even jokingly, without considering every meaning of every word."

Great. We're going to the land of fucking Scrabble to match wits with magical Batman villains. That's exactly my idea of a good time.

"And remember, they're bound to the oaths their rulers took even in their lands. Disobeying the Society's rules about the unemerged would ripple their kingdoms as well. We *all* have to abide by the treaties or it'd be chaos."

Doyle sighs and I imagine him stretching out with a pout. "Don't I know it. My auntie and the rest of the feckin' assholes up there hold us to their edicts *and* the bloody Society rules, so it makes getting anything done an effort one of my dear cousins would have had trouble with."

"That was a hint, wasn't it?" Presley says in an amused voice. "You love flaunting those rules, Haggerty. I think you're a bigger wildcard for this brief trip than Magpie is."

Unfortunately, I'm not sure he's wrong.

WORRY

WOLFGANG

My anxiety has been ramping up with every minute we get closer to Dublin. I haven't been here since I located my mother when I was younger. I only entered Faerie briefly on that visit—just long enough to realize I wouldn't find my father easily because he didn't *want* to be found. Callie, as my sugarplum is calling her, wasn't hiding as much as she simply didn't give a shit about what happened to me. The paternal side of my lineage was actively trying to cloak himself in shadows.

That kind of asshole didn't deserve my presence in his life, anyway.

However, all that means is that although this land is my birthright, I don't have contacts or strong ties to anyone who can help us. Theoretically, I'll have a species advantage that may be useful; the Fae are my people and I should be able to suss out their horseshit. But what I can't do is give us solid leads or a good place to start. It makes me feel useless and I don't like that, either.

Doyle seems pretty familiar with the culture, though, and I wonder for a second if he's considered that his own father might be tied to the Celtic pantheon. He slips into the persona of an Irishman well, and his mischievous bent certainly mimics the tricksy smugness of many of the various Fae who live there. It's not a stretch, but since we don't know who his mother is, I can't put my finger on who his father could be.

Like calls to like, after all.

The biggest problem about this outing is Jolene—both her natural outspokenness and dancing around the oath because she's unemerged. She's smart and curious, which the Fae will love, but she's also prone to telling people where they can stick it if they make her mad. That won't play well with some species, especially royalty. It will make everything harder, even with me, smooth talking Teddy, and placid guys like Benjy and Prez. Fuck only knows what Doyle will do, so he's my second worry.

"Lucy, you can't control this. You know that."

Prez's murmur in my ear makes my cheeks heat. He knows me so well. "I do, but I can't help worrying. Everyone knows how they … are."

I have to be careful what I say now because we're in the car heading towards the outskirts of Dublin where the entrance to the Veil is. Sugarplum is in the front seat with the judge, but she sees and hears more than people realize. I'm sure it's part of her law enforcement training and I know it's not to be intrusive. None of us can take chances, though, because we have her and our family to live for. Risking death when we've found our mate isn't an option.

"Relax, wee pup. I've been here more times than Boone's bent the rules." Doyle winks, giving me an unconcerned smile. "I know how the story goes once we're escorted into the… estate."

Jolene turns to look at us, frowning at me. "Do you think your father is bad?"

I sigh, shrugging. "No idea. The one time I went looking for him, he was a ghost. I got the sense that it was on purpose. Since Callie was a definite bust and he was purposely making himself scarce, I gave up. One asshole mother and one damaged one was enough for a lifetime."

"I'm sorry," she murmurs. "It's hard when the people who are supposed to take care of you turn out to be not what you thought they were or should be. The flashes of memory I've been getting have made me reevaluate my own parents. They aren't as bad as most of yours, but… I'm still having a hard time with it."

Benjy leans forward, grabbing her hand when Teddy growls in the driver's seat. "I think what Edgar would say if he wasn't focused on driving is that we didn't realize you were having flashbacks, Princess."

My brow furrows as I nod in agreement. "You didn't tell us. Why?"

"I don't know… I'm not even sure if what I'm remembering is real. Some of it comes to me while I'm sleeping. What if it's just weird dreams?"

My sugarplum bites her lip and I know why she's hesitating. Whatever she's seen—awake and asleep—has challenged her entire worldview of her childhood. She's struggling with the same feelings I had when I discovered Aurelia wasn't my mother. They only got worse when I met my bio mom and failed to locate my bio dad. It makes you spiral through the stages of grief while also wallowing in self-worth issues.

"Usually people don't dream while they're awake, sugarplum." I look into her eyes, trying to convey that I know what she's going through.

Presley squints at her. "You're having blackouts again?"

"Small ones. Mostly long enough to have these fugue dreams where I see and hear things that definitely feel like genuine memories. Like… I can place the scenes and see it through my eyes with complete confidence that it happened."

"*Tilly,*" Edgar growls and I see his fingers tighten to white knuckles on the steering wheel. "That's important. You should have shared it with us."

She dips her head for a moment and when she raises it again, I feel her holding back tears. "I'm still figuring out how to deal with hearing that they adopted me as some sort of… career move, Teddy. If it wasn't real, I didn't want anyone stomping around trying to uncover more of that truth when I wasn't ready."

Even I know he would move Hell itself to make her happy, but this isn't something he could have pushed; it's Society business.

"I might be a bulldog when cornered, Tilly, but I wouldn't force you to do anything you weren't ready for." His voice is soft, and I know he means it.

Jolene may not know that many of the children and grown adults in the Hollow were all adopted for similar reasons, but someday, she will. Abandoned hybrids like me, her, and so many others have long been sent to enclaves like the Hollow so Society members can raise them until their supe sides emerge. It's their way of making sure the world isn't full of lost ones walking around, causing chaos.

Ones they missed have fairly ugly places in human history; it never ends well for anyone.

Our girl turns back to the front for a moment, putting her hand on Teddy's arm. "I know you wouldn't. However, I also know you'd happily curb stomp anyone who stood in the way of me finding out what I need to know. I'd prefer not to risk you ending up in prison because some bureaucrat wouldn't release records Eli could hack with his eyes closed."

"Have you spoken to Thorn about this?"

The question sounds casual, but Doyle's testing the water. We need to know what shit she has him and his pet hacker looking into. Obviously, he won't break the oath, but he's not exactly skilled at hiding shit from her, either. Their time together at State U complicates the situation more than he'll admit. Jolene learned to read him, even by voice, and he refuses to acknowledge it.

"No," she sighs. "We've got Eli chasing the cop leads, Aurelia's info, shit about those club drugs, and digital breadcrumbs about my stalker. I feel bad asking about too many things at once. Jackson has other clients besides me."

Teddy snorts. "Like that fucking bloodbath up at SU in the hockey rink. The news says he's repping the rich hockey douche accused of killing his rival."

"Seriously? Why?" Presley says with a frown. "He doesn't seem like the criminal law type."

"Uh, maybe because the idiot being questioned is the heir to the Wolfenberg fortune?" The judge pauses as he listens to the GPS for a moment, then continues. "Also, because that rogue chick got made Dean and everything there is up in the air, I'd assume. It's playing hell with the odds on all of their sports teams because they could lose accreditation. I've had Billy up there watching it unfold so I can adjust things as needed."

Benjy scrubs his hand over his face, then shakes his head. "Boone, I'm not sure if it's genetic or if you can't help yourself. You've got Billy Remington running around spying? He's as thick as a tree trunk, man. Who's running the gym?"

"Billy's always my boots on the ground. *Better Booties* pretty much runs itself since I helped him replace the staff and management. His talents are *not* in business, as you know. They're much more suited to collection and intel gathering through less savory negotiations."

"Pan's hairy nutsack, I really am turning into a complete criminal since I got home." Jolene glares at Edgar, then Doyle, and lastly Benjy. The latter holds up his hands then thinks better of it. "Don't give me an innocent look. You run an illegal, unlicensed speakeasy, Benjamin Louis Foster."

She's got him there.

"Do we need to worry about any of this shit going on at the school you all attended?" Doyle sounds amused, but I wouldn't be surprised if he does his own poking around now that it's caught his attention.

"No." Teddy waves his hand as we turn onto another small dirt road. "I'm only watching because of the book. Nothing there—to my knowledge—affects what we're seeking. I'm sure Thorn will tell us if he finds anything pertinent—the last thing I saw on the gossip columns was one of his corporate planes landing in the city with an entire team."

"See? He's busy with some case," Sugarplum says. "Eli is probably helping, so I'm not adding anything about adoption to their list until I'm sure that wasn't just a weird dream."

"That's probably a good idea." Her eyes meet mine and I give her a small smile. "Finding out the truth is freeing, but it's also a field full of landmines. You'll question everything you knew about the parents you had and start aching to track down the ones who weren't there. That's a big distraction when we're already beset by bombs, puzzles, potential murders, secrets, and all this other shit. Maybe not adding it until you have to is the best decision."

The Irishman clears his throat, commanding our attention. "We're almost there. I think it's time to discuss how we're going to handle this one more time. I know it's vague, Tíogair, and that vexes you. But it's *imperative* to your safety that you're crystal clear about complying."

Her nose wrinkles, and she gives him a dirty look. "I'm not stupid, Lucky. You're all in the know about some dangerous shit I can't know and if I don't behave like a good girl, I'll get hurt. It doesn't have to be repeated over and over."

"I beg to differ, Tilly. You may not be stupid, but your head is hard as a rock." Edgar's voice is full of amusement and fondness, which makes me smile. "We're all aware you do shit just to piss me off sometimes. The cheeky idiot is trying to make sure you don't dig your heels in to spite me."

"Fair," she sighs.

You could hear a pin drop when she admits it. I'm the first to pick my jaw up, so I get the first word. "Holy shit, sugarplum."

"What? I have flaws, little Wolfie, and I know what they are. Something deep inside of me *adores*, trampling all over Teddy's fucking orders until he snaps. It makes me tingle and we have a good time afterward. Denying it would be silly and I get why you all think I'll struggle with this now."

This woman amazes me at least once a day with her self-awareness.

"Yeah, that sums it up, Tíogair. So you'll do your best *not* to make poor decisions based on pissing the doggy off?" He gives her a smirk and she shrugs.

"I'll *try*. That's the best I can do." Tilting her head, she listens to the GPS calling out directions, then pulls that weird pair of glasses out of her messenger bag. "I want Wolfie to get answers and hopefully, that helps us get more information about our search. So I'll behave until I can't. Deal?"

Doyle groans and throws his hands up. "What did we say about deals?"

This is going to be a pain in the ass for certain.

What's This?

Jolene

We pull up to a large, ornate looking house not long after my declaration. I squint through the glasses, surprised no one else is commenting on it being way out in the country-side like this. I almost ask, but a voice in my mind whispers to stay quiet. It's not my own, but I don't recognize it, either.

Jesus twerking Christ, I'm going to have a hard time with this trip; I can feel it in my bones.

"This is our destination?" I say instead, scratching my chin. "It must be bigger on the inside, like the fucking T.A.R.D.I.S. or something."

Doyle snorts, then coughs when someone elbows him hard. "Fuck, you animals. I'm only agreeing with her."

"It's a sprawling estate, Tilly." Teddy turns the car off, opening his door to hop out and head for the back of the vehicle. The trunk opens and I hear the animals grumbling discontentedly.

Isis got to stay with me as usual, but the cats and dogs were perched like sentries among the light luggage we packed. A thud on the roof of the car tells me Eury has arrived and I let out a breath. I've gotten so used to their presences that I don't know if I could deal with leaving them behind no matter where we're going.

"How long will this take, do you think? I mean, we only burned a couple days in Istanbul and another few with Wolfie's bitch egg donor, so we've got three more weeks. I'm just curious what the plan is."

Presley appears at my car door, yanking it open and holding his hand out to me. "Out you go, Magpie. To answer your question, we're not sure. Since we *have* time, we'll stay until we settle this or run out of time, I suppose."

I'll have to walk around looking like a rave kid for weeks. Great.

"I'm sure we'll be greeted with some… fanfare," Wolfie murmurs. "It was the last time I came, though no one would explain to me why."

Frowning, I walk over and take his hand, squeezing it. "Maybe it wasn't because of your father, but because you're so damn pretty."

Teddy's head pops out from behind the car. "He sure as fuck is."

That makes our darling vet blush furiously and Prez laughs along with me. "Don't get shy now, Lucy. You know you're beautiful. Besides, it's more likely they greet anyone with an unknown heritage in that fashion. It allows them to get a read on the visitor and decide who in the… house… should be informed of their arrival."

They really suck at this and I'd love to tell them, but I'm not brave enough to peek and see what they're hiding yet.

"Stop it, guys," he mumbles as he walks over to round up the four-legged companions. "I know you're trying to make me less nervous, but I don't know if that's even possible."

"Pup, it doesn't matter what they say or do in here. Hell, it doesn't even matter if we find your bio dad. You have all of us, even the Irish jackass, and that's all that matters." Teddy's voice is a soft rumble, but I guarantee Wolfie is melting into him gratefully.

I don't know why, but it suddenly occurs to me that Teddy and I are the heads of this rag-tag family that's forming. We keep everyone focused and cared for without a second thought. And if you'd asked me if I thought this shit was possible when we knew each other in the past, I would have asked how high you were. Edgar Olivier Boone III is turning into the man he had the potential to become if he hadn't been surrounded by toxic assholes when we were young.

"Guys, we should probably get moving. Something is making me *anxious*," Benjy says as he joins us by the side of the car. "Like making *my hairs* stand up."

I have no idea what that means, but all of them pause in place.

"Yep, time to move," Doyle says as he slings a bag over his shoulder. "The welcome wagon is definitely waiting now."

Wolfie tugs a small rolling bag behind him as he emerges from behind the SUV. Jekyll, Hyde, Kali, and Hecate follow him towards me, all of them sporting pinned back ears. Cursing internally, I let them surround me as I head towards the enormous mansion with Teddy in tow. There's something wrong, and it's making my animals wary as fuck, but I know I have to trust the guys.

"These fuckers better have a *nice* welcome wagon waiting or I'll need someone to help me with controlling my fiery tempers," Teddy mutters to the group. "I'm getting fucking tired of all the damned surprises everywhere we go."

"Agreed," Benjy chimes in. "The feeling in my... gut... is not something I'm sure I can handle. I haven't felt this way in a long time, so I'm not used to it."

Fucking riddles. I hope to hell this place has good alcohol or I'm going to lose my temper at some point.

"Guys, I'm feeling a little left out. Can we just get to the door and find out what's behind it instead of talking in circles about it?" My voice is full of irritation, but I can't help it. The woman in my dream told me I had to trust their clumsy fibs because they're only doing it to protect me. That's simply easier in words than in practice because they really suck at it.

Doyle skips in front of me, winking playfully. "Come now, Tíogair. We're on an adventure to a place full of interesting things. You may not understand all of it, but you *will* have fun if I have anything to say about it."

"Have you been here before?" I almost smack my forehead when it pops out of my mouth. I know he has, but they don't know I overheard them on the plane.

"Mmm, yes, I have. This is a grand meeting place for people like me." He jumps up, clicking his heels together like an old timey musical character. "But don't feel bad—only the vet and I have visited the illustrious halls of our destination. Everyone else is a virgin, so to speak."

"Gross," Presley groans. "Why did you have to make it weird, Haggerty? We're all *long* past that particular rite of passage. Plus, the way people make it some big deal has always seemed strange to me. It's sound and fury, signifying nothing."

I blink. "Actually, I've always agreed with that. Down with the patriarchy and shit."

"Look what you started, doc. Now she's going to be 'I am woman; hear me roar' for the rest of the day." Teddy shoots a glare at him, his eyes dark. "That makes it *much* harder to get her pliant in the bedroom."

"*She* is right here, asshole, and we're coming up on the door. Can we *not* discuss our sex life in front of those frowning gentlemen standing next to it? They look as though they haven't gotten laid in a decade or more." I look up, making sure Eury is above us and when I see her, Isis squeezes me. They all seem to know how on edge I am about this shit.

It's damn near impossible for me to blindly trust anyone, especially so close to a betrayal.

"Everyone get ready. The first obstacle to finding out anything we want to know will be here. Remember: think about every word before you say it," Wolfie murmurs. "It matters."

This is going to be a disaster, and it will probably be my fault.

"Who approaches? Announce yourselves and be assessed for entry."

The man and woman standing on either side of the door to the immense house look tall and attractive, but not threatening. However, their scowls are almost indented in their faces. I guess this is a serious job and they have responsibilities—even if it seems like overkill to me. The woman spoke, but her companion is watching us like he'd be happy to toss us across the yard on our asses if we don't comply.

"Allow me to introduce our family," Teddy says smoothly. The guise of the perfect Southern gentleman radiates from him as he gives them his most charming smile. "This is Miss Jolene Whitley of Whistler's Hollow and her companion animals. It will be her first time here and we need to ask for your *discretion* because of her *late arrival*."

Both of the guards' eyes widen as they look at him, then at me in the ridiculous glasses, then back at Teddy. Finally, the female speaks again. "Your words are well chosen and we understand. Continue."

"I am Edgar Boone, also of Whistler's Hollow. My father, Senator Boone, has likely visited here on diplomatic trips." That gets their attention again, and I roll my eyes as he goes on. "The bespectacled gent is Dr. Presley Hamilton and his partner is Dr. Wolfgang Fletcher, both from the same town. Wolfgang has been to his homeland before."

"I see," the male grunts as he eyes Wolfie in a way I don't like. A soft growl echoes in my chest and the guard laughs. "Ah, we found the one they protect, Fiannula."

"Shut up, Lorcan."

Teddy clears his throat, sending Lorcan his own glare. "The redhead over there is Doyle Haggerty, currently of the Hollow, but of many other places prior. He, too, has been to this house—many times, I've been told. Benjamin Foster is the last of our group and he grew up with Jolene and I."

The woman straightens, reaching her hand out. "Present your hands one by one and we will determine whether we will grant you entry."

"Lorcan doesn't get to touch her."

I roll my eyes as Teddy snarls. "As if I'd want him to."

"Aye, lass. You've got enough cock to stuff a Dark Court whorehouse as it is."

Before I can shut Lorcan down, Doyle is on him, a knife at his throat as if it's a completely reasonable reaction. "Apologize to the lady or I'll get very clumsy."

"You can't…"

My Irishman looks at me. "Close your eyes, Tíogair. Just for a moment."

"But I…"

"You promised," the crazy ginger sing-songs and I groan. My eyes shut and I put my hands over the glasses. It sounds like there's a scuffle, but all Doyle says is, "Now do you see the bloody light, idjit?"

A muffled scream almost makes me peek, but suddenly, there's a warm hand at the small of my back. "Don't, Sugarplum. You promised."

Having a moral code sucks ass sometimes.

"Fine," I mutter. "Someone tell me when I can stop hiding from whatever the hell crazy pants is doing."

"You can open now, Tilly. I believe the jackass has made our point."

When I comply, I note Lorcan is still alive, but it smells like he might have just shit his pants. There's no blood on him, but even Fiannula looks spooked. *What in the fuck did he do and why does it smell like… sulfur?* Shaking my head, I let out a long breath.

"So, do we pass or what? I'm tiring of standing here like morons. We've been traveling for days and it's getting dark."

Fiannula cocks her head, looking at me with a slow, knowing grin. "Oh, yes. I definitely think I'll grant you all access to the…finest home in all the realms. How long you'll last is a toss-up, but the idea amuses me to no end."

"Great. Thanks. Glad to be of service," I mutter. "Can we go in now?"

The guard moves aside with a glare, holding a hand out as a door opens. I don't know what the hell that's about; it's not like I said something offensive. Shaking my head, I look at the other guard. Lorcan is still cowering, staying as far from my group as he can while all the men, animals, and I step inside one by one.

Something about the way she said that tells me we're in for a rough ride… but what else is new?

New World

Edgar

My eyes dart around the corridor that serves as a funnel to the portal to the Faerie. Everything inside of me—all three supe sides—are screaming at the danger this puts our mate in. I'm sure the pup and the doc are feeling the same, the tension is radiating off them in waves. Benjy doesn't get it yet, but that damn snarky demi-god does. He's fueled by the prospect of chaos and this unease is amping him up.

That's why he flashed his true energy at that smart mouthed guard and damn near blinded him.

Gods, even demi-gods or half-breeds like Doyle, are a reckless bunch. Their immortality makes it impossible to see things clearly in the short term. So when provoked, it's a toss-up whether they will cause a giant fucking mess for the Society to clean up. The Fae are equally long lived, so adding that to the mix is about as combustible as you can get until you factor in an unemerged supe.

"Haggerty, I'm going to need you to think with your damn brain, not your dick. You can't start a war here with your careless behavior. The balance is as volatile as ever." I shoot him a dark look, but he shrugs.

"Boone, old boy, that is none of my concern. I'm not far enough up the ladder to care about that shit, nor am I responsible for it. What I care about is our girl, and I'll do whatever it takes to make certain she's safe. Don't you feel the same?"

Before I can answer, Tilly grabs my arm and squeezes. "There's no need for you guys to fight. We didn't come here on some diplomatic mission like your father, but we don't need to piss our hosts off, either. I may not know why you're all so afraid of these people, but I assume it's money and power. I spent years in that world and they'll smell fear on you."

If only she knew how accurate that was.

"Aye, Tíogair, they will. They'll smell division as well, so it's best we only squabble in private once we're through this last door."

The faux Irishman stands at the gilded double doors, his lips curved up as he smirks at me. Tension dances in the air as he waits for me to nod, and when I do, he yanks it open with a flourish. "Welcome to Fair Lands, fellow misfits."

We walk inside, most of us looking around like Wonka just led us into the damn chocolate factory. The Fae certainly allow people to travel between their courts and Earth, but they've gotten stricter since that virus ran around the planet. It didn't affect most supes much, but the amount of expats flowing in to escape the craziness in our world overwhelmed them for a few years.

Hence, the idiots guarding the doors being such hard asses.

"This doesn't look much different from any other fancy retreat I've been to," Tilly murmurs.

Wolfie covers a laugh as the rest of us look at the lush foreign foliage and traces of magic floating through the air. "I suppose not, sugarplum."

Her head whips around and she nails him with a glare that would shrivel the balls off a fucking Minotaur. "Don't you patronize me, Wolfgang Lucien Fletcher. I might be a goddamn Magoo right now, but I can *feel* how amused you are."

"It's okay to feel left out, Princess," Benjy says as he steps in, putting an arm around her shoulder. "They're being dicks because they can't help themselves. I won't tease you; I promise."

I hold my breath for a moment, hoping she'll believe him. Since he's a recent addition to our motley crew, she's not as suspicious of his motives as she is with us now. Tilly chews her lip for a moment, squinting at him through the glasses, then sighs.

"I *hate* this, for the record. Being compliant without an explanation is going to give me hives." In contrast to her bitter words, she lets my friend pull her close. "Don't get any ideas about this being a permanent behavior—especially you, Teddy."

"I wouldn't dream of it."

She snorts, shaking her head. "*That* I do not believe, but lead the way. I'd like to get settled before we hunt down our prey."

"Shit, shit, shit."

Giving Benjy and our girl a little push, I wait until the animals follow them before turning around to see what's going on. I smile when I see Wolfie cursing under his breath as he tries to get control of his fully manifested Fae side. His wings flutter as he stomps his foot in frustration—something that makes him look even more delectable. Prez and Doyle are watching in amusement as he has a miniature tantrum, which means I need to intervene.

"Pup." I wait for him to look at me, tilting my head. "Did this happen the last time you came home?"

He rolls his eyes and pouts. "Obviously not, or I would have warned everyone. How the hell am I going to hide *wings* from her?"

I blink, realizing why he's making a stink. As long as Tilly is wearing the glasses, she won't see his iridescent skin or the pointed ears. The second she touches him, however, it will be impossible to conceal his glittery birthright. "I don't know, but we'll figure it out. Give her a bit of space until we know why you're reacting this way. I know that's not what you want, but you can cuddle Prez or I if you need tactile input."

"Boone's right, Lucy. This is only the second time you've been here and—"

"The first time he appeared with mates."

My head swivels to look at Doyle as he shrugs. "You think that's why?"

"Fuck if I know for sure, mate, but that's the difference, isn't it? Little cub changed nothing else, right?" Wolfie shakes his head and the demi-god nods. "See? The bloody land has something to say about it. We'll have to listen closely to suss out what."

"Great," Wolfie mutters as the doc pulls him to his side. "Benched by my damn homeland. Not a good start to this stupid mission."

Walking over to him, I look down and kiss him softly. "Shush, pup. It will be okay. We're going to be fine. It's just a bump in the road. Don't worry."

If we're lucky, it's not false hope because he's right—this isn't a great beginning.

WE GET ONLY TEN STEPS PAST THE SIGN WELCOMING US TO THE capital city of the Daybreak Court when a cadre of gorgeous, glittery Fae appears. They're all dressed in filmy pastel colors with layered armor and carry various sharp weapons. I blink at the variations of their wings; aside from the pup, I've never had much dealings with their people. Of the five serious looking soldiers standing in front of us, the first male has one's like a dragonfly, the smaller female has delicate moth wings, the next male is huge with bat style wings, the next male has huge ones like a bird, and the last Fae is obviously non-binary, but their wings are big butterfly-style wings. They arch a brow at me as I look, and I realize I'm probably being rude.

Shit.

"See? Something you like?" The bird man asks with a smirk. "You seem to have plenty of options already."

A growl echoes in my chest as his eyes run over Tilly first, then the pup, and finally over the Irishman, Benjy, and the doc. "None of them are available. Who are you?"

"Pardon us, weary travelers! We are the *Laochra Na Peitil*," the petite woman gives me a bright, sunshine-y smile as she claps her hands. "The Royal Family is pleased to welcome you to our home. Think of us as your official guides and escorts to the—"

"Stop." Wolfie's urgent plea makes her pause and look at him in confusion. "We have an uninitiated visitor among us."

The girl's eyes widen, and she slaps her hand over her mouth. While she panics, the dragonfly guy steps in with a sigh. "Please forgive Aoife. She's very excited to have a group such as yourselves here to visit, as is our employer. My name is Sítheach."

I nod, holding my hand out. "I'm Edgar Boone."

"Who's the lovely lass, then?" BirdMan interrupts me to look at my family again, his eyes twinkling with mischief.

Ah. He's the Doyle of their group.

"Feck, Ciarán. You'll piss them off before we get them back to the palace and the Queen will be angry again. Rein it in." Frustration radiates from the lithe butterfly Fae on as they look at me apologetically. "That asshole is Ciarán and I'm Daire. The silent dick over there is Taranis."

"Nice to meet, y'all," Jolene says as she steps in front of me. She's laying on the Southern awfully thick and I tilt my head, watching her as she bats her lashes behind those silly spectacles. "I'm Jolene Whitley, and I suppose they're calling me the uninitiated. Left to right, that's Wolfie, Presley, Doyle, and Benjy. My companions are with us, obviously. They answer to Jekyll, Hyde, Kali, Hecate, Isis, and Euryale."

Taranis looks up at the eagle, then at each of the animals. His eyes are dark for a moment before he nods at the group. "Truth."

"Bloody hell," Doyle mutters as he crosses his arms over his chest. "Of course, they send one on their welcoming committee. And this will be the *least* irritating version of this test."

Presley nods and shakes his head. "Violation of Article 3256.890123 and you know it. I don't care who you work for. We should share that tidbit when we return home."

"No, no!" Aoife says quickly. "It's not what you think. Taranis is very fond of... *animals*, not people."

I hate this fucking place already. Everything is a mind fuck.

"Ah. Very smart," Wolfie murmurs. "Someone like me is a tricky addition to their team. It doesn't break laws, but it can be very helpful in identifying threats."

Once I understand what he's implying, I glare at the group of Fae preventing us from moving. They aren't here to welcome us as much as size us up for their royals. I can grasp *why* they'd want to do that, especially in a large, powerful group like my family, but I'm not interested in human politics, much less that of Fae courts.

"Now that you've skirted the rules to figure us out, we'd like to move on. Relay our thanks for the welcome wagon, but we want to find lodging and eat before we explore your city." I put the power of the alpha hound behind my words, hoping to get their attention.

Taranis smiles faintly. "Powerful hound. Over two."

What the hell?!!

"Oh, no, just the two," Tilly says with a smile. "They're Teddy's, but they've sort of adopted me. But don't worry! All our animals will behave. I have the paperwork for them in my bag if you need it."

I turn to look at her, confused why she's suddenly playing the role of a Southern bimbette. This isn't like her at all, and I have no idea what to make of it. "That's... true."

"You won't need to do that," Daire says with a tight smile. "Our illustrious king and queen will host you during your stay. They have prepared a wing in the guest villa on the south side of their palace gardens for your group. You'll have time to get settled and freshen up, then they're hosting a small court dinner in honor of your arrival."

That's not suspicious at all.

"We appreciate your hospitality, but—"

The pup shakes his head and cuts me off. "That will be wonderful, and our family is very grateful for their kindness. We would love for you to lead us to the royal guest quarters so we can ensure we're prepared for such an auspicious occasion."

"Oh, you will be!" Aoife says excitedly. "Once we drop you off, you will have two hours before the royal tailors and merchants arrive to help outfit you for tonight and the rest of your stay. Isn't that fabulous?"

Oh, yes. It's fucking perfect.

Make A Bet

The group of oddball soldiers leads us to a pearlescent pink SUV parked down the street while Aoife chitters away to Presley. He's the most approachable outside of Wolfie, but my darling boy is unusually quiet. I look at him, trying to understand why he's staying on the other side of Teddy and biting his lower lip. Sure, Teddy's right about how damn suspicious it is that we're barely a mile into this place and we've been accosted, but it's not his fault.

Unless he's upset about something else?

I've been using malicious compliance to amuse myself while I'm forbidden from questioning the stuff going on around us. Being ridiculously syrupy and dense is fun, especially since the guys don't seem to get why I'm doing it. But I can't enjoy myself if Wolfie is this freaked out. The need to comfort him is slowly making my chest ache and that prevents me from snarking about the fancy ass Barbie Escalade we're piling into.

"What's up with him?" I point to Wolfie and elbow Teddy in the ribs as he waits for the others to get in. "And why are you so damn tense? I'm behaving as promised."

"Tilly, that's not something we can discuss at the moment." He sighs when I growl, leaning in to look at me with a rueful expression. "You know, I'll have to keep saying shit like that while we're here. Don't make me spank you."

Rolling my eyes, I huff as he helps me into the spacious SUV. "This thing is much bigger on the inside. If you're trying to keep me from being curious, this kind of crap isn't helping. I'm not stupid and you all know it."

Wolfie leans forward, taking my hand and whispering as the car lurches forward. "Please, sugarplum. You have to just… go along with it. No one thinks you're dumb—if we could show you, you'd do better than Teddy without question."

"Hey," the judge says as he tugs the vet back between him and Prez. "I'm doing a fucking great job reigning in my shit. Diplomacy is in my blood, pup."

"Then you need to have a transfusion," Wolfie says with a grimace. "You can't… apologize… to my people. They don't like it. Take criticism and move on—that's how it works."

Well, that's never going to happen. Southern folk apologize more than they breathe —even if it isn't sincere.

"Good thing you have me," Doyle says as he winks. "I almost never need or want to express that sentiment. I should be the designated diplomat for dinner tonight."

"Uh, how about no?"

He pouts at me, making my skin heat. "Are you saying I *can't* behave like a refined gentleman when I choose, Tíogair?"

I snort. "That is *exactly* what I'm saying, Lucky. You can't hold your temper or your need to sow chaos long enough to be a negotiator. You'll get us arrested."

"That, my lovely, sounds like the beginning of a bet." Doyle stacks his hands behind his head, his eyes twinkling with excitement. "Anyone care to get in on this? We'll have to set the terms carefully. I don't want our friends up there to think I can't set proper boundaries."

To my surprise, Benjy raises his hand. "I want in. I'll put fifty on you screwing up in the first hour. I might be new, but I've seen how you operate. You'll give in and Jolene will win."

"No way. He's stubborn as a mule with bets. I hate to side with the jackass, but I'll see your fifty and add another." Teddy smirks, watching the guys with a hungry expression. "I want to know what besides cash is on the line, though. Cash I've got plenty of."

"Ooh, we're adding favors?" The redhead leans in and I can feel the testosterone amp up in the vehicle. "Now that makes it really interesting. It should have a cost and reward for our beautiful girl."

Snapping my fingers, I wave at them. "Shouldn't your beautiful girl get a say in this? If I didn't allow bets on the plane, why would I allow it in Barbie's First SUV?"

A hand lands on my knee, and I look at Presley. His expression is fond, but there's a hint of something else behind it. "You do get a say, Magpie, but I think a distraction from the things you can't say or do might help. I also think that's what this dick is trying to do, not that he could ever admit it."

My eyes dart to the bet-maker and he shrugs. "It also amuses the hell out of me when people underestimate me. I feel like proving my point. Being right is *almost* as fun as being mischievous."

"Not as fun as being in charge," Teddy mutters, and I laugh. He shrugs, leaning his forearms on his knees as he looks at all of us. "So this better be good if you're asking me to back off and let this play out."

Now we're getting to brass tacks.

"What are the real stakes? You guys can call and raise like we're playing poker all you want, but it's obvious you want to pony up more than cash. Hell if I'm going to step into that as blind." Crossing my arms over my chest, I glare at them expectantly.

Teddy gives me a knowing look. "Good girl. We told you not to get cornered in a deal without making sure it was fully explained. If you win, you get to be in charge for an entire night."

"*You're* going to be submissive?" My jaw drops as I stare at him. "I don't believe you."

"Fuck no," he laughs. "However, I will let you call the shots. The rest of these clowns can submit."

Of course, that's what he meant—alpha dominant to the end.

My adorable docs shrug, looking at Benjy and Doyle for confirmation. Benjy nods, but the troublemaking ginger takes his time. "I suppose I could agree to that if we can come up with a suitable option for when you lose."

"If I lose, you get to move back into the house when we get home." Batting my lashes, I try to appear nonchalant. I planned on letting them do that anyway, but if I can make them think it's a big concession, then I win this silly bet no matter what.

"Oooh. That's an interesting offer," Presley says as he looks between the two more dominant men. "I like it."

"Me, too," Wolfie says softly. "I miss you, sugarplum."

Always the soft one making my walls crumble. Fuck.

Edgar sighs, looking between the softer three, then does some sort of 'dude eyebrow conversation' with Doyle. After a few moments go by, he looks at me again, his lips curved up. "Acceptable, but mostly because the leprechaun's place is creepy."

"Oi!" Doyle grumbles before he points at Teddy. "You've been well cared for, you spoiled dandy. I won't have you slandering my hospitality."

I roll my eyes at them both. "So you agree, Lucky? The terms of the deal are simple: if you can't maintain diplomacy for the entire group tonight, I win. If you do, you win. Teddy's books aside, the side prizes are a night of me in charge or you all get to come home. Is that accurate?"

Wolfie reaches out, squeezing my hand. "Good job, Sugarplum. You have to re-state things and make sure there aren't any loopholes."

"It's more difficult with people actively trying to mislead you," Prez adds. "But you're doing well so far."

My eyes cut to the partition separating us from the crew of royal assholes, and I frown. "Do you think they can hear us?"

"Likely." Teddy waves his hand. "Back to the deal. Haggerty, is this satisfactory? You started this little wager."

"Aye, I'll agree to it."

Grinning broadly, I stick my hand out for him to shake. "We have a bet, Mr. Haggerty."

When his hand clasps mine, his eyes seem to flash with satisfaction. "Oh, it's more than that, Tíogair. We have a pact."

Why do the rest of the guys suddenly look extremely uncomfortable?

BY THE TIME WE REACH OUR DESTINATION, I FEEL LESS ON EDGE THAN I was when we got into the car. I didn't expect to get scooped up by a fancy welcoming committee, and knowing that everyone around me was hiding shit from me made that chafe worse. The motley crew of soldiers ushers us out of the vehicle, then opens the back for the animals to follow suit. When Jekyll and Hyde place themselves under my palms, the residual nervousness coursing through me subsides slightly.

"This way. We're on schedule, so as we explained before, you'll have two hours to relax, then you'll be visited by our staff." Aoife bounces on her toes in front of me and I can't help but smile.

This chick is a lot like Seer, and it makes me miss my bestie.

"Be mindful of your animals and your surroundings. This is one of the most honored guest lodges and it would be an insult to our employers if anything is broken or missing when you leave." Sítheach's voice is serious, and it's obvious they've had issues in the past.

Doyle opens his mouth like he's going to shoot back a sarcastic remark, but he pauses, then winks at me. "Of course. My family will show the housing the utmost respect while we are here. Please extend our deepest gratitude to the King and Queen."

Our escorts don't look surprised, but that might be practiced indifference. The rest of my group hide snickers as Doyle puts on the air of a reasonable person, and I see Benjy slip Teddy another bill surreptitiously. They think he's going to win, and they have conned me, but I'll show them. There's no way he can hold on to that placid exterior when we're among snooty, rich dickheads tonight.

"Follow me," Daire says as they crook a finger. "We're wasting time."

As we walk behind them, all I see is a fancy looking guest house with lots of greenery and flowers surrounding it. I know there has to be more than this—otherwise why would I have to wear these fucking glasses—and the rebel inside of me itches to look beyond the frames to see it. I won't be able to escape my curiosity forever, but I have to last longer than the first few hours. The woman in my dreams was very adamant that I could put everyone around me in danger if I didn't follow the rules.

That doesn't mean I can't do it when they're not *around, right?*

I chew my lip as Isis squeezes my torso comfortingly. She might agree or she might try to get me to behave; I'm not sure. It's not like I speak Parseltongue and she doesn't give me easily interpreted clues like the feathered and furry companions. "I wish you could talk," I mutter to myself.

"What was that, Tilly?" Teddy says as he puts his hand on the small of my back.

"Nothing," I sigh. "It's very frustrating that I can't ask questions and I have to walk around pretending. I'm a trained investigator, Teddy. Before I came home, I went through an entire program designed to enhance those skills. I don't enjoy being in the dark and having no recourse for it."

"Tilly, if I knew a way to get around this shit, I promise I would have after you tossed us out. None of us enjoy having our hands tied anymore than you like being in the dark. We're lucky the leprechaun hasn't thrown caution to the wind, hoping to ask for forgiveness later."

The tour guides stop in as we come to a large lounge area with an open-air kitchen and dining room on one side. Daire pauses until everyone is still, then smiles blandly. "This is the main room. Down the hall to the left are the rooms and bathrooms. You are free to decide how those are distributed. Out the doors behind me is the back lawn, which you should be able to give your companions free roaming as long as they understand to stop when they hit the barriers. It's safe within them and less so outside of them. We'll leave you for now, but please use the paging system if you have needs."

I paste a smile on my face as I look around. "This is lovely. Thank you for everything, sugar. I'm much obliged."

Teddy knocks my shoulder with his and nods at the soldiers. "Agreed. Will we see you at the festivities this evening?"

Taranis snorts. "You will see *everyone* at the dinner, hybrid."

With that, they turn on their heels to leave, and I'm left gaping.

What the fuck is a hybrid?

Far From Hom

Doyle

They think they're so smart, but I have a lot more bloody control than any of these young supes think. After all, I'm older than damn near anyone they've ever met; it takes a lot of skill to stay on this side of the Styx for that long. I can't be killed, but an angry relative could have us locked in some ridiculous prison if they chose. Demis like me don't have the raw power our full bloods do and I've run afoul of every type of deity in every pantheon over the millennia. Some I have no quarrel with and some I'm lucky to have survived their…attentions.

I refuse to let the sneaky-ass Fae beat me at my own game.

Luckily, the royalty of the Daybreak Court are as over-the-top as my Olympian family. This place looks rustic, but everything in it is hand-crafted or expensive as hell. There are enough rooms for us to have our own if we choose, but the docs grab one to share and the judge and his buddy take another. I'm fine with having my own; it makes it easier for me to let Odie free without our girl noticing. I'm not hiding him because I don't trust her, but I don't want her ruining his cover by glancing at him if he shows up places.

"Off you go," I mutter as I open the window in my room. The raven takes off, his wings spread as he ascends. Unlike the other compan-ions, I've given him instructions to defy the boundaries of our supposedly generous hosts. If we're going to find the vet's father, we need eyes on the city outside of the palace grounds.

Once he disappears into the sunlight, I flop on the bed, stacking my hands behind my head. The urge to break rules and foment chaos rides me hard; I don't like being constrained by the Society's archaic bullshit. I chose my Tíogair's little bargain, so I can live with that. But not being able to show her what this world truly looks like is pissing me off.

Jolene is an artist, and she would have loved seeing all the bright, colorful flowers and plants. The outside of this building looks like a fancy, rich people hunting lodge to her, but if she wasn't wearing those damn glasses, she'd see a miniature Fae castle accented with all the fantasy flora and fauna you'd expect from movies. She's missing the best parts of this place because a bunch of people older than the fucking Crusades decided we have to stay secret until we emerge.

We know *she's a damn supe, and they do, too. What's the point?*

Kicking my boot heels against the mattress, I grunt in irritation. There has to be a damn way around this. I don't have the patience for waiting like the rest and I actually think it's dangerous that she doesn't know. Boone agrees with me, but he's in too damn deep with the whole brotherhood shit to do anything about it. Hell, I'd ask my auntie to give me permission to shove their silly rules down their throats, but she'd think I was weak for even asking.

Unfortunately, I'm not totally on my own dealing with the consequences of my rash bullshit now. I've got this menagerie of people and animals, plus the ones coming. The thought of causing them all pain or getting them put on trial is distasteful—something I've never experienced before. I actually *care* about what happens to these people in my wake.

By Apollo's oiled balls, I might be growing up!

Snorting, I shake my head. That's doubtful as hell. I don't think I'm made to be quite that serious; it comes from my absent, dickhead father. My mother is perfectly happy floating along like the perfect representation of our kind and the avatar of her powers. The most rebellious thing she's ever done is get knocked up and have me—look how well that went for both of us. I don't count on her support or help with anything because she's what the humans call a narcissist.

Still amazes me they honored that mirror licking tool with a word used around the globe, but they're not the brightest crayons in old Gramps' box.

"Haggerty, where the hell are you?"

My door opens and I arch a brow as I hold my arms out. "Right here, as you can see. Why are you whispering?"

The feathery doc looks sheepish as he rubs the back of his neck. "Magpie fell asleep in her room and we're trying to let her rest before the Fae tailors get here. Wolfie says that's going to be a pain in the ass of epic proportions."

"It is. Probably second only to visiting one of the deity strongholds, if I'm guessing. Fae palaces are just as rigid and grandiose as Olympus, Asgard, or even a pyramid. I can't imagine the King and Queen of Daybreak will allow us to walk around as their guests dressed like humans."

Presley puts his hands over his face. "She's going to lose her shit. I still don't understand why we couldn't call the pixie back to help us wrangle this."

"Were *you* willing to do a spell to contact the women of the tapestry? I sure as hell wasn't in the mood to argue with them. The last time I had to visit, they took me for every dime I had on me. Never play Go with witches who can see the bloody future," I grumble. "It was a bloodbath until I used my special talents. They wouldn't have been happy to see me."

His eyes squint behind the thick frames. "Do they owe you money? Are you *serious*?"

I shrug, unconcerned with his shock. "The list of people who owe me money or favors is *significantly* longer than those who don't."

"Mother of gods," the doc mutters and I smirk.

"*She* doesn't owe me. Good guess."

"Who doesn't owe you?" Boone arches a brow as he comes up behind the healer. "You were supposed to bring him to the living room right away, Hamilton."

"As I said, very few people don't owe me. And I'm coming, keep your bloody britches on, doggy." Rolling to my feet, I make sure we cracked the window for Odie before I walk over to join them. "But don't worry… I wait to collect until it's most advantageous to me. That will be helpful at some point."

"It better be," Edgar growls as he glares at me. "Otherwise, I'll kick your ass myself. We haven't had a rematch since that street brawl."

Giving him a gleeful grin, I flip the snarly hound off. "Anytime, pooch. You, me, and a wide open space."

As long as I don't kill him, I'm sure the rest of them will forgive me.

"I'M CONCERNED WITH HOW 'SOLICITOUS' THE DAYBREAK COURT IS. As far as they know, we're nobody. We didn't request a Council clearance specifically to fly under the radar," Boone says as he scratches his chin. "I made sure we weren't tagged as diplomatic or mission-based in the system."

I frown, considering that for a moment. "Do you think Nelia or your father spoiled our cover by accident? You mentioned the Senator."

He shakes his head. "Pops isn't remotely concerned with what the hell I'm doing until it affects him negatively. I learned that as a teen. Throwing around his name doesn't really draw attention to his end."

"Then they're catering to someone else," Wolfie says softly. "Whether it's stroking an alliance or rankle a rival, the royals in this court are playing Fae politics, not supe politics."

"Your dad." The doc grimaces at his lover, stroking his hands through his hair. "It'd have to be him."

My brows furrow as I think about that statement. Supposedly, no one knows who the fuck his dad is, least of all him. How would the King of the Daybreak Court know and how would he benefit from acting like he doesn't? The Fae are known for this shit, as are my relatives, so I probably have the most experience with immortal grudges and games. It's always some sort of long con to best the other player— even when the person isn't aware they're playing.

We need to know more about how the Courts are interacting and what their treaties are.

"I believe we won't be able to suss this out without more information on current alliances *and* some popular gossip. Many times, with beings like my family or the Courts, their machinations are so far-reaching that it's hard to nail down intent. We need facts, both current and past century, paired with the rumor mill to find the truth in the middle." I steeple my fingers as I let scenarios run through my mind at light speed.

"You think they're manipulating us to get the pup on their side before he figures out who his dad is? What good does that do? And if they know, who else knows?" Edgar frowns, looking pissed as he watches the vet curl up more.

"Possibly none. Possibly quite a bit if his resentment or birthright could gain leverage in some internal bullshit. Keep your enemies closer and all," I say with a shrug. "Most of my mother's family amuse themselves by causing trouble for one another and then watching the chaos with glee. Their reason could be as simple as boredom."

Wolfie sits up, his wings fluttering as he looks at us in alarm. "Sugarplum needs us."

That stops the conversation. We all spring into action, rushing to the room where she was supposed to be sleeping. I hear nothing, but I yank the door open anyway, letting Boone take the lead. It's dark and since her animals are taking a break outdoors, she's alone. The silence is deafening and unnatural, so I let some of my power slip out so I can test for magic.

Holy fuck, look at this place.

It lights up like a feckin' Christmas tree when I turn on the juice. There's so much magic in here that it's cloaking the space, keeping the sounds coming from my Tíogair ensconced inside. She's mumbling and groaning in her sleep, but it's garbled. I walk over to the pup and shake his shoulder. "Oi, lad. Turn it on for a moment. You have to see what I'm seeing. The others won't understand."

His eyes widen and I watch as the glow envelops him, wings shimmering and his visage transforming to full Fae within a blink. Wolfie looks around and takes a step back. "Holy. Fucking. Shit."

"Anyone want to share?" Boone sighs dramatically, but the big guy and the birdman nod in agreement.

Licking my lips, I try to find the right words to explain to the shifters how big a deal this is. "The room is *saturated* with magic. It's dampening the sound of our girl having very involved dreams—not sexy ones, unfortunately, but also not bad ones. The amount of power in the room suggests this land is affecting her as much as our vet here; however, since she's not emerged, it's almost hiding itself."

"Doyle, I don't even know what that means," the doc admits. "That damned old fool who worked in the Hollow before me let these hybrids run amuck and I've never heard of shit like this. It shouldn't be possible, but then, neither should Magpie."

The judge tilts his head, his expression interested as he watches Presley. "What do you mean?"

"I mean, nothing anyone who lives in this damn town says makes any sense! There's far too many unemerged and lost ones popping out, not to mention the way you all described your emergence is absolute bullshit. You all should have been prepped and coaxed through it like I do to the kids now. That jackass let you all fend for yourself and it's not surprising shit like this happens."

He straightens his glasses and rakes his hand through his hair, seething. Wolfie walks over and leans into him, making a calm feeling flood the room. The little shit is using his empathy, but I don't blame him. A magical, sleeping Jolene is far more dangerous than shit that's already done and dusted.

"What do we do?" Benjy asks. "All this is fascinating, but blame doesn't do shit. We need a plan: wake her, leave her be, check for outside influence… pick one. Pick them all if need be; just do something."

I knew I liked him—no wishy-washy bullshit with that simian.

"Alright, Boone. What does the great and powerful *tripleskia* think?"

CHANGING

JOLENE

The bright light above hurts my eyes. I'm crying, and I don't know why. There are sounds in the room, then shadows fall over me in a tight circle. I can't see who's looking at me, except there are a lot of them. Somehow, I know they're worried; I can feel it.

I don't know why they seem so fearful until one more person leans in. Her voice croons in a language I don't understand, but the emotions behind it coast over me soothingly.

"We'll have to do it soon. Look at her; we can't hide it much longer."

That man sounds very upset, and I know he's not an enemy. The room fills with tension at his words, and I start crying again. I don't understand any of this, but I know it isn't good for me.

"I just need more time." Her voice trembles and I want to help calm her, too, but I can't.

"We've had two years to come to terms with it. It's for her safety and the greater good." This man sounds stern, but not angry.

She sniffles. "You're far too calm about this, Calix."

"He's only being pragmatic. We all knew this day would come."

All of them speak at the same time, and the tension ratchets up around me. I can't handle it, so I hide within myself as they argue. This isn't how it used to be, but *now it's common. I don't know what it means or why everything has changed. Finally, the noise stops and a pair of arms scoop me up.*

"It's decided. We will travel to the nearest enclave at the end of the week. We cannot risk sentiment further pushing our sacrifice out."

My eyes pop open and I let out a wail as I sit up. Once my brain catches up, I slam my eyes shut before I see something I'm not supposed to, but that makes the pain radiating through me worse. Within seconds, there are hands on me, warm bodies moving in to touch me as I try to stop yelling like I've been murdered. I don't know what's wrong with me—it's like I don't have control over myself.

"Shhh. It's okay, Tilly."

Teddy. He's on my right side; I know by the scent of dragon's blood and sandalwood with a hint of cedar. My brows furrow as that pops into my head unbidden—that's a very specific scent profile, and it came to me without a second thought. I sniff, testing out my theory, and it's like my brain is assaulted with so many smells I can barely focus.

What the hell is going on with me?

"Grab her glasses, doc. She's trembling, but she can't open her peepers until we get her covered, yeah?"

That musical lilt is Doyle and I feel him flank my other side, filling my nostrils with a spicy scent—black pepper, cloves, lavender, and Tonka bean. Confusion floods my mind as that knowledge settles because I don't know what the hell a Tonka bean is, much less what it should smell like except… him.

Am I having a stroke? No, that's burned toast. I think.

"Here you go, sugarplum," Wolfie murmurs as he lifts my chin and slips the rainbow frames on my face. "You can open those pretty green eyes now."

I give him a grateful look when I comply, hoping to reassure him. His anxiety about my state is needling against my skin; it's making his typically outdoorsy scent of allspice, patchouli, and vanilla even stronger. Swallowing hard, I clear my raw throat before I answer. "Thank you, darling boy. And… all of you… for coming to check on me. I don't know what happened."

Presley is frowning. He's not the worrier of the group, nor the gate-crashing alpha. Seeing him look less than placid makes a lump form in my gut. His fists are clenched at his sides, fingers flexing in and out as if he's trying to control his reaction subtly. I inhale, focusing on him and the fresh cedar, vetiver, and ylang ylang wash over me.

This shit is fucking weird and I'm going to have a panic attack if someone doesn't explain.

Oddly, Benjy is the one to approach, his eyes dark as he drops to the floor to kneel in front of me. "Princess, are you having trouble with something? Besides the yelling and shooting up in your bed like it electrocuted you, I mean."

He smells clean, like lemon, sage, and rosewood. Biting my lip, I murmur, "The dream wasn't... a nightmare. It was weird. Some-times, the parts of my past that have been hazy since I was in middle school come back in bits. It used to be in my black outs, but since I came home, it's in dreams, too."

His brow arches. "I'm glad you told us that, but it doesn't answer my question. I can see your mind working. What else?"

"We don't think you're crazy, sugarplum." As if he can read my mind, Wolfie allays my greatest fears about the weird shit happening to me these past few months. "You can tell us."

I nod, raking my lower lip through my teeth again as I gather my courage. "A lot of unexplainable stuff has been happening since I came home. Most of it seems like oddball, small town shit or maybe paranoia. But... I've never had the blackouts and woken up injured or covered in brush. That's new, and suddenly, my emotions and senses randomly get super heightened."

The room is quiet and I worry I've said too much until Teddy cups my cheek to bring my gaze to his. "Tell us more about that, Tilly. What do you mean by heightened? Be specific."

"I feel shit much more keenly than before. Rage is like a burning ember inside me and pleasure is like liquid fire. Other people's feel-ings smack into me and, depending on what they are, it's like they're fueling mine. I react and reflect maybe? That's not normal for me. I can't lock shit down like I used to."

Wolfie tilts his head as he studies me. "Do you feel like their emotions are tangible? The stronger they are, the more substantial they become and sometimes too much in one place is overwhelming?"

"Yes. Yes, that's it!" I look over at Presley hopefully. "Is it a stroke? Or maybe a tumor? Hell, anything that won't require me to call my therapist and tell her all her work has been ruined by my hometown."

He rakes a hand through his hair, shaking his head as he chuckles. "I have never in my life witnessed someone seriously ask if they have a tumor in excitement. Magpie, you're… just one of a kind."

Pouting, I lean into Doyle. He's quiet, but it's comforting. "I don't *really* want it to be that, Prez. It's just… I spent years working through my trauma about Trevor and Antigone and dissecting all my crap from high school. My parents died while I was still sorting out the repressed past shit, and I decided I was going to leave well enough alone. Now that's amping up and I seem to be losing my marbles one by one while we're chasing murderers."

"Tilly, you're handling a lot and doing it with the grace of a true Southern woman. Don't let anyone suggest otherwise, or I'll make sure they regret it." Teddy's thumb strokes my jaw as he continues. "What did you mean by your senses? You haven't gotten to that part yet."

I wrinkle my nose when he says that, and they all chuckle. "Don't laugh, but everything stinks. Well, no, it doesn't stink. I mean, it's like my nose went into overdrive. The same thing happened a couple of weeks ago with my ears. I'm hearing shit I never heard before. It's all hyper-focused and intense. That's why I started wondering about a brain problem."

They all look at Presley, and he groans, scrubbing his hand down his face. He says nothing for a few minutes and I worry that he's trying to figure out how to say I'm fucking dying. My pulse spikes as I wait, and suddenly, Doyle finds his tongue.

"Doc, I think our girl is going to have an actual heart attack if you don't say something soon. Work it out, lad."

I don't know where chaotic, trouble-making Lucky went, but I dig this silent, supportive side, too.

"Jolene, sometimes when we're extremely stressed, our bodies go into fight or flight mode. They have tossed you around like a canoe in a hurricane the past few months. On the surface, you're doing fine, but your body may overcompensate to keep you level. Visual and auditory quirks can absolutely be symptoms of acute anxiety and stress pushing you to the limit. You only need to worry if those things become hallucinations rather than passing symptoms."

His voice is calm and his words make sense, but that same emotional awareness I mentioned earlier is telling me he's not telling the whole truth. Fear, worry, and regret are buzzing off of him like a swarm of bees prickling my skin as I focus on my sexy physician. Whatever he's hiding, it must have to do with the stupid oath I want to shove up the ass of whoever invented it.

If I find out, I just might. It would serve those motherfuckers right.

"Tilly?"

Teddy brings me out of my violent reverie and I blink up at him. "What?"

He chuckles, his lips curved in amusement. "You blanked out for a minute and your eyes had this…fire… like you were planning someone's doom."

I shrug, trying to make light of my dark thoughts. "Maybe I was. I don't back down from fights anymore, Teddy. After Trevor, I vowed to never let people steal my agency again. I spent too long running from what the catastrophe shit and my ex did to my mental health. Now, I finish shit even if I didn't start it."

"Amen to that," Doyle crows. "I'll happily join you in destroying someone if it will bring a smile back to your face, Tíogair. I don't have a single fuck in all of my fields to give, and I'm known for being a dick."

Teddy snorts. "Amen to *that* as well."

"Oi!"

"Doyle, you can't give him openings like that if you don't expect him to take it," Wolfie chides. "Be fair and take your lumps."

They bicker amongst themselves for a few minutes, eventually including Prez and Benjy as well. It makes my chest ache in the best way, watching as I slowly wind down from the tension. I feel better knowing I shared my worries about the weird symptoms, but I know I glossed over the bits about my dreams.

I have no idea how to tell them I'm recovering tiny pieces of that past that scream my mother adopted me in a promotion campaign. Or that I just had a dream about weird fuzzy people doing something with me as a tiny child. Science says I shouldn't *have* memories that far back, hazy or not. The dream with the mystery woman and her glasses that magically appeared on my night stand makes me afraid I *am* having hallucinations.

What if I sleep-walked and stole or bought them damn things?

There were cases of people on zolpidem doing shit like driving and running around while asleep a couple years ago. Did someone slip me a sleeping pill to help me rest, and it backfired? No, I don't think Prez would do that to me. I'm stubborn as hell, but one of them could convince me to take medicine if needed—especially Wolfie.

"Magpie, what do you think?"

My eyes widen as I look at them all, waiting for my response. I zoned out, completely trying to muddle out my damn snippets of history and now I've missed what they were talking to me about.

"Um…I'm sorry. What do I think about…?" My cheeks flush, but I know better than to agree to *anything* I didn't hear around these jackals.

Teddy's grin widens. "Good on you, sugar. You didn't agree to anything you weren't paying attention to every word of. That's what you have to do tonight at dinner."

"You knew I wasn't listening and pretended?" They all look sheepish, and I point at them one by one as I glare. "Strike one, assholes. Clean up your act before we come home tonight or none of you is hitting a home run on this field."

Wolfie blinks. "Did she… just chastise us with… a sports metaphor?"

"Maybe she is having a stroke after all," Doyle jokes.

Mr. Smartass returns in time to call me out. Great.

It's Time

It's obvious some of Jolene's supe powers are breaking through the binding spell. Despite how firmly it was reinforced by the caster, her supe sides —whatever the hell they are— have mated with some of us and the magic is weakening. If pressed, I'd say each time her inner power claims someone, the enchantment will crumble a bit more until she emerges in one hell of a burst of energy. None of us are common, weaker supernaturals and she's been able to handle everything thrown at her unconsciously.

Magpie is going to be extremely powerful and mighty pissed when it all shakes out.

"It's not a tumor or a stroke, Haggerty," I chide as I walk over to our girl. "But I will monitor you and the others will let me know if they see something worrisome, right?"

A chorus of mumbles makes me roll my eyes. Some help these clowns are—they can't even put a show on to help me sell this anxiety shit. I start to speak again, but a loud tinkling sound fills the room, obscuring any other sound. It chimes four times and I realize it must be the royal Fae version of a cuckoo clock.

"Sounds like it's time to get up anyway, sugarplum," Lucy says as he rubs his ears. The noise must have been different for him, because he looks slightly pained. "The dressers will be here soon. That was a not-so-subtle warning."

Not a clock, but an alarm. Good to know.

"We should all get showered and cleaned up before they get here." Teddy rises, holding his hand out to Benjy, then to Lucy. "We don't want to be 'travel grimy' when their snooty tailors come to outfit us. I get the feeling it would definitely be dinner conversation."

Lucy nods, his eyes serious. "*Everything* will be fair game for mockery, trickery, or snobbery this evening. They will analyze every word, looking to make themselves appear smarter, more cultured, or more powerful. It's the games played at court and being visitors makes us fresh meat. Sharp wit and an unflappable demeanor will impress them, not outbursts. That is, unless you're prepared to back it up."

Boone meets my eyes and I know he understands what 'back it up' means—combat.

Hera help us if it comes to that.

A SHARP KNOCK AT THE FRONT DOOR OF THE GUEST HOUSE PUTS ALL of us on edge. We gathered there after freshening up, choosing to hang out comfortably while the animals gorged on the dinners Lucy made for them. The fridge was fully stocked, so only my secret favorite, Eurayle, took to the hunt outside. They'll be joining us at the event tonight and Magpie wanted to ensure they had food. Hungry wild animals are harder to tame and we're going to have enough trouble keeping alpha Boone and mischevious Haggerty from fucking everything up.

Fuck only knows how our family ended up with three stubborn, powerful dominants vying for control.

My lips curve as I think about Jolene. She's a switch like me, but she definitely leans more towards the top while I lean towards the bottom. Those two do their level best to keep her in line, but she proves they'll cave for her every single time. I actually enjoy watching the three of them duke it out and I'm not usually one for conflict. I prefer calm, easy going vibes—something Benjy and Lucy have in spades. Our girl's spark of defiance makes her irresistible to me; I would have never predicted it if you'd asked me.

"Prez? Yoo hoo?"

Blinking, I smile as Magpie waves her hand in front of me. "Yes?"

"Teddy went to answer the door. Get ready for whatever the hell is coming." She looks at each of us, her expression stern. "I haven't said it yet, but I don't trust *any* of these fuckers, by the way. Something feels off about this situation and I don't like it."

There's the bit she's getting from Lucy—it cranked her natural intuition and empathy to a million.

"Princess, I think we're all in agreement—holy shit." The simian shifter cuts off as a crew of people decked out like they're attending the fucking *Hunger Games* appear in the lounge area.

Boone's lips are pressed together tightly and I can tell he's trying like hell not laugh his ass off. A snort comes from where Haggerty is lolling about and, even with his Fae blood, Lucy is fighting a grin. The designers standing before us are almost Seussian; that's how insanely they're dressed.

"Um, not to be difficult, but I'm definitely not wearing anything like *that*," I say as I gesture in their direction. "Leave me here if it's required."

Hell if I care about cultural requirements—I'm not letting Haggerty get pictures of me trussed up like a goddamn Sneetch.

Doyle bobs his brows and I know he's figured out why I'm protesting. "Relax, doc. I promised to behave this evening."

"I doubt that extends to *after* the completion of this wager," I reply drily.

Before we can start bickering, the tallest of the magical Muppets claps their hands. "Gentlemen, gentlemen... I beg your attention. You needn't be worried about how we plan to outfit you for this royal ball. We are *expected* to appear outrageous to set trends by virtue of our positions. The selections we have available for you are much more suitable for visitors."

Adjusting my glasses, I nod as relief floods me. "Good to know."

"What do you need to get this over with?" Teddy asks. He's leaning against the wall watching them, and I see the sliver of fire surrounding his cornea. He's using the hound to sniff out what he can and if he doesn't like what he finds, he won't hesitate to shut this shit down.

"Oh, excellent question!" The tall leader with spring green hair claps again and I groan internally. Of course, they'd send a damn cheerleader to do this. "My name is Deirbhile, and these are my assistants Ríordán, Aimhirghin, Ealadha, Draighean, and Áinfean. We will each take one of you to style in your quarters. I will, of course, be working with your female companion."

That's a relief. Two of them are male and we would have had a riot if this chick assigned them to Magpie.

Deirbhile cocks a brow when no one moves, then sighs in exasperation. "Off with you, men. The lady seems capable and there are plenty of companions in the room. Shoo, now."

"Go on, guys," Jolene says as she tilts her head to the hallway. Once we move, she glares directly at the assistants, zeroing on the one called Ríordán. "All of you keep your hands to yourself, understand? I won't hesitate to put a bullet in someone who misbehaves."

Boone chuckles, ruffling her hair and dropping a kiss on her head before he leaves. "That's my girl, Tilly."

"Not exactly the subtle we were going for, sugarplum." The pup is smiling though, so he's not exactly mad.

She shrugs. "I am being subtle… just not about what's mine. People should pass my lack of humor about the subject along. It might prevent awkward situations later on."

Doyle's grin practically splits his face as he follows the group. "Ha! I'm not the one planning to fuck up tonight. You're all going to lose your bloody shirts."

Who knew getting him to agree to behave would pass the shit-stirring position onto our girl? Not me, that's for sure.

I'm pleasantly surprised when Ealadha finishes measuring me quickly, then selects a damn fine suit in a deep forest green. It's not a perfect fit, but he rectifies that within minutes using a spring blossom smelling magic. I tilt my head at the silent tailor, realizing he will not speak beyond grunts unless I do.

"I don't recognize your magic. Not to be rude, but I'm the town caladrius and it's rare for me not to tell pretty quickly."

He snorts and rolls his eyes. "Otherworlders and their healers. You don't know everything."

Isn't that what I just said?

"True. I definitely don't know you." I don't move so his work isn't interrupted, but I'd like to cross my arms over my chest in irritation. "Educate me. I'm willing to learn."

"Not my job, birdie. But if it will quiet your curiosity, I'm a hybrid, like much of your group. Druid and brownie—we don't visit your lands much. Only the Fae and pixies enjoy the Otherworld. The other species in the Veil stay out of the reach of humans."

I blink as I think about that. He's right—I don't see brownies or fairies or goblins or druids at all. There are more species than that across the Courts, but the only Daybreak dwellers who frequent our world are the two most humanoid. I suppose that makes sense. It's harder for the others to hide their natures and the laws of the Society are strict about it.

"That makes perfect sense now that I think about it. It also explains why I've never felt your magical blend before. I didn't think there were any Druids left. My mentor said you were all gone," I reply apologetically.

"Humph." He walks around me, examining the suit carefully. "Gone because we're all here. Not dead yet, thanks."

This guy must be a gas at parties—sheesh.

Looking down at myself, I grin. It really is absolutely exquisite now that he's made his adjustments. "You could make a lot of money in my land. It's obvious how talented you are."

"There isn't enough money in the human world to replace the honor I receive for being part of the royal family's cadre. I want for nothing, birdie. Our group travels the realm similarly to rock stars, designing on commission for the most elite in every kingdom." His eyes find mine as he pauses. "You and your family know very little about my world. A word of warning: the Fae are ruthless in their treatment of Otherworlders. Be cautious."

I nod, shooting him a grateful look. "I will be."

"Let's go see what my team has done with your mates, caladrius."

Guess that's the end of the conversation.

Following the stocky hybrid out of my room, I notice it's quiet. The lounge is filled with the men in our group dressed in varying styles of suits, the same color as mine. Teddy's has a vest and muted tie, making him look very billionaire chic. Benjy's has an open shirt and pinstripes, while Doyle has tails and a bow tie. The only one of us who doesn't fit the theme is Lucy—he's outfitted in a brighter emerald with a shine to it. His wings are on full display again, but somehow, the longer jacket and flowing shirt work perfectly with it.

"Where's our girl?" I murmur. "Not that I missed how hot everyone looks, but she's—"

"Right here," an amused voice behind me says.

Spinning on my heel, I turn to look and almost have to hold my jaw in place. Deirbhile has completely outdone herself; Jolene looks like she should be a fucking advertisement for Faerie, not a visitor.

The strapless top is some sort of delicate lace in emerald green that flows down to her hips, then the bottom is made of layers and layers of filmy material like the petals of flowers. There are hints of various greens along the edges, along with random sequins dotting the fluffy bottom. Magpie has long, shining opera-style gloves with no fingers and there are matching nails on her fingers. A vee shaped choker with a fat emerald in the center has delicately beaded tendrils leading from it to lacy shoulder caps that sit above draped strands of the same beads. They pinned her raven hair up in messy curls and her makeup is light and springy, with scarlet lips.

And they put fake, filmy fucking wings that match my love's on her damn back.

"I..." No one else is talking, either, so I'm not the only dumbfounded moron in the room. "Magpie, you look stunning."

"Good enough to eat," Boone growls in agreement.

She wrinkles her nose under the silly rainbow glasses as she peers at us. "The wings aren't too silly? I don't want everyone to stare."

Doyle snorts, then coughs as he gets control of himself. "I don't think anyone will think that, Tíogair. You look delicious, more so than usual. Right, pup?"

Lucy swallows hard and I can tell he's struggling because his wings are practically vibrating with his emotions. "Truly statuesque, Sugarplum. The team has us looking like a vision and I'm certain they will be praised highly by the royals."

Deirbhile claps her hands again, a smug smile curving her lips. It's more calculating than her cheery enthusiasm earlier, and I narrow my eyes. "Excellent! I'm so happy to hear you are all satisfied. We will take our leave now, and your ride to the front entrance will be here shortly."

The rest of her team gathers their things quietly and I frown as I try to work out what I'm sensing.

"Oh, and have an *illuminating* evening. May the road rise to meet you all."

I don't like her tone one bit; something is off and we'd better figure it out fast.

Anticipating

Jolene

As we exit the big SUV, I hold on to Wolfie's arm tightly. Ever since Deirbhile finished dressing me, I've felt this odd sensation crawling all over my skin and it's worse now that we're standing outside the big Tudor-style mansion they call 'The Castle.' Rubbing my free arm, I look around at the immaculate gardens and pristine grounds of the building, trying to figure out what's bothering me. They *filled* the air with an aromatic blend of floral and spring-time scents, but nothing that hints at danger. Yet I can't stop myself from reaching out to grab Benjy's arm and threading mine through it, so I'm flanked by my men.

It's like there's something just out of reach in my mind— like a word you can't remember on the tip of your tongue.

"Are you okay, Princess?" Benjy murmurs. His brows are drawn in concern and I instantly feel bad for making him worry when it's likely only anxiety about meeting some power couple who liked to be called the King and Queen.

Giving him a small nod, I continue following Teddy and Doyle as they stride towards the entrance. Prez is behind us with the compan-ions surrounding him and I feel his discomfort at the servals to his left. He's doing his best not to show that they make him skittish, and it makes my chest ache. Everyone in this group is making certain I'm protected, despite being able to take care of myself, and I hate to admit it feels good. Outside of Seer, I haven't allowed myself to depend on anyone for a very long time.

I just might be healing, inch by inch. My therapist would be proud.

"Halt and present yourself for inspection!"

The booming voice comes from one of the serious-looking security personnel at the door. There are six of them, all dressed in tuxedos, with earpieces just like the Secret Service. I suppose if you've got enough money to claim the monikers these clowns do, you can afford a cadre of fucking beefcakes protecting every single doorway. It reminds me of how the uber-rich in Europe or the juntas in Asia set up their protection teams. That means the money comes from mostly or entirely illegal gains—a fact that changes how I'll look at every person inside.

"What do you need?" Teddy growls as he stops the group in front of them.

A lilting voice comes from behind the wall of muscle and I tilt my head to peer around the two alpha males standing in front of me. "Don't worry, American prince. We mean your family no harm. Our search will be gentle, only taking a few moments to find out what weapons you possess and your intent is."

American prince? Barf. The Boones might be a Southern version of Camelot, but that's a simpering description if I ever heard one.

"The primary ma—er, we will examine the leaders of your family first, then we will continue with the…" The loud make from the announcement pauses, clearly unsure what the hell to say.

"Brutus means we will begin with you, fair prince and your princess. After that, your Irish rogue and lost son, then the healer and the friendly giant. To every family, there is an order and it must be respected, so we will."

Wolfie and Benjy let go of my arms reluctantly, and I step out from behind Teddy. It takes every ounce of my F.B.I. training to school my features when the guards come into view. My smile stays pasted on and I keep my eyes trained on the faces of the people before me, not wanting them to see the panic that now floods my veins. I was right to worry about the prickling feeling; it was a harbinger and I'll never ignore it again.

Standing in front of me are the same tuxedoed security men and a woman who must be the calm, lyrical voice. But now, the detail doesn't look like big, beefy ex-military types from some private security firm as I'm used to. The two biggest men who stand on either side of the female are enormous tusked orcs so muscled they might burst the seams of their suits. After them, I have to guess what I'm seeing based on playing D&D in college, but they *seem* to be a pair of gorgeous, ripped Fae men, a werewolf, and a bear shifter. The woman is petite and delicate, with dragonfly wings and multi-colored skin and hair. Fairy, maybe?

Fuck if I know. I'm wondering if someone spiked the damn food in that place.

I count slowly in mind, hoping to slow my pulse until I'm under control. Whatever is going on here, I can't let anyone know right now. This moment feels important, even without the damn hallucinations, and I can't screw it up for Wolfie. So I square my shoulders and hold my hand out, palms up. "Feel free to check me first. We are only here to enjoy your generous hospitality."

"Excellent!" The fairy woman claps her hands, then places them above mine, hovering as she closes her eyes. "Close your eyes as well, and I will determine what we must know."

Teddy literally snarls like an animal next to me, but I don't dare look at him. Instead, I close my eyes behind my glasses and focus on breathing deeply. Whatever hippy-dippy shit this chick is doing will be over soon, and I doubt it will—

Ow.. ow… ow… holy fuck… ow… ow… ow…

It takes all of my strength not to let the pain slicing through me show in my body or expression. I don't know if this is a test or if something is seriously wrong with me, but it feels like I'm peeled open layer by layer from the inside out. My teeth grit, but I force the smile to stay in place as I wait for it to stop before I pass the hell out.

Suddenly, a flash echoes in my head.

A cold room. Bright lights. Everything is hazy.

There are people hovering over me, but they're shadows. I can't see their faces, but one has weird instruments in their hand. They're all holding their hands over me and it feels like I'm being burned now from head to toe.

My mind can't handle it. I float away, leaving the cold steel below me and molten heat inside of me as they continue to mutter words in a language I don't know. In the cloud, separate from the pain, I'm safe. Nothing bad can happen to me here. This is where I can hide from what's happening. I can stay here and I won't have to feel any of this ever again.

I watch the mysterious people work covering my body in odd drawings and colorful light. None of it looks like it's hurting me, but I know the searing of each and every symbol is making the body below jerk and twitch. It doesn't leave a mark on my skin; I can't see one scratch or scar. But beneath…

Beneath that layer, an intricate mural of art lies, glowing with power.

Why? Why are they doing this to me?

They speak in hushed, fearful tones and it's confusing. How could I scare people so badly they have to do this to me?

What am I, a monster?

The second the tiny woman pulls her hands away, the vision stops and I freeze in place. She doesn't look worried; no, she beams at me happily as she nods. "You are quite truthful, Miss Jolene Whitley of America. You have no ill-intent for our royals or our kingdom. You are cleared to enter the Castle."

Stepping aside, I carefully avoid letting anyone touch me so they can't feel the trembling of my limbs. That vision was important and so is whatever the hell is going on with my brain. I lick my lips and finally raise my gaze to look at Teddy. The purple-haired tester is holding her small hands over his large ones now. His body tenses and I swallow a gasp when his visage flickers—first, a huge fiery dog that smells of sulfur, then a gorgeous man that smells like cherries and sin, and then an enormous bird that has the scent of clean air and spices.

What. The. Actual. Motherfucking. Fuck.

I whip my eyes to the others in the group and let out a slow breath when I see nothing weird—until I hit my darling boy. *Oh, sweet baby Jesus wept, look at him.* Every cell in my body activates at once, and I have to lift my hand to surreptitiously check for drool. Wolfie is always a gorgeous runway model, almost pretty, but now… His undercut, dirty blond hair is now long, sparkling silver framing pointed ears and pale, iridescent pink skin. The green of his suit perfectly compliments the pale coloring, and the gorgeous blue, purple, and pink ombré-d butterfly wings curl at the ends, fluttering bits of glittery dust as he waits his turn.

"Done! You, too, are cleared to enter, Edgar Boone the third, son of the lawmaker and upholder of human laws in America."

The irritated growl he lets out tells me Teddy is already tired of the pomp and circumstance of our hosts. He spent most of his life following his father and mother around to this kind of shit, so I'm not surprised that he can endure it, but wants to smash something. "Hurry this up. I don't like standing in the doorway like we're selling Amway."

"Patience, young prince," she chides. "Join me, Irishman. It is your turn now."

Doyle looks even *less* pleased than Teddy, if that's possible. Nothing about him looks unusual—until the woman places her palms over his. The minute she does, a blinding light flashes out and surrounds him like a goddamn painting of an angel. He doesn't grow wings, which makes me let out a secret sigh of relief. I don't know what the hell my hallucination is assigning him beyond power, but thank hell, he's not an angel. I'm the right age for a schizo-affective break and religious iconography would be a telling sign that I'm not just drugged.

Relax, Jolene, there's no history of that in your family. Even if there was, you know exactly how to manage it. Don't be ridiculous.

The logical part of my mind is working overtime at the moment, and I have to listen. Obviously, with my training, I know how to manage a multitude of mental issues. There's not a damn thing wrong with having medical conditions like that. It's just a knee-jerk reaction to thinking I'm having serious problems I wasn't ready for. But… something in my gut tells me that's not what this is and the sooner I accept that, the sooner I'll understand what's happening.

"Hurry it up," Doyle says impatiently. "You're lucky I'm even allowing this nonsense. I don't have to and you know it."

"Ah, yes. Your kind are given so many exceptions," murmurs the fairy woman. "You are now cleared, Doyle Haggerty of lands farther than even ours reach. Mind your agreed upon tenets while you enjoy our homeland."

He waves his hand at her, then gestures for my beautiful Wolfie to step up. "I will do what I've agreed to, Captain. Now, do the pup so we can get on with this fucking circus."

The second Wolfie's hands are below hers, she gasps, pulling back briefly before she gathers herself. "Oh! My goodness! You, son of winter, are exempt. You may enter."

What? The son of a senator is suspect, but not a vet?

"She must know Callie," Teddy mutters next to me. "I don't blame her for avoiding that fucking psycho's wrath."

I don't turn to look at him; I watch Wolfie frown before he walks over to join us. He seemed hopeful the woman would have some other reaction. *Maybe he thought she'd know his father?* My brows furrow and I try to reason out why I think that. It *feels* true, and his disappointment is flowing over me as he gets closer.

"It's okay," I whisper as I reach for his hand. Everything is a mess in my head and I'm not sure if I'm losing my mind, but nothing can keep me from comforting him. The smile my darling boy gives me is even more brilliant than usual, and I almost swoon.

How in the hell did this goddamn drug haze make all *these assholes even hotter?*

I'm never going to survive this night.

Bad Feeling

Wolfgang

While the guard checks out Benjy and Prez, I watch Sugarplum out of the corner of my eye. She's fidgeting and tense, though she's trying desperately not to show it. I don't know if that's because the woman doing the testing is odd or because something else is wrong. There was a split second while their hands were together that I caught the tiniest pulse of pain from our girl, but since she didn't even grimace, I let it go. But now that she's holding my hand, my natural empathy is kicking in.

Jolene is walling herself in, keeping her emotions and thoughts to herself.

She hasn't done that since she allowed us in the house again that night before we left. I've been able to sense how she's doing and gauge when she needs support. Whatever happened between those two has her throwing up shields, and she doesn't even understand what she's doing. Of course, being bonded to more of us than before has only increased that power, so even I'm struggling to find a way past what she's doing. That's not good on so many levels, and Teddy's going to be pissed when I tell him.

My gaze flicks at the other alpha mate—a term that idiotic orc almost said out loud in front of someone unemerged. Orcs aren't particularly cunning, which is why this kind of job is perfect for them; unfortunately, this one inserted himself into a delicate situation. Luckily for him, Jolene was too focused on the psychic fairy to question what he almost spilled. That's another conversation to have with one of our hosts later, but it still made my entire body freeze until we got past it.

How do you explain that mated groups almost always have an alpha pair that leads their mini-packs that authorities defer to in this kind of situation?

You can't if they don't know what the hell mating means, much less how supernatural diplomacy works. Jolene probably thought they were being jackasses about size or something much more *human* than shifter vibes. We're not all shifters, but we've formed a family and that will often be treated just as a pack would. Without a doubt, Teddy and Jolene are at the top of our food chain. Doyle would never admit it, but he knows it's true.

For some reason, they put *me* equally with him, and that I can't fathom. I'm as submissive as they come and no one's ever accused me of being in charge of shit. The look in the fairy's eyes when she assessed me was curious, though, and I don't think it was entirely to do with my mother. I wonder if she could sense something about the other part of my heritage that she couldn't say. It wouldn't be surprising; I'm obviously not Daybreak Court, but there's Fae in me. They all have a myriad of agreements and promises made to keep their fragile peace over the centuries.

Perhaps identifying anything about my lineage would violate one of those clauses.

Looking down at my feet, I let calm flow over me so I don't show the turmoil inside. Sugarplum's glasses keep her from seeing my true nature, but the others can plainly see when I'm agitated by this form. I need to hold it together until they let us into this damned castle. Once we're away from the royal contingent, I can bounce ideas off of Prez or Teddy. One of them will have something useful to say about my experience with the court fairy.

"You are now cleared to enter the castle, brave barkeep!"

Teddy lets out an annoyed breath, then turns to us. "Let's get this show on the road. I'm already tired of being gawked at."

"Don't be such a sourpuss," Jolene murmurs as she wraps her other hand around his. "Maybe if we find our seats, we'll get to eat before anything else odd happens."

There's a tiny tremor in her voice, as if she's worried something *will* take place before we can sit down. I squeeze the hand I have, hoping to pass some reassurance to her as our brash hound leads the way past the hulking guards. I'm glad she can't see them, to be honest, because they're all huge and look like they'd enjoy tearing someone apart for fun. Their power level is lower than mine, but truthfully, we're walking around in a fairly overpowered group at the moment. I hope it warns off the more aggressive types that hang around court functions in this land.

"Psst."

I arch a brow as Doyle sidles up to me. "Hm?"

"She seem off to you, lad?"

Biting my lower lip, I decide to be honest. I'd expect the same from him, so it's only fair. "Yes. Since the woman checked her, Sugarplum has been shut up tighter than a diamond vault. Is that what you mean?"

"Mmm no. Good to know you're sensing something, too, though. I meant more like… unease. Something is making her feel very nervous and I can't suss out what it is. She's using that wall thingy you mentioned keeping us from noticing, I'd wager."

I nod at the demi-god. "She is. But it could be her reacting to not having control here. Much like you and Teddy, she hates being out of control and out of the loop. It might make her edgy."

"Not like this, pup. She's running cold as ice and just as sharp." He shakes his head and looks around, watching the elegantly dressed species from the Daybreak Court mill about. "Keep your eyes peeled for more signs. We may have to get her alone to get it out of her."

"Okay," I breathe.

Intrigue isn't my forte, but I also refuse to let something hurt our girl; I'll have to suck it up.

AS WE WEAVE OUR WAYS THROUGH THE GLITTERING THRONG, I'M NOT sure which of our goals is more impossible: keeping Sugarplum in the dark or finding my father. My mother is a self-centered bitch that enjoys causing others pain, so she could have lied about damn near anything I've been told or started the rumors I've caught over the years. Aurelia knew nothing, even before her mind broke. It's clear I have Fae heritage from my shifts and powers, but nothing in the Daybreak Court calls to me. Our first stop on this vagabond tour is likely a bust—unless we can get someone to talk.

But getting people to talk when we have to keep things secret from Jolene is an obstacle itself.

Teddy finally stops at the long table in front of the dais where the King and Queen look down from their thrones. There are several males and females on smaller thrones on either side of them, which I assume are the favored children *du jour*. It's common for the Fae to have large families; they take 'heir and a spare' to new levels. Most of them will end up married off in political alliances, but not until the definite heir has ascended. The six princes and princesses we see now are likely only half of their family 'stable'.

"We're not seated with *them*, are we?" I hiss as I let go of my sugarplum's hand to approach him. My wings are fluttering with anxiety and I know he can feel the tension in me when he tucks me into his side and presses a kiss on my head.

Prez comes closer as well, then all of our family is circled around me in a group. Jolene smiles softly as she brushes her fingers over my jaw. "Don't worry, little Wolfie. We'll make sure they don't do anything to hurt you."

"It's not hurt that I'm worried about," I mumble. "It's misleading me to amuse themselves. I don't feel like this is where we'll find my father; it's far too light and hopeful in Daybreak for my mother. She'd never choose someone with this much… sunshine in their soul. So they may have rumors and riddles to give us, but they'll also enjoy sending us in the wrong direction because they can. Royals bore easily and they're immortal, remember?"

Benjy gives me a serious look. "Man, I don't know jack about this. The doc is right in saying they were really keeping us in the dark about some shit and who the fuck knows why. But I know that we have one of the trickiest motherfuckers I've ever met with us and he's agreed to a bet that ties his hands. Perhaps if we think his talents will be useful, we need a signal to relieve him of that burden?"

I swallow hard, waiting to see what Sugarplum will say. After all, this was her bet and her bounty if Doyle fucks up. I can't ask her to release him 'just in case'—can I?

"Oh, for fuck's sake." Our girl rolls her eyes and puts her hands on her hips. "Doyle can do his thing if it's going to get us information for you. Why the hell would I stop him because of a silly ass bet? Really, you boys have no faith in me at all."

Teddy grins, his eyes dark with gratitude. "Good choice, Tilly. You'll get a reward for that later."

"Stuff it, Coach," she mutters as she looks around. "There are more pressing matters than our bedroom Olympics at the moment."

Maybe, but she just sent all our trains off the track with that comment.

I clear my throat, getting the guys back as I tilt my head at the table. "We should probably sit down before we offend someone."

When the circle breaks, a smug-looking troll approaches us, bowing before he speaks. "Ah! You are ready to be announced now, yes?"

"Announced?" Presley says as he looks up at the raised thrones. "To... the royal family?"

"Yes, yes! It is a great honor to be seated here and we must announce you, then ascend to greet our most generous rulers. Once that happens, they will call the reel, and the family will join one by one. You will join as the princes and princesses do. Hopefully, you will not disgrace them with your performance."

Oh, shit.

"We'll be asked to dance... with them... in front of the entire room?" I clarify as I look around.

"Of course! Again, you are being afforded the *highest* honors for visitors from the Other Realm. I don't know why, but it is my job to prepare you. So, please, line up in the reverse order that our door sentries granted you entrance to the castle."

Jolene sighs when he moves away. "When I was little, I wanted to be a princess. Every girl does, right? After my escapades in Europe, I saw what kind of constant bullshit women like these have to endure and was suddenly glad as hell to be a lowly commoner. This needless pomp and circumstance is keeping everyone from eating, and I'm going to be hangry soon."

"Then let's get it over with before the monster gets loose," Teddy says with a chuckle. "Benjy, you're first, man. Then the doc, then Wolfie, and so on. Line up so they can call us, bow or curtsey, be polite, and we'll get through this shit. Everyone knows how to dance, right?"

"You're asking the Cotillion Catastrophe if she knows how to dance?" Sugarplum grumbles. "You've got nerve, Edgar Olivier Boone III."

"I'm not asking *you*, Tilly. I know you went through all the cotillion practice. Foster did as well. I'm asking the docs and the dick."

Doyle snorts. "I've graced many a salon with my quick feet over the years, doggy. More than you'll ever be able to claim."

"I know. I escorted someone during my time at WHFS," I admit. I would never have been considered for that part of high society like them, but I could attend with a girl who did.

"I can dance." Presley shrugs. "My mentor was a stickler for doctors presenting themselves as part of the town fabric. The damn balls and shit have different names in different parts of the world, but it's all the same. I should do fine."

"Good," the hound says as he looks up at the haughty royals. "Because I get the feeling they will judge us."

ROYALS

JOLENE

G*reat.*

Teddy's prediction hit me like a brick to the face and now I'm gripped with old fears about being judged at a stupid formal event in front of an entire town. It's been so many years since that damn night, yet when the anxiety from it is triggered, I still have to fight my way through an electric light show in my mind and body. The snooty Fae in this room aren't very different from the most elite townsfolk in the Hollow. Guaranteed, there are more than a few bitchy women and their male counterparts milling around. If I make one wrong move, they'll go for the kill simply to impress the royals.

They'll come for your men.

I frown, unsure where that thought came from. Before my goddamn glasses started malfunctioning, I didn't even believe this world existed. Now my mind is filling in gaps with information I can't possibly have a basis for. What the shit went on between the guest house and here that nullified the dream woman's efforts to keep me in the dark? I assume she was attempting to protect me and this has something to do with the 'big secrets' the guys can't tell me. Clara Whitley may not have been the best mother, but she didn't raise a fool.

The reality of a hidden world shouldn't be possible, yet here it is. Not only that, but my guys are part of it, which means… This place isn't a one-off. The cheerful broad at the entrance to the castle revealed all of them have… forms… I didn't know about. But she didn't seem surprised, and only Wolfie had something that appeared to connect to this world. The others had animals or glowing auras; I assume that means every myth and fairy tale I've ever been told is possibly based in fact.

Life was so much simpler when I was dealing with contrary despots and CEOs.

While I've been noodling the fucking bizarre turn my life has taken, the dance floor in the middle has cleared and guests are lining up. I hold on to Wolfie, counting in half time in my head to prepare for the quick steps. They can choose a wealth of music for this, and for all I know, there are specific Fae tunes they'll use. But reels are traditionally in a faster 4/4 time and if I just keep count, I'll be fine, regardless. Hopefully, the guys know that, too.

I don't have time to remind them, though, because we're ushered into formation and the uptempo beat begins. The beat climbs as we all move in unison, and I dart my eyes away from the crowd of multi-colored Fae to make sure the guys are doing okay. Even Benjy is moving gracefully and I let out a small sigh of relief. I can't imagine what would happen if—

As if by magic, the reel music stops and everyone stands in place. I wait for the bow and curtsey, but it doesn't come. No, the music begins again and everyone moves to lines divided across the space.

Shit. They're switching to a contra.

My eyes flutter closed briefly as I wing a prayer to whatever mother-fucker is listening that none of them were lying about remembering the damn cotillion training. This shit was one of their main events and I'll be damned if no one mentioned switching dance types mid-stream. This isn't a strange dance for people who have gone through what Teddy and I have, so we're able to get into position quickly. His palm faces mine as we circle, and I lift the edge of my dress with my free hand as we circle. I can feel the intensity of his gaze burning into me and for a second, I almost whisper that I know.

But I can't. If this really is the crap they aren't allowed to speak of, I don't think we've hit the flash point yet. Doyle, at the least, would have whooped for joy if whatever trigger they're waiting for got pulled. None of them have acted like they expect me to know Wolfie has fucking wings. For that reason alone, I'm keeping my damn mouth shut. I don't know what punishment they'd get, but it has to be serious for Doyle to obey.

We haven't even spoken to the royal fuckwits yet—this night may never end.

The lines move and I frown, watching Teddy slide in front of a tittering Fae woman with blue hair and an enormous dress. My gut curls in, a dark sensation sliding through me as I dance with my new partner instinctively. A soft cough brings my attention back to the male in front of me and I blink owlishly. One of the indolent princes from the stage has his palm centimeters from mine as we move through the steps. He has flowing black hair, huge raven wings, and a smirk that says he finds me lacking.

"Good evening, your highness. Pleasure to make your acquaintance," I drawl as I bat my lashes. I'd prefer he thinks I'm a clueless idiot from our world than looks too closely.

His eyes narrow, and he throws his head back, laughing as he moves in time with me. "Cute. You seek to disarm me with this guise, but I see through it. I will not break the accords by telling you how I know you are not the simpering belle you pretend to be. However, you will meet far less scrupulous royals in the other strongholds."

Isn't that grand?

"I'm sure I don't know what you mean, Prince…?" I let the question hang, ignoring the eyes of my men on me as we speak in hushed tones.

"Prince Eógan." He grins a bit as he looks around and leans in again. "Your men are very nervous about my proximity to you, especially the one who seeks his line."

"We're here on vacation, nothing more," I reply casually. "Genealogy isn't one of my hobbies, I'm afraid."

The prince huffs, bowing as our turn ends. He gives me a saucy wink as we switch to the next partner, and I roll my eyes.

Hera, save me from the tsunami of hot, asshole men who have become a daily trial in my life.

Each one of the male royals took a turn with me in the contra, playfully bantering about what they knew that I didn't. I parried to each of their verbal thrusts, not breaking character for a second. Somehow, I knew letting even one of them know they'd gotten into my head would be a dangerous proposition.

By the time we make it to the last partner, I stare at Wolfie in relief. Strain is clear in his eyes as he smiles at me and I realize he's having the most trouble with tonight. His transformation probably started when he set foot in this land, and he's had to keep me at arm's length to protect me. That can't have been easy on him—my darling boy craves touch to balance out his emotions. Teddy and Prez did their best, I'm sure, but if the pull to his mates is similar for him, he's suffered.

"Well, hello, little Wolfie," I say as our palms hover together. "Fancy meeting you here."

He snorts and I see several people glare at him. I search their faces, something deep in my gut whispering dark things about what I should do to all the Fae involved in this fucking circus. The longer they have forced us to dance and endure their royal brats, the easier it was to see that this entire night is a set-up. The Daybreak Court is beautiful, but far too light and springy for Callie. We've been held hostage by tradition simply so they can gather intel or maybe just for their amusement—and I don't like it a bit.

"Um, Sugarplum?" Wolfie says quietly. His voice breaks my concentration and I turn back to him with a smile. "You're getting awfully hot. Are you overheating in your gown?"

Tilting my head, I consider that for a moment. I feel warm, but nothing alarming. "Perhaps. I think this will be our last goodwill dance. Our hosts have imposed on our desire to follow tradition for long enough."

His eyes widen, and he shakes his head. "No, we have to—"

My lips curve and I step out of the formation. I dust off my old favorite as I look directly at the bored-looking King and Queen. Seer would be proud if she could see me doing the most sarcastic, overly exaggerated curtsy I can before I walk back to my table. The Queen looked pissed, but I honestly don't give a hairy possum's ass. At home, expecting your guests to perform while you hold dinner for ransom for an hour would get you kicked so far back over the Mason-Dixon line you'd turn into a Yankee.

Once I'm standing by my chair, I see Doyle jump out of his spot, covering his laughter with his hand as he joins me. The look on his face is one of pure excitement as he leans down to murmur by my ear.

"They underestimate your sass every time, Tíogair. You don't suffer fools and you've got as much stubborn dictator in you as the doggy."

"I can't abide rudeness," I say as he pulls out my chair. "There's something rotten in Denmark here, Lucky. Nothing about tonight is what it seems, and I fucking hate subterfuge. If these dicklickers want to come at us, we won't go down like whimpering pansies."

His eyes narrow. "Amazing. Your lips are moving, but I'd *swear* I'm hearing the judge. Did you do a Vulcan mind meld?"

"Don't be ridiculous. Everyone knows aliens aren't real," Prez scoffs as he and the others take their seats.

I look around the table for a second, taking in the fantastical sights. My hand flies to my mouth as a giggle escapes, then another, until I drop my head on the table as I laugh. Shoulders shaking, tears leaking, gut clenching, laughter rolls through me as the irony of his statement hits me.

As if Fae, magic, winged dudes, royalty, and fucking shifters are so goddamn normal.

"Uh, Princess? Are you okay?"

I lift a hand, waving it as I try to calm the slight insanity in my mind. The blackouts and flashbacks I've had most of my life always made me think I had a screw loose. Now I'm embroiled in some plot worthy of a TV show, running around a world full of things that shouldn't exist. I continue laughing, wiping my eyes to keep my face from being ruined, and I wonder if I'm going to wake up one day in a mental hospital surrounded by dudes in white coats. They'll tell me I've been in a coma for ten years after falling off a horse and suddenly, all of this shit will make sense.

A tight squeeze under my gown gets my attention and I blink.

Nope, not a coma, because those don't involve an eight-foot snake wrapped around your torso like a straightjacket.

Sucking in a deep breath, I get myself under control. I just have to get through the rest of this fucking trip without toppling off the deep end or stabbing someone. It's been a long time since I've had to do that and I should be able to control myself. A sound from the dais floats down to us and I whip my head around. The first dark haired prince is grinning like a madman at me as I gather my wits. A pink haired sister is whispering with him as they stare down at our table, and I know it means trouble.

"Sugarplum, you should probably calm down…"

Picking up my silverware, I unfold the napkin, only to see my hands are on fire.

This can't be good.

POISON

EDGAR

Thank fuck for those stupid glasses. I still haven't figured out where they came from, but I knew what they were for the second Tilly put them on. It's hard to control the protective instincts of *all* my goddamn sides as she's casually chowing down on her weird Fae salad with flaming hands. The pup tried to calm her down when he noticed, but she's obviously too worked up to be soothed with words.

Doesn't mean I'm not going to try.

"Tilly, your hands look red. Did you touch something unusual while we were dancing?" I put on an innocent expression, hoping she won't notice the strained edge to my voice.

"Other than fuckfaced rich guys? No," she says before she takes another bite. "They do feel itchy. Perhaps their gallons of weird cologne are triggering an allergy."

Doyle squints at her, his eyes dark as he watches her eat. It's hard to tell what he's thinking when he's not being a brash asshole, and I don't trust the quiet a bit. "Itchy, huh? Perhaps a rash?"

She shrugs and gives him a sweet smile. "Maybe? Who knows what those dipshits did while they were interrogating me? They sucked at it, by the way."

Holy hell, I get it now.

Tilly's hands are on fire, and her aggression has ratcheted up a thousand percent. She has to be drawing on... me. Our connection is stronger here and even though the mating isn't completely sealed from her end, somehow, she's accessing one of my powers. *Not good, not good...* It took me a long time to mostly master the hellhound, and he's the easiest of the three sides. I whip my head around, looking at Benjy, then cut my eyes to her hands. It takes him a minute, but I see when he remembers the first time my fire manifested at a football game in late elementary school.

"Princess, slow down before you choke," he says as he takes a sip from the large tankard of fizzy shit the Fae servers placed at each of our seats while we were dancing. "You're practically inhaling that stuff."

"S'good," Jolene says. "Plus, it's been a dog's age since we ate and I'm trussed up like a fluffy swan. *And* I had to dance for an hour straight. It feels like I could eat an entire hippo, honestly."

All the guys share a knowing expression—she's getting closer to emerging. Her appetite will double or triple depending on how large or powerful her form is. That might be hard for her since she's got trauma about eating, so we'll have to be very careful not to trigger that unintentionally. The fire on her palms leans towards being like me—her scent even has a trace of sulfur right now.

"Then fill up, Sugarplum. We don't want you all worn out by the time we get home."

I smirk as the pup hiccups. This Fae mead shit must hit him harder than it does us because he's giving our girl intensely flirty eyes. The doc grins at me, clearly noticing the same thing I am, and I lean back in my chair. Once we're back in our little guest house, it's going to get wild. No matter what happens here, we have that to look forward to. All we have to do is make it through dinner and whatever formal introductions these asshats want us to go through, then we'll escape.

"What are you making that face for, Teddy Bear?" Tilly asks as she pauses to take a sip down some of the mead. "You look like a cat that caught the canary and—wait, where the hell are the cats? And the others?"

"Hunting, love," Doyle says smoothly. "They're getting a read on the room for us. Don't worry; she's watching." He points up to a high railing where Euryale is glaring at the room as if it offends her. "Your feathered friend is making certain the furry ones are safe, just like your scaly companion is secretly helping you."

Little on the nose there, you idiot. What's he playing at?

"Oh! That makes perfect sense. Jekyll and Hyde are particularly sneaky when they want to be. It's cat nature, I think." Tilly nods and my eyes narrow again.

She's being quite easygoing for someone whose damn hands are flaming. I know from experience it means my hound is fucking furious when the fire moves from my veins to the outside of my body. Our lovely Jolene is playing a game of her own and I don't know who it's with—us, the royals, or everyone at the ball. There's no way she'd have magical flames dancing over her without actually burning anything, if not.

Disturbingly enough, it means she's controlling their effects somehow, too.

I was almost sixteen before I figured that shit out. The Senator had to cover up quite a few incidents when my temper blew and I accidentally committed arson before I learned how to tell the flames what to do. That fact makes my gut clench in anticipation; Tilly will be a formidable mate. We'll have a pack that possibly dwarves every group of supes within the States. Outside of Guardians, I'm not sure there's even competition.

Presley clears his throat and I look up. "Penny for your thoughts, Your Honor."

"I'd say that's overpaying, birdie," Doyle mutters.

Ignoring him, I shrug. "Considering what all of this means for the future." My gaze flicks to her hands quickly, then back before Tilly catches on. "The control being shown is not common, in my experience. It's very powerful and hard to manage."

He looks thoughtful for a moment. "I see. Perhaps it will be revealed soon, then?"

"Fuck, I hope so," Tilly mutters and we all look at her in panic. She frowns at our gaping, waving her hands around. "This formal bullshit is tiresome. I'll drink this yummy fizzy shit and eat whatever desserts they bring, but I want out of this dress. You might have to roll me home like a blueberry."

The imagery makes me snort and I lean in to nip her jaw. "Tilly, I'd happily roll you home if you're getting naked when we get there. I enjoy *all* types of juicy fruit."

That gets the attention of everyone at the table, and our girl turns bright pink as she smacks my arm lightly. "Don't be crude, Edgar Boone. We're at a ball… I think. What would your mama say?"

"Tilly, you know for fact I don't give a toad's bumpy ass what my mother would say anymore. I'll yank this tablecloth off and fuck you over the damn table if I want. Not one motherfucker in this room will stop me, I promise."

Jolene sucks in a breath, and I can scent her arousal floating in the air like perfume. Her typical magnolia and plum fragrance, with the hint of my burning embers mixed in, makes my hound thrash against the cage inside of me. I blink, feeling the heat in my eyes as the ring of fire surrounds my iris. Knowing our mate is going to emerge with our powers makes it hard to control the giant beast, but I tamp down hard. I can't do this here; even if the Court knows what all of us are, they do *not* know about the rest of me.

Only my pack—my family—knows about the rest of me, and it needs to stay that way.

"Princess," Benjy says loudly, pulling us out of the intense stare we were holding. "Have you noticed the rest of the room seems normal and we're all… tipsy, maybe?"

His words make me freeze in place. *That can't be.* Looking around quickly, I note all the other people chatting and eating with no kind of commotion at their tables. No one is ready to hop on one another and rut, nor are they getting feisty enough to have fire hands. My old friend is right; we're the only ones teetering on an emotional cliff. I suck in a breath slowly, working to process that information without all of my short-tempered supe sides losing their shit at the same time.

"We've either been drugged, poisoned, or this stuff interacts with *our kind* differently than the other guests," Presley says quietly. "Two of those options are concerning and the last is simply unfortunate. The first two would be extremely unwise on the part of our hosts. It would certainly break… laws. And it will cause a lot of… paperwork."

Snorting, I look around again. When I don't see our companions right away, I whistle low. It takes mere seconds for the cats to leap up to our table, taking seats at the small stools that appear in-between Tilly, the pup, and I. Kali and Hecate arrive next, posting up on their seats as Euryale touches down behind the doc. We need their help and I hope the Irishman's raven is somewhere nearby as well.

"Sniff the food. Scent the people. We may have eaten something dangerous. Report back."

Our girl's companions take off with mine in tow, scattering across the room to do my bidding. Jolene tilts her head at me curiously, but doesn't ask me what the hell I was doing. She's probably a bit more off than the rest of us because we encouraged her to chow down and she's been drinking the mead. Lucky for me, it's made her a lot more complacent towards me; unfortunately for the royals, she was pissed at them before this discovery.

I'm worried what she's going to do if we find out this shit was intentional.

"We need to pack up and get the fuck out of this Court tomorrow morning," Doyle says mildly. "Even if this is a mistake, it's a dead end and we shouldn't waste anymore time playing their little games."

"Agreed," Wolfie says as he looks at me. "I don't trust them. This probably isn't poison because it wouldn't affect me like it does you. But it could be some sort of drug or serum used to loosen us up before the big introduction. That's definitely against the accords and they're taking a tremendous risk."

"I have supplies in my luggage," the doc says. "I'm taking samples from everyone when we get to our rooms. I want to test them later, just in case we need proof."

Presley Hamilton is a fucking genius, and he does not *get enough credit.*

"Good idea, doc," I murmur. "We'll want evidence for Nelia and Jackson if they need to help us pursue things."

Tilly beams at me, her eyes dancing. "Jax and Eli are up at State helping that hockey player avoid getting charged with murder. It's super scandalous. I can't *wait* for him to tell me the entire story."

I scratch my neck as I consider how to answer that. We talked about this earlier, but I didn't go into detail. Being part of the Society and an alum, I'm aware of the turmoil going on at our alma mater. My father is on the board that replaced that misogynistic old fart who used to run it. The Senator was furious that they almost cost State their ability to play D1 sports and he's neck deep in all that shit. But I don't know how much of what I know has been made public.

"There's some crazy shit happening everywhere, it seems, Tilly." She nods and I breathe a sigh of relief. "Even your bestie got called off for a job instead of meeting us for this trip."

Mentioning Seer will distract her, even if it's a gamble.

"I know! I wanted her here with me, but she said she had to meet up with Julia and her fam to do something important." Her pout is adorable and I almost snicker. "I *hate* that she's missing this. She'd help me kick their rich, snooty asses for sure."

"Perhaps it's better she's *not* here then, Sugarplum? We don't want to break laws ourselves," Wolfie says cajolingly. "We just need to survive tonight and get the hell out like Doyle said."

Jolene's lip curls as she looks up at the group of fancy fuckers on the dais. "I doubt that's how it's going to work out, little Wolfie. I have a bone to pick with our gracious hosts; they won't be happy when I'm done, either."

Dionysis, save me from Fae drugged women and men tonight.

"Can we *try* not to start a war?" I ask drily.

Our girl sneers like the green Christmas thief as she shrugs. "Depends on how I feel by the time they finally call us up there, Teddy. I'm mighty fucking tired of being the bigger woman."

Just. Fucking. Fabulous.

Run The World

Jolene

"Attention, everyone!"

Turning my attention from the increasingly hot flirting at our table, I look up to see the troll from before standing in front of a microphone. An air of practiced calm has replaced the smugness. If this isn't our time to be called before those damn lazy royals, I'm taking another stand. We're leaving this ridiculous excuse for intel gathering in the next hour or I'll take Teddy up on that table fucking plan.

Zero fucks given is my new mantra with the Fae—they underestimate me and that will change.

"It is now time for our honored guests to be introduced to their hosts. If our guests will please head for the right wing in the order they entered the reel, we will begin."

I pinch the bridge of my nose, trying to rein in my irritation. This is one humongous waste of our time and these asshole Fae are doing it on purpose. What I don't know is *why* they're keeping us captive with pomp and circumstance. Dropping my napkin, I stand up, waving at the guys to follow. It's hot as hell here. You'd think royals would at least be as smart as Southern humans and provide the ladies in enormous dresses with fans.

Teddy takes my arm, his brow arching as he looks at me. "We need to cut this shit off, Tilly. You look like you're on fire."

Oh, he's hilarious tonight, isn't he?

I nod as I approach the dais, lifting the bottom of my skirts to ascend. When I'm halfway up, I look each of the assholes in the eye as I repeat my patently sarcastic curtsey. The troll looks scandalized when I don't dip my head or avert my eyes, but I want these people to know I'm serious. If everything I've figured out so far tonight is true, they're aware they can't tell me this stupid secret outright or they will be in trouble. But I believe from the bottom of my sugar and spice Southern soul that the woman who dressed me did something that fucked with my glasses or my eyes. That's when I started noticing little shit and by the time we were inside this place, it was all revealed.

The question is still: why and who does it benefit?

"Miss Jolene Athena Whitley, Whistler's Hollow, United States of America," the troll finally says.

Mustering all the saccharine coated steel I can, I smile and say, "Charmed, I'm sure."

The snicker behind me says Teddy is amused as hell. This is the first time he's seen me use the assumptions about our roots to fool people, but it's not the first time I've used it. If Seer were here, she'd be bouncing with glee; turning on the 'Miss Scarlett' always made her giggle. A glance at the Queen says she's unimpressed, but the King nods at me like I've passed inspection.

"Welcome to our home, Miss Whitley. May the road rise to meet you." His wife sniffs, looking down her nose at me for a moment before ogling my men again.

Nope. Absolutely not.

"Thank you, sir. May I be so bold as to introduce my family? We're growing weary from our travels and would like to extend our gratitude before we must take our leave."

"Leaving your own party before it's over?" The first prince I danced with gives me a predatory look, his lips curved up as lounges in his chair. "I can't imagine that's acceptable in your land."

Batting my lashes, I tilt my head at him. "A lady must excuse herself if she cannot maintain a suitable demeanor in public. I merely offered to expedite our introductions so we might express our gratitude for your gracious treatment before it becomes necessary to take our leave."

"That was a lot of fifty cent words for 'I'm tired.' It's impressive," the second prince says as he shrugs. "Perhaps we should allow her to do it. I'm interested in her… point of view."

"Fine, fine," the King interrupts. "Let the girl speak."

Unsurprisingly, the princesses and the Queen haven't been asked their opinion. This may be my least favorite stop of the trip.

"Thank you again," I reply quickly, dipping in another curtsey before gesturing to Teddy. "This is Judge Edgar Oliver Boone III, son of Senator Boone, Whistler's Hollow, United States of America."

Teddy steps up beside me, standing close enough to make it obvious he's not simply a friend. Before he can open his mouth and fuck things up, I gesture to Wolfie and Doyle. Wolfie stands at my left and Doyle joins him as I continue. "This is Dr. Wolfgang Lucien Fletcher, also of Whistler's Hollow, and Doyle Aloysius Haggerty, Ireland."

I ignore the loud snorts from the princes as I continue. They clearly have more information than me, but at this point? I'll get it from someone else. These motherfuckers have their heads so far up their own asses they can see teeth and I'm over it. Waving my hand, I see Benjy and Prez come up next and paste a smile on my face. "Finally, we have Dr. Presley Hemingway Hamilton and Benjamin Louis Foster, of Tokyo and Whistler's Hollow, respectively. Together, my family would like to formally thank you for your hospitality."

Teddy steps in front of me, dipping his head once as he looks at the assembly on the dais. "I'm sure my father and our associates would love to express their gratitude as well. Please excuse our absence now that we've had the pleasure; we have check-ins to complete with our Guardians."

What the fuck is he talking about? Does this have to do with their secret shit?

The word seems to send a ripple through our hosts, though. They've been holding us hostage with formality, but now they actually look worried. The Queen is the one who sits up, nodding at Teddy as if she's been on his side all along.

"You are all excused, Mr. Boone. Please send our deepest regards."

I frown as I realize all the women are sitting up straighter, their expressions serious, and the room has gone silent as they get involved.

Son of a bitch. They're the ones in charge, not the idiot men.

Of fucking course, they are

AS WE EXIT THE CAR THAT SHOWED UP TO TAKE US BACK TO OUR guest house, I look at the outside. I can see it—the real facade—for the first time and it blows me away. It's a smaller version of the castle we were just trapped in, made for the guests of the royal twats. I guess it's supposed to make us feel important, but all I feel is pissed. I don't know the rules of this game, but I recognize that until the 'right moment,' I'm not able to let my men know their secrets are out. Jekyll was studying me the entire ride back and I'm pretty sure the fucking animals have figured it out.

Luckily, they can't talk—as far as I know.

Isis squeezes me and for the first time since she arrived, it occurs to me that no matter what I'm wearing, this big ass python fits under it. I almost facepalm as I walk towards the door; I couldn't have been more blind if I tried. Seriously, what the hell was wrong with me? The snake practically sinks into my skin, two wild cats adopted me, Teddy's dogs never leave my side, and a big ass eagle from another continent took up residence in my backyard. That *alone* should have tipped me off to something being off, but I walked around like a dumbass in front of everyone.

Shit, does everyone *in the Hollow know? No wonder the Nip/Tucks are snickering behind their hands.*

Fury boils up inside of me and I stomp past the guys, heading down the hallway to my room. Even if everyone is bound by this fucking oath, I'm still the village idiot. I passed *F.B.I.* exams, for fuck's sake! My observational skills were in the top one percent, but I didn't see that my hometown was some sort of Mystic Falls wanna-be. Pacing back and forth, I rub my temples, feeling the migraine pounding in my head like a band of gnomes banging out a Sousa march.

"Why me? Why was I singled out? What the hell is going on with my memory?" I growl under my breath, looking down at my flaming hands in exasperation. "Why doesn't this shit burn me?"

"*Mow!*" Jekyll says the cats hop up on the bed, sitting perfectly straight like statues.

I frown, looking around the room to see all the animals perched in various spots as they look at me expectantly. "Guys, I don't fucking know how to answer you. Hell, I don't know if you can talk or under-stand me. Can you understand me?"

Kali barks, then sits back on her haunches. My gaze roves to each of them, pressing my lips together as I think about this. They've always seemed to get what I'm saying, so that might be a 'yes.' Euryale makes a soft screeching sound, her wings flapping open, then closed before she settles on the dresser.

I'm probably losing my mind. They also listen to—

"Oh. Wolfie. You understand him, too." I wait, and none of them snuff like I'm stupid, so I assume I must be right. "Okay, so that's part of his… power… or whatever. He's obviously Fae and whatever his bitchy mom is. She's not Fae, for sure. Something old and power-ful, though, right?"

Hyde's tail twitches as she bobs her head. "*Mow.*"

I pull the sparkling shit out of my hair, letting it fall down my back with a relieved sigh. That helps more than I'd like to admit. "Right. So he's here to figure out his dad, who definitely isn't part of this Daybreak thing. But I bet that hybrid comment was about someone like him that's… half and half?"

This time, Hecate barks and I grin. *This is sort of working, but it's a shame I can't just talk to the guys.* While I think about my next question, I pull off the wings and undo the tight ass dress, looking down to see Isis emerging from my skin like a living tattoo. "What in the actual… goddamn it. How am I supposed to handle all of this at once?"

My snake squeezes me, and I know she's trying to help me cope with all the new knowledge being flung at me. That's *her* function—keeping me calm and even when I'm about to lose my shit. It's probably a shared duty and the fact that I need six animals here to watch me *should* frighten me, but it doesn't. If all this magical shit is real, then I suppose Fate is as well. That means everything that happens is…

Nope, not ready for that *realization yet. Putting that shit away for much later.*

"Wait a minute." I blink as the whole Catastrophe thing flashes in my mind. Why would the Richie-riches organize something that could possibly reveal them? Did they have that little control over their teens or…? *No.* "Son of a bitch. There *are* people in the Hollow who don't know about this shit. That prank was intended for that Lorelei girl, not me. Dad was *so* angry about mom for not pursuing it more…"

A brief memory makes me groan as I smack my forehead. My mother was part of this shit and my dad wasn't. She didn't go after the girls or even the boys because their families aren't just rich—they're neck deep in some supernatural hierarchy. That also explains Teddy and Benjy having odd shadows that seem to say they're like… weres? Shifters?

Fuck if I know.

But now I get why my parents were fine with me taking off and not coming back to town. Eloise decided I was a disappointment and my dad couldn't convince her otherwise. That's what that dream meant —I was supposed to be more, and I turned out to be nothing. She was always angry at me, just like I thought growing up. She'd adopted a damn lemon and couldn't return it.

My eyes prick with tears as I finish stripping off all the layers and walk to the dresser to pull out something to wear. There's a silky set of pajamas that looks like heaven, so I put them on. Once I'm no longer bound in girly shit, I look at my servals sadly. "I guess I'm more of a failure than I thought."

"*Mrrrrp,*" Jekyll says as he stares at me.

"You can disagree all you want, but obviously, whatever special shit I should have gotten isn't coming. I'm a dud," I grumble as I wave my hand at him. Then the fire on my hands interrupts my pity party and I blink. "Wait…"

This isn't the first weird thing that's happened since you came back.

Licking my lips, I listen to the voice in my mind as I consider the months since I returned to the Hollow. The dreams, the blackouts, the missing time, even the guys… Jesus Christ in a bourbon bottle, the sticks in my hair and leaves in my bed I couldn't explain. Something was happening and no one could tell me. I *am* changing; I'm just a late bloomer.

"But what am I going to do about this? I can't ask for help because I can't tell anyone I know. What if I hurt someone?"

There's no one to answer that, so I drop onto the bed next to Jekyll and Hyde, stroking my hands over their backs.

I need to figure out how to get information without putting anyone at risk, even if it means I don't tell anyone what the seamstress helped reveal.

Jolene Athena Whitley isn't human and the world just got a whole lot weirder.

Twin Peaks

Wolfgang

There's something going on with Sugarplum, but I can't put my finger on it.

She's been acting resigned since we arrived here, and it's not like her. Until she squared off with those Daybreak ninnies, I was worried she might sink into a funk. Jackson warned Teddy about that from her college years and seeing her look so tired had me concerned the weight of our secrets was making her spiral. But she stood next to us and damn near gave them the finger in the most polite way possible—behavior that's right out of her typical playbook. It made my chest loosen up, despite her angry retreat to her room alone last night.

Breakfast was lighthearted, though, and we packed up our shit quickly. I remembered how to use the Flit app to call a car to transport us from Daybreak to our next stop, and we took off. I was glad to leave this section of Faerie, to be honest. The royals seemed to have ulterior motives, which isn't odd for our species, but they seemed far too interested in causing trouble for us.

I can't help feeling like they knew something they held back — something important.

"What do you know about our next destination?" Doyle asks me as he lounges on the bench seat. He scratches his chin as he thinks. "It's been more than a dog's age since I've been there."

Pressing my lips together, I consider how to answer him. The Daybreak and Autumn Courts are both Seelie, which is why we started with them. They're not likely to be where my dad hails from, but they are the less devious Fae. I spent little time in Harvest on my journey here when I graduated from college. It's a beautiful place, but it didn't feel like *my* home, so I moved on. "If I remember correctly, the folks who live in this part of the countryside aren't as fanciful as our previous hosts. They're the quieter version, if that makes sense."

"I don't care if they're chatty; I only care if they act like douche canoes," Sugarplum says grumpily. "This is your notice, boys. If these fuckers try what the people at our last stop did, I will not be held responsible for whatever diplomatic issues I cause."

Teddy smirks as he tugs her closer, moving her onto his lap entirely. "Tilly, I've spent most of my life making as many headaches as I can for the Senator. I will not stop you as long as you're willing to accept the consequences."

Has he lost his damn mind? She doesn't even know what the consequences are.

"Uh, Boone? I'm not sure you should—"

He rolls his eyes, waving Prez off with a grin. "Our girl wants to make her own decisions. The bullshit we endured at the damn mansion last night made me re-evaluate our 'lie low' tactic. Perhaps we should throw a reverse Uno in the mix?"

I pinch the bridge of my nose as I think about his suggestion. Out of all the courts, Harvest is the least likely to take affront at bold, stand-offish behavior. They're calm and logical, with fewer airs than Daybreak and less power than the Unseelie courts. If there's a place to try the aggressive stance, this might be the one that doesn't get us killed. "We could try being more direct here. Compared to the next two stops, it probably won't cause a global incident. I think."

"You *think*?" Benjy says. "That doesn't fill me with confidence, doc."

"It's been a while since I was here, and I haven't followed the… changes. If their leaders have changed, I might be wrong. The leader was quite old when I last set foot in this place, B. One of her children may have taken over—worse, one of her children may have been married off in a treaty and someone unexpected is in control. That's how these people work."

Jolene frowns. "Arranged marriage is bullshit."

Finding out about the thing with Jamie has made her bitter, and I don't blame her.

"Not here, Sugarplum. It's just a part of life. Think about how old families at home twine the branches of their trees, or even the royals in monarchies like England. Sometimes kids grow up knowing it's part of their duty and they accept that."

"Or they don't, Wolfie. Look at Prince Harry. He gave them all the finger and I approve," she says firmly. "He never looked happy at all that royal shit when Seer and I were running around. I say good for him."

Doyle tilts his head, his eyes twinkling with mischief. "What if Fate has their own idea of arranged marriages, Tíogair? Maybe some people come together because the stars said it was so long before their bodies existed."

"Don't be a Miss Cleo weirdo," she mutters as she bends to stroke her hand over Hyde's head. "Obviously, there's no such thing as Fate. It's all butterfly wings flapping in China and the other stuff Jeff Goldblum said."

"What if both chaos and Fate can exist?"

I frown at the Irishman, unsure what the hell he thinks he's doing. The last thing we need is to play with the lines of our oath and he's drifting closer to No-man's-land by the second. "Maybe they do, but I don't see how that makes a difference. Arranged marriages are cultural, particularly to families like this, and my only point was if a princess ended up with someone from another land, it would complicate our plans."

Sugarplum grins as she looks up at me, and the glimmer in her eyes surprises me. "I'm not sure how anything could complicate this shit more than it already is. But if it does? Bring it on. I'm ready for whatever these people want to throw at me."

Unfortunately, I'm not sure I agree.

OUR ARRIVAL IN THE CENTER OF THE HARVEST CAPITAL CITY ISN'T AS auspicious as when we crossed into Daybreak. We didn't have to pass through an immigration check and our car rolled through the quaint, picturesque city without being accosted by an envoy. I'm not sure if that's a good thing or if it doesn't bode well—do the royals here not give a shit or are they biding their time? Given my admittedly thin amount of information on them, I presume the latter is the case.

"This place looks sort of like the Northeast… like Vermont or New Hampshire," Jolene murmurs as she looks out the window. "It's very Norman Rockwell and maple candy."

Prez gives me a knowing look as he nods. "Sure is, Magpie."

It's a pity she can't see all the burnished hues of glimmering copper, gold, and pewter covering the trees and gilded stone buildings.

"It seems less Hunger Games here than our first stop," Teddy says as he strokes his fingers through my hair. "The outfits at the ball, the behavior of the high and mighty… it was all a bit too pretty dystopian for me. Is everything there like that, or was it a facade for guests?"

Sighing, I ponder that. Everywhere has class systems, but humans have damn near everyone beat on the divide they've cultivated. "There are less fortunate parts of all the lands. But nothing as starkly obvious as we see in our big cities at home. At least, nothing I've seen or heard about. You know cities like the Hollow have disparity, but not at the level of other places. It's similar for our hosts here."

"While I was traveling, I was most shocked to find out how much the rest of the world is not what gets taught in our schools. Seer and I went all over—small to large nations—and it was so obvious we'd been fed bullshit. I remember being so disappointed that most people would never know any of it, you know? Is it like that?" Jolene looks at me seriously, her emerald eyes glinting with a cunning that feels out of place.

"Aye, lass. It's a bit like that in the places we'll be going. People love to tell stories about things they don't know about and once your eyes are opened, the world becomes a very different place."

I glare at Doyle, then cut my eyes to the rest of the guys. This jackass is really doing a tango along the lines and I'd prefer *not* to be called to a trial for violating one of the biggest tenets of the Society. "Knowledge always changes your perspective. If it doesn't, you're not really learning anything."

"Sometimes information changes the course of your entire life, so I agree."

Out of all of us, Benjy's the poster child for having his world turned upside down; finding out he had a fated mate made him up-end his entire life.

"How are you doing with that, man?" I squint at him, wondering how he found the courage to enrage a beast like Sherilynn and do what made him happy, regardless of the consequences.

His smile is genuine as he shrugs. "I'm happy where I am now. Boone helped me get the demon off my back long enough to escape with you guys. What I'll come back to is totally unpredictable—Mom's buried in her research up at State U with that Shadwell woman. My dad is… well, he's no better than Edgar's, as you know."

"Are they pissed at you?" Presley asks softly. "My parents haven't been an active part of my life for a long time, so I forget what it's like to have meddling bio donors around."

"At least you know who the fuck yours are," Doyle grumbles. I hold my fist out to him and he bumps it, grinning a bit. "Pup and I are chasing raging sociopaths around. Though I suppose the judge has his two a bit close for comfort."

"Mine are dead." I blanch at Sugarplum's blunt words and she shakes her head. "No, it's fine. I made my peace with that a long time ago, guys. I wasn't playing 'who has the worst sob story.' We're hunting down info on what really happened to them, but it doesn't… I'm not opening old wounds or anything."

I wonder if she knows her aura is vibrating with blues and blacks that reflect her genuine emotions.

"No one would fault you if it did. Making peace with their deaths differs from finding out they might have been killed on purpose." I reach over my head, holding my hand out to her. When our palms touch, a zap of energy flows between us, filling me with her confusion, sadness, and anger. She's not nearly as okay as she wants us to believe.

Teddy's eyes meet mine and I nod slightly. He rests his chin on Jolene's head, murmuring low. "Just because they weren't perfect doesn't mean you don't love them. The Senator and my mother are the only parents I've ever known even if they're dicks. That shit scars you in ways it's impossible to predict."

Closing my eyes, I project the roiling emotions hanging in the air to the companions. Kali and Hecate move to Prez and Benjy, while Jekyll and Hyde flank the two of us that Teddy's commandeered. The screech above the car tells me Eury would like to join, but the space here isn't conducive to the large eagle. She'll have to wait until we arrive at the hotel. It shouldn't be much longer now.

Everything quiets and by the time the car stops, the bleakness has faded from the group. I smile as I feel the vibe even out, glad I could help. Teddy ruffles my hair, making me blush, but when I catch Sugarplum's eyes, she's watching me like I'm a puzzle she's trying to figure out.

Shit. That might have been too obvious.

"What's wrong?" I venture carefully.

Her eyes crinkle, and she gives me a gentle smile. "You're just a wonderful person and you don't get enough credit for your big heart, darling boy. I feel like all of you have… roles in our family and it's why we work. Yours is the soft underbelly and warm heart."

"And yours is the center of our world, Sugarplum. Never forget that."

Before she can respond, the door to the car opens and a tall set of ginger-haired twins are giving us wide, jack-o'-lantern grins.

"Welcome to Harvest Grove, land of cozy fires and spiraling towers."

Great. We've been met by the damn Tweedles.

Slow Me Down

Jolene

Blinking at the twins, I take a second to gather my wits. They seem harmless enough—not at all like the serious Fae in our welcome wagon in the last Court—but I don't trust anyone here as far as I could throw them. There's too much at risk to fall into a trap like I did with that friendly designer who messed with the glasses. Hyde makes a low growling sound next to me, and within seconds, the rest of the animals are flanking me.

Quite a merry band of protectors I'm amassing.

"Thank you for meeting us. I'm Jol—"

"We know," they chirp in unison. "Word of your arrival came through the grapevine."

Teddy grunts, muttering under his breath, "Fucking spooky."

He means their twin bullshit, not the gossip, and I agree. Pressing my lips together, I try not to get annoyed and have fire pop out of my hands. It's hard enough to cover up my newfound knowledge in front of the guys when we're in private, much less with an audience. Once I'm calm, I paste a smile on, cloaking myself in the Southern belle persona I've been using to deal with the wily jackholes in this land.

"How convenient! I find repeating myself tiresome, especially after traveling." Batting my lashes, I tilt my head like I'm curious. "And who might you be?"

They smirk and I can tell this twin thing must really work for them with the ladies. "We are the regents of your hosts in the city. Mick and Mack Stuart, at your service."

Okay, that was kind of impressive.

Doyle steps up, rolling his eyes at their antics. "Alright, lads. We get it. You have the twin mind meld going for you. It's not as charming or special as you think."

The twin on the left—I *think* it's Mick—gives him a wicked grin. "We know who you are, Haggerty, and it's not one of us. But I believe you *do* know about twins."

"Aye, he does. Not his mum, but in the same ballpark," Mack adds. "Sadly, none of them want to claim him, so he pretends."

I hide a grin as I tuck away new information about my chaotic lover. Despite not understanding what the hell it means, I know it'll be useful later. I reach over to grab Doyle's arm before he shoots back a response. I refuse to stand here all day and play games. "Great. Now that we've agreed twins are fucking annoying, can we please head to our rooms? The animals are hungry and frankly, so I am. I'd be happy to give them permission to find a snack right here if we're going to be detained."

Wolfie chuckles as he ruffles Jekyll's fur. "Not a bad idea, Sugarplum. They look big enough to feed them all. I'm sure Isis will clean up the leftovers."

As if summoned, the large python slithers her head out of my sleeve, flicking her tongue at the ginger bastards menacingly. I grin as her head fills my palm. "She definitely would."

Instead of looking concerned, the duo sigh and gesture at the large hotel we're in front of. "Be our guest. We would hate to make our new friends uncomfortable. Take your time and we will send an envoy to discuss your audience with our employers this evening."

My eyes narrow. "It had better not be a team to fucking dress up like dolls again."

Their eyes dance as they shrug and I groan internally. If this shit is going to happen in every new location, I might scream. I've let Seer use me as her personal doll for many years, but as far as I know, she's never tried to cause an international incident while doing so. Unfortunately, I also realize that if I don't *pretend* to play their games, I won't get to the people who might give us intel on Wolfie's dad.

I'm good at politics, but I fucking hate them so much.

Luckily for me, His Honor steps in smoothly. "Your envoys will find us much more amenable after some rest. Please pass on our gratitude for your welcome and we look forward to speaking with your employers later."

"Exactly," I add, as I smile prettily. "Teddy said it perfectly."

"Understood. Please enjoy your suite," they chirp before saluting and heading off down the street.

"So fucking weird," Benjy says as he grabs the bags out of the trunk. "Can't say I'm a fan."

"It's worse when they're male and female," Doyle says as he takes the rest of them out of the trunk. "I can attest to that."

Shaking my head, I wait until the redheads disappear around a corner before I respond. "I get the feeling they won't be the only troublemakers we run into—just the most obvious ones."

"Why's that, Magpie?" Presley says as we walk to the doors of the hotel.

"Just like animals, these folks are hiding the real dangers behind the pretty, colorful things they throw in our faces. We have to look deeper than the peacocking the flunkies do if we want to get what we need and not get hurt."

"I think she's right," Teddy rumbles. "We'll adjust our strategy when these 'envoys' show up. And this time, no one is to be alone with them. I have a bad feeling about being divided."

As well he fucking should—that's why I'm in this damn mess.

"MAGPIE, ARE YOU TALKING TO THE CATS?"

My face turns bright red as Prez wakes up, shifting to reach over me to get his glasses. Realizing the movement will wake everyone up from the much needed nap, I scramble to put my frames on while he yawns and stretches. I didn't mean to wake any of them; I just have so many things to run past my companions, so I have a better chance at winning the game they keep insisting we play.

"I might be bouncing things off the animals. It's not crazy," I grumble as Wolfie stirs at my waist. "They can't talk back, so I get to untwist things in my mind without being interrupted."

"What do you need to untwist, Princess?"

I smile as Benjy looks over Teddy's shoulder, his big brown eyes soft. "Not you guys. I'm… slowly making my peace with that. More like, I'm trying to figure out how we can find out who Wolfie's dad is." I pause and shrug. "I'm also a little worried about Seer? She hasn't checked in for a bit and it makes me worry."

"We can call her," Doyle says as he pops his head up next to Prez's. "Boone's got an emergency phone for that sort of thing in his bag. Should work and then you'll have one thing off your plate."

"Think it'll work to call the Sheik and Hugo, too? They have to be wondering what the hell we're doing by now." I frown for a second, not liking that it didn't occur to me until this moment. "I hope they don't think we're leaving them out."

"I doubt that's the case, Sugarplum. You can call Seer first, while we rotate through this tiny shower. Then you get clean and while the rest of us finish, you check in with Amiri." Wolfie smiles as he drips a kiss on my belly button.

The location makes me flush pink and I grumble a little. "Alright, none of that. If you start that shit up, none of us will be ready and no phone calls will get made."

"I mean…"

My glare is sub zero as I look at Teddy. "Not an option, Your Honor. The Chair moves the committee gets their asses out of bed and moving before their supply chain is subject to budget cuts."

The room is silent for a moment, then Doyle howls with laughter. "That might be the fanciest way I've ever heard a woman say she's cutting me off. Good on you, Tíogair."

"The judge from the great state thinks the Chair has let power go to her pretty head." Teddy winks at me as he wiggles out of the pile and stretches. My eyes glaze as I watch the taut abs and bobbing cock like I'm hypnotized, then I snort.

"Good try, but we really do have shit to do. We can role play procedural shit later," I retort. "Move it, boys. Mama needs the bathroom before you all steam it up."

"You just said mama," Wolfie calls as I speed walk to the closed door.

Absolutely fucking not.

"Don't even *dream* that shit or I'll make you wake up and apologize!"

I have to keep these assholes in line every second or they'll push their way past my barriers for sure.

And that's one I'm not budging on.

I SHOWERED ALONE, WHICH HELPED ME FINISH MORE QUICKLY, BUT also gave me time to inspect myself without anyone noticing.

What a goddamn revelation that *was.*

It says a lot about your mental resiliency when you can find four bites, two burned brands, and a bunch of sparkly fucking tattoos you don't remember receiving and shrug it off. Honestly, it's a credit to my therapist and I probably owe her a spa gift card. All these marks having been hidden by whatever the fuck bullshit magic is swirling around the Hollow, me, and everyone else I know.

I'm not stupid—I've watched enough shows like *True Blood* or *Buffy* to understand these are some kind of claiming mark. They obviously correspond to the guys, but not all of them, and that I'm unsure about. The sparkly shit is clearly my darling boy, and at least one bite must belong to my canine alpha counterpart. Aside from that, I haven't figured out what is what because I *think* more than one may belong to each of them.

This constant sleuthing is getting exhausting and I'm going to nut punch the person responsible.

"So they can see this shit… but can everyone else?" I make a face in the mirror as I dry my hair. "Can that cuntmuffin Sherilynn *see* these boys are mine and *still* come after me? I bet she can; she's fucking deficient that way."

I sigh as the possibilities tumble through my mind. I will not figure it all out today, nor is anyone going to help me until this big 'moment' they're waiting for happens. I have to keep gathering info and be patient—something I'm not known for doing.

Picking up the phone Teddy left me, I punch in the numbers for my bestie. I'd love to muddle this out with Seer, but she's neck deep in this shit and banned from helping me. So much for guarding me or whatever the hell she said her job was. I wonder if people with that job ever lose their charges? Seer has definitely almost lost me a couple times because of my shit, so I'd bet they have.

It would suck ass to figure out you have weird supernatural powers with no explanation or people around you to help you cope—probably fuck your brain up for good.

"Go for Saoirse."

The chipper tone of my friend makes me smile and warmth spreads throughout my chest. Even on the phone, hearing her helps me find my center. *Is that magic or just friendship?* I don't care, but I never want to lose it. "Seer! I miss you. Where the hell are you?"

A pause on the line trips my wires and I hear muffled shuffling around before she answers. "I'm on an assignment overseas. Where are you, Peanut? Still in bonny Ireland?"

"Mmm hmm. We're at the second stop on this Magical Mystery Tour of the old country," I say carefully. I know she won't give anything away, but I want her to wonder what I know. It feels like appropriate vengeance since everyone but me is allowed to know what's going on.

Her laugh is soft. "Always the jokester, Peanut. I've been running around for weeks trying to get cut loose so I can come see you. The bosses just won't let me go, and you can't really say 'no' to their clients. So I'm stuck, but you can catch me up. Tell me about the people you've met and everything that's happened since you met with your puppy's mum."

"It started with these jackasses who gave us crap at this customs gate…"

I Would Do Anything For Y

Benjy

Thinking you're sheltered and *knowing* it are two very different things.

My mom married old Vlad when I was five. No one ever discussed my bio dad and I'm not sure she even knew who he was—that's why the only person I consider my father is the asshole incubus who adopted me after they got hitched. He's never thought I lived up to his expectations, especially because he's the town prosecutor and a retired agent for the Society. In contrast, I went to college, played ball, and didn't go to law school or take the agent qualifications. I married Sherilynn as agreed, which he was all for, but then I used my business degree to open the restaurant and the bar.

Vladimir Simon Foster thinks we're above 'small town pizza and beer,' so he practically ignored me after that. In fact, he stayed away right until he was in the thick of convincing me to adopt the kids with Sherilynn. The twins and their older sister aren't related by blood, nor are they any combination of supes that fit with Sherilynn or I. But my 'dad' was gung-ho and Sheri just wanted to make him happy so he'd include us in Society shit.

Before my best friend convinced me to tag along on this trip, I'd only ever left the Hollow for college and the games I played there. I sure as hell didn't come to Faerie or journey across Europe. For all her worldly affectations, my ex-wife preferred being queen bee at home rather than a tiny fish in a big pond elsewhere. Plus, someone had to keep the businesses running. Her interest in Derby Pies only piqued when it was part of the divorce settlement—not a second before.

All of this shit is brand new to me, despite emerging as a teen, so I get why the Princess is so stressed out.

"Fucking unbelievable," I mutter to myself as we walk into a large throne room surrounded by *walls* of bookshelves floor to ceiling.

If I'd thought the over-the-top fancy crap in the Daybreak Court was a bit much, this place is even worse. It's different: huge cozy fireplace crackling, large overstuffed chairs for thrones, thick rugs, and an atmosphere of crisp autumn permeating the air. But it's also insanely ornate and full of random people milling about with wine and cider as the royals look down from their perch in front of the flames.

Princess grabs my arm, squeezing it, and I smile. Her eyes glitter as she looks at all the books, and I know she's thinking about how much information they store here. Even when we were kids, Jolene was smart as a whip. The years since college, all her education and experience, have only increased her ability to look at shit in ways others don't.

That's why I've always known her secret—she knew taking that girl's place at the cotillion would end in horror, but she did it anyway.

"You're awfully quiet, big guy. That's not unusual, but your brow is furrowed like you're working out a play."

Blinking in surprise, I tilt my head to look at our girl. "Princess, how would you know what I look like when I'm working out a play?"

She rolls her eyes, sighing heavily. "Benjamin Louis Foster. There was literally *nothing* to do in the Hollow on Friday nights if you didn't go to the game. I didn't give a fuck about winning, but I enjoyed watching people. Figuring out how people will behave has been one of my talents for a long time."

"Ah, but you weren't just watching the QB like he assumes," I tease as we walk around the big room. "He'll be crushed."

"There is *nothing* that could dent Teddy's ego. Pull on the other leg before they get uneven," Jolene snorts, then hides her mouth with her hand as a snooty-looking Fae gives her a glare. "Why is this place set up like a library? Are the people up there our hosts? And where are those blasted, annoying twins?"

"Whoa, there, Princess. That's a lot of questions for one breath." My eyes cut to her hands, making sure she isn't getting too riled. Edgar might touch that without getting hurt and maybe his pet vet, too, but I'm not taking the chance I'll get accidentally crisped. "Close your eyes and let the calm flow through you. That's what your yoga boyfriends keep saying."

Jolene draws in a slow breath and breathes it out of her nose loudly. When I chuckle, she wrinkles her nose. "The docs are good yoga partners because they're very placid. That's true. But you're not easily riled yourself—not like Lucky or Teddy."

"Uh, we don't need more than the three of you with short fuses. I'm pretty sure that's enough plastic explosive in the group. Plus, I never would have survived a decade with Sherilynn if I was easily angered."

Oh, shit.

Instead of being mad that I mentioned my ex-wife, Jolene simply laughs and squeezes my arm again. "I don't think you could have said that any more nicely than you did. She's the worst and I admire your ability to talk about it without resorting to nastiness. It's very mature, Benjy."

I stay quiet for a moment, thinking about that as we stop at the bar. She orders us each a bourbon—thank hell they have something normal—and I sip mine before I answer. "Sheri and I were the product of old-fashioned parents playing weird politics. We were both told we should be together as teens, then stayed together at college. After that, we made the leap to marriage because our parents said it was the right move. Neither of us were strong or smart enough to question that premise once we were old enough to do so."

"I don't think—"

"Give me a moment, Princess. You'll agree once you hear the rest. I know you'd like to defend me, but I was honestly dumb as a post with blindly following what my dad said." She nods and I sip again, then continue. "Even as young as middle school, he held up the idea that him and my mom are proof that two different people can come together for a purpose and be happy. I believed him and although Sherilynn and I were never actually happy, I obeyed because I wanted him to be proud. Obviously, it never worked."

"But why? You have two great businesses, people love you, and I can't imagine you not being a good spouse or dad." Princess frowns, her expression frustrated as we head over towards the far end of the room where the docs are chatting with two scholarly looking Fae.

"I didn't go into law and Sheri couldn't conceive and give him grand-children. Not my fault, but he acted as though it was. He recruited my mom to help push adopting the kids. I gave in to that demand as well, which was a bad idea, given the state of our marriage. She's raised those kids to despise me as much as she and my father do."

Her eyes narrow, and she stops in place, whirling to look at me. "That's not right, and I won't stand for it."

"Jolene, it's okay. I mean, it's not, but it is, you know?" Pulling her into my arms, I hug her close, figuring out how to express this without saying something I'm forbidden to. "I'm not a big believer in a lot of woo-woo shit, but I think things happen for a reason. You came to town, and the world filled with color. I quit ignoring things I should have dealt with long ago. Now, I'm halfway around the world with you, my best friend, a bunch of zoo animals, and a squad of fellow oddballs. My life is changing for the better, so I don't want to focus on the hurt from the past."

She licks her lips, looking thoughtful for a second before she nods. "Yeah, I think I get that. There are things I know will upset me coming—you told me so. But... I don't know if I want to trade right-eous anger for the good things I feel now."

I smirk at her, knowing what she's talking about. "I think you'll give us all hell—which we deserve—but you'll also realize we only want to protect you. It doesn't leave us with a lot of appealing choices, but life is full of times where the only options are bad ones. That doesn't mean you can't be upset; it only means you have to weigh your anger against what you truly want."

"What I want," she grumbles as we move again, "is alone time with all of you tonight. So these motherfuckers had better wrap up their welcome party early or I'm going to ruin their night like I did the last hosts. And for the love of Dionysius' pet goats, *someone* better have info on Wolfie's dad. I'm tired of wasting time on dead ends."

"I can promise you the first part if everyone behaves, but the second might be above my paygrade. You might have to see what the hell Boone and Haggerty are doing before we confirm that one."

Our girl winks at me as we join the docs and I feel my chest expand with happiness. As long as I get to stay with her, I'll be able to move on from the bullshit of the past. Together, I think our family will get over the big secret when she finally emerges, but that's only if all the players do their part.

Unfortunately, that's not entirely within my control.

"Thank you for the invitation to this... salon?"

I hide my grin behind my hand, staying at the back of the group as we're introduced to the Harvest Court royals. The irritating Tweedle Twins—as Princess calls them—homed in on us as soon as we joined the docs. It took a few minutes to locate Edgar and Doyle, but once we did, they immediately escorted our group to the raised platform by the fireplace.

"Yes, we *adore* bringing together the most interesting minds to mingle and share ideas. When Mick and Mack informed us you were journeying to our home, we simply *had* to arrange a get together. Isn't that right, Hieronymus?"

The little old man in a tweed suit with elbow patches looks like a college professor, not the King of the Harvest Court. But he beams at us as his much younger wife gushes at our girl in a very familiar way. I'm not sure what the guy knows about the cougar he married, but if she doesn't quit eye-fucking the docs, Princess is going to dig them right of the sockets for her.

"Quite so, pumpkin," the short royal says as he nods at us. "I am excited to learn why we are graced with such an impressive group from across the pond. I'm sure Allora will be as well."

"Yes, she fawns over new people," the dark-haired queen mutters.

Huh. She doesn't like this chick, so given my experience, I'll assume it's the step-daughter.

"Is Allora your daughter?" Jolene looks at the Mr. Magoo wanna-be like he's a kindly librarian and a bad feeling lodges in my gut. "Will she be joining us tonight?"

"Very subtle, Tilly," Edgar says as he glares at the Queen. She's ogling Prez and Wolfie again, but it's getting more obvious. He might be more trouble than our girl if the woman doesn't knock it off.

"Why, yes, she is!" The King claps and hops down from his immense chair. "Come, Miss Whitley. I'd love for you to meet her. She's with her new fiancé amongst our brilliant guests. Allora prefers not to sit in her rightful chair; it's the youth these days. Always rebelling against traditions, you know."

Jolene's eyes widen as he offers his arm despite his head only reaching her ribcage. I'm about to intervene when I see the old-fashioned breeding kicking in. Her eyes soften and she accepts his arm graciously, even adding a small curtsey before allowing him to lead her down the stairs. Turning to my old friend, I murmur, "We need to follow her."

"On it," Doyle says as he brushes past us. "Anyone else coming?"

I watch as the sparkling wings of our vet flutter. He mumbles an excuse to the Queen, ignoring her disappointed clucking as he pulls Presley along with him. Once they join Teddy and me, we make our escape. Doyle's bright red hair isn't as good a beacon in this land; there're gingers everywhere, as well as many people with various yellow and orange tones. It makes sense for the Harvest kingdom, but it's also annoying as hell when you're tracking someone.

"There she is," Teddy growls as he drags us throughout a knot of people blocking the way. "I can smell her. And... something else familiar."

The laughter of our girl and a tinkling giggle are our greeting as we finally get through the group of Fae. My eyes widen as I look at a gorgeous woman in a very similar dress to the one they gave Jolene, except hers is in deep gold and reds. The king is looking at them both fondly, which I take as a good sign until I see the man standing off to the side. I feel the growl of my friend as it leaves his chest, and I know we've found at least one thing we were looking for: a clue about the pup's father.

"Gentleman! I would like to introduce my daughter, Princess Allora, and her fiancé, Alistair Silkshine of the Midnight Court."

"How very *interesting* it is to meet all of you." The wicked grin of the fiancé is a dead giveaway. He's tall, muscled, and has hair like a raven's wing that tumbles over his shoulders onto his deep purple suit. The look is supposed to evoke mystery, but given his bone structure and the pattern on his sparkling wings…? It doesn't.

There's no doubt in my mind Wolfgang Fletcher is Unseelie and this motherfucker knows something.

The question is… what will we have to pay to find out?

Girl on Fire

Jolene

A flutter of anxiety beats its wings against my ribcage as I look at Allora, her gown a cascade of fiery autumn colors pooling at her feet. The dark Fae, Alistair Silkshine, is leaning against a marble column like he's part of the architecture—sinuous and permanent. His smirk makes me want to smack it off him and I have to pull the reins on my temper once again.

Pretending I'm not aware of everything going on gets harder with every moment, especially because some of these people are determined to fuck with me.

"It's an honor to meet you both. I'm Edgar Boone," Teddy says as he extends his hand, taking the Princess' and kissing her knuckles. I dislike him touching someone other than our family, but I realize he has to follow the protocols. "May I introduce my companions? This is Jolene, Benjy, Doyle, Wolfgang, and Presley. We're visiting your land on a research trip."

"Charmed," she replies, her voice the tinkling of crystal in a still room. She gives us all a bright smile, but I can see her intelligence sparkling in her green eyes. Allora is downplaying herself much like I am and when I realize why, it makes me grin at myself.

The Princess wants her fiancé to believe she's less capable than she is—their marriage must be very strategic to her future rule here.

"Enchantment's in the air tonight. Or, perhaps, that's the effects of a new presence in our midst? The allure of the Southern belle has always fascinated me, I must confess. The movies make your people seem so… captivating," Alistair drawls with his eyes locked on me. His words are both a caress and a slap—a velvet glove over an iron fist used to taunt my companions.

"Bless your heart, Alistair. You shouldn't believe everything you see in the media. If I did that, I might make very inaccurate assumptions about gentlemen without knowing their true nature," I return tersely, ignoring the itch under my skin that threatens the fire I'm trying to hold in. "That would be a grave tragedy, I'm sure."

Teddy smothers a snort behind his hand and I feel the tension in my guys' release slightly. "Excellent point, Tilly. As always, you know how to set the record straight in the most elegant way possible."

"She is lovely," the tiny King says with a clueless smile. "Don't you agree, Allora?"

The Princess eyes me for a moment, arching a brow as she studies me closer. "Oh, I agree, Father. Miss Jolene is quite the addition to our soirée."

Shit. She's going to be harder to fool than any of the men here.

"Perhaps Alistair would enlighten us," Doyle says as he narrows his eyes at the gorgeous Fae. "He looks keen to share his vast knowledge."

I tilt my head as I look at the cagey male, making sure I project the doe-eyed belle he accused me of being. "That would help our search. Alistair, do you have information you think we'd be interested in knowing? I'd be obliged to know anything you think is important."

"Information on what, exactly? My dear, you wound me with your directness." The Fae laughs, the sound low and wicked as his eyes dance with glee. "I'm merely an honored guest in this house, much like the lot of you. I'm not privy to any secrets or coveted knowledge in this place."

Allora purses her lips and I catch the look of annoyance she gives him. While the King is happily doddering along, she's likely keeping this court afloat and having to marry a smarmy son of a bitch like this to claim her birthright *has* to chafe. I feel she'd like to jump in and correct him, but her dim façade is preventing her from doing so.

I get it, girl. Being a woman sucks rocks when you live in a world built to cater to men and their fragile egos.

"How disappointing," Benjy says as his fingers touch my elbow lightly. The contact helps calm my sparking nerves and I breathe slowly while he diverts their attention. "Hieronymous' introduction made me think you were more integral to their family than a simple guest."

Smart, smart man.

Alistair bristles, and Teddy's grin turns absolutely feral. That tell gives him a weakness and as long as I've known Edgar Boone, he's never been one to ignore an opening. "Obviously, we've journeyed a long way and mere pleasantries aren't enough to capture our attention. Allora, thank you again for gracing us with your companionship, but we'll be—"

"Ah, but simplicity does not preclude substance," Alistair interrupts with a mischievous expression. "There are many truths I am aware of —not all of them can be shared. Your family has not asked the right questions, I fear."

I can see the gears turning in his head and the glint of malicious glee in his eyes. He'd love to violate the guys' oath for them, but they have not given him an opportunity to do so without implicating himself. If we press him to get information about Wolfie's dad, we need to be *very* careful or he might complicate our lives even further just to amuse himself.

Like all the royal Fae I've met so far, beneath the sparkling, pretty outside lies a conniving, chaos loving troublemaker with minds as sharp as thorns.

"He's enjoying the game," Wolfie murmurs as his fingers lace with mine. His jaw is clenched as he lifts soulful blue eyes to mine. "Be careful, Sugarplum. We don't know what he'll reveal—including things we'd prefer to remain in the dark."

"Games are the spice of life, *pup*," Alistair taunts.

Wolfie winces and the irritation rolling off Teddy slams into me like a wave of hot lava. If I didn't realize it before, I definitely know now—

the fire has something to do with the man who broke my heart as a teen. When he's angry, my blood heats and the itch ramps up inside of me.

And he absolutely wants to beat the shit out of Alistair for calling Wolfie 'pup.'

I lean into Teddy, looking up at him for a moment until the temperature cools a little, then I turn back to the irksome Fae. "It's very bold to assume you can use a nickname with one of my beaus, Alistair. I highly doubt you'd like one of them to call Allora 'sweetheart,' now would you?"

His dark eyes narrow at my barb and he opens his mouth to retort when a loud tinkling fills the room. King Hieronymous claps his hands, looking giddy as he hops in place a bit. Allora smiles softly as she watches him and I immediately understand why she's taking part in this bullshit arranged crap. She adores her father, and whatever they need from Alistair's people is desperate enough to force her hand.

"That's the call for dinner?" Presley says, pushing his glasses up as he glances at our hosts. "I hope so, because I'm absolutely famished."

"You are correct," Allora says as she turns back to us. "You'll be seated at the head table with us once the staff is ready. Perhaps you'd like to head for the washrooms briefly while they set the room?"

Her eyes cut to the guys, and I have to bite my lip to keep from giggling. Obviously, she wants me out of this room while magical shit happens and she doesn't know how else to tell them to yeet me out of the space.

"I think that would be perfect," Presley replies. "Come, Magpie. We'll freshen up while they get ready, and then we can feed you. It's been a long time since lunch."

He's not wrong about that, but I feel dinner will not sit well with any of us.

WHEN WE RETURN FROM OUR SOJOURN TO THE MOST LAVISH bathrooms I've ever been in, there's a long table at the front of the room set for ten people. It's perpendicular to the immense chairs where the King and Queen were sitting when we arrived and the rest of the room was dotted with circular tables for the other 'salon' guests.

I'm not excited about round two of 'Guess Who's Not Going To Get Dinner,' but I don't think we have a choice.

"What a lovely table," I say as we approach the table. The King looks chuffed and Allora smiles gratefully, but I notice the Queen is still looking down her nose at us. She's certainly part of why the princess is playing a role, but I'm not sure how yet. Truth be told, it's not my circus, so I shouldn't care, but… I can't help but empathize. Allora's surrounded by sharks and she's clearly the only one concerned about it.

Alistair pulls the chair out for his fiancée, but his gallantry ends when he shrugs. "They have a quaint notion of grandeur here; I agree."

"Quaint enough to warrant your attendance," Teddy grumbles under his breath and I smother a laugh. He definitely does not like this asshole, and I don't blame him. We have more than enough problems without a smirking fuckwad trying to weasel his way to a big reveal.

"Indeed, it is." Alistair joins Allora at the table, gesturing for the rest of my guys to sit. "Sit and be merry with us, friends. I'd hate for you to miss all the fun."

"Fun's one word for it," I mutter as Wolfie claims the seat to my right and Prez flanks him. Benjy takes Teddy's right, winking at me as Doyle plops down beside him.

At least the most volatile men are surrounded by calmer heads—that is, if I can keep myself from flaming out.

"Jolene has a fiery spirit," Alistair observes, his voice low and teasing.

My head pops up and I look at my hands surreptitiously before glaring at him. He's full of shit—I'm not on fire—and I have no idea how this dickwaffle knew to push that button. A surge of warmth comes from Teddy again and I place my palm on his forearm to help him center himself. I'm not sure if he's always had this much trouble quelling his… powers… or if this place is making it hard on him. Either way, the jerk in front of us is just dying to make him lose his shit.

"Careful, darling, wouldn't want to burn down the castle."

A soft growl rumbles out of my dominant lover, but I ignore it to snap at the taunting royal. "Wouldn't dream of it. This library is far too amazing to risk, especially since we have had little luck finding useful sources of information for our research."

"You wound me, Miss Jolene," he says as he laughs. "I promise to be much more candid after the food is served. I'm sure you'll want to wait until your bellies are full before we get into the meat of our discussion."

Doyle gives him a pointed look, finally speaking up as he points a sharp knife at the smug prince. "I'm quite certain our girl isn't interested in anymore meat. She's got a veritable smorgasbord to choose from as it is."

I blink, my face turning bright red as the princess muffles a giggle, and the King looks at us all in confusion. My gaze flicks to the satisfied looking Irishman, and he shrugs as the knife spins on his palm like he's a goddamn circus performer. "I... uh..."

"Don't worry, Jolene. I'm told all men are like dogs. No matter how hard you try, some of them never learn not to piddle on the carpet." Allora gives me a tiny grin as she picks up her water glass to take a sip and I damn near choke on the laugh that tumbles out.

Maybe this girl isn't so bad, after all. I think Seer would like her a lot.

Come At Me

Edgar

The ceiling of the Harvest Court's dining hall stretches above us like a cathedral to decadence, garlands of golden wheat and ruby-red apples cascading down stone pillars. The tiny absent-minded King presides at the head of the table, his eyes crinkling with delight as he listens to Doyle recount an absurdly embellished version of our experience in the Daybreak Court.

His daughter is eyeing the Irishman warily, but I think it's because she knows he's full of shit.

"By the roots and berries!" King Hieronymous exclaims, utterly oblivious to the undercurrents swirling beneath the surface of our polite conversation. "You lot have had quite the adventure!"

"Indeed we have," I reply smoothly. "But everyone has shown us generous hospitality, even if it's sometimes difficult for us to navigate in the circumstances."

Alistair leans back in his chair, a silver goblet poised at his lips. His gaze rests on Wolfie, who fidgets beside Tilly, his knee bouncing like a metronome of anxiety. I reach out and place a hand on his thigh, feeling the tremor beneath my touch. I don't like how this fucker is purposefully torturing him and it's making all my supe sides riot. It's been a long time since I felt this out of control with my powers; I spent a great deal of time in my teens with Bane learning to tamp down the hound and applying that knowledge to the other two.

However, an ill-intentioned fuckknuckle using my family for his amusement is activating the alpha protective mode.

Cracking my neck as I check on the others, I note Benjy is actively trying to keep the demigod from overloading. That helps and I'm grateful to my old friend. Tilly can take care of herself whether I want her to or not; that much is becoming more obvious by the day. But Wolfie is a far more damaged soul than her and the vibes coming off of him make me want to shift and pin this motherfucker to the wall until he cries 'uncle.'

"Your mother must be quite the character," Alistair says to my pup, his eyes glinting with mischief. "From what I understand, you didn't make her acquaintance until late in life, but her infamy casts an enormous shadow, I imagine."

Jolene's nails dig into my arm and I know she's telling me to keep my cool. Alistair told us he wasn't aware of gossip and intrigue among the courts, but knowing who Wolfie's mother is betrayed the lie in that statement. If he knows that tidbit, he also knows we're looking for his dad, and that's why the jackass is toying with us.

He's got information we need—whether it's rumors or fact doesn't matter.

"Callie has her moments," Wolfie responds in a tight voice. He doesn't look at the smirking Fae; instead, he pretends to fiddle with his napkin.

I catch the other doc putting a hand on his leg to help ground him and once again, I'm thankful for the less dominant members of our group. They provide a balance we sorely need, especially as Tilly hasn't found her true nature yet. I don't know if the two missing suitors will add to that or tip the scales, but for now, I'll take what I can get.

"You seem to be an enigma," Alistair continues, swirling the wine in his cup with a casual flick of his wrist. "I assume you don't share her heritage? One can't help but wonder about the origins of such a fascinating person."

"Origins can be very... personal, don't you think?" I interject, trying to keep my tone light despite the gravity of what he's insinuating.

This dick is edging awfully close to discussing what powers our pup has, and he knows full well he can't do that in front of Tilly. If he continues, I'll have to make a scene to distract her, and I'd prefer not to. The King and the princess seem like decent people—especially the princess.

She might make an excellent ally for our girl once she emerges.

"For some, yes," he agrees, a smirk playing on his lips. "For others, tracing the threads of their lineage might lead to unexpected places. That's also exciting."

"As long as it's not harmful," Presley chimes in, his eyes narrowed in a silent challenge. The typically placid doc sits up straighter as he leans forward on his forearms. "The unknown has an element of danger to it. Discovering secrets before you're ready to grasp their magnitude has grave consequences, especially if they have hidden the truth for a reason."

Jolene sips her wine, humming under her breath as if she is bored with the conversation. When the sharp tongued Fae continues staring at her, she gives him a saccharine smile. "In America, particularly in the South, it's considered quite rude to question people's heritage in mixed company. Families often have secrets twined throughout the branches of their trees—exposing those to sunlight for one's own amusement is not something we'd consider polite."

"Perhaps not in the court of public opinion, but in courts that convene under the cloak of night or reap what others have sown, it would be looked upon differently," Alistair muses. His words are carefully chosen, tiptoeing around the secrets that hover like specters between us, but it's clear he will not back down.

My eyes cut to Allora, but she's watching her stepmother fuss at the King. Sighing, I scratch my jaw as I let Alistair's statement hang in the air. He was hoping to get a reaction from one of us and I don't want to give it to him. I can't let it sit unchallenged, though, so I look him directly in the eyes when I reply. "Courts are such mysterious entities; if you aren't familiar with their procedures, you might end up on the wrong side of the law. I'm grateful I have a thorough understanding of all the various law systems that affect our everyday life. If I didn't, I could see myself making an idiotic mistake meddling in their intrigue and—"

"Darkness?" Alistair finishes for me, arching an eyebrow.

This idiot has no sense of self-preservation.

"Darkness, light..." I shrug, feigning disinterest. "It depends on the time of day and location of the proceedings, doesn't it?"

"Or the phase of the moon," he retorts smoothly.

That gets Doyle's attention. He joins Prez and me as we lean in, his eyes flicking between Tilly and the asshole determined to fuck shit up. "I doubt the moon phase influences trials. That's a bit... out there, isn't it, Judge?"

I grin. "Some folks claim destructive behavior amps up during the full moon, but I've never seen evidence of it. People do stupid things regardless of outside forces; it's within their nature. Right, Tilly?"

"My experience with people all over the globe agrees with you, Teddy. Of course, some irresponsible fuckwits make excuses for their lack of sense, but no one takes them seriously." She looks over at Allora and tilts her head. "Particularly men with more swagger than brain cells, right?"

Allora chuckles softly as she nods. "So I've been told, Jolene. Those afflicted should rein in their baser instincts and show the decorum we have taught them as children, in my opinion."

I knew I liked this chick.

The King is still blissfully unaware of the conflict brewing at our end of the table, but when forks clink against plates, he mutters to himself. "Moon phases. Ah, that reminds me of a poem I once forgot. Something about cheese, was it?"

"I'm sure it was something memorable," Benjy assures him with a kind smile. My friend rarely passes up an opportunity to be kind and like the rest of us, he's figured out the princess is stuck managing an addled father and greedy stepmother. His dad is a real fucking treat and his mom is lovely, so the dynamic makes sense to him, even flipped by gender. "You'll tell us when it comes to you."

"Cheese," Alistair scoffs softly, a taunt not-quite-hidden in the curve of his mouth. "Very quaint."

Wolfie looks at Tilly in a silent plea for strength, and she smiles softly, trying to send reassurance to him without it being noticeable. My mind races as I consider how many ways I'd like to rip this idiot to pieces, but I have to keep my anger simmering below the surface. The Fae prince knows more than he lets on, twirling truths and lies with the finesse of a master weaver while he dances around the lines that could get us all killed. I don't know what his motivation is, but the continued pressure feels like it's about more than simply toying with us.

Does the prince have a death wish? Or is he beholden to someone even more powerful than himself?

"Quaint can be charming," I counter as I meet Alistair's challenging stare. "I'm sure many find it less taxing than your games."

"Games?" King Hieronymous looks puzzled as he speaks up. "Are we playing a game? love games!"

"We certainly are," I say to him with a forced smile. "Your future son-in-law enjoys very dangerous pursuits, and he's engaged us to join him."

The clatter of cutlery punctuates the tense air like an erratic heartbeat, as Alistair's eyes glint with mischief—a predator toying with his prey. I fight the urge to let my inner flames lick at his smug façade once again as he pauses for effect. When he finally speaks, he's swirling his wineglass with a languid motion that suggests everything and nothing. "As I was saying before we sat down, family trees can be so convoluted, don't you think?"

"Especially when the roots are tangled in secrets." The quiet words from Allora get all of our attention and it makes the annoying jackass beside her bare his teeth. She's gotten to him; I can't help but think she did it on purpose. Maybe it was to explain why she's holding back or maybe she wants to help—it's impossible to tell because Allora isn't meeting anyone's gaze.

"Ah, but the discovery of one's lineage can be quite..." He pauses again, putting deliberate emphasis on the word, "... strategic and very enlightening."

Doyle shifts beside me, looking like a storm cloud ready to burst. I sense his power crackling beneath the surface, the angry deity magic seeking release in retribution for Alistair's casual remarks. I catch his eye, willing him to rein it in.

He probably won't listen, but it's amazing he's held in his natural penchant for chaos as it is.

"Enlightenment is overrated," Doyle replies through gritted teeth, his gaze fixed on Alistair with thinly veiled contempt. "Many of us can go through life without it and not suffer any consequences."

"Perhaps remaining in the dark is acceptable for some," Alistair drawls. "However, I believe there's always merit in fully understanding one's... heritage. It opens so many doors that were previously closed."

"Heritage isn't everything. Who we are now trumps the past every time," Wolfie whispers to Tilly, his voice filled with a tremor I can feel.

I slip my hand to my lap, reaching across our girl to find his under the tablecloth. Our finger knot together in silent solidarity as I bite the inside of my cheek. The cheeky Fae from the Unseelie is making him scared to find the answer we came here to seek because of his malevolence. He's worried his father will be worse than Callie, and it's not an unfair concern. If someone as arrogant and brash as Alistair is holding back, especially given his title, the man responsible for impregnating the Cailleach has to be fearsome.

"Speaking of being more than your lineage..." I say with a smirk. I'm trying to steer the conversation away from dangerous waters, so I'm going to piss this fucker off. "There's something precious about self-made legacies. Earning respect is more impressive than gaining it through association, I think."

"An odd opinion for the son of a senator, don't you think?" Alistair shoots back, his lips curling into a knowing grin. "But I suppose you have distanced yourself from him since you left the nest. Your name carries weight on its own, granted, but we must never forget where we come from—no matter how high we rise."

"Or how far we fall," King Hieronymous chimes in, chuckling absentmindedly at his own joke. Allora looks at him in concern, but lets out a breath when she realizes he's mostly oblivious to the undercurrents lapping at the edges of the conversation.

"Exactly," Alistair agrees, his gaze flicking back to the King, then to Allora before he focuses on me. "Some falls are destined by blood, wouldn't you say?"

"Destiny is a tricky thing," I counter in irritation. "Fate is never so capricious as when people tempt its edicts."

"Ah, but rarely do they change the tapestry for a single being," Alistair says, leaning forward slightly. "The proof of that is all around us. It's present in the way we move, the power we wield, the fires we…"

His voice trails off and his eyes dart to the flickering candle between us. I'm not manipulating it, but someone is. I take a slow, steadying breath, feeling the heat within me pulsate in response.

Calm down, Tilly. Don't give him the satisfaction.

Before I can respond, Doyle is sneering at him in contempt. "Sometimes, fires are best left unlit. Some embers shouldn't be fanned for fear of the wildfire that will rage in their wake."

"Indeed," Alistair concedes with a tilt of his head, "but where's the fun in being so cautious?"

"Fun is subjective," I say, my voice steady despite the raging torrent inside me. "And some games have higher stakes than others."

"Life's a high-stakes game, Judge Boone," Alistair whispers, as if sharing a secret meant just for me. "Despite the risks, I do so love to play for big pots."

"Even pawns can checkmate kings," Tilly cuts in, her voice darker than usual. When she looks at me, I have to press my lips together because her eyes aren't emerald like normal. There's a litany of things flickering in them one by one—a flame, wings, a sparkling darkness, and a ring of red.

This is very, very bad.

Just Like Fire

Jolene

A muscle in Doyle's jaw twitches, the only warning before the storm breaks. "I've had enough of these cryptic games," he growls, pushing back from the table with a scrape that echoes off the gilded walls.

"Wait, Doyle—" He's gone before I can get the words out, a redheaded blur of anger and frustration weaving through the throng of oblivious guests beyond the head table. I glance at Benjy, his eyes already tracking Doyle's departure.

We can't allow him to lose his temper, even if it's not with the royals.

He nods to me in unspoken understanding. "I'll make sure he doesn't do anything rash."

"Thank you," I murmur as I watch him retreat. Doyle's outburst pulled me out of my inner fury and I blink when I realize he might have done it on purpose to keep me from exploding on the arrogant dipstick who's watching me like a hawk. When his reaction confirms that the Fae was hoping to push one of us over the edge, my irritation simmers like coals waiting for a breeze.

I knew we would not get to eat dinner. Son of a bitch.

"Your friends are quite... passionate," Alistair observes, his voice as smooth as the silk shirt clinging to his lean torso. He's looking at his nails and the eye roll I give him damn near sends them into the back of my head.

"Passion fuels more than anger. My men's temperaments keep me more than satisfied in other ways," I reply with a saucy wink and Allora coughs again as she tries not to giggle. "But if you don't comprehend that, I'm not sure I can do more than express my regrets to Allora."

His eyes narrow and I see the first crack in his impenetrable armor. Alistair doesn't like when I win her favor, and he likes when she makes sure we know she agrees with me even less. I know how to win this battle; like any other male, I need to break his ego into tiny little pieces until he cries for help or admits his actual intentions.

That's child's play for a woman with my background.

Before I begin, a soft sound to my right draws my attention. Wolfie's shoulders shake ever so slightly, and he shakes his head. The sight triggers a protective surge within me and I turn to my darling boy. This is hurting him more than it's helping and since that fucker knows where we're heading next, it's bound to get worse. I wouldn't be surprised if he showed up, nor would it shock me to find out he'd tapped allies to make our journey more difficult.

"Teddy," I whisper, as I watch Wolfie. He stands, ignoring Alistair's huff of derision, and moves behind him to lay a hand on Wolfie's back. It's a simple gesture that speaks volumes about how much he cares for him, but my heart does funny flips, anyway.

"Easy, pup," my grumpy alphahole murmurs. His voice is a low rumble that resonates over both of us, and I sigh happily. His confident presence is palpable, and dominance always anchors Wolfie and makes me feel stronger.

"Is the doctor okay?" Alistair asks mockingly, his gaze flicking between Wolfie and Teddy like a predator scenting vulnerability. "Does he need smelling salts?"

"He's more okay than you'll ever be," I snap, my words laced with venom. Teddy's oddly calm composure contrasts with my fury. I watch as Wolfie lifts his head, the pain in his eyes replaced by a quiet gratitude as we defend him.

His grateful look is a reminder of what's at stake—our family, our secrets, our safety.

"Such loyalty you all show," Alistair muses, leaning back in his chair with an air of nonchalance that fools no one. "I can't imagine having to defend weaker stock all the time. Is it burdensome?"

"Only to those who don't understand the value of empathy," I counter, meeting his gaze squarely. "Either stop dancing around what you know, Alistair, or you'll see what loyalty truly looks like."

He tilts his head, considering me like I'm a puzzle to be solved. "My dear Jolene, knowledge is a currency. Why should I spend it so freely? Because you put on your big girl bloomers and ordered me to? I hardly think that's a likely outcome."

"Maybe," I lean in, lowering my voice to a dangerous whisper, "you owe a debt you're not aware of yet."

His eyes narrow, a glint of challenge flashing within them. I don't respond, holding onto my power by being the silent one. I'm honestly not sure what I'm bluffing him with, but I'll figure something out. I just need him to back off Wolfie and let us get out of this room gracefully.

Though I doubt it will hurt to have him wondering what I might do when we head to his fucking court.

"Touché," he concedes with a slow clap. "You might hold cards I'm unaware of; you certainly have the connections amongst your harem to get information. But as you know, debts can be paid in more ways than one."

"Consider this a down payment on what's owed," I say firmly. "I want answers. Whether it's tonight or within the next few days, you will give me something to work with. Understood?"

Wolfie's gaze flutters to me, seeking reassurance, and I catch Teddy's eye as he subtly flexes his fingers in a silent reminder of the strength we possess together. Once Benjy's gentle influence returns Doyle to us with his fire tempered, Teddy will make our excuses with the King and I'll handle Allora. The way he's looking at Wolfie and the sadness emanating from our empathetic vet means he's struggling as hard as I am. I seem fearless, but I know this is my last chance to force his hand.

The tension in the air is a tangible thing as the quiet stretches, wrapping around us like the creeping vines that snake their way up the palace's ancient stone walls. Alistair Silkshine toys with his wineglass, his smirk deepening as he watches me. "Perhaps there might be some merit in... exploring old texts for your answers."

"Go to the library? Is this mother fucker serious?" Presley's grumble is so unusual for him that I have to bite my lip to keep from bursting into laughter.

"We must always consider the veracity of the sources, of course," the Fae says as his eyes roam over the overwhelming amount of bookshelves lining this room.

"Books don't lie—unlike present company," I quip as I follow his gaze carefully. I don't think he'd give me clues that way, but who the hell knows with this asshole?

"The victors write much of history," he counters, his eyes twinkling with mischief. "There are those who would dispute your simple assessment."

I bite back a retort, clenching my fists under the table. This game could go on forever, and I'm done wasting time on this smug piece of shit. My hand slaps the table and the King jolts awake. The sound distracts me and I frown when I realize the Queen is gone, having left Hieronymus to snooze and their guest to pick fights with us.

I guess it doesn't matter where you go, royalty is full of snobby idiots who don't deserve the chairs they sit in.

"On that note," Presley interjects smoothly, rising from his seat with a grace that belies the power coiled within him, "we would be most appreciative if we could peruse the library archives. Tomorrow, perhaps?"

Allora smiles, giving him an appreciative look before putting her faux bimbette mask back on. "Oh, we have such wonderful scrolls and tomes. Father, wouldn't that be grand? I could give them a tour."

The sleepy King is as adorably oblivious as ever, but he peers over his spectacles with a bemused expression. "Hmm? Oh! Yes, yes. Quite right." He waves a dismissive hand, the jeweled rings catching the light. "Open the archives to our guests, Allora."

"Thank you. We deeply appreciate you allowing Allora to assist," I say, allowing a smile to soften my features. The relief that flows through me is echoed on Teddy's face, a silent thank you for Presley's intervention. I nod at the princess, hoping she knows how helpful her alliance tonight has been. "We should go, though. I'm afraid travel is still catching up with us."

"I suppose it's settled then," Alistair concedes, though his voice holds a note of reluctance. "Tomorrow, the past shall speak to those with ears to hear."

"Let's hope it screams," I mutter under my breath, catching Wolfie's eye and offering a wink to lift his spirits.

Before the jerk can start another round of bullshit, I rise and curtsey at the remaining royals. Turning on my heel, I whistle low for the companions, hoping they pick it up as we make our way out of the opulent chamber.

The heavy doors close behind us with a resounding thud and I let out a sigh of relief as I realize we're alone in the dimly lit corridor. The last thing I need is a confrontation with anyone else in the fucking place. I just want to get back to our room and order room service while someone rubs my damn feet.

Fuck this day and the horse it rode in on.

"Where'd they go?" Teddy asks, concern etching lines across his brow.

"Knowing Benjy, somewhere quiet," I reply, scanning the hallway. "He probably had Doyle breathing like a yoga master in no time."

"Found them," Wolfie says softly, his voice a blend of relief and affection as he spots the pair down at the end of the hall.

Doyle is leaning against the wall, his chest rising and falling in a measured rhythm, while Benjy rests a hand lightly on his arm. They turn towards us, and the newest person to join my family winks at me. I tilt my head, waiting for the Irishman to acknowledge our presence. When he stays quiet, I give in.

"Ready to head back?" I ask Doyle.

He nods, a grateful look softening his features as we close the distance between us. "More than ready," he replies in a steady voice. "Sorry I almost lost it, Tíogair. I didn't like how he was treating you or the pup. Made my system overload."

"Don't I get it, man," Teddy chuckles as he shakes his head. "Prez, warn *him* this time."

I arch a brow at them, but Dr. McNuggies just gives me a mischievous look. By the time we get out of the castle, it's dark out, and I realize we're going to have to navigate through the twisting streets of the Fae city. "Please tell me if one of you paid attention to how we got here. We have to get back to the hotel and back here tomorrow."

Despite the gnawing uncertainty about returning to the lion's den, there's a flicker of excitement within me. Answers are close—I feel them, as surely as the fire coursing through my veins now.

"Don't worry, Tilly. Your eagle flew above us."

Prez whistles, and the giant bird flaps in front of us, screeching as she looks at me. "This is your moment, girl. Take us home before our woman gets us all kicked out of the city."

Very funny, Birdman.

Helpless

Doyle

The great bloody bird pulled through and led us back through the disturbingly quaint capital of the Harvest Court. I'm still furious at the entire situation that forced us to endure the little shit's games all evening. I've never understood why unemerged supes who are part of the program aren't given the info they need before they leave their enclaves. Even if they don't develop powers, they're going to have shadows following them forever, watching to see if they do.

It's secret supe parole and puts them in more danger than it keeps them out of.

But we're all bound by the same fucking oath no matter what level of the Society we're part of, so we dance to their tune like good automatons. Organized shit is the worst and I hate being part of any system that takes away people's free will. My stance on that shit is why my 'family' on Olympus dislikes my presence and it's definitely why I've stayed on the fringes of the town almost the entire time they have stationed me in the Hollow.

As we head upstairs in the elevator, I notice the pup is getting less anxious by the second. Both the doggy and our girl have his hands while the doc is standing behind him, so he's well guarded. That doesn't mean I'm satisfied that no one is going to attempt to fuck with him again during this trip, especially since his marked mates are unaware or unable to use their gifts. I, however, am less hampered than they are if I do it subtly. It's not my style, but much like my tricks at that trial, I may have to surreptitiously fuck people up if they behave like the dark Fae did tonight.

"You better now, man?"

I give Benjy a wry grin, shrugging. "Never been a fan of hiding my light under a bushel, and this trip is making it hard to honor my promises."

Jolene lets go of Wolfie's hand, walking over to me. She places her palms on my chest and looks up into my eyes. "You're doing a good job reining in your temper, Lucky. I know we all appreciate the effort, but we also like that you want to protect everyone. That's what family does."

Snorting, I lean in, resting my forehead on hers. "You lot are the first people I've made an attempt for in a very long time, Tíogair. However, when this jaunt to the old world is over, I plan on wreaking havoc on every idiot who gave us shit. You can take that to the bank."

"I would expect nothing less," she says with a smile.

The elevator dings and we file out, heading to the suite with less tension arcing through the group. Boone waves the key at the door and the second we step inside, he snarls as though there's an enemy at the gates. Sighing, I push through the crowd, leaving our girl in the middle so she's covered. When I see it, I roll my eyes and pinch the bridge of my nose.

"Pull it back, you idgit," I hiss at the judge. Calling a tiny fraction of my power, I check the room out to make certain no one is hiding out of sight or in the connecting bedroom. Once I'm sure, I turn to our family. "He's a wee bit put out that someone was in our space while we were gone. It doesn't appear too malicious, but we'll have to be cautious until we inspect everything."

As we enter, the scent of roasted meats and baked bread fills the air. They parked a gargantuan cart laden with platters of food in the center of the living area with a note that reads:

"With sincerest apologies for any discomfort. Until tomorrow."

"Looks like someone is trying to butter us up with a feast," Presley says as he looks over the spread. His eyes are twinkling with amusement as he pretends to examine the food, but I catch him running his fingertips under the edges of tables and furniture as he goes.

Not much gets past our resident scholar, that's for bloody sure. I wouldn't have considered conventional spy methods.

"Or trying to poison us," Wolfie snarks. He looks like he's joking, but there's an edge to his words that makes me pause.

His words silence everyone, but I shake my head. I don't think they're trying to kill us—not even the prince would survive an inquiry from the Society involving this many inductees. It's like the princess is trying to apologize for her objectionable choice in men, especially since we didn't get to eat a bite before we had to leave. She seemed like a good sort and the King, though addled, also didn't trip my wires.

My gaze flicks to Boone, then to the half-Fae holding his hand. "I'm sure many suspicious additives would have scents. I don't smell almonds, for example."

Their eyes widen as they get my insinuation. Between the doggy's nose and the Fae's natural gifts, they *should* be able to suss out if the food has dangerous shit if they focus. We'll need to distract our girl, but that won't be hard. She hates being trussed up and the dress they sent her still has her bound up tight.

"Princess, why don't you get out of that thing so you're comfy? We'll check out the food, and if it's not up to snuff, we'll pack it up and order something new. Sound good?" Jolene looks over at the gentle giant and it makes me smile to see how easily he can guide her without being overwhelming.

I grin. "Benjy's got it right. Put on those adorable yoga things that make your ass look biteable and we'll handle this."

Her eyes narrow, but the desire to shuck the finery wins out. "Fine. But I don't like people in our room leaving notes, even if it comes with food that smells like the goddamn heavens beamed it down."

Sharp as a tack, that's our girl.

"Understood, Tilly. Now, shoo."

WHEN SHE RETURNS IN A WELL-LOVED, OVERSIZE GUNS 'N ROSES TEE and yoga pants, I grin. Jolene's hair is down and the makeup is wiped clean, leaving her looking dewy and soft despite the sharp edges she loves to put on. Her feet are bare and when I squint at the pants I love so much, I see that she's got a knife clipped in one of the side pockets.

Wonder where she hid that in her tight autumn colored gown tonight?

"Clipped between the girls," she says as she catches me staring. Her lips quirk and I chuckle as I flop down on the couch. "Did you guys make sure this stuff isn't full of death spices?"

"Bit dramatic, but yes," the pup says as he meets her in the middle of the room. "We're as sure as we can be. Apparently, that's good enough for Teddy."

The hound whips his head around, giving Wolfie a look before he sighs. "We can't be any more sure about things brought up from the kitchen, either. So we did the best we could to verify, but we can't starve."

Jolene's stomach growls, and she flushes when we laugh. "Oh, fine. Make fun of the girl who hasn't eaten and got strapped into a stupid dress for a formal dinner. Very 1865 of you all."

"Before she makes garments out of the curtains, we should dig in," Teddy says wryly.

It doesn't take long for everyone to attack the various dishes. We're starving, and the day's frustrations have left us ravenous and cranky. I grin when I catch Boone adding helpings to her plate and have to swallow a snort when Benjy brings a few extra small plates with desserts to the coffee table with him. They're both mother hens, but from different ends of the spectrum.

I slide to the floor when the rest of them take places next to one another around the low crystalline block we're using for the food. My

Tíogair is between the pup and the dog, so Prez, Benjy, and I scoot in to flank them. Our girl smiles when I pass her a glass of Fae wine, wagging a finger at her to make sure she doesn't gulp it. The ruby liquid swirls hypnotically in my glass as I watch it, content being here despite all the people pissing me off. This vintage tastes like wild berries and summer nights, leaving a hint of something exotic dancing on my tongue.

"Damn, this is good," I murmur, feeling the first tendrils of warmth unfurl within me. "I forget how good alcohol is when you're not in… the United States."

Benjy snorts, and Boone has to smother a chuckle. They both know I was about to say 'the human realm.' I need to be careful how candid I get when we drink this shit. It can loosen the tongues of the strongest supes.

"You… are being silly." Jolene points at me with her food filled fork. When I wink, she chomps the meat with a groan that makes every one of us grunt in response. "This shit is good. I think I don't care if it's poisoned."

Wolfie pinches her side before he snitches a carrot off her plate. "It's not. Everyone needs to quit saying that."

I finish my wine before I dig in again, finally feeling myself relax. "Just a bit of dark humor, doc. It's hard not to be sarcastic after the past couple of days. This was supposed to be the easier portion of the trip."

"Christ on a cheez doodle," Jolene mutters. "What the hell are the rest of the flighty fuckers going to do? They have already forced me to bind myself up twice. You know what? That's it. I'm done. No more fancy dresses. I'll go in ripped jeans and a band tee if I want. *Viva la France!*"

"Everything okay, Princess?" Benjy asks. He's very perceptive to shifts in moods, though not as good as the little vet. "You're awfully rebellious suddenly."

Our girl holds up a skewer of sizzling vegetables wrapped in a leaf I can't identify. "Better than okay. I'm re-asserting control over my fucking life. Burn the corsets and all that rot."

Mmm hmm.

"While I applaud your desire to be less constricted and suggest you take a step further to go commando…" I pause as she giggles. "I'm not sure antagonizing the hosts at the next stops will help us get what we need."

"Since when does my lack of underwear make a damn bit of difference to people who can't see my naked ass?" She waves a potato that seems to be a variant of a French fry at me, chastisingly. "It's my party and I'll free ball if I want to."

I have absolutely nothing to say to that, so I shake my head and let her go. It's nice to see her looking happy, even if it's odd timing. Laughter and conversation ebb and flow around the room as we eat. By the time we've cleaned our plates, the air feels thick with an energy that's tantalizing and dangerous.

"Is it hot in here, or is it just me?" Teddy asks, tugging at his collar.

"Maybe you ate a weird pepper, dude," I reply as I loll on the floor, sipping my wine. "Some of that stuff was spicy as hell."

"Definitely not just you," Benjy agrees, his voice dropping an octave as he looks at our girl.

"Guys," Presley starts, his usual laid-back demeanor slipping. "I think we've been—"

"Drinking too much," I cut in as realization dawns on me. The food and the wine must have been laced with something that won't kill us, but it sure as won't make us complacent.

"I suppose we should be angry that they served us jacked up booze but…" Jolene's sentence trails off as her gaze travels over each of us with a hunger that has nothing to do with food.

"Angry later. Bed now," Boone growls. He rolls to his feet, holding his hand out to her. His pupils are dilated with a cocktail of desire and whatever aphrodisiac they spiked our shit with, but I think he simply doesn't care.

"Bed," I echo as I mirror his stance. My thoughts are growing hazy around the edges, leaving only a singular focus on the surrounding bodies. "Sounds like a bloody brilliant plan to me."

"Everyone okay with this?" Benjy, ever the gentleman, checks even as he helps haul the docs off the ground.

"Oh, I'm *more* than okay," our girl says as she sashays towards the open door to the bedroom. "And if I'm not better than that soon, you're all getting your asses kicked."

Yes, ma'am.

Dangerous Woman

Jolene

Clothes are flying as we enter the room and I laugh softly when Teddy grabs my waist to toss me on the bed. It's been a shitty couple of days and I'm not even upset with him manhandling me. My butt bounces on the mattress as I scoot back, my eyes glued to the muscles and skin being revealed by my guys. They're eager to burn off some of this frustration and helplessness, too, even if some Fae pheromone shit predicates it.

"Tilly, if you take those damn glasses off, you'd better have your eyes closed or you'll get three every time I catch you." Teddy gives me a stern expression and though I'd fight him on that normally, I know why he's being stern. He's worried we'll knock them loose in our haste and something bad will happen. So I nod, giving him a playful wink. Pointing out that he's admitting there's something special about my new eyewear would ruin the vibe and I'm not ready to have that conversation.

See? I can be reasonable.

"She's definitely hungry for more, Boone. You didn't even have to fight her," Doyle says as he crawls onto the bed next to me. He gives me a cheeky grin and hooks his fingers into my yoga pants. "I'm suddenly sorry I demanded these, but we'll remedy my error quick enough."

"Don't tease me," I growl as I bury my fingers in his flaming locks and tug lightly. "I'm fresh of patience for games, Lucky."

His chuckle vibrates over my skin as he kisses his way down my torso, working my pants over my hips along the way. "Tíogair, I think you'll find we're all a bit on edge tonight. It's a toss-up whether you or Big Doggy will be in charge, though."

My eyes roll up as he nips and bites his way across my stomach, trying not to groan in response. Benjy climbs on the bed from that side, his gentle smile making me melt even though he's not touching me. He's gorgeous as he kneels next to me, his bulky frame contrasted by the softness in his eyes. It doesn't hurt that he's got a beautiful dick mere centimeters from my mouth, but he's waiting for me instead of pushing.

"Why not both?" I murmur as I lick my lips. "Doyle, stop fucking around down there while Benjy fucks my face. Wolfie, take care of Daddy and Prez until I'm ready for you."

Teddy turns, his perfectly sculpted athlete body in sharp profile as he gives me a wicked grin. "Why, Tilly, I thought you said you'd never…"

"Shut. Your. Mouth." My eyes narrow at him and I flick my hand to Prez and Wolfie before I turn back to Benjy, reaching out to stroke his cock lightly. "Come here, big guy. Give your Princess a taste."

He scoots forward and I wrap my lips around his tip first, suckling gently. I use my free hand to give Doyle's hair another tug and he finally moves below my belly button. At the first wet swipe of his tongue along the seam of my leg, I moan. Sliding Benjy's length into my mouth, I open wide until I hit the root. It takes a second for me to adjust and breathe out of my nose, but once I do, my playful Irishman flicks his tongue over my clit. A surprised sound vibrates over Benjy's shaft and his hands wrap around my head to hold me in place.

"Fuck, Princess. Do that again. Holy shit."

I'd grin if I could get my mouth any wider, so instead, I do as told and repeat the high-pitched hum. He shudders and pulls back, then slams in again with his big palms guiding me. I rarely let someone have this much control over me when I give head, but it's hard to complain when my fiery lover is writing a long ass sentence on me with his tongue. I'm caught between my pussy leaking on his face while my hips writhe and my typically gentle giant picking speed as I suck him deep.

Are the others…?

A dark snarl echoes off the walls, and I ache to grin again. That sound means Wolfie has Teddy balls deep in his mouth and the whimper that follows tells me Prez is rewarding him. The noises make my skin heat and I feel my blood follow suit when Doyle's tongue slips inside of me. I suck in a deep breath through my nose and the scents that mingle in the air make my gut clench.

Beyond the normal musk of sex, there are delicious aromas emanating from my men as the lust in the room gets thicker. My eyelids flutter open to see the vague shadow on Benjy and the golden glow ringing Doyle again. The fire on my hands is flickering from orange flames to an odd pink mist as I swallow my newest lover down every time his hips pump forward. There's something just out of reach, I feel it, but the waves of pleasure pushing me towards a peak make it hard to focus.

"You're almost there, Tíogair," Doyle's voice is almost a purr and his tongue swipes roughly over my clit again as he thrusts three fingers inside of me. My walls squeeze him and I accidentally scrape my teeth over Benjy. I try to pull back when I realize it, but his fingers bury in my hair and he grunts as he continues thrusting.

"Keep going, Princess. I like it rough."

Teddy's chuckle is low and raspy from the other side of the bed. "He really does, Tilly. Mark him up; he'll like it. Benjy never lies."

Spank my ass and call me Charlotte—I can do that.

Lifting my hand from Doyle's head, I grab the big guy's hipbones and hold on tight. My nails dig into him as I renew my efforts. I suck harder, nip lightly when I can, and scratch my teeth along his shaft as his pace picks up. I feel the tension in his body build when I do and something deep inside of me unfurls. They don't know I can see the flames and mist alternating as I grip Benjy, but I know the dark satisfaction in my gut is tied to it. Every time he moans or Doyle adds another finger to slam inside of me, it spreads.

"Stop, doc," I hear my alphahole growl before he sniffs the air like an animal. "No one comes before her and she's close. Haggerty, make her come or I'm taking over."

I flick my tongue over the tip of Benjy's head, then deep throat him again, getting the vein underneath with my bottom teeth. He jerks and lets out a surprising rumble. "Fuck, Doyle, tip her over before she…"

The minute a full fist pushes inside of me, my hips buck hard and the pressure on the right spot makes me gush as the orgasm crashes over me. The cock I'm sucking on muffles my loud moan, but I don't let go as my brain leaks out my ears. Benjy thrusts one more time, then hot fluid shoots down my throat as I rock on Lucky's hand. I don't know if I've ever felt anything this intense in my entire life, but from the flood downstairs, Doyle knows it.

These sheets are definitely ruined; housekeeping is going to love us.

When the shudders cease, the big guy pulls out and closes my mouth. "Swallow it all like a good girl, and I'm sure Big Daddy will reward you."

My eyes widen, and I want to retort, but I've got a mouthful of jizz. *I'm going to kill these motherfuckers for feeding his ego.* Instead of dribbling cum out of my lips like a fool, I look Benjy right in the eyes as I swallow the rest of him down, then lick my lips clean. He groans and flops back against the pillows, his arm above his head as he looks over at Edgar.

"Brother, that was the hottest fucking thing in history. Our girl can take me like a champ."

Don't do it. No one say it and I won't have to—

"That's why we're calling him Big Daddy from now on."

Springing forward at the waist, I push a snickering Irishman off of my lower half and open my mouth to let Prez have it. Except he's the one sucking Teddy down and Wolfie is sprawled out with my dominant ex-bully's hand circling his cock possessively. I blink for a second, taking that new situation in as the rest of the scene gets clearer.

Teddy has the same flickering flames and mist in the aura surrounding him, as well as colorful feathers. Wolfie's gorgeous wings are fluttering as his hips wiggle, sending sparkles into the air. And Prez... He has the shadow of huge white wings behind him as he works his mouth over Edgar.

Even a monster orgasm isn't making this any easier. Just breathe, Jolene.

I tilt my head, pasting a satisfied smirk on my face as I arch a brow. "Big Daddy? Are you out of your goddamn minds? His head is big enough to get stuck in the doorways as it is."

"Relax, Princess. You can keep calling him asshole if it makes you feel better."

Benjy's easy quip hits just right and I cover my mouth as a giggle escapes. I want to stay irritated, but one giggle turns into two, and before long, tears are running down my face. Teddy shrugs and runs his hand over Prez's head gently, his expression full of swagger.

"Fine. Big Daddy Asshole, it is," I say when I finally get control of myself. "Although, if you keep collecting my boys, you're going to have to figure out what they're going to call me when it's my turn to be in charge."

"Tilly, get your sweet ass over here and ride my dick so the doc can fuck your ass while I suck the pup. Once you get off a few more times, we can discuss titles." Teddy pulls Prez up, winking at me as the lithe doctor scrambles across the room to our bags.

I'd bristle at the order, but it sounds like a good fucking time.

"Two in one night, Big Daddy Asshole. Don't let this shit go to your head," I whisper as I hover over his cock. When he laughs, I sink down on him, spearing myself on his dick with a soft moan of pleasure. "Holy fuck, that feels good."

"Woman, you're so wet I can't even..." Teddy trails off as his hand tightens on Wolfie. "Pup, you'd better get ready. This is going to be a rough ride."

"Aye," Doyle says as he moves up the bed. "Because she's got one more hole to fill and I aim to get our girl airtight."

My eyes move to Benjy, noting he's hard again and stroking his hand over himself with a lazy grin. "Don't worry, Mama J. I like to watch sometimes and I have a feeling this is going to be hot as fuck."

If I wasn't trapped between a dick in my pussy and one pushing at my lips, I'd strangle them all.

That's when Prez comes back, and I hear the bottle opening. I shift on Teddy, squeezing his dick until he growls at me, and lean forward to take Doyle into my mouth. His ragged breaths pick up as I take him deeper, and the golden halo around him gets brighter. I wait for Prez to line up and slide home, filling me full enough to draw rough sounds from everyone, then I move.

Presley's hands on my hips and smooth thrusts help me rock on Teddy and the forward motion brings Doyle to the back of my throat. The rhythm consumes me as the tasty scent permeates the air, and my cunt grips Teddy with every downstroke. My eyes are closed just in case the stupid glasses fall off, but I *know* all the weird shit has to be getting more intense. The stuff I saw when I was with Benjy and Doyle was a precursor; I feel the intensity in my body building to another out-of-control peak.

Something is coming… something beyond an orgasm that will make me black out…

With Doyle in my mouth, I can't warn them, but as our bodies move and skin slaps, the sensation gets bigger and bigger until a loud cry escapes. The climax explodes within me like an atom bomb, and my eyes stay squeezed shut as the feeling of being ripped apart slams into my consciousness.

The last thing I hear before I pass out is an unearthly howl, the beat of wings, and a pounding sound.

Then it all goes black.

HALF A WORLD AWAY

DHAMPIR

My eyes pop open, and I sit straight up in my bed.

Something is happening.

The oracle awakens immediately, looking at me with concern from the couch. "Amiri, what is it?"

I close my eyes, connecting to the universe that only ancient powers can. Once I sort through the threads, I see it clearly. My smile is genuine as I look at Hugo. "It's begun, my friend."

"Shit," he says as he scrubs a hand down his face. "I didn't think it would start until she was home. The visions were murky, though."

His position prevents him from sharing much regarding his gift, but I know he is trying to give me what he can. We've been traveling around, using my wealth and status to open doors the others could not while they searched for the Fae's kin. Our mission has been moderately successful and when they return to Whistler's Hollow, I plan to share the information we've gathered with our fated.

But we both believed this process wouldn't begin until she'd marked all of us—the Fates must be playing their little games again.

"The others will help her. They have the good doctor to guide them and our fated through the beginning phases. It will be okay," I tell him. "We cannot lose focus; our tasks are vital. This turn of events makes me feel more than ever that we must solve the mystery of Jolene's adoptive parents' death. Once we do that, we will follow the clues to her true heritage."

"Why is this so important?" Hugo asks softly. "My kind rarely get mates and my entire body is screaming that we should be there while she's emerging."

Ah, the short-sightedness of youth.

"Patience, my future-seeing friend. I feel the pull as well, but we are not as tied to her yet, so we can use that to our advantage." I run a hand through my hair as I consider how to explain what the stars are telling me. "I do not have visions like you, but my first tie to Jolene was through granting a wish. That connection twists us together even further than mating—it twists our threads together in the great tapestry. I feel a distinct urgency around uncovering her past, so it must be irrevocably tied to her future."

He stays silent for a moment, then nods. "I understand now. Your magic is tied to the fulfillment of those desires. It must have mistakenly given you access to the Fates' plan—or part of it."

"Perhaps. We both know they enjoy being cryptic, but they enjoy reweaving things to teach people a lesson even more. I do not want to upset the balance by acting outside of the current bounds."

"Then we continue on as we have been?"

I nod, stroking my beard. "We do, and we trust that the rest of her mates will keep her safe among the sharks they are swimming with. Our purpose has not changed, nor has that of her friend."

"Saoirse checked in with her when they were at Daybreak. She was worried that Jolene seemed distracted. Perhaps this started there?"

"A sound assumption, Hugo. We will call her tomorrow and have her fill us in on what the weird sisters have demanded. For now, we should get some rest."

He huffs, thumping his pillow as he lies down. "As if I'm going to be able to sleep now. Just make sure when the damn visions come I don't swallow my tongue, please?"

I chuckle, giving him a thumbs up. "Agreed, friend. I'll safeguard your person and keep Isra from bursting in like we're being stormed by invading Huns."

"Thank hell. That woman is terrifying."

"Are you certain the man they have asked you to guard is human, Saoirse?" My brows furrow as she squawks about her current assignment like an angry goose. "The Sisters have you and your cadre babysitting… a human criminal?"

"I didn't stutter, Prince Ali." Her tone is irritable, and I truly can't blame her. "They rerouted me after Budapest, told to meet Julia and the guys at their safe house in London. They'd been keeping some dude they scooped up there since they left after Halloween. He's been sedated, so he won't need his memory wiped, but whatever sign we're supposed to wait for hasn't come yet. I'm pissed as hell."

"Do you know who this unlucky gentleman is?" I frown as I try to understand why in the heavens a team of Guardians would be asked to guard a human. "Have they given you any hint as to be why he must be protected?"

"Not a word. He's too doped up to ask, and none of our magical probing has indicated a link to our world. He's a computer guy, and he got injured in a bombing—they picked him up afterward. That's all I know."

The frustration in her voice is understandable; They trapped Saoirse far from her best friend and charge at a crucial time.

"Don't worry about Jolene. I promise we will keep in contact with you and I am certain the others can help our girl through her transition. If the Fates deem this crucial enough to tie up four Guardians, it will become clear eventually. Do your job so you don't tempt them." I look at Hugo and he nods. The visions he had last night were unchanged from the last time, so we believe everything is still on course.

Saoirse sighs heavily, and a loud crash behind her rings out. "Fine. I have to go see what's going on, anyway. Tharin deals with being cooped up *really* poorly, and he's been a nightmare to deal with, especially since Zasha is amusing himself by torturing him."

My lips curve and I chuckle softly. It seems no matter what year it is or where one is located, there will always be a troublemaker and grump within a group. Saoirse has her work cut out for her someday, I fear. "Go deal with your cadre and we will look for the next location we need to visit. We must find the team that killed the policeman and his family, just as you must guard this charge."

"Be careful, yeah? My girl likes you and that other one a lot—she might not know how much yet, but if you get hurt, she'll be upset. I don't like how involved these ancients are and how little the Society has to say about it."

On that point, we are in absolute agreement.

"We will. Keep in touch."

"Always."

Turning to Hugo, I sigh. "It is very odd that the ladies have that many supes watching a human. Even more odd is that their handlers have not made noise about tying them up with something any agent could do."

"It's very strange. Four Guardians to a full human is like using a nuke to drive a nail. What value could this guy possibly have to warrant such heavy artillery?" The oracle frowns, shaking his head. "Maybe we could run his information past Jackson's tech geek?"

Arching a brow, I give him an amused look. "Do you not think I have resources of my own? We do not need him contacting Jolene and worrying her. Although, until Saoirse and her team figure out who their charge is, we have nothing to research."

Sighing, he nods. "Then we should pack up and move on. The last clue I got was in Brazil. We'll have to head there if we want to track down the people responsible for the massacre in Turkey."

"Then Brazil it is. Allow me to speak with Isra and Fazal, then we will take the easy way across so many miles. I don't relish the thought of a flight that long, even in a private jet."

"The easy way?"

I grin and wink at him. "You'll find out soon enough."

Morning Light

Jolene

My eyes flutter open only to be greeted by the aftermath of indulgence. The morning light filters through the curtains, casting a warm glow over the tangle of limbs sprawled across the bed. The scent of musk and sweat lingers in the air, a remnant of last night's revelry.

"Morning," I murmur, my voice still hoarse with sleep. I'm not sure who's awake—if anyone—but I'm feeling so damned good that I can't help saying something.

"Hey there, Princess," Benjy replies, his voice a low rumble that resonates through my bones. He leans in to press kiss to my temple and whoever he squashed to do so grumbles good-naturedly.

This is my idea of Paradise and knowing we have to get up and move sucks rocks.

I stretch, the sheets slipping to my waist. The damn glasses perched on my nose are a necessity for keeping the illusion that I don't know about their world. Surprisingly, they didn't budge during the night's escapades. When I look at the warm bodies on the bed, it's obvious something's different this morning. My vision isn't just clear; it's... revealing more than ever before.

"Guess hot sex turned up the contrast while I wasn't looking," I mutter to myself as I marvel at the change in scenery.

The guys' still look hot as hell, but I can see vivid auras surrounding them that show me the full extent of their supernatural natures.

Sniffing delicately, I shudder when their scents tickle my nose, provoking a visceral response from my body. *Holy fuck that's potent; is that what they smell all the time?* I shake my head a little, trying in vain to clear the tantalizing aromas from my brain. They make me want to stay here all day, luxuriating in my boys until… something happens. I don't know what, but the dark spot in my gut has blossomed into a voice that whispers to me.

"Not good, Jolene," I mumble as I shift. I need to get up and pee, but more than that, I need a fucking minute. I feel like I've stepped into a paranormal romance show; it's wigging me out. Wiggling a bit, I untangle my limbs slowly so I don't disturb everyone.

Teddy lifts his head, concern etching his features as he frowns at me. "What's wrong, Tilly?"

"Just need the bathroom, Teddy," I lie smoothly. He arches a brow and I know he must not be buying it, but my guileless expression makes him pause.

I hate having to keep my knowledge a secret. When the hell will I be able to let them know?

Benjy stretches and I watch as the silhouette of a gorilla flickers around him. His strength has always been apparent, but now it's almost tangible in its intensity. It's more than human—primal, powerful. Yet his eyes and his touch are so gentle that I can't see him doing some movie magic shift into King Kong.

Does Sherilynn know about this? I bet she does and that's completely humiliating.

My gentle giant stretches again, rising from the bed to walk over to the bar. The lines of his back, the muscles, and the power in his form are so magnified now that I can see him as he truly is. I can't believe it took me this long to see how fucking gorgeous this man is; it's almost a crime that it took this long.

"Wow." The breathy comment escapes my lips before I can help it and I feel my face heat.

"Like what you see, Princess?" he teases as he turns to look at me.

He's unaware of the depth of my newfound perception, so he doesn't realize I've got a view of the full monte, plus the extra bits.

I shrug and give him a soft smile. "Always, big guy. You're damn near sculpture-worthy."

Teddy chuckles, stretching his arms out above his head. I tilt my head as a combination of flames, pink mist, and feathers swirling through his aura. So far, he's the only person I've seen with three competing signatures and I wonder how rare that is. His presence is usually so solid, but the multiple pieces make him enigmatic and mysterious. I'm not sure what it means, but I'd like to know. It feels important that our alpha hound has more going on than most and I wonder how many people know about it.

Teddy's known for being strategic, particularly when it's to his advantage.

I reach out to trace the line of Teddy's jaw, my fingers passing through the mist but feeling the warmth of the flames beneath. They don't hurt me, much like the ones on me don't harm me or the others when I touch them. That, too, must mean something important. "You look like a cat who ate a canary, Judge Boone. So much for your legendary poker face."

He snorts, rubbing his cheek in my palm. "I promise, no poker face for you, Tilly. As much as we can, we will be honest with you, even when it's painful."

The room is silent save for the soft breathing of Wolfie and Presley, still lost in slumber. I smile at the two of them curled together at Teddy's waist. They were draped over both of us, but I moved to alleviate the pressure on my poor bladder. I'm struck by an overwhelming urge to stay in bed again and the dark voice whispers more.

"Speaking of pain… How are you this morning, Tíogair? We were a bit rough, so it would be natural if you're a bit achy." Doyle's eyes meet mine, and I'm caught in the radiance of his golden light—an aura that speaks of powerful magic and secrets. It's breathtaking, and for a moment, I'm lost in it, wondering at the source of his power.

"Um, not too bad, really." That's absolutely true and I'm kind of surprised by it. My limbs move and my girly bits don't feel like I need to hobble, so I'm taking it as a win. I expected to be damn crippled this morning after that intense romp.

"Good dreams?" Doyle asks, his voice laced with something akin to curiosity. He's watching me closely and I get the feeling he expects to see something specific.

Scooting to the edge of the bed, I put my feet on the ground and stand, then stretch up to the ceiling. My back cracks loudly, but my muscles don't even pull. In fact, I feel pretty damn good. "Who needs them when you have wild orgies?"

The Irishman laughs, his eyes dancing as he props his face in his hand. "Good answer, love."

Wolfie stirs first, his blond hair a stark contrast to the golden sheen of his skin. He's opposite in every way in comparison to the dark fae of fairy tales we met last night. While he has an ethereal beauty, especially when he's fully Fae, Wolfie doesn't look like you'd think someone with his heritage would, nor does he look cold and pale like Callie. I'm not sure where on earth my submissive vet got his Cali boy looks in his human form, but I love both versions of him.

He's model-gorgeous and the fact that he's mine is as astounding as the other sexy men here. What the hell do they all see in me?

"Sugarplum, you're staring again," Wolfie chides playfully, though his eyes sparkle with mischief.

"Can you blame me?" I challenge, my heart swelling with a mix of affection and awe. "You're all sprawling or strutting around like a fantasy calendar. It's scrambling my brains—all before I've even had my morning coffee."

Prez opens his eyes, sighing as Wolfie hands him his glasses. He's been the least readable in terms of the secret power shit, but now his aura sports the feathers of the caladrius. I'm not sure I'd ever heard of the mythical bird believed to heal the sick and dying before, but that flash last night seemed to upload the knowledge directly to my brain. It's a revelation that leaves me breathless in its simplicity.

How could I have missed the signs when he's so talented at taking care of everyone in town?

"Presley," I start, but words fail me because I can't admit I know what he can do. "You're absolutely lickable in the morning."

"Thanks," he says with a shy smile. "I'd share my thoughts, but you seem to be having enough trouble tearing your eyes from us as it is. And you did say you needed to.."

"Oh!" I turn red as I remember and the pressure is obvious again. "Yes. Damn. Be right back."

With that, I run to the bathroom, cursing my idiocy in my head.

Why can't you just be normal, Jolene?

Once I've taken care of hygiene, I stand in front of the mirror looking at myself. I'm surprised to see a myriad of marks that don't look temporary dotting my form from neck to hips. Each one is a little different and when I touch them, a rush of desire floods my system. I pretend not to hear the groans in the other room because that's enough evidence to confirm my suspicions.

I'm not sure if I want to be mad about this or not—it may not have been a conscious choice.

My nose wrinkles as I roll around all the fictional information I have on supernatural shit. I have no idea what's myth, what's truth, and what's a load of bullshit. It's not fair, but life rarely is, so I have to suck it up. We don't have the luxury of wallowing in philosophical tripe—not when we have a deadline and specific goals for this trip.

"Discussion about possible mating marks *later* then," I mutter as I put my hair up in a high ponytail. "Dealing with egomaniacal Fae now."

Of course, the list of questions about this situation is far *longer than that, but I'm keeping them filed away until it's time.*

Looking at myself in the mirror again, I fight off the never-ending urge to cover myself before I go back into the room. Body dysmorphia isn't something you get over and move on from. It's a constant battle with yourself and it's for the rest of your life, even after you've done the work. I *know* there's nothing wrong with my body in my head and the guys didn't have a single complaint last night. But I hate the thought of walking out there nude in the daylight where they can see every imperfection clearly.

"Are you coming back, Magpie?"

Prez's voice brings me out of my head and I close my eyes for a moment, murmuring my mantra until the anxiety in my veins dies down. When I'm calm, I answer. "Just a minute…"

One more look in the glass has me straightening my spine. These men may have fallen out of the pages of a damn Playgirl, but I'm Jolene Whitley. I partied my way around the globe like a rockstar and not once did *anyone* make a remark about what I looked like. That trauma belongs to high school Jolene and though two of my guys remember her, they've both admitted they liked her.

My past pain does not define my future happiness.

I smile, squaring my shoulders, and head out the door into the room. The hottest men I've ever known all look at me with hunger in their gazes and my gut flutters with pleasure. "Here I am."

"We can see that," Teddy growls softly.

My gaze travels over them, taking in the nuances of their true forms. They're more than men; they're legends brought to life. Suddenly, the sexy factor seems less important than knowing I'm a part of a world so vast it threatens to swallow me whole. I wish I could let them know what I can see; I want to share that with them, but deep down, I know I can't. I have to wait for whatever the sign is or everything will get much more complicated. Instead, I distract myself by bringing up another topic.

"Last night was… " I trail off, not able to find an adjective that feels accurate.

"Definitely one for the books," Benjy says as he pulls on a pair of jeans.

Having some of the skin on display covered helps and I laugh softly. "Indeed. Sorry I did that passing out thing. I swear, this shit only happens with you guys. Seer never had to find me blacked out after sex in Europe or anything."

The growl coming from Teddy makes me smile and I walk over to perch on his leg as he sits on the edge of the bed. He buries his face in my neck for a moment and I sense the struggle he's having with not being a super possessive dick. "We're the only ones it will *ever* happen with, so don't apologize."

Presley rolls his eyes as he heads for his bag to grab clothes. "You know that's not entirely true, Big Daddy, so get yourself sorted."

Ugh, I'd forgotten about that for a few, blissful moments.

"We aren't *really* going to keep feeding that monster ego of his, are we?" I laugh as Teddy nips my neck in response, rubbing my cheek on his hair. "I thought you guys were joking."

"Nope," Benjy says in a sassy voice, popping the last letter for emphasis. "We decided we're all in with you two being the big dogs, Princess."

I scrub my hand over my face, knowing this is going to bite me in the ass at some point. "Great. I can't wait for that to come out today."

"It's going to be a tough day," Teddy reminds us as he lifts his head. "We only have a certain amount of time to browse and that assface is definitely going to be there, hovering like a wasp."

"No shit. Alistair Silkshine is the epitome of the spider his name suggests," I quip. I ponder for a moment, wondering if that's some sort of clue or I'm just reading too much into things as I try to make sense of this world.

"He's something else, that's for sure," Wolfie says, his expression unusually feral. "I don't like him and I definitely don't trust him. He knows something about me and what's worse, I think he knows something about Doyle, too."

We all stare at the typically passive vet in shock. He's normally not so vehement, nor is he quite as anxious as he was at the dinner. Could this be why he was having such trouble with Alistair's taunting?

"I didn't catch that," I confess, my heart racing with the thrill of the unknown. "Did any of you?"

The rest of the guys shake their heads and the shining golden man in question glares. "Well isn't that fucking peachy? Now I'm going to have to actually deal with the smarmy shite until I figure out what his game is. Nothing to do with my family is simple and their secrets have quite the price."

"Does it mean we're in more danger?" I ask quietly.

Doyle snorts and rakes his hand through his hair. "If we don't find out who he's been bargaining with, it leaves us very exposed in ways I can't tell you. But I will say it's not something we want to risk."

Just when I thought we might make progress, we're in the middle of yet another mystery.

Who did I piss off in another life?

Family

Wolfgang

The scenery flies by as we head for the palace, but I'm trapped in my thoughts. I wasn't joking when I dropped that bomb this morning; I'm just not sure *why* I believe it to be true. So much about my empathy is cloaked in vibes and feelings that sometimes I feel like I'm a seer predicting a nebulous future. I'm not, but there's a certain amount of big picture shit that I can sense without knowing what the tiny pieces that formed my view are until everything comes together.

It's the Cassandra effect, Prez says, because most of the time, people don't believe me.

But my family does and they accept that I can't give them solid reasons why I think that jackass knows a hell of a lot more than he's letting on. I spent most of that dinner curled in, but it wasn't about his taunts in regards to my father or Callie. I'm not stupid—I realize my bitchy mother wouldn't stoop to fuck around with someone she considered beneath her. That means the bio dad is a big kahuna of some kind and he's stayed hidden for a good reason.

Who knows what that reason is or even if it's as valid as he thinks, but having to hunt him down makes me believe I'm right. Callie's reticence about details also confirms their union would not have been acceptable. She's not one to give a flying fuck about that shit, so the secrecy must be at my father's demand. To get her to comply, he's either *very*powerful, *very* connected, or has something *very* bad on her. The Cailleach isn't known for doing anything out of the kindness of her heart.

If she has one, it's frozen like the tundra.

"You okay, darling boy?"

Jolene's voice brings me out of my thoughts and I give her a soft smile. She's perched on Teddy's lap in the back of this damn limo, looking completely at ease despite all the challenges we're facing. Once she made her decision about not playing people's games anymore, she pulled on the ripped jeans that hug her like a second skin and shoved her feet in worn combat boots like she was declaring war on the Harvest Fae.

Our girl doesn't do anything half way and I fucking love it.

"Yes. I'm just pondering my theory from earlier. I hate that I can't give you guys better clues as to why I think Alistair knows about Doyle, too." Running my hand through my hair, I give her a sheepish look. "I'm also not used to anyone but Prez believing my weird not-premonitions."

"If you say you have a feeling, we believe you, pup," Teddy says with a shrug. Like Sugarplum, he's dressed more casually than yesterday and we all followed suit. He's a natural leader like his dickhead father and the constant support is more of a balm than he realizes. Even Prez has let go of reins because he knows our alpha dog and our girl have it covered. "I don't give a shit if you can't hand me courtroom proof. There's something to be said for instincts and your gut."

Benjy nods, giving me a thumbs up. "Exactly. You guys aren't really sports folks, but we always trust our captain even if he's running on vibes. This family is our team, so if one of us has a theory, we support it."

"The scary part is none of you realize how often Lucy is right," Prez says with a grin. "It's downright eerie how good he is at reading shit when he can focus. That's why I didn't bother him yesterday; he always looks like a sad panda when he's doing that shit."

Pressing my lips together I give my lover a *look*. "I do not."

"You do, but it's adorable. Shush. I'm trying to be supportive."

I give him another look then turn back to Jolene. "Are you ready to kick some snooty rich guy ass, Sugarplum?"

Her lips curve up and the sparkle in her eyes answers before she speaks. "Today is all about 'come at me, bro.' I'm not seeking out trouble, of course, but I'm done letting that twat fuck with us. If we don't find anything before lunch, we're going back to the hotel to pack up and move on. As cute as this place is, we don't have time to dawdle."

Teddy arches his brow, running his eyes over her with a smirk. "Not looking for trouble, huh? Dressed in… that."

All eyes go back to the holey jeans with her torn Clash tee-shirt and knee-high Docs. She shrugs, one shoulder of the tee slipping to reveal her creamy skin. "I'm wearing normal clothes for a normal errand. Anyone who doesn't like it can catch me outside, how 'bout that?"

I almost choke on the snort that escapes my lips and within seconds, everyone is howling with laughter. She's chosen her armor for its battle cry and her attitude this morning is right in line with the genre. "Prepare for parking lot fist fights…. got it."

"Damn straight."

Doyle squints at her, his hand dropping to pet Hyde absently. "Are you sure you want to provoke them this thoroughly? They have the ability to be very indiscreet about our stay to our future hosts."

Jolene shrugs, looking at us as if waiting for someone to correct her. When we don't, she grins at the mischievous Irishman. "We're sure. If you feel the need to be… *you*… we won't stop you, Lucky."

That gets his attention. Doyle sits up straighter, tilting his head as he studies her resolve, then nods. "Right then. We're here to show them when you fuck around, you find out. Message received."

"Damn," Prez says before he whistles low. "You're *asking* for a showdown letting him off his leash, Magpie. You know that, right?"

"Was she unclear?" Teddy asks mildly, his big hand squeezing her knee. "Tilly said we're done playing nice, so we are. That means within certain boundaries, we're all free to do what we need to in order to get our information or defend our family. Saddle up, gents. This dog and pony show just got interesting."

THE DOUBLE DOORS TO THE PALACE FEEL MORE FORBIDDING TODAY than yesterday, but I think that's because I know Sugarplum's let everyone loose. It felt right when she did it, but standing here, I have yet another flash of intuition—something is going to go awry here. I don't know if it's a good or bad thing yet, but I *know* this visit is going to go off the rails in a major way.

"Let's not keep them waiting," she says as she grabs my hand and squeezes. "I don't want that idiot to think we're scared to see him again."

I lick my lips and nod, but I can't help adding, "Be on your guard, though. I have an odd feeling that this won't go as planned."

Teddy nods, striding up to the doors and pressing the button on the intercom. His posture is full of that 'big dick energy' he and Doyle have going for them as he waits for someone to answer. It makes me smile and when I look at my Sugarplum again, she's doing the same.

Big dogs are gonna strut no matter what, I suppose.

"State your business," the voice snaps.

A wave of irritation rolls over the group and that bad feeling digs into my gut again. Not a good start, especially when we've all been pumped up by our coaches.

"Jolene Whitley and family. We're invited guests of Allora. I highly doubt she forgot to inform you of our imminent arrival this morning."

My eyes widen when the charming, diplomatic Edgar takes his leave completely and puts the barking bully in charge. "Holy shit."

"Guess we're not waiting for them to fire the first shot, Lucy. Prepare yourself for a lot of spiky anger when we get inside," Presley says as he comes up behind me.

I'll say—unless we get the Princess herself, we're going to be greeted by pissy ass staff after that declaration.

The doors open and our leader winks at us, holding one as he gestures for us to precede him. As we step into the corridor, my pulse throbs in time with my footsteps. There isn't any opposition so far, but I can't imagine the steward will be pleased when they get to us. Sugarplum squeezes my hand again and tugs me forward, her gait confident as her ponytail bounces.

I suck in a deep breath, schooling my features like I've watched her and Teddy do, then straighten my spine. Benjy and Doyle are following with their heads held high, eyes moving over the hallway as they take in our surroundings cautiously. It might be the same way we entered last night, but we're not here as compliant guests today. Our family was invited to peruse the archives by the princess so we're not here to kiss anyone's ass.

"Was that tone necessary, Your Honor?" A short Fae appears in front of us, his arms crossed over his chest as he glares up at Teddy. He's obviously required to observe protocol and use the honorific, but he doesn't want to. The expression on his face and the ramrod posture he's projecting make that abundantly clear.

Jolene steps forward before he can answer, looking down at the brownie. "It was. The greeting was rude, which I doubt is normal for someone who works for such gracious people as the Hieronymous and Allora. It makes me wonder if you knew who was there and *chose* to be snide. Is that what happened or did you make an error on a bad day?"

The mustachioed man looks even more furious at her question. He huffs, then turns on his heel. His voice is less aggressive when he calls over his shoulder. "Follow me to the archives. Do not dawdle or deviate from our path. You have not been cleared for any other area of the building."

I get the feeling this fucker works for the Queen; she seems like the type who would employ a nasty little weasel to greet people.

We follow the steward down a hall, around a few turns, and down two separate staircases until we reach another large set of double doors. He sneers at us as he pulls a big key ring out, using it to unlock the doors. The room he reveals is *not* the book filled hall from last night—no, it's an enormous, dimly lit underground room with row after row of ancient looking tomes and scrolls.

"Allora will join you shortly to review the archivists' guidelines for using our treasured library. You may wait inside until she arrives, but *do not* touch anything. There are…" he pauses for a moment and looks as if he's searching for a word. "…*security measures* in place to ensure none of our most valuable records are used or taken. It is a rather aggressive system and I do not recommend trying your luck until she disarms it."

Excellent. He's telling us this is guarded by nasty magic that will hurt or kill us if we get impatient.

"Thank you for informing us," Jolene says as her eyes roam the room curiously. "It must have been difficult not to leave us to our own devices without relaying that knowledge. You made a good choice."

The stout Fae gives her a sour look, then marches off, leaving us standing in the room alone.

"You really are ready to do battle today, aren't you, Princess?" Benjy says with a soft chuckle. "I thought you were going to curb stomp that little dickwad when he mouthed off to Big Daddy."

Her head whips around and she gives him a venomous glare. "Shh-hhh. If that nickname gets around, you'll be the one in my hot seat, Benjamin Foster. We'll see just how much *you* like a red ass."

He shrugs and gives her a bright grin. "For you, I'll try anything once, Mama J."

What the hell life am I living right now?

Jolene Whitley has torn every one of us down and we're all building back up together and I am *here for it.*

Secrets

Jolene

The air is thick with the scent of old paper and dust, a perfume that stirs an odd sense of reverence within me. My gaze drifts over stacks on stacks of ancient tomes, their bindings etched with time's tender caress. It's like stepping into a world where history pulses through the very walls, whispering secrets of ages past. I've always loved libraries and one of the extremely geeky, touristy things I made Seer do in every city we visited was to go places like this. It always feels like knowledge is just pouring into the air, waiting for you to grab on to it.

The guys haven't seen this side of me yet, though I know Teddy and Benjy remember how much time I spent in the library as a teen.

"I'm so happy you were able to return," Allora's voice is melodic yet hushed, as if the library itself demands a certain solemnity. She moves with an ethereal grace as she enters.

I step aside as she walks over to a pedestal by the wall, glad we have at least one ally in this damn place. She places her hand on a piece of glass above it, and a series of intricate symbols glow with a pale blue light. Her fingers are quick as she pushes various fast moving things on the screen as if playing a very high tech version of Simon. A tinkling sound echoes through the room and I hear something that sounds like a pop before she turns to us again.

"There we are. The security systems are quite particular. It's keyed to certain people and requires a light touch," she explains vaguely.

She doesn't meet my eyes, so I simply nod. Feigning ignorance is my only option until I'm allowed to know shit, but my mind reels with curiosity. That seemed like it might be magic mixed with tech—something that fascinates the hell out of me. I don't know that I have innate abilities that would allow me to work with such a fancy system, but I'd love to feel that secure in my house.

Damn the assholes who put this stupid ban on telling people like me what the hell is going on.

"Over there, you'll find the handling gloves and special cloths for the more delicate pieces," Allora continues, gesturing towards a neatly organized cart.

Bottles of what I assume are preservation liquids line the top shelf and various instruments gleam even in the dim light of the library. They obviously take their stuff seriously, so I shoot Doyle a narrow eyed look. He smirks, holding up his hands in surrender and I turn back to the princess, satisfied none of my crew will fuck around with their important shit.

"Thank you," I say, plucking a pair of white gloves from the pile. They're softer than I expected, almost like they're woven from clouds. I pull them on, and they fit perfectly, as though they were made just for me. No way *that* isn't magic and now I'm even saltier about this situation.

Imagine what that kind of power could do for sheets…

As we walk, Allora points out the different sections, her words carefully curated to keep from violating my silly ban. "This area holds volumes of political history—power struggles, alliances formed and broken over centuries—including with other families and peoples." Her fingers trace the spines of bound leather, the embossed titles indecipherable to my untrained eye.

"Social and practical histories are through here," she gestures towards another row, lined with scrolls sealed with ribbons and wax. "You'll find accounts of cultural practices, economic developments, and other significant societal evolutions."

I can't help wondering who they're significant to, but I keep the question to myself. I don't want to fuck anything up and get her in trouble, either. She's doing us a huge favor allowing us into this vault of knowledge. We can't make her life any more difficult than it already appears to be.

"Of course, we have our mythological annals as well." Her smile is tight as she nods towards a section that seems to hum with an energy all its own. "Tales of heroism, tragedy, creatures of legend... they provide essential context for understanding the broader picture."

"Sounds fascinating," I reply, my throat dry. I'm itching to dive into those stories, to see the hidden threads of magic and Fae that I know must be interwoven in the text. I can't let that show, though, because nothing she's describing would warrant that enthusiastic response. If I look like I'm going to lose my shit, she'll suspect that I know—Allora's not dumb.

"Lastly, newer information from the last century is stored here," she says, indicating a set of shelves less burdened by the weight of time. "It includes various interactions and events involving multiple groups, even some pertaining to sister courts."

Sister courts? Was that slip on purpose?

My heart skips a beat. I'm so close to the knowledge I crave, yet it feels just out of reach, veiled in Allora's careful phrasing. There's a dance happening here, one where every step and turn is measured, deliberate.

"Allora," I start, trying to sound casual, "have you ever come across something in these histories that surprised you?"

"Constantly," she replies, her eyes finally locking onto mine. There's a depth there, an ancient knowing that sends a shiver down my spine. "History has a way of unfolding in unexpected patterns. Sometimes what we believe to be true is merely a fraction of the story."

Her words echo in my mind, a puzzle begging to be solved. But for now, I simply nod, my hands itching to peel back the layers of the past hidden within these walls. I follow her lead, each step taking me deeper into the labyrinth of knowledge, the threshold between what is known and what is meant to remain secret.

The scent of ancient leather and dust fills my nostrils in the next part of the library. The air is cool and still as if it too is holding its breath in anticipation. Allora's slender hand traces the spines of books so old I fear they might crumble under her touch. Something about the way the tomes here are displayed gives me a hint and my eyes widen when I figure it out.

"Genealogy?" I ask, my voice a whisper amongst the towering shelves. "We're hoping to find something on lineage."

Teddy grunts and I note him putting a hand on Wolfie's shoulder. They've been quiet as our guide led us around, but I imagine they're concerned what would happen if I were to be allowed to dig into this section.

"Ah, yes," she replies, her gaze lingering on a heavy tome bound in dark green leather. "There is a section for that, but Wolfie will need to go through it with Teddy." She pauses, her cough delicate like the flutter of moth wings. "You understand, such materials require... specific clearance."

"Of course," I say, nodding even though frustration knots my stomach.

Everyone around me plays their part perfectly, faces schooled into understanding. I know better. It's not about clearance; it's about keeping secrets from my 'human' eyes. The same secrets my now useless dream glasses are supposed to shield me from. I bite back a bitter smile – if only they knew how clearly I see through their charade.

"Benjy, Doyle," Wolfie calls out, "you take ancient history. Teddy and I will handle genealogy."

They nod, making their way toward the dustier end of the library where time seems to have stilled, leaving whispers of the past clinging to the air.

"Magpie, you're with me," Presley says, gesturing toward the newer archives. His eyes glint with a scholar's fervor, unaware of the unease tightening my muscles.

"Let's get started then," I reply, trailing behind him.

As we approach the sleek terminals set against the stone walls, the juxtaposition of old-world charm and new-age tech strikes me. I sit down at a computer, my fingers hesitating over the keys.

This is where I'll either find answers or more riddles.

"Look for anything related to notable figures in the last century, especially if they seem to be avoiding the media," Presley instructs before he gets absorbed in his own search."I think that's where we're going to find this guy—in the shadows, not in the spotlight."

"Agreed," I murmur, my heart pounding as I delve into digital records.

The screen illuminates my face as I comb through an intricate web of sites and services. There's a whole other world of communication sprawling before me. *How could I have been so naïve?* Supes have their own networks, thriving and pulsating right under human noses. No wonder everyone from my past was scrubbed clean from the mundane internet.

They're keeping the profile low where they can't be seen as extraordinary without drawing attention.

"Anything interesting?" Presley asks when I sigh in annoyance. He doesn't look up from his screen and I see him navigating all these unfamiliar windows with ease out of the corner of my eye.

"Somewhat," I answer, careful to keep my tone neutral as I stumble upon a website for message boards. Once I navigate to our home town, I blink in surprise. My men are talked about as if they are celebrities in the Hollow messages. Fame and adoration drip from every post, painting some of them in a light I never considered. The fawning over Teddy isn't shocking, nor is the ire for Benjy because of his split with Sherilynn. But the thirsting over Prez, Wolfie, and Doyle is… intense.

"You seem to be getting the hang of this pretty easily," I comment. Using a half-truth to mask my real discovery is the best I can do. A lot of the gossip on the Hollow board is salacious or downright nasty, so I'm wading through dreck to hunt for nuggets of gold.

"It's pretty simple. I've had to deal with programs like this before at school," he says with a shrug. Prez is too focused to notice my distraction and I know it's because he's assuming the glasses are doing their job.

Too bad that designer chick fucked with them and now I'm getting all the tea I've wanted since they admitted they're hiding shit—or least, some of it.

My curiosity propels me deeper, past the innocuous pages, to forbidden territories. Hybrids, Andromeda Bane, the schools— they're all pieces of a puzzle that's slowly clicking together as I surf their internet. Memories from my childhood align like stars in a constellation, revealing a picture too grand and terrifying to fully comprehend. I lean back in my chair, the weight of knowledge pressing down on me.

"Are you alright?" Presley finally looks at me, a look of concern creasing his brow.

"Fine, just... I'm overwhelmed by how much there is to go through," I admit, offering him a strained smile. "Our hosts and their reciprocal families have lots of connections and get a shit ton of attention online. More than I ever would have realized."

"Do what you can for now," he says, turning back to his work. "We have visits to the last two families left before we jet home. I have a feeling we'll pick up things while we're there, too. This is more like extra credit, you know?"

I grin, looking at him as he pushes his glasses up. Prez is so adorable and so damn easy going. He and Wolfie made the first couple days I was home much more tolerable, especially since I was still fighting Teddy. *Speaking of which...* "Prez?"

"Hmmm?" he murmurs from his computer.

"Not that I'm complaining *at all*, but what the hell happened with you and..." I make a face at my screen as I choke it out, "...Big Daddy Asshole last night?"

He bursts out laughing, swiveling his chair towards me. I do the same, my cheeks flushed as he grins. "Surprised you, didn't I?"

"I mean, yeah?" I tilt my head as my eyes dance. "You're hot as fuck together—in a different way than he is with Wolfie."

"Probably different than Doyle will, too," he says as he takes my hands. "And don't tell me you can't see *that* cause you're not blind, Magpie."

I laugh softly as our fingers twine together. "I'm not dumb enough to think that putting those two tigers in a cage won't result in fighting, fucking, or both. Doyle's about as fluid as they come. He does whatever the hell he wants no matter what anyone thinks."

"Yep," Prez murmurs as he lifts our hands to kiss my knuckles. "I, however, choose people based on emotions. And making Lucy happy is *always* a good way to worm your way into my good graces and perhaps, eventually, into my heart."

Now I get it—the way Teddy takes care of Wolfie made him more attractive until Prez couldn't help himself.

Wrinkling my nose, I lean forward to whisper to him. "I get how you arrived at what happened last night now. What do you think went on with Teddy?"

He snorts and shakes his head. "Oh, Magpie. That man is a sucker for people who love you as much as I am for people who love Lucy. And he's likely always been curious but had no way to explore it before you demanded he accept us. Now he has an entire room full of people to boss around and protect. Edgar Boone is living his absolute *best life* right now."

"You're pretty smart, you know. It's really sexy," I whisper before kissing his lips lightly. "But we have to get back to it or someone's going to come in and threaten to spank us."

"I'd literally *pay* to hear that conversation."

Prez winks at me and scoots back to his computer, leaving me grinning like an idiot as I spelunk my way through the supe internet looking for clues.

I'm living my best life, too.

Destiny

Edgar

The air in the genealogy section is thick with dust and the musty scent of ancient leather, a tangible reminder that history is more than words—it's a living, breathing entity. Harvest Court's secret archives aren't as vast as the Society's, but they're focused on a species determined to keep much of their internal history and strife to themselves. Tilly can't appreciate how rare an opportunity this is until we can be completely honest, but she's going to love it.

The amount of people allowed into this kind of place within Faerie can't be more than a handful a year—less than the Vatican archives, I'd bet.

"Do they feel different to you?" The pup's eyes scan the spines of countless tomes with a mix of reverence, his fingers trailing over the embossed titles. Despite the time crunch, I've noticed he seems wistful at times when we look around these lands. Perhaps a vacation with the family where things aren't so urgent? I file that away in my mental notes for later.

Considering his question, I shake my head. "No more so than the rest of the room. Does it feel different to you?"

"Very. They're humming with energy until I touch them. Once I make contact, they sing."

My brow is furrowed as I take in his words, then I squint at the volumes. "Do they all sound the same, pup?"

"Nope. Some are louder, some are soft, and some are almost silent. Do you think that means something?" He pauses, looking at me with unsure eyes as his hand hovers near a shelf.

That damn doctor wasn't wrong about the submissive Fae—once his hooks are in, you're a goner and I already went down with the ship.

"Probably," I scratch my chin as I pull out a thick book on the history of the Unseelie Courts. "I'd look at the loudest ones first; they might be trying to give you a hint."

Carrying my chosen book to a nearby chair, I leaf through the ornate volume looking for sections that stand out. We don't have time to read everything, so I pull out my phone to snap pictures of anything that catches my eye. We can print this out later and add it to Tilly's board at home if we need to. I doubt the Fae are involved in the mysterious cover-up involving her parents' death, but I think the clues to who and what she is could be anywhere. There's too much unexplained about her and the way she's emerging for it to be anything simple.

Wolfie finally settles on two books, bringing them over with him as he settles on the ottoman to my seat. He curls up on the wide, cushioned footrest, leaning against me as he opens his books. My lips curve up and I drop a hand to run my finger through his hair as we read.

If someone told me I'd be gallivanting through Faerie with my mates and family a couple months ago, I would have laughed in their face.

"Look at this," Wolfie murmurs, pointing to a faded painting of a being shrouded in shadows. The text below the image says it's an advisor to the court known for his cunning, discretion, and power. "Do you think this might be him?"

"Maybe." I squint at the image, then the page, noting there's no name associated with the figure. The book he's flipping through is definitely old as hell and even I feel the buzz coming off of it. It's not calling to me like it did the pup, but there's magic in that book. "We need more than speculation, though. Can you find more references to this advisor?"

"I'll try." He goes back to scanning the text and I watch for a minute. The kid reads so fast it's like the pages are going by in blur. He's so unassuming that I forget he skipped grades and flew through vet school like a blur because he's a damn genius. Looking at him in his element, though, it's impressive as fuck. Wolfie researches like that skinny kid on the crime show Tilly likes and for a moment, I grin when I think about it.

She's forming her own team with a hard-nosed leader, a boy wonder, a kind muscled alpha, a troublemaker, a wizened old soul, a visionary, and a laid back doctor. No wonder she enjoys that shit so much. Hell, now that I think about it, there's some of her in the dark haired chick.

"Teddy?"

Whoops. Got distracted thinking about whether she'd let Benjy call her 'baby girl.'

"Did you find something, pup?" I ask as I return to reality.

"Maybe. More of a question…" Wolfie's voice is laced with frustration as he taps the book page. "If the Society made strict rules about interbreeding, why did they allow people to break them? Why create havens to take care of the results of breaking that edict? I mean, why not hunt down the people who were thumbing their noses at the decree?"

"Rules are for those who fear consequences, not for those who write them," I reply as I turn another page of my book. "Most species aren't forbidden to inter-breed anymore, as you know. There's some historical shit, probably in Benjy and Doyle's section, that will clarify who those rules apply to now. The program was designed to keep lost ones whose parentage might be dangerous from being dropped in the middle of humans to live their lives like normal people. I mean, there are lots of human tales that likely describe that very situation still happening. Look at shit like Hercules or X-Men or Superman."

"So they created the program specifically to monitor the kids who might emerge with multiple sides or powers that would be dangerous. That means the only supes or beings dropping kids at the assigned spots have to be… extremely powerful," Wolfie says, piecing together the history. "Deities, demi-gods, ancients, overpowered shifters, magicals… Anyone who was adopted through the program has the potential to become a huge issue if they aren't watched. That's why they have the Guardians, especially for adoptees who don't emerge when they should."

"Exactly. The Society inducts or employs the unpredictable ones, like us. They monitor the ones who haven't broken their barrier spell because they didn't emerge." Teddy agrees, glancing toward the door as if expecting someone to overhear. "Nelia said there was one a few years ahead of us that seemed like a major concern, but according to her Guardian, she disappeared off the face of the planet. The chick reappeared with suspicious skills that can't be explained, which is why they're so worried about Jolene."

"The Hollow was never just a town," Wolfie whispers as it dawns on him. "It was a crucible for something bigger."

"Likely. They had to wait until the opportunity was right to get control of the town so they could increase cloaking and barrier spells for the humans and non-emerged. The Senator was part of swinging that deal; I remember him being so damn proud of it. Even as a kid, I knew it was a big deal. Whistler's Hollow was the last enclave they got full control over and it was the most important one, he said."

I pinch the bridge of my nose, feeling puzzle pieces slot together from my life, our current situation, and my work with the Society. The people who are pulling these strings aren't evil; they're trying to protect everyone. By the lengths they're willing to go, it stands to reason that there are beings out there that everyone needs protecting from.

They must be working with the Fates to prevent something; that's the only thing big enough to span this many centuries and the entire globe.

"That's why they have Bane in the Hollow," I breathe. "The woman is ancient as fuck and she's been in charge of making certain the emerged here are trained and developed. But lately, they've been sending her on away missions again, which says to me that they feel it's safe to have her absent from town. Why?"

"They've got some chick with powers and no info running loose, as you said. Plus, there's been a lot of Society chatter about supe activity in other parts of the country." Wolfie looks at me for a moment, his brows drawn together as he thinks. "If they were worried about a specific being or events, they'd send their strongest people to deal with it. Andromeda is one… and Saoirse's team must be another. They're being directly instructed by those wacky sisters."

"Christ," I mutter as I scrub my hand down my face. "This shit is hitting the bottom of the ocean. It feels like they've all been moving chess pieces for centuries—or longer."

"Maybe they have," he whispers softly. "So many supes *never* find their mates, Teddy. All of us have landed smack dab in the same town—right at the time our unemerged girl comes blowing in like a hurricane. Doesn't that feel… coincidental? Like *too* coincidental?"

Well, now *it does. Fuck. Me. Running.*

"To be clear, we're surmising that we are all part of a millennia-long experiment—a test to see how much we could change the game without breaking it. But now whatever the fuck they were worried about is happening, so they're scrambling to 'Avengers Assemble' and make a team?" I shake my head. "Too surreal, pup. This is tin foil hat level shit."

"Maybe," Wolfie says quietly. "You have to admit it's weird. You being the only *triplásia* we've heard of, Doyle and I having mystery dads, Prez being a healer, Jolene reacting to all our supe sides, all being fated… all of that is a lot. And that's without throwing in the companions, a fucking *djinn*, and a *male* seer. It's too much to be random. Mathematically speaking, random isn't…"

"Either way," I sigh, closing the heavy book with a decisive thump, "we're far more entwined than we imagined. All of us might have been drawn here—bound by a secret destiny or some shit."

"Bound by fate," Wolfie muses. "Not something you can plan for, huh?"

I snort. "I spent most of my life rebelling just enough that the Senator couldn't force me into some world-shouldering responsibility. I definitely wasn't looking to get recruited for a Scooby team. Can't we just… run off to the Maldives and buy a fuck hut? I could get Tilly on board; I know it."

He blinks then bursts into laughter. "A fuck hut?"

My eyes narrow and I give the pup my best version of a pout. "Yes, that's what I said. We all chip in and buy a hut on the water. We'll laze in the sun all day and fuck and eat delicious shit. No dangerous world saving fuckery involved."

"You don't like the idea of anyone being in danger," the Fae says with a soft smile. "I get it. Making sure you're not responsible for anything is a reaction to the disappointment your father expressed and—"

"Pup?"

"Hmm?" he asks as he pushes his hair out of his eyes.

"Shut it," I say with a fond grin. "We've got more research to do on your sperm donor before we leave. I want to get as much done here as possible so we don't have to keep working when we get back to the hotel."

Tilting his head, he gives me a serious look. "We didn't talk about what happened last night and even if we can't include Sugarplum, we need to."

I frown. "Because of the doc?"

"No, because I had to magic away a pound of faerie dust, feathers, fluids, and that weird solid dust your mist turned into once our girl passed out." Wolfie makes a face and points at me. "*You* didn't tell anyone your... mist... is solid."

Uh-oh. Admission time.

"That's because it's *never been* solid before," I mutter. "Jolene is changing us in ways we aren't aware of until it happens. I mean, you haven't released that much glittery shit before, either. The doc doesn't leave feathers everywhere. I highly doubt Benjy left sheds like that at home or Sherilynn would have thrown him out long ago. This is *all* new."

"We're getting stronger as she bonds to all the parts," he murmurs. "And she's definitely bonding to them more deeply each time. Did you see her eyes?"

"Yep." I lean back in my chair and look up at the ceiling, blowing out a breath. "We are so fucking screwed, pup."

His head rests on my lap as he responds, "On the bright side, no one's trying to open a Hellmouth, so we have that going for us."

Oh, well, I suppose everything's peachy, then.

Wish That You Were Here

Hugo

The world folds like origami, edges sharp and sudden, before it bursts into new shapes. I stagger as reality solidifies around us, the air thick with the scent of salt and humid earth. Temporal magic has always had its quirks, but nothing quite compares to the prince's brand of travel.

"Welcome to Brazil, my friend," Dhameer says, a hint of amusement in his voice. He's used to this, as is his staff, but moving through time and space by accessing the object where he exists outside of time is rough.

Not that I have any idea what that object might be—djinn guard those secrets like the Society does the identities of their highest ranking members.

I nod, trying to keep my balance and dignity intact. The once-familiar sensation of ground beneath my feet now seems alien. My words come out shaky, mirroring the tremble in my legs as I finally reply, "That was... intense."

"Quicker than a flight, though, wouldn't you say?" He sweeps an arm grandly, indicating our lavish surroundings, the sun casting glimmers over Rio's skyline visible from our penthouse suite.

"It's perfect if you don't account for the migraine." I press my fingers against my temples, hoping to quell the pounding behind my eyes.

My visions, usually a trickle of foresight, are now a deluge of images, crashing over me with no regard for my sanity.

"Ah, yes, your gift can be... inconvenient at times," Dhameer acknowledges, his concern peeking through his usual stoicism as he watches me closely. "You should rest. We have time."

"Rest, he says," I mutter under my breath in half amusement, half exasperation. Those who don't have the 'gift' of sight rarely comprehend what a physical toll it takes on your body. The mental weight is enough to destroy lesser beings, but the bodily symptoms wreck even immortals like me. "As if lying down will stop the kaleidoscope in my head."

"Sometimes, Hugo, you must allow the body to catch up with where the mind has been thrust." His tone brooks no argument—the prince's natural imperiousness ever present in his demeanor. "Do as I say or we won't be able to achieve our goals when you break down."

"Fine." I relent—not because I want to, but because arguing with an ancient royal when I feel like I've been tossed in a cosmic blender is futile. I sink into the plush king-sized bed that looks like it belongs in a museum rather than a hotel room. Closing my eyes, I pray for relief, but the darkness only serves as a canvas for the flashes of places I've never seen and people I've never met.

"Let me know if there's anything you need," Dhameer says, worry creasing his brow. "We could call for a healer—"

"No healers. Just time." I force a tight-lipped smile, opening my eyes to meet his gaze squarely. "It'll pass. Always does."

He nods, though I can tell he's not entirely convinced. The prince moves toward the door, pausing to glance back. "Remember, we have all the comforts of Olympus here. Use them."

With that, he steps out, leaving me to wrestle with my own turbulent senses. Finally alone, I focus on breathing.

Inhale. Exhale. Repeat.

My thoughts drift despite my efforts to anchor them. I try to piece together any coherence from the maelstrom of my visions, but it's like grasping at smoke. All I manage is to catch glimpses—a street carnival exploding in color, a woman's cry, the flit of a shadow just out of reach.

Hours pass, or minutes—it's hard to tell. Slowly, the flashes subside, and the migraine dulls to a persistent throb. I sit up, testing my equilibrium, relieved to find the world holding steady. I rise, steadier now, and walk to the window. Rio sprawls before me, lively and vibrant. I watch the city pulse with life, and promise myself that I'll partake in it—as soon as I'm truly able. For now, though, I am content to observe from this quiet refuge, gathering strength for what lies ahead.

THE SUN DIPS BELOW THE HORIZON, SPILLING MOLTEN GOLD ACROSS the opulent room. I stand by the window, a silent sentinel, fingers tracing the chiseled marble of the windowsill. Outside, Rio de Janeiro hums with unceasing energy, but within these walls, there's a different kind of intensity brewing.

"Any improvement?" Dhameer's voice ripples through the stillness as he enters, bearing a sheaf of papers that whisper promises and secrets.

"The visions are clearer," I answer, turning to face him. "No more riddles from the ether—for now." Relief is a tangible thing in my chest, yet it's laced with caution; my gift never allows for complacency.

"Good. We need clarity if we're to unravel this mess." Dhameer spreads the documents on the mahogany desk, his brow furrowed in concentration. "Our thread leads here, to Brazil. The assassin—or assassins—who executed that officer in Istanbul and decimated an entire family... they've left traces. Infinitesimally small traces, of course, but Isra was able to track them down for me."

I join him at the desk, my gaze flitting over the pages, each one a breadcrumb on a trail we must follow. "Human criminals?" I muse aloud, the notion foreign yet plausible amidst the chaos we've encountered.

"It would seem so. Saoirse's intel suggests they're operating under the noses of human law enforcement with ease. Though in the Society's defense, I can understand why no one understood this particular assignment had bearing on the supernatural world. We don't interfere in human affairs without just cause, so this group hasn't been on the agents' radars, either." He taps a photo of a group of people in black with obscured faces gathered in shadows, and I feel the weight of their deeds like a yoke around my neck.

"Then we'll shine light into those shadows to see what they're hiding." Determination steadies my voice even though getting involved with humans gives me pause. Oracles don't interact with them much anymore, except for me, and my assignment has always been to observe and report. I've kept myself apart from the citizens in the Hollow purposefully to honor that agreement, but this skirts the line of what my people are allowed to do.

I could get in a lot of trouble for taking part in this—maybe even be recalled to the temple—but it's worth it for her.

"Exactly." Dhameer's agreement is fierce, a warrior's pledge.

He rifles through the stack, showing me a few more clues his faithful guard gathered. Isra found records of their individual entries into the country, a few clues about where they might have gathered after they arrived, and the last part is what led us to Brazil—four separate identities that left Turkey. They snaked around the globe before ending up in Brazil, but their trail is here in black and white.

I look around, taking in the lavish surroundings—the villa is grandiose, sprawling. It's hard not to feel dwarfed by the scale of luxury, by the sheer opulence that seems to mock my Spartan tendencies. The Temple of our lady is luxurious, but the acolytes who live there do not stay in that environment. Our quarters are nearby and virtually barren to prevent clutter from clouding our visions. My apartment in the Hollow is similar—it's what I know and feel comfortable in.

"Is something wrong?" Dhameer catches my gaze, a corner of his mouth quirking up in understanding.

"Olympus wasn't built in a day," I quip, trying to shake off the discomfort. Riches have never been something I sought; I've always found more value in the unseen, in the visions that guide me.

"Consider our journey practice," he says with a chuckle. "This is nothing compared to the halls of gods and heroes you've tread. I'm aware of the Greeks' love of exorbitant surroundings."

"True," I concede, a smile tugging at my lips. "Though I doubt Zeus concerns himself with air conditioning glitches or Wi-Fi passwords. He's more of a delegator."

"Ah, but does he have a view like this?" Dhameer gestures towards the panoramic vista of Rio's night skyline, winking with endless lights.

Olympus moves, so he could if he chose. But that's information I definitely cannot share.

"Point taken." I allow myself a moment to marvel at it all—one does not simply overlook the beauty of the mortal realm when you have the chance. All the work various deities put into this world as it developed is breathtaking, even after so many years on this plane.

"Come, let's focus. There's much to do, and time, as ever, is a fickle ally." He turns back to the papers, his demeanor shifting to that of the general he truly is, mapping out the terrain of our investigation.

As I lean over the desk, poring over maps and notes, I can't help but feel a surge of gratitude. For all its strangeness, this journey, this mission—it binds us together, a fellowship cast against darkness. And in the heart of this gilded cage, we forge our resolve, ready to confront whatever may come.

THE HUMID AIR OF RIO CLINGS TO MY SKIN LIKE A SECOND, STICKY shadow. Fazal and Isra have already melted into the throngs outside, their silhouettes fading among street vendors and pulsing samba rhythms.

"Think they'll get what we need?" I ask Dhameer, watching the crowd swallow his two closest advisors.

"Isra's instincts are sharper than a viper's fangs," he replies without looking back at me, his eyes scanning the sea of humanity with an analytical gaze. "And Fazal has a way with words that could sell sand to a desert."

I nod, the weight of the mission nesting uneasily in my stomach. We need connections, threads to pull us closer to the web of assassins we're hunting. The thought of what those threads might lead to sends a chill through me despite the sweltering heat.

Once we put together all the intel Isra gathered, Dhameer called Jolene's Guardian and she insisted we wait until she arrived. She's been losing her mind cooped up with her family and the human; I think the prince took pity on her, so he used the same method of travel to bring her to Rio while Fazal procured earwigs for us. The careful inquiries Isra made in the marketplace this afternoon gave us the time and place for a private party at a villa in the hills we believe will help us make contact with an informant.

Now he and I are on the guest list of the affair, which allows his staff and the Guardian entry to snoop around the mansion.

"Got it," Saoirse's voice cuts through my reverie, her determined tone ringing clear even over the din. "Lead confirmed. I'm on it."

"Alone?" Isra's voice is cool, but the disdain for an operative so opposite of her isn't lost on me. The lesser djinn does not like all the new people in the Prince's life and I suppose after centuries of working for him, I don't blame her.

But Seer knows what she's doing or the Society wouldn't have her guarding an unemerged lost one.

"Listen, grumpy. I can handle myself. Besides," Saoirse retorts in irritation. "Hugo and Dhameer will see me safely to the rift once I accomplish our mission and you'll be rid of me. Don't get your armor in a bunch."

"Let's make haste, then," Dhameer says, breaking the tension. "We have a party to attend."

The castle looms before us, its walls steeped in history and secrets. It reminds me of *Schloss Neuschwanstein*, but any whimsy is snuffed out by the realization of its dark past. I feel a shiver travel up my spine as we pass under the archway, the sense of walking through a portal into a time best forgotten.

"Escaped Nazi legacy in full effect here," Saoirse mutters, her eyes flitting across the grandeur, the opulence built upon the bones of atrocities. She speaks for the ghosts who can no longer cry out. "This shit makes my skin crawl."

"Tomorrow," Dhameer whispers to her, his voice a low growl of promised vengeance. "Isra will return, and the past shall fear the future."

"Good." Her lips curve into a smile, but there's no joy in it—only the sharp edge of a blade thirsting for righteousness. The Valkyrie in her has never been quite so obvious as right now—Dhameer's promise of justice for the innocent makes it shine like a beacon.

I watch the two fierce warriors, cloaked in the finery of a gala but armored with conviction stronger than steel. As I stand beside them, I realize that while I falter amidst the luxury that feels foreign to my touch, I am anchored by something far greater— faith in the visions that guide us.

"Let's not linger any longer than necessary," I suggest, the mansion's tainted legacy weighing heavily on me.

I do not want to get trapped in visions here; the rancid atmosphere is crawling over me as it is.

"Agreed," Dhameer says, his eyes briefly meeting mine before returning to the task at hand. "We dance with wolves tonight, but we do not join their pack."

With my friends by my side, I step further into the lion's den, ready to face whatever beasts may lurk within.

Hopefully, the risk is worth the reward.

QUIET

JOLENE

The air in the digital archives hums with a kind of static energy, as if the magic vibrates through the cables, connecting us to the outside world. Silver-blue screens cast an eerie glow on Presley's determined face as he methodically captures the last bits of data. I'm saving photographs of scroll after ancient scroll like a thief of knowledge in a treasure trove that stretches back centuries.

Too bad I have to continue this ridiculous charade of not understanding what I'm screenshotting.

"Do you think we've got enough to piece together what we need to know?" Presley's voice cuts through the silence.

Suppressing the urge to roll my eyes at him—because how the fuck would I know since I'm not supposed to be able to see the real texts—I push back from the table with a sigh. "More than enough. Their past is written in more than just words. It's in their actions—the deals they made and broke."

Presley nods, tapping his phone before he frowns at his screen again. "Allora mentioned the 'sister' courts, right? Hopefully, you found references to them. I think our current and previous hosts pretend they're the sunshine twins, but I bet their shadows cast just as darkly as the others when it comes to politics."

"We're about to walk into part of that shadow later today. I don't know if this will help us, but I made sure to get anything that seemed noteworthy." My mind races as I reflect on our next destination—the Midnight Court. Home to Alistair, with his eyes like twilight storms and a demeanor just as unpredictable, it's not known for being the most vicious, but it's a close second.

We're willingly entering the belly of the beasts despite being hampered by that damn oath; I don't like it.

"Jolene," Presley leans closer, lowering his voice, "these families play the game differently. Like our snooty friend from dinner, they craft confusion until you're trapped in a labyrinth of your own making. We all need to be more cautious with what we say and do—even in private."

"Gee, I was hoping we'd go somewhere that makes me worry I'm being spied on while we fuck. It was on my 'to-do' list for next year," I quip. I sound like I'm joking, but based on the tricks and traps I've been reading about, it's not outside of the realm of possibility. It's not like they'd release revenge porn, but they will use shit they have no right to in order to get ahead in negotiations. Every court dances around truth as if it were a flame—beautiful to behold but perilous to touch—but the next Fae we visit seem to have mastered intrigue.

That is, if you believe everything you read online—which I don't.

"I'd say fuck this, but we need them." His reminder is like a pin to a balloon, deflating any illusion of avoiding their bullshit. "We're more likely to find details about Wolfie's father or perhaps even the man himself in these destinations. It's important to him, so we have to make it work."

"The risk is why most people avoid them entirely unless they have specific needs. It's pretty clearly outlined in everything I found— don't fuck with the dark houses." I shrug, leaning back in my chair as I try to dance around what I know again. "But they have a big industry and whatever it is they provide is in demand, hence all the tales of *caveat emptor* about making deals with them."

"Big gains," the doctor muses, "big risks. People know what they're getting into when they come calling. That doesn't make it right, but it does help us figure out what to watch for, I suppose."

"Exactly." I exhale, the weight of what lies ahead settling on my shoulders. We're about to dive headfirst into a world where even the flora may have fangs and every bargain is a beast waiting to pounce. I thought the crap the rich people in the Hollow put me through was bad, but I have a feeling this is going to much worse.

No room for mistakes with this one, Whitley.

"Ready to pack up?" Presley asks, glancing at the clock. Time has slipped away from us, hiding in the crevices between each revelation and secret we've unearthed and we definitely need to get moving if we want to arrive in the next place before dark.

"Ready as I'll ever be."

My affirmation is a battle cry tinged with trepidation. As we gather our devices and exit our section of the library, the light shifts, casting long shadows that mimic the ones we're stepping towards. I squint, tilting my head as I watch them change in the flickering light. They grow, mimicking horrified faces, then change back to our normal profiles.

Hell, even this damn place knows we're heading into the great unknown... fantastic.

THE ANCIENT HISTORY SECTION OF THE LIBRARY IS A SANCTUARY OF hushed whispers and the musty scent of time-worn pages. This looks like some of the old libraries I toured throughout Europe more than the section we just left. I close my eyes, inhaling the scent of lignin with a smile. No matter how many people try to make candles and shit that carry its scent, there's nothing like the real thing.

Hovering between rows of towering bookshelves, I run my fingers over the texts carefully. Some are well used—their spines are cracked and faded. Others look as if they've rarely been touched and I wonder if the royal library takes donations or if they simply gather copies of everything they can like literary hoarders. I'm all for it either way, but a girl could get lost for weeks in this damn place.

How do they get anything done when they could be down here?

"Over here, Magpie," Presley calls out softly. His voice is barely more than a whisper in the quiet atmosphere, but it echoes through the large section. The dimly lit historical archive has architecture that amplifies sound and I haven't the foggiest idea why anyone would do that.

As I ponder that odd feature, I navigate toward his voice. He's gone deeper into the stacks to find our companions and though my steps are muted on the thick carpet, he turns as soon as I get close. Benjy is at a big mahogany table, poring over a pile of scrolls so ancient, I fear they might crumble under his touch. He doesn't look up, keeping his hands steady on the equipment he's using to ensure he doesn't damage them. Doyle, however, is the picture of idleness, sprawled out on a high-backed chair with one leg lazily thrown over the armrest.

"Did you wear yourself out lounging about while we were all working?" I ask drily as I peg Doyle with a disapproving glare.

"Appearances are deceiving, Tíogair." The Irishman flashes me a roguish grin and lifts his phone, the screen aglow with images of text in languages that twist and coil like serpents. "I snapped these while you two were digging into digital dirt. These scripts are relics, but we can unlock their secrets with the right tools."

"Show-off," I mutter. His brows bob and I walk over to peck his cheek in apology. "Sorry for jumping up your ass without any proof. I know you're trying to contain the chaos as much as possible."

"Ah, but you weren't wrong to suspect me. I have been doing this the easy way while Foster took the worst of it," he admits, eyes twinkling with mischief. "But I didn't sit around with my thumb up my ass, so I'll accept your gracious apology."

The Universe is testing me, I think as I pinch the bridge of my nose. *And I'm going to fail eventually because my patience snapped.*

"Found anything juicy, Benjy?" Presley distracts me from strangling Doyle as he leans over the giant's shoulder, looking at his current focus curiously.

"Legends and lore," Benjy rumbles. "Tales of ceremonial… wedding things, cryptic references to original treaties... It's like piecing together a puzzle without the picture on the box."

"Sounds about right," the doc says as he blows out a breath. "Most families like this are so intertwined that they're almost incestuous. It changes the dynamic from strictly political to a very dangerous familial one. That means what you find will include influences beyond the normal business of the land intrigue—it's tainted with interpersonal shit as well."

"Family secrets are difficult to uncover when people want them buried badly enough," I murmur, my thoughts drifting to the truth about my mother. "People will do anything to keep some things from becoming public knowledge. That's pretty true in the normal royals around the world, too. Europe is full of random people connected to old royal lines through adultery or marriage. They only trusted people of their own station."

"Those people made powerful allies or formidable enemies—many leaders will choose the former. That's why there was so much inbreeding going on." Prez grins, pushing his glasses up as he looks at me.

"Often that led to finding out the object of their alliance was both, if they were not careful," I say thoughtfully. "Alistair's family are like sirens luring sailors to their doom for Allora's family. Their beauty masks the danger beneath, but the risk involved must be worth the price."

"Charming analogy, love, but that can't be our concern right now," Doyle says grimly. "You may like the girl and I do, too, but our biggest concern has to be getting what we need. Once we do, we can go home and leave the expert level bullshit here."

"There's still bullshit to deal with in the Hollow," I correct him as my gaze flicks over the snaps of foreign script on his phone. "We're not going back to a rose garden, Lucky."

Benjy puts down his work, looking up at us with a sigh. He rolls the scrolls carefully, his large hands gentle as he puts them into the casing. "You're both right. However, we can't stand around and argue because we have a date with a bunch of manipulative asshats tonight."

"He's right," I whisper. "We have to get on the road in time to arrive before dark; that was a very stringent recommendation in the things I read today."

"Then let's not keep them waiting," Prez says with a wink. "We'll grab Boone and Lucy, then get back to the hotel to pack up the animals. We're not going to give these fuckers anymore advantage than they have before we get there."

His resolve steadies my nerves and I nod. "Let's blow this joint."

WOLFIE'S VOICE CUTS THROUGH THE DENSE SILENCE OF THE genealogy section as we walk in. "Honestly, this is a mess, Teddy. Alistair's marriage to Allora is all political maneuvering. Dumb crap about heirs and lineage that the royals care about far too much."

"Isn't it always that way with your kind?" Teddy mutters as he flips through a book that looks like it's going to fall apart. "I mean, sometimes there's other stuff like—"

"Money," Wolfie continues as he looks up at him seriously. "They don't want to join forces with Midnight, but the Queen seems to be pushing the King. I wonder why." He pauses, eyes narrowing, as if seeing the chessboard of intricate politics in his head. "Hieronymous isn't exactly in good health, particularly mentally. If something happens to Allora, there will be a fight. I can smell the greed coming from her stepmother."

"Charming family dynamics," I say when they notice we're here. "It's almost like we're not the only ones with fucked up relatives. Oh, wait… that's everyone."

I think I'm funny, but apparently none of them do.

"Tilly, you spent a shit ton of time with lots of rich assholes and celebs. Do you think their problems are the same as normal folks?" Teddy grins and shrugs. "Everyone's family has issues, but when you throw in money, fame, and politics… dysfunction takes on a life of its own. As much as I'd like to write off this stuff as 'not our problem,' I worry it's going to affect our time in our future locations."

"You're right," she exhales sharply.

"Alistair is the oldest of seven siblings—all sisters. His mother died young, and his oldest sister is the heir apparent. He never had a chance when it came to taking control of their family. That definitely means he's up to something," Wolfie says softly as he looks up at me.

"Alliance through marriage," I muse aloud. "That's why his father offered him up—to cement peace between the courts—but I doubt it's why he agreed. He's got other motivations and he'll screw with us simply to see if it helps him get ahead."

"Exactly," Teddy says grimly. "Neither Alistair or Allora are thrilled, but it's a union meant to strengthen their bloodlines, not their hearts."

I can't imagine being stuck with fucking Trevor now that I know who he is; having to deal with Alistair has to be no better for Allora.

The door creaks and I wave my hand, hoping to quiet them without saying anything. When no one shows, I frown and make a slashing motion across my throat. If someone's listening in, they can't hear us speculating about this topic.

"Tell me we have something to eat in this trove of knowledge," Wolfie grumbles as he rises to his feet. His eyes dance as he winks at me and I have to cover my mouth so I don't laugh.

Definitely never assigning him any undercover duties.

"Later," I promise. "We've got to make tracks if we want to hit the next stop by nightfall."

"Night travel isn't wise where we're going. You guys ran into that advice, too, right?" Teddy asks as he runs a hand through his disheveled hair.

"Speaking of which," Allora appears out of nowhere to interrupt us with a smile. "I've arranged transport for you. My driver will ensure your safe passage."

"That's more than kind of you," I say, studying her face for any sign of deception. I don't find it, but there's a feeling of something unsaid that prickles the back of my neck.

Could she have overheard Alistair plotting to mess with us?

She smiles again, looking me in the eyes. "I'd feel terrible if something happened to people who were under our care when traveling through such difficult terrain. It's my pleasure to ensure your safe arrival."

The way she's looking at me speaks volumes even if she's not saying it out loud. We need to be cautious on our way and she's hoping her staff will deter any shenanigans. I hold out my phone, giving her a knowing grin. "We should keep in touch. Share your contact with me and I'll do the same before we go."

"Excellent idea, Jolene," she replies as she whips out a device to do so.

Of course the weird iridescent, winged thing she thrusts forward is not a damn thing like my iPhone, but I have to pretend I don't see it hovering mid-air.

"We'll head out now and gather our things. Will your cars know when to meet us?" Prez asks as he extends a hand to help Teddy up.

"Of course. They'll follow you to your hotel and wait for you to come down with your animals," Allora says. "Though I am sad I did not get to meet them properly. Perhaps in the future?"

Teddy snorts. "Perhaps if you're alone."

Allora does her best to hide a laugh and I wink at her. "Enough jokes, guys. Super un-fun assholes await."

That's about as much as I can say about our future hosts without wanting to smash something.

Rise

Benjy

The hotel room is a stifled mess of suitcases and animal gear when I step in.

Teddy's hovering over the King Danes, whispering last-minute instructions that sound more like pep talks. "Stay close to Presley, you two. We're in for a bumpy ride," he murmurs, stroking their glossy coats with a gentle hand. The servals are less compliant, their golden eyes flashing with mischief as they swat at the judge when he tries to dangle leashes in front of them.

I doubt that's going to work; Jolene never makes them wear that shit.

"Ready, Benjy?" Presley calls out as he steps back from Euryale. The giant bird is even bigger inside a building, but he acts like it's tiny parrot. It's weird until you realize his shifted form is a bird that dwarfs the eagle in size by leaps and bounds.

"Almost," I reply, zipping up my duffel bag with a final tug. "Just need to grab my —"

"Your what? Your sense of impending doom?" Teddy interjects, his voice laced with dark humor as he eyes Allora's cars outside the window. To anyone else, they are sleek black SUVs, but through our knowing gaze, they shimmer with enchantment, transforming into majestic royal carriages waiting to whisk us away.

"Can't forget that. We're going to need it," I shoot back grumpily. My gut churns with the kind of apprehension that precedes a storm, and Jolene's obliviousness only amplifies it. She sits on the edge of the bed, scrolling through her phone, the very picture of calm, but that's only because she doesn't actually understand how dangerous our next two visits will be.

This bullshit about not telling her has made everything ten times more difficult and I want to strangle someone every time I think about it.

Once everything is settled, we head downstairs to the cars. Doyle and Presley lost the rochambeau, so they get to take up the rear with our menagerie and luggage. Allora's guards nod to us, their faces unreadable masks as they takes the reins up front. I wonder what Princess sees when she looks at this crazy Cinderella-esque get-up? Probably some Secret Service SUV bullshit, I suppose. Shaking my head, I climb into the damn thing, settling next to her on the opposite side of Teddy.

"Teddy," Jolene says firmly. "I appreciate your skepticism, but I really believe Allora is our friend. She didn't have to offer this, nor did she have to hint that something might be coming on the horizon. She took a huge risk, I bet."

"Forgive me if I can't simply accept it at face value, Tilly," Teddy grumbles. He understands Allora's plight: forced to marry Alistair, used as a pawn in a game we're all too familiar with because the Hollow politics aren't much different. That doesn't mean my old friend is going to entrust someone we just met with our girl. "I've learned to question everything and it's kept my ass out of the fryer many times."

He's not saying that if she were less trusting, she would never have become the Catastrophe years ago, but it's true.

"I get it; I really do," Jolene says softly, "so are these night family folks —are they really as cutthroat as the forums say? Do you think they actually do the whole mafia-style make them disappear shit? If so, I know how to deal with it, but I need to know if you believe it so I can prepare myself."

"Cutthroat?" Wolfie laughs without humor, pushing up from where he'd been lying with his head in Teddy's lap. "They'd consider that a compliment. They're masters of manipulation, always angling for the upper hand. And yeah, I absolutely think they kill anyone who crosses them or gets in their way."

"Think of them as ultimate chess players," I say, trying to keep my voice light. "Every move calculated, every bargain a trap disguised as opportunity. The history books make them feel more like psychopaths, not sociopaths. They play the game because they enjoy it and they don't care if everyone involved knows the rules."

Of course, now's probably not the time to mention the only folks who have managed to best them are the Court of Reaping and the Society.

"Sounds like Alistair's got competition, then," she muses, unaware of how close to home her words hit. "He won't be the only one trying to fuck with us while we search. Maybe that will work in our favor."

"Maybe," I mutter, looking out the window to see Odie flit between shadows above us, a silent sentinel ready to alert us to danger. Euryale soars higher, her keen eyes fixed on the road ahead. I wasn't keen on Doyle sending them ahead as sentinels, but maybe he was right.

"Are we safe as their guests? I mean, I assume the whole diplomatic stuff should keep them from really trying to harm us, right?" Jolene asks, a slight furrow in her brow as she looks at Teddy.

"Safe as one can be when dealing with the night families," Teddy says as he watches her run her fingers over Isis. "Rumors say their hearts are as dark as the night sky they adore—which explains a lot about Alistair. It also makes me nervous about Allora because aligning with them is... problematic. Her stepmother has hidden schemes up those designer sleeves."

Princess frowns, stroking the python wrapped around her thoughtfully. I can tell she doesn't like Teddy's train of thought and that means she's already considering taking Allora under her wing. That protective streak is the other reason she got humiliated in high school, but even the trauma hasn't made her less willing to stand in front of the cannons if someone's in danger.

That's part of why we all love her, even if we can't say it yet because she gets wigged out.

"Problematic," she echoes, rolling the word around like it's a puzzle piece she's trying to fit into place. "We'll just have to be smarter than them, won't we? It shouldn't be too hard with our darling boy genius, the clever troublemaker, and our slick son of a senator, right?"

"Smarter, or luckier," I mutter under my breath. "Though good to know you, the doc, and me are just here to look pretty."

Jolene rolls her eyes at me as she bumps my shoulder with hers. "You *are* pretty, Benjy, and so is Prez, but we're gifted in other ways."

"Such as?" Teddy smirks as he preens about being named a smooth operator with the damn Irishman. "Tell me what you see us all as, Tilly. We have plenty of time."

"For the love of…" I give him an annoyed look. Edgar's always loved praise, though he enjoys giving it even more. "She doesn't have to do that, buddy."

"I don't mind," Princess chirps with a sly look on her face. "Benjy and Presley have a lot of very useful jobs, but one of the biggest is being the calm center of our little family. When the big dogs are going off the rails—even me— or the tension is off the charts, they help us come back to Earth. And that's so necessary that I don't know how we'd survive without it. Plus, they're pretty, kind, strong, and gentle."

My smile is broad as I look my friend smugly. "We're the center of her storm, dude. Suck it."

"Don't tempt me to start shit in this car," Teddy rumbles. "Our girl will get mad when we make a mess of her friend's vehicle."

"I will once I stop screaming; you're right," she says happily. "So don't get him started until we get to our destination. I don't want to arrive grumpy about the mess, even if I would be satisfied in other ways."

"Fine…"

I settle in, stretching my legs in front of me as I get comfortable. Jolene smacks my leg, her eyes dark. "Don't start flexing, either."

Laughing softly, I bump her back and we all sit back to watch the road that stretches before us, winding towards a destiny shrouded in uncertainty and shadow. As we drive, I can't shake the feeling that we're heading straight into the belly of the beast.

And we simply don't have the food to bait the damn thing.

A SCREECH SPLITS THE AIR, A PIERCING ALARM THAT HAS US ALL snapping to attention. Euryale's cry is urgent, and as I struggle to wake up, I lean forward to look out the window. The eagle is circling above a snarl of twisted metal strewn across the road ahead.

I have a bad feeling about this.

"Dammit!" Doyle's voice crackles through the intercom from the other car. His tone is laden with disgust and resignation as he growls, "It's definitely 'wounded gazelle' setup."

I'm about to ask what that means when our vehicle shudders violently beneath us. It feels like invisible forces are slamming into us with the intent to crush. Teddy's eyes light with fire as he snarls and I know we don't have a choice—we have to get out and fight. Within seconds, we're spilling out of the vehicles in a wild cascade of bodies, fangs, fur, and fury.

"Tilly, stay back." Teddy's command is sharp, his eyes shooting daggers of warning her way. But she's already moving, dashing past him with an unapologetic look and dual middle fingers extended.

"Try and stop me," she shouts over her shoulder, and there's fire in her eyes that rivals anything Teddy could conjure.

I shouldn't encourage her, but hell yeah, that's our girl.

My heart is hammering as I watch her dive headlong into the fray. One hand is brandishing the knife she always carries and the other is gripping the polymer gun she managed to sneak in under the Fae's noses. I'm not sure which will be more useful to her, but since she has no idea she's going to be fighting magic, it's a toss-up.

"Shit," I breathe out in irritation. We've been so damn careful to keep things under wraps, but now, there's no room for caution. I feel the change rippling under my skin, a call to something ancient and powerful.

We're all going to shift and whether she'll figure things out afterward, I don't know.

Teddy explodes into his hellhound form, massive and monstrous, flames licking around his maw like tendrils of the underworld reaching out to claim souls. Smoke coils from his nostrils, sulfur tainting the air as he jerks his head at me then takes off into a group of black clad assholes in masks.

"Cover our girl, B," he roars in a sound that vibrates through my bones.

Despite being the soft compliment to our group, Wolfie doesn't hesitate to let loose. His transformation is fluid—dark fae majesty made flesh. His wings unfurl, vast and shadowy, while his ears sharpen to lethal points. The air around him shimmers with magic, a pink iridescence that paints the world in shades of danger. He looks both beautiful and deadly, making me realize he's never really shown any of us the extent of his full form before.

This one makes it impossible to believe he's from the lands that spawned Alistair.

"Let's dance," Wolfie growls softly, and there's a gleam in his eye I haven't seen before. "I don't like people trying to hurt my girl."

Before I can pick my jaw up, I see our other friends coming out of the second car. Doyle's aura pulses with a golden light so bright it almost blinds me. The power he wields is raw, unbridled—a force of nature that refuses to be leashed any longer. He moves with a purpose, his every step a statement of divine wrath.

"Benjy, now!" Doyle commands, and I don't need telling twice.

Muscles bulge and my body stretches until I'm an eight-foot tower of primal strength. My fists are hammers and my roar a challenge to the very sky. "Let's bash some heads," I bellow, giving in to the gorilla within.

The inner beast is thrilled with this shit because I almost never let him out and definitely not like this.

Presley leaps skyward, transforming mid-air into the majestic caladrius, his cries echoing Euryale's. Together, they dive towards the melee, two sharp beaked birds bent on tearing into their enemies. No wonder he has such a rapport with that eagle; they look like a perfectly matched squadron of predators in the air.

"Watch it!" I yell as one of the black-clad assailants produces a bow, aiming at Presley. A swipe of my massive hand sends the attacker sprawling and I run for the next one before they can find their own weapon. We're a storm of supernatural might, but even storms can be unpredictable.

That's when it happens—the twist none of us saw coming.

I stop dead in my tracks, almost dropping the dickhead I'm shaking when my Princess shifts. Unlike new shifters, her body snaps into the form of an enormous hellhound like Teddy, her body wrapped in blue flames and exhaling mist the color of his incubus. Quetzalcoatl feathers adorn her tail, but dark fae wings sprout from her back. The glitter flying as they flap is black as obsidian, sparkling in the air with unknown power.

"By my maiden auntie's dusty panties," Doyle whispers. "I've never seen anything like it."

For an ancient demi-god, that's saying a lot.

Her transformation isn't just shocking—it's a revelation, a display of raw potential that none of us anticipated. When one of the attackers lands a lucky strike, drawing a line of crimson across her side, we all freeze, our battle-lust replaced by sudden fear.

But then, a soft, gentle golden glow radiates from her wound, spreading outwards in waves of silent fury. The attackers, previously so confident in their numbers and skill, turn to ash before our eyes, crumbling away like shadows at dawn.

"Did you see that?" Wolfie's voice is tinged with disbelief, his normally unflappable demeanor shaken.

"Impossible..." The word is a whisper from my lips, my thoughts racing.

What does this mean? How did she...?

"Focus!" Teddy snaps us out of our stupor, his fiery gaze sweeping the scene. "We have to keep moving."

"Right," I say, shaking off the shock. "Let's get out of here before more show up."

We glance at Tilly with trepidation as it hits us that while she's going to be an amazingly powerful supe, that won't come without even more challenges. Until she's fully emerged and aware, the news of this event getting out would have put her in serious danger. It still might if anyone managed to zip out before her atom bomb of god-like power cleared the field.

She's out again, a sure sign that this still isn't the final leg of being emerged, so Teddy picks the now human form in tattered clothes gently. As we pile back into our battered carriages, my mind whirls. We're all going to have to keep this secret, especially if she wakes up not knowing what happened.

I don't know how much longer that gambit is going to work, especially in a court where they delight in revealing weaknesses.

Nightmare

Jolene

My eyelids flutter open just as the car shifts from the smoothness of the road to a gravelly ascent. The sky is bruised purple and orange as we pull up to the castle that looms ahead. The giant, gleaming structure is less a building and more an eruption from the very bones of the earth. The style is unsurprisingly gothic, draped in a verdant shroud of vines and flowers that whisper concealment. Fae creatures, their eyes like shards of moonlight, skitter across the blackened masonry. It's an odd paradox: dark yet sparkling, as if this realm has purposefully decided to don night-time regalia and forsake the warm cheer of summer.

I suppose it has—that was one of the oft repeated rumors I came upon while reading from the digital forums.

"Overcompensate much?" I grumble as I stretch my limbs. My sarcastic quip cuts through the thick aroma of night jasmine and lilies that saturates the air within the car. Patchouli and myrrh linger underneath—darker scents that feel like warnings. I press my palm against the window, half expecting the glass to frost from the magic outside. When it doesn't, I breathe a sigh of relief.

There's only so much I can take at once.

"They really went all out with the 'midnight' vibe," Teddy agrees.

He's making light, but his laughter sounds hollow, like he's trying too hard to make this seem less daunting.

"Eccentric rich people are so over-the-top," Benjy adds as he gauges my reaction. He's very perceptive because he's often quietly observing, so I have to be careful how much he sees when I'm not paying attention.

"I bet this place is a hoot at Halloween," Wolfie chimes as he smiles at me. His expression doesn't reach his eyes and the solemn undertone in this car makes me worry about what shit happened while I was supposedly asleep.

I study them all through my lashes, noting the scrapes on Teddy's knuckles and the way Benjy's lip is split at the corner. Wolfie's jacket is torn, like he's been grappling with more than just his inner demons about his family. My stomach knots because now I know for certain something serious happened while we were driving here—something they're keeping from me.

That can only mean one thing and I don't like it at all.

"Guys," I start, my voice betraying the edge of anxiety. "What aren't you telling me?"

"Tilly, it's nothing. Let's get inside and—" Teddy begins, but I cut him off.

"Nothing? You look like you've gone ten rounds with a boxing champ." I point accusingly at his hand, then to the others, piecing together a story they refuse to voice. "What did I miss?"

"Bad blow out on the road. We were in a rough area and some jackasses tried to mug us while the driver changed the tire. Can we talk about this later?" Benjy pleads, but there's a firmness in his tone that says it's not up for discussion.

"I'm not an idiot, Benjamin Louis Foster." My words are sharp, laced with rising fury. They exchange looks, and I know—it's got something to do with this place and our so-called hosts.

"Sugarplum..." Wolfie says, trailing off as he catches sight of the disquiet in my eyes. He knows I hate being left in the dark, yet here I am, blindfolded by my own mind's gaps. "Just... let it go. We're all safe and no one is truly hurt. You have to trust us until we can be more specific."

Of course it would be him that asked—I can't say no to his big blue eyes.

"Fine," I relent, folding my arms as a defensive shield around myself. "But when I *can* be let in on the secret, you assholes are going to tell me everything you know even if it takes a fucking *week*, got it?"

"I promise we'll share everything when we can. In fact, I swear on my bottle of Pappy, Tilly." Teddy gives me a serious look and I believe him—mostly because that's a five thousand dollar bottle of bourbon he looks at like it's made of gold.

As we approach the gates to the creepy disco castle, the sparkles from the castle's embedded gems catch the dying light, flinging prismatic colors across our path like a mocking celebration. I snort. "Can't wait to see what they've got lined up for the welcome party. Maybe a diamond studded platinum carpet instead of red?"

My grumbling gets a genuine laugh from Benjy, and even Teddy cracks a smile. They know I get more sarcastic when I'm irritated, so the jokes tell them I'm not worried as much as ready to stab someone. Sadly, I doubt I'm going to get the chance, but a girl can dream.

Especially when we'll be seeing that fucking tool, Alistair.

"Knowing these folks, it'll be woven from the fur of an endangered species or a goddamn unicorn," Wolfie adds, shaking his head. "People who need this much bling to feel good about themselves make me uncomfortable."

"Even if they were real, unicorns would be off limits," I retort, trying to find solid ground in humor. "Even fucking rich people have standards."

He arches a brow at me. "You know they don't. There's assholes racing to send themselves to the moon for street cred out there, Sugarplum. Bored people with more money than sense will always push the boundaries of acceptable behavior; they lose touch with reality after the seventh zero."

I chuckle at his assessment as we come to a stop. The engine dies and the silence feels heavy as we all prepare for whatever nonsense is in store. Finally, I crawl over Teddy and Doyle to step out of the car with my back straight and chin high. I'm ready to face whatever waits inside this twisted place, even if it pushes me to the edge of my boundaries. I look determined, but inside, I'm stoking a small fire of rage.

Even if I accepted their fake ass excuse about the injuries, I know the motherfuckers in this castle are responsible for whatever happened.

I swear on my dying breath if this castle's masters are behind the attack that hurt my guys, they're on my list. While I may not be able to act on it today, I will keep it locked up tight inside of me until the time is right. When it is, I will unleash everything at my disposal to show them exactly why people don't want to piss off a Southern woman.

Bless their hearts, they just made an enemy, and they better find someone to pray for them, because I'm coming.

IT TAKES A FEW MINUTES FOR THE GUYS TO GET OUR LUGGAGE AND the animals out of the cars. As they thank the reluctant chauffeurs Allora provided, I take in our surroundings. The four men who rode in the front of the vehicles have grim expressions on their faces as they look around and I take note of it. We're not the only ones who find this place off-putting.

"Thanks," Teddy grunts to one of the men, his voice strained through the courtesy. "We couldn't have made it without your... expertise."

"Ours is but to serve," the man replies with a bow so shallow it's almost an insult. I narrow my eyes at him, but I let it slide.

After all, Allora's private guards have no reason to be loyal to us and I have far too many enemies on my chessboard to add disrespectful idiots.

The air is a tangle of animal excitement and apprehension, mirroring my own emotions. Jekyll mrrps as Hyde follows him to my side and I smile. I miss them when we have to split up and this trip has been a *lot* of separation from my furry companions. Eurayle traces circles in the sky, her silhouette cutting through the thinning light. Kali and Hecate bark, eager to escape confinement, and I snort as they run for a place to relieve themselves. I kind of hope they piss on something important; it feels like a fitting tribute.

"Keep watch," I murmur to my servals, hoping they understand. My eagle's sharp cry is comforting, even as I spot the raven tracking her every move. *Déjà vu* prickles my skin; I've seen that bird before. It has to be someone else's shadow masquerading as a friend. I press my lips together, not liking the possibility that we're being followed.

Would one of the people who demanded that stupid 'oath' send a bird to keep watch on us? Fuck if I know.

"Sugarplum?" Wolfie's voice breaks through the hum of my thoughts. "Are you okay? You… slept pretty hard."

"Never better," I lie with a tight smile. Poor Wolfie struggles with the lies even more now that I know they have to do it. It's not in his nature to be so secretive, I think, and he hates it. But he can't stop himself from worrying about me, so he had to ask.

"Come on," Teddy says with a sigh. "Let's face the music."

We turn to face the castle as a group. Its opulence is a stark contrast to our disheveled appearance, but I don't give a fuck. Whatever happened on the way here was arranged ahead of time and our survival is probably more surprising than the state of our attire.

Within seconds, a group of men exit the huge double doors. They're dressed to kill and look like a fucking fantasy calendar lineup. Alistair stands out because he's smirking like he owns the place—which, unfortunately, he does. I assume the others are his sisters' suitors. They range from the casually confident to the brazenly brawny, but not one has a single hair out of place or crease unpressed.

Fantastic. We're being greeted by the Fae mafia.

"Welcome," Alistair drawls, stepping forward, his designer clothes whispering of wealth and indifference. "I'm so glad you made it to our home safely."

"I wouldn't miss it for the world," I say, pouring sarcasm into each syllable. My eyes narrow behind the glasses as I look at each of the seven men who are courting Alistair's sister carefully. There wasn't a lot of information on them, which I found shocking, but I suppose keeping their assets under wraps is what criminals do.

"Delighted," says one of the smaller Fae. His eyes gleam with an intelligence that suggests he's more dangerous than his stature implies. The others nod in agreement, a chorus of predatory smiles shining at us in the waning light.

"Tomorrow night will be... enlightening." There's something about the way the largest Fae—part orc if I had to guess by his short tusks—grins that sends a shiver skittering down my spine. He looks like a mountain with a vendetta.

"Can't wait," I manage, my words edged with faux enthusiasm. So far we've heard from the smallest and the largest, plus the biggest dickhead in town. I'm not sure what the others in the rainbow of rich douchebags bring to the table, but this is a lot of treacherous people to manage at once.

"Please, follow us," the medium build masked man offers. He doesn't say another word as we look at him—not even an explanation as to why he's wearing the half mask over the top of his face.

Fucking weird ass Fae, I swear to Hades in a hamper.

These men are all different shades of threat dressed in silk and arrogance. Alistair may be the devil I know, but the rest of them are question marks. They could be from anywhere in the four kingdoms, with any powers, and any connections. Until someone actually introduces us and gives me something to work with, I have to consider them all threats to me and my family. I'm sure Teddy feels the same way because he's shifting towards me as we all stare one another down.

"Lead the way," Benjy finally says. He shoots me a look that tells me he's as wary as I am, but we can't stand here all day.

Our band of misfits moves forward when our hosts do, but my mind is racing faster than my feet. *What kind of special event requires such an ominous invitation?*

Tomorrow night might hold answers, but I'm not sure I'll like what we find.

AS WE WALK DOWN LONG STRETCHES OF HALLWAY, MY KNUCKLES ITCH with the need to give Alistair a piece of my mind the old-fashioned way—right across his smug nose. He made the purpose of the event tomorrow clear while we traversed the miles of castle to the wing we're going to be staying in. They're throwing another fucking ball and I'm fresh out of patience with this shit. As a woman who grew up in the damn debutante world and then traveled the world as a fixer, I've been to a shit load of fancy events. They're not my favorite thing, but I can bend when it's necessary.

But we've been in this place for a little over a week and I've had it up to here with these high-society shindigs where they treat me like some kind of dress-up doll. I'm here for one thing, and that's to dig up dirt on Wolfie's elusive dad, not to waltz around in glittery gowns.

I am not their Barbie girl in their Barbie world.

Before I can open my mouth to let these asswads know how I feel about *another* formal event full of bullshit, Alistair stops the group. The men face us, all giving us a different form of creepy smile.

"I'm Lucien, husband to Elara," says a Fae who looks as if he could charm the scales off a snake. His eyes glitter with mischief and I can *feel* the trouble wafting from him. I don't think he's fully Fae, but I haven't the foggiest what else he could be.

Another one bows, his voice as smooth as the velvet cloak draped over his shoulders. "Julien, betrothed to Celestina," he says as nods at each of my men.

Note to self: That one doesn't think women should be in charge. Restrain yourself, Jolene.

One by one they introduce themselves, each name tied to a sister like a badge of honor—or a shackle, depending on how you squint at it. Then Alistair steps forward, and I can almost hear the air sour.

"Alistair, intended of Allora," he declares, an edge of defiance in his tone.

The snickers from the rest are almost imperceptible, but I catch them —little ripples of contempt across a very exclusive pond. When they turn their backs, Alistair's facade cracks for a fleeting second. His eyes darken, his jaw tightens, and that smirk? It slips away like it was never there.

How very odd. Why do they find the alliance lacking and why does he look like he actually cares what they think of Allora?

"Let's get you settled, then."

A maid pops out of nowhere and I almost scream. I was so focused on this clown car of men that I wasn't paying attention to anything around me. *Bad Jolene*, I think as I jerk my head at the guys. The animals gather in close, and Hyde gives the bevy of buttheads the stink eye as we look at the staff member waiting for us.

"Thank you," I mutter, my brain churning with fresh suspicions. There's more to this Allora-Alistair alliance than meets the eye, and I'm itching to unravel it. Once this stupid oath shit is behind me, maybe I'll come back and help Allora—if she really is a friend to be had.

"Right this way, esteemed guests," the small woman chirps as she leads us down a corridor that looks like it was ripped straight out of an epic fantasy novel.

"Esteemed, my ass," I mutter to myself. "These dudes think we're rubes."

Teddy shrugs and winks at me. "Perhaps that's not a bad thing, Tilly."

He might be right.

Walk Through Fire

PRESLEY

The door to our suite swings open, revealing a scene plucked from a dream—or a particularly inventive hallucination. Starlight dances across the ceiling, casting a soft glow on the colossal bed that sits like a throne in the middle of the room. An enchanted forest mural wraps around the walls, so lifelike that I swear I see the leaves fluttering. In the corner, a spring bubbles merrily, its music a soothing counterpoint to the chaos of my thoughts.

Jesus salsa dancing Christ, how are we going to keep the damn oath if these shit-heads keep throwing our girl into situations like this?

"Wow," Benjy breathes out, his awe echoing my silent admiration. "This is the most swank set-up yet."

"Of course," the pixie maid nods, oblivious to the frustration on most of our faces. "Should you need anything, please do not hesitate to ring the bells. The cord is over there by the…jacuzzi?"

I snort as she fumbles for a normal word to describe the bubbling spring without letting our unemerged mate know what's really going on.

"Thank you," Teddy swoops in to save me before I crack up. "We appreciate all of your hospitality."

The maid curtseys and scurries out, leaving me to look at the rest of our group. Jolene is walking around oblivious thanks to the weird glasses. Benjy is still gaping at the spread as Wolfie eyes every inch of the place. The only one who seems relaxed is Doyle. He's heading for the couch at the sitting room end of the giant suite with a skip in his step.

I have no idea how that idiot maintains such a happy-go-lucky exterior right up until he bursts into a rage.

"We should check for bugs," Teddy whispers, already scanning the room with trained eyes. Given his less than legal side hustle, I'll bet this isn't his first rodeo with that particular challenge.

"Every nook and cranny," Magpie confirms as she nods at him.

The weight of exhaustion pulls at my limbs, but we can't afford to let our guard down, not even in this fairy-tale sanctuary. "I'll take the en suite."

"Sitting area," Doyle says as he drops to his knees.

So that's what he was doing; I'll be damned.

"Tomorrow's another day, as the belle said, but tonight isn't over yet," Wolfie sighs as he lowers himself to the floor by the bed.

"Another day, another firing squad," I grin. "At least this one seems to have cracks." I wink at them, heading for the room I claimed.

"Let's get to work, then," Benjy says, rolling up his sleeves as he passes me on the way to what I assume is a large closet.

"Then we sleep," Jolene says firmly, "because gods know, we'll need our strength in the morning if we want to get through this without murdering anyone. We can dismantle spy equipment and double-check shadows now, but after that, we're on geezer time. I want to be alert as hell when we have to face that squad of fuckwits."

"As you wish, Princess," Benjy replies.

I knew he picked that nickname for a reason—how clever.

THE GROWL THAT WAKES ME IS LOW AND GUTTURAL, A WARNING THAT ripples through the predawn silence like an ominous breeze. My eyes snap open, heart pounding in the stillness, and I'm immediately aware of the tangled mass of limbs around me—my arm thrown over Wolfie's waist, Doyle's calf draped over mine, and Magpie's fingertips touching mine as she snuggles into Boone. We're a jigsaw of bodies, interlocked in an accidental intimacy that only a night spent in the same bed can create.

"Prez," Wolfie whispers, nudging me with his elbow, "something's at the door."

"Ugh," Teddy grunts, his voice groggy as he disentangles from our human knot, gets up, and pads barefoot across the room. The animals are all standing with their hackles raised, ears pinned, and lips curled back to reveal an arsenal of teeth. It's a canine and feline chorus of distrust aimed squarely at the unexpected interruption.

"Easy, guys," I murmur at the group, though I'm not feeling particularly calm myself. Pushing myself up on one elbow, I watch as Boone opens the door to reveal a stack of neatly wrapped packages. They sit innocuously enough, but in this place, even gifts feel like thinly veiled threats.

"Looks like Alistair decided to play dress-up with us," Teddy announces as he hauls the boxes inside with a wary eye.

"Great," Jolene mutters. "Because nothing says 'Welcome to our home' like complimentary yet also obligatory wardrobe choices."

It didn't occur to me that sending clothes was a way to control us, but I'll be damned if she isn't right.

"Stylish spies, that's what they are," Doyle says as he climbs out of the pile. He pokes a box with his toe suspiciously, frowning at us. "Guaranteed these wankers know we found all their surprises and mucked them up."

Disengaging from Wolfie reluctantly, I rip open the packages aggressively to find clothes that are my size while also comfortable with a touch of elegance that doesn't sacrifice mobility. The rest of the wrapped boxes have similar contents for each of us, including a pair of pre-worn, punk rock looking jeans for Magpie with a faded Sex Pistols tee shirt and Union Jack flag combat boots.

"It's fucking creepy how well they have us nailed," Benjy says as he pads over, "but then again, Allistair's probably got the staff wired to snoop better than the NSA."

"Maybe he asked them what sizes we wore at the Harvest Court," Wolfie offers reasonably. He sounds casual, but his eyes are tight with concern, mirroring Benjy's unease.

"Either way, it's unnerving," Teddy agrees as he grabs his parcel of clothes. "I don't like them knowing this much, especially because it gives them an advantage we don't have. Hell, they didn't even give us everyone's name yet."

We dress quickly, each lost in our thoughts until a staff member knocks on our door. Their impeccable timing has us exchanging glances laden with trepidation.

Did we miss a fucking camera? We'll have to check again.

"Breakfast is served," the lady says when we open the door. The maid gestures for us to follow her and I look to the rest of them.

"Let's go," Magpie says with a sigh. She crooks her finger at the servals and dogs, grinning as they jump to flank her.

Teddy's expression hardens when we head out. "I'm interested to find out what kind of circus awaits us today."

"Keep it cool," I murmur, knowing some of their 'pre-coffee' tact is about as refined as a sledgehammer. "Remember, we're in their house and we have to play by their rules for now."

"Doesn't mean I have to like it," Magpie grumbles. "I get the feeling I'm going to want to beat the shit out of them no matter how much caffeine I suck down."

"None of us like it, Princess," Benjy reminds her as he herds the dogs through the doorway.

Though, unlike the rest of us, her, Teddy, and Doyle are the most likely to get us arrested.

We make our way down to the dining room through an open court-yard where Euryale disappears into the morning light immediately. I don't blame her; I wish I could take to the sky and get a better view of this shit. There's so much going on in front of our faces that I think we're missing a bigger picture, but I haven't been able to put my finger on it.

"Are we ready for whatever this breakfast charade brings?" I ask, as we approach another set of double doors.

"As ready as we'll ever be," Benjy says, a forced smile on his face as he corrals the dogs with practiced ease. "We have no idea what they're hiding or even what they want with us. It feels like we're going in blindfolded; I don't like it."

"Guess we'll find out if the food's as good as the fashion," Doyle adds, a dry edge to his voice.

"Or if it's poisoned," Wolfie says, half-joking but his eyes are scanning for exits and potential threats.

Why did he have to say that? For that matter, how did it become completely normal for that to be a serious question?

"I just want to get through this meal without any casualties," Magpie says as she shoves her hands in her pockets. "I wouldn't mind kicking someone's ass, don't get me wrong, but I'd prefer to do it when I have a clue what I'm up against."

"If we can make it through the meal without one of you volatile folks lunging across the table at someone, I'll be surprised as hell," Benjy teases.

"Hey, I'm always a lady," Jolene retorts, "even when I'm plotting murder. Maybe more so then, actually, because I like to bat my lashes and simper to distract them."

"Can we keep the plotting to a minimum?" Wolfie sighs as he adjusts his new jacket. "We have to learn as much as we can about them before we try to play their game better than them."

"Fine," Doyle acquiesces, "but only because you asked so nicely."

Apollo help us.

With a final look shared between us, a silent agreement to stick together no matter what, we step into the fray, ready to face the courtly masquerade that waits beyond the dining room doors.

THE MOMENT WE STEP INTO THE DINING HALL, THE AIR THICKENS with tension and unspoken questions. The prince and his 'brothers-in-law' are already waiting for us. An array of Fae masculinity that spans the spectrum from Lukas's diminutive elegance to Julien's towering presence looks up at us with interest when the door opens. They're clustered at the far end of a long table, their conversation halting as if snipped by shears when we enter the room.

"Where in the world are the sisters?" I whisper to Wolfie. It's weird that we haven't heard or seen a thing about them, but they're the entire reason these clowns are here.

We're seated by staff at the close end of the table, facing the eight men like chess pieces poised for a game neither side knows how to play. No one says anything, we all just stare as servers bring out food and drinks like they're feeding an army.

Alistair finally takes charge, introducing us one by one, his voice carrying an odd note of formality. "Jolene Whitley and Judge Edgar Boone," he begins. "Drs. Wolfgang Fletcher and Presley Hamilton," he continues before pointing to the last two members of our family. "And Benjamin Foster and Doyle Haggerty."

"You've met Lukas and Julien, but the others are Finn, Declan, Riordan, Keegan, and Angus." Alistair's voice trails through the introductions, naming each Fae man in turn. Their eyes are curious, watchful mirrors reflecting back our own wariness.

"Where are your sisters this fine morning?" Doyle can't help but ask and I have to hide my smile. His voice is laced with sarcasm he doesn't bother to hide, plus he's starting to lay on the faux Irish charm.

"Off having new gowns made for tonight," Lukas answers with a smile that doesn't quite reach his eyes.

When I turn my head to look at my Magpie, she looks like she's fighting the urge to slam her forehead on the polished wood of the table. Teddy puts an arm around her shoulders, keeping her place as he whispers in her ear.

"New gowns," she mutters before Doyle steers the conversation towards safer waters.

When asked by one of the predatory looking Fae, he explains our land tour is inspired by finding out more about Lucy's heritage. I catch snippets of interest flickering across their faces—that is except for Alistair, who seems to be pretending he's clueless for some reason.

It's probably time to get their attention off Lucy before Alistair pounces again.

"Tell us how you met your respective princesses," I say as I lean forward. "I'm dying to know."

Julien answers first, recounting a tale that has more gloss than truth, and one by one, they chime in with stories of encounters orchestrated by destiny or clever matchmaking—tales from all corners of the dark lands that were featured in some ridiculous reality TV show.

"From nobility to business families," Lukas adds, his voice tinged with pride. "The search was... extensive."

"Sounds romantic," I comment dryly, and from the corner of my eye, I see Alistair's lip curl as he gazes off into the distance, no doubt recalling the spectacle.

"Indeed, it was quite the event," another chimes in, oblivious to Alistair's disdain.

"Event," Jolene echoes, her tone heavy with irony. She glances at me, then Wolfie, her concern clear.

I know she worries about his sensitivity, but there's something about Alistair's irritation that feels significant. "What, no comment, Silkshine?"

He glares at me and I hear Doyle snort. The Irishman clears his throat, giving the princes a charming grin. "Obviously, he was overcome by your grand overtures for his sisters."

"Aw, but it's your turn, Alistair," Teddy says, unable to keep the edge out of his voice as he taunts the Fae. "How did you and Allora cross paths?"

The smirk he gives us is infuriatingly familiar. He's put his mask back on as he leans back in a picture of arrogance. "We met in the most romantic way possible: our parents decided we were a good match."

Guffaws erupt from his brothers-in-law, their laughter echoing off the vaulted ceilings. I can't imagine why that's any less admirable than a fucking televised audition tour, but for some reason, these dimwits think they're better than the real prince of this land.

"Didn't have to strut your stuff on the marriage market like us, right, Allie?" Finn teases, elbowing Alistair.

"Unlike some, I didn't need to audition for love," Alistair retorts sharply, his eyes flashing with something that might be anger or pride —I can't tell.

But he's echoing my sentiments rather than making a shitty comment about Allora, which I find odd.

The room falls silent, those around us suddenly finding their plates fascinating.

"Love is so... unpredictable," I mutter, trying to defuse the tension.

Unfortunately, it's too late; Alistair stands abruptly, his chair scraping loudly against the floor. "Excuse me," he announces, his voice cold enough to chill wine. He strides out, leaving behind a wake of awkwardness.

"Guess that's our cue," Benjy says, standing up as Kali and Hecate whine. "We should take the animals out."

Before they can protest, Teddy nods and rises to his feet, holding his hand out to our girl. The rest of us join her as the watch us herd our zoo out of the dining hall quickly. In the hallway, we nearly collide with Alistair.

His eyes are stormy, his jaw set as he glares. "Watch yourself. This court is more than it seems."

"Is that a threat?" Teddy growls, pushing him against the wall with surprising force. "Did you send those black-clad goons after us?"

"I have no idea what you're talking about."

"Right," I chime in, not fully convinced but seeing the truth in his bewildered expression.

"Believe what you will," Alistair bites out, regaining his composure. "But know this—there are layers here you don't grasp. If you want insight, watch the show. It's... enlightening."

Frowning at him, I try to work out what the hell he wants us to know. My gaze flicks to Doyle, who shrugs, and then to Wolfie, who shakes his head. Finally, Magpie blinks and I see it dawn on her.

"The tailors will come by tea time," Alistair adds before shoving Teddy away and stalking down the corridor.

"Looks like we've got some binge-watching to do," Jolene says, a wry twist to her lips.

My mind churns over what we've learned, what we haven't, and what lies beneath Alistair's carefully constructed indifference.

Jolene is right; there's a puzzle here, and we need to put all the damned pieces together in order to survive this shit.

Everybody Wants To Rule The World

Jolene

"I never watch shit like this at home, you know. I'm making an exception because there's something hinky about the way Alistair told us we needed to see it." I look up at Teddy, who arches a brow at me.

"Sure, you don't, Tilly," he says as he drapes my legs over his lap. Benjy picks up my feet on the other side of him, his strong hands massaging them and they both chuckle when I groan.

Wolfie scoots closer on my right, making me grin as Prez runs his fingers through my hair with the arm resting on the back of the couch. Doyle returns with the tray of drinks he made at the in-room bar—a luxury I'm extremely grateful for, despite the time of day—then settles on the floor in front of me. His head leans back against my hip and Teddy's leg as he rolls his eyes up to look at us.

"I sent the beasties on an exploration trip. Seems best if both the winged and furry ones get the lay of the land inside and out just in case we have to sneak out or hide."

I've been on my own for years, outside of Seer, so I don't think I'll ever get used to these guys simply doing shit before I even think to ask. It's eerie.

"I'll admit I'm curious about how they handled this," Wolfie says softly. "It's odd for these kinds of families to allow the kind of access a show like this would require. I mean, half the things we read about in our research were based on rumors and speculation because they're all so secretive."

"Politicians are, too, pup, but I know the Senator allowed ridiculous access to our family during the last campaign. Everyone is looking to go viral—getting famous without doing anything. Regular people don't get how painstakingly orchestrated much of that 'viral' fame is. The ones benefiting from it put large investments of time and money into being declared an overnight sensation. It's all rigged and I'm sure this is no different. It is reality TV, after all."

He frowns at Teddy, then looks at me. "All of it?"

"Most things, darling boy. It's fairly common knowledge in the circles I traveled in that awards, bestseller lists, some elections, and more than a few romantic liaisons are simply business deals. You, too, can have a number one album or book or movie if you've got the cash flow to back the launch and continue promoting afterward. Sorry to burst your bubble," I say as I lean in to kiss his cheek.

"That sucks," he says as he wrinkles his nose. "It's not surprising, but it's also pretty disillusioning. I hate that we can't trust a damn thing anywhere."

"Only us, pup," Doyle says as his hand comes up to pat Wolfie's knee. "Everything else you should question. I sure as fuck do and it's kept me from getting boxed in over the years."

I'll bet it has.

"Shhh," Teddy scolds us. "The damn show is starting and we have to pay attention or we're wasting our time. Behave, children."

Benjy huffs a laugh and mutters something that sounds a lot like 'Yes, Big Daddy,' which sends us all into peals of laughter. My grumpy alpha pauses the TV, narrowing his eyes at all of us imperiously until we're quiet, then unpauses it when we're quiet again.

The glow of the screen casts a pallid light across our faces as we sink into the depths of 'The Princess Games.' Nestled in with the guys, I watch the first season begin curiously—will I be able to see the real deal or will my glasses magic hold up with something on video? I don't know, but I hope like hell the shit that the first designer did will help me unravel this mystery. I'm relieved when the first few episodes

introduce Elara, the eldest princess of this court, and the fifty supernaturals who are vying for her hand in marriage.

*She's a more patient woman than me because five is straining my ability to cope.
Fifty would make me homicidal.*

Luckily, the episodes of 'Princess Games' aren't too long and we
speed through her various dates and challenges with ease. But when
we get to the second to last show of the season, I find myself
enthralled with the story—even rooting for a competitor that I know
won't win. Suddenly, Elara's laughter is cut short by a screech that
sends a shiver down my spine—an ugly avian creature with talons
sharp as nightmares and cries that curdle blood swoops on screen.
The weird Fae animals focus on the carriage she and Lukas are
riding in immediately. In a flurry of dark feathers, engineered chaos
unfolds as the bird things continue to batter the vehicle.

The breath in my lungs freezes and I stare at the show in horror. *Why
does this feel familiar? Why am I humming with the need to punch something?* I
look around at my men and note they've tensed, but they aren't
nearly as wired as me.

"Real or rigged?" Prez asks, skepticism lacing his tone.

"Does it matter?" I counter, not taking my eyes off the ensuing
melee. "I doubt Elara was aware either way. She looks absolutely
terrified and I'm an excellent micro-expression reader."

Lukas leaps into the fray, dispatching the creatures with practiced
ease, but it's the cloaked figures emerging from the treeline that draw
our collective gaze—black-clad attackers that make my pulse spike
even higher.

"Those can't be extras," Doyle says, his voice low and dangerous.

"Definitely not local theater troupe material," Teddy agrees, his
frown deepening.

I gasp when one of the people pull Elara out of the carriage and a
fight ensues as Lukas battles to get her back. It's obvious the fucker
who yanked her out was going to take her, but the smallest of the
princes fights like a man possessed until he's able to get her free.
Then a blast comes out of nowhere, knocking Elara to the ground
and I know in my gut this is serious. She's barely breathing and

Lukas launches himself into the fray until he scatters their attackers to the wind.

Our group exchanges loaded glances, a silent consensus forming that there's more to Lukas than meets the eye. When he drops to Elara's side and starts working some sort of emerald tinged magic on her, it becomes obvious that he's a healer of some kind, though I don't know enough about this to identify what kind. Elara shoots up, coughing up blood, but breathing and the episode ends. The one that follows is the last and she obviously chooses Lukas despite favoring another suitor for most of the season.

I don't know if that's because he was always supposed to win or if it's because no one but him was there to save her.

But as soon as one mystery begins to unravel, another spins onto the screen. Celestina, the vibrant second oldest princess, is introduced at the beginning of season two. Unlike Elara, it's not clear who she's leaning towards picking because she seems quite unhappy to be taking part in the show. In fact, most of the episodes depict her being annoyed and sarcastic as they primp and polish her, as well as her shooting down the men with a bored expression. It makes me grin and for a second, I think I could like Celestina if this is the real her. But yet again, tragedy strikes near the end of her season, when she's successfully snatched during the merriment of a Harvest Court festival. Julien—a mountain of orc-ish might and Fae cunning— storms after her, a relentless force plowing through fields and foes alike.

"Staged fights," Benjy scoffs, crossing his arms over his chest. He's easily as massive as the current prince on-screen, but his lip is curled at the way the hunt for Celestina is playing out.

"Look closer," I urge, pointing at the screen where Celestina's terror is palpable even behind the mask of reality TV drama. "That's not acting."

"Security's tighter this season," Teddy observes. "They're playing for keeps now."

The pattern continues, each season a variation on the theme of peril and providence. Finn's rescue of Aubrette from the clutches of a unpredictable storm on a lake in Daybreak; Declan's tussle with a pack of fae wolves keen on tearing Nissa apart in Reaping; Riordan and Marin's disorienting dance through a portal mishap on their way to our world for a trip to Disney.

"Every suitor's challenge is just outside their reach," I muse aloud. "It's almost like they're being tested beyond their limits."

"Or set up to fail," Doyle adds, stroking his chin thoughtfully.

But why? What could anyone hope to accomplish with so many others, including Alistair, left to pick up the pieces if one of the sisters is gone?

THE LAST EPISODE LEAVES US WITH ANGUS AND FLORA, THEIR JOYOUS banquet in Midnight turned sinister as they unwittingly consume enchanted edibles. The healers who rush to help them barely manage to keep them alive before the cameras go dark and I swallow hard.

"Poisoned at their own table," I whisper, the realization cold in my stomach.

"Seems like someone's playing a very long game," Prez notes, his eyes narrowing.

"Whatever's happening, it stinks of desperation," Doyle concludes.

"Or ambition," Teddy counters. "Whoever's behind this wants power without the spotlight."

"Power..." Wolfie whispers. The word hangs heavy in the air, leaden with implication and dread.

"Let's remember why we're here," I say, trying to anchor myself to the present. "Answers about my parents, Wolfie's dad, and maybe... maybe something bigger."

The last flicker of the 'The Princess Games' season finale dies on the screen, and we sit in a loaded silence. I can feel the weight of their eyes on me, but it's the unspoken words hanging heavy in the air that press down on my chest.

"Right," I start, breaking the hush. "So, that was... educational." My words feel clumsy, like trying to tiptoe through a minefield with clown shoes. The truth is unwieldy, especially because I can't let them know I'm seeing everything they do. But I am, and it's damn clear someone is trying to fuck with the Midnight Court and possibly the others as well.

Is it a coup? I don't know what de-stabilizing all four would accomplish besides chaos.

"More than that, Tilly," Teddy says, leaning forward earnestly. "That damn show told us something we should have already admitted to ourselves. We're painting targets on our backs by poking around." His hands move as if gesturing to the entire world around us being an enemy.

"The stakes are higher because someone thinks we're getting too close. They may be right or our search may have nothing to do with their machinations," Doyle adds in a low rumble. "But until we know more, we're stumbling around in the dark."

Wolfie, who's been quiet for too long, finally speaks up, his tone so soft it makes my heart ache. "Maybe our presence here isn't just about finding what we lost. Maybe it's about seeing the bigger picture —the one we've been missing."

"Seeing or being led to a specific conclusion?" I say absently. "It's not like events haven't cropped up that didn't seem random."

"Exactly." Benjy suddenly stands, decisive, as if casting off doubt like an ill-fitting cloak. His eyes cut to Teddy's and I wonder what he's trying to tell him without words. "Someone—or *several someones*—thinks they can play us."

I nod, feeling a sliver of determination wedge its way into my thoughts. "Alistair knew what he was doing when he pointed us to this show. It's like he's trying to clue us in without actually telling us. Do you think he's got some kind of... oath... like you guys he can't betray?"

Teddy frowns and looks at Doyle, who nods. "It's quite possible he's been forced to submit to a geas."

"That means," I say, ignoring the word he used as my gaze drifts over each of them, "we need to look at this from every angle. Question everything and trust no one."

"Especially those closest to the throne," Teddy adds, the suspicion clear in his steely gaze.

"Or those who stand to gain from the purposeful chaos," Doyle interjects, always the strategist. "We need to figure out who that might be. What we found in Harvest isn't enough to form a complete picture."

"Chaos..." I murmur, rolling the idea around in my head. Like pieces of a puzzle, events and warnings begin to click into place. "A butterfly's wings in China..."

Prez laughs, shaking his head. "Yes, Magpie, life finds a way. I don't know if that theory applies here, though."

Rolling my eyes, I look to the ceiling for patience before I respond. "I didn't mean someone's breeding hyper-intelligent dinosaurs—though if they are, I'm *so* in for the first tour. I'm much smarter than those idiots."

"Tilly, focus," Teddy says as he laughs and scrubs a hand down his face. "I can't believe you still have a thing for fucking extinct reptiles. It's been decades, woman."

I cross my arms over my chest, wishing I could shoot back that if I have to believe in goddamn Fae, orcs, were-animals, magic, and any number of shit that would get me thrown in an asylum, I should be able to hope someone resurrects T-Rexes for me to ride. "Fine. My point was that there's too much coincidence in this chaos for it to actually *be* chaos."

"She's right about that," Doyle says as he rolls to his feet. "I can *feel* that it's not right."

"Whatever's coming our way, we have to trust each other and no one else. That's how we keep people from manipulating us into dancing to the tune. Besides," I add with a wry smile, "we've dealt with worse bullies than those grumpy princes."

"Sherilynn, for one," Benjy cuts in with a grin. "Their machinations can't touch her and that band of harpies she hangs around with."

"Exactly. We can't forget our purpose for being here, even if we're caught up in Alistair's games," I caution them, even as warmth floods through me at their confidence. "His marriage to Allora might be more than it appears, but he could have told us before now. The bullshit is layered thick in this stupid place."

"Then we cut through it," Teddy declares as he joins Doyle, then holds his hand out to me.

"Let's not get ahead of ourselves," Prez cautions, though his eyes hold a spark of rebellion. "If we don't step carefully, we could end up in a web similar to the one we believe Alistair's caught in."

"Forward is the only move we have, Prez. It's not like leaving will erase our names from anyone's minds." Wolfie sighs and I have to pretend I can't see his wings fluttering nervously.

"Then we keep going until we get answers," I say firmly. "I'm not about to tuck tail and run. That's not something I do anymore. Let the assholes slinking around in the shadows bring it."

Glory

Edgar

My gaze wanders around the room as I take in my family. I was worried that the talk of this formal event would end up with us dressed like something out of *Interview with a Vampire*, but the designers who accompanied the tailors were actually less outlandish than the previous ones in the other courts. Midnight seems even more concerned with protocol than Harvest or Daybreak, but somehow more relaxed at the same time. However, what we got wasn't a bunch of plumed and ruffled weirdos, so I guess I should be grateful.

"When is she coming out?" Doyle asks as he fiddles with the dark plum vest. "I'm not putting this stupid hat on until she does. I feel like the git from that sailor cartoon—masks, tails, and fucking top hats."

Notice I didn't say we weren't dressed in something ridiculous—just not in crazy Gothic costumes.

"Soon, I'm sure," Wolfie replies as he straightens the doe's bow tie. "They always take longer with her than us. There's a lot of crap involved in dolling up women."

Prez snorts, batting his hands away to tug at the jacket. "She doesn't *need* all that shit, babe. Magpie's gorgeous just as she is."

Time to redirect or we'll wander off topic discussing our girl's attributes when we need to focus.

"Tonight," I cut in with a sharp tone, "we're going to need eyes and ears on everyone—the princes included." My eyes flick to the door as if expecting a staff member to waltz through it at any moment. "One of them could be part of this... whatever it is."

Benjy leans against the wall, looking large and in charge in the black and maroon tuxedo they sent for him. "Even if they're not, the likelihood of someone attempting shit at a big event like this is high. We thought the other courts were messing with us by giving us amped up booze or putting aphrodisiacs in our food. It might not have been them fucking with us at all."

I nod, feeling the weight of his words settle in my stomach like stones. He's right; we can't afford to overlook anyone, especially not those bathed in the spotlight of royalty. "Question everything," I murmur, "and trust no one's story without scrutiny."

Wolfie stands by the window, his silhouette outlined by the departing light. The perfect cut of his emerald and onyx suit makes him look both delicate and wicked at the same time when he's fully shifted. It's sexy as hell and I catch Prez looking, too.

The pup is a magic of his own and we're all entranced by him.

"Are you thinking it's a coup?" he asks. At my nod, he frowns, then shakes his head. "Fae courts are brutal in their transparency. This.." He gestures vaguely to the space between us, encompassing the unseen threat with a sweep of his hand, "... is shrouded in secrecy. Whoever's playing this game wants the power shift unnoticed until it's too late."

"Secrets within secrets," Doyle says, pacing back and forth like a caged animal. "That's how they're moving—like shadows in the moonlight. That's how deities work, but I don't think this is any of their doing. They'd have to contend with their brethren here if they played games in Faerie."

A chill runs down my spine as his words make the wheels in my mind turn. "Whoever it is might want people to think the gods are involved somehow. They obviously wanted us to blame the courts previously," I say slowly, reluctantly voicing the fear that has been gnawing at the edges of my mind. "What if someone who knows how all the players operate is involved? Someone who can see the whole board would know how to manipulate all the pieces, even the Fates. Hell, what if Wolfie's father is involved? What if he's aiding our unseen enemy?"

Doyle stops pacing and Benjy's grin fades. A heavy silence falls over us, thick and suffocating. It's as if the suggestion has deflated all of us. I had to say it, though, because the only thing about our trip here that could have drawn attention to us is looking for the guy. Even traveling with an unemerged like Tilly shouldn't have made this so hard. We're being sucked into things we don't understand but it doesn't feel personal. This shit is more clinical—distract and disarm us rather than kill anyone.

What better way to discourage us from continuing to look for the missing bio dad than waste our time?

"Then we'll deal with it however we have to," Wolfie says, his voice barely above a whisper. His words are brave, but the doubt in his eyes speaks louder. For a heartbeat, no one moves or speaks. We stand frozen, each lost in our own thoughts of betrayal and the painful decisions that might lie ahead.

"Guys, we don't need to borrow trouble," Benjy finally says, but there's a tightness around his eyes that belies his casual tone. "Worry is a misuse of imagination and we've got more immediate issues to consider."

"Right," Doyle adds, though his hands clench and unclench at his sides. "We stick to the plan. Watch, listen, and learn—that's all we can do for now."

Our raging Irishman isn't usually an advocate for self-control, but I think he's trying to keep Tilly from doing whatever the hell she did when we were attacked in public.

I glance at the fading light outside. The first stars are starting to prick through the velvet sky in a beautiful but deceptive calm. The view confirms why the land of summer is choosing to embrace the night; it's stunning . The staff is preparing the huge outdoor area where the ball is being held. Everything trimmed in midnight blues, silver, and black with sparkling accents and lights outlining the lavish gardens.

"I'd ask if you're ready, boys, but it seems like I'm last to the finish line again."

"Holy hell," Benjy mutters as we turn to look at Tilly.

The gown is beautiful, but it doesn't hold a candle to the woman wearing it.

I'm still gaping as she steps out like a celestial phenomenon, her gown a cosmic burst of midnight blue, black, and silver sparkles that contend with the dimming light. A crown of stars is sitting on her dark raven waves and the silvery mask draws attention to her darkly rimmed emerald eyes. The mating tattoos on her skin shine, rivaling the luminescence of her dress, casting an almost divine hue around her.

"Damn," Benjy murmurs from beside me, his words barely a whisper. We both stumbled through our teen years, tripping over reckless decisions, yet here we stand, united in our love for the incredible woman Jolene turned into.

"Is it too much?" Tilly asks, her voice laced with self-consciousness. "I *hate* letting these people treat me like "Dress Me Up Barbie,' but I have to admit this damn dress is almost worth it."

"Never," I assure her as I continue staring. I can't stop looking at her and I chuckle when I figure out that Wolfie and Prez are similarly struck. Their expressions make them look like love-struck fools who'd follow her to the ends of any realm—which probably isn't too off-the-mark. Doyle's eyes narrow slightly, assessing her like a man who's been alive long enough to classify the most beautiful things in history.

"You look…" he starts, a tremor of hunger in his voice, "… astounding. A vision worthy of the women in my family for certain."

Considering his known relatives are goddesses, Tilly has no idea how flattering that sentence is.

I feel a hum in the air, as if the essence of her power is sending shivers down my spine. It's a siren's call, even to the demi-god blood coursing through Doyle's veins, and I don't blame him for struggling not to answer it.

Jolene rolls her eyes, a gesture so like her that it cuts through the enchantment of the moment. I know she's trying to hide the blush staining her cheeks with assertiveness, but even that is so damned attractive I can't help but grin. She strides forward, the fabric of her dress swishing audibly as she twirls before us. "Pockets!" she exclaims, her face lighting up with childlike glee. "For my phone and of course, my knife."

"Of course," I say solemnly.

Laughter bubbles up among us, a release of tension in the revelation of such mundane concerns. I'm not that sheltered; I know women adore garments with functional pockets, but most of them aren't looking to slip a weapon in them—except our woman.

It's why she's goddamn amazing.

"Wait, you're all unarmed?" Her brow furrows in disapproval. "We know this thing will be filled with snakes. You can't go in unprotected." A head slithers out from between her breasts, letting out a hiss that almost sound affronted. Tilly looks and sighs. "Not good snakes like you, Isis."

"Relax," I say as I walk closer, reaching out to smooth the line between her brows with my thumb. "We've got it covered. Sometimes you've gotta trust the rest of us to watch your back."

The snake hisses at me and I glare at it as Tilly's lips pout up at me. When I arch a brow, the stubborn set of her jaw softens and Isis backs off. "It's just—" she starts to explain when Doyle interrupts her.

"Just because you need to be battle-ready in your ballgown doesn't mean we have to be weighed down with armor, Tíogair."

"You hush," she warns, her tone playful yet edgy.

She walks over to him, giving his lapels a yank to straighten him out, then quick as a viper, her heel comes down hard on his foot. His grimace speaks volumes, but he doesn't chastise her. Instead, he chuckles—a sound that holds a tinge of respect for her spirit.

"Okay, okay, truce," he concedes, lifting his hands in surrender.

"Calm down, you two," Prez, ever the voice of reason, finally speaks up. "We have specific goals tonight. That doesn't mean we can't have fun, but it does mean we need to be aware of what's going on around us."

I nod at him, grateful for the injection of logic. "Stay sharp, everyone. The night is young, and this place is full of secrets waiting to be uncovered."

"Real secrets draped in jewels and masked by fake smiles," Tilly muses, her eyes flickering towards the entrance where our evening awaits. "We'll have to be careful where we dig."

The grandeur of the outdoor ball unfurls before us, the scene drenched in opulence that even rock stars would envy. As we enter via the sparkling path that leads to the party from the patio, Jekyll and Hyde slip away, all feline grace as they slink among the sparkling throng of people. Kali and Hecate stand sentinel at the periphery, their dark eyes vigilant as they watch every one who leaves the palace. Eurayle, the embodiment of predatory elegance, soars overhead as she keeps tabs on the movement around the vast borders of the party under the stars.

Our girl's entrance is nothing short of majestic, walking into the crowd with Isis coiling around her arm with an air of possessive warning, in a gown that seems to mimic the night sky. Doyle chuckles as we follow behind her, his slight limp a testament to what happens when you cross our woman, even in jest.

"Always the dramatic one," he says with an approving nod. "She knows how to get everyone's attention on what she wants them to see without being obvious. It's a useful skill."

"The best way to make a statement is loudly," I reply as I scan the crowd before I head to the bar. The setup encourages mingling—staging a perfect opportunity for us to weave through the whispers of the court in search of clues about Wolfie's enigmatic father. "Remember, we're looking for someone who can match Callie's years—and her cunning."

"Got it," Benjy says, saluting as he follows Tilly towards a cluster of elder Fae.

Wolfie and Prez veer off in another direction, their senses tuned to the undercurrent of gossip that might lead us to our quarry. They're looking for younger, but less tight-lipped prey. Doyle winks, walking backwards away from me before disappearing into thin air.

That motherfucker and his slipping in and out dimensional pockets—what if Jolene saw? Reckless.

Once I get to the bar, I place an order. It arrives quickly and my hand wraps around a chilled glass of Gooseberry Whiskey. This shit is expensive as fuck and I'm surprised they're serving it. I'm about to comment on it to the bartender when he gets distracted by a man who sidles up beside me. The newcomer is quiet, but his presence commands my attention—a picture of weary aristocracy, clothed in a pinstripe suit that whispers of wealth and power. The purple sparkle of Phantasm swirls in his glass and I wince. That is not a drink meant for the faint-hearted or light-walleted.

"Careful with that," I comment, nodding towards his drink. "Phantasm is known to reveal more than some wish to see."

"Ah, but sometimes revelation is exactly what one seeks," he responds in amusement.

I study him closer now, noting how the silvery threads of his suit glint with a magic signature that sends a shiver down my spine. It clicks suddenly—those are no ordinary pinstripes. They're spells, stitched in silver thread from collar to hem. Something like that had to cost enough to set back a small state budget.

Could this be the elusive Midnight King? No one has even mentioned the patriarch or matriarch of this court.

"Interesting choice of attire," I remark, keeping my tone neutral. "Protection spells?"

"Observant," he replies with a tired smile. "One must always be prepared, don't you think?"

"Indeed." The dance of riddles between us is a subtle duel of wits, but there's a hollowness to his gaze that suggests his true target might not be me. We sip in silence for another moment until I finally excuse myself, leaving the king—or whoever he really is—to his devices.

I need to find Tilly and Benjy; the royals might be mingling amongst us in disguise.

I locate them deep in conversation with two couples whose elegance is striking. One pair shimmers like moonlight, the other dark as pitch, and their masks obviously conceal more than their identities. As I approach, my hound's instincts kick in; these strangers bear the same scent as the king I just left. The men are princes, which means the women are two of Alistair's sisters.

"Teddy!" Our girl greets me, radiant as ever as she sparkles in the moonlight. I lean in and kiss her cheek, drawing curious stares from our company.

"Your... family structure is unique," one of the women observes. There's a mix of fascination and puzzlement in her voice, so I know she's not being nasty, but I dislike nosy questions.

Tilly's easy laughter rings clear as crystal. "We're polyamorous. There are three more guys wandering the party. We're all very happy together, I assure you."

"Quite the modern arrangement," comments the darker of the men. His tone is unreadable, but I wonder if any of the competitors for that stupid show had considered a family like ours.

Probably not. Despite monogamy not being the norm in supe communities, the old guard of a lot of species still encourages it so we blend in.

"Our love doesn't follow outdated rules," Benjy adds and I grin at my friend. He's really coming out of that shell he was stuck in for so long.

I kiss Tilly's knuckles, sealing our explanation with a gesture of endearment. The couples look a bit ruffled, so we take our leave not long after.

The air is thick with unasked questions until we get far enough away that I feel safe murmuring to my companions. "Did you learn anything useful?"

"Maybe," Benjy says, his brow furrowed. "Though I feel like it was more about how unhappy they seem."

"Trouble in paradise? How could that be when you enter a relationship based on a TV show contest?" I feign surprise and they both snicker.

"The glitz has definitely faded," Tilly snarks as we encounter Wolfie and Prez. "Those women seem about as sexually satisfied as a group of nuns."

"Guys, listen," Wolfie starts, urgency lacing his words. "We might have found something."

I close my mouth, letting my response to Jolene's quip fall away. "Tell us, pup."

"We heard about a fae who tried to unite the kingdoms a long time ago. He moved through all four, advising the royals and trying to stop a lot of the petty bullshit wars. When it became obvious it wasn't working, he vanished for a decade. When he returned, he was a different person—cold, manipulative, and power hungry."

"Sounds like a delightful chap," I muse. "I suppose that could be your dad, Wolfie."

"Having to fuck Callie would do that to anyone," Tilly muses and I give her a look.

Wolfie dips his chin and shrugs. "I mean, she's not wrong, Teddy."

"We should keep digging," I say with a sigh. "There's more to this court than meets the eye, and we're going to uncover it all."

Legendary

Jolene

Everything here glitters like a constellation of nobility and deception swirling in dance. I watch from the outskirts, my eyes scanning for clues among the fancy people drinking and mingling. My heart thuds a rhythm that matches the undercurrent of dread in my gut. I don't like hearing that we're probably hunting a bad guy, especially because it will disappoint my darling boy.

He's had enough bullshit in the parental arena and I'm ready to tan someone's hide if it doesn't stop.

Wolfie's profile stands out from the group he's in, his expression etched with growing concern. Once he sees me, he excuses himself, making a beeline for me. His voice is steady as he speaks, but there's a tremor there—fear, anger, or maybe both. "Any luck, Sugarplum?"

"Snippets of stories, but nothing solid. It's like trying to catch smoke," I reply as a frustrated sigh escapes me. "Some say 'he' moves through shadows; others claim he's waiting for war. There's no substance, only specters."

"Same here," Prez chimes in, his brow furrowed as he joins us. He tries to lighten the mood with a wry smile, but it falls flat. His hands land on Wolfie's shoulders, squeezing them gently. "It's like this dude is their Boogeyman."

"Or a ghost story," Teddy adds as he comes over to pat Wolfie on the back. I smile as the vet turns to lean into both of the men, loving how they take care of him. "We'll get to the bottom of this if it kills me. I hate feeling like we're in an episode of Scooby Doo, though."

Wolfie nods, but I can tell his mind is racing with possibilities. He's far too sensitive and kind to not feel bad if both of his biological parents are complete psychopaths who get off on torturing people.

"Hey," I ask, lowering my voice to a softer tone. "Are you okay?"

He shrugs, a gesture meant to be nonchalant but laden with sadness. "I just hoped for... something different." His gaze flickers downward, then towards the regal and detached Fae court, and then back. "I guess madness runs thicker than blood."

"Lucy," Prez says as he pulls him closer to press his lips on his forehead. "We have you—all of us. You're not alone and you're not crazy, even if all your bio-donors are."

Teddy nods as he joins them, his protective instincts palpable as he rumbles softly. "The doc is right. You're ours, pup, and nothing is going to change that—especially not asshole parents."

"Thanks," Wolfie murmurs before pulling away to straighten his tux and gather himself. "I don't want to be needy, but this shit is harder than I expected."

"Tilly," Teddy says, turning to me, "stick with the women. They talk more around you."

"And even more when she walks away," Doyle snorts. "They're as bad as the belles back home with the mean girl shit. Our girl should watch for a knife in the back from damn near anyone in this garden."

Fucking fabulous. I just make friends and influence people everywhere I go now.

"I'll go back out there," I say with a sigh. "But keep an eye on our boy or I'll be pissed." When they nod, I nod and turn away to weave through the throngs of guests. Now that I know what to look for, I see when the princesses flit by. Their smiles are tight and their eyes betray the sadness lurking beneath. I also catch glimpses of the princes with stoic masks firmly in place. Both seem equally out of tune with the grandeur of the ball, but I can't figure out why.

"Something isn't right with them," I mutter under my breath as I pass a group of teen girls who titter at my proximity. "Obviously Doyle was right about the fucking rumor mill, too."

An older woman hears me growling and pauses, her lips quirking as she looks me up and down. "Darling, this whole thing's a sham. Ever since the show started, it's as if the entire court has been bewitched."

Ooh. Now this *is interesting.*

"Perhaps they're enthralled by their own misery?" I suggest, baiting her to see if she'll bite.

"Or cursed," she returns. Her voice drops to a fearful hush, and I tilt my head as I pretend to think about that.

"By whom?" I gasp, feigning ignorance as I put my hand on my chest. "Wouldn't that be very dangerous to attempt?"

"Who can say?" she replies, her eyes darting around nervously. "They whisper of a shadow, a phantom advisor who vanished and returned to pull strings from behind a veil of darkness. It could be him."

Paydirt.

I have to hide my grin as another woman scurries up, giving my new friend a reproachful look. "Those are tales for children," she scoffs. "It's more likely the royal family are embroiled in a power battle between the new princes and the true heir. Alistair is known for his vicious temperament; it's why they're sending him to Harvest."

"Do you think it's only a fairy tale or are you scared it could be true?" I challenge. My mind races as Alistair's words echo in my mind '*That's when shit started going wrong.*' He meant the show and the pairing off of the princesses.

He must think a guiding hand was messing with all of it.

"Perhaps you're right," I concede with a smile that doesn't reach my eyes. "But if not, your rulers have a serious problem on their hands."

"They're royals, darling. They always figure it out," the second woman says with a shrug. "We're not responsible for their troubles. Come, Priscilla. I see a fresh tray of hors d'oeuvres circulating."

I frown as they walk off, disliking their snooty dismissal of troubles in their land.

All it takes for evil to win is for good people to do nothing, after all.

"I'm going to riot if we don't actually get to eat this time," I declare as I slide into a chair at our secluded table.

From our table, the royal family's grim faces are on full display—a veritable theater of quiet despair. The man Teddy suspected to be the King sits with the weight of the world bowing his shoulders and his wife is beside him, her face masked but her expression unmistakably hollow.

What the hell is going on in this damn place?

"It feels like we're dancing on a knife blade, doesn't it?" Doyle murmurs as he takes a seat across from me. "Our hosts have been nothing but gracious, but they're treated like pariahs among their supposed sycophants."

"Maybe it's not what they've done," I suggest, picking at the bread in front of me, "but what they're expected to do that scares them."

Before any of my guys can respond, an unnatural shadow blankets the stars above. My heart rate kicks up as a swarm of winged beasts darken the sky, their shrill cries drowning out the music and laughter. Panic ignites the ball, a fire fueled by fear of the shrieking monsters diving from above.

"Tilly, get down," Teddy growls as he leaps to his feet. He shoves me toward Prez, but I'm already ripping away from his grasp.

"I'm not helpless," I spit out with my teeth clenched. I give him the fingers and stomp away before he can get his hands on me. Pushing through the chaos, I feel my dress billow around me in an impractical sea of fabric. Cursing, I consider ripping it away, but I don't have a damn thing on under here that wouldn't be humiliating to show off in public.

I'll be damned if I'm letting these motherfuckers watch me fight in goddamn Spanx—that's a line I won't cross.

"Damn it. This is going to be really hard to explain later," Prez mutters somewhere behind me, but his words fade as I spot Alistair under attack—from Prince Finn, whose form is monstrous and covered in white fur matted with blood he didn't shed.

"Yo, Fuzzball," I yell, drawing the beast's attention long enough to dart forward and jam my knife deep into his shoulder. Finn's pained roar confirms he's still in there somewhere, but trapped in his body as it betrays him. I have to do something or he's going to get killed and I *think* Princess Aubrette might be upset. I don't hesitate, swinging a fist with all my might, connecting with a crunch.

I don't have many options, but here it goes.

Gathering my fury at every stupid thing going on in my life right now, I swing my fist in a vicious right hook, grinning when it connects with a sickening crunch. Finn collapses, and I'm left panting over Alistair, who's more vulnerable than I've ever seen him.

"My sisters," he croaks, blood spilling from his lips. I'm pretty sure he'll be okay, so I nod.

"Stay alive," I shoot back before turning on my heel to find the next afflicted couple. Grumbling, I head for the next fight on the stage. "I can't wait to blast you for this fucking mess, you absolute goddamn biscuit."

"Tíogair, get back," Doyle shouts as I approach him and Celestine. She's dangerously close to receiving a fatal blow from her prince in his hulking orc form. My cheeky Irishman is clearly holding back, causing a desperate dance of evasion as he fights the green monster man. "I'm going to finish him off."

"You can't kill him," I breathe as my mind races for a solution. Closing my eyes, I feel a strange surge crawling up my spine as I stare at the two men fighting. When wings unfurl behind me, I try not to freak out. Doyle doesn't look surprised when they sprinkle the air with black sparkles that settle like a whisper over the chaos.

Son of a bitch. Am I fucking fairy like Wolfie?

The feral prince and terrified princess slump to the ground, suddenly enveloped in slumber. Doyle's wide-eyed shock mirrors my own pounding heart, but before I can process it, he's pulling me away, hand locked with mine.

"Nobody can know what you just did," he hisses as we dodge through the fray.

"Over there," I point, spotting Benjy in gorilla form giving Keegan the elf a thrashing that might end in death. I don't know what to do except reach out to touch the primal fury in him. It takes a moment, but I see clarity return to his gaze. He stills, panting heavily, his fists unclenching as he looks at us in confusion.

Benjy doesn't have a lot of human in him when he changes—good to know.

"It's not just the princes," Doyle says as realization dawns "Something—or someone—is driving the men wild, stripping them of control. That's why I almost… and Benjy… Fuck, who could wield that much power? I'm not exactly easy to…"

He looks frustrated as he mutters to himself, obviously trying to keep his full thoughts from me as he works through this newest complication.

"I think the better question is: why turn it against the Midnight Court?" His eyes meet mine and he shakes his head. My brows furrow as we look over the people fighting all over the lawn. "Whoever it is, we need to put a stop to this… fast. Otherwise, someone is going to die, Lucky."

I have a feeling our secret enemy has a fall guy lined up to take the blame—it could easily be someone in my family.

I'll be damned if I'm going to let that shit happen on my watch.

Cello Suite No. 1 in G Major
Dhameer

The clink of crystal and the murmur of the elite weave into a symphony of decadence. Here, in this ballroom awash with golden light and laughter, we are hunters cloaked in the finery of our prey. Hugo stands beside me, his posture relaxed but eyes keen beneath the low glow of a chandelier. Saoirse's elegance is effortless, her gaze sweeping the room with a predator's precision. I can't help but admire how she carries herself—like a blade sheathed in silk.

It's very different from how she typically presents herself; her Guardian training is more apparent tonight than I have seen in the past.

"Patience," I whisper to myself, scanning faces and fine jewels, searching for one particular glint of auburn. She appears at last, the *Reina Pantera*, slinking through the crowd. The woman from the horse show in Turkey materializes like an enigma wrapped in emerald velvet, her famed red locks a fiery contrast to the subdued hues around her.

"Found her," Hugo murmurs, his voice barely audible over the chamber quartet's crescendo.

"Let's not rush," I counsel. "She's dangerous and easily spooked. My experience with her was not typical; most do not survive being the center of her attention."

We glide through the throngs of guests until we stand before her. There's a weariness to her eyes that wasn't there in Turkey—a shadow beneath the blaze. It's jarring to see such fatigue on a creature known for her ruthlessness. I cannot help but notice the change and wonder if I'm picking it up because she allows it or because she cannot conceal it.

What could possibly have this serious effect on such a powerful supernatural?

"Good evening, *Reina*" I greet, masking my emotions with a diplomat's smile.

"Ah, you've arrived. And you're traveling in a charming trio this time," she responds, her voice a melody laced with hidden notes. "You've been busy since our last encounter—building an alliance, Your Highness?"

"Simply enjoying the company of good friends. Are you here with your companions this evening?" I ask as I look around discreetly. "Or is this meeting an extension of an assignment?"

Her lips curve in the ghost of a smile and she shakes her head. "No guests this evening, Prince. I am far too busy to pause for revelry at the moment. But your associates' probing for answers drew my attention and I decided to handle this situation personally."

I arch a brow at her, my expression curious. "How would our subtle digging show up on your radar of all people, *Reina?*"

"Just as you have your sources, I have mine." She sips the martini in her hand, twirling the stem in her fingers with the dexterity of a master thief. "You've shown up on reports you don't want to be on. Eyes far less understanding than mine have noticed your efforts. So I made time that I did not have to meet with you."

"Saoirse," I say as I turn to her. "Is your family as discreet as Isra?"

"Always," Saoirse replies smoothly, the corner of her mouth ticking upward.

Reina smirks and shrugs. "They likely were, but the people I'm referring to have more resources than you can imagine. Which, given your wealth, isn't a small feat, I know. You do not want to continue fumbling around and catching their eyes, Prince."

She's trying to help us, but I have no idea why—that worries me.

"How do you know this and why would you risk coming to tell us?" Hugo cuts in. His face is a mask of distrust as he studies the lethal woman.

"Especially since I *technically* still owe you one," I mutter. That gets a laugh out of the woman and she shrugs, but it's not enough for me. "Why can't we locate this team of assassins who slid in and out of that house without leaving a trace? We've been looking everywhere, even in human circles."

"I suggest you search for those who dwell where your sun's fingers cannot pry," *Reina* advises cryptically. "It takes more than mere mortals to bypass the wards that protected that officer's home."

I feel a chill despite the warm air. *What are we stepping into following this lead?* My face reveals nothing of my concern; I've learned to school it into impassivity over countless negotiations. She tilts her head, her bright blue eyes flashing emerald for a moment and I have to hide my reaction again.

Reina Pantera is not human, either—a fact I doubt many know since the Society has never mentioned her.

"An intriguing suggestion," I say as my mind already sifts through possibilities while discarding the impractical. There could be a team of supernatural mercenaries operating outside of the Society's purview, but it seems unlikely they wouldn't at least be aware of them. I wonder if the cover up we're tracking isn't one orchestrated by our people, but one purchased by an outside party from skilled criminals.

But how does she know?

"Consider it a free piece of advice. You can take it or leave it, Prince. Now that I've warned you, my responsibility is done," she says cryptically, then drifts away like smoke, leaving us to ponder her words.

"More than mortals," Hugo echoes thoughtfully, glancing at me with a frown creasing his brow.

"A surprising piece of information indeed," I reply, watching the space she vacated. "It makes you wonder what sort of darkness hides within her own silhouette, especially since she comes and goes with such skill."

Saoirse touches my arm lightly—our shared signal to regroup later. None of us want to be seen entering or leaving as a group for fear of drawing too many eyes on where we'll end up afterward. I'm particularly well known, so keeping my staff with me while the other two slink off allows them to disappear into the crowd easily.

We disperse among the revelers, and I'm lost in contemplation. This night has yielded more questions than answers, which is not my preference. Our hunt for the killers continues, but now we must pursue phantoms that slip between worlds, it seems. I wasn't prepared to hear that, nor to find out that we've been pinning our efforts on a conspiracy that may be coming from another source. I will have to contact our family and let them know there are more enemies than we were aware of.

Especially since somewhere, behind tired eyes, the Reina Pantera watches, a puppeteer holding strings we have yet to see for reasons we cannot fathom.

As I make my way through the party, pretending to mingle with the guests, the music pulses like a heartbeat in my ears. The thrum of urgency quickens my heartbeat as I continue to mull over the possibilities. While I have to stay a bit longer to keep my cover, I'm barely able to focus on the banal conversations of the elite around me. I lean closer to Isra, the din necessitating proximity as much as secrecy does.

"I'll delve into the *Pantera*'s advice," I tell her, the words nearly lost amidst the cacophony of laughter and bass. "You and Fazal can gather leads on these shadowy supernatural criminals."

Isra nods, her golden eyes reflecting the strobe lights, giving them an otherworldly glow. "I'll consult with lower beings and leave more respectable ones to Fazal. Your friend should speak with her handler. The Guardians know much about beings that prefer obscurity; some of their teams monitor them."

"Supes were sent to erase that human family because other supes were protecting them with wards. It feels as though there is a problem in the Society's ranks," I muse aloud.

Humans aren't the only ones who are corruptible, but it's disappointing when any of our kind go rogue.

We move slightly, allowing a couple laughing drunkenly to stagger past us, their carefree antics a stark contrast to our grave conference. My faithful general shrugs as she scans the crowd to make sure the people who bumped us weren't a precursor to something darker.

"A lot of money is involved then, Amiri," she says in a low voice. "A team of killers who can do that and make everything disappear, a mole high enough to have the right information… I do not believe this is the work of an individual and it surely is not last minute. This reeks of a very long term gambit."

"Too many coincidences lately," I respond thoughtfully. My mind paints the recent chaos in vibrant, violent strokes. "The witch disturbances during Halloween in Salem. A mafia upheaval shaking the West Coast. Northern Europe's Snow and Ice Kingdoms rattling sabers over trade routes. The death of that elder dragon. Young heirs being accused of murder."

It didn't occur to me until now that the small eruptions I've seen in the supernatural news might tie together.

"None of those issues intersect," Isra frowns. Worry is etched into her fierce features momentarily before they smooth into practiced calm. "That sounds as if we have discovered a much larger plan beginning to unfold."

"Agreed." My jaw tightens. "An unseen hand agitating the supernatural world's chessboard. But to what end, old friend?"

"Let Fazal and I do our jobs once you are safely ensconced in the hotel." Isra jerks her chin at him as he joins us. "We should take our leave, Your Highness."

"Of course." I reach out, focusing my energy. The air around us shivers, reality bending to my will as I open a pathway for us. "We will regroup with Hugo and decide what happens next."

THE MOMENT WE ARE BACK IN THE HOTEL, MY CLOSEST ALLIES CHECK every inch of the suite until they are satisfied that we are safe. Hugo watches in amusement, but I know they are simply doing the things that have helped me stay both alive and free for many years.

It's difficult even for him to understand the life of a djinn.

Once they complete their sweep, my staff do exactly as promised—they head out into the night to see what they can glean from the local supernaturals. Hugo arches a brow as I retrieve my laptop, beckoning him to join me in the sitting area.

"Time to report back to Nelia," I say as I dig through my valise to find the files we've been compiling.

He nods, his face set in lines of concern as touches my arm when I'm about to hit the call button. "Are we certain she can be trusted?"

"Yes. Nelia isn't quite as ancient as I am, Hugo, but she's been part of the Society for longer than you. Her loyalty is unquestionable, which is why they put her in charge of a town like the Hollow."

"Okay. I'm just..." he trails off for a moment, then continues, "... feeling a bit paranoid after this evening."

I nod, understanding his hesitance. "As should we all."

When I hit 'call,' it only takes a few seconds before Mayor Nelia's face flickers onto the screen.. "Dhameer, Hugo. Any progress?"

"Only cryptic hints so far," I admit, watching her expression carefully. She's trustworthy; I didn't lie about that. But I'm not one to show all my cards to anyone until I know what I'm looking at.

"Have you heard anything from Jolene's family? They're still in Faerie, last I heard and they've only got about two weeks left to accomplish their goals before Jolene has to be back here."

"Harvest Court was their latest stop when I spoke to them. No luck finding Wolfgang's father yet though." I keep my tone neutral, but the news clearly troubles her.

"Things here are... unsteady," she confides, glancing off-screen as if expecting eavesdroppers. "The Hollow's balance is teetering with so many strong citizens out of town. The more... ambitious... towns-people are causing quite the stir with their gossip."

"Will this affect Jolene when she returns?" Hugo asks, his concern mirroring mine as he leans in.

"Undoubtedly." Nelia sighs. "She'll have to navigate a sea of old grudges and fresh whispers. I'd put a stop to it if I could, but mean spirited gossip is not a crime—especially not when it's shielded by influence and heritage."

"We'll prepare her as best we can," I say firmly, feeling the resolve steel within me. "I appreciate you making us aware of the increased pettiness and venom, Nelia. I know it's not your job to monitor this sort of nonsense."

She sighs and rubs her hand over her face. "Unfortunately, this is part and parcel when you live in a small town. I just don't want to see the girl harmed again. I wasn't there to help prevent it the first time."

"Understood," I rumble as my frown deepens. "I will send you any pertinent findings before we head to our next destination tomorrow. Have a good night, Nelia."

The mayor returns the sentiment and our call ends with the click of a button.

Hugo looks at me, his gaze unsure. "What now?"

I think about *Reina*'s words, my determination a match for any darkness we may face. "We follow the shadows, and we brace for the storm to come."

He nods as I close the computer, ending our duties for the evening. We will sleep while my associates do their work and in the morning, we can regroup. I have faith that Isra and Fazal will bring us something we can use to determine our next path.

They haven't failed me in over a thousand years and I highly doubt they will start now.

MORNING LIGHT SLICES THROUGH THE HALF-DRAWN CURTAINS, casting a geometric glow upon our belongings strewn across the room. I'm bent over my valise, methodically packing the materials I do not wish to have leave my person when we travel.

When Isra and Fazal gave their report this morning, I decided we would head to Argentina next then back to the States. My general heard rumblings about a facility off the coast of the nearby country, while my assistant caught wind of a possible lead in the Midwest at some bar. It was hard to decide which one would yield more results, but since Argentina was close, I chose to stop there first.

We're about to leave the suite en masse when the sound of voices coming closer tugs at my attention. I poke my head out the door, frowning as I wait.

"Keep it down, assholes." A woman's voice hisses the rejoinder as she turns the corner to come into view. Her electric blue hair is long and it sways around her hips with each step she takes.

I shake my head, turning back to pretend to zip my bag shut as they near our open door. They don't need to know I'm watching or listening to them as they walk by.

The girl is flanked by a woman and three men—one of whom's face tickles the back of my mind as if I should know who it is. The tallest man is rough around the edges—clearly the type who knows the back alleys of the world all too well. Another companion leans heavily on crutches, the clack of his progress rhythmic and steady as they head toward us. He trails behind the first two with the other woman. Their incessant stream of chatter spills from their lips as if words were currency. That's who the leader was chastising, for sure.

It's almost too distracting, in fact.

"Hey, isn't that—" Hugo begins, but his words falter, his eyes glaze over, and I recognize the distant look that precedes his visions.

"Damn." I reach out to steady him, my gaze still locked on the group now disappearing down the hall. "Is it over?"

"Many heads... animals..." Hugo's voice is a hoarse whisper, his brow creased in concentration. "A darkness—so vast it devours the light. And there... the hooded figure from the trial."

"Do you have any idea what it means? Is that even something you can share or is it going to violate your ethos?" My question hangs in the air, heavy with the burden of our unknown adversary.

Hugo shakes his head, frustration etching lines into his face. "Not yet. But it's vital, Amiri. I feel it in my bones."

"Visions are never just smoke," I sigh. The unrest, the supernatural undercurrents, the hooded figure—it's a puzzle with pieces scattered across a shadowy board. I love puzzles, but this one has parts flung around the globe and possibly throughout the years.

We need to catch up.

"Let's get moving." I sling my bag over my shoulder, determination fueling my stride. "We have a lot of ground to cover, and I don't intend to let these threads unravel without us holding the ends."

"Right behind you," Hugo replies, though his eyes remain clouded with the remnants of his vision.

As we leave the room, I glance back once more at the corridor where the blue-haired girl vanished. There's a story there, another piece waiting to be placed.

I'll be damned if I let it slip through my fingers.

Dead Man Walking

Jolene

"**D**amn it, Riordan!" I shout, the words torn from my throat as another bolt of magic sizzles past my ear, singing the ends of my hair. The air crackles with energy as the half-Fae prince charges up again. I dart to the left while clutching Princess Marin's arm to keep her behind me. "Stop it, you idiot. You're going to hurt her."

This cannot be my life… ducking magic bolts with Fae royalty was not on my goddamn bingo card this year.

The fae prince grins, his eyes wild with some rogue spell or enchantment. He looks completely off his rocker and I have no idea what the hell to do about it. My heart pounds in my chest, each beat echoing my rising anger. My hands are ablaze again, flames licking up my wrists, turning my internal fury into scorching heat.

"Tilly, watch out!" Teddy's deep growl reverberates through the mayhem. He's enormous – a monstrous black hellhound man with thick fur flickering with fire. Once I nod, he pounces on Prince Angus, holding the squirming scaled fae beneath him. Water sprouts from Angus's fingertips in a futile attempt to quench Teddy's inferno and I realize he must be part mer… something.

Fuck, I'm so behind when it comes to this shit.

"I think he's trying to dampen your spirits, Teddy," I mutter under my breath. I'm trying to find levity in the horror, especially since I get the distinct feeling I'm not going to remember a damn bit of this when it's over. The more I think about it, my inconvenient blackouts feel like they're a protective measure. It's like they're meant to help me stay sane until that one moment when everything makes sense the guys keep referring to.

"Focus, Tilly! He's behind you," Teddy barks, voice rough with the notes of the canine he's shifted into.

I steal a moment to glance upward where Prez, now shifted into the huge white bird again, clashes with winged beasts that darken the sky. Euryale is striking at anything that comes too close to him; my girl is fierce as hell as she works alongside my adorable doctor. Their aerial ballet is a desperate fight to defend those of us on the ground while we try to temper the hyped up men.

"Your men have Angus and the sky covered, but Riordan's coming!" Marin's voice trembles as she rushes closer to me, her gown dirty and torn from the fray.

"Shit. These damn women can't keep themselves out of trouble for a second," I grumble as another blast from Riordan narrowly misses us.

Note to self: Alistair needs to get his sisters some fucking self-defense classes.

Grabbing her hand, I tug Marin out of firing range while I gather myself. I see my sweet, dependable Wolfie, weaving through the throngs of possessed partygoers. His wings shimmer, dusting the air with fae dust that I think is meant to soothe the savagery surrounding us. I watch as a couple, moments ago locked in a vicious duel, now cling to each other. It's effective, but for every pair he calms, ten more are still fighting as if they want to end one another.

"Come on, Wolfie," I whisper under my breath, "we don't have all night."

"Princess, duck!" Benjy's command snaps me back to reality just in time and I take Marin with me as I hit the ground.

I'm tired of this dick trying to fry me and I don't care if he's Marin's fiancé—the motherfucker is done.

"Enough," I grit out as the burn creeps up my forearms. *I have to end this, but how? How do you stop a tidal wave with a teacup?* "One cup at a time, just like eating an elephant, Jolene."

Marin frowns at me as she dusts herself off. "You want to eat an elephant?"

I shake my head, looking around for a second to get my bearings, then give her a crooked smile. "Not literally. But we have to do something about this mess; it's getting bigger and more out of control by the minute. So, how do you eat an elephant?"

The princess looks confused for a moment, then gives me a grim look. "Ah. One bite at a time, yes?"

"Yep," I say as I wipe the blade of my knife on the ruined gown. "You stay over here while I try to remove your prince from my plate. I'll do my best not to maim or kill him, I promise."

"Be careful," she pleads, reaching out to grip my wrist for a moment. "Please. I don't think anyone knows what they're doing right now."

I know that, but if you can't stop a rabid animal, you may have to put it down to protect everyone else.

"Careful went out the window three princes ago. I have to stop him, Marin, but I'll try," I reply.

With a feral cry, I rush toward the magic-wielding Fae. It's him or me —and I didn't put on this ridiculously elaborate dress to be outshone by a man, even if he is a sparkling fairy prince.

I have to dodge and weave around the stupid magic blasts—which sucks in a dress—but I finally see my opening when he spins to look at a loud sound from above. Euryale is flying above him, taking swipes with her enormous claws, and I could kiss my damn eagle if I wasn't busy.

Now's my chance.

Leaping onto Riordan's back with a force that knocks the wind out of him, I hold on tightly as we crash to the ground. The impact jars my bones, but I twist until I can clamp my thighs around his neck like a vice. He flails beneath me, sputtering desperate words in a language I don't know while I squeeze. He starts to go limp and I feel a vicious satisfaction when I finally get the upper hand. Slamming the butt of my knife against his temple, and I pant while Riordan sags into unconsciousness.

"Yoga isn't just for chanting wusses. I've got thighs of steel, baby," I mutter as I push the hair sticking to my forehead away from my eyes. The heavy fabric of my dress is in my way, so I gather it to free my legs. Once I do, I frown in sadness before using the knife to cut a ton of it off so I can slide out from under the fallen prince.

That was a damn fashion crime and I'm adding whoever made me destroy that thing to my 'getting their shit stomped' list.

I look around, seeing the world around me is still in chaos. The entire garden is a cacophony of screams, spells, and wingbeats. My heart hammers against my chest as I try to figure out what bite I need to take next to help end this thing.

~Jolene,~ the voice in my head begins—her tone oddly serene amid the turmoil. *~Use the mist.~*

"Are you kidding me? *Now* is when I lose my marbles? *Here* is when the voices in my head start? Very funny, universe," I mutter, more to myself. "What the chicken fried *shit* is the mist? How do I use it? Why are weird voices in your head so damn vague?"

Note to self number two: Call your therapist when you get home.

~Look inside of yourself. Find where you are connected to your canine. Push aside the fire to find more..." the voice instructs with infuriating calm.

Rubbing my eyes as I make peace with the fact that I may be having a psychotic break, I flick my gaze to Teddy, fully in the form of a colossal hellhound made of shadow and flame. He's battling the watery wrath of Prince Angus still. The voice says the mist is connected to Teddy, which means like some of the Fae, he's got more than one supernatural part. He's a man, a beast, and... something else that I need to figure out quickly.

"Okay, okay. Fine, weird dream lady. I'll give it a try." I take a deep breath, focusing on looking inside of me without closing my eyes to carnage around me. "Push away the fire..." I envision the flames licking up my arms, the heat that mirrors my anger, and mentally shove it aside.

A shiver runs through me as I reach deeper into the bond I share with Teddy, toward a soft pink glow. When I realize it's the odd pink mist I saw at the Harvest Court, I feel like a dumbass. The mist swirls around, pulsing with a warmth that I didn't notice before because it happened at the same time as the flames. When I reach out to touch it, the vapor soaks into my skin immediately.

Well, okay, then. I am one with the mist.

"Here goes nothing," I whisper as I look at the fighting Fae surrounding me. I take a deep breath and hold my hands out, reaching for the mist with trepidation. "Hopefully, you don't kill everyone. That would suck and I'll be very cross."

The mist unfurls, shooting out of my fingertips and spiraling out into the night. At first, it's just a wisp—a tendril curling through the air. Then it grows bolder, spreading its influence across the garden party in pretty pink curves of smoke that curve around the warring factions.

"What. The. Actual. Fuck?" I murmur to myself. I'm awestruck as the mist caresses each frenzied guest, altering their behavior almost immediately. Every being it touches stops the fighting, and replaces their grunts with ones of a different nature.

Everyone is no longer kung-fu fighting—they're kung-fu fucking.

"Hooooooleeeee shit," I breathe in shock. My eyes widen, taking in the results of my experiment. Across the garden, couples are entwined as their aggression transforms to lust. The effects are hitting everyone except for my guys. They're all standing, frozen as their expressions range from shocked to bemused.

"Sugarplum, what did you do?" Wolfie asks, his voice tinged with concern.

"I don't know," I admit as the strange heat from the mist swirls inside of me. I feel like I'm the conductor of a symphony I barely recognize the music for. "But it worked, I guess."

The moans and grunts around us are better than screams of agony—marginally.

"Tilly, do you know why suddenly everyone is fucking?" Teddy says sternly. He's shifted back, which means he's standing with his arms crossed and his Dom face on—stark naked.

Wolfie chokes and I have to smother a very inappropriate giggle before I answer. "Apparently, I'm Cupid? Hell if I know, Big Daddy Asshole. This shit seems to just happen to me."

"Sugarplum," Wolfie scolds before he snorts, covering his mouth as he looks away. I know he wants to say more, but he's struggling to keep the laughter in.

"Quite the party trick, amirite?" I bob my brows at Teddy, who looks ready to turn me over his knee. Prez lands and walks over—*naked*—to scan the crowd going at it around us. His gaze cuts to me and I shrug. "I don't *know*, Doctor McNuggies. Trouble follows me like a bad penny."

"Speaking of bad pennies," Doyle says as he saunters up. He's not naked, but the gorgeous man following him is. Benjy just winks at me and I feel like I'm going to over heat on the spot.

Too. Much. Sex. And. Candy.

"Magpie, are you okay?" Prez asks, but his words are distant, echoing as if from another world.

I blink, feeling the world tilt a bit and that's when I know it's coming. I'm going to fucking blackout *again*, and I'll be lucky if remember *any* of this shit when I come to.

"Tilly? Tilly? Are you okay? Guys!"

And then my body surrenders to the void, leaving my allies to untangle the aftermath of this nightmare while I float in nothingness.

Someone in this damn universe has a sick sense of humor.

So Suspicious

Doyle

The air is thick with the stench of sex and sweat as people continue humping all over the damn lawn. I normally wouldn't object to the way it clings to my nostrils and coats my throat, but it's not my family producing it—it's a fucking arse load of random Fae. Trudging through the piles of bodies, my boots stick in places where blood from some of the fighting has congealed with… other fluids. My irritation simmers just below the surface, threatening to boil over at any moment as I make a disgusted face.

I've been alive a long fucking time and this might be one of the grossest outcomes of battle I've ever seen.

"Breathe through your mouth and it will get better, mate," I mutter to myself as I sidestep a healer. The woman stumbles past me hurriedly, her mask fogging up with each labored breath. Jolene's borrowed incubi mist remains like a stubborn specter unwilling to release its grip on the castle grounds. It's a miracle most of the royals avoided a worse fate. Getting by with scrapes and bruises that seem to be immunizing them against the lust fog is a pretty light punishment considering what could have happened.

Teddy extricated my Tiogair from the chaos as quickly as possible. Her dress was in tatters, skin smeared with grime and flecks of someone else's blood as he carried her to our room. We decided to clean her up while the castle staff cleared the grounds little by little.

Prez handled her with care that belied his shaking hands, stripping away the ruined silk and washing her wounds with water that turned pink before swirling down the drain. She was unconscious, blissfully unaware of the result of her tapping into Boone's power.

While she was out, Benjy and I came outside to look around. I wanted to see the bodies of the damn winged motherfuckers Hamilton took out in the air, plus we were all curious how long this weird orgy would last. The answer is nebulous, obviously, because it's still going despite an hour going by.

"Man, these things are ugggg-ly," Benjy says as he kicks the corpse of a buzzard thing. "And they stink to high hell."

I snort. "How can you tell? All I can smell is jizz and blood, mate."

The big guy laughs, shaking his head. "You're not a shifter. I can smell… everything out here. If you think jizz and blood is the worst it could be, you're sorely mistaken."

Before I can fire back a retort, my phone buzzes in my pocket. I don't bother to answer; I know who it is. "We gotta split. Our girl must be moving."

"Shit, let's go. Watch your step over there," Benjy says, pointing to the pile of Fae writhing on the ground behind me.

"I never thought I'd see the day when I was turned off by a garden-sized fuck fest. This is surreal," I grumble as we walk toward the back of the castle.

Benjy just grins. "Our girl's just that special, man. I didn't feel a thing out there."

Neither did I—not even a spark of excitement about the chaos.

How very unusual for me.

WE'RE ALL STANDING OVER HER WHEN MY TÍOGAIR FINALLY FLUTTERS her eyes open and gives us a confused look. I tilt my head as she pushes up on her elbows, groaning low.

"My head feels like a brass band and a group of tin men are having a slap fight," she says as she blows a hair out of her eyes. "What the hell happened?"

"Tilly, do you remember anything at all?" Teddy asks gently. He's closest to her, and he takes her hand as we all wait with baited breath.

"Not a damn thing," she replies with a disgusted look. "This is getting *really* old. I've had these blackouts for most of my life, but never this often. It's getting worse."

Honestly, it's probably better that she doesn't remember, but I can't say that out loud. Every one of us knows we can't talk about this shit until she's done emerging. Based on my theories, she's not done and won't be until the others join us. I'm not sure what the fuck we'd do if she had memories of the battle.

I don't want to gaslight the shit out of the woman I love just to please those stuffed shirt Council dicks.

"Where is Alistair? And the princesses?" Jolene frowns, rubbing her temples again. "I feel like I need to check on them, but I don't know why."

Wolfie's eyes go wide and he moves closer, putting a hand on her shoulder carefully. I know what he's doing—he's reading her emotions. A small shake of his head at Boone tells me that he believes she doesn't know. "I think some of them are in the infirmary, Sugarplum. They needed medical attention."

"Medical attention?" she squawks as she spins to put her feet on the ground. "Are they okay? If one of you doesn't tell me what the hell is going on right now, I'm going to be really pissed."

Teddy sighs and rolls his eyes toward the ceiling before he turns back to her. "Tilly, something poisoned the whole damn party. When everyone started getting… sick… a group attacked and tried to harm all the leaders. There was a lot of fighting and some people got hurt while others are still not well."

Her brow furrows and she looks at us suspiciously. "Okay. So you assholes swept me away when I passed out, cleaned us all up, and waited until I woke up?"

"That's about it," Prez says. "You were out for about an hour, so I assume they've got most of the family triaged by now."

The truth isn't too far off from her summary, so I don't feel like a rotten fuckwad.

"Do you want us to take you with us to the infirmary?" I ask. The words pop out of my mouth before I realize what I'm saying and I find every eye in the room on me. "She's going to insist on it, anyway. You know I'm right."

Heaving a frustrated sigh, Boone nods and holds his hand out to her. "Come on, Tilly. As much as I hate to admit the Irishman's right, you'd be throwing a hissy fit the minute we tried to leave. Let's cut out the middleman by just taking you along."

"I'm never going to let you forget you said that," I say as I wink at him.

Jolene lets go of his big paw and comes over to kiss me on the jaw. "Good job, Lucky. You're my favorite today."

THE CASTLE INFIRMARY IS A SYMPHONY OF GROANS AND WHISPERED comforts with harried healers flitting between beds like hyperactive toddlers. Alistair catches my eye from his cot, a grim smile pulling at his stitched-up side—a fate much less painful than what my Tíogair could have handed him. As we approach, he clears his side of the room with hushed commands, leaving only our tight-knit group at his bedside.

"Start talking," I demand once no prying ears remain. "What the hell happened out there?"

Boone is standing behind Jolene and he looks at the injured Fae with a menacing expression as if to remind him of our girl's handicap. "Carefully."

Alistair winces, and I can't tell whether it's from pain or the difficulty in explaining the situation without revealing things he shouldn't. He nods toward Jolene, who folds her arms defiantly, as he asks, "If you want to know, why bring her? It only makes this harder."

"Because *she* has a mind of her own and refuses to be left out," my Tíogair says firmly. "Danger doesn't discriminate here and I'm not staying in our room alone like a sitting duck when there are kidnappers running around."

I have to hand it to the asshole—he didn't even twitch at our big ass lie.

"Convincing her would have taken longer than we were willing to wait, " Prez chimes in, a smirk playing on his lips. "And her… companions… are occupied with their own pursuits, so she's not wrong about being alone."

The animals are all outside sniffing around the battlefield for clues at Wolfie's behest. Since the flying tank helped Prez ward off the ugly air beasts, I can't really complain about having the circus around. They're watching our backs and helping us keep Jolene calm, so they're okay with me. Plus, Odie's watching them as well, so we've got even more eyes on what's happening at the sex fest.

"Since you were injured in the line of duty, we thought you might be more amenable to our questions, Alistair," I add as I wink at Jolene. "Are the painkillers not very good? I'd think your people would be lauding your name and giving you the very best shit."

"Doesn't sound like they think he's a hero," she says with a mix of sarcasm and genuine amusement. "Maybe it's his sparkling personality."

Every time she plays along with my need to poke and prod, I realize again how fucking perfect this woman is for me.

Alistair gives her a rueful expression, accepting the narrative we've painted and her snark with a surprising grace. "You're not wrong. I don't have the most… gentle reputation. But since you asked, my pain medicine is more than adequate."

"Damn. I was hoping if I poked that stab wound, you'd feel it," Jolene mutters. "Whoever got a piece of you did a great job."

The prince chokes, coughing as he tries not to laugh. "Yes, the woman who stabbed me in just the right place to incapacitate me but not damage any organs was quite skilled. And maybe a little merciful, though you wouldn't know it now."

"Watch it," I warn him as he looks at her in amusement. "We don't know who attacked the party, so we can't assume they had mercy on their mind." My irritation simmers below the surface like a beast waiting to pounce. This entire scene is a farce, and I find myself not in the mood for the amount of playacting we need to do to keep it up.

Stupid rules have always been my downfall—the need to flaunt them drives me insane.

"Calm down, Haggerty," Teddy interjects, slicing through the tension with the precision of a surgeon. "What's your take on the attack, Alistair? How could someone have gained access to the grounds to… poison… the affected people?"

Alistair's eyes flicker over to Jolene for a fleeting second before landing back on us. His fingers twitch against the linen sheets as he tries to figure out how to respond. "This mess is bigger than any of us realized, including me."

"Mutiny always is," I mutter under my breath before I can stop the word from coming out. Everyone looks at me and I shrug. "We're not pirates, but it's the same shit, right? This is some betraying mother-fucker giving your enemies what they need to accomplish a coup. The target was the entire next generation of your family, mate."

"You're right, of course," he says finally. "But I believe we're mere pawns on a chessboard so vast we can't see the edges."

"Or who's moving the pieces," Wolfie agrees as he looks around. "That's how I feel about our journey here as well. We're dancing on a knife's edge and there are people constantly trying to push us off."

"Let's not slip, then," Jolene replies, her voice a beacon of resolve. "I say we should be the ones who move first so we surprise the hell out of whoever's orchestrating this nightmare."

Says the woman who has absolutely no idea what's going on, but is willing to jump into the fray without hesitation.

Her determination is infectious, and I feel a reluctant smile tug at the corner of my lips. We've been through a lot of shit since this trip began, but somehow, she always manages to pick herself up and keep moving. It's admirable, if not a bit naïve, and I'd follow her straight into Hades if she asked right now.

"Right," I say, clenching my fists. "We can do this together. Tíogair has the right idea."

The rest of our crew give me proud grins and I shrug. *Even an ancient demi-god can learn new tricks.*

"Into the fray together," Benjy says. "Has a nice ring to it, Haggerty."

For a moment, I let myself believe that it's enough—that our united front will shield us from the storm that's brewing just beyond the horizon. But as I steal another glance at Alistair, the furrows in his brow tell me that the tempest is closer than we think.

"That's great, but I don't think you understand the breadth of this issue," the prince says with a sigh.

"Before you say anything else, I have to know," Benjy starts, breaking into my thoughts, "At the Harvest ball, were you just putting on a act? If so, you're a damn good actor. I wanted to knock your block off."

Good question because I did, too.

Alistair sighs, the sound heavy with fatigue. "Yes. To protect Allora and our people, I have to pretend to be what everyone expects me to be." He pauses, his gaze flickering to our girl for a moment. "There's a rot setting in among the families, and it's spreading fast. Allora and I made certain to convey that our arrangement was unwanted and motivated by parental pressure."

"Parental pressure," I echo, snorting. The absurdity isn't lost on me. "Here I thought those smiles were a bit too tight. You both looked like you had poles shoved under your fingernails and that seemed like a bit much to me."

Wolfie leans against a wall, arms crossed and expression thoughtful. "I don't think your mole is any of the princes from the show. To be certain, I'd need to dig deeper, and they'd sniff me out before I could uncover anything."

"Then we keep our noses clean for now. Good job, pup," Teddy interjects then peers at Alistair with concern. "Anyone else aware of something off-kilter?"

"Daybreak's women rule from the shadows," Alistair reveals, a note of respect in his voice. "It makes their men visible targets and I think it's why they've had the least trouble with this shit."

"Ah," Jolene mutters, her lips twitching, "that explains the peacock display." Laughter ripples through us, a brief respite from the gravity of our situation due to our woman's undefeatable sass.

Prez steps closer, scrutinizing Alistair's injuries like he's assessing the state of a prized fighter. "They've got you stitched up well, it seems."

"Luckily, your lady is quite the blade master," Alistair retorts, a glint of mischief in his eyes before he winces. Tíogair's brow furrows, but before she can question it, he clears his throat. "The poison must be muddling my head still."

Teddy smirks proudly, exchanging looks with Prez and Wolfie. "What's our next play, then?"

"You need to head for the Court of Reaping. They're insular and secretive. If there's a scheme brewing, they'll have the least leaks," Alistair says, conviction steeling his tone despite his weakened state.

"Spies, plants... bloody garden of treachery," I mutter under my breath. Suddenly, it occurs to me that I love that kind of atmosphere. "That should be the most fun we've had since we got here."

"Those closest to me, like Allora, are working to contain this... internal blight. But if these conspirators seize control—" Alistair doesn't finish the sentence, yet the implication hangs heavy in the air.

"Then we'd best help you root this out before it strangles us all," Teddy says. "Otherwise, the effects might spill into other places."

"Exactly," the injured prince says. "That's what I've been worried about."

Well, isn't that bloody great.

Good Riddance

Jolene

I watch Teddy and Doyle , the silent communication between them almost palpable as they play the eyebrow talking game. When I get tired of being an odd man out, I put my hands on my hips and glare at them both. "Doyle, what the hell does finding Wolfie's biological father have to do with any of this? Why do the two of you seem to think that it's putting us in the middle of all this crap?"

Alistair shifts on his hospital bed, grimacing as he re-settles. "I don't know who he is exactly," he starts with his gaze locked onto Wolfie, "but the resemblance is striking. I've seen those features before – in our history books. I can't imagine there wasn't at least one person at Daybreak who recognized them."

There's a weight to his words, like each one is a piece of a puzzle we're not seeing clearly. I look at Doyle, but he's solely focused on Alistair, his expression intense. Teddy crosses his arms over his chest, sighing as he waits for the injured prince to elaborate.

"During dinner, I pressed you because..." Alistair trails off, squinting like he's thinking hard about something before he glances at me. "I knew it would make you more likely to believe my ploy and I could give you what I knew when you came here. Doyle, I felt the same about you. Your attitude, your signature—it's familiar. It reminds me of someone who once visited our homelands quite some time ago.

You know I can't name him, though. Your kind don't take kindly to being outed."

His kind, huh?

I roll my eyes, throwing my hands up in exasperation. "Great, yet another taboo topic. As if we needed more secrets to prevent us from actually figuring anything out."

Alistair nods solemnly at us, his expression grave. "Be ready to leave for Reaping under the cover of darkness. We must move swiftly, before dawn exposes more than just the light of day. I fear your presence will cause those looking for answers to point the finger at the convenient outsiders."

"Trust is a luxury we can ill afford," Teddy says as he takes a scrap of paper Alistair pulls from under his blanket. The gesture feels like an anchor, a lifeline in a sea that's determined to swallow us whole. Between him and Allora, we have at least two people who aren't trying to kill us. "Don't make me regret extending you the courtesy."

Doyle, ever the one to find humor in the abyss, snorts as he rolls his eyes to the ceiling,"Looks like destiny decided to dump its entire burden on our doorstep. We're adding your shit to the load we're already hauling now."

Alistair lets out a brittle bark of laughter and we join in, the sound echoing around us—a chorus of discomfort. Deep down, I know the stakes have to be impossibly high for him to risk sending us away like this. As much as we try to fend off the creeping dread with humor, it still clings to us like a second skin of unease.

After all, we seem to be fighting something much bigger than my parents' death or finding an absent father—when did that happen?

"Go and keep in touch with the information I gave you. You don't have much time."

People keep saying that.

THE STERILE TANG OF ANTISEPTIC NIPS AT MY NOSTRILS AS WE LEAVE Alistair to his staff. His warning hangs like the sword of Damocles in my head, swinging back and forth until the rope snaps. I'm pretty good at juggling a lot of balls—see my bedroom for proof of that—but this feels like more than I can handle. In the past few weeks, I've gained another man in my family, two more seem to be headed for joining us, and then the whole supernatural thing hit me.

It's a lot. I don't know if I'm ready for destiny level responsibility right now.

"Time to pack up again," I murmur, more to myself than the guys as we enter our room. "I can't wait until we're home. Moving around like we're part of a traveling circus is fun when you're in your early twenties—not so much in your early thirties."

"When we're home, Sugarplum?" Wolfie says quietly. He gives me a soft smile and I feel my chest tighten.

Goddamn cheaters—always sending in the adorable one.

"Yes, when we're home, darling boy." My brows furrow and I tilt my head at Benjy. "I don't know what that means for you, big guy."

He shrugs, winking at me. "I hope it means no more apartments over the store for me. That place is cramped as hell."

Teddy whistles low, his lips curved up. "Sparks are gonna fly in Dixie."

"Oh, stuff it, Your Honor," I grumble. "We have to get moving. Everyone stop farting around and help me get us ready."

Prez straightens up, the ever-ready spark in his eyes as he nods. "I'll locate our animals," he says, heading for the door.

Doyle's gaze latches onto him, but he just nods. It's another silent conversation, and though I catch it, I decide to release it into the ether. We're about to slink our way from one dark haven to another cloaked in shadows. There's no room for petty mysteries right now; I simply don't have the spoons.

After he leaves, Teddy goes back to pacing in front of the window and the others help me fold, stuff, and pack the things. We didn't bring a lot, but it's getting a bit rumpled as we move through this damn place. I wasn't lying when I said I can't wait to get home. I'd like to have more comfortable clothes than dress up ones available and I miss my damn bed. It's a really fucking good bed and my back is feeling the lack of support.

What? I'm over thirty—even if I have superpowers, my damn back hurts like everyone else's.

"It feels like we're fugitives, doesn't it?" Benjy's voice pulls me back to the present..

"Doing the time without the fun of the crime sucks," I reply as my hands work methodically to stash our belongings. Escape is a strange bedfellow when you haven't actually done anything wrong; he's right about that. However, I also agree with Alistair that we're convenient scapegoats and anyone looking to avoid attention on themselves would sell us out for a fucking Snickers.

Or whatever the Fae equivalent is.

My eyes flick over to my ex-bully. Teddy's brow is creased deeply with worry as he continues brooding. He's determined to be our rock, but even boulders feel the weight of the world. I watch him for a moment longer, the tension in his shoulders speaking volumes about what's going on in his head.

"Teddy?" My voice is soft as I wrap my arms around his waist from behind. His body stiffens for a second, then melts against mine. "You're wound tighter than a spring. What's wrong?"

He exhales slowly before he responds. "It's nothing."

"Nothing doesn't look good on you," I counter gently, feeling the thrum of his heartbeat against my cheek. I grin a little, pinching his butt. "And not much looks bad on this ass."

His chuckle is a low rumble, but he doesn't elaborate. I splay my hands on his abs, humming a little as he leans into me. After a few moments, the others join us, forming a fortifying wall around my grumpy alpha. Wolfie steps in front, a protective barrier, while Benjy and Doyle flank us.

Their silent solidarity is a pact without words.

"Hey," I say, squeezing Teddy tighter, "whatever it is, you know we've got your back, right?"

There's a pause—an uncommon moment where Teddy's vulnerability shows—and then he nods, his hand finding mine. "Always," he says, and though the word is simple, it carries the weight of our shared history.

We stand there quietly for a few minutes until the urgency of our departure presses upon us once again. Finishing up the last bits of packing, we wait for Prez to return with the furry and feathered contingent. When he does, I wait for Teddy to grab his things and join us. With our gear slung over our shoulders, we step out into the inky embrace of the night, ready to face whatever lies beyond the threshold of the Court of Reaping.

Whatever the hell that might be.

THE WEIGHT OF OUR PACKED BELONGINGS PULLS AT OUR SHOULDERS as we stride out a back entrance to the castle. I can't help but break the silence, my voice barely above a whisper, "Are you guys that worried about this next stop?"

Wolfie's eyes are distant, reflecting a storm that's yet to break. "Alistair's info about my dad has me on edge," he admits, running a hand through his hair. "We don't even know what side he's on."

Doyle rolls his shoulders back, a defiant tilt to his chin. "I stopped caring who my father is a long time ago," he declares. There's a hardness in his eyes that tells me he's protecting himself. "Anyone who'd get involved with my mom is trouble. He'll be better at hiding than Wolfie's old man and ten times as dangerous. So no, I'm not worried about locating the git."

My eyes move to Benjy, who shifts from foot to foot with a rare unease. "I'm not scared, but I am worried," he says, his voice steady despite the confession. "It's more the people we care about... There's so much that could happen outside our control—things we might not be able to fix."

That's legitimate and pretty logical—which is why Benjy seems to be the eye of the storm lately.

Teddy just grunts, shaking his head—like a boulder refusing to roll downhill. His silence pricks at me until I can't stand it anymore.

Poking him in the side, I prod, "Come on, Teddy. We're family. You need to share, too."

He looks down at me, his blue eyes a turbulent sea. "I'm worried I won't be able to protect everyone," he finally says. There's a crack in his voice that mirrors the fault lines in our situation. "Not from our parents, the wacky shadowy villains, or the chaos snapping at our heels. I can't fail you again, Tilly, especially when there's even more at stake."

Silence blankets us, heavy as the darkness that shrouds the house we're about to leave behind.

Prez snorts, a smirk playing on his lips as he looks at our leader. "You can't control everything, Teddy. But that's okay. We look out for each other—that's how family works."

I think Teddy's going to slap the smug look right off Doctor McNuggie's face for a second, but he finally gives him a rueful grin. "Doesn't mean I don't *want* to control everything, you jackass. But I know you're right."

A line of cars greets us ahead, their engines purring softly as they wait. This is Alistair's people, ready to spirit us away. The ghostly gray vehicles seem almost spectral in the moonlight, the shine in their silhouettes promising both sanctuary and peril.

We have got to get out of this weirdly Gothic nightmare before I turn into Poe— what is with me?

Climbing into the car, I nestle against Teddy's side, his arm a comforting weight around my shoulders. I want to help him come to terms with the unpredictability we face as we head towards the last destination in our journey. Unfortunately, the steady rhythm of the road and the stress from whatever the hell happened last night hit me all at once. I know I'm getting sleepy and I can't help it.

As the miles unfurl like ribbons behind us, I'm passed from embrace to embrace—each one keeping me until I'm almost out. Eventually, exhaustion claims me, and I drift into sleep cradled between Benjy and Doyle, their steady breaths lulling me deeper into dreams.

Preparation for the final family can wait—we have time, even if people keep saying we don't.

Unsteady

Wolfgang

We've been on the road for hours, the hum of the engine a constant companion as landscapes merge and shift outside the window. Now, as we approach the border between the Midnight Court and the Court of Reaping, the world takes on an otherworldly glow. The sun cresting the hills is devoid of its usual fiery palette; instead, it's a glowing white orb hanging in a sky painted with grays and slates. Frost clings to every surface, icicles dangle like daggers from branches, and the ground is carpeted with snow that sparkles with crystalline accents.

Yeah, this feels like a place my twisted bio mother would be fond of.

"Looks like something out of a twisted fairytale," I murmur as my breath fogs up the glass.

Prez, ever the steady presence, nudges my side to get my attention. I lean into his warmth, feeling the coiled tension in my muscles ease just a fraction. He's doing his best, but there's no real comfort, not when I think about what—and who—lies ahead.

"Callie's always had a taste for the dramatic," I muse aloud. My mother is the infamous Cailleach and she could care less that she broke sacred laws when she and my bio dad conceived me. Hell, I wouldn't even put it past her to have done so on purpose to corner a powerful being. That would explain why they had to dump me in an enclave once I was born. Regardless of their arrangement, I'm here now, chasing down the specter of a man who could be steeped in rebellion and treachery.

My genetics aren't looking very promising at this point.

"Maybe he's just a hermit," Doyle offers out of nowhere, his tone laced with a wryness that doesn't quite mask his concern. "Sometimes rich, powerful people like to disappear into the ether to keep all the sycophants and sponges away."

"Or maybe he's playing a long game," I counter, pressing my palm against the cold window as the landscape rolls by. This journey isn't only about unearthing family secrets—it's about untangling a web that could ensnare us all.

Unfortunately, I've pulled Sugarplum right into the heart of all this drama.

"Sleeping dogs, Wolfie," Doyle says, glancing at me in commiseration. "Sometimes they're better left undisturbed."

"Right, because avoiding fleas is so important when you're dealing with a potential coup," I scoff. I know there's a kernel of truth in his words—some stones are best left unturned. But I've never been one to walk away from a challenge, especially not with stakes this high. Being the youngest person in high school, then veterinary school, and then in the Hollow's induction pool taught me that you can't simply let some things go.

I'm not a fan of conflict, but I know when it's necessary.

"Whatever's waiting for us," I say, pushing off Prez to sit up straighter, "we'll face it together. No one's going into this blind."

"Damn straight," Doyle replies, and I can hear the unspoken pledge in his voice.

The car begins its ascent up the final hill and the view expands before us. My heart beats a staccato rhythm against my ribs as we get closer. This is a precipice, and I'm poised on the edge. Jolene's strength, Doyle's loyalty, Benjy's calm, Prez's quiet care, even Teddy's brash courage—they're the anchors in this sea of uncertainty. With them along, I know I can face whatever the hell it is I'm going to find when we locate my dad.

"Here goes nothing," I whisper, more to myself than to anyone else, as the Court of Reaping comes into full view.

As the first light of their false dawn spills over the edge of the world, it paints everything before us in a ghostly luminescence. It's like we've stepped into a fairy tale penned by a madman—beautiful and eerie all at once. I press my forehead against the cold window, watching the frozen landscape unfurl before us.

"Tilly," Teddy's voice cuts through the silence as he nudges Jolene awake. She blinks slowly, dragging her slender fingers through her tousled hair, pushing up her glasses with a practiced motion.

"Wha—?" Her voice is groggy, but she's alert in seconds, attuned to the tension that coils around us like a serpent. Her attention shifts toward me, and I can't help but lean into her warmth when she wraps an arm around my shoulders, her chin resting atop my head—a silent anchor in a sea of disquiet. "It's okay, little Wolfie. We've all got you."

I nod, smiling against her warmth. She didn't have to think of me before she even had time to fully awaken, but that's the kind of woman our girl is. "I know, Sugarplum."

"Worried about your dad?" she murmurs, reading me like one of the smutty books she and Teddy like to share.

"Something like that," I admit, my voice muffled against her jacket. "Thoughts of a father I never knew, hidden agendas... It's a lot."

"Join the club," Doyle chimes in, his eyes meeting mine as he stretches his legs out. "My dad's probably a grade-A asshole, and my mom isn't winning any Mother of the Year awards."

"Family's complicated," Teddy adds with a half-smirk, though his gaze stays fixed on the castle coming into view. "I'm an asshole with or without parental guidance. But change? That's the real bitch."

"Guys, really, you don't have to—" I start, but Jolene cuts me off with a soft chuckle.

"Let them bleed out some of that testosterone, Wolfie. Sometimes showing a bit of vulnerability stops them from being complete alpha holes. Helps make them more useful with our hosts, especially when they're being dicks to us."

"Point taken," I concede, a reluctant smile tugging at my lips as I sit up straighter.

The car slows, and we're suddenly face-to-face with the full spectacle of the Court of Reaping—an immense, glistening castle of obsidian and ice, carved into the very heart of the craggy cliff. The structure shimmers under the unearthly light, the trees surrounding it adorned with ice crystals that gleam like jewels.

Holy fuck, it's like Frozen and Nightmare Before Christmas had a baby.

"Damn," Jolene breathes out, echoing my thoughts. "These guys are *not* screwing around."

At the foot of the castle, a giant man waits for us, his sapphire attire offset by a raven beard laced with frost. His crown, a twisted amalgamation of dark stone and ice, sits heavily upon his brow. Beside him, the woman who must be his spouse radiates warmth despite the chill —a stark contrast with her fiery hair and crown bedecked with vines and gemstones. They are definitely the royals of this court, their lineage unmistakable in the faces of the four princesses and two princes beside them, gazing at us as we arrive with their partners a step behind them.

"Looks like they rolled out the red carpet for us," Doyle comments dryly, earning a grimace from Teddy.

"Should've known Alistair would send us into a den of wolves without so much as a how-do-you-do," he mutters as he pinches the bridge of his nose. "You all need to be on guard. Do you have your blade, Tilly?"

"Relax, guys," I say softly. I can't shake the feeling that every glittering eye on us is out to do us harm. "We don't know that Alistair told them. In fact, I'd bet he didn't; I think it's the work of the mole in Midnight. Regardless, they're just people standing there waiting right now."

"Huge people with unknown… influence," Doyle retorts with a sharp look at me. " who also come with a pet polar bear."

I blink, then I see the enormous white bear lumbering out of the snow to sit by the King's side with a suspicious look at the cars. "Could be worse," I offer weakly.

"Could be better, though," Prez says ruefully. "That's more threatening than I'd like."

"It could be exciting, though," Sugarplum says, her eyes alight with a spark of mischief that belies the gravity of our situation. "I've always wanted to pet a polar bear. Think they'll let me?"

Everyone groans and I smile a bit. 'Exciting' isn't the word I'd use—not when each step toward this castle feels like a descent into the unknown. But we've come too far to retreat, so we steel ourselves as Teddy shakes his head.

"Tilly, I am fully convinced you'll die trying to pet something you shouldn't. And since I don't want that to be anytime soon, she stays behind us until the animals are unloaded from the other car." He winks at her and she gives him a dirty look as we untangle our limbs. "Pup, I expect you to keep her from doing anything stupid while we deal with this formal nonsense, okay?"

I doubt anyone could stop Jolene Whitley when she has her mind set to do something, but I'll give it a whirl.

THE AIR FILLS WITH AN ICY TENSION THAT SEEMS TO CRYSTALIZE between us and the awaiting assembly. As we exit the car, I watch Jolene's shoulders tighten. Her breath mists in the cold as she peers out at the gathered crowd. "Someone definitely sang like a canary," she whispers.

"Or maybe a stool pigeon," I add, my eyes tracing the stoic faces of the younger royals. Their fear is a tangible shiver in the air—one they poorly mask with brittle smiles. Benjy catches it too, his head canted as he observes them from the corner of his eye.

"Scared heirs and their dates are becoming a familiar sight," he murmurs under his breath.

Teddy's gaze follows mine, landing on King Darragh and Queen Eabha, their expressions oddly mismatched to the gravity of the situation. "It feels like all the elder generations are puppets on strings. They haven't had a clue things are amiss—not in any of the courts so far. Some sort of… drug," he says as he looks at Prez and I. His tone suggests he's pondering that magic might be at play, but he can't say it in front of Jolene.

It's certainly possible, but that means this conspiracy goes much deeper than a few snitches in the courts.

"Let's not jump to conclusions," I caution, even though I'm already considering potential spells in my head. I'm not a caster —more of a 'natural magic' user. We'll need to talk to a more proficient spell user to get a better idea. Maybe we can text Alistair and Allora to look into it.

The frigid air bites at my skin as we wait for the animals to join us. What sends a chill down my spine isn't the temperature—it's the implicit understanding that every eye upon us has been watching since before we crested that final hill. Alistair's people unlatch the other car and release our animals, drawing the attention of everyone as they alight.

Jekyll, Hyde, Kali, and Hecate saunter out with a regal nonchalance, only to be met by the intense scrutiny of a massive polar bear. The stand-off is brief—Euryale swoops down from above to land beside Prez. Her screech echoes off the ice, commanding respect from the bear, which begrudgingly backs away.

I'll be damned.

Our girl chuckles at the exchange, a sound that softens the severity of the scene. King Darragh grins at her, a spark of mirth dancing in his eyes. "If you're as brave as your companions, the hunt will be quite the spectacle," he booms, his voice carrying across the frost-laden grounds.

"Nothing says 'welcome to our home' like chasing after wild beasts. Fucking Fae," Doyle mutters, the sarcasm dripping thicker than the icicles from the trees.

"Careful," I hiss at him. I don't want him offending the royals or breaking our damn oath just to get in a one-liner.

The King's laughter rumbles through the air, rich and deep, a counterpoint to the chilling silence that had preceded it. *He definitely heard and we're fucked.*

Queen Eabha steps forward while he chortles, her demeanor the blend of light and dark that seems to permeate this court. "No balls and gowns in the Reaping," she explains, her smile warm despite the cold. "We favor the thrill of the chase and the skill of the hunt."

"Thrilling," Teddy deadpans, exchanging worried glances with the rest of us.

It should concern me. A hunt here presents so many issues: what beasts they'll chase, what we'll have to ride, what weapons we'd use, and a multitude of things Jolene can't know about. I know all of it, but I can't help the grin that tugs at the corners of my mouth.

This is their game, but Sugarplum? She's made for this.

I know how she handles a horse, her ease with weaponry, and the way she moved with predatory grace in the battle at Midnight. She could outshine them all if given the chance—even without her supe sides fully emerged.

"Consider it a challenge," I say, feeling the adrenaline stir within me. It's a test, perhaps, but one we might turn to our advantage.

Jolene, undeterred by the audacity of asking your guests to compete, strides up to Darragh. She extends her hand in a gesture of good will rather than curtseying. His lips curve up at that, delight written all over his icy features.

"I look forward to meeting your hunt master once we're settled," she says, her confidence unshaken. "I hope your quarry is ready for me. I won several fox hunts during a stay in England."

That declaration makes me tilt my head—I'm fairly certain Sugarplum wouldn't kill an animal unless she had no option. *What's she playing at?*

As her fingers wrap around the King's, I feel something shift—a strong sense of readiness. This hunt may be unexpected, but so are we. And if they think we're the prey in this twisted game, they've got another thing coming.

The crowd all watch as the staff takes our bags and leads us toward the entrance to the castle. I look at Jolene, checking to make sure no one else is near us and whisper, "How did you win fox hunts without killing anything, Sugarplum?"

She gives me a wicked grin. "It's hard for anyone else to beat you if you gather up all the prey and take it back to the finish line with you. Sometimes, the best solution is around, not through."

Damn, she's clever.

Landslide

Jolene

I knew this place was swanky when we walked inside and it had a double staircase with an immense, intricately carved chandelier in the foyer. The place looked like it was designed for a fairy-tale LARP by an egregiously wealthy yet eccentric billionaire. I've been in three castles here and many at home and nothing I've ever seen prepared me for the Court of Reaping.

No wonder they let people call them ruthless killers—they want thieves to think twice before setting foot anywhere near this monument to opulence.

The door to our suite swings open, and I'm blasted with a gust of cold air that's somehow warmer than the icy chill in the hallway. My breath catches—not from the temperature shift, but from the sheer spectacle of our new quarters. Comfortable yet stunningly beautiful décor sprawls before us like a frozen kingdom, each corner meticulously carved from ice, yet emanating warmth. A monstrous four-poster bed commands attention, its icy pillars jutting up to support a canopy that glitters with encrusted jewels. Onyx, aquamarine, and diamonds wink at me as if they're in on my secret.

"Damn," Teddy murmurs beside me, his eyes wide as he scans the room. "I've heard of ridiculously wealthy homes built by movie stars and sultans, but this is…something else entirely."

"It's well past a bit much and on its way to offensive," I mumble, forcing myself to blink away the magical allure. My tame reaction is part of the act I still have to go through—despite the fact that pretending not to see the enchantments is getting old. Having to play blind when every detail screams to be acknowledged is harder than it sounds, especially with a group of men so attuned to my emotions.

For fuck's sake, there's a hot spring simmering inside of an icy whirlpool in the floor!

"The setup looks comfy, though," Wolfie chimes in, his attempt at casual undercut by the furrow of his brows as he strides toward the closet.

The sitting area boasts snowy white, fur-covered furniture so large and plush you could get lost within its depths. I take a whiff, my nose twitching until relief floods me when the synthetic scent confirms no animals were harmed for our comfort. It's a strange comfort, knowing we're lounging on faux luxury curated by someone who seems to know us intimately.

"Check this out." Wolfie emerges from the closet, his frown deepening into a scowl. "Clothes for all of us. Perfect sizes. Everything from casual to formal to night time included."

"Oh, wonderful," I say dryly, watching as the others poke through the selection. "Heaven forbid we look anything less than royal when we're sleeping."

Teddy is prowling now, his irritation tangible. "They've been tracking us closely—too closely for my comfort."

"Maybe asking ahead was someone's idea of hospitality?" I counter, hoping to calm him despite my gut twisting with intuition. This isn't just someone being thorough and I know it. Detail this intimate is invasive—a silent declaration that our supposed secrecy was nothing but a pipe dream.

"Look at this," Wolfie continues, gesturing to the sideboard adorned with a feast worthy of kings. Meats, cheeses, fruits—an entire perishable spread that would make Bacchus envious. Next to the Fae-style charcuterie display, there's crystal glassware and various types of drinks and on the floor, beds for our animal companions, complete with trays of food and water.

Okay, now *I can't pretend it's someone being a good concierge.*

"This is beyond stalking," I breathe, the words slipping out before I can stop them. "It's the work of the mole, for sure."

"Yep," Teddy agrees, his jaw clenched. "Time to check in with Alistair. Maybe we'll find out the douche bag gave this info to one of his 'spies' here and everything will be a little less creepy."

"If so, he's definitely as clueless as he claims. Anyone who gives up that much info to possible double agents is lucky they haven't been shanked yet. That's still better than being a traitor himself, though," I add as I frown.

The seed of doubt takes root as we continue looking at the items in this room specific to our family. I don't *think* he was lying; his worry for Allora was real. It's hard to trust anyone in this damn world, though, because they simply don't play by the same rules as the rich people in ours.

Big fucking surprise—supernatural elites are even more annoying than human ones.

As Teddy pulls me over to the comfy couches, I watch the shadows dance over the icy crystals. This place is so beautiful, but lots of pretty things are deadly once you scratch the surface. At least the ugly threats are honest. I turn to look at my grumpy ex-bully, tilting my head at him. "Are you just going to ask him point blank?"

Teddy's fingers fly over his phone, the screen a rectangle of blue light in the cavernous room. "Of course not, but Alistair better have some answers," he growls low, as much to himself as to me.

"Or you're going to kick his ass, I presume?" I lean in, trying to peek at the conversation unfolding on-screen. "That will be a feat all the way from here, Teddy Bear."

Prez laughs as he finishes stowing the rest of our things with Wolfie. The two of them join us on the big couch, dropping down on my other side. The doc's strong hands run over my shoulder and I groan low.

"Keep it PG, Tíogair, or we're going to make a mess before we get the answers we need," Doyle snarks as he flops on the big ottoman in front of us.

"Leprechaun's right, Tilly. Oh, and the prince claims he's clueless," Teddy snorts after a moment. There's an uneasy line between his brows as he responds to the next text. He's not letting this go at a simple 'wasn't me.'

"What else is he saying?" I ask as I peek over his arm. His damn privacy screen is blocking me and I punch his arm in annoyance.

"He's promised to check with his sisters to make sure they didn't contact anyone trying to be nice," Teddy continues, reading aloud the prince's response that flickers across the chat. "If they're not behind this, he'll send his own people to sniff out the traitor."

"As if that's any consolation," I grumble. "We're walking around blindfolded here."

Guilt gnaws at me—I'm withholding truths as heavy as the stones encrusting our ridiculous bed. So far, trusting the dream woman's advice about keeping them in the dark for their own good has worked out. Despite being attacked, the guys haven't let me out of their sight for a minute, and I think it's keeping us *all* safe.

At least, I hope so. I've never had dream woman hand down edicts before, so fuck if I know.

Before we can dissect Alistair's potential innocence further, a knock on our door shatters the stillness. The guys all jump to their feet as the animals bound towards the door. Growls fill the room and I rub my hand over my face, rising from the couch to greet whatever fresh hell is coming.

The door swings open to reveal a motley crew straight out of frost-bitten myth. A giant man looms, tusks protruding from beneath his bottom lip and eyes glinting with a chill that rivals the décor. Beside him, a fairy no larger than a child sparkles darkly, her wings a blur of shadow and shimmer. An earthy woman with a scent that speaks of wild forests and moonlit transformations nods curtly, while a stout Elven man, thickly dressed, clutches a ledger like a shield.

Dude, these people aren't even trying *in the Court of Reaping. What the hell would I be seeing if the Daybreak woman hadn't messed with my specs?*

"Evening," the giant rumbles, his voice like gravel tumbling down a mountain. "My name is Njord and we're here to prepare you for the hunt."

Teddy walks over, his scowl deepening as he looks at them. "We were told we'd have time to settle before you were sent."

"Preparation starts now, whether ye be ready or not," the elf says, his tone apologetic but firm. "Our skill is great, but not so much that we can sit around fiddling the day away."

"Alf is correct; our time to get you ready grows short," the shifter woman says, "and we aim to outfit you properly."

"Royal guests deserve nothing less. But do not fret! Both Bodil and I are as skilled as our fierce counterparts. You can ask anyone," the fairy chimes in, a twinkle of mischief in her eye.

"Revna speaks true, but we must take you in groups of two. We can focus more efficiently that way. Choose those who will follow us now, for we must make haste in order to finish for the late night hunt this evening." Bodil's eyes light on me and I try not to sniff the air to see if I can figure out what she is.

Doyle steps forward first, but Prez right beside him. They share that look—the one that means they're taking point to assess risks before they allow anyone near me. "We'll go ahead. We can speak with them about our specific…needs."

That translates to make sure they know our girl is currently under an information ban that's tying our hands behind our backs.

"I am not—" I protest, but Benjy's hand lands gently on my shoulder.

"Haggerty only means we should accompany you and the pup," he says, silencing me with a reassuring smile, "And not because you need protecting. Unfamiliar animals don't react well to me and Big Daddy over there."

Okay, that actually makes sense given what I shouldn't know about them.

"Same for Doyle," Prez interjects with a snort, folding his arms. "He can charm the pants off an old dowager, but animals look at him askance until they know him. It's probably his chaotic vibes."

"Please," Doyle huffs, a smirk lighting his features. "I've tamed more beasts than you in my lifetime, Hamilton." The doc rolls his eyes and they turn to follow the hunt team. His voice drops into a mutter, and I swear I catch the words 'Poseidon' and 'bastard horses' before the door closes behind them, leaving the rest of us to stew in a mix of concern and curiosity.

ONCE THE GUYS HEAD OUT, WE'RE LEFT TO LINGER IN THE OPULENT sitting room. Unease fills the air and I wrinkle my nose at the oppressive atmosphere. We can't sit around and worry, so I plop down on the couch again, gesturing for the others to do the same.

"Okay," I start, shifting the focus away from the gnawing concern for the others. "We've got one shot at getting the lowdown on Wolfie's dad during the hunt. Who has the best idea on how to approach these fuckers?"

Teddy rubs his chin thoughtfully, stepping into his element. "Diplomacy first. We keep it casual—feel them out during the ride. People love to talk about themselves, especially nobles. Maybe one of them will let something slip about the powerful people they know."

"True. You'd be amazed at the shit people say when they're drinking at the Speakeasy. The need to look important outweighs common sense all the time," says Benjy, nodding. "That's why I think we'll have more chances at dinner. Between toasts, small talk, and mingling—they're all opportunities to pick up clues."

"Exactly." Teddy paces, hands clasped behind his back. "We can't afford to spook anyone, so subtlety is key. I know most of us can do this, but someone will have to keep tabs on Haggerty. His natural inclination will be to cause trouble and that might seal lips."

"He's about as subtle as a flaming unicorn," I murmur under my breath, eyeing the abundant sideboard in distrust. "But he does have his strengths. He's excellent at loosening tongues when he's in his element."

"What an odd choice of words," Teddy murmurs, reaching for a piece of cheese and popping it into his mouth. His eyes widen, and he pauses mid-chew, turning to look at me.

Shit. Bad move, Whitley. Back it up before he figures it out.

"Is something wrong?" I ask, trying to sound nonchalant as I drift closer.

"Uh, cheese shouldn't taste this...rich." He watches me as I grab another piece and pop it in my mouth before he sighs in relief. "But it seems as though you like it. Should we venture out to that market we heard about so we can take some home, Tilly?"

I squash the impulse to blurt out why I have no desire to do that by biting my tongue. Crafty asshole thinks he'll trick me, but he's dead wrong. I pluck another piece off the tray and chew it enthusiastically. "Mmm. It's tasty as hell, so maybe we should. I'd like to see that place from the show."

Turning my back to the guys, I realize my face must betray my true feelings. Jekyll and Hyde perk up from their corner, tails twitching as they look at me. Their duet of delighted noises fills the space and I have to stifle a chuckle.

Obviously, they get my conundrum and sympathize—as much as cats can.

"Rich people are so fucking weird," I grumble as I contemplate whether to share this ludicrous luxury with my feline friends. The guys are still talking, but I'm stuck on this damn cheese like a skipping CD. My mind churns with the practicalities—or rather, the impracticalities—as I shake my head.

How rare are unicorns? How do you milk one? And how much does this shit even cost?

"Should I ask about the market tonight, then?" Teddy asks, oblivious to my inner turmoil over mythical lactation. "I think it would be a good place to look for clues, too."

"Maybe," I deflect, hoping I didn't miss too much when my brain took a curdled vacation. "We need to focus on finding out what we can about Wolfie's dad and anything we can about the people trying to kill the younger family members."

"Agreed," Benjy says, plucking his own piece of cheese but hesitating before biting into it. Teddy chuckles at him and the big guy frowns as he catches the words on the card. "We have to focus on our primary mission."

"Right," Teddy nods, his procedural mindset snapping back into place. "No distractions tonight. All our efforts have to be on getting what we need before we leave this place so we don't have to come back for a *long* time."

As if our collective will can conjure answers from this icy castle, we huddle together again—strategists plotting in the shadow of unicorn dairy treats and shadowy secrets.

If this damn cheese is the weirdest thing that happens today, I'll be a happy woman.

Protectors

Benjy

Tension prickles my skin as we walk back to the prep area with Bodil and Revna. Prez and Doyle are leaving their fittings, their expressions grim like bad omens. Their eyes lock on us—no, not us, Princess—and what I see isn't their usual bravado or laid back ease, but a flicker of something darker.

It's a warning for me about what's to come and I need to take it seriously.

"Something's got them spooked," I mutter to myself. "This isn't good."

Jolene is looking around the hallway curiously, watching as they approach her. She must have heard me because she scoffs as we get closer to them. "Spooked? Those two? Never. They look determined, sure, but we have to be, right?"

"I don't think it's that simple." I rub at the nape of my neck, feeling the prickly heat of unease. Doyle has seen a lot in the insane amount of time he's been on this planet; making him grimace like that isn't easy. The fact that neither stopped to fill us in means they couldn't figure out a good way to communicate without breaking the rules.

That's all bad fucking juju, as my mom would say.

Doyle throws me a glance over his shoulder, his brow furrowed in a way that would have sent lesser creatures scurrying. I catch it, but luckily Princess is oblivious. She's back to chatting away with Bodil and Revna about the Huntmasters' need to separate us into small groups. They're struggling to follow the rules—I can tell— so I distract our girl with a question.

"Are you looking forward to showing off, Princess?"

"Of course I am. But did you see their faces when I mentioned mounts?" she asks, amusement lacing her tone. "They acted as if they're asking us to ride unicorns or something."

"Unicorns might be less of a worry," I mutter to myself again.

My mind races with potential scenarios, each more unsettling than the last. These Fae could have any number of terrestrial or airborne mounts to hunt with—the myths and legends of what Fae do are so damn broad. Not one of us saw anything about this fucking hunt shit in the research we did at Harvest, so it must be a *very* well-kept secret. We couldn't prepare ourselves; hell, obviously even Alistair didn't know. Teddy would wring his neck for not warning us and he knows it.

Doyle probably wouldn't leave anything for my friend to strangle, but his temper is straight from a power that none of us really understand.

"Benjy, you're frowning like you're trying to solve a riddle," Princess teases, bumping her shoulder against mine. "What's got you brooding like Big Daddy Asshole?"

"Nothing," I reply as I force a smile. "I'm obsessing about the hunt and what it will require of us more than anything."

"Don't think too hard, big guy. We've got skilled riders and people trained in weapons since they could walk. Bless their hearts, we're from the South; they won't know what hit them." Her words are confident, but the sentiment doesn't quite reach her eyes—she knows something's up.

I may have overestimated my ability to wrangle our girl as well as Big Daddy can.

The image of Prez's worried gaze makes me feel like something big is coming, that involves the beasts we'll be riding. Teddy's words echo in my head—Jolene's skill set is as lethal as any weapon she wields. But how do you prepare someone for a monster when they're expecting a horse?

"Princess, you know whatever happens in this stupid game, you should stick close to one of us, right?" The plea slips out, wrapped in a half-joking tone, but it's real. I just found her and I can't bear to think about her getting hurt or worse. It's eating my gut like a damn virus as we take our final steps to the prep room.

"I will because I trust you guys to help, *not* because I need anyone protecting me," she replies in a strident tone. "We're a team, Benjy, and I'm doing my best to remember that after a long time where I took care of myself because I didn't have anyone else. It's not easy to unlearn that kind of hyperindepedence."

Just like that, her words lift my spirits and place the weight of responsibility on my shoulders at the same time. I have to keep her safe, even from things she can't see.

Hell, especially from the shit she doesn't know about yet.

"Benjy?" Her hand finds mine, her grip warm and reassuring as we approach the door. "We'll handle it together—whatever 'it' is."

"Of course, we will," I say, though the drumbeat of my heart tells a different story. We step inside, and it's all I can do not to let the fear show on my face.

Whatever 'it' is, I get the feeling it's going to be one hell of a ride.

The scent of leather and oiled steel mingles with the tang of magic as Revna, the fairy seamstress, circles us with her measuring tape. She's a whirlwind of efficiency, her fingers dancing along the fabric like nimble spiders spinning silk.

"Deep purple for you, my dear," she declares, draping material over Jolene's shoulders to inspect it. "It'll complement your complexion splendidly."

Princess's face lights up, a stark contrast to her usual disdain for finery. We should have known she'd react this way to being given pants rather than a ballgown.

"Finally something practical," she mumbles as she admires the rich hue. "I was born to wear shit like this, not those ridiculous poofy things."

"I don't know, Princess. I think you look sexy as fuck in both." I wink at her and she wrinkles her nose. Guaranteed she would have flipped Teddy off, but somehow, she's okay with my statement.

Revna smiles, her eyes twinkling with mischief. "And for Benjy, black. He'll be a striking shadow to Jolene's vibrant flame."

If only she knew…

"Sounds perfect," I reply distractedly. We're being dressed for a hunt, but there's an edge to this prep that feels more warlike than sporty. That makes my animal twitch and I feel like I need to pace to work out the excess adrenaline.

Njord stomps in as I consider moving, his imposing half-orc frame casting shadows across the stone floor. His grunt is noncommittal as he sizes me up with expert eyes.

"Stand still," he rumbles, jotting down notes with a hand that looks capable of crushing stone.

"You don't seem like the kind of dude I want to irritate," I say, trying to lighten the mood. "Just tell me what you need and it's done."

"I'm not," he scoffs without looking up. It's hard to read him, but I sense tension in his posture. There's an unspoken warning in every mark he makes on his parchment and I have no idea what it's about.

Did Doyle piss this enormous motherfucker off?

"Alf will take care of your armaments," Njord grunts, finally stepping back with a satisfied look.

I didn't realize he was assessing both of us at the same time, but I nod. "Sounds good."

"This is my kind of fitting, big guy. I can't wait to see what they've got for us to choose from." Her excitement spikes again as we enter the armory. The walls are lined with an arsenal fit for gods, and she's like a kid in a candy store. Her gaze lands on a compound bow, sleek and deadly, its limbs whispering promises of power and precision.

"That's the one. I can *feel* it on my bones," she breathes out, her eyes never leaving the weapon.

"Are you sure? You have to use it while you're riding Princess, and—" My voice barely hides my concern. "That's a lot of weapon to use while you're moving unless you're from the Rohan."

"I've got this. Trust me." She throws me a look that's all fire and defiance and I crumble like a cookie.

Boone's going to fucking murder me when he finds out.

"If you're sure, then I won't try to talk you out of it," I relent. Holding my hands up in surrender, I smile before I head to the wall to look for myself. I select an ornate spear, noting that something makes it feel *right* to me as well, just like she said. Its heft is good in my hands—a balance of reach and lethality that suits my style.

"Now you come with me to the stables," Bodil urges, her voice a lilting song that can't quite mask the undercurrent of anxiety. I figured out she's a wolf shifter the second her earthy scent mixed with canine and pine hit my nostrils and I wonder how she's able to manage their animals with a predator inside of her.

Jolene catches up to her, chatting animatedly about the stables back home and what she does for Percy. It doesn't help my anxiety about this situation a bit, despite hearing how good she is with the Prince's horses. This isn't going to be high-strung thoroughbreds or show horses; that's obvious by the distance between the prep room and the damn building the animals are housed in.

I squint at the dark, brooding building Bodil identifies as the stables. It's a stark contrast to the polished grandeur of the prep area, both outside and in. As we enter, I see rows of stalls housing creatures that seem conjured from nightmares. Their fiery breaths puff out in angry clouds, and their red eyes gleam like coals.

"Jesus Christ on a boogie board," I mutter under my breath, hoping the Princess sees nothing more than impressively large horses.

"Look at them, Benjy. Aren't they *magnificent?*" Her squeal of delight cuts through the tension as she claps her hands. Our girl is enchanted by the entire group, but she's moving toward the most formidable of the lot—a jet-black steed with piercing blue eyes.

"Careful, Jolene," Bodil warns. "Antiope is not a normal beast; she's wilder than the wind."

"Wild suits me just fine," Jolene retorts with a grin. She's fearless as she steps into the stall without an ounce of protection. To my horror, she reaches out a hand, stroking Antiope's mane as if the beast is a gentle mare.

They're all going to kill me when this thing kicks her ass across the barn; I can see it now.

"Give her this," Bodil says, passing a carrot to our girl with a hesitant hand. "None of us have been able to get her to take anything from us, so that would be an accomplishment."

"See? She's a sweetheart," Jolene coos, feeding Antiope with a confidence that borders on insanity.

'Sweetheart' isn't the word I'd use for a creature bristling with power and malice that's huffing sulfur at us. But somehow, Jolene's touch calms the steed from Hades enough for her to swing up onto it's bare back.

"Looks like I've found my mount," she grins triumphantly. The horse glares at Bodil and I, her piercing blue eyes and snowy white mane eerie in the low light of the barn.

"Great," I say as I imagine the look on Big Daddy's face when he sees this damn thing.. "Just fucking great."

What the hell have we gotten ourselves into?

I GRAB TEDDY'S ARM AS SOON AS WE GET BACK TO OUR ROOM AND steer him away from the chattering trio. Jolene's animated voice fills the space, recounting her conquest of Antiope with a gleam in her eye that only adventure can ignite. She doesn't notice us peeling off; her focus is all on the hunt.

"Bro," I whisper urgently, "we need to talk."

His eyes lock onto mine, dark pits of concern that tell me he's already halfway to guessing what I'm about to spill. "What's up, B?"

"Princess chose the one damn horse in the entire stable no one has been able to hand feed, much less ride." I shake my head, still reeling from the audacity of it. "She's riding the beast no one in this court dares to approach, much less hop on. I couldn't stop her, man."

He grimaces, pinching the bridge of his nose as he lets out a long breath. "Prez suspected she'd do something like this. As soon as Wolfie told us he believed this 'wild hunt' isn't just a game or tradition, I knew the mounts had to be fearsome. This is the real thing—the hunt of legend—which makes it a survival test."

"Survival?" My voice pitches higher than intended, and I glance at Jolene, who's now wielding an imaginary bow, her movements fluid and deadly as she shows them what she plans to do. The hits just keep coming and this fucking oath is keeping us from warning her.

My gorilla wants to kill someone and he's usually not very 'King Kong.'

"All of this is what Wolfie feared," he continues. "And there's more."

"More?" I echo hollowly.

"Devil dogs." His voice is barely audible. "If the legends hold true, I'll have no choice but to shift and lead them. It's part of the hunt—a part I hoped was myth—but it means I won't be able to resist."

"Jesus, Teddy..." A cold shiver races down my spine. "Princess can't be part of this. Not when..."

He cuts me off, raking a hand through his hair. "We need to speak with the Huntmasters. We've got to find out what we're hunting and try to control the narrative. If it's humans, this could go sideways fast."

"Control the narrative? Have you lost your mind?" I scoff. "With hellhounds and whatever else they throw into the mix running around?"

"If I can keep the devil dogs in check, maybe it won't spiral out of control." Determination hardens his features. "I've sure as hell never met any of my kind before, but I've always been an alpha. Maybe I can wrangle them."

Dude's ego is writing a check his ass can't cash, no matter how rich he is.

And what, exactly, are you going to do to get them to follow you? Do you plan to gnaw through the prey in front of the Princess? Have you ever even *done* that Edgar Olivier Boone"

"I'll do whatever it takes to protect her," he says, the steel in his tone leaving no room for argument. "Doesn't matter if I'm fond of the idea or not."

"Mr. Boone," Revna's sharp cough slices through our hushed exchange. "We must leave. It's time for your fitting with Mr. Fletcher."

"Go," I urge, swallowing the knot in my throat. "We'll figure this out."

"Benjy..." He hesitates, his gaze flickering toward Jolene. "Keep her safe."

As Teddy strides away with Revna's fluttering presence guiding him, Wolfie follows. They both look like men marching toward their doom. I turn back to Jolene, whose laughter dances around the room as she continues to talk with Prez and Doyle.

"Benjy saw the way Antiope looked at me. It was like she knew I was the one to tame her. It's my specialty, you know," she boasts, oblivious to the darkness creeping at the edges of our reality.

"I saw you step into that stall without a lick of fear and the devil horse responded to you," I manage, my voice strained as I plaster on a smile that doesn't reach my eyes. "Together, you and that eerie looking mare are going to rock this hunt."

"Damn right," she replies, her confidence unshakable.

I watch her, the sinking feeling in my gut growing heavier.

Doyle's eyes meet mine from across the room, a silent understanding passing between us. The twinkle in his gaze tells me he's ready to revel in the chase. If anyone will be able to help us corral our enthusiastic mate, I think it's him. He's been alive far longer than us and he loves to pretend he's from this region.

Maybe he knows more than he's letting on; hell, I hope so.

Because Teddy and I?

We're bracing for a battle of a different kind—one that could very well change our entire lives in one fell swoop.

Yellow Flicker B...

Jolene

Our room now smells of leather and steel—a sharp tang that nips at the inside of my nose. I'm hunched over our latest delivery, a collection of kits and gear laid out before us like a merchant's treasure. The armor from Njord gleams with an anticipatory luster, and Alf's weapons whisper promises of battles to come.

I feel like I'm gearing up for some real Games of Thrones shit and boy, did I never anticipate saying that sentence unironically.

"It's hard to believe this doesn't even phase us now," I murmur, my voice barely above the rustle of fabric as I run my hand over the sleek surface of my purple kit. The shining armor that will go over it is lightweight but promises durability, and I'm certain it will fit like a second skin for the hunt ahead.

"Best get used to it, Sugarplum." Wolfie chuckles from the other side of the room, his eyes scanning his own pile of equipment. "Every time I think I've seen it all, the world throws another curveball."

Benjy and Prez are just waking up, rubbing sleep from their eyes as they shuffle over to join us for dinner. We're nibbling on dried meats and hard bread—nothing too heavy; we can't afford to be sluggish tonight. After we all finished our time with the hunt masters we took naps in shifts to make up for the sleep lost last night. No one wanted to get tired by the time this thing started.

"I still can't get over their amazing horses," I say to Wolfie, and Teddy's eye twitches. Across from me, Doyle grunts, his attention fixated on sharpening a large sword. Its blade curves menacingly into a sickle-like protrusion. My frown deepens; it's foreign, not like anything I saw in Alf's armory.

Where the fiddling fuck did he get that *from?*

"How come he gets some weird mega sword?" I nod towards Doyle's weapon, my voice a conspiratorial whisper intended for Wolfie's ears alone.

He shakes his head in warning. "Don't ask him," he replies quietly. "Doyle and his mysteries are not safe topics on the best days, but he's been almost as grumpy as Big Daddy since he got back from the fitting."

"Revna and Njord took some liberties with his kit," I observe, watching as Doyle sets aside the sword and reaches for the ancient-looking helmet beside him. Its design speaks of old wars and older gods, which matches the weapon he's sharpening methodically.

"Everyone has secrets," Wolfie responds before he shifts the subject. "What do you think of your compound bow? Are you sure it won't be a hassle on the move? Benjy was really fussed about that."

I chuckle softly. "Darling boy, I've had my share of wild rides and most weren't on cowboys. Seer and I spent a couple months with travelers running a carnival in Eastern Europe. I picked up stunt riding while Seer dabbled in acrobatics."

"Is there anything you haven't done?" He blinks in surprise, and I shrug nonchalantly.

"Running around the world tends to fill your pockets with stories," I confess. "Especially when you're running from something and hoping it never catches up to you. One gets a bit… cavalier with mortality when they haven't worked through their shit yet."

As we talk, my gaze lands on Teddy. Unlike the rest of us armored to the teeth, he's traveling light, carrying only a curious bag clinking with metal. Its purpose is a mystery and I want to solve it. I open my mouth to question him when Bodil strides into the room, authority etched into every line of her face.

"Time to gear up," she announces. "The hunt begins within the hour."

We spring into action, each movement a testament to our strategy for surviving the night. I slip into my armor, feeling its familiar embrace, and grab my trusty bow. Tonight will be a test of skill—a dance of death and honor under the moon's watchful eye.

As much as the others may worry or keep their silence, I know one thing—we're a family.

And family looks out for each other, secrets and all.

THE STABLE IS A SHADOWED HIVE OF ACTIVITY AS RIDERS GET THEIR mounts ready. Anticipation and the musky scent of the creatures within fills my nose as we enter. I don't know if I'll ever get used to how much sharper my sense of smell and hearing are getting. I can't ask if it's a side effect of whatever the hell is going on with me, but I assume it is.

I glide among my companions as we find our horses. Each of us is clad in our colors and my armor hugs me like a second skin. The armor's design allows me freedom of movement, and the hue... well, it's always been a favorite. So I feel just as good in this battle gear with my hair tied back in a fat braid as I did in the glittering ball gown at Midnight.

Plus I get rocking fucking boots instead of stupid heels.

"Where's Teddy?" I ask Doyle as I squint at the empty space beside him. His emerald gear makes him look like a warrior from ancient myths, especially with that helmet casting his eyes into pools of mystery and the blade that pulses as if its alive.

"He'll be around soon enough," he says, his voice rough. "Just remember, Tíogair... stick close to us, but don't meddle in our fights. This hunt—you've got to prove your own worth."

I snort, pushing back a stray lock of hair. "I didn't come here to audition for these twats, but I guess we don't have a choice."

He grins, the metal of his gear catching the dim light. "You make it sound like a talent show."

"Isn't it though?" I shoot back, the corner of my mouth twitching upward despite the tension coiling inside me. "Just—" I hesitate, lowering my voice, "make sure we all get through this, okay?"

"Trust me. I've got your back." His words are more than a promise; they're an oath spoken by someone who understands what's at stake.

Internally, I catalog the silhouettes of shapeshifters as we line up at the edge of the forest. Their forms ripple between man and beast—a reminder of the hidden layers of this world and its inhabitants. Doyle shines like a beacon amongst them, Wolfie's aura flickers with enchantment, and the rest—the warriors—are an eclectic mosaic of danger and grace. The royals have provided us mounts that defy normalcy and their sides heave like bellows as their eyes glow with fire.

Keeping the fact that I can see all this damn nonsense silent feels like hoarding a cache of weapons so I can wield them when the time is right.

Then, the horn's call slices through the night, deep and resonant as it echoes off the hills.

An inferno leaps forth—an enormous armored hellhound, followed by a legion of smaller devil dogs. It takes me a minute to register that it's Teddy and that's why he didn't have the supplies the rest of us did. He's unmistakable even in this form as he leads the cacophony with howls that pierce the soul.

"Dammit, Teddy," I mutter, annoyance flaring hot in my veins. He should be here, where we can guard him as one of our own. "That jackass always has to be a show off."

Antiope snorts beneath me, her coat ablaze with ethereal flames. With a terse nod, I drive my heels into her sides, urging her forward. She responds with exhilarating speed, racing after the royal vanguard in a spectacle of fire and power.

Okay, I could totally get used to this shit. I feel like a goddamn Valkyrie.

Wolfie appears beside me, riding with the ease of a man born in the saddle. We're at the front of the pack with the elites simply because we ride better than most of the horde of hunters. But it's Doyle who surprises me most, charging ahead as if the very act of riding these hellish steeds was his birthright.

In the moonlight, his figure is outlined with an otherworldly glow. Helmeted and brandishing that bizarre sword, he's transformed. An epiphany crashes over me as I see the golden glow emanating from him: Doyle is not a mere mortal. No, he's touched by divinity itself— a god or demigod hidden in plain sight.

I'm going to flay him alive with a paring knife when I get a hold of him.

"Focus, Jolene," I chide myself silently, shaking off the shock as the hunters flow forward en masse, reaching a vast clearing.

Again, the horn sounds, a clarion call to the wildness within us and it's echoed by the chorus of Teddy and his devil dogs.

The hunt has truly begun, and with it, the unspoken challenges we each must face.

THE GROUND HEAVES BENEATH ANTIOPE, CRACKING WITH OMINOUS finality. Our large party has finally made its way through the forest to the Field of the Wild Hunt, but as soon as we cross the border, the earth began to shake.

I pull my horse up short as the soil beneath us ruptures, and from those jagged fissures, the lichs emerge. I don't know how I know what they are, except that they're a grotesque parade of decay. Their hollow eye sockets burn with malignant hunger as they seek anchorage in this world. My heart jolts against my ribs; these are not mere ghosts to be banished with a chant or a charm.

Even if I knew one—which I don't.

"Gods above," I mutter, a prayer or a curse—I'm not sure which.

The sky darkens above as if it heard me, and fae beasts come cascading from tears in the stratosphere like dark ink dropped into water. Their shrieks tear through the calm, and for a moment, it's all I can do to keep Antiope from bolting.

"Shhh, girl." I stroke her neck, and she steadies, fire in her eyes reflecting my own resolve.

My gaze swings across the clearing where a swarm of black clad riders approach like an omen of doom. It's a sight that chills me to the bone and for a second, I wonder what in the fuck we're going to do this time. I sure can't predict another burst of stuff like at Midnight. I look around at the hunters desperately, and amidst the fray is Doyle looking both radiant and terrible, his sword a beacon in the tumult.

"Dammit, Doyle." I spur Antiope toward him, the ground churning beneath us. When I reach him, I hiss. "Do something or we're all dead."

He whips around, his helmeted visage unreadable but for the flash of his eyes. He sees me—really sees me—and in that instant, recognition dawns. I know his secret, the divine blood coursing through him —not fae forged, but something far older. And that means I know my secret, too.

Come on, Lucky. Figure it out before they attack.

"Tíogair," he growls, the timbre of his voice resonating with an ancient power I've only read about in the dusty corners of libraries. "Take Antiope. Help Wolfie and Benjy with the royals."

"Like hell! You're—"

"Go!" His head jerks toward the others, his command leaving no room for argument.

I grind my teeth, fury roiling within me like a storm, but this isn't the time for our clash of wills. With a resentful nod, I wheel Antiope around, her flames blazing a trail through darkness and doubt.

"Stay alive, you stubborn asshat," I whisper to the wind, hoping it carries my words to him.

Antiope moves with otherworldly grace, parting the sea of combatants as we reach Wolfie and Benjy. The former is stringing arrows with lethal precision while the latter twirls his spear, a dancer among the dead. I wouldn't have believed it a few weeks ago, but I'll be damned if this isn't our goddamn life now.

"Need a hand?" I call out over the din, loosing an arrow from my compound bow with one fluid motion.

"Always," Wolfie replies, a wry smile on his lips despite the encroaching peril.

"Focus!" Benjy shouts, parrying a strike from a skeletal adversary. "We have to protect the king and queen and their children. That's what this shit is about."

"On it, big guy." I let another arrow fly then look over my shoulder for a moment.

Behind me, Doyle engages his foes with a ferocity that belies his usual calm. He moves like myth made flesh, every swing of his sword cleaving the shadows. That son of bitch is acting like a fucking hero and he's spent all his time convincing me he's a freaking bad boy.

He'll never live this down if I have anything to say about it.

"Alright, Antiope. Let's show these motherfuckers who they're dealing with," I say, drawing back my bowstring as I spur her on.

Together, we rocket across the field in a streak of black and purple. Once I get the feel of her gait, I push to my feet, standing in the saddle as I fire at one beast after another. The old fortune teller at the carnival we traveled with used to say I was born to do this kind of stuff and I always said my bruises told a different story.

But right here, right now? I kind of wonder if she wasn't crazy after all.

THE GREATEST SH...

DOYLE

I can't help but pause, the chaos around me fading into a blur as I watch Jolene. She's a comet of fury and focus, her form outlined against the darkening sky. Standing tall in her stirrups, she becomes part of the steed beneath her—her movements fluid and precise. Arrows fly from her bowstring, singing their deadly tune as they arc toward the fae beasts that swoop down maliciously. Without missing a beat, her aim shifts to the lichs scuttling around her horse, cursing at them as she takes them out.

It's not in the stars to hold our destiny, but in ourselves.

"Damn that bard got it right every time," I mutter under my breath as an incredulous chuckle escapes me. How did the Fates stitch all these different souls together into this unconventional family? We're a smorgasbord of supes, each more different than the last, and all broken in various ways. It *should* be an absolute disaster.

My gaze is drawn westward when a howl echoes off the hills and I see Teddy has erupted into a monstrosity of wrath. He tears through flesh and bone as if possessed by a hunger for destruction. "I wouldn't have pegged you for a beast of Armageddon, Boone," I whisper to myself, admiration lacing my words.

A flurry of movement to the east catches my eye. Wolfie gallops over the field with his wings unfurled, trailing fae dust like cosmic breadcrumbs. His arrows cleave the air with deadly precision, finding their marks in the horde of advancing enemies.

"Nice shot, pup!" I shout, but my voice is drowned out by the cacophony of battle.

That's another one I didn't think had it in him, but look at him go.

My gaze moves to Prez as he wields his crossbow like an artist with a brush, painting death upon the undead skeleton men who dare advance. Next to him is Benjy, his gorilla roaring into the night and his spear a blur as he impales anything within reach. Those two don't shock me—I think they've had it in them all along, much like Edgar. They may be the calm in our family's storm, but their fierce love for our girl is fueling their rage.

"That's it, mates. Keep pushing them back," I mutter as I take in the rest of the field carefully.

Together, we're a symphony of mayhem. Yet, my Tíogair hasn't even tapped into her true potential. Her powers are lying dormant as she relies on her fighting prowess alone. She's beauty and grace… right up until she punches you in the face.

I think that's from some movie they made me watch…shit.

Focus, Haggerty.

"Time to even the odds." That decision sparks my inner desire to bend the world around me to its knees and I shudder in pleasure. Energy coasts over me as I tilt my head back in preparation.

I close my eyes, drawing deep from the wellspring of power handed down from the ancestors I know. The glow envelops me then spreads across the battlefield slowly. My horse, sensing the surge, grows restless beneath me. With a firm pat to its flank, I dismount, landing squarely in the midst of the fray.

"Now we'll show them why prayers are said on their knees," I chuckle darkly.

The air hums with energy as Harpe vibrates in my grasp. The famous sword of my relatives is hungry for release. I let the power swell within me, thrusting the sword's tip into the earth. A shockwave erupts sending vibrations through the ground. Lichs stumble and fall like puppets with their strings cut, while my comrades ride through the tumult unscathed, their mounts surefooted amidst the upheaval.

"Yesss," I hiss as the field is cleared in one fell swoop. "Score one for cheating like the bastard you are, old boy."

Lifting Harpe, I press the blade to the golden helmet I borrowed. "Thank you, Auntie," I whisper, knowing she can hear me wherever she is. The gratitude is a fleeting touch, a moment of softness in the heart of battle.

Unlike my mother, she mostly gives a shit about me.

Once I pay my respects, I let out a cry that splits the heavens, then unleash all my pent-up fury. Golden magic arcs from the blade, striking out at the fae beasts like divine retribution. They plummet, one after another, in flaming spirals to their doom.

"Fuck yeah, you scraggly sons of bitches. Take that," I roar, my voice ragged with triumph.

Their bodies crash to the ground, and I can't suppress a savage grin. This is what I was born for—the clash of steel, the rush of power, the dance of death. The battle is far from over, and now that I've let loose the parts I keep shadowed, I'm thirsty for vengeance.

WHEN I FINALLY BURN THROUGH THE FURY BUILT UP INSIDE OF ME, sweat clings to me like a shroud. The rush of power that surged through me ebbs away, leaving an all-consuming fatigue in its wake. I tug the helmet off; it's suddenly suffocating. Tucking it under one arm, I lift my weary gaze.

"Damn," I mutter under my breath as I inspect the grim aftermath.

Supes and Fae are busy around me, their weapons rising and falling in deadly arcs, finishing off the remaining lichs and beasts in a cacophony of final screams and guttural cries. The air is thick with the coppery tang of blood and the sharp scent of burned magic.

We won, but at what cost?

Teddy's not far off, looking like hell in his canine form but moving with purpose. He corrals the devil dogs, his own wounds forgotten in the face of duty. Beyond him, the King props up the Queen, both battered but unbowed. My lips press into a thin line as I take them in; it's their fault we were all out here in the open. Despite their vicious reputation, the Court of Reaping was infiltrated as easily as all the others.

"Prez!" I shout, my voice cracking with strain. He's over with the royals' kin, playing medic and assessing injuries with a keen eye. The people in the Hollow trust him implicitly and the injured here seem to do the same. It's the gift of his kind and he wields that power with amazing efficiency.

A sob splits the night, pulling my attention to a wretched sight. One of the princes is kneeling, his form shaking with grief as he clutches a fallen figure. I swallow hard. The sight of his loss is too raw. I knew eventually these attacks would lead to something like this, but now it's real.

It's not even the first time I've seen someone die this year, but somehow, it hits differently now.

"Benjy? Are you okay?" I ask when I spot my comrade. He's pale as death, clutching his side, but nodding affirmatively. I know he'll live, but my relief is short-lived.

"Shit. Where are...?" My heart hammers, a sudden panic slicing through the numbness in my limbs. "Pup! Tíogair!"

"Find her," Teddy barks, his eyes wide with the same realization. We all fan out, urgency propelling our exhausted limbs. Prez and Benjy are kicking their way through the piles of bodies, checking to see if there are people underneath who might be breathing.

"Jolene!" I call again, my voice hoarse as we navigate the littered field.

Teddy's beside me, his nostrils flaring, sniffing for a trail or sign of them. He stops, then darts forward, leaving me to sprint after him. "Over here," he growls, his voice tight with dread.

We reach the forest's edge, where two hell horses, one of them Antiope,stand sentinel. Their riders are conspicuously absent.

My words catch in my throat. "Fuck, no..."

On the ground, Wolfie's and Jolene's weapons lie discarded. A nearby patch of earth tells a tale of struggle, the soil torn and trampled, and blood staining the grass.

This cannot be happening.

"They're gone. Jolene, Wolfie—taken, hurt." I can barely breathe the words without wanting to scream.

"Who would dare?" Teddy's voice is a low snarl of disbelief and rage.

Whoever did this has no idea of the storm they've just invoked.

"Someone's going to pay." My promise is ironclad, forged in the heat of my fury.

Teddy's immediate transformation is explosive,—a violent eruption of feathers and scales. His body elongates, snaking up into the sky, wings unfurling with a snap that echoes like a thunderclap. The giant Quetzalcoatl, soars above us, trailing flames and fury in its wake. My heart clenches watching him—this is his rawest form, the embodiment of his wrath.

"Find them," I growl, my voice barely audible over the beat of his massive wings. The bird glares at me as if it would like to peck my eyes out, but his head bobs before he streaks into the air.

Prez sprints over, his eyes wide as he takes in the form our leader never takes soaring through the air. "I'll go with him." His shape morphs into the white brilliance of his caladrius. Its healing light is stark against the darkened battlefield as it follows Teddy into the night.

A surge of helplessness swells within me. *I'm earthbound, so I can't join them.*

Benjy hobbles to my side, grimacing with each step. He's a mess of blood and determination, but his eyes stay locked on mine, searching for a plan in my gaze. "Dammit, Doyle, what do we—"

Before he can finish, the air sizzles, charged by an unseen force. Lightning cleaves the sky, striking the helmet under my arm. In a blink, it's not the same helm I'd tucked away. This one gleams sinisterly, its presence alone menacing. My skin prickles at its touch and I caress the curves and points with a wicked grin.

"Holy shit." Benjy's face blanches, his voice hushed as he stares at me. "Now we know who your fucking father is, bro."

Emerald and gold swirl in my vision, the colors of my heritage igniting within me. A smirk tugs at my lips; it feels foreign yet fitting. "Yes, we do," I muse, relishing the dread that ripples through the air.

Whoever has dared to take mine has unleashed the tempest.

"Did you have any clue? Do you think the people who took them know it's…"

"Someone they'll regret crossing?" I reply to the simian. The helmet in my grasp pulsates with a power that feels ancestral, divine, and diabolical all at once. "Likely not."

My mother's lineage may give me the divine power of persuasion, but my father's blood is a different beast altogether. It yearns for destruction—no, it revels in it. And right now, it's calling me to scorch the earth, to make ashes of whoever dares harm those under my protection.

"We hunt," I command, my voice echoing with newfound authority. "Now."

Benjy nods, swallowing hard.

Together, beneath the vanishing trails of Teddy and Prez, I smile as Odie and Eurayle herald the arrival of the animals.

The croaking raven doth bellow for revenge[2]… and so do I.

Read just a little bit more in the Revealed in the Hollow Bonus Scene!

Preorder Revenge in the Hollow now!

Realizations in the Hollow

Awaken

Jolene

We appear in a blink on a field of dead bodies and raging storms. The wind is whipping like it's trying to destroy the entire realm, and lightning is flashing like the pulse of a heartbeat. I look down to see Wolfie still knocked out, but safe, on the ground beneath the tree covering us. This isn't a great place in a storm, but I also know my job is to get out and stop this shit before everything gets worse. My inner voice is telling me that revealing all of my men's secrets is just as bad as letting mine come to light before its time.

Right. Time to pull your big girl panties up and go rope some wild horses, Jolene.

I close my eyes for a moment and look inside of me for the source of the random shit that's popped up over the past few months. It's a chaotic mess, and I'm not sure what I need to do to make anything happen. Licking my lips, I speak in my head, hoping it will work.

~Listen. ~

The swirling mayhem in my center stops as if it's doing exactly what I said, so I try again.

~Help me get them to stop. They cannot tear Faerie apart. ~

This time, I feel warmth spread through my limbs from head to toe. Various sensations seem to compete for control until one cohesive rope of power floods my veins. Sparkling energy dances over my skin and my eyes pop open to look at the terrifying scene where my men are going off the deep end. Confidence fills my mind as I flip my hair in a way the Hollow 'mean girls' would envy and stride onto the field with my spine straight. My dress is ripped and filthy, my raven locks in knots and tangles, but my bare feet sink into the earth with the surety of someone who is used to commanding respect.

Once I'm standing in the middle of the storm, shifters, and magic, I plant my feet on the ground to get a solid base. Lifting my arms in the air, I look up at the sky and boom an order that I can't even understand, "*Teleióste ti máchi sas, moiraía.*[1]"

My jaw drops when everything—and I mean, *everything*—halts immediately. The storm withdraws, the shifters melt to humanoid, the wind pauses, and even the magic flooding the area disappears. When I look around, I see Teddy, Prez, and Benjy standing naked as the day they were born, covered in mud and battle wounds. Doyle is still shining like a fucking glow stick, but he's not surrounded by fire, lightning, a slew of random dazed looking Fae, and snakes. However, I can't help but notice that his form is flickering like an old TV that's having trouble with reception.

What the bloody fuck *is with that?*

I scrub my hand over my face, trying to take in all the input without blacking out, as usual. If I can just get my body to keep *listening*, I know I'll be able to put the pieces together. The power inside of me shocks me a little and I take the hint, pausing my perusal to speak again. "*Epistrofí stin eiríni. Therápefse ti gi. Irémise ta thiría kai ta stoicheía.*"

Doyle storms across the field, his eyes golden as he gets in my face, then grabs my arms roughly. "Are you real?"

I arch a brow, twisting to the side and using my leverage to throw him over my shoulder. He hits the ground with a mighty rumble, and I turn to grin down at him. "Feel authentic enough?"

His features blink again and he goes from blond to red to black shaggy hair as he lets out a breathless chuckle. "Then we've got a real problem. You know that, right?"

"Someone's going to be madder than a cat being baptized?" I give him a shrewd look as he finally picks himself up to dust off the dirt.

"Indeed," he replies as he looks around. "I don't know how much the others saw because you fucking forced a shift and that's disorientating. Let them come to us and we'll see what they say first. You found this out on your own, but if we keep them quiet until you come into the full monte, we might avoid some very boring meetings and a lot of yelling."

Blinking, I grab his arm and look deep into his eyes. "I'd do a lot of sketchy shit to avoid boring meetings, Lucky. I'm in."

His lips curve for a second before he frowns. "Where's the pup?"

"Still out over there under that tree. I think he was given a bigger dose than me. It kept him out while I… learned some heavy stuff." Pressing my lips together, I think about whether I should share the news about meeting his dad or wait until a better moment.

~You need to wait. ~

Goddamn it, that wasn't *my* internal monologue. It was the damn dream lady. If people don't stay the hell out of my skull, I'm going to look like a looney tune. Wolfie will freak out because of his mom and I know for sure it will worry control freak Teddy. I shake my head to clear it, pushing away any stray jerks trying to take up residence there. At least, I hope so.

"You look worried, Tíogair," Doyle murmurs as we watch the others hobble over to us. "Did someone hurt you while you were gone? I swear to Ares' rusty codpiece, I'll—"

"I wasn't hurt, nor was Wolfie," I reply quickly. "It was really more of a… heads-up kidnapping than a sinister one."

He frowns, but drops it when Teddy sees me and picks up speed. The tall ex-football player damn near barrels us both over as he scoops me into his arms and spins us around. I feel the pain underneath his façade and tap his shoulder until he puts me down. "Tilly, if you ever do that again, I'll tan both of your hides. Where's my boy?"

Dropping a soft kiss on his lips, I look at him fondly. "I'm fine; not a scratch unlike you tantrum-throwing babies. Wolfie's asleep under the tree over there. He's fine, too."

"Princess, I don't understand why someone would go to the trouble of stealing the two of you, not harm you, and then return you within a couple of hours." Benjy comes over and pulls me into his arms, resting his cheek on the top of my head as he hugs me. "It doesn't make any sense, but that doesn't mean I'm not relieved as fuck that it's true."

Prez ignores him, pulling me out of his embrace to drop to his knees and examine me from head to toe. Teddy snorts, shaking his head as he heads towards the spot where Wolfie is sleeping peacefully while Benjy and Doyle snicker. Every time I try to move, my doc bats my hands away, clearly needing to satisfy his own mind regarding my safety. Once he's satisfied, he stands, pushing his glasses up as he flushes. "Sorry, Magpie. I had to make certain everything was kosher."

He means he wanted to make sure I wasn't bespelled, so I can't fault him for being thorough.

"It's okay, babe," I say as I shrug. "I understand needing to know the people you care about are in good condition. That's why I'm working my ass off not to bite all your heads off—you guys are covered in wounds and blood. I don't know what the hell went on after I was gone, but it looks like all hell broke loose."

Doyle sucks a soft breath in through his teeth, but I'm tired of pussy-footing around this. I need to know if they saw my reciprocal tantrum or if I need to keep what I know to myself. Not a single one of them has given me a damn clue yet.

"Well, that's because you and Lucy are more important. All of our shit is superficial," Presley replies stubbornly. "And Teddy is fetching him, so I checked you over."

My eyes narrow as I look between Benjy and Prez, finally deciding they have no idea what happened when I forced the shift. Whatever my powers did, they kept everyone but the golden boy over there from knowing it was me. Was that as a cover for the stupid oath or because I truly need to stay under wraps still? One glance at Doyle says he doesn't know, either.

"Where's the rest of our hosts? This was a damn ambush, and I'd like to know how those people got through their security."

No sooner than the words leave my mouth, King Darragh and Bodil come bounding up. They've obviously had some kind of healing because when I got back here, no living supernaturals on this field were unscathed. The former gives me a bright grin as we've just played a vigorous polo match and won.

"Jolene, as angry as I am about The Hand of Morrigan invading my gathering, I'm ecstatic about this fantastic match-up. As usual, all's well that ends well in our land, but your companions were stunning."

I blink, trying to understand why the man is damn near gleeful about a field full of dead…. things… and holes in his security that almost got us all killed. "Uh… thanks?"

Teddy glowers as he carries Wolfie over to the group, his eyes looking red and fiery. "I have a dimmer view of this outcome, sir. The losses were unnecessary, and the risk was far greater. What the hell kind of circus are you running?"

The King looks at my alphahole as if he'd like to strangle him, but Doyle steps in between them. He nudges Teddy back, facing the royal with a determined stance. "His words may have been harsh, but you'll find mine disrespectful as fuck, Darragh. You have a duty of care when visitors from our lands are in your kingdom and you've failed miserably."

He can't argue with that, even if it's surprising that my tricksy Irishman is the one questioning him.

"Well, I… You see… We couldn't have…"

Bodil sighs, rolling his eyes. "What the King is surely trying to say is that perhaps our trials drained too many resources and brilliant individuals took advantage of the gaps. We will, of course, help you all get cleaned up and give you a place to heal until you are ready to continue with the visit."

"Fat chance," I mutter. "We're getting out of this goddamn Temple of Doom."

Teddy chokes back a laugh and I see Benjy doing the same. Even Presley looks amused, but I'm not joking. We're going to clean up and heal, then get Wolfie out of his trance, but afterwards, we're on the first portal the fuck *out* of Faerie. My hometown is filled with vipers and waspy women, but at least they're in your face about it. Random attacks from bands of whatever the hell aren't common in the Hollow and I like it that way.

Something niggles at my brain and I furrow my brow for a second as I play back the conversation in my head. I'm missing an important piece of info that I have to make certain I get. When it pops back in my head, I grin broadly as I push between Teddy and Doyle to face the puffy chested royal. "Darragh, what in the ever-loving *fuck* is The Hand of Morrigan?"

His face pales and he must realize he's the one who mentioned it. "I don't know what you're talking about, Miss Whitley."

Bullshit.

I open my mouth to protest his lies, but Doyle shakes his head. He must have a plan to check it out on our own. I guess that makes sense, as Darragh is likely to lie his ass off, anyway.

Fine. We'll do it ourselves—just like always.

HIT THE ROAD, JACK

DOYLE

My Tiogair never ceases to amaze me. Her performance on the battlefield only confirmed my suspicion that she's figured out *some* of what's going on in her life. That she waited to see if the rest of our family remembered it made it crystal clear that she's carefully keeping her knowledge secret to prevent us from being reprimanded. It also explains why she had those damn glasses—someone is helping her and I hope whoever it is has her best interests at heart.

I won't ask her to tell me if she's not ready, though.

Jolene walks over to Boone, smiling as he carries the pup over to us. "He's still out, huh? That shit must have been really strong."

"What stuff?" Prez asks curiously. "It might help us counteract the effects, if you know."

She shrugs, shaking her head. "I have no idea, Doc. Our captor didn't tell me, but I know he used it on me, too. I haven't croaked, so it will not hurt him. I guess he's just more susceptible to it?"

"Mmmm," the doc says, making that face again. He doesn't believe Wolfie has a lower tolerance and I agree with him. It's much more likely our girl has burned the shit out of her system because she's more powerful than any of us know.

"This isn't the place to have this conversation," Teddy finally says. "We need to go inside and get cleaned up. Curiosity and suspicion can wait until later."

With a bright smile, Jolene nods, turning on her heel to look at the royal contingent. "Who's taking us to our rooms? Chop, chop, people."

Benjy snorts as a small Fae hurries over, bowing before gesturing for us to follow them.

Back to the suite, it is.

"I don't *KNOW* WHO THE MAN WAS, GUYS," JOLENE SAYS, HER VOICE full of exasperation. "No amount of meditation or trauma informed interview techniques are going to help me if he didn't say. I didn't recognize him at all. He was definitely from around here, good look-ing, and older. That's what I got."

She's lying—I can feel it in my bones.

The sensation is annoying, but I feel like since the battle, I've had some sort of…upgrade. My power was nothing to shake your fist at to begin with, but demi-gods have a few pieces missing that our parents don't pass on. It doesn't feel like I'm missing anything now and that's going to be a *big* problem the next time I have to go to the Mount. My auntie will know, though she won't be mad so much as curious, but the others? There's definitely going to be a fight.

"We're not trying to make you feel bad, Sugarplum," the pup says softly. He finally woke up a few minutes ago, but he's still groggy as he sprawls in Prez and the judge's arms. "But it's weird as fuck that the man didn't harm either of us and then let us go."

Benjy nods, looking down at our girl while he braids her hair. "It is. Like what half-assed villain shit is that? Was it to prove he could? Is he not a villain and if not, what the hell is his game? I don't like it."

Boone sighs. "I don't know, either, B. Darragh acted *very* weird when we asked about The Hand of Morrigan, though. Alistair was right about the royals keeping the rebels under wraps from the rest of the world."

"I suppose the royals at home would, too," I offer. "If we had one of those pretend do-gooder groups trying to upset the balance of things, we'd want to deal with them quietly before their message got out."

The room is quiet for a moment as the others consider it. Before anyone can speak, there's a knock at our door. Every supe tenses, even Jolene, until the big guy ambles over to open it. The brownie on the other side squeaks in surprise, but he gets it together long enough to herd our animals in. The cats and dogs were filthy from the battle, so we let the staff take them to shifter pools to get rinsed clean. They weren't happy with leaving us, but Jolene whispered to them and they trotted off without another complaint.

"Look how clean you guys are," Jolene says as they immediately surround her. "And someone decorated you, too."

That's a word for it.

The servals have flower rings around their necks and the Danes have some sort of sparkling shit singing in their fur. I'm glad Isis and the bird didn't go along for the ride because I can't imagine what they would have done to the enormous snake or the huge eagle. Neither pair of animal seem disturbed by the Fae bling, and Jolene is giving the scared looking brownie a delighted smile. I arch a brow at the pup, silently asking if this is an issue, and he shakes his head slowly. He's still coming out of the haze from the kidnapper's doping, but I trust his instincts.

"They saved several ladies-in-waiting while the rest of your group were busy," the staffer says softly. "My colleagues wanted to thank them for their heroics."

My eyes narrow as I make sure the guy sees me warn him to be careful of his words. He swallows hard, then fidgets a little before clearing his throat. "We appreciate your efforts. If you don't mind, we'd like to finish gathering our things so we can leave."

"But... the king said... we believed you'd be staying the night..."

Teddy snorts. "Absolutely not. I'm making some calls and we're heading to the nearest exit as soon as possible. I believe we have over-stayed our welcome in your lands."

No shit, Sportsboy.

"Yes. Okay. I will… inform the family. Thank you," the brownie says nervously, bowing before he skedaddles like his feet are on fire.

Once the door closes, my Tíogair rounds on the lounging men on the couch. "We're not waiting until morning? I thought this place was dangerous to travel at night."

"To be fair, Magpie, it's proven to be dangerous in broad daylight." Presley gives her a half-grin, obviously hoping to cushion the news.

She gives him an exasperated look. "I'm not falling for that, McNuggies. You guys made some sort of executive decision while I was in the shower, didn't you? I *hate* being left out of the conversation."

"As do I," I say as I walk over and drop into a chair. "This new plan was made while I, too, was cleaning up. What gives with you four?"

Surprisingly, Wolfie is the one who answers. "I had a slight flash of memory while you were gone. I think… I think maybe my father took us. I'm not sure because it's all hazy, but it would explain why he didn't hurt us. He's part of something or knows something—and he wanted to make sure we knew. But… I can't remember anything else."

"And I think that means we need to GTFO," Teddy says quietly. "I don't know if the pup's right on any of those accounts, but if there's a chance he is… The information the kidnapper wanted to relay had to be *extremely* critical to yank them out that situation. I don't know why it's been obscured, other than maybe it will come back after the drugs and trauma fade."

He's being careful not to say maybe a spell will unlock at the right moment, but I get it.

"Fine," Jolene sighs. She looks around, noting the same thing I have. They packed everything while we were gone. My money's on the doc and the bartender because the judge is in Uber alpha protective mode with the vet. His distance from our girl tells me how much he *actually* trusts her to take care of herself. "Then who are we calling for the escort to the exit?"

Teddy smirks. "Our good friend from the Midnight is headed out way with some of his security. They'll be here shortly to join us on the route. Once we're out of these lands, the airport is our next stop, then home to the Hollow."

Jolene snorts. "I'll be damned. I never thought I'd be so glad to hear those words."

That makes two of us, Tíogair.

ALISTAIR'S CONTINGENT TAKES ABOUT AN HOUR TO ARRIVE AND AN interminable amount of time to clear the King's security. Darragh couldn't prevent the fuckers from attacking his trials, but he's set on looking as if he's taking our safety seriously now lest the Society get involved. I think it's less about us or the Society in the end; he doesn't want anyone looking into this Hand of Morrigan thing.

Of course, that means it's the first fucking thing I'm going to poke around about in my circles.

"Miss Jolene… I heard you survived yet another tragic challenge," Alistair says with his trademark smirk.

Our girl rolls her eyes at him, dismissing his swagger as she calls the companions. "Nice to see you again, too, Silkshine. You're a treat, as always."

"You wound me," the dark Fae flutters his lashes as he pretends to be hurt. "I'm here on the figurative white horse. Allora would have come as well if the guards hadn't blocked every escape she tried. She's very fond of you, but it's far too risky for her to be on unplanned jaunts."

"At least you're not stupid." I shake my head as I grab two of the bags and jerk my head at the others. "Let's get the hell out of here before anything else happens."

Jolene chuckles as she walks past Alistair to the door. "He's very bossy lately. Almost as much as the other one. I don't know what I'm going to do with them all."

"I have suggestions," Boone mutters as he follows her. "But they'll have to wait until we're out of here."

Silkshine arches his brow, but says nothing. That makes me suspicious, so I wait until the others are following our girl down the hall. When they round the corner, I back the shithead against the wall, pressing the knife that appeared in my palm to his neck. "What the *fuck* was that look for?"

"Bloody hell, *leanabh nan diathan*. What are you doing? I'm on *your* side," he wheezes.

"Why did you give the hound that look? The others missed it, but I didn't." The last thing we need is more fucking surprises. This kind of shit is why people have a love/hate relationship with Faerie—it giveth and it taketh away.

"I merely thought he wanted to avoid the legends," Alistair says as his eyes flash. "After battle, our kind are frequently… fertile. Jolene has triumphed in *two* challenges in as many days. She's likely full of light and life, so waiting until you're away from lands would negate that possibility."

I blink, then throw my head back, laughing. The Fae looks puzzled, especially when I disappear the knife and let go of him. When I calm, I pat his shoulder, shaking my head. "Sorry about that, mate."

He frowns at me. "You're not bothered by the prospect? It's clear none of you know what she is, but all of you are powerful in your own ways."

"Not that it's any of your business, but that's not an option for our girl. Some terrible incident as a child. I doubt Boone even knows about that version of your lore." I chuckle as my eyes dance. "The pup is more likely to get pumped full than our girl."

Alistair rolls his eyes. "Your orphaned Fae is *not* part demon. Those bastards are the only ones who can do that kind of shit."

As we turn to walk in the direction the others went, I shrug. "Not only them, you know. Your princess probably knows this, but some deities, demons, a few of the watery types… there's more who can… cross-pollinate. I've met some of them in my many years. Gets no less odd each time."

"That's probably something you should ease Jolene into when she finally finds out what our world really looks like," he says with a grin.

"I think she'll be okay with the basics, but the really weird stuff in the supe world will take a bit to digest. Give her time and be patient."

If only he knew how little time we really have…

PATIENCE

JOLENE

We exited Faerie without incident—a minor miracle, in my opinion. I was prepared for an attack of some kind and another blackout, but now we're on the road to the airport. Euryale is flying overhead and the animals are unhappily cooped up in the second car with Doyle and Wolfie. Teddy wasn't thrilled with letting our darling boy ride in a separate car, but Benjy and I calmed him down enough to make him see sense. It's better for the vet to be near the animals while we're on the road so he can make sure they're ready for the long flight. He didn't like it, but Prez's insistence that he be close to me to keep watch helped grease the wheels.

Aphrodite, save me from these ridiculously over-the-top men and their growly shit.

"Will Hugo and Dhameer meet us at home?" I ask. It occurs to me that our group has been split up for almost a month and I miss seeing them. Most of all, I miss Seer, but she said she won't be back until mid-January. Something about the assignment she's helping Julia and their men with is keeping them tied up.

Teddy looks over at me, his expression fond. "They will be back not long after we get home, Tilly. The Prince said they had one more lead to follow up on and both were eager to wrap it up so they can get home."

My cheeks flush as I think about the way the word 'home' has changed regarding Whistler's Hollow in the past few months. When I came storming back to find out what happened with my clearance, I meant to resolve the problem and head to the next place once I had it sorted. Sure, I set everything up as if it might take a while because I had no idea what I was walking into. But my goal was to solve the riddle and GTFO. But now…

Now I've put down roots and even if I figured this shit out tomorrow, I don't think I could pick up and leave.

The town that was my traumatic past has come full circle to being my future and I'm surprisingly okay with it. Outside of a few buzzing gnats who won't go away, I'm making in-roads to healing the wounds of the past. The Jolene who ran after high school, the one who was betrayed in college, the jet-setting single girl, and the serious F.B.I. applicant have all morphed into a woman who's found what she was always missing: a family. It's surreal as hell, but I'm actually looking forward to seeing what is in store once we get past this whole 'secret' thing.

"I'll be damned," I mutter to myself. My therapist is going to have a *field day* with this shit. I'm almost excited about the future. We've been working on not simply focusing on the here and now to avoid my past and not fret about the future. All it took to get here were seven men and an army of animals—who would have thought?

"Why?" Benjy says as he turns around in his seat to face the three of us. "What's going through your head, Princess?"

Shrugging, I give him a small smile. "I was mulling over all the changes since I rolled into town and how I've recalibrated my entire trajectory in just a few months. It's not a bad thing—in fact, I think it's fantastic. My shrink sure as hell will."

He nods, his expression shy. "Thank you for saying that. I've been seeing a virtual therapist since the divorce, but you know how that sort of thing is frowned upon around our parts. I didn't tell anyone because I was worried it would make me look bad. But since you shared, I feel like it's not a big deal."

Teddy snorts. "Dude, it's *so* not a big deal. I know everything in the Hollow is about appearances, but we know half the people who run the place are on some sort of chemical substance to make their lives run smoothly. At least you're addressing your issues from Sherilynn, so you don't have to carry those bags forever."

"Edgar Olivier Boone III, every time I think you can't surprise me more, you say shit like that," I say as I shake my head. "I don't know what kind of magic mirror you've done all your reflecting in, but damn, it's good."

"Right?" Benjy chuckles. "The dude has evolved into a whole different species since high school and I didn't realize it."

"I don't feel the need to share my innermost shit with people unless it's necessary," Teddy murmurs. "There's value in allowing the masses to believe your armor is your skin, especially in a town like ours. Since I don't give a fuck what they think of me, I'm happy to let my freak flag fly now that it's worth the bullshit."

Presley winks at him. "We definitely enjoy that part."

"Amen," I mutter and they all laugh as they give me smug looks. "Guys, I have zero problem admitting that you're all hot as fucking hell and I enjoy watching you… but that's not all of it. I also *love* feeling the emotions that come out when everyone is together—both in the bedroom and outside of it. We're this big, warm family that takes care of one another even while we're giving one another shit. I didn't think it could actually *be* like this."

Benjy reaches out, taking my hand to kiss my knuckles. "Same, Princess. People who didn't appreciate us broke you and me. It takes work to accept the support we're getting now."

"That's exactly it. I keep waiting for the other shoe to drop. It's probably why I went ballistic about the big secret shit; it hit one of my trauma wounds and reopened it."

Teddy slides his arm behind me, pulling me to his side. "It absolutely did, and I regret having to do it. But if there was another option, Tilly, we would take it. Trusting us all when we told you our side is a big step towards our family becoming a true safe place."

My eyes narrow as I settle into him. "Don't you dare say soft stuff and make me cry, Teddy Bear. You know how I feel about that shit."

He chuckles, pressing a kiss to my temple before he gives the other two a knowing look. "I do, but I can't help wanting you to understand how I feel about you. I doubt the others can, either. You'll have to learn how to take compliments and emotional declarations, I'm afraid. I think the Prince is probably going to put us all to shame in that arena someday."

That makes me wrinkle my nose and scrunch further into the seat. "I really *cannot* talk about being involved with someone whose title is Prince again. It's such a fucking pain. Seer and I swore no more royals, especially sheiks. What the hell am I thinking?"

"You're not thinking, Magpie. You're feeling, and it's a good thing."

Humph. If you say so.

LOADING UP ONLY TOOK A FEW MINUTES AND JACKSON'S CREW WAS already running through their checks by the time we arrived. I assume one of the guys contacted them and, once again, I marvel at not having to arrange every damn thing on my own as we take off. The past month has been a rollercoaster of revelations—emotional and world-rocking reality ones. I haven't checked in with Nicey or anyone, preferring to keep myself removed from whatever shenanigans ensued after my departure.

The one thing I'm not looking forward to is facing the whispers and stares that will follow me when we're home.

It's inevitable; the word that everyone, including Benjy, took off to Europe for a winter break getaway will have spread like wildfire. Even if we didn't tell anyone, the gallery, the docs' offices, and one of the local judges were unavailable. That's not to mention the Speakeasy being run by Benjy's staff—it would have been noticed immediately. I'm sure my gaggle of women with nothing better to do than harass me over things long past will champ at the bit to get in my face.

"Why the frown, Sugarplum?" Wolfie looks up at me from his spot lying across the couch between Teddy and I. "You seem worried."

I hate *having to keep the father thing from him, especially since I think the guy might not be a bad guy.*

"I'm just thinking about how much shit I'm going to get from the Nip/Tucks when we get home. It's exhausting to always have to be on guard," I admit softly. "I wish they'd either fuck all the way off the planet or just grow the hell up and *leave me alone.*"

His lips quirk up. "Of course you do. But we all know people like that can't let shit go. They're so miserable in their own lives that they desperately try to fill the void by ruining things for others. Standing up to them only makes them dig in further—and you, Jolene, have definitely shown them you're ready to fight."

"I say let loose, Tíogair. Beg forgiveness later, but show them what they'll deal with if they keep coming. And I don't mean words, I mean action."

The look he gives me is pointed, and I roll my eyes. I can't use powers I'm not supposed to know I have to teach these whiny narcissists to cut the shit. "Mayor Nelia would be pissed if I caused another scene like in the Hollar."

He shrugs, looking as if he'd enjoy it. "Who cares? Those people are a cancer eating away at you. Everything you do gets tainted by having to worry about what's coming from behind you afterward. You can't really live if you're always looking over your shoulder, love. The time has come to rip the band-aid off. Show the town who they are."

"The town *does not* care," Benjy snorts. His fingers are scratching Hecate's head as he leans back in his chair. "Outside of Nelia, most of the dicks in charge raised their kids to act like fools. The success rate being what it was, you'd face more backlash than one would expect. Remember, we had a lot of clean-up when Isis appeared."

"We?" Doyle says in an amused tone.

Benjy flushes and I grin. "Okay, you guys did, but I had to hear about it—both from you and the people at the bar. It was a hot topic for a bit before and after. A great deal of them were not satisfied with the decision that was made, either. You can't expect any help if you choose to meet it head on."

Scrubbing my hands down my face, I press my fingertips into my eyes as I think. Both sides have merit, but Benjy's is more logical.

Enraging the entire town isn't a good plan if I want to stay under the radar.

~ You deserve to feel safe in your home. ~

That damn voice is back and I scrunch my face up in irritation. I don't know who or what it is, but all the shit inside of me agrees. I feel fire and slithering and howls like they're happening in real time echo in my mind. "Just great. You're all aggressive freaks."

"I am not," Prez and Wolfie say in unison.

Their grins make me chuckle, and I relax a little. Luckily, I have a few family members who aren't ready to rip off heads when someone upsets me. That's going to help when I have wrangle the *very* furious parts of me that aren't entirely ready to show their faces yet.

After all, someone has to be the one to talk us all out of murder, right?

Small Town

Edgar

Yawning, I ease myself out from under the pile of people crammed in the big pile of the floor. This damn jet has a perfectly serviceable bed, but it's too small for Tilly and me to allow our family to snuggle in. The trip to Faerie brought everyone closer and the protective instincts of *all* my surprisingly possessive sides prefer them as close as possible. My hound thinks of the five people sleeping on the floor as our pack and he's restless about what kind of danger might lurk back home.

Jolene's stalker didn't follow us to Europe, but they're likely waiting at home.

A low growl echoes out of my chest as I pad to the galley and pour myself a bourbon. I sent the flirty attendant packing on a first-class ticket home rather than tempt the Fates by having her make Tilly pissy mid-air. It felt like the right plan and Wolfie's handled keeping us fed, so I think I made the right choice. Taking a sip of the single barrel Blanton's, I sigh as I think about the challenges we face in the Hollow.

First, Jolene is still emerging, and she's not aware what the hell is going on. Our theory about her having more sides has to be kept quiet, so the Society doesn't make her a bug under a microscope, but it limits our ability to keep weird shit from happening. It also creates a very dangerous balance that the Hollow Mean Woman squad, led by Sherilynn, will seek to take advantage of. Managing them while making sure Tilly is safe will be a pain in the ass. Luckily, we have enough people to keep someone nearby most of the time.

She won't allow us to trail her like guards at home—that I guarantee.

"Penny for them, Boone," Doyle says and I whip around, glaring at the faux Irishman.

"Poseidon's fucking seaweed jockstrap, Haggerty. I damn near jumped out of my skin," I grumble in irritation. My hound doesn't like that he can do that shit with his 'god powers' or whatever. Usually, we can sense an approach, if not smell it, but this dick is like a damn shadow when he wants to be.

His smug grin doesn't help, but he finally shrugs. "It's harder to control since the battlefield. I've never had this much raw energy flowing through me. I leveled up or some shit. That might not be as drastic for you, but it's making me volatile."

Interesting. I noticed a minor power up across the board, but I figured it was a mating thing. I wonder if the pup and the doc got one?

As if he's reading my thoughts, Doyle nods. "We all have so far. I notice it more because mine is *very* drastic and my magic was already over-powered. You four may not see as big a difference until you are forced to use the boost in a big way. I filled that role in the last battle, but you'll likely get a chance."

I snort. "Because our woman can't help but draw psychos and power hungry fuckwits like a bug zapper?"

"No, because our woman is important in a way none of us under-stand yet, and that kind of destiny frightens those who see it coming. They know there's someone out there who can foil their plans and seek to destroy them before that's no longer an option." Doyle gives me a withering look. "Unless you've read none of the mythos of the gods of any flavor? I mean, she's a damn Hercules or some shit."

Sighing, I brace myself on the counter. I've had that thought before, but since there are quite a few lost ones being monitored who seem to harbor a lot of power, I dismissed it. By the nature of the supe hybrids left in enclaves, they're all stronger than normal supes. That's why the Society gives them Guardians and watches so closely. But Jolene is very different and I think that's not a surprise for our bosses.

They know something they aren't ready to share, and Jolene plays into it.

"Yeah, I think there's hinky shit going on, too," Doyle agrees as he moves to pour a Jameson. "Especially with Seer and her gal working for the crones. Some cosmic fucking chess game. But what the hell do my Tíogair's parents have to do with it? Or the pup's mum? It's bloody complicated."

I pause, tilting my head as I study him. "Can you hear what I'm fucking thinking, you asshole?"

That makes his face turn bright red and I blink. He clears his throat, then admits, "Well, I couldn't before, but I woke up because you were thinking so damn loudly it woke me. This is new; I swear."

"Turn it off, dick," I growl softly. I'm not thinking anything he can't know, but it feels ridiculously violating to have someone in your mind all the time.

"I will when I figure out how?" His grins is charming and I roll my eyes. He might and he might not, but at least I know he's there now.

Fuck, I hate the goddamned deities; they never give a straight answer to anything.

"Hey! I resemble that remark," the demi-god says as he raises his glass. "*Slainte.*"

"Cheers to you, too." I raise my glass and clink it with his, deciding his snooping is way behind the other worries on my list.

Doyle takes a hefty draught of his whiskey before he looks at me again. "We have to make sure the new guys understand how this town fucking works. People will gun for her simply because she's taken a handful of the hot eligible bachelors. Not to mention Bitter Betty that was married to your friend."

I think about that for a moment. He's probably right; Dhameer is from another culture entirely, and Hugo has never taken part in our community other than school. He's an odd duck, always ending up in places he shouldn't looking like he's run through a ringer. It's weird and I haven't really unpacked everything we don't know about his gifts and mandate. The Prince comes with his own challenges and that I can't wrap my mind around.

"You think she'll have the girls from school on her heels, but they'll also set every other single chick in town after her?" I arch a brow, waiting for him to confirm.

"Fuck, yes, I do. And we have a shit ton of research and travel to do. I want to know what the shit happened to her at the doctor in the city and *why*. I want to know who had the fucking cop killed. We have to find out what drove Aurelia over the edge and if her parents were murdered. There are far too many random pieces hanging out to even form an outline of what's going on."

I dislike having to admit this asshole is right this often.

"We need to know what my dad has to do with this and that Faerie rebel group," a soft, sleepy voice says behind me.

My lips curve as I turn to yank the pup into my arms. It still makes my supe natures upset he was taken—more than Tilly because deep down, I know she can handle herself. Wolfie might have mates and emerged years ago, but he feels… unfinished. Maybe it's the lack of knowledge about his dad and that side of his biology, but he's not as powerful as he should be. It makes him feel breakable and delicate, which sends the hound in particular over the edge. "You should be asleep."

Doyle snorts. "Don't be a mother hen, Big Daddy Asshole. The pup probably woke up for a reason—like your internal strife over the mess we're flying home to."

Wolfie nods as he looks up at me. "That's true. I felt like I was needed and so I wiggled out to come here. But… we definitely have a lot of strings to untangle on the board. Your father may be part of it, too, Doyle. Hell, there's probably a fuck ton of other stuff in the bigger picture we can't even see yet."

That's not comforting at all.

"You're likely correct," the demi-god muses as he leans against the counter. "But we can't focus on the parts of the board we can't see yet. The only thing we can do is continue working through the clues and questions we have now. Parentage, murder, cover-ups, lineage, powers, timing… all of it is part of the strategy we aren't seeing."

"Like how Sugarplum spent years getting cleared to be everywhere— including the human president's damn plane—and suddenly failed a background check for law enforcement?"

I blink, never having thought of it that way. *How* did *she get clearance for all that other shit without so much as a blip?* Sure, we're not allowed to be higher in law enforcement than local cops, but... the Secret Service vets people for that damn thing. Her hometown should have crossed her off that list faster than someone could bat a lash. Yet until that moment, in that place, she suddenly threw up the standard supe trail shit.

"Damnit, you're right, pup," I rumble as I sit my chin on his head. "Someone either unflagged her in the past and waited until it was useful to flag her... or they knew when she'd start becoming a threat and added the flag then." I frown, unsure whether I'm talking about some Society toadie or someone much more sinister.

Is there someone watching the lost ones who might know when to pull triggers like that to set off courses of events?

"The sisters don't do shit like that. They plan ahead," Doyle says. "But that doesn't mean they aren't aware of everything happening now and moving their pawns around."

"Is anyone higher than them? I mean, gods are, but also... they can't interfere, right?" Wolfie asks. "So... who's bigger than the weavers?"

Hell if I know. Obviously, no one teaches that shit.

The Irishman sighs, raking his hands through his hair. "Honestly, perhaps some primordials types, but many are locked up and others choose to stay in the background. I mean, you all know the story of my fuckwit, philandering uncle... he locked up some of them. His version is questionable and I'm not sure they deserve it, but who wants to find out? Not me."

"But there might be others like them who aren't buried in a volcano cave?"

He rolls his eyes at me. "Of course there are. There's always a beginning and an end to everything—an alpha and omega. Things come from other things; we just don't know all the origins of the Universe because no one can—not even the sisters. My relatives have counterparts with stories about other primordials; they're ancestors of the gods, if you prefer a more straightforward explanation. But not every branch of belief had to put theirs on ice. And some belief systems died without leaving written records to tell us about their shit."

Scrubbing my hands over my face, I groan. "We could be part of some bazillion year old prophecy. Is that what you're saying?"

"Sure. We also can be simultaneously part of some jackhole's brilliant plan to prevent the damn thing, too. Both things can be true, and a handful of other options. Time and patience are the watchword of destiny, Boone. I've been alive too long to discount even the far-fetched possibilities."

"Shit," Wolfie says as he pulls away. "The Fae are old as hell, too. And there's some rebellion going on. Doesn't it seem weird that's happening while Sugarplum's going through this stuff, plus the Guardians had to quell witch stuff in Salem? And uh… other stuff, but I haven't been paying close attention."

"If we're part of some ancient deity's shitty world domination plan, I'm going to be pissed," I growl softly. "It's too cliched to even consider. I fucking refuse."

Doyle smirks and shakes his head. "As if you get the choice because you're the great and powerful Edgar Boone III."

Of course I do. This isn't ancient Greece… free will is a thing and I'm not conceding a damn thing.

"Wakey wakey, Princess," the voice says. It's soft and gentle, much like the gentle giant who owns it. Benjy isn't the type to startle me awake as a joke like Doyle, nor is he the type to surreptitiously work me up and leave me hanging playfully like Teddy. He simply gave me a soft shake and a calming tone to come back to reality in.

The many facets of my men constantly amaze me.

"Ugh," I grunt, as I stretch and yawn. I notice no one's surrounding me at the moment, which means they all got up first to take care of shit. "What time is it?"

Benjy smiles, his face lighting up as I look at him. "We're heading towards the final descent into the private landing strip, gorgeous. You need to hop up and have a seat."

Blinking, I swivel my gaze around, seeing the guys sitting in various chairs with the cabin cleaned up and ready for landing. "Damn. I slept like the dead. Why didn't you guys wake me up?"

"Because, Tilly, we felt you needed the rest to be at your best." Teddy grins at me as he finishes his last sip of bourbon. "It's mid-day here and we're headed to drop you at your place, then go to Haggerty's to pick up our shit before we return the vehicles. If anyone shows up while we're gone, it's better if you're not half-asleep, mm?"

He has a point.

"Yeah, I'm not in the mood for someone to show up and give me shit about our vacay. You're right, Teddy. Thanks." I push up to my feet, bending to grab the pillow and blanket. Folding the soft fur, I walk over and stow it in the closet we found it in before I head to the couch.

All five of them are blinking at me and I roll my eyes. *So dramatic, these men.* Flopping on the cushions, I settle in with Wolfie, letting him curl around me. I refuse to acknowledge their pretend shock at my simple apprecia-tion. I'm not always going to fight him; this wasn't worth the energy.

"Um, Tíogair? Are you feeling okay?" Doyle ventures.

"For fuck's sake," I mutter as I wrinkle my nose. "I'm not *that* stub-born that I'd have to be ill to accept he has a point. Yes, I love to fight Teddy Bear, but some things are just *not* the hill to die on."

The judge grins in his hungry hound way, teeth flashing as his brow arches. "Ooh, does that mean you'll stop fighting me about *all* the plans all the time? I know you bought us those fancy collar thingies, but I could—"

My eyes narrow and I jut my chin out as the plane begins its descent. "Edgar Olivier Boone III, you three belong to *me* and if you want to challenge me on that, I'm your Huckleberry."

That gets a snicker out of Wolfie first, then Prez, and soon, everyone is laughing. I beam at them, happy I've asserted my dominance with little argument.

Take that, Big Daddy Asshole. Mama J is in charge now.

"When do you think Dhameer and Hugo will be back?" I ask as we speed down the highway towards the Hollow. The private strip was closer to the City and there was a lot of uproar in security about some group of big wigs flying back from New York City later in the day. I almost poked around to see who the hell everyone was worried about, but we needed to get home.

There's only four days before school starts up again and I have to unpack, get the guys settled, get my studio aired out, and organize shit for the upcoming semester. Much to do and little time to do it in, which is why I texted Nicey to make sure we had plenty of groceries and supplies in the house early in the flight. She was happy to hear the guys would be returning and promised to make certain everything was prepared for our return, including the stuff my animals required.

You know someone loves you when she runs out to procure raw meat, frozen critters, and other icky things for your exotic pets to eat.

"I'm not sure. They said shortly after we arrived, but we've been so out of touch on our trip that I worry time will differ from they assume," Doyle says absently. "Their last location was South America, but I'm not sure where they were headed afterward."

Prez grins as he looks back at me from the front. "They'll probably come see you as soon as they get back. Don't worry, Magpie."

I frown, trying to figure out how to respond. Those two are supposedly part of my puzzle and I agree that's true, but… I just don't know them well enough to really put a label on how I feel. I worried—but that's because there are dirty motherfuckers hiding in every shadow lately. I don't want *anyone* to get hurt because of me. But I don't have a good bead on how to organize my thoughts around the history teacher and the Prince.

I fucking hate *that shit.*

"Why the frown, Sugarplum? Do you not want to see them yet?" Wolfie whispers.

"No… it's not that. I can't get my hands around what to think or feel about them. It's very odd to have this certainty from you guys, but my own insides are in turmoil." I give him a sheepish smile and shrug. "That probably sounds crazy."

"Not at all, Tilly," Teddy says from the driver's seat. "I've gone through it a couple of times recently. You've got a disconnect between brain, heart, and lady bits."

"Lady bits? Gross," I grumble as I wave at him like I'm shooing him off. "Teddy, you're much smoother than that."

His laugh is soft. "Perhaps, but I let that persona slide with my family. Haven't you noticed?"

His family.

I gulp, feeling a big knot in my chest that's swelling like it's going to burst out like in *Alien*. When I can speak again, I rasp, "There it is, you grumpy sweet talker."

Wolfie beams as he reaches up to squeeze Teddy's shoulder. "He's doing good, huh? Now if we can get the surly Irishman to play along…"

"Oi," Doyle grouses. "You're not picking on the Doc or the bartender."

"Because we don't have the emotional range of a grapefruit," Benjy counters as we swing onto the one road leading off the main highway into the Hollow. He sighs as we pass City Hall, Atwater's and the garage. "Plus, you do more joking than emoting, man."

Presley ponders for a moment, then nods. "That sounds about right. You're a closed book most of the time. I don't know if it's different when you and Magpie are alone, though."

I watch Doyle screw his face up, then let out a breath. "You might be right. I keep to myself more than the rest of you because I stopped getting close to people a long time ago. My… posts were always temporary and I dislike having to see people left behind."

Why do they all look so understanding now? Fuck, I want this secret shit over, so I'm not lost.

"I guess that makes sense," Wolfie says softly. "But it's obviously not the case now, so you'll have to re-learn how to be part of a group. It's especially important for more people joining, eventually. We all have to have each other's back if this conspiracy stuff goes beyond Jolene's parents' death."

"Agreed." Teddy nods as we glide past the bank, florist, and even my gallery. "It's important to present a completely united front in town. That will help eliminate the threat of the girls… maybe."

"At least calm it down," Benjy mutters.

I snort. "Uh, no, it won't. Those women are out for my blood, and Benjy joining our team makes it a million times worse. Nothing you guys do will stop them; they perfected the art of stalking me until I was alone in high school. But… I can handle it. You need to trust me."

"Tíogair, we trust *you*," Lucky says carefully. "But we do *not* trust them. They might notice changes and… ignore the laws of the town if they think they can get away with it. You don't understand."

Oh, I very much do.

My adorable jokester is saying they'll corner me alone, figure out I know something, and use that as an excuse to unleash whatever they have on me. Since I know jack and shit about this place and what people here can do by design, I'll be unprepared and vulnerable. What he doesn't know is that I'll happily shoot every one of them right between the eyes before they can do enough damage to count. I have *zero* problem with that and I'll be contacting my guy for more of the smaller, illegal 3D printed weapons to carry.

"Tilly…"

I shake my head. "No, Teddy. I can bring the animals with me every-where and they'll do what is needed. But I can't let you guys stalk me around all the time or it will become obvious there's something to worry about. That makes people reckless and I'm not about to have some dipshit poison my fucking milkshake."

"Hazel would never allow——"

"Of course she wouldn't, Wolfie, but shit happens and people are very smart when they need to be. I've dealt with some really clever motherfuckers in my fixer days. You'd be surprised how intelligent a normal human can be when they have revenge on their mind. It's part of how Seer and I almost ended up in prison in Thailand."

"It's not fair that you won't tell us that story still," Doyle grumbles. "I guarantee I'd find it hysterical and sexy, but you're irritatingly tight-lipped about that jaunt."

"Seer has to be here *and* agree, it's time. I promised her no revealing our ridiculously dangerous improv without her present." My brows furrow and I pout a little. "I want her home. Having her this far away for so long without contact sucks."

"She has important work to do," Teddy says as we finally pull into my driveway. "You know that. Besides, I'm sure she'll come back not long after the Prince and MacAuley get here. Her assignment isn't supposed to be long term as far as I know."

The SUV stops and we all scramble out, stretching our limbs as we move to get the bags and the animals out of the back. We took one vehicle because no one felt safe in a multi-vehicle caravan. That probably should have clued me into how nervous the guys were about coming home, but I just enjoyed everyone squished together.

Euryale screeches from the sky as she swoops past, then heads around the house to her perch. I grin, knowing the dogs and cats will follow her to the backyard the second the trunk is open. Teddy springs it and I'm proved right as they barrel out, knocking things to the ground as they bound to the grassy open space happily.

"I could have told you that would happen," I tease, as I look at him with a fond smile. "They've been cooped up far too much this month."

"So have we, Tilly. But I promise we'll do our best not to smother you. Okay?" He tilts his head, holding his arms out.

I walk into them and squeeze him tight. "I'm going to hold you that, Mr. Speaker. Otherwise, you'll be a daisy if you do."

He laughs, recognizing my movie reference immediately. "You wound me, my love. I'm not daisy, despite you being absolutely as clever and self-sacrificing as your pick of anti-hero."

"Get me a cowboy hat and some chaps and we'll see about that," I reply as I sashay toward the house.

That should keep them all busy for a little while.

FROM NOW ON

BENJY

After we get our travel shit settled into the rooms upstairs, Jolene let each of us take a turn saying goodbye so we can retrieve our things from the Irishman's house and my apartment. I worry about my turn more than I feel comfortable telling them; my employees are loyal, but Sherilynn has pixie in her. She's not above using her powers to get what she wants out of people, despite the very specific laws around using magic to control others.

I didn't know that when I married, but I certainly found out quickly that she had no compunction about it.

"We're going to my place first, big man. I'd like to have the pup, the judge, and the doc's stuff loaded up and ready. I don't trust the people in this town and their grapevine as far as I can throw you," Haggerty says as he looks in the rearview at me.

I sigh and give him a grateful smile. "That's a good plan. I bet some people had eyes at the damn airport waiting for us to land. It's unlikely we've snuck back into town unnoticed." Biting my lip as I watch the scenery go by, I squint at Derby Pies and Bottles' N Cans. They're both open as they should be, but that doesn't mean my ex-wife is on premises at either. She's rarely where she should be and always where the drama is.

Teddy turns in the shotgun seat, looking at me seriously. "It'll be okay, B-man. We have plenty of secret weapons to use if Sherilynn calls her little coven into action. And all the animals are with our girl —which you may not know, but those damn cats will gut a mother-fucker for her. They came after *me* once."

That would have been pretty fun to watch.

"He's right, Benjy. Between the servals, dogs, snake, and eagle, she's got early alarms. Plus, our girl is a goddamn dead shot. She shocked the piss out of Prez and I when we first met her. Her basement is an *armory,* and she's not afraid to use it."

Remembering when she greeted us with a Desert Eagle, I chuckle. "Alright. You've convinced me. The girls might have magic, but Jolene won't be caught off-guard." I scratch my chin, pondering for a moment. "She went to take a shower. You think she's covered there?"

Presley snorts as he shakes his head. "I'd be surprised if there aren't spring loaded weapon hidey-holes everywhere in that house. She was very specific about her security system when it was installed."

We all consider Jolene sprinting through the house, unlocking guns and sliding around like a badass. It takes Doyle clearing his throat to bring us out of the reverie and I laugh. "Well, that's a fun roleplay idea. She'd make a hot as fuck assassin. Someone get on buying a catsuit?"

Wolfie flushes bright red. "Make sure it has tall boots and a choker. Be awfully hot, don't you think, Daddy?"

My oldest friend grins as he reaches out to ruffle the Fae's hair. "It would, baby."

Our live have taken such a turn in the past month that their play doesn't even faze me anymore—not that I was judging, mind. It was just different to see Edgar like that.

"Come to think of it, we should probably find Lucy some kind of sidekick outfit, don't you think?" Prez grins like he knows he's being naughty as he bobs his brows.

It amazes me how easily this family is sliding into a functional unit without an ounce of jealousy or pettiness. There's teasing and elbows to the ribs, but it's just so damn drama-free in terms of relationships.

I've never been around people who genuinely support one another like this. And I don't know if it's because they all had the capacity before or if our girl simply made it possible because of how much she cares about everyone.

"You look deep in thought," Doyle says as he looks at me in the mirror again. "Penny for them? Suggestions for the pup's outfit? Requests? I'm not partial to masks, but I'll make an exception if it floats your boat."

I blink. "Uh, no. No masks needed. Well, I suppose they could wear little eye covering superhero ones and it'd be hot, but not like… gimp shit. That gives me a shiver."

"Me, too," Prez agrees as he bumps my shoulder. "But I don't mind a secret superhero look… I'm just nerdy enough for that to do it for me. Point of fact, I could get behind Leia and Solo, too. Or maybe beautiful elves…"

Teddy groans. "Fuck, now we've entered geek out land. You realize that annoying friend of hers will have a whole fucking closet of costumes piled up if you tell her about this, right? I swear to shit, we'll have to build another extension to house the vault for it."

"Would more rooms be a bad thing?" Doyle tilts his head. "We have enough for the coming members, but maybe we could use another building with offices and playrooms and such."

"She'll kill you," Wolfie says in a forceful tone. "Don't you dare start arranging more buildings or extensions without talking to Jolene again. She'll wig out about us paying for things and get all weird. We should bring our stuff back and then discuss it like a family."

My lips curve up, and I nod. "The pup's right. We all agreed to be united when we got back here, and that means no unilateral decisions that cause cracks. Those will help all our enemies slither in to cause havoc."

Teddy grimaces as he turns to look at the driveway to Doyle's place. "And the last thing we need is any discord for people to exploit. I grew up here, and I honestly didn't realize how bad it is —probably because people are afraid of me and the Senator. But being with Tilly has opened my eyes to the rot at the roots in my hometown."

I saw it the night of the Catastrophe, but I was too chicken to do anything—not anymore, though.

ONCE THE REST OF THE GUYS LOAD UP THE STUFF THEY TOOK WHEN Princess gave them the boot, I lean back in my seat and blow out a breath. I texted Cerise and Evangeline that I'd be stopping by once I peeked at the schedule. I didn't get a response, but if they're getting the lunch time drinkers, it wouldn't be unusual. Hopefully, it's hopping in there and I don't have to answer too many curious questions about my absence.

It's not the first time I wished I could be invisible, but this time seems fairly important.

"You ready to face the music, man?" Teddy asks as he hops in the front seat again. He notes my worried expression and laughs. "Just kidding. I highly doubt your employees at BnC will join your ex in her angry bullshit. Maybe at Pies, but you split that to her in the settlement. You can't worry about these folks anymore, B."

"I know. But some kids are good people and I know how she treats people. I know the kind of manager she'll hire, so she doesn't have to interrupt her busy spa schedule. It won't go over well with the staff, but they may not have a lot of in town options—at least, not the human kids who are clueless."

He hums under his breath, looking thoughtful. "Well, we'll have to figure something out to help. Maybe I can talk to Percy and Jamie. Those places have lots of staff and might finagle something if your soul sucking ex goes on a rampage."

"Thank fuck," I sigh gratefully. "That worried me because, with Reese, Jillian, Amy, and Ophelia behind her, Sherilynn will spread her bile around. The humans who work alongside us will take the brunt, I fear. She'll equate it with the weakling she thinks our Princess is supposed to be."

Presley pops into the backseat next to me, scooting to the middle to leave room for the other doc. "If she does, we'll deal with it together. We've got a judge, the town doctors, and the liquor supplier. I think put together we can find a pretty compelling fix via cutting off the booze flow for… *reasons*."

Teddy winces, chuckling as Wolfie and Doyle get in. "Ouch, Doc. That will definitely get their backs up. It might even stop the girls' campaign of terror in its tracks. How are we all supposed to watch the NCAA and high school hoops without bourbon?"

"Exactly," the bespectacled caladrius says. "Sherilynn can play hardball, but we can, too. Atwater's doesn't have a liquor license and there's nowhere else that will let them carouse during games like your place."

"You realize I'm not as… well off as you guys after the divorce, right?" I ask, arching my brow. "Basketball season is very kind to our coffers."

That gets a snort from the Irishman as he finally starts pulling out of his driveway. "You don't have to worry about it. We're all family now and that means we have joint financial support. As old as I am, I'd likely to yeet myself into a bloody volcano if I wasn't obscenely well off and able to help people."

Wolfie grabs my arm. "Did he just admit he's a billionaire? Sugarplum will *not* like that at all."

"For fuck's sake, pup, I help more down their luck people a year than most people do in a lifetime. Trust me… my need for chaos is often slaked by bringing fortune to those who need it and misfortune to those who deserve it." He grins smugly and I shake my head.

Only Doyle would assume that's enough.

"I may have made a wee error in that regard about twenty-seven years ago," the demigod continues. "I thought I was rising a downtrodden, homeless British chit with a dream and I'll be buggered if that hasn't turned out to be a fucking nightmare now. Makes me wish we could mess with time—I'd tweak a few things, but alas, the flow of time has to continue forward, not backward."

I lean over to whisper in Presley's ear. "Did he just admit to helping…?"

He laughs and nods. "I think he did. I'll be damned, Haggerty. That was a chaotic mistake. You couldn't have seen it coming, man."

As we pull into the lot behind my store, he growls, "The three ladies did, and I had to trade them one of my loveliest Degas in payment. The middle hag said she felt a weird vibe, and I was too drunk on that stupid mead/ambrosia small batch shit they'd won off my uncle in a poker tourney in the underworld. Regardless, I'm too distracted by our current issues to bother with trying to fix my mess. Someone else can step in; most of them barely do a damn thing, anyway."

We all exit the car on that note, and I watch my best friend as he wraps his arm around the vet. He's grown into a much more mature and caring person since Princess came back to town. Hell, I suppose I have, too. Now we need to pay her back by keeping her from suffering the same fate she did her first round in the Hollow without breaking any rules. It shouldn't be hard, but with a stalker and a murder cover-up on the table, I don't know if we can manage it.

"Oi, Benjy! Come unlock the door before we all freeze our asses off," Doyle grumbles. "I want to be in and out of here in less than a half hour. Anything else you want, we'll make a separate trip for. I'd like to make sure we all get home in time to chat with Tíogair and relax until bedtime."

"That's a really odd way to phrase fuck her until she can't walk…"

Presley smacks Edgar on the shoulder, shaking his head. "Focus, Coach. We have a mission; lead us through it so we get home to our girl."

"Fine, move your ass, Foster. We're on deadline."

Sir, yes, sir.

Just My Luck

Jolene

Once I dumped my bags in the living room, I head straight for the kitchen to fix myself a 'welcome home' milkshake and sort through the mail in the basket. Gene and Niccy did a fantastic job of making sure everything was ready for me once again and I make a note to give them a bump in their quarterly bonus. Not coming home to an empty fridge and a mess is absolutely worth an extra bit, especially since the guys will move back in tonight and over the next few days.

My space won't feel desolate again, and that is surprisingly comforting.

Shaking my head, I pull a big glass out of the cabinet and gather my ingredients. Once I've got the mango dragon fruit vanilla bean concoction going, I flip through the mail. The stack of junk grows as I blend out the lumps, but one envelope stops me in my tracks. The return address is Lakewood House Recovery Center and for a moment, I think it's for Wolfie. But it's not—the name on the envelope is mine, written in a small, spidery script.

"Holy fuck," I whisper. The only person we know in Lakewood is Aurelia Fletcher. Obviously, I never met the woman personally, which is why I find this even more odd. Wolfie's description of her current state wasn't what I would call optimistic. Receiving correspondence from someone who can accurately be described as 'off her rocker' wasn't on my bingo card this month.

I'll have to wait to open it until the guys get back. There's no way this is a coincidence.

My thoughts drift back to his dark Fae father, frowning as I consider the possibilities. If Callie and the mystery Fae dropped Wolfie off at an orphanage and he was sent here, being adopted by Aurelia and his full Fae dad was pretty lucky. There had to be more than Fate involved in that decision. It seems like they'd have to have some kind of… testing? Maybe something that would tell whoever works at these places where to send the kids and who to allow to adopt them? Can they actually tell or do they just… get a sense and hope for the best?

"I need actual information, not guesses. No one can tell me because of some stupid rules and I'm flailing around, hoping not to fuck up. This is bullshit of the highest order." My blender stops and I walk over to pour my deliciously fragrant shake into the glass. Sipping slowly, I savor the quirky comfort drink while I think about the possibilities.

If I have these powers, it means I was ditched somewhere, too. That explains the dream flashbacks where my mom was complaining about a raw deal.

Sighing, I sort the rest of the mail, leaving the letter from Lakewood in the middle of the counter. As I head to the living room to brood, I open the back door and let the animals in. Eurayle comes screeching in first, tearing around like she's starring in a crazy horror flick.

"What the fuck is going on?" I ask the cats as they trot in with Teddy's dogs. None of them seem quiet right, and I frown. I do not like this one bit. Animals are the most sensitive to weird shit and ones that live in the Hollow should have a pretty high freakout threshold. "Why are you guys being weird?"

"Mow!" Jekyll grumbles as he jumps on the couch. Hyde follows him, her eyes darting around in suspicion.

Okay, seriously, what the fuck?

Frowning as I suck on the straw, I look around the room, but I see nothing. Isis tightens around my ribcage, then lets go. I know it's her signal to be wary, so I walk into the living room slowly, placing my drink on an end table. There's something wrong here and the animals sense it. Eurayle is particularly bothered, but the others seem less concerned. They're annoyed; I can tell that by the furiously swishing tails on my servals. The Danes are sitting at attention, their ears up as they take in the scene.

"Okay, whatever you are…" I say as I reach behind me to click the hidden compartment on the buffet table I'm standing in front of carefully. "…we're not big on uninvited guests in the South. It's rude and being invisible makes it that much worse. Show yourself before I'm forced to show you how we handle visitors who have overstayed their welcome."

Silence.

I take a slow, measured breath in as the compartment on my furniture slides open without making a sound. My fingers curl around the compact .38, lifting it up so I have a good grip on the barrel. When there's still no answer, I whip my arm around, dropping into a balanced stance with both hands. "I guarantee your day won't improve with an injection of iron, buddy. And I *will* shoot you; don't assume I'm bluffing. *Where* I'll hit you is the only question right now."

Not a word.

Hyde hops on the back of the couch, her eyes meeting mine as she walks pointedly to the right. I assume she's trying to redirect my aim, so I spin to that side with the gun aimed at the empty space in the hall. "Seriously. I don't know who or what you are, but I'm not even supposed to *know* you can actually be invisible. If people get home and find out I know before it's time, it will be a shitshow. Show yourself so I don't have to shoot my goddamn house."

Growling in frustration, I fire a warning shot at the ugliest vase in North America. I figure it's a fitting casualty in this war of quiet rebellion. My mother loved it and I've never liked it. Despite wanting to solve my parents' murder, I'm conflicted about the secrets they kept. Shooting the damn thing is a win-win all around.

"Did you see that? I assure you; I didn't miss. I'm close enough to be deadly accurate with this baby gun. Time to show yourself, dickhead."

Still nothing.

I make a furious face, firing another shot into the ugly heavy crown molding. Maybe this damn see-through invader isn't so bad—I'll definitely have to remodel after this uncharacteristic tantrum. I blame it on the time change and my fucking head being full of stupid secrets because I'm never this cavalier about weaponry.

I'm also scared that it's someone with powers I don't know exist who can fuck me up with very little effort.

A low growl echoes from behind me and two more join in. Eury swoops past me, landing on the upper bannister with her enormous bulk, and I wince. Fuck, I hope she doesn't break the damn railing. Her eyes are focused like lasers on the small table by the door where I keep bits and bobs I might need as I leave. There's nothing there, but she looks like she wants to murder the damn thing.

"One last chance, motherfucker. If you don't… uncloak… or whatever… I'm gonna let the bird have you after I put a cap in your ass. On the count of three, I'm firing again. One… two… thr——" My jaw drops and all the air is sucked out of my throat, rendering me unable to do anything but make a Shemp noise.

Shimmering into being before my eyes is a small, golden monkey with dangerously intelligent eyes. It tilts its head at me and I swear to Hippolyta's belt, it's *smirking* at me. With a swish of its oddly fluffy tail, the monkey waves its hand, and the gun disappears from my hands.

"Hey! I don't know who the fuck you are, but no one takes a Southern girl's weapon," I yell as I fumble for the knife tucked in the back of my pants. Huffing with relief when I feel it, I flick it open as I tense in place. The blade is pointed at the goddamn simian intruder as I look around wildly, hoping this isn't a precursor to something much bigger and angrier. "You're a rude little shit and I hate hurting animals, so if you make me fucking stab you, I'm going to be so fucking angry…"

A soft chitter that sounds a lot like laughter comes from the damn thing and it rises to stand almost bi-pedal as it looks at me with its bushy old Zen master whiskers. Waving its hand again, a flower appears, and the creature holds it out to me.

I blink, trying to comprehend what I'm seeing. *It's a magnolia; I've always loved magnolia and jasmine.* As I continue to hold the big knife out defensively, Hyde saunters over to the table, going up on her back paws to get closer. The monkey sort of raises an eyebrow——I think——

and waits as my cat sniffs it thoroughly. When she finishes, Hyde turns to look at me with big eyes.

"Mow…"

I guess that means this little shit is safe.

Suddenly, a thought occurs to me, and I groan. "Oh…. no. No, no, no. Don't tell me."

Eury lets out an annoyed screech as she glares at the mischievous intruder and I roll my head back on my shoulders, looking up at the ceiling pleadingly. When I don't wake up and an enormous banner with 'Just Kidding' doesn't drop from the sky, I make a strangled sound of frustration.

This isn't just any monkey—this is my *goddamn monkey.*

"Am I not doing something right? Have I offended some tight-assed relative of Lucky's? *Why* do I own a monkey now?!"

As has been the theme tonight, silence falls over the room as I stomp over to the buffet. I pretend I don't have to explain a god's blessed jungle creature to the men who are likely on their way back now as I pick up the gun. Checking it and rendering it safe without even looking, I stow it back in the secret pop out hatch then slide it closed. Not only do I have to reconcile a furry asswipe, they'll want to know about the bullet holes and the broken vase.

My life is an enormous cosmic punchline, I swear to Bobbi Jo's Lilly collection.

"What do you eat, dude?" I ask the golden newcomer. It chitters and takes off toward the kitchen like a streak. "Fuck, that asshole is fast. I wonder if that's normal or if it's magic?" The other animals just give me a disgruntled expression and I throw my hands up. "It's clearly here to stay; what do you want from me?"

Of course, they can't answer anymore than the monkey can, so I'm the only nutter talking to herself.

"Great. I enjoy being on my own and spend a decade doing it and after three months in the damn town, I have two cats, two dogs, an eagle, a python, a monkey, and seven men in a fucking pear tree. This is getting ridiculous."

I Wanna Be Like

Wolfgang

Sugarplum: Holy shit. Holy shit.

Doctor Asshole: What's wrong, Magpie?

Lucky Asshole: Did your friends forget milkshake fixings?

Cute Asshole: Tell us, sugarplum.

Big Daddy Asshole: What. Is. Going. On.

Sugarplum: I cannot believe this.

Lucky Asshole: Did your eagle kill a gopher again? I believe that.

Cute Asshole: Of course you do. They eat them, dummy.

Sweet Asshole: Guys, don't tease her…

Big Daddy Asshole: I don't like waiting, Tilly.

Sugarplum: There's a fucking monkey in my house.

Cute Asshole: *blink*

Lucky Asshole: No, he's with us.

Doctor Asshole: Shut it, Haggerty.

Big Daddy Asshole: Who changed my name again?

Sweet Asshole: I think she's serious.

Sugarplum: I am serious, you nitwits!

Cute Asshole: An actual monkey? Or it is an ape?

Sugarplum: It's got a goddamn tail.

Cute Asshole: Okay, definitely a monkey.

Sugarplum: Thanks, Dr. Doolittle.

Lucky Asshole: Where did it come from?

Sugarplum: Just south of your ass; Jesus, Doyle, I don't know. That's the point.

Lucky Asshole: Touchy, touchy.

Big Daddy Asshole: It just appeared, Tilly? Like the cats?

Doctor Asshole: And your snake? Who maybe you should…

Sugarplum: Oh, shit. Just get back here now. Gotta run.

I blink at the screen, turning to look at the others in surprise. Teddy just shakes his head, grabbing a few duffels of the big guy's stuff to sling over his broad shoulders. Doyle can't stop snickering and Benjy looks at us in surprise.

"So her cats… weren't her cats until they showed up out of nowhere?" he says as he scratches his head.

"Yep," Prez confirms as he continues loading a box. "After she met you at the diner, right, Lucy?"

Nodding, I shake myself out of the stupor and help my mates. "I think so. She brought them on our first date so I could check them out."

"And Boone's dogs took to her right away, too, yeah?" Benjy asks.

"They stick to Tilly like peanut butter to jelly," the judge says as he piles a few more bags on. "Have since the first time they saw her."

"The eagle?"

Prez grins, his face looking smug as he adjusts his glasses. "Showed up right before Lucy brought me over the first time."

"Uh-huh. Isis?"

Doyle snorts. "Fell out of the ceiling in the Hollar office when the mad women went after her. I was nearby, and these idiots let her leave your place alone while they talked about sports."

I pause my packing, the train of thought Benjy's following becoming crystal clear. "You think the animals are tied to her mates somehow? Personalities or whatever. They show up as she finds or accepts them."

He shrugs, looking unsure. "It's only a theory, man."

"But it fits," Teddy says as he scratches his jaw. "They're all exotic and obviously not from around here, except for my girls. She couldn't mistake them for strays, and the timing is spot on. Plus, they seem to guard her. No, you may be onto something, Foster."

Frowning, I think about it and then snap my fingers. "Mehdi. She showed up with instructions for only Sugarplum to train her right before Dhameer did."

Presley wrinkles his nose. "Then what the fuck is coming for MacAuley? I assume we're missing one, still, right?"

"Zeus on a scooter," Edgar mutters as he heads for the door. "We're going to have our own goddamn zoo soon."

"We have to get over there and figure out what kind of monkey this is," I reply as I lift the stuff I was working on. "Because we know the animals tied to her seem... special. They can definitely understand her, which is weird, but also that the snake disappears. Each new one seems to have more... unusual traits."

"Great. What the hell could this blasted simian do?" Doyle grumbles as he finishes and grabs his pile.

We all look at each other, but no one answers.

I guess we'll find out soon enough.

WHEN WE ARRIVE AT SUGARPLUM'S HOUSE, THERE'S A GIGANTIC crash we can hear through the open windows. Boone throws the car in park and we tumble out, leaving the boxes and shit where they are as we rush up to the front door in one big pack of panic. I step inside first, hoping to help her calm the animal before the more predatory shifters scare the hell out of it.

"Sugarplum, what—" I stop talking as I realize the crash wasn't caused by some wild, out-of-control monkey.

No, it was caused by our girl throwing blueberries at a crowd of excited cats, dogs, a giant bird, and a small monkey and laughing when they crash into one another, trying to get to them first. She's rolling with giggles as the monkey zips past Hyde by swinging from the fancy light fixture, then runs flat into the King Dane glaring at it. There's berry juice and knocked over shit everywhere, but her face is full of delight as she pitches another berry and they all clamor across the wooden floor of the foyer.

One thing I adore about Jolene is that she doesn't take herself too seriously, and this is one example.

Teddy growls, moving me out of the way by lifting me up and setting me aside, then stops as suddenly as I did. "Tilly, what in the world is this?"

Sugarplum looks up, wiping the tears off her cheeks as she beams at us. "You're back! Excellent." Whistling loud enough to make *all* of us wince, Jolene wipes her hands on her yoga pants and stands. "Hey Genghis, get back here and meet the guys."

I watch as the mustachioed monkey seems to poof in and out while he travels across the room to land in our girl's lap. She must not have seen the magical bullshit we did because of the binding, but I sure as hell did. My gaze flicks to the others, who grimace, and then I walk over to examine the little guy. "Genghis, huh?"

She gives me a look as if I'm dense. "You see that bad ass 'stache, right? I mean, it's epic, even for a monkey."

Chuckling, I nod as I look at the obviously magical being over carefully. "It *looks* like an emperor tamarin."

"Looks? Why say it like that, darling boy?"

Because I'm pretty sure the damn thing is a signifier of Eleuggua, which means it's going to be as much trouble as Doyle.

"Because I need to be sure, Sugarplum. We should take him to the office tomorrow and I'll check him out properly," I reply with a forced grin.

Presley, Doyle, and Benjy elbow their way in, jaws dropping when they see the mess that was once the living room. Doyle smirks, taking it all in, and I know he's proud of our mate for indulging in the moment's mischief. Benjy, however, swipes his big hand over his face and groans. Falling in between them, my handsome doc just smiles and shakes his head.

"This is a mess," Teddy says with a dark look. "Why would—"

I lay my hand on his arm, looking up at his thunderous expression. "She was having fun with her new friend. I think that's worth a little grace, mm?"

He blinks, tilting his head as he watches Jolene playing with the damn monkey in her lap. Finally, he sighs, rolling his eyes up to the ceiling. "*Fine.* But we have to get it cleaned up so we can move the stuff in."

"I'll help," Sugarplum says brightly as she rises with the new pet on her shoulder. "Genghis can stay with Jekyll, Hyde, and the others."

Doyle busts through the crowd, saving us from having to explain how we shoved everything into a car far smaller than the amount of shit we brought back. He knows the answer is his bullshit Mary Poppins magic, so we can't let Jolene go outside to help. "How about you and I work on the mess while they do the heavy lifting? I bet we can even call for a massive amount of takeout for us to eat afterward, then feed the bestiary in the backyard."

Sugarplum beams as he approaches her and holds his arm out for the new simian. It takes one look at the demi-god and sniffs, clutching at her hair as it snubs him. "Genghis, that's rude."

Odds are it's going to attach to Benjy, given we think it's because of her acceptance of him, but she doesn't know that.

"No worries, Tíogair. Your other beasties like me well enough. It's okay if the little shit isn't fond of me yet." He holds his arm out for her. "Shall we go order the food, then come back in here to clean up?"

"We shall," Jolene says with a grin.

Waiting until they're out of sight, I move closer to Prez, Benjy, and Teddy. With a quick mutter, I cast a silencing enchantment before I whisper, "That thing is definitely not just a pet, nor is it just a familiar. It's a mythical creature in its own right—I think."

"What the hell, man?" Benjy says, and I sigh.

"I think it's a signifying monkey and they're like… messengers. It probably showed up because of you, but also to remind us that something is coming. I don't know if that's just the other two mates or if it is all the shit from my realm."

The tall football coach that loves to cuddle rakes his hand through his hair as a growl rumbles out of his chest. "Not just the trouble in your realm, pup, but the shit here, too. We know there's something big rumbling about because of all the memorandums from the Society. Shit's going down all over the country and the globe. One by one, it wouldn't mean shit, but…"

"Put together it's concerning, right?" Prez says. "I noticed that, too. Crap in the city, in Salem, in Tenerife, in Europe, in Argentina, in Bay City… There's a lot of weird stuff happening to Guardians. Do you think it's tied to our girl and her family?"

Teddy shrugs. "I don't know. Neither Eloise nor Andrew were Guardians. Eloise was a recruiter, and he was human. But the Irish bestie and her crew keep getting re-routed and there's fucking odd things happening in too many places at once, don't you think?"

"Especially when it's crossing the Veil to Faerie," I mutter. "That's really goddamn odd. Normally, shit from here doesn't even cause a ripple over there."

"Should we interrogate your mother again?"

I give my sexy Dom a look like he's lost his faculties. "*Hell* no. We are *not* inviting Callie anywhere *near* our home."

Benjy gives me a sympathetic look before he says, "She's not a vampire, man. She could come whenever she wanted, anyway."

No shit, Sherlock.

"I know. That's how we met. I just… I'm trying not to let her get a claw-hold on me again. She's not good for me."

Prez tugs me into his arms, sitting his chin on my head. "That's true, Lucy, but if we end up needing to call her, are you going to be okay?"

"Yes," I mumble into his chest.

"Guys…"

We look over at Teddy as he holds up an envelope that was on the buffet table. He passes it to Prez and when I see the address, my eyes fly wide and I step back in shock.

That's Aurelia's facility—what is my mom doing sending mail to Jolene?

"Speaking of mysteries and mothers," my lover murmurs as we hand it to Benjy next. "How did Aurelia stay lucid long enough to send anything and then how did it get past the mail embargo there?"

I shake my head because I don't know. The last time I visited her, my foster mom could barely string a sentence together like that dark-haired vampiress in the TV show. "I have no idea."

"We need to find out quickly," Teddy says, his face a mask of concern. "But we won't know how serious it is until Tilly opens it."

How are we going to get her to do that without getting suspicious?

Fear

Jolene

My hands actually tremble a bit as I sit on the couch surrounded by men and animals, staring at the envelope. I'm not scared of what's inside, other than its ability to hurt the Fae curled between Teddy and me. Prez is sitting in front of us, his head leaning against Wolfie's knees as he looks up, and Doyle is next to him. Benjy is on my other side, reluctantly letting my new simian friend perch on his shoulder.

Hyde rubs her face against mine, then against Wolfie's head as she and Jekyll lounge on the top of the couch behind us. "Mrrp."

I chuckle softly, noting the attentive pose of all the companion animals. "I guess everyone is as nervous about this as I am."

Teddy arches a dark brow, his expression gentle as his fingers comb through our darling boy's hair. "No one wants to see the pup hurt. Difficult parent shit is hard, especially if you have to open old wounds."

Exactly the reason only Doyle knows what happened in the goddamn cave with Wolfie's dad.

"Just rip it open like taking off a Band-Aid, Sugarplum. You can't let my issues keep us from finding out what we need to know," the vet says softly. "Aurelia has been there since I was a teenager. I've had time to come to terms with it."

Blowing out a long breath, I nod and put my fingernail under the flap. If I were still in Richmond, we'd be handling this shit with tweezers and gloves, but now I live in a world of magic and Faeries. It doesn't seem to matter if the envelope has prints or DNA on it; that will probably lead nowhere if the sender can fucking spell the damned thing.

Fuck, my life has taken a hard left into Crazytown.

"Okay, here we go," I say, hoping my voice projects more confidence than I feel.

The paper is basic parchment, nothing fancy, but I sense there's power humming in it. My eyes cut to Lucky and he nods slightly; he can feel it, too. Unfortunately, I have no idea what the hell to do with that knowledge and he definitely can't tell me with everyone else so damn close. I'll just have to wing it and hope for the best.

Unfolding the letter, I frown as my eyes take in the spidery writing, littered with symbols and drawings that make no sense. It looks like the ranting of a woman who has been in an asylum for a psychotic break for ten years, for sure. Wolfie sighs and Teddy grunts as he presses the Fae tighter between us. There's a light tremble in my boy's body and it makes my heart ache as I sift through the pages, seeing more of the same.

"It's a dead end," Presley whispers. "That's all some odd code or language she's made up in her head. It's not uncommon, but I don't know how or why she would send it to you."

My gut is screaming that he's wrong, but I can't say that out loud. I'm bound to keep my new knowledge of the supernatural to myself until the binding is fully broken or they'll be punished. But whatever power I have inside of me is literally humming with anticipation as I scan the sheets. There's something here and there's *definitely* a reason it came to me—I just don't know how to unlock it.

"The doc's probably right," Teddy says with a frustrated sigh. "Maybe some nurse or orderly from here was gossiping. If Aurelia heard it, she could have been lucid enough to get someone to help her send a letter. That would explain it."

Nope. That's not it. I don't know why or how I know, but that's not all of it.

I close my eyes, trying to find the parts of me that respond to all the weird events that have been happening since I came back. Breathing slowly, I find the palace in my mind my therapist had me create years ago. Inside, there are many doors leading to memories, information I need to remember, and emotions I have and have not dealt with. Everything is labeled, just like my boards in the basement, and I take stock of what has changed in the past few months. The landscape looks like an enormous library—my escape when the problems of Whistler's Hollow got bad as a teen—and the sections are different aspects of my life. It's gotten bigger, almost unrealistically so, and I imagine myself standing in the space.

"Help me find what I need," I murmur to myself.

"Tilly—"

I hold up my hand, not opening my eyes as I focus on the mind palace. There's a blur like the rapid turning of pages flittering through my vision, and I wait. Finally, a spark of light appears and, like a good girl, I follow it through the tall shelves and immense space. I don't know what I'm doing, truthfully, but my gut tells me it's necessary if I want to figure out what the hell Aurelia sent me. The spark stops briefly at a corner where Jekyll appears, then Hyde. Once they join us, it keeps moving until I've gathered all the animals, even the monkey who perches on my shoulder.

Guess I know why the damn animals keep appearing for sure now—and that I should expect another at some point.

When we've picked up all the pieces, I'm left standing in the middle of the space in front of an immense stone wall with an ancient Greek looking carving. I'm not familiar with it, but it almost looks like a damn logo. The female head is adorned with some sort of decoration and surrounded by a snake eating its tail... I think the Greeks called it an Ouroboros. I have no idea why the hell that would be in my palace, nor why I'm standing in front of it with my companions, like I'm waiting for it to talk to me.

"What the hell does it mean?" I mutter as I stare at the relief on the wall in frustration.

I'm so deep inside of my mind I don't hear exactly what the guys are saying, just hushed murmurs and hands touching me. But I can't pull myself out until I follow this thread to its end, so I let that go in favor of immersing myself even further into the construct in my head. Once I sink into it far enough to be completely oblivious to anything else, the room fills with a power so huge it terrifies me. The energy dances over my skin, zapping me occasionally as colors and sound dance around like a scene in a fantasy cartoon.

My inner self closes her eyes as well, opening up to everything, hoping it will direct me. The scent of sulfur and brimstone assault me first, flaying me with the heat of fire. When it fades, I don't have time to process that before the rich smells of the ocean and dragon's blood press into me. The combination is heady, but it morphs to musk and patchouli that tingle through me. Normally, I'd be worried that I'm getting far too much for me to handle—like in a fucking Bath & Bodyworks—but each time a new scent appears, the old one feels like it's embedding itself into me. So when vetiver and cloves swirl through the air, I inhale it deeply and sigh when it infiltrates my senses. The last pairs bring peach and bergamot, then sage and hemlock, and finally, cedar and myrrh.

As the whirlwind of smells dies down, I open my eyes inside my head to see the carving glowing brightly. I lick my lips, approaching it carefully as my body thrums with all the input coming from this place. When my hand touches the stone, the glow gets blinding, and I gasp as I shield myself from what feels like an explosion within.

"Oh, fuck, what's happening to her?" *Benjy.*

"Lay her down; it looks like a seizure." *Presley.*

"Sugarplum, come back to us, please…" *Wolfie.*

"Do something, Hamilton!" *Teddy.*

"Just chill out, ya ninnies." *Doyle.*

As their voices penetrate the haze of my meditation, reality seeps back in, and I find myself sprawled on the floor, surrounded by faces looking down at me from men to furry and feathered. It almost makes me jump, but my muscles are locked in place and aching. Blinking, I force my heart rate to lower by breathing slowly and unclenching my jaw. I take a few minutes to regain control of my faculties, but once I do, I can *feel* the relief in the room.

Shit, that's new.

"Tilly, can you talk?" My dominant alphahole's voice is filled with strain and I know he's having trouble keeping himself calm for the others.

"Yes," I croak. "But not much."

Presley leans in, putting a cool cloth on my forehead as he shines a light in my eyes. I know he's checking me out like a doctor—and not in a fun way—but it's a bit much after the light bomb in my head. I cringe and growls fill the air, telling me the others are angry. To his credit, Doc McNuggies just rolls his eyes at them and continues his gentle exam.

"I need to make certain she doesn't need a healer, or worse, a hospital," the easygoing doctor says absently. "Don't be stupid."

That only earns him irritated huffs, but at least the snarly shit stops. I swallow, my throat dry as I clear it. "Water?"

Wolfie's up and gone like the damn Flash and it gets a chuckle out of Presley. Even Teddy cracks a smile as he runs his hand through his raven hair. "He'd fight a goddamn tank for you, *drugar*."

"Please, Boone. We all would, and you know it. Give us a smile, Tíogair. He will not back off until he can verify that you will not die."

Flicking my gaze to Doyle, I try hard to convey that something important just happened, but by the smirk on his face, I think he already knows. I have no clue what the hell it is, mind, but I'm not stupid enough to dismiss what seemed to be magic and meditation fusing inside me. "I'd love to sit up and look at the letter again."

Benjy shakes his head, looking unsurprised. "Princess, you're ridiculous."

I think I narrow my eyes at him, waiting for the rest of them to get their shit in gear and help me up. "I'm not… joking."

Staring at them mutinously, I wait for someone to move. Teddy throws up his hands as Doyle finally gives in and helps me sit up. They maneuver me to lean against the couch, each one positioned where they can touch me and I sigh in relief. I needed to be in a position where the world wasn't off-kilter. Wolfie comes back with a glass of water on the rocks with a straw and three fingers of bourbon in the other hand. The corner of my lips curls up as I accept them both carefully.

You know you're in the South when you ask for water and it's assumed that it's supposed to be next to your Booker's.

After I take a sip of each, I hand the glasses to Wolfie and gesture to the guys. "Give me the letter, please. I need to look at them again."

They all look at one another and I almost roll my eyes. I know they're trying to speak with their eyebrows—as dudes do—but if they were this obvious before I had the curtain lifted, I'd be a little ashamed of myself. They are *not* good at group subterfuge in the slightest.

"Fine, but I doubt having a seizure is going to allow you to speak some pidgin language made up by someone in a dissociative state," Presley says carefully. "This is pretty common for people in Aurelia's condition and—"

"Just give it to me, please," I say firmly. "I want to look at it."

Teddy hands me the sheets and I take a deep breath, hoping the universe sent me tripping through the coolest library of all time for a reason.

Here we go…

Waiting on the World to Change

PRESLEY

I'm not thrilled with Magpie insisting she immediately be allowed to return to normal activity, but Jolene is nothing if not in charge of herself. For better or worse, she's determined to make her own decisions and we have to respect that.

I'm still not happy with this; I think she accessed magic, and it blew her off the map because there are two more bonds left.

Regardless of my opinion, the raven haired woman who captured all our hearts is sitting between Wolfie and me, clearing her throat. The water and bourbon helped, but she's a little husky as she reads out loud.

"Dearest Jolene,

For many years, I have kept my silence on the matters that affect Whistler's Hollow in the gravest manner possible.

Those involved are beyond the reach of a star my size, and my mind has been forfeited in exchange for the privdege of knowing.

I did not consent to that outcome; the shadows were

dark, and they took without mercy or permission. What was once a simple check, a balance, a preventative measure grew to proportions that no one understood.

The prophecies were not clear—not from the beginning or to the end of stars in your sky, nor long past that day to now. It's a silken web of lies woven by the one who thrives upon the ancient injury they cannot bury with the bones of their dead.

As time moves, whispers come to me and hear things that have passed or will come. I cannot say which is real and which is planted to make me believe the eventual demise of our world has been averted.

I know that time continues to flow whether we want it to or not, and this, much like the River Styx, cannot be dammed. Some levers have been and will be pulled to divert the rush until the moment is right, but I am not cognizant enough to figure out who is doing that or why.

My access to your world is so limited—visits from my one true love and the best thing I ever did, even less than that, is all I know outside of the call of the winds. I try to negotiate with the trees and flowers, but they are not inclined to give me much information.

You need to gather them all, and once you have, the twists and turns will lead to the next phase. I am bound by powerful knots and cannot reveal to you the truth I know, nor enough to help you get further with your own tree. However, you might find answers in the land of Nod should you care to explore.

It is so very difficult for me to focus on communicating to you when the words have been stolen and my vision is so fuzzy. You deserve to have peace as much as I do, yet those who are older than the clocks keep that from us like misers.

Use the blocks and build the wall. You must protect the Princess, my dear, or we will all suffer in the end.

Let them help and when the moment arrives, accept the tale you are told and continue.

It all lies within.

Regards,

Aurelia Fletcher"

Wolfie swallows hard and turns to bury his face in Boone's shoulder. It's so hard for him to reconcile Aurelia's broken mind. I don't blame him; he grew up watching her descend into madness like a slow drip. He believes if he'd been stronger or more powerful, he could have saved her. But I've never believed that and this letter confirms it for me.

Yes, it's made-up of incoherent riddles and metaphors, but there's substance underneath.

"Lucy, your mother clearly did *not* just go crazy on her own," I whisper as Jolene stares at the letter intently. "These are the words of a woman fighting to get reality back."

"That's what happens sometimes with her disease, Prez," Wolfie mumbles. "The doctors tell me that all the time. She goes in and out of clarity constantly."

"Pup, maybe the doc is right. If she was clear enough to ask for paper, write this out, and find someone to post it… maybe she's in there fighting when it's necessary." Boone smiles gently, rubbing his big hand over our boy's hair, then looks at our girl. "And she sent this to you to help, so we need to decipher it."

"How does she even know me?" Magpie says as she bites her lower lip. "I was out of here long before Aurelia's trouble got bad."

"Could she have known your parents, Princess?" Benjy's question is good and I flash him a grin of approval.

"That sounds like a promising trail to follow." I take the letter from her carefully, folding it up. "But one we have to follow tomorrow. We have things to put away and we need rest. While Benjy, Wolfie, and I can fob off work if we choose, Teddy and Magpie have school in the morning."

"Stupid trip taking longer than expected," Jolene mutters petulantly.

Doyle snorts, his face alight with mischief. "I notice you didn't mention me, and I assume that's because Nelia allows me a great deal of latitude with my work, eh?"

"I said it because you do whatever you want regardless of what anyone else wants, Haggerty. If you want to skulk around town following leads in the morning, you will. The Mayor will have to do without you as far you're concerned. It's a nice gig if you can swing it."

His grin only gets wider. "I am appropriately rewarded based on my valuable contributions, Hamilton. Never forget that."

Jolene slaps her thighs, a sure-fire Southern sign that she's going to end this shit. "Your bickering is adorable, boys, but Presley had a point. We really need to get this shit unpacked and get some food before we crash."

"Watch us fly through this, *drugar*," Teddy rumbles as he looks around at our gang. "Get shit put away, put in the laundry, whatever… and get it done in thirty minutes. Now, break, gentleman!"

Fuck if we don't all leap into action—Coach Teddy saves the day.

THE MORNING COMES FASTER THAN I WOULD HAVE PREFERRED, BUT when I put my glasses on, everyone is out of bed. Delicious smells fill the air and I grin broadly—Lucy is already settling into our home. I roll up to my feet and ruffle my hair as I pad to the bathroom. My first appointment isn't until ten, but the clock said six forty-five.

Not surprising, given the Coach and our girl have to be at school before seven.

"Guess I'll have time to do some laundry before I head over," I mumble.

After I brush my teeth and get cleaned up, I head downstairs to greet the early birds. They're all sitting on stools at the counter while Lucy cooks at Jolene's stove. Magpie smiles, leaning in as I peck her cheek on my way to my seat. Boone grunts, Doyle smirks, and the big guy holds his fist out for a bump.

"Morning sunshines."

Jolene groans into her coffee and Edgar chuckles as he gooses her lightly. "Stop it, Big D. The time change shit is my Kryptonite. No matter how many times I moved from place to place, I've never gotten right with it."

Wolfie keeps him from retorting by placing a stacked plate of food in front of him. "She's right, Daddy. You guys have a long day today. The calendar on the wall says there's a staff meeting afterwards."

The Coach pushes up with his arms, leaning over to counter to claim a kiss and even I'm impressed. Lucy and I are in great shape, but he and Benjy are fucking stacked as shit. Maybe we should let them train us? Shaking my head, I watch my boy flush with pleasure, then go back to retrieve the plates for the rest of us.

You'd think it would chafe that Magpie and Boone get theirs first, but it doesn't— not even Doyle is complaining.

"These pancakes are delicious," our girl says with a groan. "I've never had them with white chocolate chips and strawberries before. This might be my new favorite."

When Lucy hands me my plate, I kiss him, too, then I'm surprised when Haggerty gives us all a cheeky grin and does the same. "What the hell" I ask around my first bite.

He shrugs, looking pleased with himself as he plops down again. "I despise being left out. I don't know about the big man, but feel free to include me in the love, you assholes."

Magpie's eyes go wide, then she winks at him. "Do we get to be in charge?"

"Maybe," he says as Lucy finally hands Benjy a plate, then goes back for his own. "Depends on what mood I'm in. Hamilton is the same, so it's not like I'm the outlier."

Boone sighs around another huge bite, then wipes his mouth. "How in the fuck are we going to keep this herd of miscreants in line, Tilly?"

She shrugs, her eyes dancing as she takes a sip of her coffee and sighs happily. "No idea, Teddy bear, but I enjoy thinking about it. In fact, I'll probably be thinking about it during that entire stupid meeting. Only Bobbi Jo would schedule one the first day back from break."

"She's a real go-getter," Boone grumbles into his eggs. "It's annoying as hell. I wanted to get the team on a run; the cold would wake them up fast."

"You make them run in the snow?" Doyle says. He looks disgusted and our girl nods her agreement.

Benjy laughs, shaking his head as he picks up his empty plate to take it to the dishwasher. "Dude, athletes with big dreams have to be dedicated. They run in the rain, snow, sun... whatever. Weights are all year round. Practices happen as much as the state athletic boards will allow. You don't make it to the big game without sacrificing some comfort."

That explains the muscles on their muscles—he and Boone played in college.

"Well, I'm not joining either of you in the fucking snow," Magpie declares as she finishes. She hops off her stool, leaning over to press a kiss to Lucy's head before returning her plate as well. "I'm going upstairs to finish getting ready. Anyone going in *my* car needs to be ready in ten."

The flap at the back door opens at her words, and I watch as the animals parade inside. Lucy must have put their food out before our was done. The giant snake and the monkey trail behind Jolene, eager to get close while the servals and dogs greet everyone at the counter.

"You're not getting any scraps, guys," Lucy says sternly and I roll my eyes.

He's definitely going to give them leftovers once the others leave. I'm not dressed, but Edgar, Benjy, and Doyle are all kitted out to leave.

"I'm going to work on the research for the Aurelia-parent connection, then head over."

Lucy collects the rest of the dishes and turns the appliance on. "I have to head out to the farm. Medhi and the other horses should be checked. I've been away for a bit. Then I'll come back and look at the appointments for the week in our office, babe."

"Going to the bar to balance inventory and go over the books from the holidays. Then I'm meeting my lawyer about the email he sent. Sherilynn's pulling some shit I want handled, so this goes through before the end of the month."

Frowning, I give him a serious look. "Better get it nailed down before anything public happens and she really loses her shit."

"I'm sure our good friend the Judge can help, yes?" Doyle tilts his head as he looks at his phone, then back at us. "I'll involve Nelia if need be, but I think the legal move is the best one to start with."

"Yes, he can and trust me, he absolutely will," Teddy says sternly. "That witch will *not* fuck with my family through you, man. I'll make sure she backs the fuck off even if I have to go to the Senator for help."

I blink. He really cares about us; Boone despises his father. Filing that away for later, I get up and fill my mug again, needing the extra boost to combat the jet lag.

Hopefully, no one uses that against us.

MISERY BUSINESS

JOLENE

I'm still reeling from the letter we read last night, but I can't show it in this shark tank. Teddy and I dropped the dogs, cats, and my brand new monkey friend off at the familiar play area. Isis never leaves me when we're out, but luckily, I figured out how she stays hidden. Eury stayed with Prez, though her sharp gaze followed us as we pulled out of the driveway. I think she's up to something, but fuck if I know what.

I don't think I can talk to animals—not really. Right?

"What are you thinking about so hard, Tilly?"

Teddy's question is soft, using that voice you'd have to be special to hear. Before our trip to Faerie, I didn't understand that he was doing it, but I do now. I look around for a moment, unsure if I can match that tone yet, then sigh. "I always feel safer with the animals around. Obviously, Isis will help if something happens, but… I don't know what we're walking into, especially at the end of the day."

"You have nerves of steel, woman. No one would know by looking at you that you're even the tiniest bit concerned," he murmurs. "I just know you better than random Hollow dwellers."

Chuckling, I loop my arm through his. "I'd hope so, Big D. If you didn't, the boys would school the shit out of you. Doyle would love to take you on; he's just that crazy."

"No shit. That dude is *loco* twenty-four hours a day, plus some that don't exist." My ex-bully grins and my stomach flutters at the wickedly handsome expression.

Damn him for being so fucking pretty.

"It's not fair, you know." I wrinkle my nose as we wave our badges at the back door to the gym and head inside. "All of you are so damn good-looking that it makes me stupid sometimes. I'd like to register a complaint, but it seems counterproductive."

He barks a laugh, his eyes dancing with merriment. "Especially since you love gawping at us. Don't think we've missed it, *drugar*. Benjy's muscles, Doyle's abs, my ass, the pup's piercings, the doc's tatts… You're not subtle."

My face floods with color as I gape at him. "What?"

I'd like to die right here on the stupidly expensive gym floor, if possible.

"You thought we didn't notice? Tilly, I'm hurt. You'd have to be blind not to see it." Teddy smirks as he tugs me forward towards the double doors that lead into the hallway.

"I… But… I…" His laughter isn't helping me get my shit together, so my snake tightens her grip on my waist. I run a hand over my stomach, letting Isis know my blood pressure spike isn't a bad thing, just a humiliating one.

"Nice Shemp."

Giving him an irritated glare, I pull my arm away, huffing as I toss my hair over my shoulder. This works for the Nip/Tuck girls, so maybe it will work for me. "Edgar Boone, you're on my shit list."

"Aw, Tilly, don't be—"

"Ha. I knew she'd take you for granted, Eddie. What were you thinking?"

My spine stiffens at the voice, and I turn slowly, like a predator looking for its prey. After Faerie, I'm in no goddamn mood to let people randomly fuck with me for their amusement. The willowy woman sneering at me is none other than Jasmine Behle, Amy's younger sister. She doesn't know me in the slightest as I'd graduated before she hit WHFS, but I'm sure her lovely sibling has filled her in.

"Ah, the welcoming committee. I wondered when the Tucks would send minions to visit." I rake my eyes over the woman in a way that she'll recognize before I continue. "Not the 'A' team, but I suppose they had to make do."

Teddy snorts, covering his mouth with his hand as he shakes his head. He's not stupid enough to intervene on this one; I'm the one who needs to handle this bullshit.

"I'm not wrong. Eddie isn't even supporting you, Catastrophe. I don't know why you ever came back." Jasmine puts her hand on her hip, glaring at me through her librarian glasses. She's obviously not very good at this female bully shit, being the less popular of the Behle girls, but she's trying.

I scratch my forehead, trying to decide how thoroughly I want to destroy her. She's one of the two teachers who clearly had a thing for Teddy from what I saw at the first meeting, despite neither of them even being on his radar. I could be very cruel if I wanted, but I don't think she deserves it. She's merely a sheep being directed by her shepherd and she doesn't know how little she matters to them in the grand scheme.

Delusional worship doesn't equal evil intent; I won't let their games change who I am.

"Look, I know you've been sent to fuck with me. You're not good enough at it to harm me, and I'm going to give you a little free advice instead of decimating your world right now." The youngest Behle opens her mouth and I shake my head. "Nope. Keep your yap shut and listen. I will be no one's punching bag in this town. I've told Sherilynn; I've told Amy. Now I'm telling you—back off or I'll destroy you so completely that you'll run from Whistler's Hollow with your blistered ass glowing in the fucking moonlight. Got it?"

Jasmine looks at me suspiciously, and I gather everything roiling inside of me, pushing it forward to back up my word. I don't have the slightest clue *what* I'm doing, but I know it's making every inch of my body sing with happiness. The influx of power dancing along my skin practically vibrates as it's allowed out of the cage. Her eyes widen and her jaw goes slack as she stares at me, so I smirk. I have to appear to have control of this, so she tells the others.

Fake it 'till you make it is our motto.

The sentiment makes me miss Seer, and I hope she and the others get back to the Hollow soon. I haven't seen her in forever. I miss her irreverence and I kind of miss the gentle Prince and Hugo's quiet. Even though I don't know them well, not having my people nearby has been harder than I wanted to admit to myself. I want everyone where I can ensure they're safe and within reach of aid if something goes sideways.

"You…. You…" Her finger trembles as she points at me and I shrug.

"What can I say? I contain multitudes, Jasmine. Now toddle off and report to your masters."

The woman stares for a second, then turns and skitters off, clutching her folders and books to her chest. I take a deep breath, willing whatever the hell I just unleashed to go away before I face Edgar again. His grin is huge when I do, and he crosses the distance between us quickly. His arms pull me into a tight embrace and he's kissing the living hell out of me before I can say a word. When our lips finally break, my hormones are clogging my brain and I gaze up at him dazedly.

"Holy fuck, Teddy Bear," is all I can get out.

"That's my girl, Tilly. Show those vipers what you're made of and we'll get them knocked off our list in no time." His expression is almost proud and I'm puzzled for a moment.

I haven't been acting like a wimpy wallflower, right?

"I always do," I say as I observe him. "How was this different?"

He shrugs, his hand squeezing my ass. "It was hot as fuck."

"I'm not usually?"

"Ha." He plants a kiss on my forehead, pulling back to take my arm again. "You will not trap me, woman. You're hot even with paint on your face and singing so off-key that it hurts the animals' ears."

My nose wrinkles and I mumble, "I'm not *that* bad."

"Oh, *drugar*, you really are, but I love it and you."

I whip my head around at him, sucking in a breath. "You are dead, Edgar Osiris Boone, the third. A walking corpse."

He knows why, and doesn't let me scramble away. "Kill me later, Tilly. We have a show to put on."

The doors to the main halls are in front of us, and I realize what he means.

Once more into the breach...

THE REST OF THE DAY GOES QUICKLY, MUCH TO MY SURPRISE. TEDDY and I don't get accosted the moment we walk into the main part of the school, and my classes go smoothly. There are a few unruly kids, but that's to be expected on the first day back after a monthlong break. Teenagers are just as bad about changes to routine as younger kids; they get used to being able to play with their tech or drift off when they're not in school. That makes their first week off break challenging, and I made sure my lessons today had activity rather than lectures.

If you can't beat them, join them, I say.

By the time the end of the day rolls around, I was tired as shit from the time change and cleaning up all the art supplies as I went. The kids had a good time creating paintings of mythical and fantastic creatures, though, and I think I could identify which ones have families that have shared their knowledge of the secret world hiding here with them. I wanted to pinpoint what students I need to be cautious of because I know well that their age group has impulse control problems, but if they're also struggling with some fucking supernatural power developing, that's twice as bad.

Andromeda hasn't shown her face yet, but that woman owes me a goddamn explanation once I'm able to share what I figured out. She's definitely one point of contact for emerging supernaturals, as is my dear Doc McNuggies. They're the two people I'd expect to be most involved and while Prez has done his best to be honest, my old confidante from school, the one person I trusted when I was being bullied, has not.

Fucking bullshit, that's all there is to it.

Inhaling a deep breath so the anger rising inside of me doesn't trigger something else, I wipe down the stations one last time. Teddy is supposed to meet here so we can walk to the meeting together, and I want everything done when he arrives. We have a history in this room and I can't trust either of us not to skip this stupid thing for other pursuits. Bobbi Jo will have a conniption fit and I'm not in the mood for that, either.

"Knock, knock, *drugar*," my handsome coach says as he leans against the door. He's posed like a fucking magazine model and I have to close my eyes for a minute while I tell my body to shut the hell up. Not getting jiggy last night was a poor plan, but damn, I was so tired.

Now I'm paying for it in spades.

"Stop acting like we're in some very inappropriate porn movie," I grumble as I head to my small back room to grab my things. "We don't have time for that, and you're still on my list."

"I could be off it so quickly if you'd just let me—"

"Nope, nope, nope," I reply as I hurry back into the room and push on his chest. "None of that. We have a boring, annoyingly cheery meeting to attend."

His eyes flash and I pretend not to notice. I know he can smell me, and it pisses me off, but I can't do anything about it. It's not like I can stop my inner shit and my physical body from reacting to these men —no, I can only mask my expression and hold firm. That's what I'm going to do because fuck if I'm going to do shit anywhere we can be caught and my 'slut' rep will be confirmed in people's eyes.

Puritan-ass hypocrites are everywhere and I refuse to give them ammunition.

"Fine. We'll go to Bobbi Jo's FunTime hour." His lips quirk and he grins hungrily. "But I'm taking you to the studio, and you don't get to send me packing since lessons haven't started yet."

That's a plot thickening right there and I'm sure it has to do with other things doing the same.

Enemy
Edgar

The minute we enter the conference room, I feel the tension in the air. There are plenty of clueless folks meandering about in the middle chatting, but there's a faction in the far corner sitting primly, as if waiting for us to arrive. Jasmine, Elyse, and Dolly are poised to strike, though their smiles are deceptively pleasant. I see Bobbi Jo working with one of the science teachers as she tries to get her presentation set-up without MacAuley to assist. For a moment, I wonder when the hell he and the Prince are getting back, but shuffle it quickly to a 'for later' list.

I have to focus on this meeting because I have a Bad Feeling ™ about it.

Tilly and I choose seats near the other coaches—even the female ones seem content to have us join them, and I sigh in relief. I've made certain *all* sports programs in this damn place get generous grants, so they *should* be loyal to me. That's not why I did it, nor is it why I'll continue to do it, but it doesn't fucking hurt.

"Just a few more minutes, please," Bobbi Jo chirps from the front and I roll my eyes.

It wouldn't have killed her to get this done during the day, so tired teachers and increasingly late coaches could get on with their commitments. But that's not how the scattered woman works, so we're going to sit here in discomfort as I wait for the vultures in this room to pick at me. My skin tingles and I grit my jaw as the second side—the very inappropriate for this forum one—raises its head. The hound always wants to rip and tear, while the bird wants to simply implode the enemies. The incubus is more devious and reminiscent of our Irish mate—he wants to cause pain and suffering via loss of control and embarrassment. Being able to feed off of it is a bonus, but I'm not in need and I don't want to fuck up our vow of secrecy.

No way I can explain away a fog-induced orgy at the staff meeting.

"Teddy," Jolene whispers as she reaches for my hand between the chairs. "You feel very off. Breathe, Big D."

My lips curve as I look over at her. This woman is afraid of nothing, not even someone overhearing her use a very private nickname. When Jolene Whitley is all in, she's *all the fuck the way in.* Every time I think I can't love her more, she does shit like this. It's intoxicating, and I'll never tire of it. "Don't worry, sugar. I'm good."

A soft chuckle and a knowing look are her answers as she tangles our fingers together. Luckily, she's the note taker and I won't need that hand because fuck if I'm letting go of it now. I squeeze her palm, pushing some of the emotion I feel into the bond. I'm not sure if it will work, but when she turns back to me with wide eyes, I know it did.

Go big or go home, Boone.

"I…"

She doesn't get to finish because our intrepid leader claps her hands at the front, looking out at us with a happy yet oblivious smile. "Welcome back, everyone. I'm excited to start the second half of our year at WHFS. I like to start each semester with a gathering so we can all get on the same page going forward."

A hand shoots up and I bite back a growl when I see it's one of the three sneaky witches for earlier. Bobbi Jo points to Jasmine and her faux sweet smile turns nasty. "What is the district policy on moral turpitude?"

The principal frowns, her brows knitting in confusion. "I'm not sure what you're referring to, Miss Behle, but obviously, we adhere to the professional standards set by the state standards board and all law enforcement agencies."

"Then a staff member caught flouncing about throwing their poor moral character in public would *not* be something the board would take action on?" This time it's Dolly Atwater, and she looks viciously pleased with herself.

Too bad for her—Percy Atwater is into me for far more than he has liquid at the moment and her error in judgement is going to be his major financial crisis.

"I-I... suppose it would depend on the specifics, Dolly. If it violates something within their contract or the by-laws set forth by governing bodies..."

I'm about to throw in my legal expertise when Tilly clears her throat. She's making that damn fake face she put on during our time in Faerie, and I know whatever she's about to say will toss a live explosive into the middle of this room. I should intervene, but I'm so fucking done with this childish crap. Like this morning, I simply feel no need to hold her back.

"I think this is a conversation best had in private, behind closed doors, because it feels very much like an accusation cloaked in curiosity. However," Jolene smiles and this time, it's a masterclass on viciously intelligent intimidation. "...if those involved are determined to press their point, I believe it would be prudent to ask whether the accused individual or individuals have extremely high-profile lawyers like Jackson Thorne on retainer. Then, were it me, I'd step back and question whether I want to invest every penny of my dwindling family fortune in fighting a slander and hostile work environment lawsuit that won't cost the accused a penny to drag out until I have to file Chapter Eleven."

Hot. As. Fuck.

Smirking, I toss my hat in the ring. "As someone with far more legal expertise than anyone in this room, I'm going to add that if the case came before me in a court, I would award damages quickly. The district audio and video cameras will probably contain *very* pertinent information about those in the wrong, which would make it impossible not to side with the plaintiff."

"What audio and video equipment?" Elyse says with a frown. She's trying to hide her fear, but I'm definitely right; they've been plotting in common areas.

I shrug, my eyes dancing with my victory. "The ones in most common areas of the school, hidden from view to ensure student and staff safety. Unlike most people, I read every line of a contract before I put my pen to paper and the consent to be recorded is buried in small print clauses. They have ten years' worth of footage stored in secure data centers offsite for legal purposes."

Gotcha, Hollow Harpies.

THE REST OF THE MEETING IS AN EXCRUCIATING BLEND OF BOBBI JO trying to keep the angry women on topic and Tilly shutting them down at every turn. My guys grumble under their breaths in their dude way about how they should just give up and I chuckle every time. I like that my woman is impressing the fuck out of the other coaches. It bodes well for her holding her own if we have to attend social events. I have no idea how they'll take the rest of our happy family, but if they don't like it, they can fuck all the way off.

I didn't allow homophobic or misogynistic bullshit before and I sure as fuck won't entertain it now.

By the time we could leave, I could feel the exhaustion radiating from my *drugar.* She'd spent so much time trying to absorb all the damn information Bobbi Jo presented while fending off the girls that the toll became a visible strain. We grabbed the animals from the companion area and they mobbed her, lifting a little of the tired look from her face. I walked her to the car, but when we got everyone loaded, I knew it was time.

"Tilly, we're not going to the studio tonight."

Her brows furrow, and she glares at me. "I need to get shit ready for lessons to start next week."

"You do, but not today." I shake my head and reach for her hand, bringing her fingers to my lips. "Woman, you were dynamite in there, but it knocked the wind right out of your sails. You were poised, vicious, and professional to a fault; it made my Southern boy's heart sing. But holding back the parts of you that wanted to wrap your hands around their throats and squeeze until they turned purple wasn't easy, was it?"

Her lips curve, and she flushes a pretty pink before her shoulder lifts. "You got me there, Big D."

"And our trip to Ireland likely helped you connect with that part of you, which is fan-fucking-tastic, but holding back the more…" I pause for a moment to weigh my words. "…primally motivated part of you takes a toll on your body. It wears you out and you're still getting over jet lag. We're going home to have an enormous meal and relax, *drugar*. Trust me, it will help you more than you realize."

Jolene opens her mouth to argue, but Hyde sticks her head through the seats. "Mow!"

"See?" I chuckle. "Even the kids think I'm right."

But our woman is stubborn, and she shakes her head. "No, Teddy, I need to—"

This time, the damn monkey scrambles over the seat and plops in her lap. It rises on its legs, holding its paw up with a look I fucking swear screams 'bad Tilly' before it shakes the small fist. Her laughter makes my chest warm and I tilt my head as I wait for her to give in.

"Oh, fine, damn it. You're all traitors, the entire lot of you." Tilly huffs and crosses her arms over her chest, but when the fluffy tailed little shit climbs up to sit on her shoulder, she sighs. "Again, you're all cheaters and traitors. I don't know why I put up with you."

"Because you *loooooooooove* us," I sing-song as I look over my shoulder, pulling out of the spot and angling towards the road to home. She grumbles under her breath and I pretend not to understand, but her ire makes my dick jump.

I love when she's fiery and fighting me more than anything, and this trip is going to be very uncomfortable.

"You know, I really don't get the appeal," she says as we pull onto the main road. "Sure, when we were teens, that kind of bullshit might hold a certain… powerful feeling that teens need to validate themselves. And I know that low self-esteem carries over into adulthood when untreated, but these chicks have money and have their own little cults of personality. Why the *fuck* don't they just… do their own thing and leave me be? I'm not even *speaking* to them, much less stoking this fire."

Scratching the back of my head, I frown at the road for a moment as I consider her question. I honestly don't know what's motivating most of the shitty behavior here. Sherilynn, I understand a little, because her perfect fake life got upended by my friend growing a pair. It doesn't justify the behavior, and it started *before* Benjy left, but... it's comprehensible, at least. Amy, Reese, their little group, and the minions at the school are puzzling to me.

"I suppose it's a lot of things, Tilly, the simplest of which is that women aren't taught to punch one another and walk it off." She gives me a dirty look and I grin. "Look, guys do that shit from a young age and it's not very evolved, I'll grant, but it often solves this problem before it escalates to this kind of shit. I'm not being anti-feminist or whatever, but women are taught to behave and suppress their urges, so they end up using softer methods to get their vengeance."

"Edgar Boone, what the fucking *hell* have I done to these morons? Sure, I was different and chunky in high school—not a reason to humiliate me, but at that time, society didn't give a shit about bullying fat kids." She frowns. "They still don't, but those of us who survived do our best to help. However, as an *adult* who hasn't lived here for over a decade, I have done absolutely fucking *nothing* to garner this shit. Even *so*, no one does a damn thing."

I wish I had better answers for her, but the truth is... people are selfish assholes, whether they're human or supes.

"I know that, *drugar*." I sigh as we drive down the street past the familiar buildings of the Hollow, seeing my home town differently than normal. "Sherilynn can claim a grievance, though their marriage has been shit from the start. But the others? At first, I thought it was falling into old patterns and it would die down."

"It hasn't—in fact, it's gotten worse. The bullshit spread from the Tucks to others, like today. That's why I have to shut it down every single time. If I let it go once, we'll be back to high school in a blink."

She's not wrong. Claiming a bunch of the most eligible bachelors in town doesn't help her case, nor does being beautiful, smart, strong, and radiating untapped power. "Jealousy is a hell of a drug, Tilly. You came back, holding your head high, and you haven't bowed down to the queens of this town, even dowager ones like my mother. That makes you fair game to people who clearly don't have enough to do."

Her snort makes me grin as I turn into our driveway. "You're saying they think I'm a greedy whore for snatching up you and the boys, right?"

"And having a job, friends, confidence, and freedom, *drugar*. Not giving a fuck what people think and being able to make your own decisions is something most of them have *never* experienced. You know how this place works. Birth to the grave, expectations and rules and appearances."

"Huh."

I park the car, cocking my head to the side as I look at her. "What does that mean?"

"Here I thought I'd been run out-of-town like a pariah, so I went on my adventures to forge my path and heal." Licking her lips, she stares out the window, shaking her head slowly. "These bitches hate I could get out, live a life I chose, and come back with no strings. That's what you're saying?"

"Yep." I shrug, not knowing what else to say. "You've got everything they ever wanted and the only people they have to thank for that is their shitty behavior."

"Edgar Boone III, you just earned yourself a one-way ticket to happy town."

Damn. I'm getting good at this boyfriend shit.

QUIET

JOLENE

"It occurs to me that we need a bigger soaking area," I say as I lean back against Teddy. My fingers flick at the bubbles floating on the surface lazily, feeling very much at ease. He'd promised a calm, quiet evening and when we arrived home to find the others not back yet, that's when he sprang into action.

The lights are dimmed, the smells are amazing, and the candles are flickering as we soak the day from our skin in the tub together. He'd read a little of the book we've been working on, but after I drifted a bit, he put the Kindle aside to let me melt against him peacefully. I've never been a bath person until he drew the one after the club disaster, but I definitely get the appeal now.

This is warm, relaxing, and intimate—something I struggle with.

"Tilly, I'd be happy to book a damn contractor to build an outdoor hot tub area first thing in the morning. I think *everyone* would appreciate it." His chest rumbles with a soft chuckle when I pinch his thigh. "What? They would and all of us can afford this shit, so stop being so damn independent."

I wrinkle my nose as I lean back and look up at him. "I'm not a spoiled princess."

"Absolutely not, *drugar*, but you have a minimum of five wealthy assholes who *enjoy* the fact that you're ours. We *like* doing shit for you." He picks up the bourbon, holding the glass up for me, and I take it with a sigh of gratitude.

"I know, Teddy, but old habit die hard, you know?" I sip the Basil Hayden's slowly, pondering his words. "And I *am* yours—all of yours, like you are mine, but…"

Oh, shit. They're all mine.

A wave of embarrassment rolls over me when I realize that while I've made certain Wolfie, Prez, and Teddy know they're mine, I haven't done the same for Benjy and Doyle. I haven't given them the cuffs like I did my original three men, and they might think it's because they aren't as important. Damn, that would hurt, even if the reason is that everything ramped up to a million before we went to Faerie.

"What's wrong, sugar?" Teddy murmurs as his lips brush my ear. "You just got tense."

Licking my lips, I shrug before I murmur, "With all the hullabaloo of the trip and the fight, I haven't made it clear to Benjy and Doyle like I did with you guys. I mean, that we're… together. Like it means things."

I'm surprised when he laughs again, squeezing me to his large frame and burying his nose in my neck. "Tilly, darlin', if you think those men don't know who they belong to because you haven't given them a token yet, you're sorely mistaken."

His teeth graze the pulse in my throat and I groan softly. "Are you sure? I don't want anyone to feel like they're not important to me."

A firm nip and a soothing suckle at the skin he bit makes me shiver as his reply vibrates over my skin. "Benjy and the hot-headed Irishman know you are theirs and vice versa, *drugar*. All of us have a bond that gets deeper every day, but if you *want* to show them through visible gifts that others will see, by all means, do so. I love mine."

My cheeks flush as I turn to catch his lips, kissing him slowly. Warmth and hunger flow through my veins as our tongues dance, and I wriggle around on his lap until I'm facing him. When we take a break to breathe, I smile. "Edgar Boone, if anyone in the universe had predicted we would be here like this… I would have offered to eat my hat. I don't know how you grew up to be such a good man with such poor examples, but I'm thankful."

"You're gonna make me blush, Jolene Whitley." His hand comes up to cup my jaw as he looks into my eyes. "I hate like hell that I was an easily led, oblivious little shit. We could have had a lot more time together—though I suspect we've got quite a bit to go as it is."

Well, that's an odd way to say that... unless he means we have a longer lifespan than I know.

"There's that tension again," Teddy murmurs as his hands land on my shoulder and start massaging. "Stop thinking about things that make you worry."

I give him a wry grin. "It's hard when every time we do anything, something pops out of the bushes to make shit more difficult."

"I'll give you that." He sighs and leans back against the tub wall. "This has been the most eventful fall semester I've *ever* seen in the Hollow."

"More so than the last State Championship?" My eyes dance as he winces. "Too soon?"

His arms wrap around me, pulling me into an enormous bear hug as water sloshes everywhere. "You're dancing on the edge, missy. How the hell could I have predicted the three best players on the team getting benched minutes before the kick-off? The entire thing was ridiculous, and I had to scramble to cover for their poor judgement."

Grinning as I tiptoe my fingers up his chest, I tilt my head. "Aw, Big Daddy Asshole is sensitive about his little sportsball team."

His growl makes my nipples tighten as he tugs me closer and rises to his feet with me in his arms like I weigh nothing. That would be sexy on its own, but he continues to hold me as he climbs out of the tub, wiping his feet on the mat so he doesn't fall, and stomps into the bedroom. Before I know it, he tosses me on the bed, then dives on top of me, his hair dripping on my face as he smirks.

"Woman, you don't know when to quit, do you?"

"Obviously not," I drawl wryly as I sprawl out on the bed. "Are you going to teach me a lesson?"

His grin is wicked as he fits our bodies together in a way that makes me groan. Our noses brush as a low rumble in his chest caresses my skin, vibrating over it deliciously. "Nope. I was thinking about something very different, *drugar*."

"It doesn't *feel* very different," I retort as I arch against him. "Perhaps you're mistaken."

My next sentence is cut off by a deep kiss, one so filled with emotion that my senses go haywire. His tongue tangles with mine, but this time, it's not about dominance. It's slow, languid, and like an intimate dance. I sigh against his lips when we break, letting the sensation of his muscled frame covering mine sink into my bones.

Safety. This feels like safety.

"It *is* different, Tilly. Everything with you is, and I love discovering every single thing," he murmurs as his lips move from my mouth to my jaw. The kisses are feather-light, and I strain against him impatiently. "Ah ah. Be still for me, just this time. Let me show you."

My hands come up to bury in his hair, holding on as he nips and suckles his way down my neck until I whine. I didn't know I made that noise, but here we are, and it definitely makes him happy. The small, raspy words of praise he gives as he moves over my shoulder and down to my breasts make me clench inside, shivering with need. The scrape of his teeth, then a soothing swipe of tongue over the marks is driving me crazy as he finally gets to my hard nipples.

"Teddy, *please*," I breathe as I arch my back.

His chuckle is dark, and he looks up with eyes that I know aren't his. This foray into the gentler side of his nature is pushing the limits of his control onto whatever he has inside of him. I don't know what it is yet, but I know my limbs are heavy and I feel like the oxygen in the room is filled with desire. My eyes flutter closed when he tugs on my right nipple with his teeth, twisting the other in his fingers.

"I like when you beg, *drugar*. It makes every bit of me want to give you everything you need and more."

Yes, please.

But my nature won't allow me to fully submit like Wolfie, so I dig my nails into his shoulders. "I don't beg; I ask politely, like a lady."

That makes him laugh, and the vibration combined with his end of day stubble makes my nipples burn and ache. He bites on firmly in response and my hips grip his, eager for his cock to fill the dripping wetness between them. "Not yet, Tilly. Behave; I know you can."

The trail he's following moves down my ribs, rimming my belly button so suggestively that I almost make that high-pitched noise again. My alpha sports man is never this slow, but he's savoring me like he would a fine bourbon—taste by taste. I shudder when his kisses hit my pubic bones, then his tongue drags along the creases of my legs one by one. He's barely going to need to touch me and I'm going to go off like a rocket.

"If you say so, sugar," he murmurs as his breath tickles over my pussy. His broad shoulders push my legs apart more and he settles in, his fingers tracing teasing patterns on my inner thighs. "But I think you're a little delulu." His fingers graze over the wetness, and he holds them up. "Look at how soaked you are."

I'd love to refute him, but before I can, he's spread me wide and his face is buried right where I need him. The soft laps and teasing nips make me gasp and writhe, grinding against his face. Long fingers trace around my aching hole and back to the seam of my ass as his tongue destroys me. As predicted, once he impales me on three fingers and suckles hard at my clit, sparks go off in my field of vision and I tremble in pleasure.

This motherfucking man, I swear to all the gods above.

"Keep going, Tilly," his voice rumbles against my sensitive parts, pulling another dreaded whine. "I want you to bury myself inside of you deep enough that you'll be marked for good."

My brows furrow at that because I don't know what it means, but I suck in a quick breath and nod. "Do it, Teddy. Mark me how you want."

His body surges up against mine at lightning speed, his cock nudging my entrance in an impossibly quick move. I swallow hard, knowing I have to pretend not to notice he moved faster than any human could. His eyes are tinted red, but they flash between colors, and conflicting smells fill the air of the bedroom. I've triggered something primal and powerful inside of him with those words, and it's about to get *very real.*

"Say it again."

I blink, tilting my head as I look up at him. A dark feeling hooks into my gut and spreads from there to my chest, then out to my limbs. The energy hums inside of me, making my veins burn and my eyes ache. "I said, *mark me, Edgar Boone.* I want you to."

Teddy lets out a savage roar as he throws his head back. My eyes slam shut, knowing whatever is coming is something I can't pretend I didn't see, and until Doyle tells me it's safe, I have to protect my men from whatever retribution they might face. Sharp stings make my arms quiver, but I notice it's not painful—no, it feels good. The body covering mine heats and I arch my hips, pleading with him to fill me now.

With one thrust, our bodies are joined, and I moan loudly. Even his cock feels different now, and holy fuck, I am *not* complaining at all. His hips pull back, swirling before he slams into me over and over. I have to dig my nails into his arms to hold on, but his rough thrusts are making it hard for me to focus.

His damn dick feels like it's ribbed for my goddamn pleasure now and I might die on the spot.

"Teddy…" I grit out as I hold on. "I…"

I have no idea how to tell him that dark sensation in my body is humming like it's set to explode and I'm losing control of my mind quickly. This has to be what happened on the battlefield in Faerie, and maybe what happens when I black out. But I have no idea what happens after it takes over.

"It's okay, Tilly. Let it go, baby. I've got you. You're taking me so well," he growls against my neck, and that's the end of my rope.

Goodbye feminism; hello, Teddy praise kink.

His hips piston faster and, for once, I just listen. I let the darkness and the power in me flow through me like an old friend as I cling to him. The pleasure builds until I hit a peak, and then everything explodes with my orgasm. A sharp, tearing sensation at my neck almost brings me back, but whispered words in my ear help me let go exactly as he asked.

And then there's only black as my consciousness flutters away once more.

I Feel It Coming

Wolfgang

When Prez and I get home, I can *feel* it. My lips curve up into a smile as I grab his hand. "Let's go, babe. Daddy and our woman are already warmed up."

"That son of a bitch," Presley grumbles as he squeezes my palm. "I *knew* he'd make sure he scented her up first."

Shrugging as I open the door and pull him inside, I drop my things on the buffet table in the entry and kick my shoes off. "Who cares? I wanna join and it's not a race."

"If you say so," my lover grumbles as he follows suit and we take the stairs quickly. The animals don't follow us, so I assume our woman or the dominant hound ordered them to stay put in the living room.

Handy, that ability.

We damn near topple over each other when we get to the doorway of the bedroom. Prez snorts, covering his hand with his mouth as he leans against the jamb. I smile because I can't fucking help it. I'm surprised Teddy didn't think this through, but it appears he got carried away. His eyes warn us to be careful about what we say, so I nod to make him relax.

"Having a problem, Boone?"

"We might have overdone it a wee bit, and she took my damn knot, which is why we're like this," he hisses at my love. "That would have been okay if she hadn't blacked out at the big finish."

"I mean, it's probably good she did because how long—"

"Too long, pup. And don't think you won't get to eventually, but I didn't mean for it to happen this time." His eyes darken and I shiver in anticipation. "It's almost done, I think. Don't give me shit, Hamilton. Do you know how many times the hound has offered that in my entire life? Zero. I was unprepared, we'll say."

That's putting it lightly.

"We should have expected it eventually," I reply as I consider it. "I mean, even if it's never happened before, your canine and your bird have claimed Sugarplum. They'd naturally want to mark her occasionally."

Teddy winces and we look at him as he sighs. "The incubus did this time, too. Come closer and look at all the markings. I doubt she can see them because she's still not there yet, but they've grown."

We shuffle closer, peering down at our unconscious mate. Teddy's right—the markings have grown, blossoming more symbols and swirls that look as though they correlate with the incubus' innate powers. I turn to Prez, tilting my head. "How thin do you think the emergence spell is now? Can you tell?"

He adjusts his glasses, squinting down at her intently, and within a few seconds, his large white wings appear. Teddy's eyes widen; caladrii don't allow people to see their shifts often because they're so rare and sought after. I smile shyly at my other mate, explaining softly, "It's easier for him to read the spells when his bird is freed. It's part of how they cast it or something?"

"That's right, Lucy," he mumbles as his eyes change color and the temperature in the room heats. "Spells on the hybrid young are keyed to the powers of my kind, though when hunters started picking us off, they altered them slightly to include a few other healer species. It doesn't work nearly as well for them."

"You can… sense the barrier?" my canine mate says, then sighs in relief. "Oh, shit, thank hell. There we go." He winks at me as he's finally able to move, pulling out of our girl and rolling to his back next to her. "Worth every fucking second, but *damn*. No wonder guys like me grumble about it."

Presley snorts, his hands ghosting over Jolene's form now that Teddy's moved. "Boone, I am continually fucking amazed at the lack of… anything that damn centaur did before me. Any knot-having species should have been taught that shit in puberty. It's almost criminal how ignorant the supes here are. I'm definitely having a conversation with Nelia about adult education classes."

The hound's eyes narrow and I rush around the other side of the bed, scooting into his other side to calm him. "Watch it, birdman. I'm not stupid."

Of course, he'd think that's what Prez meant.

"No, Daddy, you're not. But what Prez means is that the lack of knowledge he's seen in the adult supes in the Hollow is actively dangerous to all of you. You all should have been trained on the needs, quirks, and care of your physiologies as emerging teens. If the Senator's *son* wasn't taught, imagine how many supes here are harming themselves and possibly others by not caring for their powers and abilities appropriately."

Teddy blinks, then his brow furrows, and finally, he nods. "Okay. I can accept that. Benjy made himself miserable for years because he knew he had a mate, but didn't think he'd find them. So he married that harpy and now here we are. Correct training would have told him to blow this popsicle stand and search, right?"

"Maybe," Prez says as he continues examining Sugarplum. "The world is pretty big. But a good doc would have suggested getting some witches and Fae to try divination or astral location rather than marrying someone you don't even like."

I lean over, looking at our mate anxiously. "What do you think, love?"

"Her spell is *much* weaker than we thought. I don't know if that happened in the Veil or after we returned, but she's primed to break through soon. In fact, I'd be surprised if she doesn't start noticing things as odd."

"We'll have to be more vigilant, then."

All three of us look up to find the smirking Irishman and concerned gorilla shifter starting from the doorway. Benjy arches a brow, but doesn't comment as he notes Teddy's nudity. I shrug, cutting my eyes to Jolene, and his lips curl up. I swear, that dude is the most placid simian I've ever encountered.

"Haggerty, as always, your powers of observation are first rate," the hound drawls sarcastically. "I'd considered shifting in front of her, but *now* I'm not sure it's the right move."

"For fuck's sake," Presley mutters as he shakes off the healer's trance. "You two need to stop acting as if you dislike one another. We're a family and sniping when we're not in the middle of a crisis. It's fine. But if things go sideways…"

"Let them spar." The gravelly voice gets all of our attention, and I smile broadly as Sugarplum's eyes flutter open. She yawns, then wriggles her limbs experimentally before arching her back. That puts her sparkly nipples on display and a chorus of groans echoes in the air. "Now, boys, I'm thoroughly trashed for a little bit. You'll have to calm down."

Teddy snickers, darting forward to press a kiss to her jaw. A rumble in his chest tickles against my skin and this time, I wiggle. "Stop that, pup. I'm not quite ready for more, either."

Doyle and Benjy look surprised, but I shake my head a little. We can go over the 'knot problem' later; for now, we should probably get our girl cleaned up and fed. As if he's reading my mind, Prez clears his throat. "As much as I enjoy seeing your body, Magpie, I think we need to get you and Boone clean, then have dinner. I'm sure everyone has things to share about their first day back at work."

Oh, I definitely do; I'd almost forgotten in the shock.

"The doc's right. Up and at them, lazy doggies. Our woman needs aftercare."

I grin at Doyle, rolling off the bed to my feet. "You herd them and I'll go cook. Benjy, want to join?"

He smiles brightly, making me flush a bit. "I'm game, Wolfie. Lead the way."

"You guys think Princess is seeing things she shouldn't?"

I look at Benjy as he sets the table for all of us, his experience in creating a table atmosphere obvious in the way he's organizing everything. "Prez thinks it's possible. I know she was more calm and compliant in Faerie than most people with her independent streak should have been."

The bar owner nods, pausing in his creation for a moment. "The two of you disappearing during the battle and then reappearing still bothers me. We took it in stride because we had to, but why was she awake and you were out? Isn't that the opposite of the norm?"

Frowning, I look at the steaks I'm marinating. "Well… yeah, it is. I mean, we just walked in on one of the normal situations. Teddy was waiting for her to come back from the blackout, not the other way around."

"And she blacks out when her emotions are high… high enough to activate her supe side or sides, right? Like sex, anger, frustration, fear…"

I blink as I walk to the refrigerator to get veggies to chop. "Whatever her sides are… one calls to the parts of Big Daddy. Something calls to my Fae and your gorilla. It also calls to Prez' bird and Doyle's godly shit. Not to mention the djinn and the oracle."

Benjy takes the bundle of carrots I hand him, moving to wash them in the sink. "She's definitely got more than one. But Boone's the only person I've *ever* heard of that's a *triplásia*. I can't imagine there's anyone with over three, if that amount is so rare."

That stops me in my tracks, and I look at him in shock. "You think she's got over three hybrid sides? It's… unheard of."

"Impossible, if you ask me."

We look at my love as he joins us, holding his hand out for a knife to help chop. "I've been around healers and doctors most of my life to train for this position. My mentor is over seven centuries old and I've *never* heard of a supe anywhere in the world having over three."

"Yeah, Hamilton, but everything is impossible in theory until it happens," Benjy says as he hands us the carrots and grabs some broccoli to clean. "Jolene's been latent so long that any trace of where she came from is likely completely gone."

Prez frowns at that, cutting slices slowly. "She's finally emerging right when a bunch of weird rebels are fucking around at various places around the globe. Not only that, but the whispers among the healer sects are that more lost ones are appearing out of the woodwork."

"And we go on a quest for my dad only to find weird shit and more questions," I murmur. "There's something much bigger going on, especially with that letter arriving from Aurelia."

"Ahem." We all turn to see Jolene standing in the entrance to the kitchen with Teddy and Doyle behind her. She grins a little, and I return it, happy to see her looking so relaxed. "While I appreciate you guys trying to figure out what that letter means, we need to talk about this stuff together. I just wish Seer and the others were back."

Doyle gives her a little push into the room, his eyes dancing as he strides over to pour drinks. "Aye, but that might change soon. Mayor Nelia said she believes that quite a few townspeople will arrive home this week—including a certain counselor we've all been eager to talk to."

"Bane? Bane's coming back?" Prez adjusts his glasses, then sighs when he gets smudges on them. I grab the lenses to clean them off for him and he squints at the others. "That would be *very* helpful. I need to speak to her about so many things—including how the students are being managed before and during her absences."

Jolene arches a brow at him. "What does that have to do with the war tax on putty, Doc? You've lost me."

I have no idea how he's going to answer that.

Bad Feeling

Doyle

The bloody fools in our family need to get their asses to this damn meeting. Nelia asked me to 'gather the troops' this morning, and since she rarely gives bald-faced commands, it's important. I know it's last minute; that's a pain in the ass for Boone on a court day, but the others can flit out of their little businesses when they want.

It's not like they have competition in the Hollow.

"Find out where the feck they are, friend," I mutter to Odie. He ruffles his feathers, annoyed with being asked to do something so mundane, but I don't yield. I want to find out what our illustrious mayor has under her hat. The look on her face when she demanded the tête-à-tête told me she's got something to relate.

"Doyle, have they arrived yet?"

My lips press together and I growl softly before calming myself. "No, Nelia. I sent Odie to figure out what's holding them up. I'm sure their arrival is imminent."

"Good. When they get here, bring them up to my office. I fear there is much to discuss, especially after your sojourn through the Veil."

Fuck. How much does she know?

Tapping my fingers on my desk, I huff, wondering how I'll be able to keep my extremely perceptive boss from figuring out the one secret I share with our girl. I don't want our deception to come out in front of the others; I'm still unsure how it will affect their oaths. I'll survive the strikes—I'm a demi, after all—but the rest? Who the fuck knows? And my Tíogair loves those idiots, so I can't let them be smited… smoten?

Whatthefuckever.

I pull my phone out, clicking away from the full family chat to the 'Dicks Only' one that I insisted on once I realized that we'd be forgiven as long as we apologized for our hidden motives. Frankly, I know they're all *capable* of behaving like they have fucking sense, but I don't *trust* them to do so. This town had a bunch of fools dictating the terms of its existence long before Nelia came and it's just become a more logical, well-run city with her hand guiding it.

Tricky Asshole: Where the fuck are you?

Big Daddy Asshole: I can't stop a proceeding to bolt, Haggerty.

Tricky Asshole: But you can stop to text.

Big Daddy Asshole: Who the fuck changed my name again?

Cute Asshole: Me, Daddy. I like it.

Big Daddy Asshole: Well… okay.

Doctor Asshole: And just like that…

Sweet Asshole: You're whipped, brother. The lil' doc has you soft as an old shoe.

Cute Asshole: *blush*

Tricky Asshole: Again, I ask, where the fuck are all of you?

Sweet Asshole: OMW, calm down, dude.

Doctor Asshole: Lucy and I are finishing the appointments. I'm almost done.

Cute Asshole: I let Jamie know I'll be late to the farm, so I'm good.

Tricky Asshole: Fine. Nelia's waiting. She hates waiting.

Big Daddy Asshole: Then she should stop telling people to take stupid shit to court rather than throwing the hammer down.

Tricky Asshole: I'm the last one to be reminding you how democracy works, but…

Big Daddy Asshole: Shut the fuck up, Haggerty. Be there soon.

I toss my phone on the desk, leaning back in my chair with a groan of irritation. Lucky for me, Nelia rarely chains me to this stupid office. I'm allowed to float about the town looking for ideas to help promote the local businesses and gather chatter for the town's PR and social media. I'm mostly in charge of keeping the goddamn morons who live here from fucking up the image of the town and either drawing suspicion from humans or dangerous elements from supedom.

It's harder than it sounds and though I don't have to try very hard, I have to pay more attention than people know.

"Get me the boss," I say as I push the button on the intercom. The perky chick who serves as assistant for the rest of the staff here gives an affirmative, and I once again thank my relatives that only Nelia has to deal with the bitter little troll downstairs. If I had to use Aldous for my work shit, I'd definitely destroy something on a weekly basis just to bleed off my anger.

The intercom crackles for a second, then I hear the impatient tones of the Mayor of the Hollow. "What did you find out, Doyle?"

"Boone's finishing a case, but should be along soon. The docs are likewise wrapping up, but Foster is on his way. We should have a full deck in not too long. Shall I order in from Hazel's?" I roll my eyes to the ceiling, eager to get up and move around, so fetching the lunch would help my hyperactivity.

There's a pause on the line, then a sigh. "Yes. Get whatever you think will work for your housemates and my usual. Bill it here, as this is a working lunch. That way, no one in the diner will question you pickup and perhaps spill the beans to Miss Whitley."

Fuck, she's sharp. I didn't think of that, but it's a genuine concern.

"Got it. I'll head over now, so I'm back by the time the rest of them drag their asses in."

"Doyle?"

"Yes, Nelia?" I say in my sweetest tones.

She snorts, and I can imagine her braids clicking as she shakes her head. "Don't start anything over there. I'm aware there's discontent, but you can't allow them to derail what's truly important."

"And what's that?"

"Your mate's continued development. It's imperative."

Guess that was clear enough, even for me.

WHEN I GET TO HAZEL'S, IT'S HOPPING. LUNCH STARTS ABOUT eleven-thirty in the Hollow and runs steadily until around one p.m. Since the diner is one of the easiest and most interesting daytime haunts, Hazel makes bank throughout the week. Weekends are slower and she's able to let her part time hires handle most of them. The busy breakfast and lunch rushes from all the businesses on the main drag net her more than enough to have extra staff for late nights and weekends.

I haven't had to do a damn thing to help the Laertes since I arrived, other than make her chuckle occasionally.

"Afternoon, Hazel. I've got a big one today. Mayor's having a meeting in her office last minute."

The woman eyes suspiciously; I'm usually not so free with information. She knows something is up, but she nods, playing along. "I'll take that paper, Doyle. Mayor Nelia always goes right to the front of the line in this diner."

Bless her for not making me place the order out loud.

I'm not sure who among the copious amount of citizens and busy-bodies in this place is listening, but I'd like to avoid them identifying our meeting roster through commonly placed orders. It seems like a stretch that would even be possible, but it didn't take me long living in a small Southern town to realize the shit they file away for later is astounding. They could form their own goddamn 'gossip bureau of investigation' and make enough money to buy a small island.

"How was the vacation, dear?"

I look at the cagey old supe with a smirk. "Enlightening, as always. Traveling to other lands is frequently a suitable method of adjusting perspective. Plus, experiencing new cultures is good for the soul."

She huffs, rolling her eyes as she bustles behind the counter, fixing drinks in to-go trays. "That's true enough, young trickster. However, if you did not gain all that you sought, it would be a shame indeed."

"Mmm. I agree. As it happens, I believe we got what we needed for the moment." I wink at her, my eyes dancing as I parry her thrust. "We're closer to the goal, at least."

"That's excellent news," she says as she pushes the two trays toward me. "It'll just be a few more minutes until you order is done. Sit a spell and I'll be back."

I nod, my eyes darting around the room. There are definitely ears and eyes tracking our conversation; I can feel the weight of their attention pressing on me. Since very few people know my *actual* origins, I'm able to lull them all into complacency when I'm around. My auntie enjoys that aspect of my residence here, but old Hazel caught on the minute I appeared in town. You can't fool the hearth and home supes; they know where beings belong like they know their own hands.

My head tilts and I ponder for a moment. I wonder if I should talk to the pup about helping my Tíogair lure a domovoy to our place. That would help immensely, especially since her very human caretakers are getting on in years. The sprite might know, too, whenever she rolls back into town with her crew.

A palm slaps the counter next to me and I look up to see good old Percy Atwater looking impatiently at the town's secret treasure.

"Hazel, what's going on today? I'm so hungry I could eat the south-end of a north-bound polecat."

Raking my gaze over his somewhat portly form, I snort into the Earl Gray Hazel left me. Percy swivels his head to stare me down, but I'm not intimidated by the arctic wolf shifter. I've got more power and wealth in one of my hangnails than Atwater has amassed through his nepotism. That means I ignore his irritated gaze as I continue sipping the tea.

"Haggerty, who the hell asked you, boy?" he finally huffs as he leans in. "You strut 'round here like a peacock, but without the Mayor, you'd be old news long ago."

Oh, the hubris lower beings have when they've been wrongfully elevated by money.

I set my tea down, smiling in what I believe to be a pleasant manner as I look at the grocery store owner. "Percy, old bean, I think you might have been hitting the Fireball in your coffee this morning. I'd suggest taking a bracing constitutional in the chilly air before you find yourself in a tight spot."

Man, everyone of those assholes in our family should give me praise for this control; I'm rocking this shit.

"Christ on crutches, you're a dimwit," Percy says as he stands, looming over me menacingly. "I told you to mosey on along."

My head tilts as I look at him in confusion. The fuck he did—in fact, *I* told *him* to fuck off. Has everyone in this town been smoking some sort of hallucinogenic plant their entire lives? This is why I avoid all of them like the medieval fucking plague; they're incomprehensible *and* stubborn as mules. "Percy, Hazel's diner is a *no-fly zone* for this sort of shit. I told you to walk it off, not the other way around, and I meant it."

He puffs up, stepping forward like he's going to challenge me, and I look around the room quickly. When I confirm none of the humans are in the house, I smirk as I duck the fast punch that comes my way with supernatural speed. He tries again, and fails, then once more before the flea-bitten lupine shifter howls in fury.

"Man, what is your *damage?* I didn't even speak to you, you great git!"

Hazel walks over, her eyes flashing with swirling power. "Percival Whitman Atwater, you are violating the laws of my hearth. Doyle attempted to curb your foolishness twice, and you did not heed the warning. You will be judged, and you will be punished."

Fuck yeah, Hazel, give it to this dickface.

"H-Hazel… I… no." Percy shakes his head, looking around in confusion for a moment. "What the hell just happened? I came in here and I had to wait, but there was this smell…"

I arch a brow, looking at the idiot carefully. "What smell?"

"I don't know. Girly, I supposed. But I smelled it and… that's all I remember."

My hands fly to my face as I rub them over my features in frustration.

"That's right, Doyle, my boy," Hazel murmurs under her breath. "Someone planted a scent trigger for your girl. There're witches involved."

Isn't that fucking peachy?

Dangerous

Jolene

Sighing in irritation, I look at Andromeda. "Doyle says I have to stay within the school, my studio, or home. Something's up."

Her brow furrows, and she immediately loses the relaxed pose. Now I see the hunter—the predator—she truly is. The tension in her posture and alert look in her eyes mirrors what I've seen in my guys, especially when I got that glimpse of what was really going on in Faerie.

"That shifty Irish asshole never shares with the class. It's going to make everything harder."

I arch a brow. "He told me, at least."

"Did he say where he was?" Bane fidgets a little and I have to keep my jaw firmly closed when I notice an aura shimmering over her that chills my blood.

What the fuck is she?

"No. But it's lunchtime, so I'd assume Hazel's." I don't mention how nerve-wracking it's been to have her back here while I taught my morning classes. She refused to leave, and I refused to cancel them, so we were at a stand-off until the first students filtered in. The compromise was her presence in my office, so I could come back and speak with her whenever the kids were occupied.

Rocking a little in the chair, I watch as the wheels turn in her head. It's fascinating to see the spikes of energy moving around her, even if I feel like I'm being frozen by whatever powers she has glide over me. "Hazel's is sacred. No one is supposed to use it for… disagreements. She'll be furious."

I nod, grinning a bit as I consider the woman smacking someone with a spatula. "Agreed. Whoever is fucking around is definitely going to find out the consequences when Hazel tracks them down."

A short bark of laughter eases the tension a little, and the formerly missing counselor sighs. "Everything about you has thrown carefully constructed traditions and rules by the wayside. The reports I've gotten while I was occupied were not what I expect from the Hollow. But then, many things in many places are not what I'd expect right now."

"That bigger picture you keep mentioning?"

Andromeda nods. "The trouble at State U, the uprising in Salem, a disturbance on the West Coast… and worse, other issues I can't speak of generally enough to stay within the limits. However, there are places that should *not* be having problems that they currently are. The place you traveled to, another darker place, an island, a European location, and even one outside of the control of our laws —all struggling with issues that are bigger than they seem. Those are only the major incidents, by the way. Small clusters of weird things are occurring all over the globe."

I don't know what it has to do with me, but it sounds fucking terrible.

"You think it's not random?"

"Correction: I *know* it's not random. The requests from the sisters are enough to verify that for me," Bane says with a grunt. "However, whatever is happening here feels local and less globally minded. It's a distraction and we need it to stop so the focus can be on things much more dangerous."

Leaning against the edge of the desk, I shrug. "I have no idea who or what is going on. Doyle just sent the message and since he's the only one who knows I know…"

"You believe it's important." I nod, and she rises to her feet. "I'm going to check it out. If I do a quick run through the town, I should be able to discern what's up his craw. If not, I'll go through the back and get Hazel to spill. As long as I don't interfere with her version of justice, she'll tell me."

"What should I do?"

Her eyes pin me. "Stay in here. Don't leave unless it's a bodily emergency. Be cautious with your students; we do not know if whatever has affected any of them is tripping the annoying asshole's wires. Keep your head on a swivel."

She doesn't have to say that twice; Doyle isn't exactly a worrywart.

"Fine. But you have to bring me something to eat and some goddamn coffee, Andromeda. I've been stuck in here all morning, missed lunch, and now I'm grounded." I narrow my eyes at her, daring her to refuse. "I'm headed towards hangry and apparently, that's not a good thing lately."

"Oh." She snorts, then shakes her head. "Well, that clarifies a few things. Proving a negative is almost as helpful as proving a positive with puzzles."

Putting my fingers to my temples, I try not to scream. As much as I'm grateful she's revealed *some* shit, it only leads to more riddles and double-speak. I'm not sure I'm even better off than before her visit to solve what the fuck is going on. "Whatever. Just bring food and caffeine."

"Aye, aye, Captain."

Before I can retort, she's gone like she faded into mist and I have grit my jaw to keep the scream of frustration from escaping.

This is not my goddamn day.

MAKING IT THROUGH THE NEXT CLASS IS EXCRUCIATING. I'M HUNGRY, on edge, and waiting for Andromeda or Doyle to contact me is like standing on a bed of nails. I'm not the most patient person on the best days, but I'm definitely not with all the fucking mystery shit. Bane's betrayal has taken a back seat to my need to know what to look out for—Doyle wouldn't have messaged me if it wasn't important.

But what the hell could be the problem with going somewhere in town?

I don't know enough—or anything at all—about how all this shit works. My lack of basic facts is handicapping me and if I knew what to do to *force* myself to 'emerge' like I need to, I'd be doing it. Even if it's as painful as passing a goddamn kidney stone, I'd hop on that train just to get clued into all the undercurrents and sink holes surrounding me. I really have no idea how I didn't see any of this when I was younger or when I first got back to town.

"Miss Whitley?"

The shrill tone of Ariel Nancy Behle almost gets a cringe out of me. While Brittania seems to have found her Zen because of our private lessons, the other Nip/Tuck children in my classes this semester have been much less circumspect. Luckily, I only have one in this session, but she's a doozy. Turning to face the pugnacious girl with a tight smile, I walk closer to where she's messing about with her canvas.

And I mean 'messing about' because she's not taking this seriously at all.

"I have no idea why it looks so messy. Pawpaw and Mama both say artists are lazy bums with no real world skills who suckle at the teat of true business people." Her lips tip up in a wicked smirk as she continues in the loud voice. "I should be able to do this with no problem; I'm *gifted*, after all."

Pausing to keep the biting retort from slipping past my lips, I look at the state of her filthy water glass, messy brushes, and lack of sketching below the globs of paint. "Ariel, you've been misled. Artists spend years, if not decades, honing their craft. While there are prodigies, most start at the beginning—where everything stinks—then practice so they get better. Painting well is a muscle you train, not something anyone can pick up a brush and be proficient at."

Her huff makes my insides flutter with glee, but I school my features as she frowns. "They also say that only people who can't succeed at selling their art become loser teachers. I guess that's true, huh?"

If she weren't a freaking kid…

"Perhaps some adults enjoy shaping the young minds of the future? That's often why they choose to teach. However, they also may have toured the globe, working for titans of industry and royalty like me, and decide to settle down somewhere less wild as they get older." Her snort burns my biscuits, so I can't help but add, "When some of your pieces hang in palaces, it doesn't feel necessary to live such a stressful lifestyle anymore."

Ariel's eyes turn to saucers as I shrug, walking away to leave her with her half-assed attempt at painting. I'd feel bad for abandoning her, but she didn't follow a single one of my instructions about her supplies, nor did she put in an iota of effort. Then she put me on blast because others in her little group are getting better results than her. I don't have to put up with abuse, no matter who is doing it, and just like with Brittania, I have to set a boundary.

Most of the kids here direly need those, I'm learning.

"My mother will hear about this!"

I turn back to the snotty girl, smiling through gritted teeth. "And Principal Ratliff will hear the recording I made of your statements. I believe some of them will fall under WHFS' stringent anti-bullying policy."

The snickers that erupt from around the room make my heart happy, but I know they're not for me. WFHS students simply enjoy *someone* getting taken down, no matter who it is. They'll joyously eat their own if it makes them look good in comparison—just like their parents. I don't acknowledge the faux show of support; instead, I start a loop around the room to see how the others are faring. Putting some distance between me and the popular girls is a good idea right now.

Halfway around, I stop to study a fairly decent rendition of the football stadium. The kid working on it is small, so not a player, and bespectacled. He doesn't look as snooty as the others and it occurs to me he might not be part of the 'Children of Corn' rich kids sect. I tilt my head to admire his work, deciding not to say anything now lest it cause a retaliation later on. Pulling out my phone, I glance at the seating chart, noting his name for later on.

Rhett Easton Barnes, you're going to be the first recipient of a Whitley Gallery Scholarship.

Satisfied with my discovery, I move on, looking at every painting and cataloguing the student in my head. Knowing what their base talent level is will help me work with them throughout the semester. All of this hoopla in my private life distracted me during the break, but I refuse to let the kids down. After all, Bobbi Jo took a chance on me and I highly doubt my name was an easy sell.

The bell finally rings, and I watch every one of the kids beside my secret favorite gather their things and jet out of the room. They've all left a mess I have to clean up and even though it's my free period next, that won't do. The first topic on the docket tomorrow will be learning to set-up *and* break-down your station daily without being late for your next class.

Sighing, I start the process while the canvases continue drying on the easels. If Andromeda doesn't get back here soon with my food, I'm going to break my damn promise. There's no way I can make it through another gauntlet with a student like Ariel if my temper is riding me. My stomach growls again and I grunt, stomping to the back room to dump the water glasses in my hands in the sink. This is such bullshit, but that's what I get for teaching teenagers, I suppose.

You could call me a masochist and you'd likely be right.

What's Up?

Presley

"I wonder what has Doyle's boxers in a knot?" I ask as Lucy and I pull into the lot at Town Hall. "He was especially dickish when he texted everyone for this meeting."

Lucy shrugs, squinting at the rest of the cars. "I don't know, but he didn't want to talk about it on tech. Looks like we're the last ones here, too."

Rolling my eyes, I hop out, waiting for him at the edge of the car. "We have patients and appointments. Foster only had to get coverage from one of his other employees, and who the hell knows what Boone does all day? His docket is pretty light most weeks, but his side business is, as always, hopping, I'd assume."

My love grins shyly, and my heart thumps at the happiness in his expression. I had no idea when we found Magpie she'd bring such a wealth of affection and acceptance to our lives, but I'm imminently grateful for it. I adore how complete the family makes me feel, but watching the confidence and joy it brings Lucy is even better. He's spreading his wings—literally and metaphorically—and it's fucking beautiful to see.

Some people might be jealous, but not me; I'm bursting with pleasure at his trans-formation.

"Are we going in, Prez?"

I shake my head, smiling ruefully. "Of course, Lucy. I just got lost in my head for a second."

He grabs my hand and squeezes, tugging me forward. "Let's see what's so damn urgent that Nelia wanted a full house, then."

I lost sight of that for a moment, but he's right—what the hell is going on that requires all of us?

"Doyle filled me in on your trip across the Veil."

Nelia is leaning back in her chair, looking regal yet relaxed as she studies our group. It's weird to be here without Magpie. Since she's not fully emerged, we can't include her without breaking our oath—something I intend to bring up in the next full Council meeting after she's fully inducted. I think that oath is outdated, and perhaps it contributes to losing those we believe have some of their powers developing but aren't emerged by the time they get to college-age.

That sends a half-powered being with zero knowledge or training into the world that needs to be constantly monitored.

It might have worked decades or centuries ago when people traveled less and the world felt smaller, but now? The possibilities are endless and the potential outcomes are horrifying. We can't continue leaving the 'lost ones' completely in the dark about our world after maturity, even if they don't *seem* to manifest their genetics. There's far too much leeway for someone to go down a destructive path.

Boone tilts his head, looking back at her as I muse. He's usually the most talkative, even with Doyle, but he's being more reticent than normal. I wonder if he's worried what information Nelia will keep quiet and what she'll take to the Society. Finally, he sighs heavily and nods. "As I put in the report, Faerie has significant issues with royal asshattery—as expected—but the more serious problem is some cross-Court rebellion. They're keeping it *very* quiet, but the leaders in all the courts definitely knew about it. Some of them were using stand-ins, I believe, and others were hiding behind their legions of children."

"Disturbing," Nelia says with a frown. "Fae royals don't prefer letting go of their spotlight. Allowing a stand-in or their kids to grab the glory of illustrious visitors means they're terrified. Yet their representatives have mentioned none of this turmoil in Society gatherings."

"Lucy's father is still a mystery—one they all seemed keen to keep quiet and bury in obscure history books," I say quietly. "I can't tell if that's a bad thing or simply the Fae being their secretive selves about their history."

"I vote history," Doyle says suddenly. "They have a lot of transitory movement between courts and their heroes or villains. None of it is well known to those outside of the Veil, and they despise outsiders knowing about scandal. If he was powerful and well known, but made a choice, like sleeping with Callie, they'd want it buried as far down as possible."

My lover turns bright red, ducking his head, and Boone tsks. "Don't be embarrassed, pup. You have nothing to do with their choices or Fae politics. Their bullshit isn't yours to take on."

"I know, but it's difficult to hear," he mumbles. I take his hand, raising his fingers to my lips. "But I have a wonderful family now, so I'm dealing with my issues slowly."

That's something I've been after him to do about most of the time we've been together, so I can't describe how goddamn thrilled I am to hear it.

"Wolfgang, you're a treasured member of this town, even if some people aren't evolved enough to appreciate you and Dr. Hamilton. Don't let the haters win," the mayor says with a warm expression.

Lucy chuckles, his face still red, but his smile genuine. "Thank you, Nelia."

"So, what else did you gather on this trip?" she asks.

Doyle tenses, and I have to school my features. He's resisting something, and I'm not sure what. After a moment, he says, "We gained an ally—possibly. I'm uncertain, so I'd be wary of reporting his name to the higher members. There was a battle on one of the Hunt fields, so some of our forms were witnessed fighting with them."

"That's not particularly concerning," Nelia says, as she taps her lips with her fingers. Zareb shifts next to her and Lucy clicks his tongue, causing the enormous lion to lope toward us. "Ah, you've always had a way with him, Dr. Fletcher."

My love flushes again, this time with pleasure, and ruffles his hand over the cat's mane. "He's a perfect specimen, Nelia, and I enjoy his presence. I suppose it's Fae in me, but cats are always a friendly balm."

"*Definitely* the Fae," Boone mutters, and we all laugh. "But he does well with the entire menagerie that has invaded our home."

A soft snort gets my attention and I turn to grin at Benjy. His avatar only recently joined, but the damn simian is already causing hijinks. It's completely contrary to his calm behavior. "I'm the least accustomed to all this subterfuge, as you all know, but it's very clear that there's a lot more going on than our superiors either know or are telling us. It feels dangerous, Nelia, and you've never been one to allow people to be exposed that way."

The mayor sits up in her chair, regarding Foster with a narrowed gaze. "You've gotten bolder with your chosen mate, Benjamin. I'll forgive that insinuation because you cushioned the blow, but I would *never* allow my people to be harmed if I can help it."

"Nelia, he's pointing out the obvious," Boone says impatiently. "If there are issues flittering about in other areas of the country and the world, plus issues rising in the Veil… this is a bigger problem than some conspirators killing Tilly's parents and covering it up. It's more widespread than Aurelia ending up out of her mind in a home. And it's more sinister than someone sneaking around her bushes."

Her exhale is resigned, and she leans forward, straightening papers on her desk before her gaze returns to us. "We aren't sure, Edgar. Chaos and butterfly wings, right? There are the sisters wielding their threads, but also the fantastical ability of the universe where those who believe in free will affect change that alters their patterns. You know this—yet you expect us to have accurate information without proper input."

"We expect you to be honest about your suspicions," I interject. "It can be a theory, but allow us the courtesy of preparing."

"Fine. But know, the upset in Faerie is more than we knew about prior to your reports. We'd heard some small rebel groups were making noise in some courts, but nothing on this scale. So we hadn't connected that to the witch clan Bane and Julia's team were handling." There's a slight pause and she sighs. "Nor to the rumbling on the west coast or the oddities at the university. Random pockets of trouble aren't always connected, but piece by piece, some of these things are making a larger picture. It's simply unfolding slowly, which reeks of long-term planning."

Lucy puts his hands on his face, and I know what he's doing. He's the only certified genius in the room and he has to block out all the other input for his brain to expand the board to include all this new information. If anyone can see the picture more clearly, it's him or our girl, but she's not here. He needs to focus, so I reach into my pocket to hand him the tiny case I keep with me. His smile is grateful as he takes it, pops the earplugs in, and goes back to thinking.

"What was that?" Teddy asks with a frown.

I grin, tilting my head. "Lucy's brilliant, which you know, but when he *really* needs to focus on something the rest of us can barely comprehend, he has to block out the world. I keep these tiny Loop things to help with that; don't let me forget to order more for the rest of you. You can tell when he needs it because he makes that exact face every single time."

The judge blinks, then his face turns bright red as he realizes something. "Got it. Definitely order a fucking boatload of them, Hamilton. For all of us, the cars, the rooms... whatever. I'll *buy* the fucking company if necessary."

Okay, then.

Benjy shakes his head at me. "Welcome to the logic of the Uber-rich and powerful, man. If my man cares about someone, he'll do whatever it takes to keep them happy and healthy. Don't let it phase you; I had to talk him out of buying a bourbon distillery because they wouldn't give me a lottery number three years ago."

Nelia blinks, and I burst out laughing. Everyone in our town and state knows what the lottery is and how hard it is to get a number for those golden bottles of the best bourbon we have to offer. "Buying the whole fucking distillery seems very rational and not at all over-the-top."

"That's what I said," Boone grumbles. "He told me 'no' and I've been getting my revenge in other ways ever since."

Doyle clears his throat, his eyes cutting to Nelia from behind. "So, what else do we need to discuss? We'll need to get moving with our days, especially the Mayor or the rest of the building is going to get very suspicious. It will get back to our girl if we're not careful. That little troll in the lobby is dying to spread your presence here around."

Nelia's eyes roll to the ceiling as if for help, then she shakes her head. "I'll deal with Aldous. If the former mayor hadn't allowed that fucking clause into the purchase of the town, he wouldn't be here anymore. Everything they did to create this place as a haven, including the barrier spell, the emergence enchantments, and the magic keeping the humans' curiosity at bay is tied together by that damn thing. I've long suspected they had someone at least partly Fae check the loopholes because I've *pored* over it to figure out how to be shed of the little creep."

I grin at her. "Have you asked Jackson Thorn to look at it?"

She frowns. "No, why on earth would I do that?"

"Because Magpie wouldn't be using the idiot if he wasn't fucking brilliant, and I'd wager fresh eyes wouldn't hurt."

"Hmmm. He's rather bust at the moment at State U, but you're right, Presley. I should have him take a gander. His team is rather thorough." She shuffles some papers again, then gives us a serious look. "Is there anything else I should know before we part?"

"There's a minor problem with magical triggers about the town I'm handling." Doyle crosses his arms over his chest and I get a dark feeling he's being vague for a reason. "I think we should craft a town announcement about legal and illegal use of various magics that is sent to the emerged to remind them of the consequences of fucking around."

Her brow arches. "Are you the one who's going to make them 'find out', as the kids say?"

The energy in the room rises as a soft glow envelops him. "They'll be lucky if it's only my wrath they face when I find the culprits, Nelia."

That's not at all subtle and suddenly, I'm feeling very vengeful myself.

Afraid of Quiet

Jolene

Andromeda finally deigns to show up an hour later, and I'm damn near ready to eat a fucking desk. My mood has taken a complete nosedive, and I stalk into the back room to tear into her when I notice she's frowning rather than snarkily gloating.

Uh-oh.

Taking a deep breath to calm myself, I face the woman I very much want to rip a new one for her betrayal. "What the hell is wrong now?"

She shoves a bag of food at me, her brow quirking. "You need to eat first. No sense in trying to talk when you're spending calories at an astronomical rate simply to stay upright."

The scent overrides my desire for information, so I plop down on the floor like a kid and dig in. Groaning at the taste of the cheeseburger, I inhale the food so quickly I barely have time to get my fingers out of the way. It's so good my body damn near quivers with satisfaction. When I'm finally done, the ache in bones is calmer, and my brain feels like it's almost functional again. "Why the fuck am I so fricking ravenous, Bane? I ate this morning; it's not like I'm starving."

She chuckles, shaking her head with a sigh. "The stupid goddamn rules… Every single time."

I frown, licking the leftovers from my fingertips. "Huh?"

"Your men have spoken of rules, I imagine. They were created long enough ago that... things were different. When this town was acquired in your early childhood, things were put in place that were best left in the past times, but... It is hard to get such long honored traditions to change. It has made my work and that of doctors in this town very difficult over the years."

Fucking bureaucracy screws people over constantly, I swear to shit.

"So? What does that have to do with me feeling like I need to eat an entire cow?"

Her lips purse, and she looks like she's weighing her next words. "Because things that people need to know are forbidden to be shared until it's no longer an option. However, with life expectancy extending and maturity ages lowering even in humans, that restriction prevents real preventative care. We have to work within the set boundaries or be punished. But it needs to change, and no one has been brave enough to affect that change."

"I'm starving because of things I can't know, but somehow need to deal with until I can know? That's what you're saying?" I glare at her in frustration, feeling the impotent fury I felt when I taught at the low-income schools or toured Europe with secretive rich idiots.

"Yes." She sighs, running her hand through her hair as she gathers herself. "It left a lot of information to older generations to sneakily impart to their youth in various ways. But America is not as solid with verbal storytelling traditions, especially in this internet age, so the children here are woefully under-educated unless specific triggers allow them to be brought into the light."

Ah, this is why the Faerie people were so smug; supes here are fucking their kids by not finding loopholes or taking responsibility.

"Is this something... anyone... is working on? Like now?" I ask curiously. "Cause it seems really stupid and potentially dangerous."

"Hence your current situation and possibly, many across the globe," she smirks. "So yes, there are people raising the alarms now. Our previous by-laws and... boundaries... need adjusting for the new era. Otherwise, it leaves room for the kind of thing we're experiencing across *many* areas."

Tilting my head, I consider the past few months. "Is that why the guys are always looking to feed me?"

"Indeed. They know from experience what needs to be done, even if they aren't certain what *specifically* you need. No one really knows that until the moment arrives, but there are some general steps you can take." Andromeda leans back in her chair, steepling her fingers as she looks at me seriously. "Your Irish friend took one when he texted you about staying localized."

"That's a general step for all this shit?"

"No. It's a general step for another concern—one he's right to have. I assume he's filling in the rest of your little group as they leave their meeting with Nelia." She grins, obviously aware she's dropping a piece of knowledge I didn't have. "Something you don't need to mention if you say I dropped by."

All these damn secrets and shenanigans under cover are exhausting.

"I really need all the shadowy crap to stop," I grumble. "I know I wanted to be an agent and I *love* mysteries and puzzles, but not in *my* life. It's too fucking much, Andromeda."

She nods, her expression melting to one of understanding. "I get that, Jolene. You aren't the first and won't be the last to struggle with this. However, there are reasons they set boundaries in the way they did—valid historical ones—and they actually helped for a long time. It's a hindrance now, but when you find out the entire story, you'll understand what everyone is protecting."

"Yeah," I reply with a frown. "I probably will. But it feels lousy now and I doubt the guilt will subside, even if there are good reasons. Hell, I know for a fact my family will have to air all this shit out, so it's not some big thing hanging over our head."

Her lips quirk up. "You've got shit to say to me, I bet. The generations born after the nineteen seventies always do. Therapy and expressing emotions to find a healthy balance is not the bad thing elders make it out to be, but that doesn't mean it's comfortable for anyone."

I snort. "Fuck, yes, I do. You lied to me for *years,* despite my struggles. My parents lied to me. Everyone knew shit I didn't and tortured me, regardless. Now some of the same motherfuckers torture me as adults—all the while having this big secret that makes me a fool amongst the sharks."

"That's true. Most of the people you know the best have kept you in the dark because they had no other option. But again, it's not uncommon; it simply used to be uncommon for someone like you to ever need the truth to be explained this late in life."

My eyes narrow on her, and I tilt my head. "What do you mean, *used to be?*"

Andromeda looks up, her expression thoughtful again, and I know she's working out how to skirt around that stupid oath. The damn thing is making my life a cosmic joke, and when I meet the idiot who enacted it, I'm going to punch them in the mouth. "There are a lot of things happening right now that are... unheard of or uncommon. It's using a lot of resources, including me, and it's causing the whispers that may enact change. However, no one can focus on that topic because, along with this irregular behavior, there's very suspicious and potentially harmful activity that must be dealt with."

If that's not a load of vague bullshit, I don't know what is.

"That's... entirely unhelpful, but points for trying." I grin a little and my stomach burbles. "I don't think that was enough to quell the beast."

Her smirk is wicked as she laughs. "Probably not. You'll have to survive until you go home—which I'd heartily advise you to do immediately after work unless you have no other option. Not only because you need to consume more food to settle yourself, but also because of what your lover told you."

"Just how much do I need to eat to deal with this, Bane? I don't know if you've noticed, but I stay very balanced since college. I don't want to regress into old bad habits." I refuse to tell her a damn thing about how bad off I was after high school or in college, but the sad look on her face makes me wonder if she knows already. "Don't you dare pity me."

"I don't," she says softly. "You were caught between a world you couldn't know and one that's very difficult for females. You were strong enough to survive with help and you don't wish to be weak again. That's not something to be pitied for—it's something to be proud of."

Damn it, she knows. Is nothing private?

"Fine. Tell me how to restructure my diet so I don't choke a student."

This time, she doubles over in laughter and I growl softly until she finally stops. "Oh, Jolene Whitley. I *do* love your mettle. Your doctor can help you—simply tell him how hungry you were and he'll make suggestions. Trust me; he knows what to do better than I."

"Do you ever answer a question straight or do you just 'riddle me this' like a fucking Sphinx?" I blink, then stare at her with a raised brow as I wonder if I've hit the nail on the head.

"No. I definitely do *not* dispense nothing but riddles. Not my thing." She winks, and I sigh in irritation. "I'm more of a vengeful type when I know it's warranted."

Rising to my feet, I dust off my ass and legs, then stretch a bit. "As fascinating as this is, are you going to give me a clue why I can't go places besides needing to eat? They sell food all over town."

Andromeda stands as well, cracking her neck. "This town is supposed to be safe for everyone. It's part of the… rules. It is not currently safe for *some people* and that needs to be dealt with appropriately."

Great. She's saying the damn city is full of 'Jolene-shaped' booby traps.

"I'll bet I know who they're going to go after, too." Pinching the bridge of my nose, I stifle the urge to scream. The mean girls from high school got their pound of flesh then and they've gotten more than enough since I returned. I don't understand why they're *still* coming for me years later. It's completely insane and despite being able to analyze it clinically, I'm flabbergasted on a normal person level.

"Jolene, some people grow up with such wrecked self-images that therapy can only do so much. They have to *want* to put the work in getting better, and though no professional wants to admit it, even if they do, some *can't* actually heal. Their psychosis is too deeply ingrained in their personality and worldview. If they let go of their anger at their 'haters' and 'enemies,' there's simply nothing left."

Tell me something I don't know.

I crack my knuckles, closing my eyes as I get my emotions under control. This topic is one I've discussed with kids many times, and she's not wrong, but it's so much harder when it's *you* dealing with the abuse. "I know that. Narcissists are particularly resistant to seeing the damage they do, and guaranteed, the leader of these sheep hasn't ever accepted culpability for her actions once in her life. But it's still a tough pill to swallow, knowing that this seething pit of childish, immature bullshit will never go away."

"Feels like one good punch to the mouth would fix it, huh?"

My eyes fly open, and I shrug. "It would set a stringent boundary. But I know that would only feed the fire."

"You're right; it would. However, in my very extensive experience, these people hang themselves with their own rope; you simply need to be patient." Andromeda walks over and pats me on the shoulder. "They will keep pushing and their actions will be more and more erratic. Bullies eventually drop the mask and reveal themselves for what they are with a grand, almost completely unavoidable meltdown in public. Yours will, too, when the right moment presents itself. Be patient."

Snorting, I shake my head. "Is it weird to say that is and is not my strong suit? I'm very good at patience with some things and others… it seems like it's getting harder every day."

"Not surprising," she replies with an amused look. "But you have a good head on your shoulders and you know what you need to do. Now, finish out your day while I get some shit done I need to, then go home. I think you'll find a better surprise than just food this evening."

That said, she stalks over to the back door, leaving without another word.

Just what the fuck does that mean?

Find out in Revenge in the Hollow (Book Four of M.P.P.) coming soon!

REVIEWS, PRINT, AND MERCHANDISE

If you have enjoyed this story, please review it.
It helps other readers find my work,
which helps me as an indie author.

Thank you!

Reviews are appreciated on the following platforms

TikTok
Instagram
Facebook
Bookbub
StoryGraph
Threads

To purchase print copies or merchandise, go to The Worlds of Cassandra Featherstone

GET A SECRET BONUS SCENE!

For another secret bonus scene that follows *Revealed in the Hollow,* click the link below, sign up for my newsletter, and get your freebie.

Get your bonus scene here!

World & Pronunciation Guide

****This could have spoilers. Beware!****

Characters

Jolene Athena Whitley 'Tilly', 'JoJo', 'Sugarplum', 'Magpie', 'Tíogair' 'Peanut' (Joh LEEN Ah-THEE-nuh Wit-lee) we don't know her supe sides yet, only that she's unemerged, was bullied in HS in a big incident that got her named 'The Cotillion Catastrophe'. Calls Edgar Teddy, Wolfie is little Wolfie and McDreamy, Prez is Doctor McNuggies and McSteamy, Doyle is Lucky.

Jekyll and Hyde- serval cats who adopted Jolene when she arrived in town

Isis- rainbow reticulated python who appeared when Jolene was threatened in the *Hollar* office

Kali and Hecate- Edgar's King Dane dogs

Eurayle- A Harpy eagle that also appeared and adopted Jolene

Edgar Olivier Boone III 'Teddy' 'Daddy' 'Teddy Bear' 'Hound' 'Doggy' (ed-gar OH-live-ee-ay bOOn) triple hybrid—hellhound, incubi, and Quetzalcoatl shifts; calls Jolene Tilly and Wolfie Pup

Presley Hemingway Hamilton 'Prez' 'Doctor McNuggies' 'McSteamy' 'Birdman' (press-lee Hem-ing-way HAM-ul-ton)- town doctor, involved with Wolfie, caladrius. Calls Wolfie Lucy, Jolene Magpie.

Wolfgang Lucien Fletcher 'Lucy' 'Pup' 'Wolfie' 'McDreamy' (wulf-GahnG too-See-n Fleht-CHUR)- town vet, involved with Prez and Teddy, subbie, dark Fae and Calleich mother, adoptive mother in asylum. Calls Jolene Sugarplum, Teddy Daddy.

Doyle Aloysius Haggerty 'Lucky' (doy-UHL Al-oh-wishus Hag-ert-ee)- ancient but doesn't look it, works PR at Mayor's office, demigod hybrid, sent to Hollow to monitor, chaotic. Calls Jolene Tíogair, Edgar Doggy, Presley Birdman.

Odie- Doyle's secret raven companion

Hugo Atlas Macauley (hue-go AT-lass MACK-all-ee) only male of his species, acolyte of a goddess, related to other acolytes, teaches history at HS

Benjamin Louis Foster 'Benjy' (behn-JAH-min loo-ee Foss-tur) Old HS best friend of Teddy, owns Bottle 'N Cans, married to Sherilynn Foster Grant, divorced her when he realized Jolene was his mate, gorilla shifter; adopted children Scarlett, Simon, and Simone

Prince Dhameer Mirza Al Sharqi 'Amiri' (Dah-MEER MearZAH AL Shahrkey) djinn; owner of Mehdi; new contender in Jolene's life

Percival Whitman Atwater 'Percy' (purr-sive-uhl wit-man at-wahtur) owns Atwater's Store

Virginia Dolly Atwater (ver-GIN-n-yuh dahl-ee at-wahtur) Percy's sister, teaches English at HS, wants to date Teddy

Andromeda Bane (ann-dram-eh duh bay-n) guidance counselor at HS, was also counselor when Teddy and Jolene in school, clearly more than that

Isra (iz-RAH) the eternal guard of the Prince

Fazal (Fie-zahl) the butler of the Prince, his family worked for theirs for hundreds of years

Mehdi (MEH-ee-DEE) gorgeous thoroughbred horse belonging to the Prince that Jolene trains

Malik (Mah-leek) The Prince's favorite Arabian mount

Randall Keynes Barrington (ran-DULL KEE-nz BEAR-ing-tuhn) human; Chief of Police in the Hollow; father to Reese Barrington; married to Elyse Lance

Reese Emily Barrington (REE-ss ehM-ih-lee BEAR-ing-tuhn) member of Nip/Tucks; one of Jolene's bullies; hybrid of a TikTok and a witch; manages Star Spangled Bank; married to Joseph Stephenson; adoptive mother to Carlotta and Cordelia Barrington

Amy Matilda Behle (AY-mee Muh-Till-duh BEEL) member of Nip/Tucks; one of Jolene's bullies; human, runs Hollow Hollar; daughter of Victoria & Reginald Behle; married to Lysander Behle; adoptive mother to Ariel, Dante, & Edward Behle

Lysander Marx Behle (LIE-san-dur MARR-x BEEL) unicorn shifter; interior designer; married to Amy Behle; children Ariel, Dante, and Edward

Edgar Osiris Boone II (ed-GAR OH-sigh-ris BOON) Teddy's adoptive father; Senator; Ouroboros agent; married to Margaret Emily Roth; human

Margaret Emily Roth (marr-GUH-ret EM-IL-ee Rah-th) harpy; Teddy's adoptive mother; married to the Senator

Eliot James Cantwell 'Jamie' (Eh-lee-ut Jaymz CANT-wel) Proprietor of Cantwell Farms, older than Jolene but a friend

Fidelia Violet Cantwell (fihd-AY-lee-uh VY-o-let CANT-wel) Percy's sister, owner of Dress Me Up Buttercup

Mina Cantwell (meenuh CANT-wel) Fidelia and Jamie's mother, retired horse farm owner

Aurelia Darcy Fletcher (AR-ale-ee-uh DAR-see Fleh-T-chur) Wolfie's mother, who has been in an asylum since he was sixteen

Aoife (ee-FUH) pixie Fae; member of the *Laochra Na Peitil* in the Daybreak Court

Sítheach (Shea-u-ch) Fairy; member of the *Laochra Na Peitil* in the Daybreak Court

Ciarán (kee-RUN) fairy/angel hybrid; member of the *Laochra Na Peitil* in the Daybreak Court

Daire (Dah-RUH) Fae; member of the *Laochra Na Peitil* in the Daybreak Court

Taranis (tear-AN-us) Fae/goblin hybrid; member of the *Laochra Na Peitil* in the Daybreak Court

Dylan Marlowe Grant (dill-N MARR-low GRANT) pixie; runs Bound Together; Ouroboros inductee; companion Nostradamus, a great horned owl; dating Detective Santos; parents Oscar and Zelda

Sherilynn Grant Foster (Share-UH-lin GRANT foss-tur) pixie/selkie; hybrid; runs Derby Pies; divorced from Benjy; companions Italian greyhounds Cleo and Marcus; adopted children Scarlett, Simon, and Simone; parents Oscar and Zelda

Zelda Louise Grant (ZELL-duh LOO-eez GRANT) pixie; owns Grant Home Furnishings; children Dylan and Sherilynn; husband Oscar

Aldous Basil Longworth (ALL-duss BAZ-UHL LAHNG-wurth) human, exec asst to Mayor; companions Sphynx cats Poe and Parker; married to Antigone Keene Longworth (deceased); children Ophelia Longworth

Ophelia Jane Longworth (oh-FEE-li-uh JAY-n LAHNG-wurth) siren/mage hybrid; father Aldous and mother Antigone; married to Beauregard Longworth; adopted children Brittania, Charlotte, Claude, and Vincent; runs Tame Your Mane; one of the Nip/Tucks

Saoirse Viola O' Flanagan (SEER-shuh VY-o-luh OH FLAN-uh-GAN) Guardian of Jolene; veela/valkyrie hybrid; cover job fashion designer; adoptive parents Annabelle and Seamus; dating Julia, Tharin, and Zasha

Dorothy Elizabeth Hale (Door-O-thee ee-LIZ-uh-beth HAY-L) married to Jason Simmon (deceased); mother to Jillian Remington; Arachne shifter; runs WAP Florist;

Jillian Marie Remington (Jihl-ee-n Mah-ree Rehm-ing-ton) one of the Nip/Tucks from high school; Arachne shifter; owner Close Encounters of the Baked Kind; married to William Christopher Remington; children are Brutus, Ernest, Blake, Octavian, and George.

Julia Isabelle Ricci (Jooleeuh Iz-uh-bell Ree-Chee) Guardian; dating Saoirse, Tharin, and Zasha; Gorgon.

Tharin Leonidas Drakos (TH-air-in Le-OH-nye-dis Dray-Kohs) dating Zasha, Julia, and Seer; Guardian; wyvern

Zasha Fyodor Petrov (Zah-shuh Fee-yo-door Pet-trawv) Guardian; dating Tharin, Julia, and Seer; Merman.

Jackson Ellison Thorn (Jahk-son Eh-liss-on Thorn) Lawyer; ex-RA of Jolene at State University; retired agent; runs Thorn and Associates; has a Grey wolf companion named Fenrir

Andrew Justin Whitley (an-Drew Justin Wit-lee) Jolene's dad; human; professor at State University; deceased

Eloise Clara Whitley (Eh-low-ez Claire-uh Wit-lee) Jolene's mom; agent; professor at State University; witch

Bobbi Jo Ratliff (Bah-bee Jo Raht-liff) principal at WHFS; human

Cornelia Sykes (Core-neel-ee-uh sigh-ks) Mayor of Whistler's Hollow; chimera; pet lion Zareb; has a harem of her own

Hazel Charlotte Thermapoulos- owner of Hazel's Diner; peacemaker; neutral zone; Laertes

Fiannula and Lorcan- guards at the doors of the Faerie

Deirbhile (DJIR vil a) part of the royal design team Daybreak Court; brownie

Aimhirghin (AV er yin) is part of the royal design team Daybreak Court; goblin

Ríordán (REE ur dawn), part of the royal design team Daybreak Court; Fairy.

Ealadha (Elatha) part of the royal design team Daybreak Court; druid/brownie

Draighean (DRAY un) part of the royal design team Daybreak Court; witch/Fae

Áinfean (AWN f'yun) part of the royal design team Daybreak Court; Fae.

Prince Eógan (OH-uhn) Daybreak Court

Mick & Mack Stuart (MIK and MAK Stew-art) regents of the Harvest Court; leprechauns

Alistair Silkshine (al IS TAIR SILk SHYn) Unseelie Fae; royal interrogator; engaged to Princess Allora of the Harvest Court

Princess Allora (UH for UH) Princess of Harvest Court, daughter of Hieronymous and former Queen; engaged to Alistair

King Hieronymous (HIGH Ron IM us) King of Harvest Court; scholar; father of Allora; married second time to Queen Rinah; first wife Magdalena died

Queen Rinah (ree NAH) second wife of Harvest Court King

Lukas (Loo KAS) husband to Elara, princess of Midnight Court; healer; from family of healers in Daybreak Court; Fae/hedge witch hybrid.

Elara (eh-LAIR-uh) eldest Princess of the Midnight Court, married to Lukas

Julien (Joo-lee-N) fiance to Princess Celstine of the Midnight Court; former leader of Harvest Court's elite security service for royals; half orc/half Fae

Celestina (Ceh-les-TEE-nuh) Second oldest Princess of the Midnight Court, betrothed to Julien

Finntan 'Finn' (fihn-Tahn) fiance to the third oldest Princess Aubrette of Midnight Court; nephew to the King of Court of Reaping; hybrid Yeti/Fairy

Aubrette (ah-BRETT) third oldest Princess of Midnight Court; engaged to Finn

Declan- (deck-LAN) husband of Nissa, fourth oldest Princess of Midnight Court; full Fae; the youngest son of a magic trader from Midnight Court

Nissa- (NISS-uh) fourth oldest Princess of Midnight Court; married to Declan

Riordan (rear-Dan) fiance of Marin, fifth oldest Princess of Midnight Court; wizard/pixie and son of powerful Daybreak magical advisor witch

Marin (MARE-in) fifth oldest Princess of Midnight Court; engaged to Riordan

Keegan (Key-GAN) fiance of Siofra, second youngest Princess of Midnight Court; Elf; son of the Duke of Elvin affairs in Midnight Court

Siofra (Seef-FRA) second youngest Princess of Midnight Court; engaged to Keegan

Angus (ANG-us) fiance of the youngest Princess of Midnight Court; merman/Fae; heir to the largest shipping conglomerate in Harvest Court

Flora (flor-uh) youngest Princess of Midnight Court

Darragh (Dare-AH) King of Court of Reaping

Eabha (Av-AH) Queen of Court of Reaping, originally from Daybreak Court

Njord (NY-ord) orc/Fae armorer from Court of Reaping

Alf (Ahlfuh) Elven weapons master for Court of Reaping

Bodil (beau-Deal) wolf shifter and beast master for the Court of Reaping

Revna (Rev-Nuh) Fairy designer of vestments for the Court of Reaping

Locations

Whistler's Hollow- town where it all comes together

The City- nearby bigger city

State U- nearby college where supes go in the city

Atwater's General Store- town grocery store

Cantwell Farms- racehorse and breeding farm at the end of town owned by Percy's family. Jolene and Wolfie work there. Dhameer boards his racehorse there.

Whitley Gallery- Jolene's studio and teaching spot

Whistler's Hollow Formative School- elementary school

Whistler's Hollow Finishing School- middle and high school (Jolene, Teddy, and Hugh work there)

Town Hall- home of the Mayor, her assistant Aldous, and Doyle's jobs

Wild Astor Plants- florist owned by Dorothy Hale

Star Spangled Bank- owned by the Barrington family

Hollow Hollar- town paper owned by Behles

Dress Me Up Buttercup- clothing store owned by Fidelia Cantwell

Bottles 'N Cans- liquor store and speakeasy owned by Benjy

Bound Together- bookstore owned by Dylan Marlowe Grant

Grant Home Furnishings- furniture store owned by Zelda Foster Grant

Derby Pies- pizza joint owned by Fosters

Longworth Family Mortuary- owned by Longworth

Tame Your Mane- salon owned by Ophelia Longworth

Close Encounters of the Baked Kind- bakery owned by Jillian Remington

Better Booties- gym franchise owned by Remington family

Thorn and Associates- mega global law firm now run by Jackson Thorn

Thermopoulos Diner- owned by Hazel, neutral zone

Howl- supe club in the city where Jolene and Seer got dosed, also where they first met Dhameer

Faerie- land of the four courts of the Fae, accessible only by gateway mounds across the world

Midnight Court- aka Summer

Court of Reaping- aka Winter

Harvest Court- aka Autumn

Daybreak Court- aka Spring

Laochra Na Peitil- The Warrior Petal; a welcoming committee in the Daybreak Court made of soldiers who handle high-level visitors to the Court (Aoife, Cíaran, Taranis, Sítheach, and Daire)

Daybreak Court Royal Guest House #1- where the gang stays in the first week of their Faerie trip

Daybreak Castle- where the reel and the royals come together

Harvest Castle- where they are invited to meet the royals

Autumn Hotel- finest hotel in the Harvest capital where the gang stays

Court of Midnight Royal Castle- where the gang stays in Midnight Court with the royals

Winter Wonderland Marketplace- huge wintery market in the Court of Reaping

Court of Reaping Castle- where the gang stays and the hunt is held in the Court of Reaping

The Fields of the Hunt- where the Court of Reaping holds the start of the Wild Hunt

SNEAK PEEK: VEILED FLAME

LOSER

Kat

The little blue icon on my app has been glaring at me all day, but I'm too damn nervous to open it. Everyone at Woodlawn High has been buzzing all day with their notifications and the squeals of joy and moans of despair were too much for me to take. My anxiety is through the roof—this is the moment I've been waiting for since middle school, but I can't seem to force myself to bite the billet and check.

Maybe it's because I don't have the support system most of my classmates have?

That's probably true, given I've always been a loner and I don't fit into any specific 'caste' here. It's hard to make friends when you get shuffled from foster home to foster home over the years. I've rarely stayed anywhere long enough to make a friend, much less a group of them.

I'm not delinquent or anything—the families I've been placed with just return me like a pair of pants that doesn't fit after a year or so. The caseworkers click their tongues sympathetically and hunt down a new placement, but I've never been given a reason *why* people don't want me around. One lady said I must be born under a bad sign and hell if I knew what that meant other than I'm not good enough to keep around.

It would be different, almost understandable, if I misbehaved or got bad grades. But I don't—I'm always in the top five percent of my class and I do everything I'm asked. I don't even lord my smarts over the other kids or adults. Being presentable and unassuming was something I adapted long ago to improve my probability of staying in a home long term.

Unfortunately, it never worked and though I should be a shoo-in for scholarships and acceptances galore, I can't bring myself to be rejected yet again.

So I wait for the last bell of the day, slinging my bag over my shoulder and trudging home to the latest in my temporary housing. I can't even contemplate looking at the possible heartache waiting for me in the college application system WHS insisted we use. The fear is too great and despite knowing I'll be on my own for good at the end of this year, I'm unable to risk the pain.

I hate being this way.

My court mandated therapist says it's some sort of attachment disorder that's common in foster kids, but I think that's bullshit. The problem isn't *me* not forming attachments; it's asshole adults not forming one to me. Being left at a safe haven in a fucking basket as a baby wasn't because *I* did anything wrong—again, fucking adults couldn't handle their commitments.

As usual, I arrive home to an empty house. There are two other kids who live here—Bryce and Blake—but they're at football practice. Of course, the Jamesons *love* them; they get to strut around at games because their strays are the stars of the team. I'm not mistreated, but I'm definitely an afterthought. Both of my 'parents' are still at work, so I drop my bag on the couch and head for the kitchen to get a snack.

Don't get me wrong. I *could* have been placed in far worse homes than any of the seven I've been in since elementary school. None of the ex-fosters starved, beat, molested, or abused me. They were all decent folks with jobs and houses that weren't hellholes, but they never liked me.

I have no idea why. I tried to be everything they wanted.

But when the end of each school year came, I was handed in like a textbook and off I went to some group home until the next contestant stepped up. It baffled everyone, not just me, but that's what happened every single time.

Sighing, I pull some fruit out of the fridge and grab a soda. I have homework to do and if I want to have time to work on my stories, I'll need to get it done before the house is full of people at dinner time. Bryce and Blake will have gotten messages about their applications, too, and I'd bet my pinkie toe those idiots got into some big sports school. Brett and Allison will be oozing happiness for them and I don't know if I'll be able to keep food down if I have to admit my failure when they ask.

Being eighteen sucks ass.

After I grab my books and tablet, I head down to the den. I have to give my current parents credit; they set up a very nice workspace for us to study in the converted basement. By the time they took me in, the Jamesons created a cozy room down here where the three of us could relax and do our work for school without being interrupted. It might have been more for the boys than me, but I appreciated it all the same. Desks, a couch, big chairs, and bookshelves fill the space, making it almost seem like our mini-library. They even put a small fridge for drinks and snacks in case we had to be up late to cram.

It's my favorite place in the entire house and I spend most of my time here.

I sink into the huge armchair, putting my drink and snack on the side table. It only takes a few minutes to arrange myself in the soft cushions and I pause to tug my headphones out of my pocket. Music always soothes my jagged edges and I need it to stay focused on the bullshit AP Calculus I need to keep my average up in. My course load is heavy, but I applied to tough colleges. I wouldn't have a chance to get in, especially on a scholarship, if I wasn't taking equally challenging classes in comparison to all the prep school kids.

As always, the sounds of Vivaldi carry me away as I scrawl equations on my screen and before long, thoughts of the blue notification completely fade away.

"Kat!"

The shouts barely register as I continue working on the problem set, gnawing on my lower lip in concentration.

"Jesus fuck, where is she? I could eat a hippo!"

"Kat!"

Thumping followed by what could pass for a stampede of elephants jerks me out of my math filled trance when Bryce and Blake come down the stairs. They smell as bad as the aforementioned pachyderm's cage, so they must have rushed home right after practice. The blond twins glare at me as if I'm the offending element despite being sweaty and covered in dirt and grass stains.

This doesn't bode well.

Usually, they're tired and hungry after practices so I'm used to cranky ass boys, but tonight, there's a light to their faces. That had to mean they've gotten their letters and dinner will be a gush fest in honor of their perfection. I'm going to need all of my strength to fake smile and nod as Brett and Allison fawn over them.

I don't begrudge them their success—not really. They work hard and play even harder on the field. It's not their fault they're the American dream teens and I'm the nerdy basement troll no one wants. But it's awfully hard living in the shadow of their bright light, especially when I'm no less intelligent or talented.

"I'm finishing the AP Calc, guys. What do you want?"

They roll their eyes at me before Blake scoffs. "It's not due until Monday. You're so hyper."

Duh. I take anxiety meds, douchebag; of course I'm 'hyper.'

"I can only be who I am, Blake." That earns me a snort from Bryce and I know it's because he thinks that's the problem. "Is dinner ready?"

"Almost. Get upstairs and set the table so we can shower—Brett's orders." Blake grins smugly.

The two of them seem to always arrange it so chores get passed to me for some half-assed reason and this is no exception. Sighing, I put my stuff aside, fully intending to hide down here after the dinner mess is cleaned up. Likely by me, but like I said, I could definitely live in worse foster homes so I let it go. Doing some chores isn't worth risking the group home for the last few months of my high school career.

They take off running up the stairs and I wait for them to disappear before I follow suit. My phone is tucked in my pocket and I feel like it's a stone of shame I have to bear. I know once the adults make over the twins' success, they will remember me, and I'll be forced to find out what disappointment lies in wait for me. The dread weighs on me, but I head into the sunny kitchen and pick up the pre-prepared pile of plates, silverware, and napkins on the counter.

Allison looks up from the stove and gives me a half-smile, nodding as I take the dishes into the dining room. Like I said, no one is mean or horrid, they just seem…obligated. After a while, it makes it hard to waste time trying to be bright and sunny. Being reserved makes it a hell of a lot easier not to feel rebuffed when they don't pay attention to you regardless.

"Make sure you include champagne glasses for your dad and I!" she calls from the other room.

The twins definitely got acceptance somewhere big. Brett must have gotten the bubbly on the way home.

Once I set the table, I return to help Allison bring out the roast and sides. I'm a little amazed at her efficiency when it comes to getting the housework done while working full time, but I suppose it's something people with real parents get taught as they grow up. My home life has been so fractured that I haven't learned how to cook more than very basic shit from YouTube videos. That may be a problem after graduation, but I've never felt comfortable enough to ask Allison if she'd teach me. I'm sure she would try, but it doesn't feel right.

"How was school, Kat?"

I look over my shoulder, seeing Brett in the entry to the dining room. He's already changed from work and smiling, but I see the distraction in his eyes. He's waiting for the boys to come down. "It was fine. I've got a Calc test at the end of the week. I'll be studying a lot to get ready."

"Good, good. No matter what happens with applications, keeping your grades up will ensure no one pulls any offers," he says.

Those words aren't for me. They are for the two wet haired boys who just appeared behind him.

"Kat's too much of a geek to ever let her grades slip, Dad," Blake says as he pushes past his brother and drops into his usual chair at the table. "Grab me a Powerade since you're in the kitchen, mouse!"

Both Brett and Bryce stare at me and I turn around, heading to the fridge despite the fact that I was *not* closer than the other twin. Out of habit, I take two of the drinks and a soda for myself. I've been here long enough to know Bryce will send me back to get him one as well. It would feel like typical sibling stuff, but for some reason, I just *know* they do it to fuck with me. I have no idea why I feel that way, but trusting my gut has been the one thing that helped me get through all the upheaval in my life over the years. It's a good gauge for knowing when I'll get booted or if people are being earnest in their reactions.

The therapist says that's some sort of trauma induced early trigger warning shit, by the way.

After I hand out the drinks, I sit down on my side of the table and we wait for Allison to come out. Brett is at his seat at the far end of the table and the twins are punching each other as they look at something on their phones. I know where this is all going but I drop my gaze to the table, swallowing the coppery taste of fear as it courses through my body.

I'm going to be exposed and there's nothing I can do to stop it.

Read the first three episodes free on Kindle Vella: https://www.amazon.com/kindle-vella/story/B0BSTMB1X3

Sneak Peek:
Bloodthirsty

QUEEN BEE

They dim the lights in the club, and the spots click on as the curtain slides open.

It's a full house tonight in the little burlesque club off the Rue Pierre Montaine.

Chez Arc En Ciel is not well known compared to the *Moulin Rouge* or *Le Lido*, but the wealthy from both sides of the Seine gather here for shows four nights a week. If you pass the various layers of security checks to even be permitted to book a reservation, you also have to be able to afford the two thousand Euro per guest cover charge. If you don't eat or drink anything, that's all it will cost; however, that would get you blacklisted.

Intro music pumps through the speakers and I stand on my mark in the opening position. My cane is resting on the wooden boards of the stage by my front foot as I pretend to lean on it. Roars of applause echo through the room as our troupe of dancers catch the lights, sequins sparkling like diamonds when the stage lights rise. We're dressed in pinstriped black pant suits and fedoras to match the big band style opening to the song. As soon as the horn-filled intro finishes, the dance begins.

I follow the routine with precision, snapping and popping my hips to the beat as we spread out across the stage. You wouldn't know by the fake smile on my face that I'm scanning the crowd. Two fan kicks later, I've rotated past the proscenium, and I think I've found my mark. Twirling, I stop in the place I need to be for the bridge, singing along as if my life depends on it. It might, to be honest, because I need to sell my cover tonight, so no one notices me.

The Guillotine moves in the shadows, but tonight, she's in the spotlight.

My ass shakes as I dance my way through the song, swinging the prop cane I'd replaced with one of my design. You wouldn't know by looking at it, but it's not the painted balsa the other dancers have for a very specific reason. I need it to complete the mission that forced me to spend two months in Paris working my way into this job at *Chez Arc En Ciel*. If I can't strike tonight, the surveillance, counterintelligence, and time spent building this cover are wasted because my mark is leaving for Asia tomorrow.

Tonight, the Cobra dies for his sins.

The break of the song slows the music and the dancers pour into the crowd to wiggle around the rich assholes. It's choreographed, but it's also to advertise each girl for private dances in the lounges upstairs.

We're not strippers—not that there's a damned thing wrong with a woman using her body to support herself—but we do bare more skin in the closed rooms. The *laissez-faire* attitude of the owners means as long as we kick them thirty percent of the fees for those dances, they don't care what any of the girls do in the rooms. I'd find it sleazy, but the girls who work here are highly skilled performers who choose to make thousands of dollars a night rather than peanuts in some ballet troupe or chorus line.

By the time I've flirted my way to the VIP tables, the Cobra is staring intently at all of us. Spotlights pin each one of us on the floor at the bass hits, and I swivel my hips as my free hand slides down to the secret spot on my jacket. In unison, we tear the jackets off to reveal rhinestone studded bras with straps crisscrossing our waists like shibari ropes. A lift of the fedora and pop of my hip, along with the beat, draws the fierce-looking brawler's eyes directly to me. I pout prettily and stalk towards his table with the swagger of a tiny dicked asshole that owns a monster truck.

His thin lips pull back over the famed curving fangs he had implanted. Dark, glittering eyes follow every move I make as I approach, and I pretend to whip my hair from side to side as I check for his guards. They're here somewhere, but I need them to be far away so I can beat my escape before they notice. When I get within inches, I tap his leg with my cane and spin around to shake my ass in his face. The grunt of approval makes me want to heave, but I turn, holding onto the prop with both hands. My feet click on the floor in a soft shoe step as I make 'fuck me' eyes at the dirty bastard. He leans back, his pants tented as he gestures towards his lap.

Fucking gross.

I don't care about his weapons trade or what happens when people get the shit he moves. I have no clue why I have to take him out. The reason they have sentenced him to death isn't part of my contract, and I'm nothing if not a dispassionate observer of the darkest parts of human desires. Twelve years at *l'Academie* ensured I care very little about anything that isn't directly related to my ability to complete my jobs.

Sighing, I dance closer and drop onto his rather unimpressive erection and wiggle. There's plenty of cloth between us to prevent him from doing anything I'd make a scene over, so I focus on the task at hand. I slip the cane behind his head, resting the wood against his neck as I tug him forward. The move reads as playfully bringing his face to my breasts, but at the last second, I click the release built into the custom weapon. One end slides open to reveal the razor sharp garotte and before he can say a word, I yank it through.

Faint gurgling is the only noise besides the end of the song, and I carefully slide the sides of the cane together. Climbing off the nasty fucker, I put my hands on his cheeks so I can pretend to flirt with him while I arrange the head so it looks as if he's leaning back in the booth. It needs to look realistic to allow me to return to the stage with the others. When I have it settled, I back away from the booth, blowing fake kisses as I walk backwards through the crowd. I almost collide with a dark-haired guy with his collar pulled high as I head for the stage, and I roll my eyes. Whatever celeb that is trying to keep their face away from the paps is doing a shitty job of it.

The entire troupe takes a few bows and shuffles off of stage left to the wings. I exhale a sigh of relief when the next group enters on the opposite side. I haven't heard shouting yet, so I don't think the Cobra's men realize he's down. Now I take this emetic pill, have a vomiting episode, and I'll get sent home.

That's when Arabella Montaigne, the burlesque dancer, will cease to exist, and Remy Arsine Benoit will re-emerge.

I smile to myself as I chew on the tablet that will have me retching my guts out in a few moments. This is a more complex extermination than I usually prefer, and I can't leave my normal calling card behind. The Cobra's head had to remain in the booth rather than get delivered to his home in a basket.

Such a shame, that. I quite enjoy the reactions my little gifts engender when they're discovered.

Walking into the dressing room, I carefully strip my costume off, putting all the pieces in my bag. Every item in the locker room that belongs to gets placed in the duffel carefully as I wait for the effects to hit me. It won't do to leave loose ends, even if my prints have never touched a single surface in this place. My gut roils and I turn, facing one of the other dancers as the vomit finally comes. Gracelia screams like she's being skinned when I hurl on her and it's everything I can do *not* to smirk through the chunks.

"*C'est la merde!*" she shouts, running for the showers as if she's on fire.

It takes less than a minute for the owner to send me home for the night. I walk out the back door of the building with everything just as the sirens scream.

Perfect timing, as always.

I jump into the first cab I can hail, directing him to the *Hôtel de Crillon*. Their suites are the ritziest in Paris, and it's my go-to hideout when I'm here. I used to only stay in the Bernstein Suite, but some rich fuckwad purchased it six months ago. If I could track them down and beat the hell out of them, I would, but I booked my schedule until late 2025. Assassins with my skill set and accuracy are getting harder to find. They forced the old guard into retirement because they refuse to adapt to the digital age. Too many cameras, crime labs, and hackers running about to do everything Cold War style.

The future of murder for hire is millennial, people. We're old enough to be stable, but young enough to be agile with new technology. Plus, most of them are broke AF from crooked ass student loans.

It's not an issue I have, but I've been in the business since I hit double digits. You don't survive *l'Academie des Invisibles* if you haven't killed someone before the end of primary school. It's unheard of.

I was eight the first time I used the weapon that would become my signature.

Shivering, I tap on the window of the cab and bitch the driver out. He's taking a longer route than necessary to raise my fare, and I'll have his guts for garters if he doesn't knock it the fuck off. A string of curses in French erupt from him when I voice the accusation, and I slam my palm on the window with enough force to crack the plexi-glass barrier. He almost drives into another car, but when he regains control, he makes the requested adjustments to our route.

We arrived at the front entrance after a few more arguments and a traffic jam around the *Champs*. I throw the euros at him in disgust, memorizing the medallion number for later. He's not worth my time, but I have quite a few contacts who might be interested in black-mailing a cabbie in town. Getaway cars are cliche in the crime world now. Most ne'er-do-wells like myself find greater comfort in anony-mous taxis or ride-share accounts hacked through the deep web accessed on burner phones. If your ride doesn't know you're a villain, there's no one to flip if law enforcement comes looking.

I never look the same for any job—ever.

I will not use Arabella Montaigne as a cover in the future, and once I move to the location of my next job, I'll ensure that she meets with a terrible fate. It's a lot more work to slowly kill off my alters once I've used them, but it's also why I've never even come close to being caught. The dancer with long wavy red hair, freckles, and big green eyes will never grace the streets of Paris again after I hop a plane. She will, however, get a minor story in the paper and an obituary when I decide how she tragically dies.

The Guillotine will rise from her ashes and be reborn.

Sneak Peek: Come Out & Prey

Just A Girl

Delores

Sighing, I look around my bedroom at the posters and decorations covering my walls. My obsession with pop music, musical theater, and high school rom-coms sickens my parents. They would prefer me to be into heavy metal and horror movies like the other kids my age.

Being the only child in a family as prominent as mine is difficult when you don't fit the mold. My parents—like their parents and all my friends' parents—are apex predators. Preds rule our world, and the division between us and prey is so severe that we regulate them to a completely different echelon of society. Prey shifters are weak and beneath our lofty abilities. The ruling class of elite predator families stretches back generations, and they've evolved into a bunch of assholes who only care about succession and greed.

My animal has not manifested yet, but it will soon enough. Luckily for me, none of my friends have manifested their inner animals, either. I'm part of the in-crowd at school, and my boyfriend, Todd, is the most popular guy in my class. While he and I aren't officially engaged yet, we've talked about it enough that I know it's only a matter of time before he puts a ring on my finger. I should be on top of the world, but I can't help but feel like my life just doesn't fit me the way it's supposed to.

Every teenager wishes their life was different, but I dream of becoming an entirely different person. Not inside, mind, because I'm pretty comfortable with who I am. I don't want to be part of this legacy, this society, or even this family. They are all focused on competing to be the richest, the deadliest, or the most powerful, and I want no part of it.

I walked over to my closet and pulled out the outfit that I had chosen for my tour of Apex Academy. My mother hired her personal designers to create a custom school uniform for today and expects me to present the 'appropriate' image of the sole heir to a Council seat.

I hate having to pretend to be like them because I'm nothing like them.

Regardless, I pull on the short, pink pleated skirt, three quarter length sleeve blouse, knee socks, and Mary Janes that comprise the uniform for my exclusive private high school. Since I'm using a 'college visit' day to tour the Academy, I'm expected to represent Shifter Secondary as well.

Shifter Secondary is the most exclusive high school for unmanifested shifter teens on the East Coast. Unfortunately for me, it was not my parents' first choice for my education. They hoped I'd follow in their footsteps by choosing to force my animal to emerge early. If I had done that, I could have attended *Apex Academy Lower School.*

I didn't have the stomach to use my body in that manner at fourteen.

Their heirs followed my lead, which made my mother and father furious and their hoity-toity council colleagues angry. My closest friends, the Heathers, also refused to force their animals to emerge, as did Todd and his friends. That was the first time the adults in our circle decided I was a bad influence. After that, I had to toe the line at every turn, ensuring that I followed all the strict rules and regulations that govern the heirs to council seats.

Everywhere I went, I had to dress in a manner befitting the next Drew to sit at the table. They forced me to take dance lessons, piano lessons, diction lessons, and other more humiliating tutorials to prepare for the day that I became a true predator. In our society, teenagers have no say in how we prepare for our animals to emerge.

Your parents make all the decisions, choose your friends, choose your mates, and decide every detail of your life down to what you eat every single day. At least, that's how it is in my family, because my mother is from the old world.

She came over from Slovenia when she was incredibly young and met my father on the society fundraiser circuit. Her idea of preparing her daughter for the future involves lessons in makeup, clothing, jewelry, and on how to keep your mate satisfied. Lucille is completely unconcerned about whether I end up happy, only that I attend to my council seat and my husband's *needs*.

Once I get dressed, I grab my vintage Vuitton bag and peek at the mirror for a last check before I head downstairs. I tuck my perfectly highlighted blonde tresses behind my ears, and the smokey eye and winged liner are on point with this year's fashion trends. I apply a quick swipe of cherry red lip gloss and open my mouth, inspecting my teeth to make sure they are pearly white. Even though once I develop threatening incisors or sharp fangs, something will inevitably cover them in blood, my parents want my smile to look like a toothpaste commercial.

It's all such utter bullshit.

I take a deep breath and turn on my heel, heading for the door. I can already hear my parents yelling in a Scotch and vodka induced rage in the drawing room. It's only eleven thirty in the morning, for Hera's sake.

Lucille and Bruno don't fuck around with cocktail hour. They are nicely sauced by ten a.m. every day, without exception. I can't remember a time when my parents didn't get drunk off their asses at an event or party, much less in our 'home'. They liquor up and fight until they part for the day, and then start again once they arrive home from their daily commitments.

I brace for the barrage of criticism my mother will subject me to when I cross the threshold. Closing my eyes, I whisper words of encouragement to myself via lyrics to some of my favorite songs, desperately trying to hype myself up before she can tear me down.

"Delores! I hear you breathing at the top of the stairs, darling. Come down this instant and let your father and I inspect your presentation."

My mother's purr *sounds* friendly, but believe me, it's not. I roll my eyes as I make my way down the stairs, knowing my mother won't hesitate to send one of the staff if I don't acquiesce to her command. Most of their staff would gleefully jizz themselves with being chosen to drag me downstairs for inspection.

At this time of day, the only servant in the drawing room will be Matilda—my ex-nanny turned personal assistant—and that request would test her loyalties. As the only person in my household who has my back, I don't want to put her in that position, so I answer. "Yes, Lucille. I'm on my way."

I'm not allowed to refer to her as 'mother' because it makes her feel old. 'Lucille' is always what I've called the woman who supposedly gave birth to me. I'd be tempted to disbelieve we shared any DNA at all if it weren't for our similar bone structure. She's about as nurturing as a rattlesnake, and if it weren't for Matilda, I might have died as a child. If the kitchen staff whispers are accurate, I have to accept that my mother neglected to feed me much of the time.

"You coddle her far too much, Lucille," my father growls. "As the heir to our family seat, Delores will come without being instructed to do so. We will not tolerate her insolence after her animal emerges. She will behave as I command or suffer the consequences."

The last of Bruno's rant echoes off the marble walls of the foyer as I step onto the hideously expensive, endangered teak floor. Schooling my features into the mask of indifference I wear whenever I have to deal with them, I enter their den of drunken fights with my spine steeled for an emotional assault.

"I apologize for my tardiness, Father. I only wished to perfect the image I will present during my tour of Apex Academy. I realize it is imperative I impress the Headmistress and her staff."

The humanoid features of his face shift seamlessly, and the hungry crocodile inside of him gives me a toothy smirk. "You will impress them, daughter, or so help me... I'll send you to Bloodstone Isle."

My stomach drops like a stone as I barely suppress a shiver.

Bloodstone Isle is a reformatory school. It's surrounded by spells and enchantments to prevent students from escaping—a feat that has only happened once in its one thousand years of existence. The most feared cat group in the shifter world—the Khan ambush—runs the school, and they're rumored to consume errant students when the Council allows it.

It's the threat both rich and poor shifter parents used to keep their children in line. Wealthy parents like mine use it as a method of controlling any heirs that refuse to conform to the rigid structure of our society. Predators don't value the lives of those who are weak, and they label heirs who refuse to take their rightful place at the top of the food chain weak. Everyone knows Bloodstone is full of criminals, miscreants, and psychos, and even they don't seem to survive.

Bloodstone is a death sentence—pure and simple.

"Y-yes, Father. I understand," I croak out. As if the pressure of touring my new school isn't enough, now I worry the Dean will relay something to my parents that gets me shipped off to Death Island.

"Bruno, darling, if you scare her, she'll frown. That causes wrinkles. Delores, chin up and smile for us."

Swallowing the lump in my throat, I flash my mother my brightest smile. Her blood-red lips curve, and her leopard fangs burst free as she all but purrs. "I will not have you sullying the family name, Delores. It's bad enough that your education gave you ideas about your value beyond breeding stock. You will take the seat on the Council when it is time, but the husband we select will control the business—as nature intended. Do you hear me?"

My eyes narrow briefly, and for what is possibly the millionth time this week alone, I nod at my mother to appease her temper. "Yes, Lucille."

"Excellent!" The leopard fades as she claps her hands. "Matilda!"

The tiny woman steps up, her eyes wide behind her glasses. She's a pred, but the smaller size of hawk shifters puts her in the servant class. I believe she genuinely lives in fear of one or both of my parents deciding to eat her. "Yes, madam?"

"Fetch Bruiser. He will accompany Delores to the academy for her tour. Tell him to take the Escalade—it won't do for her to arrive in a tiny car—it will draw attention to her extra weight. We must make an impression."

Matilda nods, and I feel the fear radiating from her, and I don't blame her. Bruiser is one of my parents' bodyguards and our frequent chauffeur. He's a Komodo dragon shifter and the house staff are terrified of him. It's hard not to be, given that he prefers to play with his food, then eat it after it's dead. The kitchen crew believes he 'handled' the gardener that looked too long at my mother when I was ten. He disappeared without a trace.

Once Matilda scurries away, I watch my parents drink and bicker about their plans for the day. Bruno is going golfing with a congressman, and Lucille is going to the spa. We all know that both outings will include stops at the homes of their current pieces of ass for a quickie, but no one talks about it. The appearance of the loving couple has to be maintained, although neither of them has slept in the same room since I was a baby.

They don't give a damn about fidelity; I learned that at an early age. Children often discover things they shouldn't because of adults discount their ability to understand the conversations happening around them.

I stopped keeping track of who they're boning long ago, because I'd need an assistant to keep the affairs straight.

While my parents' marriage is a sham, I remind myself that my boyfriend, Todd, isn't like them. Yes, his parents only own half the live entertainment industry, but my father allows me to see Todd. The other parents will force the Heathers to accept an arranged betrothal, and I'm grateful I'm lucky enough to have found the perfect match on my own as my high school sweetheart.

"Delores, Bruiser is ready to escort you to Apex. He's pulling the car around now," the hawk shifter says softly.

Snapping out of my reverie, I smile at the trembling woman. Bruiser must have scared the living hell out of her. For no other reason than it amused him, I'm sure. He's as much a brute as his name implies, and I don't look forward to riding alone to the academy with him.

Something about that shifter gives me the creeps…

About Cassandra Featherstone

Cassandra Featherstone has channeled her lifelong passion for writing into a flourishing career, a journey that started when she first grasped a pencil as a gifted child with ADHD.

Her debut novel, born during the solitude of COVID lockdown in March 2020, draws on a tapestry of personal encounters and insights that resonate deeply with her readers.

An international bestseller, Cassandra has topped Amazon charts in categories such as LGBT Anthologies, LGBTQ+ Mystery, and Bisexual Romance, among others. Her works navigate the complexities of bullying, PTSD, body dysmorphia, mental health struggles, personal reinvention, and the empowerment of claiming one's own space. Importantly, Cassandra offers a thoughtful and respectful portrayal of LGBTQIA+ relationships, subtly reflecting her own connection with the community through her narratives.

Her literary repertoire spans sci-fi fantasy, urban fantasy, paranormal, and comedic genres in academy whychoose settings, with a strong commitment to portraying consensual, safe, and accurately depicted BDSM and kink lifestyles. Her books are an invitation to explore transformative stories that are both inclusive and engaging.

Often affectionately called 'The Muppet' for her wacky theater kid personality, she resides in the Midwest with her tech-savvy husband, their creatively inclined college student, a literary-minded dog, and four scheming cats.

READ MORE AT CASSANDRA'S WEBSITE OR HER FACEBOOK PAGE. SIGN UP FOR EXCLUSIVE CONTENT AND UPDATES HERE.

FIND HER ON ANY OF THE SOCIAL MEDIA BELOW AS SHE *LOVES* TO CHAT AND *NEVER* SLEEPS!

ALSO BY CASSANDRA FEATHERSTONE

THE MISFIT PROTECTION PROGRAM SERIES

Road to the Hollow

Return to the Hollow

Home to the Hollow

Rejected in the Hollow

Revealed in the Hollow

Healing in the Hollow

Revenge in the Hollow

AUDIO OF THE MISFIT PROTECTION PROGRAM SERIES

Road to the Hollow

APEX ACADEMY CAPERS

Come Out and Prey

Let Us Prey

In Prey We Trust

Oh Holy Spite (3.5 novella)

Eat. Prey. Love.

Prey It Ain't So (4.5 novel)

Prey It By Ear

AUDIO OF THE APEX ACADEMY CAPERS SERIES

Come Out & Prey

Let Us Prey

In Prey We Trust

TRANSLATIONS OF THE APEX ACADEMY CAPERS SERIES

Come Out & Prey (German)

Let Us Prey (German)

In Prey We Trust (German)

DISCORDIA UNIVERSITY

Veiled Flame (Book One)

Quiet Burn (Book Two)

Zero Spark (Book Three)

Hell for the Holidays (Crossover Holiday w/ SSU & FA)

Obsidian Inferno (Book Four)

AUDIO OF THE DISCORDIA UNIVERSITY SERIES

Veiled Flame (Book One)

Quiet Burn (Book Two)

Zero Spark (Book Three)

SECRETS OF STATE U

Blood on the Ice (Book One)

Suspicions on the Stage (Book Two)

Fatality on the Field (Book Three)

FAETAL ATTRACTION

Hell on Wheels (Book One)

Jammer in the Box (Book Two)

Ghosting the Pack (Book Three)

F.E.A.R. ACADEMY

Failed State (Book One)

Trigger Protocol (Book Two)

VILLAINS & VIXENS

Bloodthirsty (Book One)

Ruthless (Book Two)

Wicked (Book Three)

AUDIO OF THE VILLAINS & VIXENS SERIES

Bloodthirsty

Ruthless

TRIANGLES & TRIBULATIONS

Hoist the Flag (PQ)

Yo-Ho Holes (Book One)

CHILDREN OF THE MOON- WITH SERENITY RAYNE

New Moon Rising (Book One)

Waxing Crescent (Book Two)

Waxing Gibbous (Book Three)

Samhain Secrets (Novella 3.5)

Full Moon (Book Four)

Waning Gibbous (Book Five)

Waning Crescent (Book Six)

RISE OF THE RESISTANCE

Ream Exclusive Prequels

Hooked on a Feline (Book One)

Peacock Me Like A Hurricane

Love The Way You Lion (Book Three)

Snake It Off (Book Four)

REAM SERIALS

Secrets of State U

Discordia University

Faetal Attraction

Rise of the Resistance

F.E.A.R. Academy

ANTHOLOGIES

Unwritten

Shifters Unleashed

Jingle My Balls

Love is in the Air

Silent Night

Snowed In

All Hallows Eve

NOTES

DON'T GIVE UP ON ME

1. Mate

LET IT OUT

1. Darling warrior
2. holy shit
3. your highness
4. Darling warrior
5. Faster, my king

LOVE THE WAY YOU LIE

1. Unleash the night within...

PRINCE CHARMING

1. Good afternoon, gentleman.

RICH GIRL

1. Panther Queen

SEASON OF THE WITCH

1. Conservation, protection, défense…the circle does not end.
2. To survive, we must protect the young.
3. Appear mother, crone, witch of winter…

MONSTERS

1. Lord Byron

THE GREATEST SHOW

1. Julius Caesar, William Shakespeare
2. Hamlet, William Shakespeare

Awaken

1.